A NECESSARY MURDER

M. J. TJIA

ISIS
LARGE
PRINT

First published in Great Britain 2018
by
Legend Press Ltd.

First Isis Edition
published 2019
by arrangement with
Legend Press Ltd.

A catalogue record for this book is available from the British Library.

ISBN 978–1–78541–646–0 (hb)
ISBN 978–1–78541–652–1 (pb)

Published by
F. A. Thorpe (Publishing)
Anstey, Leicestershire

Set by Words & Graphics Ltd.
Anstey, Leicestershire
Printed and bound in Great Britain by
T. J. International Ltd., Padstow, Cornwall

This book is printed on acid-free paper

A NECESSARY MURDER

Stoke Newington, 1863: Little Margaret Lovejoy is found brutally murdered in the outhouse at her family's estate. A few days later, a man is cut down in a similar manner on the doorstep of courtesan and professional detective Heloise Chancey's prestigious address. Meanwhile, her maid, Amah Li Leen, must confront events from her past that appear to have erupted into the present day. Once again, Heloise is caught up in a maelstrom of murder and deceit that threatens to reach into the very heart of her existence.

SPECIAL MESSAGE TO READERS

For Dave,
You are gold to me

"With what wonderful wisdom has George Eliot told us that people are not any better because they have long eyelashes!"

Mary Elizabeth Braddon, *Aurora Floyd*

Prologue

The heavy slop-pail bumps against Ruth's leg as she walks down the path to the privy.

She holds her breath, careful that its malodorous contents don't spill over the sides. She wishes the master would lay off the claret. The wire handle cuts into her fingers as she takes quick, short steps over the cobblestones and, keeping her nose averted from her burden, she fails to see the sparkle of dew on the heather florets that line the path, and the dawn rain that washes the dust from the wisteria leaves. A feathery, cool mist lights upon her upturned face, as she espies the brick outhouse at the bottom of the path.

She admires its sturdy lines just as she always does each morning when she empties the household's chamber pots. Much more handsome than the servants' privy, set a long way into the orchard, within a rickety, splintered structure. And most certainly fancier than anything Ruth's grandmother experienced when she served up at the Dodds' farm — leant up against a tree, was all, according to the old woman. Ruth shakes her head at the thought.

But, despite its promise of gentility, the household's privy retains the sour stench to be found around any outhouse. Its pong mingles with the sweetness of the honeysuckles creeping up its walls, and the flowers' rosy buds and thin, white tongues reach for her skirts as she brushes past to pull open the door.

There are two seats, one for the adults, and off to the left a smaller hole for the children of the house. Ruth sees that young Miss Margaret is on the smaller of the seats, and she apologises, starts to back out, but stops herself. The girl's small feet are bare, not in her silk slippers, and Ruth notices that her nightdress neatly covers her legs, and is not drawn up to her waist as would be expected. She pauses, confused, and steps closer, peering in the dimness.

There is a dark stain down the front of the Miss Margaret's linen nightdress.

Ruth feels bile rise to her throat, even as she reaches forward, and says, "Miss Margaret, have you had a nose-bleed?"

The girl falls to the side, jaw slack, her head at an awkward angle, exposing a raw, livid slice to her throat.

Ruth stumbles backwards into the fresh sunlight, the breath so heavily drawn from her body she thinks it will never enter again. She drops the pail, the master's shit seeping into the earth, trickling a path through the pebbles into the last of the marigolds.

Finally, after moments of what feels like a vacuum of riotous clarity — the stench of the outhouse, the shivering of the flowers, the horror to be found slumped on the privy — Ruth's breath returns, and she opens her mouth so that what trembles forth as a forced, harsh screech, transforms into a piercing clamour.

CHAPTER
ONE

I peer into the mirror and run my tongue along the ridge of my teeth until it catches on the tiny chip in my right canine tooth.

"Stop worriting at it, Heloise," says Amah, lifting my hair from the nape of my neck as she brushes. "You can't even see it."

"Yes, but I can still feel it." A reminder of that ghastly day. Each time my tongue catches on that chip, something slips in my stomach. I see the knife's blade, as mottled as an old shilling piece. I feel the sting to my lip, the strain upon my limbs.

"Well, Sir Thomas paid you handsomely for clearing up that mess, so go to a dentist, have it fixed."

I know she's not serious. She has that smirk on her face, knows I won't have some hairy brute of a dentist gouge around in my mouth. I've seen the pictures. She wouldn't either, the old mosquito.

I bare my teeth again in the mirror. It's true what Amah says. I can't even see the chip. My teeth are bright and even. Maybe that Marie Duplessis was right — telling lies whitens the teeth. I smile, bunch my cheek so the dimple fades in and out.

"Stop admiring yourself." Amah parts my hair down the middle, taking the left side of my hair to roll back from my face. Her hands are cold — have always been cold. I remember those winter evenings in Liverpool when I was small, when she'd pull my bloomers up for bed, how I used to hop away from her chilly fingers. "Who do you have coming tonight?" she asks.

"Well, Hatterleigh, of course, and Cunningham."

"Naturally." She twists the roll tight at the back of my head, and forces it into place with a hairpin. I'm sure my scalp curls away under the force of that hairpin, like potato skin under a peeler. "Who else will there be? Agneau hasn't prepared all that food for only three people."

"Well, the Pidgeons." I smile, as I dust pearl powder across my forehead. Sir Henry and his daughter.

Amah's brow lifts. "I do not like them."

"What are you talking about?" I think of dear Isobel Pidgeon. Of her sweet-serious countenance, of her pretty, flaxen hair. And her father, with his long face and kind eyes. "They're two of the nicest people I know." Of this I am certain. How many other respectable ladies would sit quietly in my house, conversing civilly with the notorious *paon de nuit*, Heloise Chancey? Of course, it's because Isobel has travelled to many other countries with her father, seen things that even I've not experienced. She's seen men, naked, except for long, long sheaths covering their cocks, and she's nibbled on fried spiders, as big as my palm. But still, in London, she could certainly choose to act differently towards me if so inclined.

Amah simply nods, with that irritating look on her face, as if she thinks she's the bloody moon goddess, Chang'e. "Who else will be here?"

"Maurice Cosgrove." Hatterleigh's friend from his time at Oxford. I feel warmth in my face. I lean forward so that Amah tuts, and pour myself a glass of sherry. Sweeping aside the curtain of hair that still hangs across the right side of my face, I take a sip. Then another. "And some of his cronies. His admirers really."

Amah coils the remaining hair back. "Ah. So tonight it is a meeting of your friends who think they've mastered the world."

I frown. "They've explored some of the world, yes."

"Explored. I can think of other words."

"Well, do so elsewhere, please. I rather like these people."

Amah breathes out through her nose, a sniff of derision. "At least they're a bit better than those pretty poets you have around — with all their languishing and posing." She scrapes more hairpins into my scalp, securing the second roll.

"How on earth would you know?"

Her mouth twists to the side again. "Sometimes I watch through the peacock tail, when I have nothing better to do. Although the stench of their cologne reaches all the way to my room."

I have another sip of sherry, and watch as a dappled blush rises to my chest. It resembles the first moments a tincture of carmine bleeds into a bowl of water, clouding it crimson. The blush is from the wine. It often happens with those first few sips. But I know it'll fade within minutes — definitely within half an hour — which is why I often have at least one drink in my boudoir before my guests arrive. Amah has told me that the same happened to her grandfather when he drank too much rice wine. My great-grandfather. I pick up the locket that was once his, that has found its way to me after all these years. It's now attached to the pearl choker I wear most days.

"He used to wear it on a gold chain," says Amah, nodding towards the gold dragon on the underside of the jade. "My mother had earrings made from the same gold."

"Where are they?" I tilt my head with the question but Amah tugs it back into line. She loops my remaining hair into a chignon at the nape of my neck.

"Lost them." Her mouth is set firm. I don't ask her to tell me more. I know she's lost a lot. More than she will ever admit.

She helps me clasp the choker around my neck as I gaze in the mirror. I don't like how Amah has done my hair tonight. It makes my face look wide.

"What's wrong?" Amah stands behind me, arms crossed.

I tease at the hair flattened to the top of my head, try to encourage a little more height. "Nothing."

"It's the same as that picture you showed me in the magazine," she insists. Of course she's right. She's done a superb job as usual. But I don't like it.

I angle my face from side to side. Maybe if I accentuate my eyes a little more. Or rub more rouge into my cheekbones.

Amah rolls her eyes, takes hold of my head to pull pins out. "I'll start again."

I duck away, laugh. "Don't be silly. Pass me that bunch of cherries I bought the other day. Or the pheasant feathers I wore to the play on Saturday night. It just needs a little decoration."

Amah's face softens. "Good idea. Your guests will be here before long anyway."

I watch her as she rummages through the trinkets, hair pieces and pomades on my dressing table. Her hands are tiny. Her fingers are thinner than mine, taper at the tips. I must have gotten my long fingers from my father.

I take another sip of sherry. Poor Amah. How bored she must be. What does she do with her time when I'm entertaining? I feel an urge to take her downstairs with me, to have her sit on the sofa with my friends. Surely they will find her stories enthralling? And how wonderful it would be to share her. But my thoughts snag. She's not simply an oddity at the fair, nor an exotic artefact from the East. And I think of how stiff my guests might be, of their shocked whispers as they climb into their carriages, how insufferably polite the Pidgeons would be to her. It can never be. And Amah would never agree anyway. Like most people in London, my guests do not realise she is more to me than a mere lady's maid. They don't realise I carry Amah's blood. How could they? I take great pains to hide it.

Amah's hand brushes some pins aside, and she picks up the newspaper. "Ghastly Murder at Stoke

Newington," she reads. She mumbles over a few sentences and then reads aloud again. "The house was locked and secured as usual by the housekeeper, but found opened upon the morning. A way was evidently taken through the drawing room . . ."

"Appalling, isn't it? Their little girl was found in the privy. Murdered."

"Sir Thomas isn't involved, surely?" Amah's voice is sharp. "He doesn't want you to stick your nose in?"

"No." I dab some colour onto my lips. "Not at all."

Amah reads from the paper again, and nods. "Ah. Well, that is good. They will use real detectives this time."

I catch her eye in the mirror. It's just like the old wasp. Right when I start to feel a little sorry for her, she stings me in the neck.

CHAPTER
TWO

What Amah Li Leen really feels like eating is a steamed dumpling — the dewy dough between her fingers, the crunch of chives between her teeth.

She can hear people arriving, two floors down, shedding their coats and talking brightly with Heloise as she ushers them into the drawing room. Amah knows the side tables are laden with cheeses, pastries and sweetmeats because she'd assisted Heloise's chef, Agneau, with preparing the menu. She helped herself to three olives and an Indian pie, but what she really craves is one of Miriam's dumplings.

She glances out her window. Heavy clouds have replaced the sun, and the red bricks of the building across the way have taken on a muddy cast. Really, though, it isn't too late to make her way to Limehouse. Taff will be too busy to take her in the carriage, but she'll find a cab if need be.

Amah's rooms are on the third floor of the terraced house and used to be the nursery suite. The damask wallpaper's faded to the colour of courgette flesh, but she still feels remnants of its velvety texture when she runs her fingers over its surface. A picture border of shrubs and fruit trees, rabbits and leaping deer, circles the room, waist high. According to the nicks scraped into the door jamb, the previous tenants' son, Tom, was over seventy inches when he escaped the schoolroom, while Eliza was almost as tall as Amah herself. But poor Will stopped short at thirty-four inches. Amah always feels a splinter of sadness when that low notch in the timber catches her eye.

She riffles through her trinket tray for the pearl earrings Heloise had given her as a birthday present. As she settles her velveteen bonnet snug onto her head, the lace netting ready to pull down over her face, she pauses for a moment, staring at her reflection. Eyes the shape of almonds and the colour of cacao beans stare back at her. Her hair is mostly black — apart from the threads that are as fine and silvery as the silk of a spider's web. Heloise has threatened to wash the white strands away with a dark dye, but Amah steadfastly refuses. She isn't sure why. Maybe as a snub to the vanities that rule Heloise's life. Or maybe it's just a feeble bid to stay true to herself. But which self? The fierce, grief-stricken girl forced out of Makassar, or the young woman, as determined and clever as a weaverbird, who had made her own way to these cold shores of England? Looking at herself now, in her white blouse with the high collar and full pagoda sleeves, Amah wonders where that young woman has gone.

Sweeping her silk gloves to the side of the oak dressing table, she pulls its middle miniature drawers out from their casings. Easing her fingertips around the edges of the cavity, she slides out the whole frame, revealing a secret drawer. She pokes amongst the silk purses filled with beads and coins until she pulls forth one pendant earring — a golden orb, with a figure of a dragon entwined around its circumference, tiny feet splayed, tail teetering from the earring's base. It's the one thing she has left of her mother's. It nestles in the palm of her hand, its smooth surface surprisingly warm, and there's a tightness in her chest.

Amah's mother always wore these earrings, even when Amah's stepfather gave her the large diamonds, as square and cloudy as shattered window glass. She'd worn those diamond earrings for one day and night, before slipping the golden dragons into her earlobes again. When Amah was young, really young, she'd lie tucked in her mother's arm, so that she could smell the sour-sweetness of the sweat caught between her mother's hairline and throat. She'd suck her thumb, gently patting at the dragon earring with her fingertip so that it swung to and fro against her mother's neck. At that time, they shared a room out the back of her grandfather's house, a room her mother had painted bright red — lacquer red, the colour of joss sticks and Chinese altars. She'd even glossed the timber flooring. A sumptuous, warm room it was, with a large, hard mattress strewn with silk clothing and jars of her mother's unguents.

Amah looks up for a moment, at her cheerfully faded room, and wonders if she should also have her walls painted red. Her lip curls into a grim smile. How Heloise would rant at her if she did. Heloise likes her rooms to be reminiscent of the stylised Orient favoured by her more artistic, wealthy friends — of peacock feathers, silk turbans and cold porcelain. She has limited humour for pork dumplings and timber that holds the scent of sandalwood.

Amah stares down at the earring again, until her eyesight blurs — at the dragon as thin as a serpent, at the gold that's deeper in colour than any to be found in London. She can't help but wonder about its twin.

A shout of laughter from the drawing room breaks into her reverie. What use is it to wonder about the past? She puts the earring back amongst her hidden treasures and replaces all the drawers. Taking up her gloves and reticule, she treads down the servants' stairs at the back of the house in order to avoid her daughter's visitors.

Once out on the street she pulls the black netting over her face so people won't stare at her brown skin, or worse. Rounding the corner, a little further on from Heloise's house, she passes a young couple. As they stroll along, they gaze into each other's faces with an openness, a tenderness, born of intimacy and care. Amah once knew that look, but never beyond a room lightened by a lamp, or sometimes the dawn's unwelcome light. The memory makes her both happy and sad.

Across the road, a man, lean and of medium height, pauses at the corner, turning sharply to glance into the apothecary's window. His black hat, peculiar in shape — wide-brimmed, but curled up at the sides — is pulled low over his brow, but there's something familiar about the slope of his shoulders, the curve of his back.

"Pardon me," says a voice, as she bundles into someone walking in the opposite direction. The rough texture of his wool coat rubs against her ear, just as her eye catches the blue and green tartan tie at his neck.

Amah takes a sharp breath as she pulls away, and her fingers curl around an iron fence paling. That voice, it's still as deep as a bronze gong. And that scent that rises from his body, the sweet pungency of *nilam* oil. She stares into his face, at the pores on his cheeks that resemble the oily skin of an orange.

McBride.

He takes a step back, bows, lifts his top hat from his head. "Please forgive me. I was searching my way and didn't see you in my path."

He doesn't recognise her. Of course he wouldn't. She's so much older now, and the veil covers her face, thank heavens.

"That is no problem, sir," she murmurs, as she veers around him to move on down the street. Her legs tremble and the skin on her neck feels clammy.

She glances back once she reaches the main thoroughfare. He's staring up at Heloise's house. Pushing the gate open, he strides up her front steps.

Seeing that horrible, orange man takes Amah back.

She presses her eyes shut in the back of the hansom cab. Ignoring the sound of carriage wheels crunching across gravel, and the call of a costermonger by the side of the road, she thinks of Makassar. The pallid men who rode through town towards the port, and the Arabs and Chinese men who hawked silks, birdcages and bamboo chopsticks. She recalls the smoky fragrance of teak and cloves, and the sweetness of rambutan, how sometimes ants hid in its spiky skin, and bit into her tongue as she slurped on the fruit's flesh.

But London's wretched cold seeps back into her mind. Months and months go by and it feels like her bones cannot thaw. Her right hand is puckered with arthritis, and her skin is papery. Not like that last night she spent in Makassar, when her skin was plump and had the lustre of an olive.

She still had droplets of Tiri's blood on her arms when her mother's youngest brother, Chee, fetched her. The blood had dried into her skin, staining it. She wanted the spots to stay there forever, a memory of revenge, a mark of her anger, etched into her like the tattoos the dark sailors had scored into their flesh.

With the servant's help, Chee made Amah pack a few pieces of clothing. He said he had to take her far away, before the governor found out what she'd done and hanged her from the persimmon tree by the marketplace. She took no notice of what the silly servant packed, but she made sure her mother's bangles and earrings were tied into a piece of silk. Chee hurried her along, so all she had time to grab from her mother's dressing table was her comb, made of carved sandalwood. Even now, if Amah closes her eyes and breathes in, she can smell its spiced fragrance. But the comb is gone. Lost on that first voyage to this chill land.

It was almost dawn by the time they left Tiri's house. The light of the moon glimmered across the slate sky, lighting the clouds. Uncle Chee held her tightly by the wrist as they scampered towards the waterfront, her bare feet wobbling across the rocks in the road. Finally, they arrived at the *Dukano*, a dark mass that rose out of the sea, blocking Amah's view of the sky.

"Come," he said, ushering her forward on the gangway. "You will be a maid for my master's wife, Mrs Preston."

A white woman's maid? Never. She did not know this Mrs Preston. She barely knew her Uncle Chee. He had only been in port for a matter of days to take care of her mother's things. "But . . ."

Again, Uncle Chee gripped Amah's wrist. "Li Leen, you come with me, or you stay behind. It is this or death."

CHAPTER
THREE

I place the bunch of Michaelmas daisies my friend Charles Cunningham has given me in the porcelain vase on the window ledge. They're a simple flower — really, lilies or roses would have been better — but I do love their warm lilac hue. As I plump them in the vase, I catch sight of Amah walking along the footpath in front of our house. She's covered head to foot in dark colours — there's only a peep of her white linen blouse at the neckline of her overcoat — but I know it's her from that tight, determined gait of hers. Where the hell is she off to?

I pick up my champagne glass again, and survey the guests gathered in my drawing room. The fashion is, of course, to entertain pretty poets and elegant men of words — I do myself, at times — but I prefer the company of these men of science, and their more intrepid compatriots who discover and conquer new worlds. I love the earnestness with which they bow their heads towards each other, discuss whatever new theorem they have formulated or reptile they have discovered. They have colour in their cheeks, their arms are sturdy and, sometimes, they carry the scent of faraway — bergamot, clove tobacco, aged leather.

Tonight there are seven men and two women in my drawing room. Sir Henry Pidgeon — who doesn't look like a bird at all, more like a spaniel with drooping cheeks and sad, sagging eyes — stands under my portrait above the fireplace with young Charles Cunningham.

I come up to them, sipping champagne. My third glass; I mustn't drink so fast. I pretend to frown at Charles. "You are blocking all the warmth, gentlemen."

"Pidgeon here was just telling me of his time in the Orient, Heloise," says Charles, not budging from his position in front of the fireplace. In fact, to speak to me, he faces his broad back to the fire even more squarely. "I'm to go to Hong Kong soon with my uncle. I'm starting out as his clerk, but he says that's how I will learn most quickly."

I can see he is about to embark on an eager litany of his father's past adventures in the East, which usually I would enjoy hearing of, but I don't want to concentrate, or nod at the right moments in his monologue. It almost feels like the bubbles of the champagne have risen to the top of my skull, floating, bursting with sweet little pops. So I pat him on the forearm and leave him with Pidgeon.

Maurice Cosgrove — explorer, some-time professor in medicine at King's College — holds court at the card table in the corner of the room. Although middle-aged now, he's as trim and handsome as ever he was; more so perhaps. His skin is still tanned from his time in India, and there's always something appealing about a man who has a fan of laugh lines at the corner of his eyes and the pepper of silver at his temple. Mostly, I like the stories of his scars: the nick above his left brow from when he clipped his head falling from a steamboat on the Ganges; the welts across his wrist from a stinging seamonster; the red line on his palm that's repeated on the back of his hand, from where a Chinese pirate ran his sword straight through his hand. I take a cigarette from the lacquer box on the table, and Cosgrove lights it for me. He smiles at me with that lazy smile of his and turns back to the others.

Three budding scientists are seated around him. I know Milly Simpson; she nurses at a dispensary in Bloomsbury, but really she wants to be a doctor. When I first met her I thought she was Cosgrove's lover, but I don't think she is, somehow. I think he admires her tenacity, enjoys her devotion to him and her work. The other two youngsters I've never met before. Cosgrove jabs his finger on the table, explains something to the chubby young man to his right. The third one ignores the conversation. He's as tall and well-built as Cosgrove himself, and his eyes are trained on me, over the top of Milly's head. He licks his fat, lower lip as he stares, as if I'm a platter of glossy steamed lobster. I want to stick out my tongue and pretend to heave, but I smile instead. I don't know who he is yet. He might be important. Rich.

I try to slide onto the sofa next to Isobel, Pidgeon's daughter, but the space is too small for my wide skirts and she laughs as she shifts over to make room for me. We're quite similar, really. Her father has dragged her around the world and society for so many years, she is at home in any situation.

"Who is that oily creature?" she whispers to me, lifting her fan. Her eyes dart to the card table and back.

"I don't know," I say, blowing my cigarette smoke away from her. "But he's a toady-looking thing, isn't he?"

I look across at Hatterleigh, who is on the opposite sofa, talking with Hunt. There's a pleasant hum in my ear from the champagne.

My butler, Bundle, ushers a tall man into the room. I've never seen him before. His hair has that gingery colour of a red fox fur, and his skin is ruddy, bodes of time spent in foreign climes. He strides straight over to Pidgeon, takes his hand, shakes it vigorously. There's surprise in Pidgeon's face, and he smiles, grips the handshake with his other hand — but is there something else? A slight shadow across his cheeks, a furrow between his brows?

"Heloise, listen to this," says Hatterleigh. "Hunt was just telling us of a dinosaur feather that's been unearthed. A *feather*. From some beast that is a cross between a bird and a dinosaur. I don't believe it can be true."

Bundle pours more champagne into my glass, so fresh its bubbles tickle my nose as I lift the glass to my mouth. This will be my fourth glass.

Through the hum in my ears, I can hear Hunt talking about his next dig in somewhere called Bernissart, but I've lost the thread of the conversation. As he speaks, the gold tip of his front, right tooth glints in the candlelight and I watch as his grey whiskers lift and separate, like the legs of a prone hairy caterpillar. I wonder what it must be like to kiss him, but only for a moment. He's a bit old, even for me. I glance across the room, catch Cosgrove's eye. He cocks an eyebrow, smiles. I smile back, only briefly though, return my attention to Hatterleigh and Hunt. I take two more sips of my champagne, and am surprised I'm at the bottom of my glass already.

Four men follow Bundle into the room, chums of Cunningham's, one of whom I've met before, but the others are new to me. I spy the bottle of champagne on the piano. I'll pour myself a glass on my way to greeting the newcomers. Pushing myself up from the sofa, I squeeze past Isobel's knees. Lovely Isobel. Her hair is so pretty, so golden. I've always wanted hair like that. I thread my way between the sofa and the low table. I'm in that nice, floaty stage, when the wine has relaxed my shoulders, mellowed my thoughts.

Isobel's father, Pidgeon, is across the room from us, still by the door, talking with his gingery friend, and as I reach for the bottle I hear his voice rise in surprise. I can't quite hear what's been said though, because the chatter in the drawing room has reached a low roar. The gingery fellow looks over towards me, and there's something in his face — is it recognition, or perhaps realisation? He turns and shakes Pidgeon's hand vigorously, rushes from the room, bowling Bundle to the side so that his tray of canapes almost slides to the floor.

Cosgrove takes the bottle from my hand. "What very strange behaviour," he murmurs, topping up my glass. His fingers brush mine as he hands my glass back.

There's something about Cosgrove, something unsettling. Whenever I'm near him I have to remind myself to be still, slow things down. I will my face to be as tranquil as that of the carved Javanese mask on the wall, while my heart judders, my breath shortens, like the time I tried belladonna drops in my eyes. I probably would avoid inviting him if I could, but he's one of this set. It'd be odd if he wasn't included. I glance over at Hatterleigh. He's laughing at something Hunt has said.

Pidgeon makes his way to the others and collapses onto the settee that is adjacent to the sofa, gestures for Isobel to join him. He takes her hand and says something in a low voice, and she gasps.

I look up at Cosgrove, pull a face. "I wonder what that's about?"

"It seems Pidgeon's Scottish friend left him with some unhappy tidings."

"Oh, yes, I've been reading about that in the papers," Hatterleigh says to Pidgeon, his voice booming above the others. He twists around, gestures to me. "Heloise and I were just discussing it earlier today."

I brush past Cosgrove, note the scent of his cologne — cedar bark, and something that reminds me of the woodlands near Paris — and lean on the back of the sofa, place my hand on Hatterleigh's shoulder. Cosgrove stands a little behind me. "What were we discussing?"

Pidgeon frowns, shakes his head. "I won't burden you with it."

"But you must," says Hatterleigh. "Didn't I tell you she's been working for that charlatan — Avery? He runs some sort of detective agency, apparently. He has my Heloise stick her nose in here and there." He looks up at me. There's pride in his eyes, but, deeper, I can see concern. "She was in quite a bit of a mess the last time he had her look into something."

Suddenly, it feels like there's a slippery eel in my guts. I think of that time in Waterloo again as my tongue finds the chip in my tooth. The gleaming, blonde curls. The chill morgue. The blood. My grip on my glass is tight as I take a long sip of champagne.

Isobel, too, urges her father to tell me about what's happened. As I make my way to a seat opposite him, he glances around the room. Cunningham and his coterie have joined the three young ones at the card table. They've set up a game of loo and are busily betting and drinking great gulps of my burgundy.

"What were you discussing?" I ask again.

"Yes, tell us of what you are talking," says Hunt. His voice has that querulous note found in those who are hard of hearing. "And speak up."

"It's Lovejoy." Pidgeon digs a finger in under his tie, loosens it. "His little girl — what's her name again, Isobel?"

"Meggie," she says. A tear hovers on her lower eyelid, looks like a bead of hot wax ready to streak its way down the side of a candle. "Margaret."

24

Pidgeon nods, sadly, swallows hard. "She's been murdered."

My eyes find Hatterleigh's. "Not the murder we've been reading about in *The Times?*" The child found in the outhouse. Throat cut.

"Yes, it would seem so."

Margaret Lovejoy, then. Only three years old.

"Not Bob Lovejoy?" Hunt looks aghast.

Pidgeon's face is ashen as he nods again. "I'm afraid so. That was McBride just then. He tracked me here to tell me of it."

"Don't tell me that was McBride!" says Hunt. "He did not greet me. Very strange. Travelled with him years ago."

We're silent for a few moments, listen to playing cards whisk across the felt surface of the card table, to Cunningham exhorting Milly to play fair.

"Cosgrove, you were in Sarawak with him, too, weren't you?" says Hunt. "That's right. Young cub, you were, arrived in town just after all the trouble. Helped patch poor Wilkins up, from memory."

"Where? What trouble?" Hatterleigh asks.

Hunt frowns. A cloud of film, as murky as a fish scale, partially covers his left iris, from too much time in the sun. "Sarawak. Must be over twenty-five years ago now."

"You weren't there during that riot, were you?" Hatterleigh looks from Hunt to Pidgeon. "I remember my father reading about it in *The Times.*" His face is even ruddier than usual. He looks more like a farmer than ever. Hatterleigh is utterly fascinated with the expeditions and adventures of these older men, but not enough to stir himself further than his own library or his club. Which suits me. What would I do if he were to wander off for some godforsaken place every few months like Cunningham does?

"Yes, that's when we were there. Blasted Chinamen, tried to force us out," says Hunt.

He's cross, but it's Pidgeon's hand I notice, how it trembles slightly against his knee.

"What is it, Papa?" asks Isobel.

Pidgeon's jowls sink low, giving him more than ever the appearance of a hound. "Remember there was that Chinese man outside our house a few days ago? I was sure he'd been trying to break in through the parlour window." Sir Henry squeezes Isobel's hand. "He moved off quickly when I called out to him, but not before I saw a damned dagger in his hand."

"You think he meant you harm?" I ask.

Pidgeon opens his mouth to say something, closes it again.

"Papa thinks the man is threatening us in some way, that it wasn't just a simple burglary," explains Isobel. Her eyes widen as she looks at me, like she thinks he's being a little silly.

Hunt snorts. "Pidgeon, you've always been too fanciful. What on earth would a Chinaman want with you?"

Pidgeon shrugs. "I don't know. I just don't know. But he gave me quite a turn, I can tell you. And now, this matter of Lovejoy's daughter . . ."

"Her murder? You can't think they're connected?"

Pidgeon leans forward, taps the table for Hunt's attention. "McBride said Lovejoy had received a threatening note. A note that warned him of a terrible tragedy. What if it was from that Chinaman? Surely it's too much of a coincidence that I'm menaced by that blackguard in the same week as Lovejoy receives a threatening letter and his daughter is murdered?"

Hunt lets out a long breath, leans back against the sofa. Looking over his shoulder to where Cosgrove still stands, he says, "And you, Cosgrove, have you had any threatening letters?"

Cosgrove lights a cigar, a plume of smoke rising about his head. "Hunt, I'm a man of science. I'm always receiving ugly correspondence from the more godly people of this town. One glance and I throw the missive in the fire."

"Nothing in particular lately?"

"No, sir, not that I've noticed."

The others turn back, resume talking, but Cosgrove's gaze holds mine. For once, his eyes are not smiling. He looks troubled.

CHAPTER
FOUR

It's dark by the time Amah Li Leen makes her way along Limehouse Causeway. With each step, she edges further away from the muddy stench of the water. On almost every corner, fish shops reek of rancid, burnt oil, the smoke adding to the smog from the chimney stacks, coating the already dark brick buildings in soot. Alleys she hopes she never need enter are heaped with kitchen waste, and as she walks along the cobbly courts, muck squishes under her shoes, but it's too gloomy to tell what she's treading upon. She passes many sailors, and dockworkers, mooching home or to one of the noisy taverns along the way. Two Malay men — there's no mistaking those high cheekbones, the neatly chiselled lips — huddle together by a baked-potato vendor. How surprised they'd be if Amah approached them, lifted her veil and exchanged a few words in their own language. Many foreign men wander these parts, but very few women — women not stuck in a bagnio or in a backroom of a public house at any rate.

Turning down a street to her left, she passes a row of dingy shops and pauses in front of one that's sandwiched between a tobacconist and a cobbler's. The glass in the shopfront window is too cloudy to see through and, in any case, is covered with a long curtain. The name Chan Chee is painted in white across the cheap panelling above the lintel. As Amah opens the heavy door to step inside, her nostrils are assailed by a mixture of body odour, incense and noodle soup.

The room is long with a low ceiling. Her heels click across rough, untreated timber and cold air seeps through the cracks in the floor where it's not covered with rattan mats. Hats and coats line the walls that are yellowed with age and smoke. At a small table to the front of the room, two lascars eat their supper and, as Amah passes them by, they peer at her through the steam rising from their soup. But the four Chinese men playing mah-jong in the corner ignore her, puffing on their pipes, coils of grey smoke suspended on the still air about their heads. The tiles of their game clack upon the tabletop.

On the back wall is a scroll covered in Chinese calligraphy, but Amah can't read the black lines and slashes. Back in Makassar she'd learnt some Latin alphabet from the Christian missionary who played *pai gow* with her grandfather — each week he wagered his allowance of tobacco against her grandfather's rice wine. And then later, Amah's stepfather had paid a young man from Holland to teach her to read a little, write a few words. He was also the tutor to the Dutch residents' children, but she'd always found his lessons such a chore, especially when there was the chance of watching a ship newly arrived in the harbour, silks and birds and pale women in heavy gowns spilling from its decks.

Amah pushes open the door at the back of the room and peeps through into the kitchen. "Miriam?"

The kitchen's much cheerier than the room Amah closes the door upon. The walls are the shade of marigolds and the timber benches have the gleam of fresh straw. A pretty girl, slender and dark, tends to a pot of boiling broth, while Miriam, majestic in a gown of blue and white gingham trimmed with lace — totally unfitted for kitchen work, Amah would have thought — rolls and pushes at some dough on the kitchen table.

"Li Leen," she says, a smile lifting her cheeks, which are rosy from the fiery ovens. "Shed your coat, dear. You're just in time to help me make these *jiaozi*."

She pronounces it wrong, always does, with a long "ee" sound at the end. Amah has tried again and again to correct her, but it has never stuck. Probably in the same way that Amah can never master the word "boot", according to Heloise. Although how she manages to mispronounce such a simple word to the point that makes her daughter mock and laugh, she isn't sure. She mouths the word as she takes off her coat and drapes it over a chair.

"Where's Uncle Chee?" Amah asks as she ties an apron over her skirt.

Miriam covers the dough with a damp cloth, pushes a curl of fair hair from her forehead with the back of her hand. "My husband is an enigma, Li Leen. You know that. He could be down by the docks trading some gold for nutmeg or he could be watching a boxing match. I won't know until he arrives home later tonight, with or without his purse."

Amah searches her face for any sign of anger, but Miriam smiles.

"Don't worry, Li Leen. Either way, he will return with a bunch of peonies for me, and go to the markets before dawn so I can have a nice lie-in." She tugs the elbow of the girl at the stove, says, "Rosemary, say good evening to Auntie Leen."

Miriam's daughter has her mother's freckles and arched eyebrows, but her skin's darker, has the tone of honey. Amah can see traces of Rosemary's father too — in her hair with its blackbird sheen and her eyes the colour of apricot kernels. Rosemary pipes out a cheerful greeting to Amah as she pours her a cup of tea.

"Have you minced the pork for me yet, Rosemary?" Miriam sets the chives onto the board to chop. "I need enough for fifty dumplings." She pauses, her knife poised over the chives. Her blue eyes find Amah's. "Were you after Chee, Li Leen?"

Amah shakes her head. "No. I had a sudden yen for your dumplings."

Miriam smiles again, and her cheeks flush darker. "Oh. That's nice to hear."

Amah pulls the bowl of pork to herself, adds some of the chives. She's embarrassed by Miriam's response. It's not often she has the time or inclination to regret the way she'd behaved in the past. What's that saying she used to admire so much? Something about a tongue being like a sharp knife — it kills without drawing blood. But, at moments like this, she feels bad. Poor Miriam. Amah had been so hard on her when they'd first met. Chee had brought Miriam to Liverpool to visit her many years before, but Amah was unfriendly to the young, skinny thing. Unfriendly or wary? Amah can't remember. Chee had married a white girl. A *gweilo* from London. Maypole of a thing, Miriam was then, all gangly and pale, and Amah's unkindness had just heightened her clumsiness over the two days they had stayed with her.

But look at Miriam now. She's able to chat with Chee in a patois of English, Chinese and Malay. And her cooking — well, Amah knows she could never cook as well as Miriam does. She watches the other woman as she ladles noodles into a bowl of soup, sending Rosemary to deliver it to the table of Chinese men. And of course she owes a lot to Miriam now . . .

"Li Leen." Miriam's voice cuts into her thoughts. "Can you finish off the filling while I take these bowls out?"

Amah rubs the chives into the cold mince, seasoning it as she goes. When Miriam returns, she flattens and cuts out the dough, and between the two of them they fill the circles with deft fingers, pleating the edges until they have a tray of crescent-shaped dumplings.

Rosemary swings back into the kitchen. "Ma, did you tell Auntie Leen that Jakub is back?" She grins at Amah, pulls a chain and pendant out from under her bodice. "He brought this back for me." An oval locket, gold, only as big as a fingernail, teeters upon her fingertip. "He said it's to keep my love's lock of hair in."

"Get away with you," scolds Miriam, an uneasy smile on her face. She turns to drop the dumplings into boiling water, but her back stiffens, and Amah wonders if a lick of pink creeps up the back of her neck.

"No, your mother didn't tell me. It must be nice to have your big brother back. How long has he been in London?" asks Amah.

Rosemary gathers up a stack of cups to take out into the other room. "He's been here for nearly two weeks. And I hope he stays this time." She nudges the door open again, leaving Amah alone with Miriam.

They're silent. Miriam continues to lower and scoop dumplings from the pot while Amah washes the bowls and pans. It isn't until Miriam sets the platter of *jiaozi* between herself and Amah on the tabletop that she finally meets Amah's eye.

"You didn't tell me he was back?" Amah's head tilts to the side as she asks the question. "How long was he on the seas for? Three, four years?" But Amah knows exactly how long. Three years, eight months.

Miriam nods. "We haven't really seen much of him. I was meaning to have you over for supper one night when he was in."

Miriam's eyes drop to the table. She fidgets with saucers and, picking up a pair of chopsticks, she serves Amah and herself two dumplings each.

Amah picks up a bottle of soy sauce, asks, "Where did you get this from?"

"Chee bought a dozen bottles a week ago," says Miriam. "From the *Coromandel*. She's just sailed in from Canton. Same boat Jakub came in on."

"He's been in China?"

"Amongst other places." Miriam splashes a liberal amount of soy sauce across her dumplings. "I think he spent most of his time in America, actually."

Amah's chest hurts a little, like it's been smeared in chilli paste. Ridiculous. It's no surprise at all that the boy hadn't contacted her. Why would he?

She bites into the dumpling. It's everything she had anticipated. Tender, delicious. She closes her eyes.

The black figure by the apothecary's. Something familiar about the shoulders, the narrow back. Jakub?

But why hadn't he approached her, greeted her?

She looks up and finds Miriam staring.

"What's on your mind, Li Leen?"

Amah considers her — the faint lines that fan from her kind eyes, the permanent furrows that etch her forehead. What a cheerful mother she must be to her children — the three young ones, to Rosemary, to Jakub. Jakub. She's a much better mother than Amah has ever been. It's true. Heloise would agree. Has agreed. Threw it at her head many years before when she'd asked why she couldn't go live with her sweet Auntie Miriam.

But Jakub — Amah always thought they had a special connection.

"Nothing important, Miriam," she says. "I was just wondering if I could sneak a bottle of this soy sauce into Agneau's kitchen. Do you have any spare?"

Miriam takes a bottle from the larder and places it in a basket as Amah finishes her last bite of dumpling. Amah had planned on staying the whole evening but her heart isn't in it anymore. She's just reaching for her bonnet when the door that leads to the back alley creaks open. Heavy footsteps tread down the short corridor towards them. A man's footsteps. Jakub's?

But no, it's Chee. As predicted, he's holding a bunch of flowers, but they're daisies rather than peonies. Amah knows he's a good seventeen years older than his wife, but really, despite several white strands in his hair and a bit of a round belly, he looks much the same as he did twenty-six years ago when he'd fetched her from Makassar. He beams at Amah, insists she sit back down, calls her his *kodok kecil*, his little frog, as he has done since she was little. Amah suspects he's imbibed in a little too much rum or rice wine with the sailors by the dock.

Along with the flowers, Chee hands his wife a hessian bag from which she brings out half a coconut. "*Masak* coco flummery thing I like, *silakan?*" he urges.

Amah and Chee chat over cups of jasmine tea, which he proudly pours from a white teapot in the shape of a resting camel, while Miriam prepares custard to go with whipped egg white and the coconut flesh that Rosemary shreds for her.

Chee tells them of a new boxer he'd bet on. "Won 15s, I did. I know he would win, because he is very angry young man. Very *marah*." He points at Amah. "Your Jia Li, he would like it."

Amah's smile is grim. "Her name is Heloise, now, Uncle, not Jia Li, and it's 'she' not 'he'." Although she concedes that he's probably correct about Heloise enjoying the boxing.

Chee waves his hand at her, repeats "Jia Li," before telling them of the newest vessel in dock.

By the time Miriam walks Amah to the front door of the shop, the night sky has taken on the gleam of an oyster shell. Miriam has tried to insist Chee accompany his niece home, but Amah's adamant. She'll be fine. A cab driver will be glad of the fare.

At the door, she turns around, nods towards the scroll on the back wall. "What does that say, Miriam?" she asks, pointing at the Chinese script. Something wise, perhaps. Like *Deep doubts, deep wisdom*, or the proverb that used to hang on the wall in her grandfather's sitting room in Makassar: *A man is never too old to learn*.

Miriam points at the scroll, her finger following the lines of ink. "If you want your dinner, don't offend the cook."

Light the colour of parchment glimmers past the edges of the drawing room curtains, marking Amah's way through the gentle mist that hangs in the air. She pulls the netting back from her face and glances up at the window. Heloise still has guests with her. A pleasant tinkling on the pianoforte reaches Amah's ears. Can't be Heloise playing then. Neither her brief time at a ladies' college or the expensive lessons she insisted upon taking a year beforehand had improved her skill. Now, if she just practised once in a while instead of gallivanting around town all the time . . . her lip twists to the side.

Amah passes the front door and continues around the corner in order to enter the house from the back. The fog's not bad, and yet the street seems darker than usual. She pauses. The rest of the street is asleep; no lights to illuminate the oak trees or the carriage that waits by the side of the road. She can just discern the faint movement of the two horses as they nod gently against their mouthpieces.

It takes her less than a second to realise what the problem is. The lamp post closest to the servant's entrance to Heloise's house isn't lit. Her eyes search the darkness, seek out further shifts in the shadows.

How very strange. They've never had problems with this lamp, not from a shortage of gas, and not from one of those explosions, thank heavens. She treads closer towards the lamp post, wishing her heels didn't click so loudly in the silence. A crunch under her left sole. Her right shoe scrapes something forward, something that tinkles. Glass. She peers up at the lamp post. The lamp's dome has been smashed, leaving a jagged saw of glass.

Amah frowns. Such a quiet street.

Dread creeps its sticky fingers up her spine.

Close at hand, hidden in the gloom, she senses something wicked. Something watching her. She feels it bursting to free itself, like a held breath. Its foulness suffuses the air, its charred eyes are upon her throat. She takes two steps backward. Swinging around, she just reaches the top of the six steps that lead down to the servant's door when she's knocked from behind.

Amah is thrown forward, wrenches her ankle on the second last step, clips her forehead hard against the door. She crumples to the ground. Groaning, she tries to sit upright. Her fingers find the fissure of skin that peels open above her brow, the hot blood gushing down the bridge of her nose, stinging her eyes. It's so dark. Too dark. She can't see a thing.

She tries to get up, find her bag, her knife, but cries out as pain judders up through her left leg from her ankle. Collapsing back, she's just about to try again when somebody lands on top of her, so heavily the breath grunts from her body.

She scrambles against him, strains with her fingers until her fingernails tear, thrashes her legs, her sprained ankle forgotten. But something isn't right. He's not moving — is as heavy as a sack of rice — apart from his head, that lolls damply against hers each time she tries to push him away. She hefts against his shoulders, shoving him aside, so that they lie crammed against each other in the confined space of the landing. She can smell the *nilam* oil, and something more gamey, raw; thinks she can feel its stickiness smeared across the skin at the base of her throat. Gagging, she pushes him away.

The servant door swings open. A lantern is held above her head, so bright she has to shield her eyes with her hand. She can't see who holds it.

She clambers into a seated position, crouches away from the body. His face is hidden from view, pressed against the tiled step, but the crown of his head faces her at an unnatural angle, almost reaches between his shoulder blades. The tartan tie she recognises, although the green stripes, and the blue, are soaked in gore the colour of cherry pulp.

McBride.

CHAPTER
FIVE

It's chilly when I wake. I squint past the shadows of my room, see dawn's pearl light glimmer through a crack in the curtains. I burrow backwards into the bed, want to melt into the soft warmth of Hatterleigh's body, search out the hard. But all I find is cool linen, empty space.

Opening my eyes, I stare at the bed's velvet canopy — at sprigs of flowers coiled around golden artichokes.

He went home after the police were called and interviewed us in the drawing room. The only guests who still remained by that time were the Pidgeons and Hatterleigh. The others had left throughout the evening, thank heavens. I don't know when. I drank a great deal of champagne.

A headache taps at the base of my skull. My mouth is dry, sour. I roll over, press my face into the pillow where I've dribbled in my sleep. Poor Amah. By the time Bundle had drawn her into the kitchen, called me down to her, she'd managed to wipe some of the blood from her face and hands. But there was one crimson globule of *something* — my stomach squelches like it did last night — teetering from the damp strands of hair by her right ear. My eyes were drawn to it as she spoke, as she told me of the dead man on the back step of my house.

Hatterleigh was already there, gazing down at the man's body when I reached the back door.

"No, Heloise, you mustn't," he said, grabbing hold of my shoulders as I tried to push past.

I frowned up at him — his face was pale — and said, "Of course I must."

The man's body lay on its side across the landing, arms and feet splayed back. But it was almost as if his head was on a hinge, pressed right back, like no circus contortionist I'd ever seen. The light from Bundle's lamp cast a shadow of my hair, feather quivering aloft, across the wide pool of his blood — ruby dark and as still as a lake.

My bedroom door creeps open and Amah pokes her head around.

"Ah. Finally. You are awake."

She limps into my room, closely followed by Abigail, the new girl who helps out during the day. While Abigail kneels, stokes the fire back to life, Amah yanks the curtains open.

I groan, bury my head under one of my frilled pillows. "It's too early. Let me sleep."

I feel the mattress dip slightly as Amah sits next to me. She waits for Abigail to leave the room, close the door quietly behind her, before she says, "Well, it's all right for you. Poor Bundle went to bed very late and was up before sunrise trying to mop the blood from your back step."

"Bloody hell. The poor thing." Lifting the pillow, I clamp it under my head. "Pass me that glass of water, would you?" As I take the cold glass from Amah, I think of the two policemen that Pidgeon had summoned, of how one stomped his great heavy boot into that pool of blood while turning the corpse over. How the corpse's head refused to follow the rest of his body, his face lolling against the bottom step.

"Sliced almost clear off," the copper said.

That sobered me up quickly, or so I felt at the time. As I look back, though, the rest of the night is patchy, as inconsequential as a nightmare. My drawing room blanched of warmth as we sat across from each other — me, Hatterleigh, Isobel and her father — answering the policeman's questions as best we could, his pencil scratching our responses into his tattered notebook. Pidgeon repeated the story of how he knew McBride from their travelling days, but he didn't mention the break-in, or his friends, the Lovejoys. Isobel's eyes were bright, but she didn't cry. Her colour was high, almost feverish. I asked the policemen if they'd found a knife or anything on the road; would they question the neighbours to see if they'd noticed anything?

It's only now I remember Hatterleigh frowning at me, the slight shake of his head. But I ignored him, kept pressing the police constables for more. My mother was upstairs in her room washing off a man's gore. I was indignant. And I was scared. It was almost a relief when Hatterleigh decided to leave with the others. It gave me the opportunity to check on Amah throughout the long night.

42

And now I can see that Amah is already dressed, as neat as an oriental magpie, but I can tell she is not herself. The fine cut on her forehead is clean, half hidden in the hair of her left eyebrow. She picks at the embroidery on my bedspread, stares at a spot on the floor. Maybe she is thinking of all that blood. I can't help myself — I glance at her hands to see if any of his blood is captured beneath her fingernails. Of course, there isn't.

"His name was McBride," I tell her. "He was with us last night. Not for long though. A friend of Pidgeon's."

The police constable had only spoken briefly with Amah, before Hatterleigh cut the interview short, allowed me to guide the shaken woman to her rooms. So she missed out on much of what we learned, and I hope that maybe if she knows more, she'll be able to rest.

"Do the police know why he was killed like that?" There are dark smudges under Amah's eyes. Her face seems older.

I shake my head. "Surely he was mugged for his purse," I say, although now I remember he still had it in his pocket. I also think of what the others had spoken of, after McBride had left my gathering — of threatening letters, of Chinamen. I think of that little girl, savagely murdered just a few days ago. How her throat was cut too. I take another sip of water, close my eyes.

"I had a look outside this morning," Amah says. "There was a smooth, grey stone in the gutter. From the garden of the house two doors down — you know the one? It was almost covered in horse dung, but I think it might have been what the murderer used to smash the glass of the lamp. How else did it find its way onto the road?"

I watch her as she stands, winces against the pain in her twisted ankle. She moves to the window and gazes outside.

"So someone had it planned? You think McBride was ambushed?"

She shrugs.

I feel sick again, and it's not from my hangover. What if Amah had been just a minute earlier? Would I then have found two bodies huddled at my back door? Was McBride's death part of a robbery or was he specifically chosen to die?

From the window in her sitting room, Amah watches as Taff helps Heloise mount her brute of a horse. Of course, she looks handsome seated upon its glossy, muscled back — she wouldn't have it any other way, even if it is a risk to her life. Amah tuts.

A wave of fatigue flushes through her and she rubs her gritty eyes. She wishes that Heloise had left her alone last night when she was trying to sleep. Her heart lurched every time Heloise peeped into her room, letting some of the hall light in. How could Amah find her balance — breathe in, empty mind, empty mind, breathe out, right out — when the bedroom door creaked open every few minutes? How could she steady her racing thoughts? How was she to forget?

And now, with each thrum of her leg, the beat beat beat that throbs up from her ankle, she tries to shut out all thought of McBride. McBride and his head . . . the blood . . .

Despite her best efforts — her eyelids squashed tight, the heels of her palms pressed against her eyeballs — flashes of memory illuminate the dark cavern of her mind.

The sea, kingfisher blue. The dirty, wide decks of the *Dukano*. The stench of burning coal that left her feeling giddy, the smokestack that coughed black clouds into the clear sky. And, of course, Mrs Preston. Jane.

Amah won't think of the last time she saw her. She won't.

But she does think of her smooth brown hair, parted in the middle, loosely pulled into a bun at the nape of her neck. Her thin fingers, almost impossibly long, with fingernails as smooth and pretty as pipi shells. Amah was with her when she first saw McBride. Amah disliked him, even then. But he was friends with Mr Preston — another foolish man — so there was no avoiding him. Just as her mind cannot avoid him now.

CHAPTER
SIX

It's early evening by the time I return from my ride in Hyde Park. I make sure to appear along Rotten Row at least three times a week in order to stoke the fire of my fame. I didn't take the phaeton this time, just Malani, a Hanoverian warmblood, my favourite horse. She's so tall and fine, I tower over the other women riding their ladylike ponies.

I slide from the saddle, rub my hand down the white blaze that marks Malani's nose and up again against the bristles. Taff acquired her for me from a soldier newly arrived back from India, who told him of Malani's bravery in battle, but also of her unpopularity there because her black coat was considered unlucky. But I've found the opposite to be true. Her inky sheen complements my own hair, which has a sable gloss, thanks to Amah soaking it in egg white, oil and honey every Sunday. Malani's assured gait calls attention to my new paletot, which is almost mannish, what with the row of military buttons down the front, although I make sure it fits snug over my breasts and accentuates my small waist. I feel almost regal seated upon Malani when I pass the cluster of people by the side of the road who wait to catch a glimpse of me. I angle my face to its best advantage, lift my chin. I pretend I don't notice this audience of mine, like I'm not aware they are there to see me, but of course I know they are. A man even wrote a letter to *The Times* complaining about them — about how they block the thoroughfare.

I leave the horse with Taff and let myself into the house. Pulling the gloves from my fingers, I rub my chill hands together. I unpin my top hat, and from its rim I unwind the chiffon scarf that has the shimmer of a dragonfly's wing. I've taken to draping squares of silk or chiffon around my riding hats, and just today I had the pleasure of seeing both Lady Rowe and the Marchioness of Beste with scarves trailing their riding hats too, aping my new fashion. I grin into the hallway mirror. I'll wear the scarf for the rest of the week, see how many more women I can goad into copying me, and then I'll never wear it again.

Bundle comes out from the drawing room and gives a slight bow. "Guests for you, madam." He leaves the door ajar.

Sir Henry Pidgeon and another man are just about to take a seat when I enter the room, but rise when they see me. Pidgeon's friend groans a little with the exertion.

"Ah, Heloise, you are home," says Pidgeon, taking my hand. The lines on his face are more present than usual. He has obviously been as affected by McBride's grisly death as the rest of us, perhaps more. "May I present my friend, here, Mr Erasmus Lovejoy. Mr Lovejoy, Mrs Chancey."

Mr Lovejoy. It only takes me a moment to realise this must be the father of the poor little murdered girl. I shake his hand and his fingers are as dry as autumn leaves. "Please, call me Heloise."

I take the armchair opposite. Bundle has left the tea things ready on the table and, as I lean forward to lift the teapot, there's the sound of something bumping to the floor in the next room. I turn and stare at the painting of a peacock that covers the dividing wall, but there is no further noise. I smile at the men. "I hope the maid didn't knock over anything too valuable."

I hand Pidgeon his tea, who says, "Thank you, thank you. You must be wondering why we are here."

"Not at all," I murmur as I pass a cup of tea to Lovejoy, who takes it in both hands. His hands shake so hard, the cup rattles in the saucer. He places it back down on the table.

Lovejoy's wiry hair is unkempt, and white, but the dirty white of snow pushed to the gutter. Even his sideburns, that creep low on his cheeks, are bushy and white. His skin is pallid, and the creases in his face have a greyish tinge. He is not a handsome man, by any reckoning. In fact, he has a bad-tempered face. And he's old, much too old to have such young children, I would have thought.

"Heloise, you once told me of a man you sometimes work for," says Pidgeon. "Runs an investigation agency, or something." Poor Pidgeon. His watery blue eyes are bloodshot. But after last night I probably don't look too fresh either.

"Yes. Sir Thomas Avery."

"Ah, yes. Can you put me into contact with him?"

"Of course I can," I say, rising to my feet. "I will write his directions down."

When I return from my study, I sense that the two men have broken off from a hurried exchange. I don't immediately hand Pidgeon Sir Thomas's card because I'm curious as to why he wants to see him.

"Has Sir Henry told you of the terrible incident we had here last night?" I ask Lovejoy. I offer them the plate of almond macaroons before taking a seat.

Lovejoy looks as though I've startled him from a deep reverie. He mutters, "Yes, yes," as he takes a biscuit.

"That's partly why we'd like to have a word with Sir Thomas," says Pidgeon.

"Oh. You think it might be connected to . . ." I glance at Lovejoy, who's staring at the macaroon in his hand.

Pidgeon sits forward on the sofa. "Have you heard anything more of McBride's death? Did the police tell you people anything at all?"

I'm tired. I've had a difficult day trying to block memories of McBride's blood trickling down the back of the steps. I think back to earlier that morning, when the lead policeman returned to my house, interviewed us all over again. As he fired questions at us, he strolled around the drawing room, gazing into cabinets, staring up at my painting. Although he asked questions of both Amah and me, he looked to Bundle, the only other man in the room, to provide the answers. As he bowed to me on his way out, I thought a slight smirk twitched the policeman's lip, and couldn't help wondering if he had heard uncomplimentary things about my former relationship with Sergeant Bill Chapman. They were from different stations, but men do so gossip about such things. Or maybe he'd heard of my successful detecting, but couldn't bring himself to believe it of a woman.

"The police think it was most probably a botched robbery," I say, rubbing my temples.

Pidgeon's eyes widen. "How did they come to that conclusion?"

"I think that, maybe, he still had his purse and watch chain on him." I shrug. "But what else could it have been?"

The two men exchange looks.

Pidgeon slumps back into the cushions. "Yes, this is exactly what we were afraid of."

"Afraid of?"

He nods. "That the murders . . ." He glances at Lovejoy, shakes his head in apology. "That the murders might be related. That the murders might be part of a larger . . ." He places his hand over his mouth, leans his elbow on his knee.

"Of a larger . . . ?" I prompt.

His eyes find mine. "Revenge plot."

"But revenge for what?"

"Sarawak."

"The riots you were talking of? All those years ago?"

He nods. "Yes. Unfortunately, when the Chinese *kungsi* attacked Kuching, we had to kill many of them just to defend ourselves." He steeples his fingers at the middle point of his forehead, presses his eyes shut. "It was very distressing." His hand drops and he gazes across at Heloise. "But, you see, if we hadn't, they might even have murdered my poor wife, God rest her soul. Slaughtered her, cut her down with a sabre, like they did to poor Mrs Crookshank."

"Poor Mrs Crookshank," murmurs Lovejoy.

"Yes," says Pidgeon. "We lost several people that day. Wilkins and the Crookshanks escaped by their kitchen door, and were trying to run across to our house when two villains rushed out from the stable. Killed poor Crookshank with a spear, and sliced through Wilkins's arm. Mrs Crookshank slipped in the grass . . . She lay like that for six hours, weltering in her own blood, before the brutes allowed us to retrieve her body. She didn't survive more than an hour after that." His voice trails away.

"And you think one of these — *kungsi*, I think you called it — has come here to exact revenge?" I ask.

Pidgeon nods again. "A couple of days later, after we'd driven them off, they sent a message to Brooke — the sultan there, you know — that stated they'd avenge all their dead, even if they had to follow us to the ends of the earth."

"And now, one of those bastard Chinamen is after us!" Lovejoy's voice is hoarse, but loud. "One of those vicious, ungodly, grasping bastards murdered my girl." The macaroon crumbles from his clenched hand. I hope Amah doesn't walk past the open doorway anytime soon.

Pidgeon pats him on the knee. "Now, now, Lovejoy. This may not be the case. We must wait to see what Sir Thomas thinks."

Lovejoy wipes his hands down the sides of his trousers, up and down.

"What do the police say about Miss Margaret's death?" I ask, my voice soft.

"They think the murder was . . ." Pidgeon looks away from the other man, "was closer to home."

"Have you told them of your suspicions? About the Chinese man trying to break into your house?"

"We tried. But they were not receptive."

"And that's why you want to bring Sir Thomas in?"

"Yes." Pidgeon drawls out the word. "But something else . . ."

Bundle stands in the doorway, announces, "Mr Cosgrove."

I feel a dip in my stomach. I sit straighter, wish I'd taken time to neaten my hair, pinch colour into my cheeks.

"Heloise. Please excuse my sudden intrusion," he says, handing his gloves and hat to the butler. He's wearing a handsome navy coat, set firmly across his broad shoulders, and grey trousers with a diagonal stripe. His necktie is held in place by a stickpin of gold, studded with a blue stone, so deep and pure, that it brings out the colour of his own eyes.

"Ah, Pidgeon," he says, taking Pidgeon's outstretched hand, "your man said I'd find you here."

He catches sight of Lovejoy, frowns. "Lovejoy, sir, you here too?" He takes a seat on a chair by the end of the sofa, next to Lovejoy. "I was sorry to hear of your daughter."

Lovejoy grasps Cosgrove's hand, says, "Terrible business, Cosgrove. It's been terrible." His bottom lip jerks.

Cosgrove's frown deepens, the sides of his mouth draw down. "Have the police found out anything yet?"

Lovejoy waves his hand. "Nothing. Nothing at all. They've ransacked the house, mucked around in the outhouse, the garden. They've even emptied the pond, in search for the . . . the . . ." His lips jerk again.

"The weapon," says Pidgeon.

"They think someone in the house did it," Lovejoy says, barely louder than a whisper.

"That's why we're here," explains Pidgeon. "We've come to ask Heloise of the private detective she sometimes works with."

"You think the police won't find the culprit?" asks Cosgrove.

"It's not so much that." Pidgeon looks to Lovejoy, whose chin has sunk to his chest. "We believe they're searching in the wrong quarter."

Light raindrops tap the window glass. A man calls for a cab out on the street.

"You're thinking of McBride's death? Of that Chinese fellow you saw. That these murders might be connected to Sarawak?" says Cosgrove.

"Indeed." Pidgeon's hound face is apologetic.

Cosgrove stares at the two men, then nods, once, as though he's made up his mind. Reaching into the inner pocket of his coat, he pulls forth a folded piece of paper. "I found this amongst my mail this morning."

He smooths out a scrap of cheap paper on the tabletop, revealing the words: *Your blood be our profit.* Under the words is a symbol, of a triangular shape, that resembles a child's drawing of a roof. The words are a scrawl, scratched into the thin paper.

I lower myself to my knees, my skirts billowing as I lean on the table to have a better look. The nib pen has been pressed against the paper savagely enough to make a tiny tear at the right-hand corner of the triangle.

I tap my fingertip near the edge of the paper, and say, "What's that peculiar mark smeared across the symbol?" It's a rusty colour, has the deep hue of an autumn maple leaf. I snatch my hand back into my lap, my eyes widening as I stare at Cosgrove. His face is grim. "It's not . . ."

He nods. "I think it might be blood. Or, at the very least, it's supposed to appear to be."

Cosgrove looks at Lovejoy, who's gawping at the letter, mouth open. "McBride mentioned something about a threatening message you received, Lovejoy. Did yours resemble this note, sir?"

Lovejoy shakes his head slowly, before turning it into a nod. "No. But yes. I don't know."

"Is it possible to see the letter you received?"

Lovejoy shakes his head again. "I threw it in the fire. Thought it was just an empty threat from a coachman I'd recently let go."

"Did it also have a smear of blood on it?" I ask.

"No, I don't think so. But it had lain in the mud for some time before I opened it. I found it by the doors that lead onto the back patio. It was the same illegible scribble though."

"What did it say?"

Lovejoy shrugs. "I can't exactly remember. Something along the lines that I'd be sorry, or repentant." He pinches the bridge of his nose, and his shoulders lift on a sob.

"Did it have this symbol at the bottom?" asks Cosgrove.

Lovejoy swallows hard. "I think it did, Cosgrove. I think it did. I took it for an 'A'. I thought it stood for 'anonymous'."

Pidgeon is even paler than before. He licks his dry lips. "Cosgrove, you recognise that symbol, don't you?"

Cosgrove's face is serious, looks almost feline. "It's the sign of the *kungsi* gang that attacked us."

"But how do you know?" Lovejoy's gaze swings from Cosgrove to Pidgeon.

"They wrote it on the wall of the house we were staying in when we were in Kuching. During the riot," Pidgeon's voice cracks. "You must remember that, Lovejoy."

Lovejoy presses his eyes shut. "Ah, yes. They wrote it in Crookshank's blood. I remember."

Pidgeon's eyes catch mine. "I'm very sorry, Heloise, that you have had to listen to this."

Cosgrove folds the letter up, pushes it back down into his pocket. "Heloise is a sensible woman, Pidgeon. We don't need to tiptoe around her."

I'm so gratified by his words I almost grin.

★ ★ ★

Amah Li Leen stands back, before taking one more swift look through the peephole. The drawing room's empty. Heloise has ushered her guests into the hallway. Amah's fingertips tingle with heightened nerves as she replaces a small oil painting over the peephole. Usually she stops to admire the painting — of dark, roiling waves under an apricot sky. It reminds her of Makassar, of its heat and colour. But this time she's too troubled by what she has just seen and heard in the other room.

Lovejoy.

She picks up the coal scuttle she'd dropped to the ground when she first saw him through the peephole. Gathering up the scattered coal, she carries it to the fireplace. She'd come in to start the fire, warm up the room for their supper, but now she can't do anything but stare into the empty, scorched grate. Lovejoy looks so much older than when she saw him last. But, of course, that was more than twenty-five years ago. He's still an ugly man though. Inside and out, no doubt.

She sinks into one of the bentwood chairs that circle the parlour table. Heloise would be surprised to see her so shaken, but the distant past is a nightmare that Amah only ever reluctantly revisits.

The door opens, and Abigail puts her head around. "I'm about to go home. Do you need help starting that fire, Amah?"

Amah stands up, wipes down the front of her skirt. "Yes, you do it. And then fill the coal scuttle, will you? Bring it back here. You're a big, strong girl."

She likes this young woman, even if she does trip over her, it seems, all around the house. Amah admires how she gets on with the job, doesn't whinge, doesn't cavil at the cleaning, the scrubbing. Not like the last miss they had in to help out during the day, who dragged her steps as she polished the banisters, and refused to clean the chamber pots properly. Abigail didn't quibble at Amah being Asian either, didn't back out of the house, saying, "No fucking way am I working with a damned chink," like the footman Bundle was thinking of hiring. Abigail said she'd worked with a family who had servants from India, who even had foreigners as guests sometimes.

As Abigail stokes the fire, Amah neatens the crystal decanters of alcohol on the sideboard. She heard some of their conversation through the air vents high in the wall. Pidgeon — yes, she remembers him well, too, from that voyage a quarter of a century ago — was terrified of some *kungsi* gang they came across in Sarawak. He said one of them was here, in London, to exact revenge, starting with Lovejoy's child. Sounded like nonsense to Amah.

But . . . a loitering Chinese man. And threatening letters. Amah thinks of how she saw Jakub standing on the corner — it was Jakub, wasn't it? She also thinks of Miriam's words, about him being back in London.

Could it be Jakub who Pidgeon had interrupted at his house? It's not like there are a multitude of Chinamen in London, after all. But why would he be stalking these men from Amah's past? Jakub couldn't have anything to do with that Sarawak business. He wasn't even born then.

Amah feels a swoop of fear in her belly. Was it Jakub who had lain in wait for McBride? Is that why she'd seen him so close to their house? Was it her beloved boy who'd cut the man's throat?

CHAPTER
SEVEN

The sip of whisky warms my chest as I stare up at my portrait above the fireplace in the drawing room. I'm still feeling rather pleased with Cosgrove's words. If only Hatterleigh could be that matter-of-fact with me. I know in some ways he is proud of my sleuthing, but, most of the time, he cannot help but try to dissuade me from such unpleasantness. Like last night, when he tried to steer me away from questioning the police, and that glint of concern in his eye when we discussed my last case. Of course, it is Hatterleigh's wish to protect me that maintains my life of comfort. When I think of this, I struggle between a preening complacency and feeling like there's a stone around my neck.

"Madam," says Bundle.

"Yes, Bundle. Supper ready?"

The butler nods. "Yes, it is. However, it's on another subject I'd like to speak with you."

I feel a flicker of concern when I see the troubled look on Bundle's usually bland, handsome face. Even that time I'd arrived home, blood smeared across the bodice of my dress, or when I'd turned up arm in arm with a vagrant, Bundle never so much as lifted an eyebrow.

"What is it?"

He leads the way into the hallway, to the mahogany display cabinet that stands against the wall between the drawing room and the parlour. He lifts the glass top so we can gaze down upon the curios collected upon the felt overlay.

"I had Abigail dust these today," he says. "That's when I noticed . . ."

My eyes take in the ivory netsukes from Japan — the glossy rabbit with flowing ears, the hunched man clutching a large fish to his chest. And the less polite netsukes, that are rather rare and precious — engorged men with spreadeagled women, who have wide smiles, their heads flung back. A woman with her intricately carved tongue poked into another's *chatte*. God, I wonder what Abigail thinks when she's dusting them. My two favourite netsukes stand in the top left-hand corner. A tiny, hardwood snake, as black as ebony, coiled upon itself. I'd bought it at an auction, because Amah was born in the Chinese year of the snake, but she wouldn't keep it, insisted it stayed in my display cabinet. Beside it is a tiger — my Chinese sign — yellowed with age, jaw snarled, front paw ready to strike.

"Has something been stolen?" I ask Bundle, looking over the pieces of dress jewellery made from cinnabar, the brass oxen, the jade Buddha.

My eyes snag on a long gap at the bottom of the felt overlay. I place my fingers on the empty space, stare up at Bundle.

"What was here?" Even as I ask, I know the answer.

A *kris*. A short sword, maybe a foot long, its keen blade a series of curves, with an intricate pattern engraved upon the iron and garnets peppered along its handle.

"That fancy knife, madam," says Bundle.

I frown. Who among my guests would swipe the *kris*? Surely if a guest or servant were after something to sell, they'd choose an easier item, like silver or my jewellery.

"How long has it been missing?"

"I saw it there just yesterday, when I polished the cabinet." His voice is as deep as usual, but I think I discern a hint of a tremor. "I wonder if, perhaps, it was taken from here last night?"

Last night.

I look in horror at Bundle.

"You think it was used to murder McBride?" The pool of blood, glistening in the moonlight.

Bundle nods.

"But who . . . ?" Who would take the *kris*? Who would want to kill McBride? "That means . . ."

Bundle nods again. "If I am correct, it means that someone — someone in this house last night — took the knife to use on McBride."

I think of McBride's head, wet, hinged backward. The damage to his throat. Amah had once told me that the *kris* has a wavy blade in order to sever as many blood vessels as possible. So the victim bleeds out quickly. The end is more certain.

I lean upon the display cabinet, my other hand clamped across my stomach. "Where's Amah?

"She went out about twenty minutes ago. She did not leave word on where she was going."

Amah's Uncle Chee is seated at a table in the corner of his own eating house, bent over a bowl of soup. He has the *Singapore Chronicle* spread before him, open at the shipping news.

She's come to see Miriam, to find out more of Jakub, but she takes a seat across from her uncle.

"You want soup?" He speaks to her in their own dialect, a mix between Malay and Makassarese. "Miriam made me some *sayur asam*. It's good." He slurps from his spoon and grins. "Not as good as your mother's, of course. But it's impossible to find tamarind here."

He ladles some soup into a small rice bowl, slides it across the table to her.

Amah stirs the *sayur asam*, watching the chopped tomato rise in the steaming soup, disappear again. She looks over at the customers grouped around the largest table, sipping tea, their voices low and urgent. Chinese sailors, in faded trousers, tattered shoes. Each has a long plait that ropes low to the seat of his trousers. Chee, although of the same blood, wears his hair short.

He shrugs. "More sailors stranded here."

"They didn't get paid?" asks Amah.

"I don't know about that. They were promised work on a voyage home, but when they got here, the company backed out. Happens all the time."

This time Amah notices the slumped shoulders of the young one nearest her, the flushed cheeks of the middle-aged man next to him. "Where will they go?"

"There are two lodging houses nearby. There's also a Chinese missionary, and the Strangers' Home."

Amah thinks back to that first evening, many, many years before, when they stepped off the ship onto Toxteth wharf in Liverpool. How chill the air was, how barren the dock. Nobody was there to greet them, no venders with food, no touts offering somewhere to stay. Certainly there was no Chinese missionary or Strangers' Home to go to. She turns back to Chee. "Not as grim as when we arrived, then."

He grunts in agreement, points at her bowl with his spoon and says, "Eat."

"Is Miriam here?" she asks, sipping her soup. "I wanted to ask her where I can find Jakub." The soup is good. But Chee is right. It's not as tasty as her mother's *sayur asam*. A bit too much vinegar, maybe?

Chee makes a sucking noise at the side of his mouth. His eyes harden. Amah has never seen him look more like her grandfather — his father. "Who knows where that boy is."

"So Miriam doesn't know either?"

"She's worried about him. I hate it when he makes her worry." Chee's spoon clatters against the bowl. "He's only ever thought of himself, that boy. Never others."

"He's not a boy, Uncle Chee. He's a young man."

"He still acts like a boy. I wonder sometimes if it would have been different if he was brought up in the old country."

"Makassar?"

"No! China."

Amah's mouth twists. "Uncle Chee, you've never been to the old country. How would you know?"

"I just know it." Chee's hand curls into a fist on the tabletop. "If someone strong like my father had him in hand . . ."

"He would have run away like we all did," answers Amah, her voice dry.

Chee meets her eye. He waves his hand, relaxes, but his mouth is still pursed in an unsatisfied line.

"But, really, Uncle Chee, do you have any idea where I can find Jakub?" she asks.

He frowns at her, takes another mouthful of soup. "Why do you want to find him so much?"

Amah's eyes drop from his. She can't tell him the truth — neither of the reasons she wants to see him. First, that she's a little hurt that Jakub hasn't sought her out after so long away. Second, that she's worried for the young man. She wants to make sure he's not involved with these murders, that he's not the Chinese man the others are talking about.

But she knows she can't get away with telling a falsehood to her uncle. This is the same man who'd caught her out when she'd smuggled the baby cuscus, with its gamey, soft fur, and its eyes as round and glossy as buttons, into her grandfather's house, and hidden it amongst her mother's bed cushions. Another time he'd caught her watching the little boy next door, laughing as he pissed on the smoked fish drying in the sun. Amah can still feel the flick of his hard finger to her ear, the residual warmth after the sting. She almost lifts her hand to her left ear with the memory.

Amah's voice is low as she says, "Uncle Chee, you know I'm always interested in what Jakub is up to."

He stares at her for a few moments. "That boy, he's very suspicious, you know." He shakes his head from side to side, makes the sucking noise again. "He should have trained to be a lawyer." He laughs, but it's not a happy sound.

"What do you mean, Uncle?"

"He found out that Miriam is not his real Ma."

Amah gapes at him. "But how does he know this?"

"I am not sure." Chee shrugs. "He asked me many questions, but I thought he was just curious about his heritage."

"Like what?"

"What boat we came in on. What year it was. Then, just before he left for the East, he told Miriam he knew the truth, that she's not his real mother."

"Why didn't you tell me?"

"Miriam thought it best not to worry you with it. She was very upset. She loves that boy. She's always been a good mother to him."

Amah hugs her arms to herself. Anxiety threads her chest tight. "Yes, she has."

"So, what do we do now, *kodok kecil*?"

Although her chest hurts, she manages to smile sadly at Chee. "Why do you always call me 'little frog', Uncle?"

He throws his head back, thinks for a moment. He smiles as he recalls the past. "I think it's because when you were small you wouldn't leave your mother's skirts. You used to peep out at me like a frog under a husk."

Another lifetime. She's almost forgotten that little girl.

"So, Li Leen, what should we do about Jakub, do you think?" he asks.

The young Chinese man at the big table hunches over and starts to cry. The man next to him clasps a hand on his shoulder, makes soothing sounds.

Amah's mouth twists to the side again. "Tell him the truth, I suppose."

As Amah trudges along the road in search of a cab, she thinks back to those first few days on the *Dukano* as they crossed the Java Sea. The pictures in her head are sepia, bright yet unclear.

Besides her mistress, Mrs Preston, there were four other families making their way to Surabaya. One end of the deck was crammed with crates containing pet dogs and birds, and furniture that couldn't fit in the hold. Three women, their pale skin gleaming in the heat, slumped to the ground, faint. After that, all the white people stayed in their cabins until the sun was low and a breeze picked up. Late at night, the servant boys slept on the floor of the saloon. Amah was never sure where the other servants slept, but Mrs Preston let her sleep in the small room where her mistress's baggage was kept.

The other ladies were Dutch and, in the evenings, they languished about on deckchairs dressed in kebayas and sarongs, like their servant girls. But not Mrs Preston. She was British. She always dressed in a blouse that buttoned to her throat and a dark skirt that billowed to the ground. That is how Amah learnt to dress the way she did. Only if it was so steamy that even Amah felt trapped in her skin, would Mrs Preston unbutton the top few buttons of her blouse.

Amah shakes her head, even smiles, when she thinks of how insolent she was when she was first in Mrs Preston's service. If Amah had a servant that acted like she did then, she would slap the servant's face until her cheek was as red as a dragon fruit. But Mrs Preston was kind, and sickly from a fever she'd picked up in Nieuw Guinea. And, of course, Amah had recently lost her mother. She was lonely. And foolish. It didn't take her long to soften. Mrs Preston treated her like her child, really. Or sister. Combed her hair after Amah did hers, taught her English words. Of course, now, Amah realises that Mrs Preston was probably just bored and starved of company, but by the time the Dutch families left the boat in Java and the *Dukano* had arrived in Sarawak, not two weeks later, Amah couldn't be pried from her mistress's side.

CHAPTER
EIGHT

Cosgrove stands in the doorway letting the cold night air in.

"Come, Heloise," he urges. "The others are waiting in the carriage."

I've been fretting about the *kris*. Amah still hasn't returned home, and Bundle has gone to the police station for me, to report the *kris's* disappearance.

"Cosgrove, something terrible has happened," I say to him, ushering him in so I can close the door. "Bundle found that a *kris* is missing from that cabinet there." I gesture further down the hallway. "You know, one of those jewelled Malay knives? He thinks it's only been missing since McBride was murdered."

I'm sure Cosgrove's blue eyes darken as I speak. "Is he sure?" He looks from me to the cabinet.

I nod. "Cosgrove, that means . . ."

He stares at me. "Someone from this house that evening must have taken it."

"Exactly."

"The police. Have you told them?"

"Bundle is there at this moment."

"Good."

He bows his head, frowning at the floor as he thinks. "Could it have been taken by one of your servants?"

I've wondered this myself, but most of my staff are of long-standing, and if Abigail wanted to steal something, surely she'd take something more easily fenced. I shake my head. "I really don't think so."

"Well, I guess we can each expect a call from the police soon, making enquiries about that *kris*."

How absurd. I feel mortified, as a hostess, that something as ghastly and inopportune as a murder has happened on my premises; that it has become an annoyance to my guests.

Cosgrove smiles at the stricken look on my face. "At least we can forget about it all tonight, though, Heloise. I overheard Hatterleigh say he was going to the Billinghams' ball tonight, so Milly thought it would be a nice idea if you came out with us. What do you say?"

A night at the theatre. It does sound enjoyable. Better than being alone, maudlin by the fireplace. But I feel a frisson of irritation that I've only been invited because they know I'm not otherwise engaged with Hatterleigh. I could cancel on Hatterleigh if I so desired, couldn't I?

I'm already pinning my hat to my hair when I ask, "But how do you know I do not have other plans?"

His lips curl into a smile, crinkling his eyes. "Well, I suppose I was hoping you did not."

I cast about for my purse and fur, in order to avoid his eye.

Crammed into the corner of the carriage is poor Isobel, who's laughing that Milly's ribbons are poking her in the eye. Next to Milly is the chubby gentleman she'd played cards with at my soiree. As Cosgrove helps me climb into the carriage, I see that I have to sit next to the tall young man, the one who was licking his lips over me the other night.

Cosgrove squeezes in next to me. "Do you remember Thatcher and Webb?"

Thatcher greets me cheerily. His cheeks are as rosy and round as apples. I glance up at Webb, to my right. Although he's not licking his lips this time, they're as wet and unattractive as I remember. His hair hangs unfashionably long and recedes from his large forehead.

"Charmed," he murmurs. His eyes gleam with what he, no doubt, thinks is a "knowing look".

"We're going to the Grecian," Milly tells me, her voice raised above the crunch of the carriage wheels. "To watch their pantomime."

"I did a season at the Grecian." The words are surprised from me. I'm usually very careful about what I reveal of my past, but really, I don't think I need to worry about this lot.

"But that's wonderful," says Isobel. "Tell us of it!"

As we trundle along the roads to Shoreditch, I regale them with stories of ponies that hauled spangled coaches onto the stage, of how the actors had to avoid stepping in the manure in their silk slippers. Of the time Dick Whittington's "cat" caught alight and streaked through the audience, screaming, and when poor Harlequin fell down the trapdoor, mid sonnet, and broke her hip.

70

"The last part I played there was as an Arabian princess in *Aladdin*," I say, just as our carriage pulls into the side of the road outside the theatre.

I'm the last to alight, and as Cosgrove takes my hand to help me climb down, he smiles, and says, "You'd be the perfect Arabian princess, madam," but my pleasure at his remark is spoiled by Webb's accompanying leer. I turn, roll my eyes, and Isobel presses her lips together, suppressing a grin.

Disappointingly, Cosgrove walks ahead, with Milly and Isobel on either side, while I'm left flanked by the younger men. Just as we enter the theatre, Isobel runs back to me, links her arm in mine.

Cosgrove pays a shilling each for us to have seats in the boxes, which are up two flights of steps. The theatre is quite full, and we're a little late in taking our seats towards the back. A milkmaid and a shepherd are singing something nonsensical yet witty, going by the laughter of the audience. Rather than disturb the patrons already seated, Cosgrove and Webb, both tall men, decide to stand at the back of the box until there's a break in the performance. The others edge into their seats, and I follow, taking the one closest to the aisle.

I'm just settling the taffeta skirts of my gown — olive green, but with a lovely burnished finish — about my knees when I feel a tap on my shoulder. A slight figure kneels by my side.

"Heloise, dear, it *is* you." Kitty, a stage hand I know from when I worked here, clutches my wrist. "You're not up for a bit of a romp again, are you? We're in a bit of a tight spot."

"What is it?"

"Well, poor Madge — remember her? Small thing, wears a different wig every day? — well, she's got somethin' wrong with her innards. Started clutching her sides and spewing. Had to call for the doctor, we did. But now we're without a Red Riding Hood."

I stare at Kitty for a moment, conscious of Isobel listening in beside me.

"But . . ." I haven't taken to the stage in over two years now. I glance along the row at my companions. I don't want to appear foolish; or, more to the point, cheapen myself in their eyes. "Surely someone else can cover for her."

Kitty shakes her head. "Everyone's performing tonight. Even Jasper, the prompt."

Isobel nudges me. "Go on, Heloise. If you don't, I will!"

Cosgrove appears in the aisle behind Kitty. "Is there a problem, Heloise?"

I laugh up at him, lightly, but I watch for his reaction as I say, "Kitty here wants me to take a part in the pantomime. But, of course, it is impossible."

"But Heloise," Kitty beseeches me, "they've finally allowed me to take to the stage. I'm to be the Wolf, but if there's no Red Riding Hood . . ."

I stare into her anxious eyes, and relent a little. "What will I wear, though? I won't fit into Madge's costume. I'm far taller than her." More buxom, too, from memory.

A wide smile lifts Kitty's face. "All you need is the red cape, Heloise. Anyone will recognise you from that. You'll do it then?"

Isobel and Milly giggle behind me, pinch my arm, whisper, "Go! Go!" Excitement bubbles in my chest. I can't deny I'm drawn to the prospect. The exhilaration of being on stage, shining brighter than the limelight. The chance to show off my acting abilities to my friends; my talent for drawing the eye with an expression or word.

I get to my feet and say to Kitty, "Of course I'll help you." As I pass Cosgrove, who looks amused, I widen my eyes, as if I don't know what I've gotten myself into, but really, in my head, I'm already applying greasepaint to my face, wondering what lines I might have to learn.

"You don't have to say anything on stage," says Kitty, as she shoves a goblin from the seat in front of the dressing room mirror. "We're just part of the general ensemble of fairy tale characters."

She's already tugged the gown from my body, and now lathers pale cream across my face, pats it out across my forehead.

"Who was that delicious man you were with?" she asks. "The last I saw of you, you were with that ugly farmer type. A lord or something."

I rub pink circles onto my cheeks. "That's Maurice Cosgrove. Just a friend."

"Nice friend," she says, winking in the mirror at me.

I grin, but can't wink back in case I smudge the black paste I've applied to my eyelashes, which now have the thick curl of chrysanthemum petals.

After I've swapped my gown for layers of frilly petticoat and a red cloak, and Kitty dons her wolf suit — which includes a full head mask of whiskery brown fur and gleaming yellow eyes — we join the others by the side of the stage. Kitty tells me that all I have to do is run from her once in a while, a game of hide-and-seek. As we wait in the wings, I'm jostled on one side by Mother Goose, who's bearded and fat, and on my other side, I think, by Sleeping Beauty. Kitty bumps into my shoulder three times, half-blind in her mask.

The fairy council flitters from the stage and Kitty pushes me forward, whispers, "We're on."

I follow Rapunzel, careful not to step on her trailing hair, golden as buttered corn, sweeping wisps of dust along with it.

For one moment I'm so dazzled by the monstrous pomp on stage, I pause, so that Mother Goose runs into me, swears under his breath. Stage lights glitter, and tall mirrors line the back of the stage, multiplying the colourful crowd of fairy tale characters. We must be a magnificent sight from the stalls and boxes — the golden crowns, the elves' green collars, the sparkling crystal chips on the Fairy Godmother's dress. Up close, though, the splendour is marred by the smell of dust, body odour and fresh paint.

Cinderella joins us, but not in a horse-drawn carriage, as I've seen countless times before. She's lowered in a basket that is attached to a billowing, golden orb that's supposed to be a hot air balloon. The audience gasp and clap. I almost do myself.

From what I've gathered so far, the fairies are mourning the loss of a precious gem from which they get their magical powers, and the Frog Prince tells us that we've been gathered to find a hero who will find it for them. I position myself towards the front of the stage. I won't peer into the boxes for Cosgrove and the others, but I'm sure their eyes are on me. I play my part by ducking behind a prince in order to hide from the Wolf, and I'm having so much fun, I wish I was cast as the hero. If only I knew the lines.

A trapdoor, not two metres in front of me, drops open and Puss in Boots springs into the air, and lands with a smart flourish at the front of the stage. In a pretty contralto voice, Puss in Boots sings of the power of *le chat*, of the cunning pussy, and while some of the audience laugh, many just nod along with the song, oblivious to the wordplay.

Puss in Boots has a lovely cascade of chestnut hair under her tricorne, and her legs . . . Oh god, I wish I was wearing tights like that too, showing off the length and curve of my limbs. I start to feel a steady tick of irritation that she's in the spotlight, and I'm hidden beneath this ghastly cloak.

Just as Puss in Boots hums her last note, Kitty slams into me from behind. I squeal, as my part requires, and pretend to run away. Hansel and Gretel are ahead of me, holding hands, and as I surge forward, I collide with their locked hands, somersault over. I land in a

75

flurry of petticoats, and the red riding hood falls from my shoulders. Pain ricochets from my buttocks, but it's worth the laugh from the audience. For one moment, everyone's watching me, not that stupid Puss in Boots.

CHAPTER
NINE

The morning air is so cold I wrench the divan a little closer to the fireplace in the parlour and lie upon it, bunching the cushions beneath my head. I actually feel quite fresh, apart from the bruise on my bum. No headache, not too weary. I didn't drink too much in the end, being caught up with the pantomime.

I'm enjoying a new book, one by Braddon. I'm up to the part where Eleanor marries Monckton but only so she can keep investigating her father's death. What a pity she has to leave off her gallivanting. Of course, Eleanor really does love Monckton, she just has to keep secrets from him. Secrets. Secrets seem to be a necessary part of a woman's existence if she is to live a whole life, it would seem. My life is so full of them, it's sometimes difficult to prise the real from the make-believe.

Abigail brings me a cup of steaming chocolate mid-morning, and a slice of lamb pie for lunch. She must've enjoyed some of it herself, too, in the kitchen, for I see crumbs of pastry caught in the downy rabbit fur on her lip.

"Madam, may I ask you, but where is Amah from exactly?" she asks me as she clears the tray.

I sit up straighter in the divan, rearrange the cushions. "Well, she's Chinese." I peep up at her face. She doesn't seem put out. It'd be a nuisance to have to find a new housemaid so soon again.

"Yes, I know that, madam. But is she from China?"

I shake my head. "Ah, no. She's from the Malaya area."

"She speaks very good English," Abigail says, but really it's a question. She's by the door, and I let her go without further comment. Amah's business is hers to tell, not mine.

For the rest of the afternoon I read and doze. The room has darkened by the time I get to the end of the novel and I angle the pages so that the light from the fire illuminates the words. I close the book and rest it against my breast. What a pity Eleanor had to sink into the vapours as well as her husband's arms, in the end. But there was such a fuss about Braddon's last book, I'm not surprised she's thrown conservative sop to the critics.

Rain lashes against the glass, so heavily the world outside is a blur. Standing, I clasp my dressing gown closer around my body, sink my nose into the swansdown ruffle. I make my way to the window and place my hand against the chill glass. The wind whistles its way through the gaps at the edges of the window frames. The street is empty apart from a slight figure making his way along the footpath and a brown brougham parked across the way. The horses are drenched, but there's no sign of the coachman.

Bundle enters the parlour with the evening paper. He pulls a small table to the fireplace and flattens out the wet sheets of newspaper to dry.

"I'm sorry, madam," he says. "The paperboy did his best."

I look back out the window. Horizontal sheets of rain drive the young man back down the street, and floods of water gush against his heels. "The poor thing."

I wonder how much longer his route is, if he has somewhere dry to bed down later. I remember one night when a couple of us took refuge from weather such as this under a bush in Kew Gardens because it was too late to sneak into the Palm House. What a miserable night that was. I shiver and rub my hands up and down my arms. I'm confident — absolutely resolute, in fact — that I will not be caught out like that ever again.

Taking a seat on the edge of the divan, I peer down at the front page, careful not to smudge my fingers or clothing on the damp ink. A picture of a fine house, its many windows blotted black with rainwater, takes up half the page, under the words, *Second Murder at St Chad's Lodge*.

A second crime has been committed, brother to the hideous wickedness so recently delivered upon the Lovejoy family of Stoke Newington. We may well remember the heinous murder of young Margaret Lovejoy, poor creature, found lifeless in the water closet. This crime, quite without parallel in our criminal records, has been repeated upon the father, one Erasmus Timothy Lovejoy. As far as we understand the story, Mr Lovejoy was locking the side gate to his property, after loosing the watchdog from its pen. The murderer or murderess had stolen upon him, either secretly or brazenly, we cannot say. Taking out some sort of blade, cunning and razor-sharp, the culprit had cut Mr Lovejoy's throat to the very vertebrae, and then thrust him face down into the horses' water trough.

My eyes run through the rest of the article, in which the reporter issues instructions on how the police should investigate the murder, and finishes with: *We must all do our part to assist the police in finding who is guilty for these foul deeds.*

Bloody hell. Lovejoy. The same grey gentleman I met just yesterday. Squishing my bottom lip between my fingers, I stare into space, remembering his trembling hands, his confused state.

I wrench the front page from the rest and leap to my feet so quickly I bang my knee against the table, knocking the rest of the newspaper to the floor. Hobbling into the hallway, I ask Abigail, who's straightening a bouquet of hyacinth in a crystal vase, "Abigail, have you seen Amah today?"

She tosses her head towards the top of the house. "Up in her room, I expect. She'd be mad to be out in this gale."

I hurry up the two flights of stairs, and I'm quite winded by the time I rap on Amah's door. I push it open, nearly knocking her in the nose.

"What is it, Heloise?" she asks, looking past me in alarm.

"Look at this." I take a seat at the round table in Amah's sitting room, spread the front page flat across the table, accidentally sweeping the silk embroidery she's been working upon onto the floor. But even as she reads, squinting down at the small print, I say, "Lovejoy. He was here just yesterday. He's the father of that child that was murdered."

Amah pulls a chair out next to mine, lowers herself slowly. She picks up the shawl she is embroidering for me, places it on the back of her chair, but it slips to the floor again under the weight of its lace border.

"Was his throat cut too?" she asks.

"Yes. The same as the girl. It says his head was almost severed altogether. Just like McBride."

I notice the colour has faded from Amah's face.

She presses her eyes together for a moment, then frowns. "Why? Why?"

"Nobody knows." I'm puzzled by Amah's reaction. I've seen her amongst the mayhem of murder, the blood, the stench. Usually she doesn't turn a hair. I wonder if the poor thing is still upset by the other night, if she has been thinking of how close she was to being a victim herself? After all, Amah usually has the upper hand in these situations — Amah and her bitey little switchblade. "But surely his death has to be connected to McBride's. They're so similar."

Amah stands up so abruptly, the chair totters behind her. She hurries to the window and, pressing her forehead to the glass, she gazes up and down the street.

I join her. "What are you looking for?"

She just shakes her head, the crease between her brows more pronounced.

I become still, then draw back behind the curtains. A chill draught ripples across my skin, which has nothing to do with the storm. Amah's watching for the killer. She thinks he might be outside.

I frown. But why would McBride's murderer return here?

A green carriage nudges in behind the brougham across the road. A man climbs down into the street, lands in a puddle. He covers his head with what looks like a magazine. As he darts across to my house, the brougham's door swings open, releasing another man who follows the first.

The rapping on the front door is so loud, so persistent, we can hear it from two levels up. I run to the top of the stairs, lean on the newel as Bundle opens the door. The voices are too low, too hurried, for me to hear clearly, though, over the rush of rain slapping against the doorstep.

Bundle shuts the door. It's quiet again, so I know he hasn't allowed the men to enter. I hurry down the stairs and, pausing on the first landing, lean over the banister until I can see Bundle's shadow. "Who was it, Bundle?"

He takes a step forward so I can see him. "Reporters, Mrs Chancey."

My shoulders relax a little. Have they heard of my turn at the Grecian last night? Maybe they've come to ask me of the crowds in Hyde Park. How very forward to hunt me down in my home. I smile. Rather pleasing, though.

"Apparently there has been another murder. Lovejoy, I believe they said," says Bundle, his deep voice as smooth, as toneless as usual. "They seem to think it is connected with the murder committed here two nights ago. Said the methods were similar."

I stare into his steady, grey eyes and then glance up at Amah who stands on the landing above. Her arms are crossed, and she shakes her head.

"Better stay in tonight, Heloise."

CHAPTER
TEN

I think I will never get to sleep. The heavy rain that drums against the bedroom windows cannot mute my heartbeat, which throbs against my ribs. I lie on my back, fling my right arm above my head — how I usually find my way to sleep. But nothing.

How on earth am I going to get rid of those reporters? The last time I peeked out the window, the carriages were still there, biding their time, like a couple of damned debt collectors. What the hell will the neighbours think? The police the other night, and now blasted reporters. I've nothing to tell them of McBride. Didn't even meet him. I slide onto my left side, then the right. Feeling feverish against the banked-up pillows, I fling two across the floor.

And I can't involve the others. The reporters must not find out about my friends — of who they are — or the Pidgeons and Cosgrove may never attend my soirees again.

And Hatterleigh. He wouldn't like this sort of publicity at all.

I lie on my back again, stare over at the closed curtains. Who did Amah think she'd seen out there when she gazed at the street? The same person who left

McBride on my back doorstep? Lovejoy's murderer? Why would he be lurking here?

I think again of the pooled blood on the doorstep, its shiny depths. As black as ink. Of drawing the ink into a well, dipping my pen in it . . . I wrench awake, clutch my throat.

The rest of the night is much the same. I feel like I haven't slept at all, yet I wake to fragments of dreams, of draping myself over Hatterleigh's broad back; of arguing with Amah until I feel a scream buzz in my eardrums. Worst — that I'm back in that room in Liverpool, the musty stench of mouse droppings, mould dappling the walls. My fingers are numb with cold, my jaw frozen shut. I weep and weep, heaving from my chest.

When I wake, the blankets have slipped off the bed and goosebumps pimple my arms. The grate is heaped with ash, barren of comforting amber embers.

"You're awake early," says Abigail, as she lumbers into the room, carrying the coal scuttle.

I sit up, watch her as she yanks the curtains open. "I don't think I really slept." Overnight, the rain has settled down to a light patter against the fogged windows.

After Abigail's conjured up a brisk, cheerful blaze, she leaves the room, saying, "I'll bring up your breakfast directly."

I lean over the side of the bed, pull the pillows back up beside me. There's a tautness across my forehead, almost a headache, from lack of sleep. I'll wager there are dark smudges under my eyes, too. My skin will be puffy. I'm no longer feeling anxious, just grumpy. What the hell did that man have to be murdered on my doorstep for? What on earth is happening?

I press my eyes shut. *Think of something else. Think of something pleasant.*

I remember I'm seeing Hatterleigh later this evening. We're going to Motts, and although it's a treat to look forward to, I feel a sliver of irritation that I'm not well rested for it. That I won't look my best.

Think of something pleasant . . .

Rolling over, I gaze towards my dressing room. I have a new Worth gown — French silk and the pretty lilac shade of a flowering betony. It has a wonderful array of frills, too, but the bow on the back, the rectangle pleats at the waist, make it look more like a walking dress than something I can wear to a dance.

I sit up, layer the pillows behind my back. So maybe I'll wear the ivory taffeta gown again, the one with moss green trim. I don't think Hatterleigh has seen me in it yet.

Amah comes into my room carrying my breakfast tray. She places it on the dressing table. "Heloise, can I dress your hair as soon as possible, please? I need to go out this morning."

I swing my legs over the side of the bed. "Where do you need to get to in such a hurry?" I take a seat at the dresser and tilt my head to the side, appraising my face in the mirror. I don't look tired at all. My eyes are a little bright, but that's not a bad thing.

"I'm going to visit Miriam," Amah says, hairpins clamped between her front teeth as she pulls the plait from my hair.

86

"Again? So soon?"

She shrugs, brushing my hair in long, smooth tugs. My head yanks back, but I know it'd be a waste of breath to complain.

I watch my mother's serious face in the mirror. Of course, her hair is neatly drawn back into a low bun, and she is already dressed in her customary black skirt and white blouse. I'm pleased to see that she has clasped the collar together with the ivory cameo brooch I gave her. But I wonder if I can discern extra shadows under her eyes, if the lines of her face seem a bit more accentuated.

"I sent a missive to Pidgeon last night," I tell her. "Asking him what he knows of Lovejoy's death. Or if there's any more news on McBride. I think the reporters must be right. They must be connected somehow."

Amah's dark eyes find mine. "And the little girl?"

I shrug, shake my head. "I don't know."

Amah presses my hair neat, pins small flowers into the braid.

"What are you doing today, Heloise?"

I take a sip of my coffee, pull a face when I realise it's not sugared yet. "If the weather settles down I might go for a ride in the park. Tonight I will be out with Hatterleigh."

Amah nods, but her eyes are fixed on the curls she's arranging in my hair.

I remember that I have a gift of perfumed soap for Aunt Miriam and as soon as Amah pats my hair neat one last time I hurry into my dressing room, find the package at the bottom of the shelves that house my hats.

"Give these to my aunt, will you?" I say, placing the fragrant package into Amah's hands. "I bought them from a sweet little shop on Tottenham Court Road. The woman said they were from France. Made with lavender."

Gazing at my vast assortment of hats, I remember my young cousin, Rosemary, swooning over my straw bonnet, the one with the cluster of silk rose buds across its curved brim. I take it from its shelf, but hesitate a moment. It's not as if Rosemary expects me to give it to her. I really love its velvet ribbons and it's a bit of a wrench to give away, but I really love Rosemary too.

I hand it over to Amah. "And give this to Rosemary. She admired it when we had morning tea last month."

Amah puts my offerings on top of the chest of drawers. "And what will you wear today?" She rummages through the top drawer, brings out a chemise and bloomers. "You're staying in, aren't you?"

I stare at her. "Maybe a ride; seeing Hatterleigh tonight," I tell her again, wondering where her mind is at. "I really wanted to wear the new gown from Worth, but it's still drizzling, and I don't want it to become ruined."

Amah glances at me and sniffs. "That purple thing? Be good if it was ruined in the rain."

CHAPTER
ELEVEN

Amah comes down the stairs, securing a woollen scarf around her neck. She tugs it a little way from her skin because, although necessarily warm, wool always makes her feel itchy.

Abigail peers through the sidelight by the front door. Looking over her shoulder at Amah, she says, "Four coaches now." She returns her gaze to the window. "And I can see at least five of those vermin reporters."

Amah reaches the bottom floor and turns towards the back of the house, passing Agneau in the kitchen, who's chopping chives with fine precision, a steaming cup of chocolate before him. She lowers the netting over her face and opens the back door. Cold air, as sharp as a knife, strafes her skin. She quickly pulls the door shut behind her, before Agneau can complain.

Bundle has done a fine job of cleaning the back steps, although, in the furthest left corner, right at the bottom, almost covered by a tendril of ivy, she can see the slightest smudge, as ruby red as pomegranate juice. But maybe she's only imagining it. She decides to not look too closely.

Coming out onto the side street, a man runs towards her, notebook in hand. He blocks her way. "Madam,

madam, can you tell me anything of the horror that happened here three nights ago?"

Over his shoulder she sees two more men approach. Across the road and three doors down, a young couple step from their house and stare at her, curious, and she recognises them from the other night — the two who had gazed so lovingly at each other, strolling arm in arm.

"Madam, tell us what happened," the reporter says, his voice more urgent as the others almost catch him up.

Amah lifts her veil, stares at him blankly. Shrugs. "Sir?"

The reporter gapes at her for a moment, his eyes roaming over her facial features. He jots something in his notebook, turning away from her.

Amah's mouth twists to the side as she pulls the veil back down.

She makes her way to Limehouse, to her Uncle Chee's. She gives Miriam the presents from Heloise, and asks after Jakub.

Miriam barely reacts to the presents and instead, looks worried. "We haven't seen him. He might be at that Strangers' Home. Down West India Road. Near St Andrews."

Amah's not sure how far it is, so she summons a cab, which drops her in front of a handsome two-storey building with at least twenty arched windows across its façade. She climbs the shallow steps to the portico and pushes the heavy swing door open.

The commotion in the expansive hall reminds her of the market bazaar in Makassar after a large ship had come in. Men cluster around neat rows of benches and tables, which are spread across the vast floor space. Lascars, and maybe a number of Cingalese, in soft tunics with bandanas swathed around their heads, are seated at the back of the room, as close to the fire as possible. More are slumped against the wall, arms crossed, waiting. Seated at the tables closest to the entrance are three groups of Chinese men, dressed in robes that hang to their shins. They appear to be arguing, but on closer inspection, Amah sees that the occupants of one table are in the middle of a noisy game of cards, while the men gathered at the remaining two tables seem to be trading clothing, nuts and pipes.

Glancing around for an office of some sort, at which she can enquire after Jakub, she's surprised to see three Indian women standing by an open doorway that leads into another hall that smells of roasting meat and boiled cabbage. Their saris — spangled blue, carnation pink, the off-white of an elephant tusk — wink from beneath their heavy overcoats. The woman in blue has a white baby cradled in her arms, while the woman in the pink sari wears sandals, her toes bare to the cold weather.

A sudden icy draught brings forth two men through the swing doors. They're taller than anybody Amah has ever seen, with skin as dark as mulberries. They're dressed in drab suits, battered bowler hats on their heads. They walk straight through the hall, disappear into a room to the right.

"Zanzibaris," says a voice at her elbow. "A ship just came in from Africa. Can I help you at all?"

A man, only as tall as she is, smiles at her. His hair is like ash, streaks of white and steel grey, and his skin is so pale she can see the spidery red veins that travel across his cheeks.

"What is this place?" she asks.

"Ah. This is the Strangers' Home. We look after foreign seamen, mostly, who need somewhere to stay between voyages. Some of these men might be looking for more work, but unfortunately some are itinerant."

"And the women?" Amah nods towards the Indian women.

"Nannies, come to hear news of relatives," he says. "The one in the pink sari, she seeks a passage home. Are you after the same thing? Because there is also an excellent agency I can point you to that looks after women from . . . China?"

"Makassar."

"Ah. Let me introduce myself. Reverend John Cadogan. I was previously a missionary in China. I can speak a little of the language, but no Malay, alas."

"Mrs Chan," Amah responds. "I'm looking for my nephew. I was told I might find him here. Jakub Chan?"

"I'll have to look in the ledger, I'm afraid. We can house up to two hundred people here, you know. Sometimes more. It's very difficult to keep track." He smiles apologetically at her, as he guides her past the three Indian women. "If you'll just wait for me in the reading room, please. I believe luncheon is to be served soon in the dining hall, and it's bedlam around here then."

He leaves Amah in a plain room that smells of dust and something like dried leaves. Four sofas, the leather worn and creased, are arranged near the bookcases that line the walls. Only one of the bookcases — the one nearest the window that faces the road — has an assortment of reading material. The bottom shelves are heaped with old periodicals, and the three top shelves are lined with leather-bound books of different shades, each one with a gold cross engraved upon its spine. Amah takes down one with a moss-green cover, blows dust from the top, flips it open. She thinks it might be Chinese script she's looking at and, slipping it back onto the shelf, she pulls down another, this one with a red cover. The script is unfamiliar, the words long. She pushes the book back between the others just as Cadogan returns.

"Please, take a seat, Mrs Chan." He's holding a thick ledger, which he balances on his knees as he sits down.

Amah perches on the sofa's edge a couple of feet away from him.

Placing a pair of spectacles onto his nose, he opens the ledger. "When do you think he might have arrived?"

Amah thinks back to Miriam's words. "Within the last two weeks, perhaps?"

"That's a lot of names to go through," he says, flipping back through four pages of the large book. His finger presses its way down the names written in the three columns arranged on each page.

A man dressed in a tidy naval uniform, turban upon his head, enters the reading room, picks up a newspaper from the pile on the table in the middle of the room. He lights a pipe, and settles into a chair to read.

"Ah, I think we have him here." Cadogan shifts the ledger around so Amah can see. "There's his name." His voice drags at the end, as if he reads something troubling.

Next to *Chan, Jakub. Dormitory 34b* is an asterisk and the words: *3 nights/departed with one Sin Hok.*

"Do you know this Sin Hok?" Amah asks, pointing to the name.

Cadogan's brow lifts in surprise. "You read?"

Amah gives a short nod and repeats her question.

Cadogan frowns. "Actually, I do. To tell you the truth, he's quite an unsavoury character, which is why Arnold, my associate here, has made a note of it."

"Who is he?"

"A Chinese fellow. Recruits for a group who call themselves The Three Lotus. Came from Sarawak, I believe."

"The Three Lotus?" Amah has never heard of them. "What do they do?"

Cadogan takes off his glasses, polishes them with a handkerchief. "They originated as three *kungsi*, I believe. The Golden Lotus, The Iron Lotus and The Fragrant Lotus. Do you know about *kungsis*?"

Amah shakes her head, although it sounds familiar. The word flickers like a warning at the back of her brain, like a shaft of lightning in the distance.

94

"Originally, they were just a collection of Chinese groups — Hakka — who wanted to strengthen their trading powers against the Hokkien Chinese in areas such as Sarawak and Montrado, but they've since branched out. One such collection has settled here. The Three Lotus. They've caused a bit of strife around here lately. The gang leaves their mark on buildings with a sign that looks like a triangle."

"What sort of strife?"

He places his glasses back on his nose, glancing to the side at Amah. "Well, let us just say, they are not a good group for your nephew to become involved with. They've been associated with both extortion and violence. I believe this Sin Hok is what they refer to as a *straw sandal*. He recruits for them."

Amah's chest is tight. Her breaths feel constricted. Why would Jakub want to join The Three Lotus when he could be at home with Miriam and the children?

"Where can I find this Sin Hok?"

Cadogan looks alarmed. "Madam, you cannot track down these men. It would be too dangerous."

"Of course I must," says Amah, her voice firm. Annoyed, even. "If I do not, who will?"

Cadogan spreads his fingers. "I do not know where they are situated, in any case."

"What of this Arnold? He might know?"

Another man in naval uniform enters the room, carrying a plate of food, and seats himself next to his compatriot.

"Arnold is not here today," says Cadogan. "He might be in this evening. I will ask him if he knows where to find this Sin Hok. But, madam, if I do provide you with his whereabouts, you must promise me that you will not search for him alone. Surely, there must be some gentleman you can take with you or you can send in your stead?"

Amah stares at Cadogan for a moment, at his earnest expression, at the cross pinned to his collar. She doesn't worship his god, so feels no compunction about lying to him. "Of course I will."

It was on that terrible day in Sarawak that Amah first learnt more of this god the British were so devoted to. Mrs Preston was to meet her husband in Kuching, and she took Amah and her Uncle Chee along with her. They travelled down the Sarawak River, until a group of native children waved them in from the banks. Several men on horseback cantered down the hill behind the children. One was Mr Preston. He was an ugly man, and his face was bad-tempered, like a sulky child's. As he ushered Mrs Preston onto the muddy banks, his voice was testy. Amah still can't understand how a nice lady like Mrs Preston was saddled with such a man. It was also the first time Amah saw McBride and Pidgeon. McBride, skin shiny and orange even from a distance, calling out to them, organising the local people to help them alight; Pidgeon, his long face, skin peeling from too much sun.

Amah only recognised a few English words back then, as the men greeted Mrs Preston and bowed over her hand. They took them to the village, with its newly constructed homes, neat and white.

Knowing they would be a while, she made her way to the bazaar by the water. There she found a familiar sight, for it wasn't so different from the markets of Makassar, just smaller. The local Iban sold leafy greens and nuts, while two Indian traders dealt in spices from other islands and colourful saris. One old woman, Chinese, Amah could tell, sold broken pieces of porcelain. As she ran her fingers over the sharp edges of a chipped teacup, she could smell the cardamom on the old woman's breath from the betel nut she chewed, the red cud wrapped in sirih leaf.

On the outskirts of this little town, she spied a simple bamboo shack with a cross on its highest gable, a cross like the one on Mrs Preston's bedside table. Amah hesitated in the doorway, peering into the shadows. At the furthest end of the room, hanging on the wall, was a statue of a thin man, almost naked. His arms were flung from his sides, but as she tiptoed closer she saw that his hands and feet were nailed to the wood and blood seeped from his wounds. He reminded her of the fish the cook prepared in her grandfather's kitchen, damaged and limp on the timber cutting board. What worship of agony was this? She glanced around, wondering where the flecks of gold were, the incense, the food offerings.

It was then that Amah heard the bell ringing, pealing across the village, urgently calling to those who were not safely inside. Women and children screamed, men shouted to each other in a mix of languages, none of which made sense to her.

CHAPTER
TWELVE

I flip through the newest issue of *Journal des Demoiselles* again, pausing at the print of a woman dressed in a white satin gown trimmed with stick-candy pink. A corsage of roses runs at an angle across the skirt, and three roses dot the bodice. Amah would hate it. And she'd be right. Looking at it again, I realise it's a bit too much. I turn over a couple more pages until I find the other gown I admired. The skirt's upper flounce is in the shape of orchid petals, but now it reminds me too much of a child's fairy costume. I toss the journal down onto my dressing table.

I consider myself in the full-length mirror, admiring my new dress, cerulean blue with smart navy bows down the middle.

"I rather like this one, but I'm not sure of this white collar," I say to my dressmaker, Mrs Shelby. I tilt my head to the side, cover the collar with my hand. "Is it too late to have it removed?"

"Of course not, madam."

My face relaxes back into a smile. "Good. Help me out of it and you can take it back with you. What was your other idea again, Mrs Shelby?"

She struggles up from where she's kneeling. "There. That hem should do it." Her chubby face is red from the exertion, and she's a little puffed. "I was saying we should increase the number of flounces on your dresses. Use lace to make them frilly."

Flicking again through the pictures in the journal, I note the neatness of the gowns, the severe lines despite the billowing skirts. Of course, the evening gowns are more embellished, but maybe Mrs Shelby is right — maybe my day dresses could be prettified too. I picture myself riding in the park, in a dress like spun sugar, despite the dirt and pollution. Yes. And what would it matter if the dress became filthy after one wear? Hatterleigh would pay for more. It'll be amusing to see who has the funds to keep up with me.

Mrs Shelby helps me get dressed again and then gathers up her sewing basket and gowns. As she leaves the room, my gaze jags on the letter that lies upon my bed. I unfold it to read again. A reply from Pidgeon. He writes of his shock at Lovejoy's death, and of how he will meet with Hunt and Cosgrove to discuss this threat that presses upon them.

Clearly he is in accordance with the reporters and thinks the cases are all connected.

The sound of male voices rises to the second floor. By the time I reach the top of the stairs, I only catch a glimpse of Bundle's back as he ushers someone into the drawing room. When he returns, he looks up at me, says, "Sir Thomas, Mrs Chancey. With an Inspector Hatch."

I pull a face at him, and smooth my hair back from my forehead as I step down the stairs. An inspector. What does he want with me?

"Ah, Mrs Chancey." Sir Thomas takes my hand in his. "How wonderful to see you again. Please, let me introduce Inspector Hatch, here."

Hatch shakes my hand. "Detective Inspector," he corrects Sir Thomas. His voice is low, serious, but a pleasant smile hovers about his lips. He's a very pale man, and his side whiskers, as coarse as straw, are almost as impressive as Sir Thomas's. The cloth of his suit is of good quality, but worn, and the leather of his boots has been polished, yet does not shine. He's much taller than Sir Thomas but seems at ease in my drawing room, so much so that he ushers us to the sofas, asks us to sit around the table where Bundle sets out glasses of sherry. It's like he's the bloody host. I tuck my grin away for later.

Hatch plucks his trousers at the knees and takes a seat himself, opposite us.

"Mrs Chancey, Sir Thomas here says that you might be able to assist me in a case."

I sit straighter. "What kind of case, sir?"

Hatch sits with his legs wide and, for a moment, he frowns and leans forward, elbows resting on his knees. "Have you been following the Lovejoy murders in the papers, madam?"

I sit back, bewildered. "Of course." Do I mention that I met the man himself just two days ago? Or no?

"Tell me. What do you know about the affair?"

"What I've read in *The Times*." I look from Hatch to Sir Thomas. "About the poor girl murdered in the lavatory. Her throat was cut." My hand finds its way to my own throat. "And then her father was murdered yesterday. In the same manner." I don't know whether to tell him of what I know. Of what Pidgeon and Cosgrove have discussed.

Hatch leans back and nods. "Yes. Well, we have our suspicions on what might have gone on, but we have yet to prove anything." He takes a notebook from his breast pocket and stares at it absent-mindedly. "The thing is, for a number of reasons, we were quite sure we knew who'd murdered Margaret Lovejoy, but then her father was killed. His murder has given me pause in my suspicions."

"Who did you suspect?"

"The nursemaid."

"The nursemaid?"

"Mmm. Nurse Marie Brown." The Detective Inspector's mouth makes an almost girlish pucker with the noise. "Yes. She shared a room with Margaret and the younger child. And Margaret's bed was not slept upon. It seemed obvious, really."

"But why would she murder the little girl? A girl in her care?" I ask, incredulous.

"Exactly what I wondered. In fact, just before we found out about Lovejoy's death, I'd sent two constables to pick the nursemaid up for further interviewing. When I first spoke to her, I could tell she was keeping something from me."

"Was there anyone else you suspected, Hatch?" asks Sir Thomas.

He shakes his head, but frowns. "Not really. But now I wonder . . ."

"Tell us of the others in the Lovejoy household."

"Well, there's Mrs Lovejoy, of course. She's Lovejoy's second wife. And there's Emily — she's fifteen years old — and Joshua, who's sixteen years old, I believe. They're Lovejoy's children to his first wife. There is also Cyril — the second Mrs Lovejoy's child, you understand — maybe three or four years old, who is in the care of the nursemaid. Of course, there are the servants, but I've counted them out by reason of alibis or lack of motive."

"And you don't believe the nursemaid guilty any longer?" I ask.

"No. No, I'm no longer totally convinced, Mrs Chancey."

"Do you think an outsider is to blame?" I ask. It looks like Pidgeon and Cosgrove might be right after all.

"Oh, no. I think it's definitely an inside job. I think the jimmied drawing room door was just a ruse. I think someone in the house definitely committed these murders."

"I have to be frank with you, Detective Inspector." I decide the only thing I can do is tell him of what I know. Sound him out. If I'm to help him in this case, he needs to know all the facts. "I happened to meet Lovejoy just a couple of days ago. He was with a good friend of mine and they were incredibly worried about some threatening letters they'd received. Something to do with their time in Sarawak? And a Chinese gang? They believed that a man named McBride and Margaret Lovejoy were murdered in revenge."

The Detective Inspector is still frowning, but smiles at me too, like I'm a gullible child that's disappointed him. "Of course I've heard all this before. Both Mr Lovejoy and Pidgeon have told me of this fantasy of theirs. You must see how ludicrous it is, Mrs Chancey." He looks from me to Sir Thomas, like he's questioning Sir Thomas's wisdom in bringing him to me. "Another detective, a very sensible fellow, is following up on the McBride murder. I do not have time to be distracted by such things, like the reporters — who may as well be men of fiction — who wait outside your home at this very moment."

He leans towards me again, and his eyes gleam like a terrier set on a rat. "Mrs Chancey, I will share with you why I think the Lovejoy murders are domestic." He holds up a finger. "One. The guard dog — and I've been assured it's quite vicious — was roaming the garden in each instance. That surely counts out a stranger." He holds up another finger. "Two. How on earth did an intruder break in through the drawing room, pass numerous servants and family members to steal away one little girl? The logistics are preposterous, in fact. And Three." He pauses, his three fingers rapping the tabletop. "According to the linen list, the cook's wrapper is missing. I believe this wrapper — which was something like a dressing gown, with long sleeves, mind you, and a skirt low to the floor — has been discarded because someone was wearing it when they murdered Margaret Lovejoy and it was covered in the girl's blood."

"You don't think the cook did it?" asks Sir Thomas.

"No. She stayed at her brother's house that night. And, really, why would she? But anyone, especially the nursemaid, with her comings and goings to the kitchen and servants' quarters, could have requisitioned it for the evening."

"The household seems to be mostly full of women-folk," I say. "Would a female be capable of Lovejoy's murder?"

Hatch's face is stern as he says, "With a sharp enough knife, or razor even, a child could have sliced Lovejoy's throat, let alone the girl's. And the women to be found in that household are robust, believe me. We've had any number of letters from the public accusing the men who found the body, but I just do not believe the Lovejoys' drunkard gardener found his way into the house, let alone the night-soil man."

I take a sip of my sherry. Really, he does sound quite convincing. His story is surely more plausible than that of Chinese marauders seeking vengeance in London?

"In what capacity would I assist?" I ask.

"I'd like you to go into the household, find out what mysteries lie abed, secrets I cannot unearth myself. Apparently Mrs Lovejoy doesn't wholly trust the children with the nursemaid anymore, so I've decided the best thing is if you can go in as the interim nursemaid. We've arranged the paperwork with the agency already."

I feel a sense of dread creep upon me. I'd been very tempted up to this point. I pick up the decanter on the table between us to pour more sherry as an excuse to think on Hatch's offer. Nanny? To someone else's children? Hadn't I chosen this life, as precarious and improper as it might be, in order to avoid the drudgery of the nursery room?

"Of course, your position as nursemaid will just be a smokescreen. Really you will be there as my spy." Hatch catches my eye on the word "spy" as I hand him his sherry. A spy. Like Eleanor in Braddon's novel, or Fouché's spies they once whispered of in Paris. For a moment, Hatch has succeeded in making the work sound exciting, perilous even, but really . . . it will be a toil.

A sharp rap on the front door catches my attention and I approach the window to see who it might be. Another reporter by the looks of it. There are now four carriages parked on our narrow street. Bastards. I roll my eyes. It won't help matters that they've seen a police detective enter my house.

Rubbing my tongue across that tiny chip in my front tooth, I look over my shoulder to the others. Sir Thomas's eyebrows are raised, waiting for my answer, but I can tell from his bland expression he's not fussed whether I take the work or not. Hatch, on the other hand, nods his head once at me, as if urging on a child in a running race.

Glancing back out the window, I realise that if I am to take Hatch up on his offer, at least I'd be away from the attention of these newspaper men. Although, no doubt the Lovejoys' home is surrounded by reporters as well. And, anyway, it cannot be. I'm to see Hatterleigh tonight, in any case, and my new lilac gown is waiting for me upstairs. Hatterleigh's also promised to take me to Brighton early next week, so I just won't be available.

"I'm very sorry to have wasted your time," I say, finally, turning back to the men. "Unfortunately, I really am not able to help you in this case, at this time." As I say the words, I feel a twinge of regret. Maybe I'm missing out on an adventure. "But I can suggest someone else for the role."

The cab drops me at an address in Tottenham Court Road, where the shopfront's window is emblazoned with the words *Bower's Servants' Registry Office*.

The offices themselves are very plain. Prospective domestic servants form a long line along the unpolished timber flooring, while others lounge upon wooden benches that hug the walls. There's nothing for it — I have to wait in line too. The man in front of me turns to the side and blows his nose into his lapel, while two women near the top of the queue quarrel loudly about who's more suited to a scullery position. I wish I'd sent Taff or even Abigail on this errand.

I wonder how Bundle had hired Abigail. Through the newspaper, through an agency such as this? Or had she approached us? I glance at the sheets of paper pasted to the wall beside me, and note the neat copperplate handwriting and sketched likenesses.

106

"Lists, they be," whispers the woman behind me. I turn to her and smile. Not a woman, after all. I don't think she could be a day over twelve years old really. "Black list of all them who've been bad servants."

I'm surprised. I look again at the poster nearest to me and read, *Max Brownley. Formerly of service at the Hare and Rabbit Inn. Roughly five foot, eight inches. Brown hair, beard, missing little finger, left hand. Stole barrel of rum, one turkey and a guest's pair of riding boots.* And then, *Paulie Sawyer, also known as Pete Sawyer. Dark hair, considered handsome. Takes liberties with young ladies of the house.* Next to this statement is a penned likeness, in which he doesn't look that handsome at all. Under this is, *Fiona Lucy Coyne. Roughly five foot, ten inches. Brown hair, smallpox scars. Extremely rude, lives above her station. Lazy.* Well. Good on her.

These lists remind me of the directory that used to be available in London, that recorded the particular charms of each fancy bird. I'm glad it's not around anymore. I don't need my "ruby tips" and "pleasing grove" described to all the leering pigs in town.

By the time I reach the stout woman at the front desk, my feet feel pinched in my new shoes, and I've received numerous looks from women staring balefully at my taffeta gown.

"What kind of position are you applying for?" the woman asks as she looks up from her ledger. She's short-sighted and narrows her eyes to peer doubtfully at my smart hat, and the onyx and emerald earrings that hang from my earlobes. "I apologise madam. I mistook you. Usually our clientele write to us of what servants they need and we send them a selection. How may I help you?"

"I was after one Bethany Bird. I've heard she's an excellent nursemaid. I was directed here."

"Excuse me a moment, madam. I will just enquire." She waddles to the back of the office and pulls a drawer out from a filing cabinet. After a search that only lasts a matter of moments, she returns to me, reading from a card in her hand. "Wet nurse. Has been in a new position for three months so far. I'm sorry, it seems you've missed out on her." Her eyes move to my stomach, trying to gauge how many months I might be.

I glance at the card that lies slack in her hand on the counter. An address in Finsbury. Simple.

CHAPTER
THIRTEEN

"What do you think, Heloise?" Hatterleigh asks.

It's quite late in the evening; an evening I'd expected to enjoy. Yet, I have to force a smile. I can't get drunk quick enough.

Instead of Motts, Hatterleigh has brought me to the top of Haymarket to a dance hall he has heard of. We had to walk past numerous oyster shops and gin palaces until we found the bar he was after. The shopfront was plain enough, covered in black curtaining, a cold fowl perched on a platter in the window. Squeezing past men squatted in the gutter and women dancing the polka on the pavement, their eyes bright from cheap brandy, I almost had to shield my eyes from the glare of gaslight that greeted us as we entered the smoky room.

"I heard a couple of fellows talking about this place at the Billinghams' ball the other night," he shouts to me over the din from the brass band in the corner of the room.

I take two more gulps of my gin and water. My elbow's jostled by a shrieking woman as she's carried to the dance floor by two men, and some of my drink slops down the front of my new gown. My mouth twists

109

to the side, like Amah's does. I polish off the rest of my gin.

Hatterleigh orders me another drink and then stands close, his toe tapping to the music, his hand warm on my back. He's rarely so intimate with me in public. He's watching the crowd bob and weave around us with a smile, and his nose is already turning puce from the cognac he has secreted in his coat pocket. He won't drink the common brandy they serve here — says it's ruinous to one's health.

And I realise something. While I am with Hatterleigh in order to experience the more refined side of life, he is with me in order to transgress the dark. What irks me about these evenings is that I feel familiar, almost comfortable, in these surroundings, yet soiled at the same time.

The sound of a drum roll barrels across the room, silencing the musicians and even hushing most of the clientele. A man snatches off his top hat and waves it in the air, whooping, while two pretty ladybirds near me clap their hands and balance on their toes. Everyone is straining to see the back of the room.

Four women, dressed in ivory frills and silk petticoats, take to the stage. They laugh and bow to the crowd, turn to the men of the band, the closest one indicating with a wave of her hand that it's time to begin. Without further preamble, the tune bounds upon the air, a rat-tat of feverish melody. The women heave up their skirts, exposing their lean, long legs encased in black stockings. The higher they lift their petticoats, the more milky thigh can be seen above the stockings. They sashay a slippered foot to the right, then to the left. They bow low, poking their pert bottoms to the back of the stage, and the crowd roar and clap with approval.

I haven't seen cancan dancers since Paris. I squeeze through the crowd so I can watch them more closely, craning up onto my tiptoes to see the women swish and twirl across the stage. If there is one thing I wish I'd learnt at a young age, it's dancing, so I too could have been a cancan dancer in some Parisian bistro.

The women sail across the stage, peeling back their chemises to shouts of delight from the audience, revealing pert breasts. A man steps in front of me, and I'm crammed in on either side, so I can only really see the dancer on the end, a tall woman with Titian hair. With each hop, the huge ostrich feathers that embellish her hat bounce in time with her full breasts.

The dancers link arms and, with a swivel of their hips, they kick their legs up in unison, and I can feel my eyes widen, even as a woman behind me gasps. I push forward, and then, yes, mid-kick, I see that I wasn't imagining it — a sliver of red hair flashes at me from between her legs. Confirming their scandalous behaviour, the dancers turn and flip their skirts up to show their bare arses, finishing on an almost deafening crescendo of music. I turn my head and search the crowd for Hatterleigh, and when I catch his eye, I grin. He smiles back at me, salutes me with his hip flask.

Later, in my bedroom, I stand facing the warmth of the fireplace. I've shed my crinoline and gown, and I reach my fingertips down and draw my slip up over my thighs, feel the silk feather against my skin. I pause a moment, my slip ruched above my hips, bend forward as if inspecting a blemish on the shiny skin of my shin. I know Hatterleigh's eyes are on my behind, which I jut out a little, wondering if beneath the apple shape of my bottom he can see some of the core.

I let my slip fall to the floor, but keep on my chemise. The linen is almost translucent, and it's open at the front so that with each movement my breasts sway, allowing him a fleeting glimpse. I reach for a large tome I've left ready on the mantelpiece and take a seat next to him on the chaise longue. I swing my legs over his, nuzzle closer so that my naked quim presses against his thigh. He puts his arm around me, his thumb caressing my back, and asks me what's in the book.

I open it against my bare thighs and peel back its pages until I come to a gouache print. "A friend of mine sent me these little paintings from India. I keep them safe in the pages of this book." I lift the picture away from the pages so Hatterleigh can see it better. The paper is fine and brittle, the fresh colours painted upon it giving it weight. Pretty branches with pink buds reach across a wall the colour of lemon, and a hill, celadon green, rests in the background. In the foreground is a man, dark and bejewelled, who stares ahead, while one of his hands holds a naked woman by the waist, her legs parted over his thigh while the fingers of his other hand toy with her nipple. The woman is arched all the way back until her hands and long black hair reach the ground, in ecstasy, in supplication.

112

"This is a painting depicting the secret pleasures of a famous prince, apparently." I let Hatterleigh look at the print a little longer before tucking it back into the pages of the book. "My friend is translating a Hindu text. A book of love."

I flip through to the next print. A woman reclines on cushions, clothed in a little yellow top and a full red skirt, below which her naked limbs are spread, revealing her neat *chatte*. The prince is poised above her. He has a cloth crown on his head and wears a smart jacket, but he's without trousers, so that the hood of his long prick is poised against her.

We laugh at the next one, of a naked couple, he on his back, she balanced above him facing his toes. She has gold bands around her upper arms, and pretty necklaces around her neck and a nose ring. I turn the picture over. The artist has scrawled the words, *The Wheel*, on the back.

As I leaf through the book for the next print, Hatterleigh's hand snakes inside the opening of my chemise. He cups my breast, strokes its curve. His thumb rubs my nipple in small swirls, presses its tip. I can feel a loosening in my limbs, between my legs.

"Oh my. I don't think I could do this one," I say, peering closely at the picture before us. She's facing away from him, so he has full access to her breasts, which I like, but her legs are curled right up behind him, tucked beneath his bent legs where he crouches behind her.

"Yes, you would have to be quite the little circus acrobat to perform some of these postures," he says. He waits for me to find the next one and his eyes trace the position of a couple joined together on a plush carpet, her leg slung over his shoulder.

"*Split Bamboo*," I read from the bottom of the picture. I pull at the top of his trousers, feel my way to his cock. He's hard, becomes more erect the more I stroke.

"This is the one, I think, that we can try." The woman rests back on a sofa. The prince has his arms about her as he presses his way in between her legs, which are hooked over the crooks of his arms. Her breasts are high and firm as he leans into her. "It's called *The Flower*."

Hatterleigh kneels onto the floor and I straddle him. He brushes back my chemise with his lips and takes my breast in his mouth. He nudges his cock into me and I gaze at the picture of the woman, the flower, who's draped in chains of gold, who stares patiently into the distance.

His arm weighs heavy across my belly and I fling it off, playfully. "Too sweaty." We've made our way to my bed. My limbs feel syrupy, and my mind billows close to sleep.

I roll onto my side towards him. "When will we leave for Brighton?" I murmur against his arm, and then peck his skin with a kiss. I love going to Brighton. The restaurants, the sea, the people. And Hatterleigh's always a bit more relaxed there too. It's our place.

"Ah, yes, about that . . ." He takes my hand and presses a kiss into my palm. "I don't think I can make it

114

after all. Why don't you ask Isobel or that Milly lass to accompany you?"

I open my eyes. "Why can't you come?"

"My wife. She's been confined. I've had word that I really should head back into the country as soon as possible."

My insides frost over like a pond's surface chilling to ice. Although I want to snatch my hand from his, I will my body to stay relaxed. "How domestic," I drawl. I smile so that my voice is light too. "God, how many brats is that now? Four? Five?"

I know it's three.

He laughs. "I'm not a rabbit."

I stay pressed against him for a count of thirty seconds. Then I roll onto my back. I fling my arm over my eyes, like I'm preparing for sleep, but my stomach has that terrible tightness I get when I'm irritated. I hate little reminders like this that our relationship is merely a fleeting amusement for Hatterleigh. I feel that familiar pang of jealousy when I think of his wife. Not that I'm envious of their marriage, but it just makes me want to grit my teeth when I think of how easy her life has been, and always will be. I bet she's never had to sponge her fanny clean from a bucket that's already been used by numerous others; or been so hungry she's eaten someone else's leftovers. And I sure as hell know she's never had to worry about money or about what will become of her in old age.

Which is all absolutely ridiculous, because I have accrued enough wealth to not have to worry either, and I don't want to be tied down to one blasted man anyway. If I really wanted Hatterleigh to stay by my side, I'm positive I could do it. I could! And not in a sneaky way, like that Tracey Greenfield who trapped Sir Neville with her belly full of arms and legs. I turn onto my side away from him and stare into the shadows. Not that that's an option for me, anyway.

Don't be such a sook, I chastise myself as I sit up and swing my legs off the bed.

"Where are you going?" He tries to catch my hand but I snatch it away with a bright smile.

"I have to take these pins out of my hair, or else they'll stab my head all night and I won't be able to sleep."

I drape a linen cloth across the plush seat of my dressing-table stool because I'm damp between the legs. I can see Hatterleigh in the reflection of the mirror as he plumps up the pillows behind himself and sits up against the bedhead.

My skin glistens in the lamplight and I can feel his eyes on my naked back as I pull my hair loose. I think of when I saw Bethany Bird earlier in the afternoon, after I'd tracked her down in Finsbury. She really did look happy as she fed that fat little baby. It was many years ago we were tails together, but when Bethany had become pregnant, she'd been talked into a life of good by the missionary who took her in. She wasn't allowed to keep her child, but she managed to find a new vocation as a nursemaid. And sometimes, between engagements, she helped me out with Sir Thomas's cases.

"But how do you still have milk, Beth? Have you had another child?" I watched the baby's pink lips suck at her nipple and knead her full breast with its plump fist.

She laughed at me as she rocked in the wooden chair by the kitchen fire. Apart from her snaggled bottom teeth, she looked like a Raphael Madonna. Always did. Sometimes that's exactly what the punters liked, especially those bastard God-bothering ones. "No, Heloise. But by keeping up this work, near babies, I can keep my milk in stock."

"But when you're away from babies?"

"Well then I have to milk myself. Something like a cow. It's nothing different from a Charlie giving them a good tug, though," she whispered to me, looking around to make sure the other servants couldn't overhear.

"So you can take on the Lovejoy position, after all?" I urged her. "The money is good, Beth. Probably the same as you'd make here in six months."

She looked doubtful. "But I like my place here, Heloise. I'm not sure I'm up to a bit of your carousing for Sir Thomas again. I nearly lost my hair that last time we tricked those fellows at that dance hall."

I cast my mind back. Ah, that's right. The amorous adventures of a gentleman we were watching on behalf of his wife. He'd become suspicious, and drunkenly fallen upon Bethany, ripping the wig from her head, along with a substantial amount of her hair. I pulled a face. "Well, it grew back, didn't it?" I teased.

I badgered her until she capitulated, and she promised that in the morning she would tell her mistress that her mother had become terribly ill and that she had to return to her home for a week.

But now, as I stare into the mirror, I think about how this is no longer necessary. I'll send Taff around first thing, to deliver Beth the message that she will not be needed at the Lovejoys' anymore. I will go.

Let Hatterleigh gallivant off into the countryside to be by his stupid wife's side. I might as well keep busy with what I enjoy.

I brush my hair, and with each stroke my breasts lift and jiggle. I catch Hatterleigh's eye as he watches. "That actually works out well, you going into Yorkshire. Sir Thomas came by today and offered me some interesting work. I won't need to turn him down, after all."

Hatterleigh frowns. "What work?"

"Oh, didn't I tell you? He came around here earlier today with the Detective Inspector who's investigating the Lovejoy murders. They want my help."

Hatterleigh's frown deepens. "But that's absurd. You'd be better to take one of your friends to Brighton."

I pout as I braid my hair into a loose plait. "No. That sounds just too boring. I will definitely take up Sir Thomas's offer."

Hatterleigh climbs out of bed and pulls on his trousers. My lips curl into a slight smile. He doesn't want to argue without his breeches on.

"But, Heloise, dear, there's a murderer at work. It will be far more dangerous than you are used to."

I twist in my chair and stare at him. What the hell does he know of what I'm used to? But then, I am a bit mollified that he's worried about my welfare too.

118

"And what do they expect you to do?" He sits down on the side of the bed again to pull on his shirt.

"I'm to pose as the nursemaid."

Hatterleigh's eyebrows could not rise any higher. "Nursemaid! No, Heloise. I forbid it. I can't have you doing menial work in another gentleman's house. What if people were to find out?"

I glare at him for a couple of seconds, then turn slowly back to the mirror. So, being in the vicinity of a murderer is slightly worrying, but the fact that I'll be posing as a servant seriously offends his senses. The sooner he rushes to his damned wife's side, the better.

I dab some cream across my face and rub it vigorously into my skin. "Sir, you needn't worry about your name or my welfare. I have always, and will always, take fine care of both."

CHAPTER
FOURTEEN

Squeezing through the omnibus door, I wonder if this is going to be the first of many times I regret taking on this case. If only I hadn't bloody quarrelled with Hatterleigh! But Hatch was right. The new nursemaid cannot be seen to arrive in a hansom cab or, heaven forbid, her own carriage.

I wedge myself between a pretty mother who has a little boy dressed top to toe in royal blue velvet draped across her lap, and a young man whose top hat is so tall it almost brushes the ceiling. Luckily my skirts are not as voluminous as usual, as I've dressed more in accordance with what is due of a nursemaid. I think.

As the omnibus trundles along, I can only see outside through the window behind the old woman seated opposite me. The window has been reduced to a sliver of glass because it's pasted over with advertisements for silverware, whisky, matches. With each sway of the coach, the old lady's basket inches across the floor against my toes and a peculiar stench wafts from her red coat. I spear her basket with my umbrella and nudge it back towards her.

I curse Hatterleigh again. I'd much rather be at home, or shopping for ribbons and pretty knick-knacks.

I'd especially prefer to be in Brighton. Maybe I should've just gone there with Milly or Isobel after all. I cross my arms and stare balefully ahead as two more passengers cram themselves amongst us.

Last night, Hatterleigh left in a bit of a humph, but it's not the first time, or last, we've had words. He'll be back.

But Amah . . . my hands drop to my lap and I fiddle with the seams of my gloves as I think of her. She's so preoccupied with something, I don't know what. She's been staying out til late, forgets to dress my hair, and she didn't even make one rude remark about my purple dress. When I'd told her of this latest caper, I'd expected her to cavil, perhaps be a little scornful, as she usually is. However, she'd just paused in her embroidery, and nodded slowly. "That might be best."

As she helped me pack a small valise, I asked her, "Why do you say that? That it might be for the best?"

She folded my Spanish shawl — although made from the finest wool, it's of a sober hue, suited to a nanny — over and over until it was a tight little square. "I wonder if it might be a bit unsafe here, after . . . you know . . ."

"You mean McBride's death?"

She nodded as her hand hovered, undecided, over my glove drawer.

Maybe she didn't hear me properly before. "But, Amah, I'm going to the Lovejoys' house. Where there have been *two* murders."

She sucked her tongue against her teeth, waved her hand. "I have a feeling whoever is doing this murdering, is finished with that household." Placing

121

two warm nightdresses onto the bed, she asked, "How will you explain your presence there?"

"I'm to be the new nursemaid."

Amah gaped at me, her eyes almost as round as when she's furious. And then she'd laughed, holding her sides, until she was reduced to a series of coughs. "You're going to look after children?"

Even now, I smile at the memory. I mean, at the time I pretended to be offended at her mockery, but really, I can see why she was so amused. It is laughable. Heloise Chancey, *paon de nuit*, reduced to wiping the nose of a brat named Cyril.

"Your stop, miss," calls the conductor from behind the coach as it lurches to a halt. "Stoke Newington. Just before the toll gate, we are, just like you said."

As he pulls free my valise, I ask, "Which direction is Lordship Road?"

He nods to the road that branches from the one we are standing on. "That's it there, miss."

I walk towards the street, lugging that heavy valise so that it bumps against my skirts with each step, making my crinoline swing like a pendulum. The air is so cold my breath puffs out before me, reminding me of how much I'd savour a cigarette.

The dwellings along Lordship Rd are more spacious than what I am used to seeing so close into town. Large houses, slick with modernity, are surrounded by expansive gardens peppered with oak and elm trees.

"Excuse me." I stop by a woman who holds a tray of puddings slung from her neck. Her apron is filthy, and she has a jaunty ostrich feather sticking out from her bonnet. "Can you direct me to St Chad's Lodge?"

"Over there, it be," she says, pointing down the road, to the right. "The house near the corner, under that there walnut tree."

I thank her and walk in the direction she's indicated. Along the left-hand side of the road, new terrace houses are going up and, as I pass a group of four men who are puffing away on their pipes as they stir up barrows of cement, I hear a low whistle. I act as though I didn't hear it, but not before I see one of them murmur something to the others with a smirk.

As I walk, I can feel their eyes inch across my body. Somehow it doesn't feel the same as when I ride in the park. The spectators who line the park lanes to watch me are there to enjoy themselves, and I'm displaying my plumage for their admiration. I've crafted the artifice. It's a performance. Here, I'm just walking, damn it. Times like this . . . it feels different. It slithers under my skin, trembles there self-consciously, reminds me of a dark night long ago.

Usually my reaction depends on my mood. In a good humour, I'll be jaunty, say thank you, catch their eye with my bold one. I'll be just disdainful enough that usually their gaze will drop away. But if I'm cranky, I've been known to do worse.

But here I'm posing as a local nanny. It might be necessary to pass them, again and again. So, no rude gestures.

Finally, I come to stand outside the Lovejoy house. Two coaches are parked by the side of the road, the horses languid, their heads dipped. A gaggle of reporters — five or six maybe — stand around under a large oak, stomping their feet against the cold. When they see me hovering, they make a start across the road and call out, but I duck through the gate, trot down the front path. St Chad's Lodge is a handsome house with a pillared front door and a fine arched window above it on the second floor. I almost approach the front door, but remember my station and move to the back. I tap at the servants' door and, upon no response, I rap on it louder. A thin woman, wearing a mob cap and apron, opens the door.

"Yes?"

"I'm the new nursemaid."

"Oh, yes, yes. The missus said you was coming. I'm the cook." Many of her teeth are missing so that her bottom jaw appears to be not unlike a piano keyboard. She stands back against the wall to allow me to enter. "I'll just let the missus know." She hurries before me down the hallway, calling out to someone named Ruth. "Hurry up and tell Mrs Lovejoy that the new nursemaid has come."

As we reach the kitchen, a girl, slight with a mop of curly hair, pops her head around the doorway. Her shy eyes sweep over me and she gulps a "Yes, Cook," and scuttles away.

"Poor Ruth has so much to do now. And the missus. We used to have a housekeeper, we did, but she left soon after . . . Well. I'll make you a cup of tea, shall I? You must be thirsty. How far did you have to come, dear?" The cook sets about the stove-top, without really

124

needing an answer from me. "I've made a lovey batch of scones too. But we won't eat them until the family have had their fill first. I was going to make a second batch, just for us, but . . ."

"That will do, Cook," says a deep voice from the hallway. "I'll see to the new nursemaid from here."

The voice belongs to a tall woman, dressed all in black, from the netting over her hair to the ribboned hem of her skirt. She's heavyset yet handsome, and her thick eyebrows are so straight and long they almost meet in the middle. It's only when she turns to the side that I realise that her skirts billow wide because she is with child.

She beckons to me. "What do we call you?" she asks as she leads the way.

"Louise, madam." We pause in the draughty entrance hall, from which four rooms open. "Louise Casey." I look to the back of the house and wonder which of the two rooms is the drawing room — the room that had its doors jimmied open, and where Lovejoy had found the note.

"We will call you Nurse Louise then, if that suits." She nods to the rooms on each side of us at the front of the house. "That is the sitting room, where the family usually gathers, and this one here is . . . was Mr Lovejoy's study." She swallows and purses her lips tight for a moment. Now that I am closer to her, I can see that the rims of her eyes are as red as raw beef, that her eyelids are puffy. "Please pay attention. There are thirteen rooms in this house, and I won't have time to repeat all of this to you." Pointing to the back of the house, she says, "That room there to the right is the dining room, and there to the left is the drawing room where we entertain guests. However, as there is plenty of space in the nursery, it will not be necessary for you to use any of these rooms down here."

"Yes, madam," I say. I nearly bob a curtsy but stop myself in time.

Lifting her skirts, Mrs Lovejoy climbs the stairs, slowly, as though a great weight pulls her back. "I'll show you upstairs."

"Was this house once a church?" I ask, as my hand runs across the smooth timber of the handrail. "St Chad's?"

"No. It's the name of the cathedral in the town my husband . . . my late husband, was born in."

Once we reach the landing, she points to the end of the hallway at the left side of the house. "My rooms." Turning to the right, she says, "The children's rooms are here. At the end there is Joshua's room — he's a young man now, you won't be called upon to care for him — and next to his room, there, is Emily's."

"Do I care for her, madam?"

Mrs Lovejoy stares at me for so long I wonder if she's confused. But then, as she exhales, I smell the spirits on her breath. Gin? Brandy? Something stronger than mere sherry or ratafia, in any case.

She turns and goes to Emily's door and knocks. "Emily. Emily, the new nursemaid is here. Can you please come out and meet her?"

I hear something shift behind the door, but the girl doesn't reply or come to the door.

Mrs Lovejoy sighs. "She never listens to me. Their mother was Mr Lovejoy's first wife, you know. Emily is just turned fifteen, so she should be under your care too, but I fear she might be difficult to persuade." She walks past me and opens the door to the room across the corridor. "And this is the nursery."

The room is richly appointed, with crisp new wallpaper featuring small posies of flowers, while the curtains that cover the three sets of windows are of a more concentrated floral pattern. Any number of expensive toys are scattered across the Wilton carpet. A crib stands by the middle window, silk brocade draped prettily over its sides. Three dolls lie side by side in the crib, staring stonily at the ceiling.

Mrs Lovejoy moves to another door, tucked behind a set of table and chairs. She opens it slowly to reveal a plain room with three single beds arranged against the walls.

"This is where you will sleep." Her stern face relaxes. She must've been truly beautiful, once. "And this is Cyril. He's having his afternoon nap."

I gaze at the little thing — at the long, long lashes that rest against his flushed cheeks, at how his blond hair catches the light, turns to gold. Really, how much trouble can a sweet little mite like this give me?

Mrs Lovejoy closes the door again and looks me over. "Well, you appear to be neat enough, so I don't suppose I'll need to order more nurse uniforms, after all. Are all your dresses like that one?"

"Yes, madam. I have brought two more with me."

Her eyebrows rise. "So many? Good enough. Please keep a list of your linen, so it doesn't go missing with the laundry. Our laundry woman sometimes misplaces things." She frowns for a moment, her hand resting on the nursery door. Maybe she is thinking of the missing wrapper. Maybe she wonders if it's drenched in her daughter's blood.

"What are Master Cyril's movements? Does he need to follow a strict routine?" I ask.

Her dark eyes find mine again. The cold expression returns to her face. "Nurse Marie will tell you what you need to know."

"But . . . where will I find her, madam?" I thought she'd been dismissed.

"She is staying in the housekeeper's room for the time being. She will help you with the children, but you must always keep an eye on her." Her voice drags on the last few words.

CHAPTER
FIFTEEN

"Where can I find Nurse Marie?" I ask Cook, as Cyril, the little beast, wails and squirms in my arms.

"She's just behind the kitchen, to your left. In old Mrs Forbes's room, she is." The cook holds my elbow for a second and says, "Let herself go, she has, poor thing. Ever since . . . well. I'll bring you both a nice cup of tea."

I carry the boy to where Cook points and, although I try to knock lightly, Cyril boots the door, then howls even louder that he's hurt his toes.

The door swings open. A sallow young woman holds her arms out to the boy, folds his plump little body to hers. She buries her face into his neck, her bony fingers squeezing his shoulders.

I think she might be crying, from the grimace on her face, but when she opens her eyes again, they're dry. "Cyril, turtle dove, why all this noise?" she coos to him, wiping the sweaty locks from his forehead. She takes a seat by the bed, settles him onto her lap.

"Her!" he says, one stubby finger pointing at me. "Her. I thought her a monster."

"Well, that's hardly fair," I say, my hands on my waist. "All I wanted to do was get you dressed into a warm jacket so you didn't freeze to death."

"She wouldn't sing me a song," he whispers to Nurse Marie, his beady blue eyes on me.

I take a seat on the bed. "I only sing songs for good boys."

He looks like he might take the bait, but then plugs his thumb into his mouth and leans back against Nurse Marie's chest.

"I'm the new nursemaid, in case you haven't guessed." I smile at Marie, to show I'm friendly, that I'm not here to trump anyone.

She doesn't reply. She looks exhausted. Her wide mouth droops, and her fringe is so long, strands teeter upon her eyelashes. There are dark smudges beneath her eyes, which are as red as Mrs Lovejoy's. I wonder if her dress — grey with a navy pinstripe — is the uniform Mrs Lovejoy spoke of. The cuffs are a little frayed and one of the faux tortoiseshell buttons is missing from her bodice.

The air is chilly, for there's no fireplace in here, and I wish I had my shawl. Nurse Marie doesn't seem to notice, though, as she pats Cyril's small hand.

Cook rustles in with two cups of tea, which she places on a small side table. Balanced on the saucers' rims are slabs of butter cake. Cook takes one and gives it to the boy. "And one special piece for Master Cyril."

Cyril scowls at her in lieu of saying thank you.

I take a sip of my tea. "Marie, might you come upstairs and help me? With Cyril? I don't know when he eats or what he does before bedtime?" It certainly looks like she misses the boy. Maybe she can come back to the nursery and resume her work; Mrs Lovejoy seemed happy enough with that. That'll give me a chance to observe her further for the Detective Inspector, and free up my time to do a bit of detecting around the house. And god knows I don't want to be left alone with the little brat for too long.

Cyril twists around in her lap and squeezes the nanny's sunken cheeks with his sticky fingers. "Yes, Nursie. Come upstairs. I don't like her." He leaves cake crumbs smeared on her skin.

After we finish our tea, Nurse Marie carries Cyril up to the nursery. I'm not sure how she does it — her arms are as thin as twigs. They look like they might snap. Surely too frail to overpower a man of Lovejoy's stature.

As we walk along the hallway, I pause to look at the pictures that adorn the walls. Between a painting of two swans in a rococo frame and a portrait of a man standing by a bull is a photograph of the whole family. At the back of the group is the nursemaid, holding the hand of a toddler while cradling the other child in her arms. Mr and Mrs Lovejoy are seated to the fore, two young people behind them, their hands resting on the parents' shoulders. Next on the wall is a large photograph of Mr Lovejoy — those snowy sideburns, the hard eyes — and above that, in a large gilt frame, is a painting of the boy himself, Cyril. Just outside the door to the nursery is a painting of a little girl, who has Cyril's flaxen hair and the pretty eyes of a kitten.

"What a sweet thing," I say. "Who is this?"

Nurse Marie turns slowly towards me, Cyril still clasped to her chest. Her eyes wander over the girl's features and her lip trembles.

"That's Meggie," Cyril says. "Emily said she's gone to heaven to be with Emily's mother."

"Emily? Your sister, Emily?" Half-sister. The daughter of the first Mrs Lovejoy.

Cyril nods. "Meggie wouldn't like you either."

I go to say something acerbic to the boy but catch the reproachful look Nurse Marie gives me.

The next two hours are taken up with the tedium of preparing a child for bed. I watch on, half-hearted in my attempts to help feed and bathe him, which Cyril also seems content with, apart from taking the opportunity to splash soap onto the apron I had the foresight to put on.

"Can you please ask Cook for Cyril's warm milk?" Nurse Marie asks me, as she settles down to read to the boy.

"Of course." I'm glad to escape. I trip down the stairs and make my way to the kitchen, where I ask Cook for the nightcap.

Cook's so busy bustling around the stove as she explains to Ruth how to turn the overripe peaches into chutney that I take the chance to slip back into the corridor. Light pours from the sitting room doorway at the front of the hall, and the gaslight chandelier still shines in the dining room, but to my right the drawing room is shrouded in shadow. There's just sufficient light for me to make out the shape of the furniture as I creep towards the French doors at the back of the room. I want to have a closer look at the jimmied door Hatch mentioned.

As I fiddle with the handle of the first set of doors, my eyes adjust to the gleam of moonlight that shines through the glass. The handle seems to be sturdy enough, as I wrench it up and down. I move onto the second lot of doors. This time I can discern a slight looseness in the handle's swing. I shift to the side to allow for the light from the dining room to illuminate the door and, bending down, I think that maybe I can see scratches in the white paint. I'm just rubbing my fingers against the grooves when the light in the doorway is blocked. Two figures, still and quiet, gaze in at me.

I draw back. "Oh my. You did startle me."

"What are you doing?" The voice is male and quite deep, yet I can tell he's still young.

Well, I've already acted guilty, so I'll pretend to be a goose. I bob a curtsy and say, "I really must apologise. I'm the new nursemaid, Nurse Louise. Maybe your mother has told you of me. I'm just waiting for dear Cyril's milk and, being of a very careful disposition, I really felt it necessary to check that all the doors and windows are secure."

They stand back for me to pass into the hallway.

"You must be Master Joshua and Miss Emily," I say, clapping my hands together. "Your mother has told me of you. She says that I shall have the pleasure of Emily's company in the nursery from time to time."

Although tall, Joshua actually looks younger than his sixteen years. A rather foolish smile is fixed on his moon-face, and his hair is unfashionably straight, flops over his forehead. But his sister is another story. She's almost as tall as he is; I have to look up at her. She's well-padded and her shoulders are broad. Her face is as pasty as a currant bun, with terrible pimples dug deep into her cheeks, several already bursting into white-peaked pustules. The expression on her face is contemptuous. Maybe a little grouchy.

"She's our stepmother," she replies. "And I am too old to need your service. I am perfectly fine in the company of my brother."

Cook calls to me from the kitchen. "Nurse, the milk is ready."

Emily's lip lifts in a sneer. "You'd better fetch up precious Cyril's milk then."

I nod and turn to go, but decide to ask one more thing, see if I can rattle this odd duo. "Those doors in the drawing room. I think I read in the newspaper that it was through them that the . . . um . . . culprit crept into the house?"

They just stare at me, the vacuous smile still on Joshua's face while an angry flush creeps up Emily's thick neck.

CHAPTER
SIXTEEN

"Nurse Marie, Cyril will be fine for the night with Nurse Louise. You may return to the housekeeper's room." Mrs Lovejoy doesn't lighten the words with a smile as she leaves the nursery.

Cyril is fast asleep, tucked up in his bed, looking as deceivingly cherubic as when I first laid eyes on him.

Nurse Marie's eyes lower as she gathers up Cyril's plate and cup to return to the kitchen. I feel a pinch of unease.

"But, Nurse, what if he is to wake in the middle of the night?" I ask her.

She pauses by the door and frowns at me. "Surely you know how to settle a child back to sleep?"

My eyes widen. "Of course I do," I lie. "I just mean because he so obviously adores you, yet has taken an uncommon dislike to me. He will no doubt kick up a ruckus."

She shrugs. "If cuddling and soothing doesn't help, there's some gripe water in the cabinet. That always manages to settle him straight back to sleep."

As she closes the door, I move to the cabinet she'd indicated and inspect what it holds. Behind a brown jar labelled with handwritten instructions and an assortment of pins and ointments, I find the clear glass bottle of Woodward's Gripe Water. Unscrewing the lid, I sniff the contents and smile with surprise. Smells just like the spirituous tipple we girls sipped before a night entertaining the gents. I lift the bottle to my lips and take a small swig. I smack my lips together. "No wonder it sends the little mite straight off to sleep." I replace the medicine and close the cabinet door.

Unlike the housekeeper's room, the nursery has a cheerful fire to keep the cold night air at bay. Leaving the bedroom door ajar so I can hear if the boy stirs, I settle into the armchair by the fireplace and open Darwin's heavy tome I have towed all the way here, tucked amongst my spare clothing. I've been especially keen to read this ever since the others' — well, Cosgrove's really — enthusiasm about it the other night at my house. That night when . . . Suddenly I see Amah's hands covered in blood that darkens at the creases of her fingers. McBride slumped across the steps. Is that how Lovejoy had looked? Head wrenched back at that ungodly angle? And young Margaret, the very first sorry victim?

I press my finger to the page and force myself to focus upon Darwin's response to those who object to his notion of Natural Selection. It only half manages to keep my attention. I gaze at the nursery door where I'd last seen Nurse Marie and I think of how Hatch had her in his sights as the little girl's murderer. Are her tears the effects of guilt? Really? That broken woman, who so obviously adores the objectionable Cyril? I can't picture it.

As I read of imported hive bees supplanting Australian native bees and the missel thrush's ascendency over the song thrush in Scotland, I listen for the sounds of the house bedding itself down for the evening. On the lower level, the servants rattle windows shut, bolt doors with a clack. Mrs Lovejoy retired long ago, and not long after nine o'clock I hear voices in the corridor as Joshua and Emily make their way to their rooms. The floor creaks as they pause outside the closed door of the nursery and their shadows dim the bottom of the doorway. I hold my breath but all I can hear is the crackle of the fire, the distant bark of a dog. My heartbeat quickens. I'm just wondering if I should open the door, ask them if they're in need of something, when they finally move on. One door after the other clicks shut further down the hall. What very unnerving children they are.

By the time the clock down below chimes eleven, the house is quiet. I think everyone has gone to sleep. I wait a half-hour longer, impatiently reading through Darwin's ideas on organisms' struggle for existence, before I place the book on the nursery table and go into the bedroom, where I don a nightgown and a warm dressing gown. It'll be much easier to tip-toe through the house without my wide skirts on. And if someone catches me, I can say I couldn't sleep, that I've come in search of a warm drink. I riffle through my valise for the silk reticule that houses my small pleasures — a silver case containing my rolled cigarettes, a flask of cognac and tissue-wrapped caramels. And there, tucked into a special pocket of the reticule, is my pistol. Glancing across the room, I can see that Cyril is still fast asleep. He's only stirred the once, turning onto his side to face the wall. He'll be fine. I won't be too long.

The nursery has sufficient light from the fireplace, so I decide to take the oil lamp with me. Turning it down low, I carry it into the hallway, first checking both left and right, to make sure all the bedroom doors are shut, that there are no glimmers from underneath. I'm pretty swift on my feet as I move down the stairs. Only one step creaks, five from the top. I'll try to remember that for later.

I move straight to the French doors in the drawing room that I was looking at when I was disturbed by Emily and Joshua earlier. The handle turns but is locked and, yes, I was right, there are scratches on the door jamb. How peculiar. If someone had broken in, the marks would be on the outside. I must see if the door . . .

I stand tall. Was that a creak from the staircase?

I rush into the corridor. I must get myself to the kitchen before I'm caught nosying around. But as I cross the hall, I can't see an answering light making its way down the stairs. I tuck myself behind the kitchen door and wait. The silence feels like it might engulf me and I bite my lip to stop from giggling.

I can't hear a thing.

Peeping into the hallway, I almost jump as that damned clock chimes midnight, each deep peal quivering under my skin. I wait impatiently for the

138

chimes to finish, for the house to settle into silence again. It's time.

I creep down the long corridor towards the servants' door. On the left is the housekeeper's room, and I wonder if Marie is still awake. Either way, she's probably trapped in the same nightmare, poor thing. I assume the last room, narrow and squashed behind the kitchen, might house Cook and Ruth. Pausing, my ear to the door, I'm quite sure I can hear a whistling snore.

I cast around for a hook or ribbon that might hold the key to the back door, but no, like many other households, the housekeeper, master or mistress of the house must have them to hand. Of course, there is no master here anymore, nor housekeeper; maybe Cook is now in charge of them. Not that it matters. I bring out a nail file and special pin that have helped me many times before. Inserting the file into the lock, I hitch it upward, feeling for the bolt. The silver grates so noisily against the lock plate, I waggle the nail file slowly, slowly, until I feel it release the stump. I pause for a moment, can feel sweat beads prickle my upper lip. When I'm sure I haven't disturbed anyone in the house, I insert the pin, turning it in the groove, and push on the spring, until the lock clicks open. Again I pause. Bedsprings squeak in Cook's room. I hold my breath. Nothing. Just the distant tick of the grandfather clock. Turning the handle, I open the door and step outside.

It's a bright, cloudless night. Cold, I shiver and I pull my robe tight across my chest. I place a stone at the door to keep it ajar, and then move swiftly across the grass to the drawing room doors. The ground near the doors is turned to sod, it needs new grass seeds sown. Rubbing the toe of my slipper against the dirt, I imagine Mr Lovejoy finding the nasty letter, trodden into the mud.

I hold the lamp up against the handle. Yes. The scratches are deeper on this side. Really gouged into the wood. I can even see the chip that'd been chiselled out in order to pry the latch open.

My eye catches a glint in the door's glass.

I swing around, but there's nothing behind me. I stare into the gloom. It's difficult to see past the glare of the lamp, so I extinguish the light and gaze again into the darkness. I don't blink for so long, my eyes dry against the cold air. Turning back, I hold my hand to the glass, peer into the drawing room, through to the corridor. Nothing.

Maybe I should just go straight back inside. Back into the warmth of the nursery. And I've been away a little while now; Cyril might be awake.

But what I really want is to breathe some tobacco smoke deep into my lungs — more so than ever, now. At least it'll serve to steady these stupid nerves of mine. I look above to where the nursery windows are. I couldn't smoke in there. If I were caught, then I'd certainly be turned away, and what good would that be to Hatch?

My eyes sweep across the yard, trying to find a discreet spot. I know, from Cook, that the servants' outhouse is further down in the back corner, under the two skeletal oak trees that loom black against a sky as shiny as a silver plate. Closer to hand, down a short path, is the family's outhouse. But Mrs Lovejoy's rooms look down on this side of the yard, so, leaving the lamp by the back door, I move off to my right towards the gardener's shed. I pass the pretty garden I have already seen from the nursery window — the neat row of hedges that meet in the middle to form a circle around a stone water feature. I walk very slowly to lessen the crunch of gravel under foot, lighting a cigarette as I go. I take cover under the spindly tree behind the shed.

The smoke lifts like fog as I stand against the wall of the shed. I can feel the bricks' rough surface catch upon the wool of my dressing gown. The house and surroundings are in shadow and, as I draw on my cigarette again, I hear a flutter above me. An owl. His tawny feathers are almost invisible amongst the dry leaves, but his yellow eyes gleam in the darkness. It looks down on me, then scratches away under its wing with its beak. I draw deeply on my cigarette again and watch the nursery window, the only one with open curtains and the welcoming glow of the hearth. My fingers are cold against my lips as I lift the cigarette to my mouth. I shiver again. Time to go back in.

I'm grinding the cigarette end into the dirt when I hear light footsteps tap across the gravel. Pressing myself to the side of the shed, I draw my arms and body in as much as possible, my reticule clutched under my chin. Nobody's going to take a stab at my throat. I slip my hand down into the reticule until my fingers touch the pistol's ivory handle.

The footsteps halt for a moment, somewhere near the shrubs, then pick up again, until they're tabbing across dry leaves, closer. Closer. So close, I can hear breathing, strained and quick.

Above me the owl rustles from the tree branch, the flap of its wings drowning out my intruder.

By the time I peep around the corner of the shed, the bulky shape that lunges for me is so low to the ground, I'm taken by surprise. I fall back, scraping my hand against the brick wall.

The dog takes a vicious snap at my leg and growls. He barks at me twice, so loudly I'm afraid he'll wake everyone up. His teeth flash in the moonlight, and I decide it may be a good thing if someone wakes and rescues me. Better to be tossed out of the house for smoking than to be mauled by this brute.

I snake my hand into the top of my reticule, my fingers brushing against the pistol handle. Digging further, I feel the rustle of tissue paper and draw out a small square. I toss the caramel to the ground and the dog draws back, as if wary of a strike. He sniffs at the sweet. After a few seconds of snuffling, he wolfs it down. He looks back up at me, expectant.

He is a stout thing and darker than the night. His beady eyes mirror the sky.

"Well, that shut you up." I try to keep my voice steady, soothing. "I forgot there was an ugly creature like you around."

I throw another caramel. After gobbling it up, he steps closer to me, sniffs at my dressing gown. Maybe he smells Cyril or Cook.

The third caramel I offer on the flat of my fingers, and he slobbers against my skin, seeking out any residual sugar.

"Not so vicious, after all." I turn my hand over so he can sniff my scent. When I think he's ready, I run my hand over his brow, tickle behind his ear. "What's your name then?"

I glance up, thinking it's time to go back inside. And that's when I see it.

Someone at the nursery window. Gazing down on me.

CHAPTER
SEVENTEEN

When Amah presses her forehead to the window, she can gaze up at the night sky above the tall buildings across the way. The sky's not black, squid-ink black, like how she remembers the Makassar sky. It's more like the metallic underside of an empty mussel shell, as barren, as cold.

That man of god at the Strangers' Home, when he spoke of the *kungsi*, Amah didn't remember at first, but now she does. That day in Sarawak. That's what they had called the group of Chinese that rioted through Kuching, brandishing poles and spears. They set fire to the new houses, destroyed the markets, cut down as many white people as they could catch. Amah saw all this from the doorway of the prayer hut with the cross over its gable.

Strong hands grasped her by the upper arms. "You cannot stay here," said Uncle Chee. "They will surely burn this place down too. Come with me."

Crouched low, they ran across the edge of the village, ducking behind huts and carts when they could. She was peeping out from behind the stables when she saw a group of white people run from the back of a house. She recognised Preston, but not the other couple. They raced for the next house, which was larger, towards a blond man with a neat beard, who beckoned from the front doorway, but before they could reach it, two of these *kungsi*, black plaits snaking down their backs, burst from the front of the stable. The first one clubbed the woman over the head, as the other swung his *kris* low and far, slicing the air until it found purchase against Preston's shoulder. He then swung the *kris* in an arc so that its blade left a crimson cleft in the other gentleman's throat. A loud crack pierced Amah's ears, then another, and the two *kungsi* fell to the ground. From a window, she could see Pidgeon as he lowered a shotgun, his mouth agape, lengthening his long, foolish face.

CHAPTER
EIGHTEEN

I take a swig of cognac and gaze down into the yard from the nursery window. I think I see the shape of the dog seated by the shed door, scratching behind its ear, but all else is still cloaked in darkness.

When I saw the face in the nursery window, I nearly stumbled over the dog. By the time I'd righted myself, the face was gone. I ran to the back door. At best, someone was checking on me; at worst — oh god — Cyril might have been attacked. On my watch.

I rushed two steps at a time up the staircase to the nursery, practising my story of a visit to the lavatory, but when I burst into the room there was nobody there. I checked the bedroom. Cyril was lying on his back, still slumbering, his chubby hands curled by his sides. Alone.

My fingers follow the engraving of ferns and leaves on the silver flask as I take another sip. Who was the dark figure in the window? Backlit by the fireplace, it was hard to tell.

Mrs Lovejoy? Surely not. If it had been her, surely she would have stayed to remonstrate with me for leaving the boy. Nurse Marie? If she'd come to check on us, I was quite certain she would've remained by the boy's side until I returned. And where was she now, in any case? She wouldn't have had time to flit back to her room. I would've passed her when I came dashing back in.

I shove my flask back into my bag and tiptoe across to the nursery door. I open it a few inches and peer into the corridor. It's so dark I can't even discern where the other rooms are, let alone the staircase.

Could the nursery's visitor have been Emily, or even Joshua? I think of his smile, of the blank look in his eyes, and my skin crawls. I pull a face as I shut the door again. I examine the handle and, although there's a keyhole, there is no key with which to lock it. I cast around for a chair to jam under the handle, but I can see that they're too short.

I position a footstool by the door, so I might at least hear it creak across the floor if someone tries to enter, and then shut the curtains. I take a seat on the medallion armchair by the doll's house and pull out my flask again.

I'm dreaming of my old friend Tilly, of how she's dyed her hair yellow, when I'm woken by a cold, prodding finger. Right in the middle of my forehead.

"Where's Nurse Marie?" Poke. Poke.

I wave Cyril's hand away and roll over in the nanny's bed, but he climbs up behind me, presses his wet lips to my ear. "Where's Nurse Marie? Where's my breakfast?"

I open my eyes and look over my shoulder at the little boy. His buttery curls are tousled, and snot crusts his nostrils, but really, he's an attractive little thing. I don't know how he could be Mr Lovejoy's son. "I don't know. It's freezing, though. Why don't you climb in here with me until she comes?" I lift the blanket for him.

He shakes his head and, as he takes a step back, I grab him by his chubby arms and pull him to me. I wrap my arms around him until I reach his sides, and I tickle and tickle, until he's squealing and trying to writhe out of my tight hold. Finally, he lies back against me, spent, and we are both smiling, warm under the blankets.

"Your feet are like icicles, Cyril." He shoves them against my shins again, and that's how Nurse Marie finds us, scuffling around my bed.

"Cyril." Her voice is sharp as she calls him. She doesn't make eye contact with me. "I have your egg and milk here. Hurry out to the table, please."

The boy scampers off and I lie in bed a minute more. I lift the curtain a little away from the window above me and the sky has the grey glare of dawn. Dawn. I'm much more likely to see first light after a night out dancing than to wake to it like this. In fact, I think I feel a bit sick in the stomach from waking so early.

I drag myself from bed and dress.

Nurse Marie is feeding Cyril, but I can see from the break-fast tray that there is no tea for me. I feel a tick of irritation. Silly woman. If only she knew I was here on Hatch's behalf to find alternative suspects to her.

"I had a bad night, Nurse Marie," I say, moving to the nursery door. "I might go to the kitchen and have a nice cup of tea. I'm sure I can leave Cyril in your capable hands."

The nurse nods, gently stroking Cyril's hair back from his forehead as he chews on a piece of toast.

As soon as I enter the kitchen, Cook hands me an apron and directs me to wash the dishes. "Nothing for it," she says. "Poor Ruth is unwell, and I can't do it all by myself. You leave that Nurse Marie with the children and help me prepare the family's breakfast."

I pour myself a cup of tea and add three teaspoons of sugar and a generous dash of cream. "What do you mean by 'children', Cook?" I ask. "Nurse Marie only seems to watch over Cyril." I'm not sure if it was a slip of the tongue — if Cook is mistakenly counting in poor Margaret — or if she means the older children too.

Cook looks at me over a bowl of egg yolks. "Ha. She's supposed to care for Miss Emily too, but that girl has always been obstinate when it comes to the new nurses." She pours the eggs into a saucepan and hands me the bowl to wash. "Ever since her mother died, that is."

In a dark corner of the kitchen, between the kitchen sideboard and the doorway to the scullery, is a family photo much like the one upstairs, but this one is lighter, overexposed. I peer at it closer. "Is that the first Mrs Lovejoy?"

Cook bustles over to stand next to me. "Yes, that's her. Pretty thing, wasn't she. She was already poorly by then." She jabs a thin finger, its nail chewed down to the quick, at a figure in the background, standing between two children — Joshua and Emily, I presume

— and whispers, "And that's Mrs Lovejoy as she was then. Mrs Lovejoy now, I mean. When she was the nanny."

"Mrs Lovejoy was their nursemaid?"

Cook returns to the stove and nods as she whisks the eggs. "Looked after them as their poor mother faded away, she did."

"I'm surprised the nursemaid is even in the family photos, actually."

There's a shrewd cast to Cook's eye. "By my reckoning, that was Mr Lovejoy's doing. Now, you get on with those dishes, or I'll never have breakfast ready by the time the family wakes."

In the scullery, I pick up a small skillet and gingerly dip it in the tub. I hope the soapy water and scrubbing doesn't roughen my hands.

I poke my head around the doorway and say, "I wonder why Mrs Lovejoy still allows that photograph to hang here. I wouldn't think she'd want the reminder."

The cook shrugs. "She's not down here much. I daresay she's forgotten about it. Or maybe the master insisted. Like he did with the one upstairs."

I mull over her words for a few moments. "So, after the first Mrs Lovejoy died, Mr Lovejoy married the nursemaid?" I infuse my voice with wonder, as though I find the whole thing terribly romantic.

"That he did." Cook glances up, watches the door. She yanks back her cap so that her hair, which is the dirty yellow of aged lacework, falls onto her forehead, and whispers, "This Mrs Lovejoy took his first wife's place faster than it took the funeral wreaths to wilt."

150

I form my mouth in an amazed "Oh".

Cook's mouth twists to the side in a satisfied smile as she nods sagely at the cooking eggs. "Had her hooks into him earlier than that, though, by my reckoning."

Inspecting some bacon fat that's been burnt onto the bottom of a pan, I wonder if I dare ask for more gossip. "Did he always . . . you know . . . with the servants?" I ask, standing in the doorway.

Cook nods and lowers her voice again. "Oh yes, I think he did. That man had unnatural urges. Not that he ever tried anything on me, mind you," she says, thumping a knob of dough onto the table. "But some of the younger servants . . . well, if he were still alive, I'd tell you to take care, believe me."

Pursing my lips, I scour the pan with all my might, but the mark seems to be seared on, so I just place it alongside the other drying dishes.

She presses her shoulder against mine as she drops a spoon into the tub. "Liked to be a buttered bun, he did."

"Even up 'til his death?" I ask, damp hands on my hips.

She gives me a meaningful look, a sly smile on her cheerful face. "Well, it wasn't with little Ruth. I kept a sharp eye on her. Promised her mother, I did, that I'd take care of her. Mrs Forbes — you know, the last housekeeper — she was an old Tartar, she was. He'd have had to have been a very, very brave man to slide a hand up her skirts, as they say. And, like I said, it wasn't with me."

Which leaves Nurse Marie. I think of her sallow face, and her thin, brittle hands and arms. I know it takes all types, but I just can't imagine it.

"You can't mean Nurse Marie?" I say, surprised.

"She doesn't look all that comely at the moment, to be sure. But she used to keep herself quite nice. Almost pretty, she was. Always wore her hair with a nice braid through it, pinned at the back with a lovely tortoiseshell comb. And she wore her uniform with pride, she did. Not like now." Cook shakes her head as she collects the clean skillet.

Nurse Marie. Playing away with the master. I wonder if Hatch knows of this.

I wander out from the scullery and, with my thumb, I bend my middle fingernail downward. My nails are already softening from all the scrubbing and I grimace at the greasy stench of suet on my skin.

Cook stares down at the dollops of lamb kidney on the kitchen table. "Master Joshua does enjoy his devilled kidneys, but I'm not sure I have time to prepare them." She glances over at me. "I don't suppose you know how to cook 'em?"

My eyes widen in alarm. Besides having no culinary skills, I'm not even really sure of how devilled kidneys are supposed to taste because I usually avoid them. I remember when I was small, Amah used to fry the bloodshot meat with soy sauce if she managed to procure some from an incoming ship. I rather enjoyed it like that, but I hardly think that's how Cook wants it prepared.

152

She sees the doubt on my face and tuts, staring down at the meat again. "Well, I'll throw them on. You watch I don't burn 'em."

I make Cyril my excuse for escaping the house for an hour or two in order to meet up with Detective Inspector Hatch, telling Nurse Marie and Cook I'm taking him for a walk, that I think his cheeks need more colour in them. For a moment Nurse Marie looked like she might join us, but I told her to take the opportunity to rest. She looks like she hasn't slept in weeks. When I returned to the nursery this morning, I found her weeping by the doll's crib, holding the doll with chestnut ringlets. I patted her on the shoulder and, although I expected her to, she didn't shrug me away.

"I miss little Margaret so much," she said, a tear teetering over her nostril, ready to mingle with the snot on her upper lip. Her hair was pulled unevenly into a bun and she was still in the same dress, the grey one with the navy pinstripe. She probably slept in it. In fact, there was a sour smell that wafted from her, and I wondered just how many days she'd lived in that dress.

Her fingers ran over the lacework of the doll's dress. "So much loss."

I patted her shoulder again and murmured how sorry I was. I nearly asked her what she thought had happened to poor Margaret, but I decided she was still too fragile. I'd wait until she was more comfortable with my presence.

Cyril tugs on my hand as we make our way to Church Street. Only one reporter remains to brave the cold, and we trot past him, ignoring his barrage of questions. "What's your name then, miss? Who's this little fellow? Are you Cyril, my little man?" Cyril looks up at his name, but I place a hand over his ear and press him to my skirts, urge him to move more quickly.

We pass the building site, but the workmen from the other day don't seem to be there, maybe because it looks like it might rain.

"Which way to the park, Cyril?"

We turn right onto the main street of the village, Cyril still pulling me along. I've arranged to meet Hatch at the gates to Abney Park. Hopefully we can find a discreet bench somewhere we can sit while Cyril chases rabbits or whatever children do at the park.

On the first corner is a little teashop and across the road is a grand building that seems to be a school of some sort. A line of ten or so girls stream from the side of the building, and with a twist in my heart, I think of another school, far from this one. We pass the open door of an inn and I can smell the malty aroma of spilt ale that has seeped into the floorboards. Next to the inn is a little rag-and-bone shop, its dark corners crammed with jars of beads, boxes of utensils and baskets of worn clothing.

Of the many shops along Church Street there is only one that catches Cyril's attention. The bakery has a pretty pink and white awning, and Cyril leaves smudges on the glass as he gazes at the sweets in the window.

154

"If you're a good boy, I will purchase you some on the way home."

He stares up at me and I wonder if he's going to have a tantrum, but on seeing that I'm resolute, he relents. "Good boy. On way home," he repeats.

The entrance to Abney Park is flanked by rather grand pillars. The interesting designs etched into the stonework are almost like something that belong in the museum. Reading the signage on the gate, I see that, actually, the park is part of a cemetery. I glance down at Cyril who's hitching up the back of his pants. I wonder if he knows what a cemetery is.

Standing by one of the further pillars is a woman selling dog collars, and two women walk past, shopping baskets swinging from their arms.

"Mrs Chancey." Hatch approaches us from inside the gates.

"Nurse Louise," I correct him, as I take his hand in greeting, nodding my head down towards the boy.

"Of course." His eyes are watering from the chill in the air. He leads us through the gates. "There's a park bench not far from here. The boy can have a run around while we talk."

He points out Abney House for us, a very handsome residence, and makes his way down a path that runs off to the left. We walk under the shade of tall elm trees that almost block out the overcast sky.

Reaching a small clearing on the banks of a small pond, he says, "We can take a seat beneath that tree over there."

As we sit down on the bench, Cyril stands by my side furthest away from Hatch and glares at him suspiciously. "Why don't you run over there, Cyril, and see if there is an eel in the water?" I say to him.

"What's an eel?" The boy's eyes reluctantly leave Hatch's face and find mine.

"It's like a long fish. Haven't you ever eaten eel?"

He shakes his head. His nose is running again, but I know I don't have a handkerchief in my bag.

"Off you go."

As he trudges off, I turn to the Detective Inspector. "Well, I've had a busy time of it. I'm quite exhausted already."

Hatch lifts his hat for a moment and pushes his straw-coloured hair back from his forehead. "Tell me."

I pick some cedar leaves from the bench beside me and rub the sprigs between my fingers. "Very late last night when I stole out into the garden to have a closer look at the drawing room door, I met the vicious dog. I'd entirely forgotten about him." I sniff the leaf's fragrance on my fingertips.

Hatch looks alarmed. "It didn't hurt you?" His eyes take in my hands, my arms.

A young couple stroll by and take up position next to Cyril by the side of the pond. They peer into its depths with the boy and seem to be asking him a question.

"No. He gave me a terrible fright, but really, I don't think he's as ferocious as you've been led to believe." I watch as the couple bid Cyril farewell and move on.

"Meaning . . ."

156

"Meaning, I'm not so sure he would be a real deterrent to an intruder. If someone came from outside to murder Lovejoy and Margaret, I think it's possible he or she could find their way past the dog."

Hatch casts his eyes to the sky and thinks for a moment. "All right. And what did you think of the drawing room doors?"

Cyril races across the grass towards us. "Nursie, Nursie. Ducks. See ducks!" He flings his arm out and points at three brown ducks that swim into view. "Bread, Nursie. Bread." I assure Cyril I have no bread, even proving my point by opening up my reticule for him to scrutinise. "Now go on and play."

As the boy runs back to the pond, I say to Hatch, "I suppose you noticed there were scratches on the inside of the door, as well as on the outside?"

Cyril crouches low, and leans out towards the boldest duck that paddles up to him.

Hatch nods. "Yes. Leading me to believe, one way or another, Margaret's murderer was trying to trip us up."

"One way or another?"

"Yes. I mean, if it was someone in the household, they've tried to make it look like an outsider broke in, but if it's an outsider who did break in, they've muddied the water by scratching up the inside."

I nod. "I see."

Cyril searches amongst the brush beneath the trees and finds a long stick. He drags it into the middle of the clearing and, lifting it above his head, he swings it down so it thumps the ground, again and again.

"What is that strange little creature doing?"

Hatch smiles. "Being a boy. My mother said when I was young I used to go into the garden and thump the tree with a plank of wood."

"But why?"

He shrugs, still smiling. "I don't know." He turns to me again. "And what other news have you for me? Any idea what happened to the Cook's wrapper?"

"No, I still need to ask her about it, although she gave me some excellent gossip this morning." I tilt my head to him as I ask, "I suppose you know the present Mrs Lovejoy was originally the children's nursemaid when the first Mrs Lovejoy was still alive?"

"Yes, that was made clear to us from the beginning."

"You might already have surmised this, but, according to the cook, even before the first Mrs Lovejoy died, Mr Lovejoy and the second Mrs Lovejoy were having . . ." I pause. I'm not sure how to put it delicately for the Detective Inspector. "That Mr Lovejoy and the second Mrs Lovejoy were already . . . romantic."

"Ha. Romantic. Is that what it's called?"

I grin at him. "Cook said he enjoyed being a 'buttered bun'."

Hatch's eyebrow hooks up. "Was there anybody lately he was being a buttered bun with?"

"Well, the cook said it wasn't with her and it wasn't with Ruth. And she said the old housekeeper was a dragon, who Mr Lovejoy would never have approached." I take my eyes off Cyril to look up at Hatch. "Which really only leaves . . ."

158

"Nursemaid Marie." He claps his hands together. "I knew there was something there that they were keeping from me. I should have known."

I shrug. "Mr Lovejoy liked his nursemaids, evidently."

"Have you asked her about it?"

"No." I frown. "She's . . . a little unhinged, I think. With grief." For the first time, it occurs to me that she has had a double loss: her ward, Margaret, and her lover, Mr Lovejoy. No wonder she isn't coping.

"I think you'd better question her next," Hatch says. He slaps his hand down onto the bench. "If only we could find that wrapper. We searched the gardens thoroughly and never found it, and no fires were alight in the grates overnight, so I don't believe it was burnt to cinders. At least not before the police were summoned." Hatch lifts his hat again to wipe back his hair. His face is troubled. "I'm afraid we don't have much time left, though, Mrs Chancey. Maybe two or three days at most."

"Why is that?"

"Have you read the latest newspapers?"

I shake my head. "No, I haven't had access to them."

A young woman leads a little girl towards the pond. The tiny thing has pretty flaxen hair that falls to the small of her back and she wears a velvet dress the shade of a violet, under a navy overcoat. Cyril drops his stick and steps closer to watch the girl as the woman hands her something.

"There's a lot of anger that the murder hasn't been solved yet. People have been writing letters. Journalists," his thin lips tighten on the word, "have been whipping the public into a frenzy of discontent. I'm afraid the Superintendent has told me that come Sunday, I will be moved to another case. And if it comes to that, I wouldn't be surprised if Nurse Marie is charged." He brushes off the back of his coat as he stands.

The girl tosses bits of bread to the ducks that waddle in the water at her feet. The woman offers a crust to Cyril, too, but he shakes his head and keeps staring at the girl. From here, I can see his bottom lip turn down. I can see how sad he looks as he gazes at her.

CHAPTER
NINETEEN

Amah reaches her fingers into the blue and white porcelain jar and brings out a piece of pickled ginger. The flesh is soft and fragrant between her fingertips and juice runs down the side of her hand. With her tongue, she catches the drip before it reaches her wrist.

Why is Jakub punishing her? What does he have to do with these men who are turning up murdered? How would he even know about them, and why does he care?

Sucking the syrup from the ginger, she thinks back to what Uncle Chee had told her. That Jakub has somehow found out that Miriam isn't his mother.

She bites off some ginger and stares down at the fibrous threads of its flesh, wondering just how much Jakub had managed to find out. She fails to taste the sweet, her appetite fading, and she tosses the remaining bit of ginger into the fireplace.

Wiping her sticky fingers on a handkerchief, she replaces the jar's lid. She will have to search for him again. Striding over to the window of her sitting room, she looks out onto the cold, grey day. She presses her palm to the glass's chilly surface, and when she lifts her hand away, she leaves smudgy fingerprints.

As she ties the woollen scarf around her throat, loosening it again, she watches her reflection in the mirror. Her eyes are bloodshot, her face puffy. Her skirt is loose, for she has had trouble eating the last few days. She hasn't been sleeping well either. Ever since Heloise left for Stoke Newington, Amah has been frozen, unable to decide what to do. The same questions swirl in her mind, in a loop, only to be repeated again when she arrives at a dead end. Where is Jakub? Who are the Chinese men he's befriended? Is he in some sort of terrible plight because of them?

But no, she knows if he is in trouble, it has something to do with the past. The questions clack in her brain like tacky notes of an old piano, until the tune makes her think she's losing her mind.

She barely notices Abigail dusting the sidetable in the corridor, and only manages a small nod as Bundle bids her farewell from the kitchen doorway, her mind is so taken up with what she must do.

She walks until her boots pinch her toes and then summons a cab, which deposits her outside the Strangers' Home, where she finds Cadogan working over a ledger in the office. She asks him if she can speak to Arnold, the gentleman he'd told her about the last time they met.

"Laid up in bed, poor fellow," he says. "But I managed to ask him some questions on your behalf, nevertheless."

After Amah assures him she has a coachman outside ready to accompany her, he directs her to an address two streets away. "You'll find various rooming houses there, especially set up for the Asian seamen who find themselves between voyages. Arnold believes your best bet is one behind a shop that has the name Kung above its door, and another run by a man by the name of Ghosh."

As Amah turns to leave, Cadogan warns her of the street. His smile's pleasant as he speaks. Fond, even. "You might find the air a little more pungent than usual and, I know I can say this to you, you must be careful you are not swindled by the characters you will find down there. They sell all sorts of potions and tokens. The Oriental Hindu or Mussulman is nothing more than a grown-up child, after all, who believes in the influence of his jinns and spirits over firm facts."

Amah's gaze finds the gold cross that glints from his collar and she holds her eyes steady to stop herself from casting them to the ceiling.

But when she follows his directions, she finds the road quite quiet. A beggar sits on the doorstep of a narrow building, his head resting between his legs, a mangy dog by his side. She pops into a shop on the corner that she knows her uncle frequents on occasion to procure the pills he takes for indigestion. The shop smells of earth, joss stick smoke and tea. The walls are covered with red and black Chinese scrolls and tablets. She studies the small pots of spices and the bottles of soy. On the counter are colourful jars of ginger and condiments and a small heap of spinach, dirt still clumped at its roots. She asks Shing, the proprietor, where she might find Kung's shop and, after checking with another man, they point the way to the far end of the street.

When she reaches Kung's, the shutters are up and barred. She bangs on the front door, but doesn't receive a response. Just as she's losing heart, she notices a group of lascars trot through a doorway further down the road. She hurries across and manages to peer into a large room packed with row upon row of bedding. Sagging sheets, like yellowing sails that can find no wind, serve as curtains to sequester the space. Three sailors dressed in uniform are seated on their mattresses, leaning back against the wall, while on the other side of the room is a youth, asleep, his rolled-up prayer mat by his side.

A dark man, his belly pushing out the front of his tunic, steps forward, blocks her view of the room. "How may I help you?"

"Is your name Ghosh?" she asks, pushing back her veil.

His brown eyes take in her face, her western attire, find their way back to her face. "Yes, that is me."

"I'm searching for my nephew," she says. "His name is Jakub Chee."

"What ship did he come in on?"

Amah stares at him. She can't think. What did Miriam say? A word that reminded her of "caramel", or "carnival". "Coronation"? "I can't recall. But it didn't come in in the last few days. Maybe two, three, weeks ago? He's been staying at the Strangers' Home. They said he might have moved here. With a man called Sin Hok."

Ghosh's chin lifts, his lips lengthen into an unhappy line. "Sin Hok?"

She nods. "Yes." Lowering her voice, she glances over her shoulder to make sure nobody else listens. "They say this Sin Hok is with a gang. A gang called something to do with the lotus."

Ghosh snorts through his wide nostrils. "He dreams!" He considers Amah for a moment more and then shrugs. "Follow me."

He leads her through the front room, which smells of sawdust and mould, to a partitioned area at the back. A Chinese man, hair as black as tar, moustache as bristly as a shoe brush, lies flat on his back, tied to the bed with metres and metres of rope. His face glistens and his perspiration has seeped into the mattress, leaving a silhouette of sweat that looks like his shadow. His eyes are closed, but he murmurs something, tosses his head.

"Here is your fearsome Sin Hok," says Ghosh.

"What is wrong with him?" Amah feels her heart peak, her blood chill. Is Jakub somewhere, unconscious like this? Or did he do this to the man?

"Too much bhang. Too much gin. Who knows." Ghosh ushers her from Sin Hok's bedside, leads her back to the front step. "Smashed up Kung's shop. That's why it's shut up. Smashed up Kung too, actually. Lucky Sin Hok hadn't found the knife by then."

"The knife?"

"Yes. Came out onto the road, swinging it around, eyes red as the devil, shouting that he was going to murder someone. Took quite a few men to subdue him.

Delirious, of course. Kung wouldn't have him back, so we tied him up here. We just have to wait for him to come around." He looks thoughtful as he pushes the door shut. "Of course, sometimes they never do."

Amah steps down onto the pavement, looking right and left. She doesn't know where to go from here in her search for Jakub. She wanders towards Limehouse Causeway and, as she comes closer, the beggar slides on his bottom down three steps until he can almost touch her skirts as she passes.

"Lady, look." He holds out his hand, which is encased in fingerless gloves, the weave unravelling at the edges. "Precious. Luck."

She peers at the object that lies in his palm. It's no bigger than a farthing, made from polished stone the colour of cypress bark. It takes her a few moments to see that the charm is in the shape of a fish.

The beggar says something in a language she can't understand, then repeats the word, "Luck."

Amah wants to back away from the beggar's odour and his filthy fingernails that are as packed with dirt as a pipe is with tobacco. She wants to back away from the empty promise the charm offers. But she hesitates. Is she really in the position to refuse an amulet that promises good fortune?

She takes out a shilling from her bag and offers it to the man, but he shakes his head, holds up two fingers. Amah shrugs, turns to continue on her way, but he catches hold of her sleeve. She yanks her arm back and glares at him. His eyes are tired, bleary as a dead snapper. His brown skin has a sallow tinge. Amah

166

rummages in her purse again, takes out a few more pennies, leaving enough for her bus fare home. She holds the coins out to the man, who almost smiles, nods, drops the charm into her outstretched hand. He settles back onto the steps next to his dog, and Amah tucks the charm into her pocket, thinking of how she will hide it in one of Heloise's bed pillows. That girl needs all the luck she can get to pass through this life.

As she trudges along, Amah wonders why the boy is punishing her like this. Has she not been punished enough in this world?

She knows, though, that on that day long ago in Kuching she was fortunate. She survived. She can't recall how they straggled back to the boat, this time with many of the Sarawak survivors with them, about ten British citizens in all.

On the *Dukano*, the gentlemen took to sleeping in the saloon. She remembers Pidgeon being there, and that ugly Lovejoy, McBride with his loud voice. Amah's not sure where the servants found to sleep then — maybe on the deck? There were only two British women left, her Mrs Preston and Mrs Pidgeon. The other one who was knocked over the head, she died, after lying in the sun for many hours. From her position behind the stables, Amah saw another *kungsi* man approach her. The white men bellowed at him from the window, but he just leant over her body, poured a little water in her mouth. He shook his head, like she was a mistake or something.

167

Mr Preston died too. He held on for a few days, but there was no doctor on board, and the heat was unbearable. As Amah held Mrs Preston's hand while she wept, she thought about how it was for the best. It would be just her and Amah now.

CHAPTER
TWENTY

Nurse Marie has been reading a boring old book to Cyril about the moral improvement of a spoilt little boy. I can see how this might be of benefit to Cyril, but damned if I'm going to sit through it too. I tuck him into bed and tell him of the book I'm reading, full of stories of exciting animals and exotic places, but I'm not very far into Darwin's work before he complains that it's boring.

"Don't be silly, Cyril," I say. "It's very interesting." As I read that "the vigorous, the healthy, and the happy survive and multiply," I feel a tweak of remorse. I'm not sure about McBride and Lovejoy, but certainly this statement can't be true of poor Cyril's sister.

Earlier this evening, just after Mrs Lovejoy's visit to her son, Nurse Marie had brought us up a tray of supper. I was pleasantly surprised, because this time she'd included a plate and cup for me, although now that I think about it, Cook probably arranged it that way.

As Nurse Marie prepared some soup for Cyril, the boy, the tip of his tongue lodged between his lips with concentration, set my bowl and spoon next to his at the nursery table. He pulled another chair close and patted it. "This is for Meggie. She really likes soup. Much more than I do."

Although my heart ached for the little beast, the pain etched onto Nurse Marie's face was frightening. She covered her eyes with her hand and fled the room.

"Nursie Marie smells funny, Nursie," said Cyril. He held a piece of bread up to me. "Butter?"

I now smile at the little boy as he lies in bed, his cheeks flushed, his eyes drowsy. "Fair enough. Let me tell you another story then."

I share with him a tale Amah used to tell me. A story of a golden eel caught by a fisherman — a magic eel that promised the fisherman a lifetime of riches. The fisherman took the eel home and his wife mistakenly cooked it up for their supper. That very night they conceived a child. A girl, who caused all sorts of terrible catastrophes.

When I was younger, I used to think of this tale often, wondering if my mother looked at me strangely, closely, as she told me that story. I wondered if she ate eel the night she conceived me.

"Cook, Mrs Lovejoy said to ask you if you had anything spare I could throw over my shoulders to stay warm while I'm tending Cyril." I'm lying. I don't know any other way to broach the subject of the wrapper.

"You mean a shawl or something?" She wipes a strand of hair out of her face with the back of her hand. She unties the apron from her waist. There are weary bags under her eyes.

"Yes, something I can wrap myself in?"

Cook takes a seat at the kitchen table, gestures for me to sit too. She pours us each a cup of tea. "All I can think of is the spare blankets in the linen cupboard. I

170

did have a very nice wrapper. Very handy. Made of a nice, crisp linen it was, just right to slip over my dress when the air has a chill to it in the early morning."

"Oh, I wouldn't take yours," I say, sipping the tea, which has gone a little cool.

"Couldn't if you wanted to," she says. "Missing, it is. Missing since . . . Well. Maybe old Mrs Warren did just lose it in the laundry, but she's sure she didn't — right indignant she was — and I have to say, she has always been reliable. But then, she has her daughter-in-law working with her now. Maybe she mislaid it."

"How long has it been gone?"

Her eyes dart to the doorway to make sure nobody is listening, but I know there's nobody around. The family retired a good half an hour ago and Nurse Marie has already locked herself into the housekeeper's room. "Since the night Miss Margaret . . . You know," she whispers, shaking her head. She takes a handkerchief tucked into her cuff and blots her mouth. "Horrible it was. Horrible. And poor little Ruth — she found the body."

"Oh dear, how terrible for her."

Cook nods, eyes wide. A ruddy flush clouds her cheeks. "Nearly swooned, she did. Lucky the nightsoil man was nearby. He caught her, he did, brought her up to the back door."

"So . . ." I pause. I want to bring the conversation back around to the wrapper. "So your wrapper has been missing since that night? I wonder why."

Cook leans in closer across the wide table and whispers again, "The police think the murderer wore it to save his own clothes from blood." She shakes her head at me, eyes wide. "My wrapper. Used in such a devilish manner. I will never get over it."

"Don't tell me the intruder crept into your bedroom in order to collect the wrapper," I say, a shocked note to my voice. "How frightening." I peer around, as though I'm searching for a prowler to jump out at us.

"No, Nurse Louise, I'd left it on that hook over there." She nods towards a row of five hooks by the kitchen door. An umbrella hangs on one, while an overcoat, faded to the shade of a mushroom, hangs on another.

"So, really, anyone could have taken it?"

She nods slowly.

It's my turn to whisper. "Do you have any ideas?"

Cook clamps her handkerchief to her mouth and shakes her head. But her eyes tell me that she does.

I'll wait. She'll tell me in her own time. She might become suspicious if I push her.

Taking another sip of my tea, which is as good as flavoured milk by now, I say to her, "I haven't seen Emily again. She hasn't visited the nursery at all. I was going to ask her to join us for a walk tomorrow. What do you think?"

"Ah. I don't know about that one. I know Nurse Marie gave up on her all together."

"Always been trouble to the nanny, has she, Cook?"

The cook frowns for a moment, squinting her eyes as she thinks back. "She's always been a quiet thing. Well, the whole household was quiet back when the first Mrs Lovejoy was sickly. I will say this for the present Mrs

Lovejoy — Nurse Kate as we knew her then — she brought some life back into the house. Ooh, she was so managing and forthright, it fair drove the housekeeper up the wall." A small smile lifts her lips. "That's right. Miss Emily adored Nurse Kate back then. You keeping up, Nurse? I'm talking about the present Mrs Lovejoy, when she was just the children's nursemaid. Miss Emily followed her around everywhere."

"And Master Joshua?"

"Oh, he's always followed Miss Emily around. Still does." Her mouth settles into an unhappy line. "I remember once I made a nice teacake for Mrs Lovejoy when she was ill, and Miss Emily came in and told me I shouldn't spoil her mother, that she was just putting on airs. Got that from Nurse Kate she did. She was too young to even know that sort of language. Another time, when Mrs Lovejoy was being taken away to visit a special sanatorium, Miss Emily wouldn't even kiss her goodbye. Broke her heart, it did. Miss Emily learnt that behaviour from the nurse, no doubt about it. And there was nothing the poor lady could do, because of course Nurse Kate had Mr Lovejoy on side too, by then."

"Are they still close? Emily and the new Mrs Lovejoy?"

"Well." She gives me a knowing look. "If you ask me, Miss Emily's now old enough to realise the games Mrs Lovejoy played with them all. As soon as the first Mrs Lovejoy died, Nurse Kate employed a new nanny for the children and married their father. Mighty cold she is to the older children now, especially after the new two came along."

"Margaret and Cyril?"

The cook nods. "It wasn't a pretty sight, I can tell you. The parents fair doting on the younger two, while Miss Emily and Master Joshua went about their own business with hardly a spare shirt between themselves."

I think of the paintings on the walls upstairs, lovely homages to the youngest two. How there are no pictures of the older children, except for the group photograph. I feel an unexpected pang of sympathy. No wonder Emily and Joshua are so odd.

The clock in the sitting room chimes the half-hour.

I pick up my reticule from the kitchen chair next to me. "I might just visit the lavatory before I return to the nursery."

"Well, I'm for bed." She picks up her apron and rummages in its pocket. "Here's the key to the back door. When you've finished, just drop it in that jug there, on the kitchen stand. I'll collect it in the morning. Don't forget to lock the back door, mind. Especially after . . ." She pulls a face at me, then shuffles off to her room.

A light fog hangs in the night air, muffling the lamp's glow, and I waste a few matches lighting my cigarette. I'm hiding again behind the garden shed and the dog has joined me once more. He sits at my feet, panting, hoping for another caramel, no doubt.

I pinch a stray bit of tobacco from my tongue and mull over what Cook has told me about Emily and her brother. Of how close the girl was to Mrs Lovejoy when she was her nanny. Of how their relationship has changed. I must find an excuse to talk with the girl, before Hatch's time runs out.

Once I've finished with my smoke, I step out from behind the shed and gaze up at the nursery window. I left the curtains closed this time, but was that a slight quiver of the curtains? A splinter of light?

Like a breath against the back of my neck, I feel a shift in the air behind me. The shed door creaks open, the sound in tune with my tense muscles as I turn. A black figure, swathed in grey fog, steps from the shed.

"That's a dirty habit for a young woman." His voice grates.

"Sir, you startled me." I hold the lamp up to his face and hope the dog will defend me if need be. But then I remember that the dog was of no assistance to either the master or Margaret. I grasp the shape of my pistol in my silk bag. "What are you doing here?"

He's hatless and has an unusually large head, and his long nose is so crooked it looks like a knob of ginger above his bushy moustache and beard.

"I'm Crossley, the gardener," he says. "Who you be?" He lurches one step towards me and that's when I see that he's very drunk. His eyes have that unsteady look about them, his lips are wet and loose.

"I'm Nurse Louise. The new nursemaid."

He leers, throwing his head back, but the movement pulls him off balance and he trips backward a few steps, lands against the brick wall of the shed. The dog pounces for him, in play or to threaten him, I'm not sure.

"Agh, git away with you, Rufus," he growls at the dog. Then he looks back at me. "Met the faithful mongrel, have you?"

"I did. Last night." I lift my lamp to see him better. "I didn't realise you lived here?"

"I don't," he said, rubbing his finger beneath his nose. "But sometimes I doss down here, when I've had a few too many ales at the inn. You want to join me?" His two front teeth are either missing or rotten black. I can't tell in the gloom.

"I'll be fine sleeping in the house," I assure him.

I go to turn away but am caught short by his next words.

"You wouldn't catch me sleeping in there with that lot. And don't you go listening to their gossip about me," he says. "Women! Always rabbiting away about something, they are."

"What gossip?"

"Those women. That there scrawny cook and her mouse of a scullery maid. They'll have you believe all sorts of things."

"Things like what?"

He folds his arms and his words slur. "That I had something to do with the child's murder, and her father's murder. Found the master, I did." He shakes his head.

"After . . . ?"

"Yer. Head near sliced off, it were." He nudges the dog with the toe of his boot. "He was there too, wasn't yer, yer mangy mongrel? Sitting by the master's body, supping on his blood, he was."

176

My eyes fall to the dog, resting at our feet. Definitely not such a loyal hound, after all. I look back up at the gardener. It's a bit of a coincidence, him being so close by for each murder. I also remember Hatch saying something about it — something to do with the newspapers, and letters to the editor that accused the gardener and another fellow who found the bodies for the murders. However, Hatch did insist he'd cleared all the servants.

I think it is time that I return to the house, nevertheless. I'd feel more assured if I had my pistol in hand, but then I'd have to put down the lamp, and at the moment I want to keep an eye on Crossley.

"Who do you think killed the poor girl and her father, then?"

He presses a finger to the side of his nose and taps it. "All's I know is I wouldn't be so eager to go back into that house, if I was you."

I take a step towards him. "What do you mean?" Closer up I can see a line of dribble that glistens in his beard like a snail's trail. And he stinks of stale piss.

"Clearing out the house, they are," he says, glancing up at the windows of the top floor. "You watch. Next it'll be that fat Mrs Lovejoy and then it'll be her wee white prince."

I close the back door behind me with a firm click and turn the key.

A prickle of fear slinks across the back of my neck. I'm not quite sure if it's from my encounter with the repugnant gardener or if it's his words that have

177

affected me. Both probably. I shake my head and shoulders like that might dispel my foreboding.

I drop the key into the jug on the kitchen sideboard and make my way swiftly through the dark hall to the staircase.

My heart judders as a shadow billows from the bottom step. I can't help but gasp and, holding my lamp high, I quickly discern that it's Emily. "Oh, but you did give me a fright. What are you doing up so late in the evening?" I ask.

She has a blanket wrapped around herself and her feet are bare. Her hair hangs limp and, despite the lack of light, the terrible spots on her face blaze painfully from her pale skin. Her eyes seem almost black in the shadows of the night.

"Why were you talking with Crossley?"

"Ah. Was that you spying on me from the nursery window?" She doesn't answer, just continues to glare at me with those eyes as flat as stone, her wide lips turned down at the edges. Nerves jangle in my fingertips. She's just a girl, I tell myself. "Was it you watching me last night too?"

Still no answer.

I brush past her to climb the stairs, but angle myself so as to keep her in sight. "I am sorry I've missed your visits. Come see me again in the morning." I smile at her. I hope it's a welcoming smile and that the wariness I feel deep in my bones doesn't shine through. With each step up that stair case, I feel her eyes pull on my back like an anchor.

CHAPTER
TWENTY-ONE

"I want sugar in it." Cyril's high-pitched demand stirs me from the slight doze I've fallen into. He's talking to Nurse Marie in the nursery, over their breakfast. Rolling onto my back in the narrow bed, I pull the blanket up to cover my shoulder. I press the palm of my hand to my nose. It's as cold as freshly caught trout.

Nurse Marie murmurs something to the boy, to which he answers, his voice rising even more, "I want sugar in my milk."

Stifling a groan, I sit up. Only one or two more nights of this, hopefully. Pulling out a little mirror from my velveteen vanity pouch, I scrutinise my face for blemishes or lines. I wonder if it's dawn's gloom that causes the shadows under my eyes, or if they are there because I've been sleeping so poorly. Last night was yet another evening I'd lost sleep. Crossley's words haunted me as I tried to drift off, not to mention how Emily had made my flesh creep. Pressing my eyes together, I apply face cream, taking a moment to enjoy its rose fragrance. I dab a tiny amount of *parfum* behind my ears and then haul myself up to dress, swapping my nightdress for drawers and a chemise.

Picking up my corset, I loosen the lacing at the back because, really, my waist doesn't need to be so uncomfortably constricted for play with Cyril; there's no call for a nanny in Stoke Newington to be a fashion plate, after all. As I draw the steel busk across my chest, lifting my breasts into position before heaving the corset together, I think of what the gardener had said about someone clearing out the house — clearing it of people, presumably. And he didn't mean the servants were doing the clearing, either. He could only have meant the two older children.

I pull on one under-petticoat, wondering if I should put on another for warmth. Plonking down onto the side of the bed, I drag my stockings over my toes and wonder about Emily and her brother. I run my fingertip over a catch in the wool, thinking of how Cook claimed that Emily was very close with the second Mrs Lovejoy when she was still her Nurse Kate. Until the nurse turned the girl against her own mother.

Maybe Emily resented that now. Maybe Emily hated Mrs Lovejoy — and her father, even — for robbing her of time with her mother. And if Cook was right about the older children being treated poorly since their mother died, well, that could lead to all sorts of grievances. Jealousy even.

A tinkle of cutlery against crockery coming from the nursery catches my attention. I must hurry and help Nurse Marie.

I step into my crinoline and my mind returns to Emily and Joshua. Could that sort of jealousy lead to murder, though, as the gardener had hinted? Could

180

Emily or Joshua really be that deranged? I think of Joshua's vacant stare, and of the malice that seems to ooze from his sister's skin as palpably as the pimples on her face. Maybe. After drawing my over-petticoat on — a plain one, no frills or stripes like I'd usually insist upon — I stare into space. Try to imagine them murdering their father. Anger driving them to incapacitate him in the garden, slice his throat. But what of their little sister? Pretty Margaret, the spoilt and loved younger daughter. Was that their first revenge upon their parents?

I know a lot about jealousy. It's as familiar to me as the smell of the back lanes of Liverpool. I know that it stabs deep and curls, heavy, in one's chest. I think again of that school in Bath, of the neat girls reading French, of the ribbons in their hair, seagull white. And, yes, there's that ache in my heart.

But could I be driven to murder? I think if I had to live with the resentment every moment, of every day . . . I shake my head. Of course not. Although there's a flicker of doubt at the back of my mind as I pull my shoes on.

As I enter the nursery, I tie my apron around my waist. "What trouble are you giving Nurse Marie?" I ask Cyril.

"I don't like milk," he says, dunking a piece of his toast into the cup.

I start to say that it'll make him strong, but he doesn't care, and neither do I. "If you behave yourself we will . . ." What? I can't be sure of what he wants to do.

"Go for a walk again?"

I consider him. I wouldn't mind visiting one or two shops in the village. "We will see."

Dipping a linen towel in the washbasin, I wipe Cyril's mouth and hands. I look across to Nurse Marie, who's laying out Cyril's outfit for the day. "I met Mr Crossley last night. The gardener. Do you know him? He's a very strange man."

She shrugs, uninterested. "I haven't had much to do with him."

I stand close to her and, reaching for Cyril's breeches, I say, in a soft voice, "He said he wouldn't sleep in the house. He said he thinks the murderer will strike again, murder another Lovejoy." I watch her closely. "Made me tremble all night. I didn't get a wink of sleep."

A flash of fear is quickly replaced with a frown of annoyance. I wonder if more colour comes into her cheeks, but I can't be sure.

"How ridiculous." Nurse Marie unbuttons Cyril's shirt. "He's just saying that because the papers are reporting that he's the main suspect in . . ." She presses her lips together, shakes her head.

It's the first time we've actually spoken for more than one or two sentences to each other. She speaks softly, almost like a child — a sweet, sensitive child who's prone to tears.

I sit on a chair to allow the boy to step into his trousers. When has she had access to the newspaper? I watch as she finishes dressing Cyril and settles him onto the floor with his blocks. Pouring her a cup of tea, I call her to the table, urge her to sit.

"Rest awhile," I say. "He'll be all right."

She sips her tea and I notice her dress, although still grey with the pinstripe, is neatly buttoned at the wrists and doesn't smell musty any longer. Either she's washed and mended her uniform or has finally changed into the spare. Her hair is still a mess, though, falling about her narrow face, while the bun at the base of her neck looks like a wren's nest.

I prop my chin onto the heel of my hand and lean on the table. "I'm not sure if I can stay here, Nurse Marie."

Her eyes widen. "Why not? You've only been here three days."

I pull my face into an anxious expression. "I'm worried about what the gardener told me. I mean, the agency warned me of what had happened here, but they assured me they were committed by a mad person outside the household. And, of course, I was offered excellent wages for taking on the position, given the circumstances. But . . ." I shake my head.

"But, Nurse Louise, you must stay. I am waiting for my agency to find me a new position. In fact, I've even considered taking on work as a housemaid, I want to leave here so badly. But if I leave, and you leave . . ." Her eyes find Cyril, who's smashing a toy horse against a prostrate soldier figurine.

Mrs Lovejoy might have to actually spend time with her son, if that were the case. But what do I know of her grief? "Before . . . before what happened, did Mrs Lovejoy spend much time with the children?"

The nursemaid stares into her tea for so long I wonder if she didn't hear me.

"She absolutely doted on them," she says, eventually.

"She's with child right now, isn't she?" The nursemaid nods. "How was she with Margaret and Cyril when they were babies?"

"I don't know. I've only been here about a year."

This surprises me. She's so attached to the boy, I imagined she'd been the family nursemaid for several years.

I narrow my eyes as though I'm remembering something. "I worked for a woman once who was a fine mother; cuddled and kissed the children. Insisted on doing everything, except for the nasty stuff. You know the type? But little Harry — the youngest — began to have terrible stomach troubles. The doctor was forever in the house. Turned out she was poisoning the little cherub. Added arsenic to his milk, the vicious thing. And she'd done it before. I didn't realise, but the family had already lost three young children." Hell, I'm too good at this lying game.

"Terrible," says Nurse Marie, placing her cup back onto the saucer. "Just terrible." Then her eyes catch mine and she stares at me, her mouth slack. "What are you saying? Why are you telling me this?"

I look towards Mrs Lovejoy's wing of the house. "Did you ever suspect that she might want to harm the children?"

184

Nurse Marie's eyes bulge and her lips gulp at air so that she resembles a fish. "I don't . . . I don't . . ." She can't finish the sentence. Her gaze drops from mine and she pushes the tea set into the middle of the table.

"But, Nurse Marie, if I am to stay, I need to know where I stand. If I'm safe." I reach across the table, entreating. "Do you have any idea what happened to Margaret and her father?"

The woman shakes her head, rapidly. "No. No, no."

"But you must have some thoughts on it, Nurse Marie."

She presses a napkin to her lips, and glances at the door. Her eyes wander towards the other side of the house — the side the two older Lovejoy children inhabit.

"Emily? Joshua?" I whisper to her, my eyes on Cyril to make sure he can't hear us.

"I don't know," she says. "I really don't know. But they seem to dislike the little children so much, I have wondered . . ." She shakes her head to show she's finished with the conversation and, standing from the table, she goes to Cyril's side, helps him gather blocks.

Emily and Joshua. So the nursemaid agrees with the gardener.

Feeling the side of the teapot, I can tell the tea is too tepid to drink. "I'll just go down to the kitchen and freshen the pot."

As I pass the dining room, I hear the familiar clink of a stopper being replaced in the crystal decanter. Mrs Lovejoy walks from the room, wiping her mouth with the back of her hand.

"Mrs Lovejoy," I say, remembering at the last moment to bob my head.

"Nurse . . ." She pauses in front of me and seems to have forgotten my name. "Nurse, tell Cyril I have to go out for most of the day, but I will visit him after supper."

I bob again and watch her broad back as she sails towards the front door. I'm surprised she's so steady on her feet, but she halts at the hallstand, rests her fingertips against it for several seconds.

"Are you in need of assistance, Mrs Lovejoy?"

She doesn't even look my way. "No, Nurse, I'm just feeling a bit tired." Her hand follows the contour of her swollen stomach, rests at its base.

I turn slowly and walk back towards the kitchen and as I reach its doorway I hear the front door close behind Mrs Lovejoy. I have to admit, I feel a little sorry for her. Despite her callous treatment of the first Mrs Lovejoy and her children, she seems to be paying a steep price now; which makes me think of those strange children again, Emily and Joshua.

"What are you pulling a face about?" asks Cook.

I laugh. "I was just thinking of the run-in I had last night with Crossley." I give an exaggerated shudder.

Cook pulls a face too, and nudges Ruth, who's back to work in the kitchen. "Horrible beast of a man, isn't he, Ruth?"

The girl nods, her eyes widening, as she stirs batter in a large bowl.

I take a seat at the table while Cook sets the kettle on to boil for me. She points out lumps in the cake batter to Ruth, tells her to whisk harder.

186

"Crossley said you think he murdered the Lovejoys," I say, looking from the cook to the girl.

"Stupid creature." Cook considers for a moment. "Although he did find both bodies, and he was the one with good reason to be outside on each occasion. What do you say, Ruth?"

The girl shrugs and spoons the batter into a cake tin.

"But did he have reason to murder them?"

Cook takes a bunch of beans from a basket on the floor and slaps them down onto a board. "Master was always telling him he'd lose his job if he was caught drinking too much brandy again. Near lopped one of the master's special shrubs to the ground, he did once, when he was supposed to be pruning 'em." She smiles at the memory. "A special plant all the way from somewhere in the Orient, it was."

Her comment about the plant, of exotic places, reminds me of my friends — Pidgeon and Cosgrove and the others — and I wonder how they're getting on. I'm reminded to buy a newspaper, see if there is any news on McBride's death. I might even dash off a quick note to one of them — Cosgrove maybe — to see if their dreaded *kungsi* has contacted any of them again.

Cook refills the teapot and pours me a cup. It's very settling watching her rhythmically chop the beans, followed by five crisp carrots. No wonder Amah spends so much time in the kitchen with Agneau. Maybe I should follow suit when I return home.

Ruth swipes batter from the inside of the bowl and licks it from her finger, smiling at me. She's just pushing the bowl across the table for me to try when Nurse Marie runs into the room.

"Have you seen Cyril, Nurse Louise?" she gasps.

I stand from the table. "No. The last I saw of him he was with you in the nursery. What happened?"

"All I did was make his bed, and then when I came out again he was gone."

"And you've checked all of upstairs?"

"Yes." She hesitates. "Except for Emily and Joshua's rooms."

Ruth joins us as we weave from room to room calling Cyril's name. Nurse Marie checks behind the sofas in the drawing room while Ruth flings open cupboard doors. I make my way upstairs and glance through the nursery and bedroom. He's not there.

I meet the nursemaid and Ruth at the top of the stairs. Nurse Marie has started to breathe heavily. Each time she breathes in it sounds like a sob. Despite the looseness of my corset, my stomach constricts. She's worried something awful has happened to him, something like what happened to Margaret, to Mr Lovejoy.

I touch the kitchen maid on the arm. "Ruth, you knock on Emily's door, see if he's there. Nurse Marie, you check Joshua's room."

I turn towards Mrs Lovejoy's rooms. I know she's gone out so I open the door, stick my head in. "Cyril? Cyril?" He's not behind the sofa in her sitting room, nor is he under the table. There are no bulges behind the curtains giving a small boy away. I peer out the window down into the gardens. I can just see the roof of the outhouse, veiled in branches from the oak tree. *Please don't let us find him there.*

I walk through the connecting door into Mrs Lovejoy's bedroom and step across the thick carpet, peep under the large bed. No Cyril. I look in the wardrobe, parting the gowns to make sure he's not hiding beneath the voluminous skirts, but he's not there either. This isn't good. Where's the little brute?

My eyes take in Mrs Lovejoy's bed linen. Far too much lace and ribboning for my liking. But tucked under a mountain of pillows, so I can just see its leather corner, is a book. I lift it out. There is no title on the front and, thumbing through its pages, I see that they are covered in spiky handwriting. *June 13 1859, Erasmus says we are to . . .* Her diary.

Hearing footsteps approach Mrs Lovejoy's room, I make a swift decision and ram the diary into my apron pocket.

"We still haven't been able to find him, Nurse," says Ruth. Nurse Marie stands close behind her. Her face is shiny with perspiration, her hair as messy as I've ever seen it.

"Just wait a little," I say, rummaging around in my pocket. Sliding the diary in there has reminded me of the bounty I bought with Cyril the day before at the bakery. I take out a bag of hard candies and rattle them. "Cyril. Cyril," I call, standing in the doorway between Mrs Lovejoy's sitting room and the upper landing. "I have a lemon candy here for you. Be a good boy and come and collect it."

The window seat in Mrs Lovejoy's sitting room flings open from the inside. Cyril sits up, grinning. "I is here, Nursie." His fingers curl in and out like he's beckoning me. "Can I have my sweet now?"

CHAPTER
TWENTY-TWO

Peachy leaves flicker like bunting against the overcast sky. We've returned to the clearing in the park we shared with Hatch the day before, but this time I've had the forethought to bring a kerchief full of bread for Cyril to feed the ducks. I leave him by the side of the pond and take a seat on the bench.

Mrs Lovejoy said she'd be out all day, but I want to be quick, in case she returns early. I riffle through the pages, and stop at a date from almost three years ago. *It's almost unbearable to go into the kitchen with that photograph there, displayed on the wall. Me in that ghastly uniform. I begged Erasmus to insist upon it being taken down, but he thinks it's a fine joke, and I don't want to make a fuss because then those scrawny bitches will think I* care. I wonder if she means Cook and Ruth. Or is it Emily she's referring to?

I continue to leaf through the diary, my gloved fingers whisking the thick pages across. I learn that the new Mrs Lovejoy couldn't stand the housekeeper, but kept her on because Erasmus wouldn't fire her, and that she resented every cent spent on poor Joshua and Emily. She's actually kept a tally of expenses the older children incur in the top right-hand corner of certain pages and, on the 12th of June two years before, she'd listed the reasons she put forward to Erasmus for denying Joshua further schooling at the expensive college he attended.

Glancing up, I see that Cyril is almost out of bread, so I flip forward to the latest entries in the diary. I take in a sharp breath. Scrawled across the page, so deeply the pen nib has scored through the paper onto the next page, is the word *EVIL*. I turn to the page before, but it's just a recount of a meeting with Hatch, and her anxieties about being left a widow.

"Nursie, Nursie," Cyril calls, running over to me. "Nursie. No bread." He points to the pond, but the ducks are already cruising away.

"I don't have any left," I tell him. I rummage in my bag, and bring out my cache of sweets. "Why don't you sit quietly for a moment, and you can have another candy."

He puts his hand out, but I shake my head, tell him he has to sit next to me quietly. He climbs onto the bench and takes his sweet, pops it in his mouth. His cheeks and the tip of his snub nose are rosy from the cold and he beams up at me, his lips pursed shut over his treat. I really don't mind the little brat.

I go back about a quarter of the way through the diary and stop at a page crammed with Mrs Lovejoy's spidery writing. She's even written in the margins, curled her text up the sides of the page.

Today I arrived home early from the village and that vile Nurse Marie, that cursed hussy, came out from Erasmus's study again. When I stopped her last time she insisted the master was just asking after the children, but I swear, I swear on the lives of my children, that she smirked at me this time. Turned her head from me and smirked!!! I am sure of it. And when I went into his study it was so warm in there, and there was a smell, I know that smell, it reeked. I am not stupid. I am not stupid. Does he think I'm stupid? Did he not play these games with me? But he denies it, looks at me like I'm mad. That's how he used to look at the first Mrs L., the stupid cow. Am I the stupid cow now? I will kill him, I will rip apart all that he loves before I become that stupid cow! I cannot believe he would do this to me but I should have known, because isn't this how he made Mrs L mad in the end, urging me to turn the children from her and to share my bed with him while she seeped away in their bed, which is my bed now my bed my bed my bed. I feel sick. I want to fall to the floor, bring up all that I have eaten, oh Lord but isn't that how Mrs L died? Am I to be next? That TROLLOP TROLLOP TROLLOP. I wish it were her breast that I lashed right now with this pen, stealing everything from me. I won't I won't I won't I won't. They don't know what I'm capable of but they . . .

What madness is this? I'm torn. I sympathise with her rage, yet I'm alarmed at the tone of the passage.

I realise Cyril is tugging at my sleeve. "What is it, Cyril?" I ask, dragging my eyes from the text.

"'Nother sweet please, Nursie."

I shake out another yellow candy from the bag, hand it to him. I flick through the next few pages and find more of the same. She's unhinged. Full of fury, paranoia. By the time the boy asks for another sweet, I tell him it's time to return home. The little beast ensconces himself further into the back of the park bench and folds his arms. That stormy look descends on his face, and as much as I'd like to ignore his wails, I also want to avoid having to carry a screaming boy tucked under my arm all the way home.

"Look, Cyril, if you behave yourself, I will give you one more candy when we get home. But not before. But if you start to cry, I'm leaving you right here. The wolves can have you." He must see in my eye that I'm quite willing to leave him behind so he hops off the seat, takes my proffered hand.

We walk through the park's gates and wait by the side of the road for a carriage to pass. Once across, Cyril presses his nose against the window of the bakery, admiring the sweet buns and pastries. I wander ahead and peer into the gloom of Sullivan's rag-and-bone shop. Looks more like a pawnshop to me, the type Amah loves, where she might find a set of bone buttons or exotic coins; refuse from others' lives. I glance back at Cyril, call him to me. I won't drag him inside. It would bore him. But I do take him into the apothecary's and he waits patiently enough while I have an ointment made up. I only have to ask him four times to stop touching everything.

As we stroll along Lordship Road, Cyril lugs on my hand as he jumps over anything he deems an obstacle, be it a stick or horse manure. The journalists have moved on, and all is quiet. We're just entering through the front gate of St Chad's Lodge when I notice a person step out from behind a large elm tree. He's wearing dark clothing and a wide brimmed hat like American men sport. He looks very familiar, but out of place somehow.

"Cyril, run ahead and knock on the door," I say to the boy.

It's difficult to see from this distance, but I think the man's eyes widen in surprise when he sees that I've noticed him, and as I approach, he turns heel, runs around the nearest corner. By the time I reach the bend in the road, he's long gone, a black figure in the distance.

My cousin, Jakub. What the hell is he doing here?

I deliver Cyril to Nurse Marie who's setting out luncheon on the nursery table. Looking right and left along the corridor to make sure nobody sees me, I creep into Mrs Lovejoy's room. Standing by her bed, I bring out her diary and have one last flick through it. I pause at the word *EVIL*, shake my head. I wonder what's on the woman's mind. I'd very much like to know if she means the evil that took her husband and child, or an evil deed of her own?

I tuck the book under her pillow again, pat the bedspread across it.

"What are you doing?"

I swing around. Emily.

"You really must stop looming up on me like this." I straighten a cushion across the bedspread. "I was just righting your mother's bedlinen. I'm afraid Cyril messed it up when he was hiding from us."

Her eyes, almost as dark as onyx, take me in. I can tell she doesn't believe me.

"Actually," I say, brushing past her, "I picked up something for you in the village."

I look back. She hasn't moved from her spot, only follows my movements with a turn of her head. "Come along," I say. Strange, strange girl.

I feel in the pockets of my coat that I've left hanging in the nursery and bring out the small jar from the apothecary's. Returning to the corridor, I find her standing by the pictures on the wall.

"Come, take a seat with me over here." I lead her to the two parlour chairs arranged neatly between her bedroom and her brother's.

She stares at me, suspicious. There's a thud in the nursery, Cyril cries out. Not until we can hear Nurse Marie murmuring endearments to the boy does Emily approach me. Even then she lowers herself slowly onto the chair, sits right at its edge.

"I bought this for you at the apothecary's." I hand her the jar. "It might help clear your complexion. The man said it was the best treatment for specks."

196

She takes the ointment, frowning, but says, "What business is it of yours?"

"Well, you are supposed to be in my care, after all."

She glares at me for a moment from under her thick brows, then looks down again at the jar in her hands. "What's in it?"

"I think he said it's camphor with a little lime water. Nothing harmful."

Emily thrusts the jar into my lap. "I don't want it. I don't trust it."

"What do you mean, you don't trust it? It's from the apothecary's. Of course it's fine."

She stares down at the jar, and I realise that she is actually quite eager to try it, but wary too.

"Here," I say, unscrewing the lid. "I'll put some on first." I dab a little on my finger, swirl it on my cheeks and smooth it in. "There. Now you take this jar, and when you see that my skin doesn't peel away or that I don't fall down in a swoon, you can try some too."

She takes the jar again, cradles it in her hands. Cyril squeals, and she looks up. "Aren't you supposed to be looking after Cyril?"

"Nurse Marie can manage for the moment." I twist in my chair, peep through the open door into her bedroom. I wonder if I'll ever have a chance to explore their rooms for the missing wrapper. Although if Emily or her brother did use it, no doubt they've burnt or disposed of it by now. "What do you do with yourself all day?"

The girl goes to stand up, but hesitates as she answers me. "Sometimes Josh and I play cards, but mostly I read."

"What are you reading? I love reading too."

"I like Dickens, and Braddon too."

"Oh, I adore Braddon. I just finished one of hers last week, in fact."

Her shoulders seem more relaxed now, although the expression on her face is still sour. She lowers her eyes and mumbles, "Actually, my favourite is Radcliffe."

I almost laugh aloud. Of course this poor, plain, bored girl loves Radcliffe.

"Do you get them from the library?" I know she doesn't have any funds to buy them herself.

"Yes." She nods towards Mrs Lovejoy's rooms. "She has a subscription."

"And she allows you to borrow what you like?"

Emily bows her head, like she's talking to the ointment. "If I do some chores for her, she lets me borrow one book a sennight."

"What sort of chores?" I ask, surprised.

"Some light mending. Embroidering the handkerchiefs and smalls. Sometimes I polish the silver, when the housekeeper is too busy. But she's gone now so I guess I'll have to do it all the time."

What an old cow that Mrs Lovejoy is, making her step-daughter do the menial work for which she has servants. But I see an opening here. "Cannot the woman who does your laundry take care of such things?"

The girl shrugs.

"Of course, the cook did tell me of the problems you have with the laundry woman, now I think on it. It's no wonder Mrs Lovejoy doesn't trust her with the

198

mending. Loses clothes, doesn't she? Lost the cook's wrapper, I believe."

I watch for Emily's reaction. Her eyes narrow and her head slides around to look at me, like a snake slithers in the zoo. There's something in her eyes — suspicion, anger, fright? I can't tell.

"I don't know anything about that," she says.

CHAPTER
TWENTY-THREE

I step out from the cab onto Tottenham Court Road. I've told the cook and Nurse Marie that I have an appointment with a dentist. I even try to bring attention to the chip in my front tooth, suck on it while I eat lunch like it pains me. In fact, I've received word from Hatch to meet him in town so that I can join him when he questions the servants' agency that Nurse Marie is with.

I find him outside Duke's Superior Servants' Registry. I can already see it's a cut above Bower's, the one I visited the other day, further down the street. The shop windows are elegantly curtained, the signage painted in refined, curling script.

"Thank you for meeting me, Mrs Chancey," he says. "Any news?"

"Actually, I think I have a few interesting points," I say, as two women bustle past us to enter the agency.

Hatch looks around. "It might be best if we have a cup of tea in the teashop across the way first. We can return here to ask after Nurse Marie once you've brought me up to date."

I'd much prefer to have a drink in the public house next to the teashop, but doubt Hatch will concur.

We take a seat at a window table, and Hatch orders tea. "I'm afraid you will probably only have the one more night at St Chad's Lodge."

Home. I can go back to the comforts of my home. Back to Amah. But I'm also disappointed that we haven't solved this murder yet. "That seems a pity. Is it the superintendent?"

"Yes." His voice is heavy and a little colour comes into his pale face. "If an arrest is not made by tomorrow, I am off the case." With that, he flips open his notebook, asks me to report all I have found out in the last twenty-four hours.

"You know that Cook said Mr Lovejoy had a penchant for his nursemaids?" The detective nods. "Well, I found Mrs Lovejoy's diary — the present Mrs Lovejoy. And she knew all about it. She was furious." I frown as the girl slides the tea things onto the table. I think of the disjointed sentences, the agony behind the words. "No, she was more than furious. I can't remember the exact words, but there was something about making him pay. Mr Lovejoy."

"You think it was a threat? Against him? Against their children?"

"I'm not sure. She seemed quite tormented." I pour the thin tea into his cup, then mine. "And there was another thing. She referred to the first Mrs Lovejoy's death." I screw my eyes together, try to recall what she wrote. "Something along the lines of how she died, and was she going to die the same way. It could just mean that she thought she might die from disappointment like the first Mrs Lovejoy, but I did wonder if she meant there was something more . . . nefarious behind her death."

He's quick to understand. "You think that they had something to do with Mrs Lovejoy's death?"

"I'm not sure." Taking a sip of my tea, I wait for Hatch to makes notes. "And I met the gardener the other night. What a dreadful creature. Are you sure he didn't do it?"

A smile hitches the corners of his lips and he nods. "Horrible man, isn't he? But yes, I've had him checked. He was at home with his unfortunate wife. Arrived at the house just after the maid found the girl and just before dawn when he found Mr Lovejoy. The nightsoil man can corroborate this."

"Was that the other person who found Mr Lovejoy?"

"Yes. On his way home, I believe."

"The nightsoil man didn't notice anything else?"

The detective shakes his head as the girl plonks a plate of soggy crumpets, already buttered, onto the table between us.

"I'll tell you what I find interesting," I say, as I stir another spoonful of sugar into my tea. "The cook, Nurse Marie and the gardener each believe that the older children are responsible. In fact, the gardener goes as far as to say he thinks that Mrs Lovejoy and Cyril are in danger of being next."

I tell him that the current Mrs Lovejoy doesn't treat Emily and Joshua well, that she's responsible for ruining their relationship with their real mother.

Hatch chews on some crumpet, wipes his fingers on his handkerchief. "And what do you think?"

202

I want to be fair, but I think of all the times they've crept up on me, especially Emily; his vacant stare and her sullen face covered in angry pustules. "They're quite disarming, I have to admit. Between the two of them, they could have taken Margaret, killed her and arranged her body in the outhouse. That'd be much easier than on their own. They could've overpowered their father too." Again, I imagine Joshua binding the old man's arms while Emily draws the razor across her father's throat. Unfortunately, it's an easy picture to visualise, when it involves those two.

"And Nurse Marie?" He takes another crumpet. "Maybe Mr Lovejoy didn't give her what she wanted."

"Such as?"

"Marriage? Money? Maybe she killed them in revenge?"

I fiddle with the handle of the teacup. Somehow, I don't think this is the case. A servant like her would know better than to expect so much. Money? Maybe. Marriage? No. I shake my head. "No. I don't think she would've murdered them for such a reason."

Hatch takes one last sip of tea and says, "Well, if you're finished here, we will go over and find out what we can about this Nurse Marie. See if there are any other reasons she might have resorted to murder."

We tread across the plum carpets of Duke's Registry, and wait at a desk for a number of minutes, while a clerk, her grey hair piled high on her head and the ruffles of her blouse clasped together with a cameo brooch, serves a couple who seem to be searching for work together as butler and housemaid. The clerk tells them they must be patient, that they might need to wait a while for a household in need of both at once.

Duke's Registry, just like Bower's, has posters on the wall. Inventories of available servants, but also those who are on the blacklist. I wander closer, my eyes taking in the likenesses drawn in graphite. I marvel at the pettiness of the charges against the servants, although one particular fellow, who has an almost gnomish face, is purported to have garrotted all his master's dogs before taking off. Further on, I smirk as I read of those who are "permissive" or "sinful", although my lips tighten as I gaze into the face of a pretty young girl, and wonder if her sin had been thrust upon her.

Hatch is talking with the grey-haired clerk now, but my eye is caught by a face that seems all too familiar. Yes, she's slimmer, younger, her black hair neat under a nurse's bonnet. But there's no mistaking those heavy, straight eyebrows, the handsome cast to the face. Mr Lovejoy's second wife, the present Mrs Lovejoy. My eyes skim over the words next to the likeness, and then I read it through again more slowly. *Catherine Chandler, sometimes Challenor. When not "baby farming", as it is referred to by the authorities, she finds engagements as a nursemaid. Beware.*

"Hatch." He's writing something down in his notebook. "Hatch," I say again, beckoning him.

He joins me. The woman is not far behind. "What is it?"

I point at the drawing. "Do you recognise her?"

His eyes take in the picture and the longer he gazes, the wider both his mouth and eyes become.

"Oh yes, her. Have you come across her too?" says the grey-haired woman behind us. "Had a man in a week or two ago looking for her. Mr Collins, Mr Collins," she calls out to a thin man with spectacles at the next desk to hers. "When was that deranged man in here? The one asking after this Catherine Chandler?"

The man scratches his head, takes his glasses off. "I don't seem to remember."

The woman rolls her eyes. "Well, it wasn't that long ago, Detective Inspector. He was very upset. I thought he might have apoplexy when he saw that picture. I nearly called for the doctor."

"What did this man look like?"

"A mop of white hair. Quite a bad-tempered face."

Hatch takes a page from the newspaper out of his pocket and unfolds it to reveal a picture of Mr Lovejoy. "Is that him?"

The woman's eyebrows rise in surprise. "Yes. I'm sure that is him."

Hatch and I exchange looks. "And what can you tell me of this woman, madam?"

"I heard she got six months' hard labour. For neglect, mind you, not murder. The shame of it. Women who are unable to keep their babies . . ." her eyes drop for a moment, ". . . you know the type — well, they pay respectable women to care for or adopt their little ones. But this Catherine Chandler kept the babies passed out on Godfrey's Cordial, I believe, and they died from starvation, poor mites, while she pocketed the mother's money and pawned the clothing. We heard she might have murdered — because, really it's murder, I think you'll agree — as many as eight children."

"When was this?" Hatch asks.

"Oh," her face wrinkles as she considers. "Quite a few years ago now. Maybe five, six, seven? Haven't thought of her in a long time, until that man came in asking after her."

"Where did she operate, do you know?"

"Moved about, of course. But she was picked up in Willesden, I believe. A doctor became suspicious by how many death certificates he had to fill for her. The local police there might be able to help you, if you're after more information."

"Can I take this?" Hatch asks, gesturing to the drawing.

"Yes, of course," she says, peeling it from the wall. "Know her, do you?"

"I think we just might," he says, taking it from her. "Thank you for all of your assistance."

We pause on the sidewalk in front of the registry. "Well, that was quite a find, Mrs Chancey. We are lucky you have such sharp eyes."

"What would you like me to do from here?" I wonder, on returning to the house, if I will be able to hide this new-found knowledge from Mrs Lovejoy. Just how callous do you have to be to allow a number of babies to die in your care? To murder them?

Hatch stares at me for a few moments. "You go back. Keep an eye on her. She's not likely to disappear, leaving her son behind. But who knows? If she's the monster we're looking for, she might do just that. Or worse." He guides me to a cab. "I'll report to the superintendent. In all likelihood, I'll be back with some constables this afternoon to arrest her. If you can, find that diary again, before she has time to spirit it away, and I can follow up on the Willesden deaths." I climb into the cab and he closes the door on me. "What with Mrs Lovejoy's pitiless character, her fury at her husband's affair and his uncovering the truth about her past life, it looks like we have finally found our murderer."

CHAPTER
TWENTY-FOUR

I have never witnessed so much wailing and struggle as when Hatch came to interview Mrs Lovejoy last night. I have been to funerals, have visited asylums, where more decorum has been shown.

As the constables dragged her into the study, Mrs Lovejoy clung to anything within her reach. She upended a plant stand, toppled side tables, scraped chairs across the floors, all the time moaning entreaties peppered with screams of protest, despite Hatch trying to assure her that he only wanted to ask her a few questions.

I'm not sure where she'd been all day, but she stank of the tavern.

Nurse Marie had to pull a teary Cyril back into the nursery while the cook and Ruth watched from the kitchen, hands clamped across their mouths. Only Joshua and Emily seemed composed, standing at the top of the staircase; Joshua as vacant as usual, head tipped to the side as he watched the show, while I'm pretty sure a slight smirk lightened the girl's heavy features.

And now, walking to the village shops, the wind is so cold and so strong, I'm sure it'll whisk Cyril's small body away if I don't hold onto his hand firmly. Oak trees rustle menacingly above us, and we need to press against the heavy gale as we stride forward. My eardrums start to ache and Cyril's eyes are watering. It's almost unbearable, but not as awful as it would have been to stay cooped up in the house.

I've left Nurse Marie in the housekeeper's room again. She's worse than when I first met her, if that's possible. Hair flopping all over the place, staring at the wall, her fingers plucking the woollen blanket I draped over her lap. As soon as Hatch left last night, and Mrs Lovejoy took herself off to bed, Nurse Marie tried to bar me from the nursery, said she was in charge of the boy. But I could tell he was afraid of her, I could see it in his wide eyes, the tremble of his lip. When I refused to fetch his warm milk, she lost her temper, stomped down to the kitchen herself. Cyril clung to my skirts as we listened to her quarrel with Cook. By the time she returned to the nursery, her composure had left her. She began weeping again, said she needed to get away, be anywhere but here in this house, so I made her a cup of tea with a slug — a very, very generous slug — of that Woodward's Gripe Water. It didn't take her long to settle down. I guided her to the housekeeper's bed to rest.

And this morning the house was freezing because Ruth was late to lighting the fires. We were lucky to get a piece of toast out of Cook, who was too busy wringing her hands over what was to become of us all, what with the master dead and the mistress losing her mind. Only when Emily came down, mild surprise on her face, asking after breakfast, like nothing untoward had happened to disrupt the morning routine, was it that Cook finally poured boiling water over tea leaves and stoked the oven.

That girl, Emily. Heart of stone. Hasn't she wondered what's to happen to her and her brothers if they find themselves without a parent?

A cab slows down, the driver asking me if we need a ride, but I shake my head. I wonder about the Lovejoys' finances. What is to happen to the children? How has Lovejoy provided for them all? I must ask Hatch to find out about his will. If Mrs Lovejoy is committed to trial . . . my mind jumps ahead — what if she's hanged? . . . Does Joshua inherit everything? Joshua, who dotes on his sister, Emily.

What do those strange children do all day? Do they sit in their airless rooms, plotting? What's really going on behind Joshua's empty eyes? And Emily's? That knowing gleam, calculating every move. I run my gloved fingers over Cyril's cap. As certain as I am that Mrs Lovejoy is our culprit, we can't leave him with those two. I'll have to bide my time until I hear from Hatch again.

We pass a tobacco shop, and I glance into its smoky depths, yearning for a lungful. I glance down at the boy and almost draw him inside. What does it matter? It's not like I'm going to be dismissed now. They might even have a bit of sherry behind the counter. But no. I'd better not. I'll sneak a cigarette at home, maybe nick some of Mrs Lovejoy's stash of sherry. I grin at the thought.

"Come on, Cyril," I say to him. "First, I'm going to look in Sullivan's rag shop over there, see if there's anything interesting, and then we're going to that teashop across the way, where you can have as much cake as fits in your belly."

We open the door, shuffle in, shutting the door firmly against a gust of wind. The shop is blessedly warm, but the air is close; has the musty smell of cast-off clothing, the staleness of unwanted detritus. It takes me straight back to the days I had to scrounge in proper rag shops, tucked away in Liverpool back alleys, looking for a decent pair of shoes or a dress without too many patches or stains upon its skirts. I remember the slippery feel of grime these searches left upon my fingertips, the itch the dust left on my skin.

"Don't like it, Nursie," says Cyril.

"We won't be long," I say, drawing him towards a glass cabinet filled with things that sparkle in the dreary light. On closer inspection, I see that it's only fishing hooks, tools I don't even recognise, and some sort of metal knobs for who knows what. On a shelf in line with my nose is a glass bowl filled with buttons made from brass, shell, wood. Next to this is an array of fans, mostly moth-eaten and faded.

"Can I ask what Miss hopes to find?"

I turn to look at the man with the gruff voice. He's big, with a barrel chest and bristling sideburns that match his thick eyebrows.

"This your shop, is it?" I ask.

He nods. "Sullivan. My father was the rag-and-bone man around these parts. Did such good trade he set up this shop. I've extended the business, I have, to include all sorts." He stands a little taller, hooks his thumbs into his trouser pockets.

"Ah, I thought it looked a little better than a mere rag shop." I cast my eyes around the small room. "I was just looking to see if you had any nice china or lacework, really. A gift for my mother."

"Step this way, Miss," he says, ushering me to the other side of the shop where clothes hang along the length of the wall. "This piece is very handsome. Bought it from a gentleman newly arrived back from Spain. He thought it was too colourful, but I think it's a very nice garment. Be perfect for a lady." His flat fingers trace their way over the crimson ribbon embroidery of the jacket's lapel.

"Very nice," I reply. There is no way Amah would wear that. "What is that coat behind it?"

He shows me a number of fur coats, but I can't bring myself to try them on. I prefer new apparel now. Clothing that has only known my skin, my scent. And Amah wouldn't wear them anyway.

"What about porcelain?" I say to him.

He leads me to a bench cluttered with gravy boats, cups and saucers, and even more saucers. I pick up a particularly pretty bowl with a willow pattern. A slight chip mars its edge, but I love the intricate pagodas, the costumed fellows crossing the neat bridge. Maybe I'll get it for myself, for I know Amah will turn her nose up at it, say it's like no Orient she knows.

I glance into a glass-top cabinet, my eyes taking in the cheap trinkets on display. Tarnished bangles and rings with dull crystals. At the back of the cabinet, though, is an assortment of quite decent snuffboxes — one with mother-of-pearl inlay — and a prettily carved tortoiseshell comb next to a silver brush and mirror set. I look around for Sullivan, just about to ask him to show me the silver, when my eyes take in the weapons mounted on the wall before me. Between a long sword with a rusty handle and a pistol blackened with age is a *kris*. I take in the wavy blade with the dragon's curves engraved into the iron, the garnets that wink dully at me from the handle. My *kris*. It's my *kris*.

"Where did you get that?" I ask, pointing. I'm so dismayed that I squeeze Cyril's hand a little too hard so that he uses his other hand to prise my fingers away.

"That?" Sullivan stares at me, calculating, for a few seconds. "A gentleman I met at the docks brought that back all the way from China. Very valuable, it is. You can see, here, on the metal . . ."

I frown at him, placing my free hand onto my waist. "As a matter of fact, it's from Java and I know exactly how much it is worth because it was stolen from my home."

He looks shocked, then laughs. "No. How can you be sure?"

"Of course I'm sure."

He's looking at me suspiciously, now. "Well, how did you come to own such a piece?"

"A gift from my uncle," I say, confident. "Who brought it here from Java. It's been in my family for many years, only to be stolen from my home a week or two ago."

His ferocious brows lower into a frown too. "I hope you're not accusing me of theft?"

I roll my eyes. "No. I'm not. But if you could just tell me who you actually had it from, then I can follow up on my loss."

"The police, you mean?" His mouth clamps shut on the last word. I fear if I say yes, I might not find out who the culprit is who supplied him with my *kris*.

"The police are of no use to me," I say. "I just want to make sure it wasn't one of my friends or colleagues."

He scratches the back of his head as he stares at the *kris* on the wall. "I hope you don't expect me to just give it to you. I paid good money for it."

"I'll pay you for it."

He hooks his thumbs into his pockets again and considers for a moment.

"I got it from Tomkins."

"Who's Tomkins?"

"Nightsoil man. He brought it to me about four days ago. Said he found it dumped by the side of Grayling Road."

My brain is awhirl as though I've been spinning on the dance floor after too many champagnes.

My *kris* turned up four days ago. Here. Just after Mr Lovejoy had his throat cut and just like McBride before him.

I pace the plush carpet of the Lovejoys' drawing room. The *kris* lies on an oval, mahogany side table with spindle legs. I gaze down at it, take in its keen edge. I peer closer, not quite sure if the dark rim that separates the hilt from the blade is a sign of age, or worse, a residue of blood.

Who brought it here?

Who was at my soiree that night — the night McBride was murdered? My thoughts are scattered, like the windswept oak leaves strewn across the footpath outside. Cosgrove? Surely not. Hunt? No, no. Pidgeon? I shake my head, take a deep draw on my cigarette. This is ridiculous. Hopefully Hatch receives my message soon so he can relieve me of this damned *kris*, once and for all.

I lift the *kris*, and its shiny blade catches what dim light comes through the window. Smoke curls from the tip of my cigarette, hangs on the still air. Jakub. I remember how I saw Jakub yesterday. I'd forgotten to write to Amah of it. What was he doing here?

I angle the *kris* back and forth, feel its heft and the cool grip of the handle, and wonder who else has held it in the recent past. Gripping it tight, I imagine how the murderer might have grabbed a clump of hair in his left hand, bringing the blade towards his victim's throat . . .

The drawing room door shifts slightly. A shadow blocks the gap at the door jamb, then is gone. I go to place the *kris* back on the table, but hesitate. I don't want to carry such a deadly thing around with me, but I don't want it to go missing again either. I slip it under a cushion on the divan and then hurry into the corridor.

I'm just in time to see Emily bound up the stairs. I follow her, lugging my heavy skirts high as I take two steps at a time. I've almost reached the landing when she rushes from the nursery, Cyril tucked under her arm. By the time I reach her bedroom door, it clicks shut in my face. I knock loudly on it, shout her name. Shout for Cyril.

"What are you doing in there, Emily?" I call between bangs, pressing my ear to the timber. I can hear voices; Cyril's high-pitched questions, low murmurs.

My heart judders in my chest. Is this how it will end? I rattle the doorknob but it's locked. What will I find in there? Crimson streaks flash across my mind. Please, no. I kick the door until my toe throbs.

"What is it, Nurse?" asks Nurse Marie behind me.

"She has Cyril." Stepping back, I stare at the closed door. "I don't know why."

Nurse Marie's slightly puzzled. Her eyes look strange, glossy. The pupils are huge, cover her blue irises. She's taken something, laudanum probably. Swaying, she lowers herself into one of the chairs.

I take to knocking again. "The police will be here soon." Was that the wrong thing to say? Will it hurry the girl along in her dastardly plan?

"Emily, don't hurt him. Please, don't hurt him."

The door is wrenched open so quickly, I lurch forward, nearly crash against her.

"What do you mean?" she demands, her eyes scanning my figure. It's the most emotion I've ever seen from her. The pimples on her face are livid, flare red from her pasty skin.

She grasps a pair of scissors in her hand.

I put my hands up between us. "I just want to know why you have Cyril." Over her shoulder, I see Joshua standing by the bed. He has his hands resting on Cyril's shoulders, keeping the little boy in place.

"I think you should return the boy to me, Emily." I'm trying to keep my voice smooth, calm, but it resonates in my ears, sounds almost childish. "He needs to go back to the nursery now."

She looks to the side, sees Nurse Marie. Her eyes harden. "I'm not leaving him with you mad bitches. He's safer here with me and Josh."

I blink. "What are you talking about?"

She brandishes the scissors between me and the nursemaid. "At first I thought it was you," she stabs the scissors in Nurse Marie's direction, "who killed Father and my sister Margaret." She swings the scissors around towards me. "But you! Turning up out of nowhere, and all your snooping about at night."

"But, Emily . . ."

She interrupts me. "And I saw you just then with that knife. I saw you! You're getting ready to kill someone else, but it won't be us." Slamming the door shut, she shouts, "You said the police were on their way. Well, I hope they arrive soon."

CHAPTER
TWENTY-FIVE

"I've explained to both Emily and Joshua the circumstances that brought you here," Hatch says, hitching his trousers up at the knees before taking a seat in the drawing room. Weak afternoon sunlight streams through the windows. "But I think they're still uneasy and feel it's best if their little brother stays under their care for the moment. At least until we know what's going to happen with Mrs Lovejoy."

I've been waiting, twiddling my thumbs, while he was locked away in Emily's room, interviewing them about our misunderstanding over the boy and our respective weapons. "You haven't made up your mind about her?" I ask.

He shakes his head. "It was hard going, last night. She was too far gone on sherry, I'd say. I'm going to question her right after this."

"And my *kris*? How do you account for its presence here?" I ask.

He takes to his feet again, and stands looking down upon the dagger where it lies on the side table. "Very puzzling, isn't it?" He brings out a magnifying glass from an inner pocket, studies the *kris*. "You're sure it's yours?"

"Yes. It went missing on the night McBride was murdered outside my house."

"Which was after Miss Margaret was killed in the outhouse?"

"Yes."

He stares across at me. "And the fellow in the shop said a nightsoil man found it after Lovejoy's murder?"

I nod.

He frowns down at the *kris* again. "So it may link Lovejoy's murder to McBride's. But not necessarily to Miss Margaret's."

I've had a little time to think on this, and have come to the same conclusion.

"I think it might be best if you follow up on Nurse Marie, while I contact the detective on the McBride case, see which one of us will question this . . ." Hatch glances down at his notes, "this Tomkins. The nightsoil man." He tears a page from his notebook. "The clerk at Duke's Registry supplied me with the directions of a special servants' home where you might find more information on Nurse Marie, although now I'm not convinced it's necessary. But I won't know for sure until I've seen Mrs Lovejoy."

The cab is buffeted by the strong wind as it pauses at a crossroads. I glance down at the slip of paper Hatch pressed into my hand as I left St Chad's Lodge. On it is written a White Lion Street address.

I decide that after my work with Hatch today, I'll return to Mayfair, finally have a full night's rest. I don't relish another evening in the nursery, and anyway, Cyril is in Emily's charge now. My eyes follow a man being driven down the street by gusts of wind, his hand clamped against his hat, and wonder what Hatterleigh is doing. Has he tried to contact me in the past few days? Has his brat been born? I turn my head, gaze out the other window. What do I care?

Finally, we pull up in front of a building made of bricks the colour of biscuit, with crisp, white window frames. According to Hatch, it belongs to an organisation that helps "fallen servants" find their way again. After paying the cabman, I rap on the brass knocker.

I smile up at the middle-aged woman who opens the door and introduce myself. "I believe Detective Inspector Hatch has written to you in regard to my visit," I say. "You had a nursemaid named Marie Brown."

"Yes, yes," she says, ushering me into the hallway. "I'm Miss Agnew. I can tell you what you need to know."

I follow her through a doorway to the right, where she asks me to take a seat. The room is cold and quite bare, furnished with hardback chairs and a table covered with skeins of wool and unfinished baby booties and bonnets. Miss Agnew's a large woman, very tall. The ringlets in her short, brown hair fall loose and her mouth purses over bucked teeth. Her eyes are bright and friendly.

"What did you want to know about dear Anne-Marie?" she asks me, folding her hands neatly in her lap.

"Anne-Marie?"

"Oh, yes. That's her full name, and how we always referred to her here. Anne-Marie Bromley. Although I have heard she prefers just Marie now. I can't think why. Anne-Marie is such a pretty name, I think you'll agree."

"That is strange," I say. "We call her Nurse Marie. And I'm sure the detective said her surname was Brown."

"Yes, yes." Miss Agnew's head bobs side to side. "Often the girls like to use new names when they leave here. The stigma, you know, if they were to be connected to their pasts."

"Their pasts?" I know what she's talking about, but would like her to clarify.

She sucks her cheeks in for a moment, so that she looks like a duck. "With child, but without husband, if you know what I mean."

"That's how Nurse Marie — Anne-Marie — came to be here?"

"That's correct. She was with us nearly seven years ago."

"And you still remember her?"

She nods, vigorously. "Oh yes. I'd just started working here, you see, and then what happened to her . . . so awful." Miss Agnew sits forward, looks around. "I forgot to bring the tea things in. Would you like a cup of tea, Mrs Chancey?"

I do, but not as much as I want to hear the rest of her tale. "No, thank you." I wait for her to lean back in the chair. "You were saying . . . ?"

"Ah yes. Anne-Marie. Well, as you must surmise, she came to us heavy with child. She was a nursemaid for a well-to-do family in Somerset, and had managed to convince her mistress that her dying mother needed her home for four months."

"Her employer didn't suspect the truth? Surely she was showing by that stage?"

Miss Agnew thinks for a moment. "She was quite a large lass, Anne-Marie. I don't think she would have looked that much different attired in a wide skirt and apron."

I think of Nurse Marie, of her sinewy arms, her gaunt face. I can't be sure we are talking of the same woman until Miss Agnew says, "The last time I saw her, though, she was a mere shadow of herself. As thin as straw. She never was her jolly self again after what happened." She shakes her head sadly.

"What happened?"

"She had a lovely little boy. Matthew, she called him, after her own father. Well, he wasn't the bonniest baby you've ever seen, but very placid, like his mama, I used to say to her. She stayed on with us a matter of weeks — maybe three, four? Usually, after confinement, the girls stay for only a fortnight at the most before they return to work, but Anne-Marie was a bit sickly, so she stayed on."

"And the babies? What happens to them when the women go back to work?"

Miss Agnew sighs. "Yes, well, that's the problem, isn't it? We are able to help unfortunate mothers-to-be through confinement, but we are not set up to care for

222

the newborns, so sometimes we send them on to church organisations we know of, or to an orphanage run by an affiliate group of ours. And, of course, sometimes, the mother is fortunate enough to find a man to marry. But that's quite rare, sadly."

"And Nurse Marie?"

"Anne-Marie was smitten with her baby. They all are, you know. People don't realise how harrowing it is for these poor women to give up their babies. Most only see the children as the bruised fruit of sin, to be discarded, hidden. But these women really want to keep their babies, they really do." She takes a deep breath. "Nobody more than Anne-Marie."

"But she couldn't?"

"No. Not if she was to return to work at her former station. And she had to. It was the only way for her to make any sort of income to support the baby. It's a terrible bind."

"So what did she do?"

"It was my fault, really. I told her of certain women who look after babies for a fee. I knew of quite a few mothers who used this type of service so that they could still be the child's mother, visit them once in a while, despite being unwed and working full-time." Miss Agnew stared into the empty grate. It was nearly a full minute before she spoke again. "Anne-Marie found an advertisement in the newspaper for just such a service and contacted the woman. A very respectable-looking woman she was, too. I saw her myself." Again she paused, shook her head. "Broke her heart to give her little boy up. But I put my arm around her shoulder, reminded her that she could visit the boy whenever she wanted. Then Anne-Marie went back to work as a nursemaid for the lady in Somerset. It was maybe four months later I saw her again. She was in a terrible state, just terrible. Told me she couldn't find the woman or her son, and asked me if I knew anything. But, of course, I didn't. I took her straight around to the police."

"And?" I begin to see the end myself. Things I've learnt over the last couple of days are coming together in a dreadful kaleidoscope.

"And," her voice is hollow. "They'd recently arrested a woman for neglecting children in her care. They took poor Anne-Marie to somewhere north of here, had her look at the bodies of two children who'd starved to death in this woman's care. Little Matthew was one of them."

My heels click along the pavement as I strive to keep up with Hatch. His strides are long, but he doesn't seem to notice how I struggle to match his pace. His chin is tucked into his chest, his hands deep in his pockets as he walks, deep in thought. What I've told him has given him much to think about.

After my interview with Mrs Agnew earlier I had the cab drop me at Sullivan's rag shop again, where I made a special purchase. By the time I returned to St Chad's Lodge, my mind was seething with notions. Hatch was still with Mrs Lovejoy in the study, which was fine with me because it gave me time to ask Cook some things while she prepared a chicken for dinner. I then checked on Cyril, who was playing in Joshua's room with his siblings.

"Are you leaving now?" Emily asked. Her tone was nonchalant as she looked at me from behind the novel she was reading, but her dark eyes were sharp, maybe a little anxious.

"Not until everything is resolved." But would it ever be for these children? I looked at Joshua, who was writing something at his desk, and Cyril, who looked up from his picture book and said, "Milk, Nursie?"

I knew that there would definitely be more trouble ahead for them, but hopefully the loyalty the two older children had shown to Cyril earlier in the day would carry them all through.

"I'll ask Ruth to bring you some, Cyril," I said. Then to his sister, "Keep this door locked, Emily. Stay together. Until you hear otherwise from Hatch, don't talk to anyone except Cook or Ruth."

Joshua glanced over his shoulder at me and Emily frowned. They both nodded, and watched as I backed out of the room.

Trotting along now next to Hatch, I ask him how far away the nightsoil man lives.

"Not far at all. I have it from the local constable that this Tomkins lives just down this alley," he says, turning to the left.

The low-set homes look more fitted to a stable yard than to a row of human dwellings. We pass five doors before Hatch stands back, looks a squat building up and down. "This is it, I think." He knocks, and then has to knock again before the door is answered.

"Tomkins?" he says.

The man squints, and his eyes are bleary. His brown hair is snarled close to his skull like sheep's wool, and his thin wrists poke out from his coat sleeves. "Yes. Who may you be?"

"Detective Inspector Hatch. I have some questions for you."

Tomkins's eyes widen a little, but he gestures for us to follow him inside. "We have to be quiet though. The missus is just trying to settle the children."

We find ourselves in a cramped kitchen so clotted with smoke it's like we're caught in a thick fog. The beams and chimney flue are as black as tar and the floor is unboarded. I take the one seat at the rickety table, while Hatch leans up against a bench. Tomkins stands by the closed door to the other room.

"Who's she?" Tomkins asks, looking at me.

"A witness of mine," says Hatch. "She's found some items we thought you might be able to help us with." Hatch lays a bundle of cloth on the table and unravels it until the *kris* lies sparkling in the gloom. "I believe you sold this to the rag shop in the village?"

Tomkins stares at it, and nods. "What of it?"

"We'd like to know where you acquired it in the first place, Tomkins."

"Well, it's mine, isn't it? Been in the family for years. Yes, years. And I didn't want to sell it, but things have been very slow for me lately. Usually I'm a labourer, earn a tidy living, what with that during the day and my nightsoil work at night. But I hurt my back a few months back, had to give up the labouring. And the

226

missus just had another baby. Have to keep the bread on the table, so I sells that there knife to Mr Sullivan." He sucks his bottom lip when he finishes speaking.

A baby mewls in the other room, and the longer I sit here, the harder it is to ignore the reek of human waste.

Hatch stands to his full height, the top of his hat brushing the ceiling. "Tomkins, we know this short-sword was stolen from its rightful owner. I do not, for a moment, believe that you ever owned such a valuable item."

"But I did, I . . ." he protests. He looks Hatch dead in the eye and it's as though the fight leaves him immediately. "All right. All right. I'll tell you the truth. It's not a family relic. I found it, long ago. On my rounds."

"Long ago?"

Tomkins nods, vigorously.

"Where?"

Tomkins screws up his face. "I think it were down on the riverbank, I found it."

"And yet Sullivan says you found it within the last week in Grayling Road." Hatch's pale skin almost glows in the dark kitchen and the nightsoil man looks up at him, fearful. "I have to warn you, Tomkins, you keep this up and I'll be forced to arrest you for theft. Now, unless I hear some truth come out of your mouth, you won't be around much longer to support your missus and children."

I'm surprised at the detective's intimidating manner, but it seems to work. Tomkins wilts, runs his hand over his face.

"I found it on the roadside. Last week."

"When, exactly?" I ask.

"Several mornings ago. Yes, Monday, it were, because I don't usually work of a Sunday night, but Driscoll couldn't work on account of being sick."

"And where did you find it?" Hatch asks.

Tomkins gulps, as though he's swallowing a lump of bread. "Lordship Road."

"Speak up. Did you say Lordship Road?"

The nightsoil man nods.

"Whereabouts on the street did you find it?"

"Well to be precise, it were at the corner, where the road crosses the next street."

"Just on the ground?"

"Lying in the grass, for anyone to see."

"Was this after or before you found Mr Lovejoy's body?"

Tomkins runs his hand down his face again. "Before, it were. The sun weren't quite up."

"But why, Tomkins, didn't you report it straight away to the police when they were called?"

"Well, it were difficult, weren't it," he says, his tone lifting. "On our rounds we often find things we can pawn or sell to the ragman. People usually give us a bottle of gin for our troubles, but that Mr Lovejoy had a tight purse. So when I saw that knife, I could tell straight away that it would fetch a pretty penny, so I swiped it, hid it in my bag, I did, so's the others wouldn't want a share."

"And later? After you found Lovejoy?"

"Do you know how horrible that was to find a dead man, his head near sliced from his shoulders? What with that and running for the police constable, the knife went clean out of my head, it did."

"And when you remembered it? It didn't occur to you that it might have something to do with the man's death? That you should hand it in?"

Tomkins sags against the closed door. Something bumps in the next room, one of the children squeaks. The planes of his gaunt, starved face catch the shadows. "I didn't think it would do any harm, me keeping it. The whole village knows it's one of them crazy Lovejoy children who've murdered the child Margaret and their father."

Hatch presses his lips together as he regards the other man. He shakes his head and says, "This won't do. It won't do at all. You might be in for some serious trouble for withholding this evidence, Tomkins."

The nightsoil man bows his head, clutches his forehead in his hand. I wonder if he's crying, and I feel a small stitch of sympathy.

"I'll tell you what, Tomkins," says Hatch. "I have one more thing to ask you about. If you tell me the truth — no prevaricating, mind you — I will see what I can do so that the authorities are lenient. How does that deal sound?"

Tomkins stares at him. "What do you want to know?"

Hatch nods to me. "I want you to tell us about this."

I reach into my bag and bring out an item wrapped in a handkerchief. As I place it on the kitchen table, Tomkins gasps.

CHAPTER
TWENTY-SIX

It's late by the time we return to St Chad's Lodge. The household's already eaten supper and Mrs Lovejoy has passed out in an armchair by the fire in the sitting room, the whisky decanter nestled in her lap.

All is quiet upstairs, and as we walk down the hallway, Ruth peeps around the corner of the kitchen door at me, only to be pulled back by Cook. I knock on the housekeeper's door.

"Nurse Marie?" I call lightly. I turn the knob, let myself into the room.

She's seated in that chair again, staring out the window into the darkness. As I draw nearer, I realise all she can really see cast against the glass by the candlelight, is her own reflection.

"Nurse Marie," I say. "I wanted to discuss something with you."

She doesn't say anything, doesn't move.

I place the tortoiseshell comb on the little table by her chair. "Do you recognise this, Nurse Marie?"

Her eyes swivel down, fix on the comb.

Something clangs in the kitchen, the back door claps shut. I can smell remnants of their roast chicken dinner and I feel queasy, for the task ahead of me is exhilarating, yet daunting. "Do you recognise it?"

Her head swings slowly side to side.

"No?" I say.

She continues to shake her head. Her lips are so chapped, I can see the keen fissures sliced into the skin.

"Cook says it's yours. She recognised it straight away," I tell her, picking the comb up again. Its teeth are spindly, more rounded than usual. Carved into the tortoiseshell is an intricate pattern of flowers and leaves, while at its centre, wings spread, is a swooping swallow. "Cook said your uncle brought it back for you from his travels and that it was your most cherished belonging. She also said she hasn't seen you wear it since . . . Well, for quite a while."

I've left Hatch standing on the other side of the door, which is ajar. I told him that I thought she was more likely to speak to me if I appeared to be by myself.

"That's not mine," she finally manages. She keeps her gaze on the comb in my hand.

"Do you want to know where it was found?"

Her eyes find mine and I think there's a flash of entreaty there and, in light of this, I almost hesitate, think of calling Hatch in to finish for me. But I pull another chair forward, across the timber floor, until I'm sitting opposite Nurse Marie.

"We — the Detective Inspector and I — went to visit a man named Tomkins."

"But why? What do you have to do with the police?" she asks.

"I was placed here to keep an eye on the household, Nurse Marie. By the police."

She's slumps back into her chair, and seems to shrink the more I speak.

"When we visited this Tomkins — he's one of the nightsoil men around here, you know, and he explained to us that he's the holeman, the one who has the delightful job of being lowered into the pit," I say. "Well, according to him, he came across this comb — your comb — in the muck of the outhouse directly after the morning Miss Margaret was found, dead. He's a very poor man, you know, open to temptation, so he wiped the blood and the mud from it and sold it to Sullivan." Her hollow eyes stare out at me. I'm becoming frustrated by her lack of reaction. "He says he knows it wasn't there the morning before because he was on duty that day too. And, of course, the outhouse wasn't used for a day or two after Margaret's little body was found."

"I lost it the day before." Her voice sounds strangled. "It must've dropped in when I was helping Miss Margaret use the lavatory."

I consider for a moment. "No. I don't think so. Cook and Ruth are quite certain it's only since Margaret's death they haven't seen your hair tucked in with that comb. They thought you'd just put it aside in your grief." I smooth my thumb across the grooves of the comb. "This is quite compelling evidence, you must see, that you took the life of little Margaret."

"Ridiculous." The nurse draws herself up for a moment, squirms her shoulders against the back of the chair. A ghastly smile trembles on her lips, and heat flushes her face. "Why would I do that?"

"We know about Mrs Lovejoy, Nurse Marie." I think of the home for fallen servants. "We know about Mrs Lovejoy's days as Mrs Chandler, about the children she took into her care."

The nurse's head rears a little and she sneers. "Care!"

I want to place my hand on her knee in sympathy, but stop myself. "We know about Matthew, Nurse Marie."

She stares into the black glass of the window, her bottom lip twitching. Finally, she says, "So you know what that woman did to my son?"

I nod. "We do. And we're very sorry for your loss, as was Mrs Agnew. But tell me, how did you find Mrs Lovejoy again? How did you come to be here too?"

"I saw her, walking along the path in the village, with the children and a nanny." She squeezes her eyes together, as though she's trying to see that day again. "I'd recently taken a post with a family in Dalston, and my mistress had asked me to come into Stoke Newington to fetch some linen she was in need of." Her eyes open. "I was horrified when I saw her — *her*, Mrs Lovejoy — strolling with the children. I thought she was up to her old tricks again. I thought she was going to harm those small innocents. But when I pointed her out to the draper, she told me that she was the very respectable Mrs Lovejoy, living in the grand house on Lordship Road." She runs her fingers through her greasy hair, clutches at the strands, before relaxing her hands again. She shakes her head in disbelief. "She told me that those healthy, beautiful children were her own."

"What did you do?"

"Left my household in Dalston and watched the Lovejoy family. The nursemaid took the children for a stroll every morning after breakfast and it only took me a matter of days and all of my savings to convince her to leave. She recommended me for the position."

I suppress the urge to look around at Hatch, but I can sense him scribbling down this information. No doubt he'll want to track down the former nanny.

"And then?"

"Then . . ." She shrugs.

"How long before you and Mr Lovejoy . . . ?" Her eyes find mine. "The other servants have told me that you and Mr Lovejoy were in an intimate relationship."

She lifts her hand to shield her eyes, but not before I see a look of distaste sweep her face. "I don't want to talk about that."

"But that was your first revenge, yes?" I push. "To catch the eye of her husband?"

Her hand flaps.

It occurs to me that she might have been planning more. "Anne-Marie, were you hoping to become pregnant to him? Was this to be your revenge?"

"I can't talk about it. I won't," she whispers.

"Ah." The awful truth of her position finally dawns on me. "But you didn't become pregnant, did you? Mrs Lovejoy did. She was going to have another bonny baby, and you were still without."

234

Her hand falls at the same time as a tear tumbles down her cheek. "She didn't deserve another child. She didn't deserve another baby to hold and love and . . ." She holds her hands out, rigid, emphatically, entreating me to understand. "She'd murdered all those babies. She'd murdered my Matthew. How could God reward her with so many beautiful children? How? And leave me with nothing?"

I take a deep breath, let it out again. She's right. Life has been terribly cruel and unfair to her. "Did you leave a note for Mr Lovejoy? On the terrace?" I'm thinking of the time Mr Lovejoy sat in my drawing room; of how he told Cosgrove and Pidgeon of the threatening letter he'd received.

She looks puzzled.

"A warning of some sort?" I prompt. Signed with a figure that looked a lot like an "A", the sign of Pidgeon's evil *kungsi*, but also the initial of Nurse Marie's real name — Anne-Marie.

"Is that where it went?" Her eyes fix onto a spot on the floor. "I wanted to caution *her*," she won't use Mrs Lovejoy's name. "I wanted her to feel that trickle of dread, the constant worry of the unknown. But the letter must've fallen from my pocket. I did better than that in the end, anyway."

My heart rate picks up pace. "What?"

"I told Mr Lovejoy of her previous life. Her former profession." Her voice rings with malice, her eyes hard. "He didn't believe it at first. But I pointed the way for him."

"To the servants' registry?"

She nods.

"What happened?"

"Nothing. I think they quarrelled about it — I heard raised voices from her sitting room, thumping on the floor. But that was it. He didn't leave her. She wasn't thrown out."

Her lips tremble again and she clamps her lips together between her teeth.

"What did you do then?"

She shakes her head.

"It must have been so difficult for you. Seeing that woman with her children. Having to follow her orders, after what she'd done to you."

"I couldn't sleep." Her voice is barely a whisper. "I couldn't sleep. Her words, her deeds, the injustice of it all. I felt I was going mad." With the flat of her hand, she taps the side of her head. "The constant thoughts throbbing in my mind." She grabs onto her hair again, close to her scalp, tugs. "She only got five months of jail time for the babies' deaths. Did you know that? Only five months! They called it neglect, but it was murder. It was murder."

"So what did you do, Anne-Marie?"

Her hands fall. Straggly strands of hair entwine her fingers. She doesn't answer me.

I wait. The clock on the mantelpiece ticks the seconds away, and I hear the slightest rustle from the doorway, maybe Hatch turning a page in his notebook. I wait half a minute, but she still doesn't speak.

"I wonder if I can guess what happened?" She doesn't answer, doesn't even look my way. "I think that you realised there was only one way you could really hurt Mrs Lovejoy. One way she would truly understand the grief she has put you through."

Nurse Marie raises her eyes to the ceiling.

"Maybe you chose the girl because you couldn't bring yourself to hurt the boy — a boy like your own Matthew who was taken from you."

"No."

"You waited until the deadest part of the night, maybe around four in the morning, and you lifted that little girl from her bed and carried her down to the lower floor." Her gaze is still on the ceiling, but tears now brim her eyes. "Maybe she woke, and you assured her you were taking her to the lavatory. That she needed to relieve herself. But going through the house you had the forethought to put on Cook's wrapper." I'm not sure if this was before or after she'd fetched the girl, but it shows a degree of planning. This was no spur-of-the-moment crime.

Still, she says nothing.

I continue. "The fire is almost always alight in the nursery, isn't it? To stay nice and warm for the children. How easy to throw the wrapper amongst the flames, destroy the evidence."

She blinks, forcing the tears to fall.

"And the drawing room doors. Jimmied on the inside and out. I think you found yourself locked into the house. Only the housekeeper and Mr Lovejoy had the keys, so you had to break your way out. And then you scraped the panelling on the outside too, to confuse the police, make it appear like an intruder forced his way in."

Nurse Marie swings her head back and forth, slowly, like a muzzled beast trying to break free. "No," she moans. "It didn't happen."

"But it did, Nurse Marie. You carried poor Margaret to the outhouse and you murdered her. You wanted her mother to know the terrible anguish she'd put you through. What did you use, Nurse Marie? When you cut her little throat? Was it Mr Lovejoy's razor? That would serve him right, wouldn't it, Nurse Marie? Wouldn't it?"

Nurse Marie clamps her hand to her face, squishing her nose and cheeks, and lets out a groan. The door creaks, and I see Hatch hovering. I shake my head at him, turn back to the nursemaid.

"Is that how it happened, Nurse Marie?" I ask her again, but she doesn't answer.

"And Mr Lovejoy? Why'd you take his life?" I'm quite sure she didn't, but I have to be certain.

The woman lifts her haggard face to me. Her mouth opens and closes, trying to force words out. She lets out a pitiful "No."

"You didn't murder him?"

She sinks her face back into her hands, still shaking her head from side to side. The sobs shudder in and out of her skinny frame, and it takes a good five minutes before she is almost calm again.

"I think you'll have to go with the police now, Nurse Marie," I say to her. "Are you prepared?"

238

"I need a drink." Her voice is hoarse as she pours water from a small jug into the drinking glass beside her on the side table. Her hand is shaking so hard, the china rattles against the glass.

"I will fetch the Detective Inspector," I say, standing.

Out of the corner of my eye, I see her lift a small brown bottle. "Just to calm my nerves." Instead of a drop or two, she splashes the rest of the bottle into the water.

I only have a moment or two to react. I know the contents of that bottle must be her stash of laudanum and she's tipped a dangerous amount into her drink. A deadly amount. Part of me sees the sense in what she is doing. Not only that, I feel bad for the sorry creature, and I understand it might be the most humane way to see this through. But what of young Margaret, robbed of life because of her mother's sins? Surely she deserves some sort of justice?

I step forward, slide my hand in between the glass and her mouth just in time. She tries to resist, but her strength is feeble, and as I wrench the drink from her hands, laudanum and water dash across my skirts.

Hatch arrives by my side. He draws the nursemaid to her feet, and leads her away by the upper arm. She's not crying anymore.

CHAPTER
TWENTY-SEVEN

It's quite late by the time Taff picks me up from St Chad's Lodge. I feel flat, a little sad, as the coach rumbles home. I left Hatch to deal with the nursemaid and, as he handed me into my carriage, he congratulated me on finding the comb. Said I made a fine detective.

Usually, after such a satisfactory ending to a case, I'm jubilant, ready to toast with a glass or two of champagne, but not tonight. As I sway against the side of the carriage, I think of how ghastly young Margaret's last moments must've been, of how her life was sacrificed because of the activities of her mother. And what of Nurse Marie? Doesn't she deserve my sympathy too? I wonder if the anguish she now lives with, having murdered such an innocent, will ever be worth avenging the death of her own baby. Remembering her trembling fingers, the lips stretched awry as she tried to speak, I think maybe not. It might've been better for her own soul if she'd just taken Mrs Lovejoy's life and been done with it.

Which reminds me of Mr Lovejoy. What with solving Margaret's murder and finding the *kris* so close at hand, his slaying continues to be a mystery. As Taff

240

helps me climb down onto the path in front of my home, I think again of how this has not been a case of three interconnected murders, after all. Lovejoy and McBride. McBride and Lovejoy, linked by the *kris*: my *kris*.

"Good evening, Bundle," I say, as he opens the door, the hallway cheerfully lit behind him. "Home at last."

"Mrs Chancey," he replies, taking my luggage from the coachman. "We did not expect you home tonight. You'll find the drawing room sadly chilly, but there's a nice little fire lit in the parlour."

"Is Amah in?" I ask, as I strip my gloves off.

"I believe she retired a couple of hours ago, Mrs Chancey."

I nod and make my way to the parlour. As I pass the display cabinet, I glance in to where the *kris* used to be, but Bundle or Abigail have rearranged the ornaments to cover the gap.

Taking a seat on the divan by the fire, I lean back into the cushions, watch the black tips of the flames lick the air. I run my fingertip over the velvet upholstery, back and forth, its soft, layered texture comforting somehow. Fatigue presses against the back of my eyes, but thoughts continue to tick away in my brain.

"A light supper for you, madam," Bundle says from behind, as he places a tray on the table. "And I'll just leave all your post here for you to read at your leisure."

I look around at him and smile. "Thank you, Bundle. Why don't you take yourself off to bed now? It's late. I won't be far behind."

He gives a slight bow and walks from the room.

The clock chimes ten o'clock before I manage to haul myself up from the divan. I inspect the soup — chicken and vegetable, cooling now — and, ignoring the tea tray, I move to the side table, half fill a tumbler with scotch. Sipping it, I sort through the post Bundle has left me. First, I pick up a package and, peeling away its wrapping, reveal a small, flat box. Lifting the lid, I discover powdery squares of my favourite sweet — Turkish delight. I dab my finger against the chalky sugar, touch it to my bottom lip where my tongue seeks it out. With it is a note. *Dearest love, I hope this small treat finds you well, Hatterleigh.* Hatterleigh. I'm so tired, I almost can't be bothered being annoyed with him anymore.

I then open three invitations to card evenings, one to a fancy-dress ball and four to fancy suppers. Maybe that's what I need to take my mind off these things: convivial evenings with women of my own sort, and the admiring men who surround us. As I drop Queenie Martel's missive onto the table, bidding me to attend her next euchre night, I notice a letter with familiar, bold, loopy handwriting. Sir Thomas. I tear it open and my eyes skim over the contents. It's dated a week earlier.

My dear Mrs Chancey,
I hope I find you well. Detective Inspector Hatch informed me that you took up the nursemaid position in the Lovejoy household after all. I won't interrupt your commission for Hatch, but thought

I'd send this letter to you in the hope you read it when you do eventually find yourself home.

A little while ago you recommended my services to a certain Sir Henry Pidgeon. He has since apprised me of the truly horrifying events surrounding McBride's death and the involvement of a group of dastardly Chinese fellows who seem set upon a path of revenge. Unfortunately, I will be leaving for Scotland in the morning with two of my employees. We are to keep an eye on a certain doctor, suspected of murdering his wife and servant. As you know, normally I do not undertake the groundwork myself, but I find this contract to be an excellent opportunity to spend some time with my daughter's family in Glasgow. Therefore, I was unable to help Pidgeon besides providing him with Bob Beveridge — you might remember Mr Beveridge? You worked with him on the Knightsbridge case. Bob will keep an eye on Pidgeon's home, and guard his daughter. My request of you, provided you arrive home in South Street before I return, is to contact Pidgeon, perhaps check up on him and his daughter? I feel it might be best if Mr Beveridge joins us in Glasgow as soon as possible to assist in this murder case. Of course, you will be reimbursed at your usual rates.

I will call upon you as soon as I am returned.
Yours Sincerely,
T. A.

Poor Pidgeon. I run my tongue across the chip in my tooth as I think of his distress. That Beveridge creature won't be much help to him, from what I remember of the man. Most of the time he was "corned", as Taff likes to refer to it, lurching from the job at hand to the nearest tavern, and back again. I really should've mentioned it to Sir Thomas, but one day Beveridge's wife turned up, a little one clutching her skirts, asking after him. I didn't have the heart to jeopardise their income.

I'm just picking up the next letter in the pile when I hear a soft rap against the front door. I frown, wonder if I could've heard correctly, but then, the sound is repeated.

Recalling that I've sent Bundle to bed, I step out into the hallway. As I approach the front of the house, a shadow falls across the glass of the sidelight. I shade the glass with my hand, peer outside. My heart lifts, races a little, when I recognise the familiar shape of square shoulders, the smooth jawline and temple beneath the top hat.

Swinging open the door, I say, "Cosgrove." I smile up at him. "A little late for a visit, isn't it?"

I move back to allow him to step into the hallway.

"Didn't your butler tell you I have come by several times over the last few days? Pidgeon let slip you were helping the police on the Lovejoy case, which made me very curious for news."

He stands rather close to me. I'm aware of his scent, how tall he is, his eyes on me. Turning away, I close the door.

244

"I was just on my way to Motts, actually. Wondered if you'd like to join our party again. I'm to meet the others there. You can fill us in on the gossip." His smile is as relaxed as ever, reaching his blue eyes.

I glance down at my dress. I haven't changed since my long day with Hatch, and I'm weary. Well, I *was* feeling weary, until Cosgrove's presence cracked through me like a sapling spark in a bonfire.

"You do look a little fatigued, however," he says. "I will leave you alone and visit again tomorrow. Maybe you can share a little of your news then." He makes for the door, places his hand on the brass handle. "It's just that I've become a bit worried about Pidgeon. I'd like to discuss it with you also, sometime soon. I fear for poor Isobel."

"Well, in that case, don't feel you need to leave immediately." It's not just an excuse to make him stay. I am interested in Pidgeon's predicament. I am. "Have one drink before you go to Motts."

He takes me in for a moment, then shrugs off his overcoat. I hang it up for him, and he places his gloves and hat on the hall table. I lead the way to the parlour.

"We can sit at the table or by the fireplace. Your choice," I say, lifting the decanter. "Whisky?"

"Yes, thank you." He takes a seat at the foot of the divan, leaving the side with the recline for me.

I sit next to him, my wide skirts encroaching upon his thigh. I try to move back, but I am quite ensconced against the side of the divan as it is. I place the box of Turkish delight on a lacquer side table. "Tell me about Pidgeon."

"Ah, yes." He sits forward, elbows on knees and gazes into his glass. "The morning after we met here in your drawing room, he received a threatening letter that was almost identical to the one I received. The poor fellow has become quite unhinged by the matter. You haven't heard from him?"

I shake my head. "No. I have only returned home this evening. I must go around first thing tomorrow morning," I say, recalling Sir Thomas's request of me. "Is Isobel not one of your party tonight?"

"No, Pidgeon has become increasingly paranoid. Won't allow her to leave the house. Has some drunk guarding the front door."

"I know. I've just read a note from Sir Thomas. I'm acquainted with the man he's put with Pidgeon. A lush buffoon." I shake my head and take a sip of my whisky.

Cosgrove turns his head to look at me. His fine lips curl into a smile, and I have an urge to run my fingertips across the texture of his face, the evening bristle.

"Tell me about your time at the Lovejoy residence," he says.

I sigh, raising my eyes to the ceiling, conscious of his gaze resting on my profile. "It was quite exhausting really." I tell him of Cyril and the drinking habits of Mrs Lovejoy. I make an amusing tale of the gardener startling me that night and befriending the vicious hound. I finish with an account of visiting the servants' registry and the information we gleaned that helped to unravel the mystery of Nurse Marie.

246

"But why did she murder Lovejoy? Why not just kill Mrs Lovejoy and be done with it?" he asks, putting his empty glass down on the side table.

"But that's the problem. We don't think she did, after all. I'm quite sure she murdered the little girl, but we can't hold her responsible for Mr Lovejoy too." I place my hand on his arm, draw it away quickly. "Remember that *kris*? My *kris*, from the cabinet in the hallway?" He nods, frowning. "It was found at the scene of Lovejoy's death. His murder must've been committed by whoever killed McBride, not by the nursemaid."

Cosgrove looks bewildered, draws back. "But I haven't seen any word of this, that the *kris* was found. In fact, the police were quite sure the Lovejoys' deaths were connected."

"Yes, but the nightsoil man found it that morning near the body, although he pawned it almost immediately. Sold it to the local ragman, without reporting it to the police."

"Outrageous. Didn't the blasted ragman make the connection between the knife and Lovejoy's murder?"

"I think he did, but he wanted the sale."

Cosgrove folds his arms, stares into the fireplace, and is silent for half a minute. "Are you quite sure, Heloise, that the *kris* went missing the night of your soirée? I'm just asking because it really does appear to be that we're dealing with that *kungsi* Chinaman who's trying to finish us off, one by one. There's no chance he could have sneaked in here that night? Nobody who works here who might've smuggled it out to him?"

I give a sharp shake of my head, a little offended. "Of course not." Surely not. Bundle's very efficient at keeping the house safe from intruders. And the staff? Why would they bother? I must remind myself, though, to question the butler regarding any tradesmen or labourers that might have had opportunity to nick it at the time.

Cosgrove brings out his pocket watch and glances at the time. "The others will be at Motts by now. I really should go."

"Of course." I feel a little disappointed at his leaving, and wonder if I should quickly change into a more festive gown, but I'd only hold him up unnecessarily. "Please, before you leave, have a slice of Turkish delight." I reach across him, and pick up the box.

As his teeth sink into the pink square, the gold pin with the blue stone that holds his tie in place twinkles in the gaslight. Feeling bold, I lean towards him, and touch the stone.

Looking up at him, I ask, "What sort of gem is this, Maurice? I've never seen such a thing."

I go to withdraw my hand, but he catches it in his. "It's called lapis lazuli. I brought it back from my time in Mandalay."

I'm so close to him I can smell his cologne, and something beneath that, something male, earthy.

"It's lovely. I must find myself a piece of this lapis lazuli," I say. A dab of powder dusts his lips. "But you must go, sir, mustn't you? Your guests wait."

He smiles. "Yes, you're right. I'm very late." Yet he doesn't make a move. Instead, he stares at me with

248

those blue eyes of his, and then cups the side of my face in his hand, his thumb softly sweeping the skin below my eye. I turn my head, kiss the base of his thumb, tracing the flesh with the tip of my tongue. With a soft choking sound, he pulls me to him, and presses his lips to mine. I taste the rose water, and feel the prickle of his stubble against my mouth.

I grin as I gaze into the mirror of my dressing table. All around my mouth, and a little bit on my chin, I have a rash from the hour or so my lips were crushed against Cosgrove's. Heat rises up through my chest and into my face as I think of his hardness pushed against me, of his lips brushing the flesh of my breasts. But I didn't take him to bed. Not yet. I have to be sure of him first.

"Yes?" I call, when I hear a light scratching at my door.

The door opens a few inches and Amah peeps in. "You are alone?"

"Amah, yes. I am. What are you doing up so late?" She does not look well. Her skin is pallid and she's taken off weight in the short period I've been away. "But what is the matter? Have you been ill?"

She stares at me for a few seconds, her mouth ajar like she might say something, but she just shakes her head. "No. I am fine. It's just this horrible cold weather. Who can rest with its nipping?" She rubs her hands together so they make the sound of rustling paper.

"Well, at least take a seat and I can tell you all that has happened while I was away." I pull an armchair close to the fireplace for her, which she ignores.

"Tell me of your case," she says, as she takes up my brush.

Taking a seat again, I close my eyes. How nice it feels, how comforting, to have her sweep my hair back from my face. Every few moments I feel her cold fingers skim my scalp, and I can smell her fragrance, something of teak tea chests and jasmine. It's not often she brushes my hair so gently, with such reverie.

"Tell me," she repeats.

"It was the nursemaid."

A sharp intake of breath. Her eyes meet mine in the mirror.

"What wickedness," she says.

I watch as she places the brush back onto the dressing table, and I see how dry and chapped her fingers are. Urging her to take a seat on the armchair, I kneel down and try to apply my special ointment to her skin. She waves me away, taking the jar, and rubs and rubs the substance into her hands as I tell her of what happened at St Chad's Lodge. The whole time I speak, she continues to massage the ointment in, as if she's polishing the silver, only pausing once, when I mention the *kris*.

"The *kris*?" Her voice is hoarse.

"Yes, awful, isn't it? So, of course now it seems obvious that whoever killed McBride also killed Lovejoy." I turn back to the mirror. "And the strangest thing, Amah, I'm sure I saw Jakub in Stoke Newington. But then I realised it was impossible." I swathe cold crème across my forehead, swirl it into my cheeks. It's made of opium and lemon water and something else that smells so sharp the rose perfume can't hide it, but I've been assured it will keep my skin pale and blemish-free. "Jakub's still abroad, isn't . . . ?" But the bedroom door clicks shut. Amah's gone.

For days Amah has hunted for that boy. She's searched the West India Docks and the shops of Limehouse. She smelt cargoes of spice, the greasy fumes that billowed from the ships, the body odour of the sailors, but all she's managed to collect are memories of a past she's striven to forget.

Towards the end of that long voyage on the *Dukano*, when they made their way across the ocean to this place, Mrs Preston was very sickly. Most of the white people had terrible dysentery — the stench, as the servant boys ran past with overflowing buckets, that mixed with the sweetness of the *nilam* oil the white men used to keep the bugs from their bedding — even now Amah's stomach recoils. She'd never seen anything worse.

Day after day, Mrs Preston lay in her bed, panting, only half in this world. Amah had to gather up all their linen, Mrs Preston's leather shoes, books, spare candles and tuck them into the bedding with her mistress, under a shroud of netting so the rats wouldn't chew on all of their things or maybe even Mrs Preston's flesh. Every afternoon, Amah lifted her mistress into a chair and turned her mattress, lined it with fresh sheets, so that when she lay down again she had some relief from the heat. While the sun was high in the sky, Amah fanned Mrs Preston's face. She watched as the woman mumbled in her sleep, her cheeks flushed. She only really found peace late at night, when the sea breeze whispered through the open doorway. It was on one such night, when the lanterns had been extinguished and the men were bedded down in the saloon, that he found Amah there.

The waves lapped the side of the boat, the timber floors and beams creaked. But still, she heard his soft tread find his way across the cabin. The dark was so complete, Amah had to blink a few times to make sure her eyes were open.

She was not sure if his plan was to attack Mrs Preston or her, but he stumbled, cursed in his white tongue, and landed atop Amah. Her breath came out in a loud huff, and she doubled over, trying to clasp her stomach. He grabbed her arm and held her pinned with one hand, while his other covered her mouth. She struggled against him. She strained to reach the knife that lay close by where she'd been slicing pineapple for Mrs Preston earlier in the day.

Amah doesn't know how long this went on for — a minute, ten? — it was like the darkness allowed no certainty, no record. But the smell of him, the feel of his flesh. She made sure that she would know this man again.

CHAPTER
TWENTY-EIGHT

Over breakfast, I open the rest of my post. Second from the bottom is a letter from Pidgeon. His handwriting is not much better than a scrawl. He writes of the threatening message he'd received, the same one that Cosgrove told me about the evening before. He complains of Bob Beveridge and how unhelpful the police have proven to be. The letter is closed with the words, *Heloise, do you trust this Sir Thomas implicitly? Something troubles me greatly, and I need to share it with someone. I think I might know why McBride had to die — indeed, why we are all marked to die. Maybe when you return, you can visit me, tell me of this Detective Inspector you have been working with.*

How very odd. I smear Gentleman's Relish across my buttered toast. But very interesting too. I need to find out what is haunting Pidgeon. I'm sure I'll be able to draw it from him.

The morning sky is so clear I decide to walk to Pidgeon's house on Derby Street. Under my cloak I'm wearing a new walking dress. The full skirt, spruce green, has a handsome Swiss waist. The white bodice is neatly trimmed with embroidered seams and has pretty, billowing sleeves. Besides my small bag, I clasp a lace handkerchief, chiefly because it matches my bodice, but also to hold to my nose if the air becomes too foul.

I pass a small bakery and it reminds me of Cyril. I smile and wonder how the little brat is doing. Pausing, I look through the bakery's window, but they only carry bread and some plain pastries, no sweets, none of the hard candy the boy enjoyed so much. My silhouette makes a smart reflection in the glass, but maybe, just maybe, it's missing his small figure by its side. My fingers curl, as I remember the boy's small hand tucked in mine. Pliable, trusting, insistent. Sticky.

Curzon Street is filled with the sounds of coachmen, carmen, and, in the distance, I can see three ladies leaving the chapel. A butcher's boy makes his way to a large house on the corner, a dog trotting along behind.

I stop short at Derby Street. The narrow road is blocked by a number of carriages and a uniformed policeman argues with a fishmonger trying to gain access.

"Sir, I won't repeat myself again," the constable says. "You cannot pass through this street until the Inspector says you can."

The fishmonger, red in the face, turns back, rolls his eyes at me. "Somebody dies, and the world has to shut down."

I glance over his shoulder to the row of houses. Anxiety taps its claw against my ribcage. "Who died?"

"They found some chap dead in his coach. Alls I wants is to deliver this fish to Mrs Poole at number 19, but I just can't get through. Tried the other side too, I did. This fish won't stay fresh all day, you know. And Mrs Poole is very particular."

The fish's grey carcase lies limp in his basket, its middle partially covered with a red and white checked kerchief. A globule of blood seeps from its gills and its mouth gapes. A whiff of its damp, raw odour reaches my nostrils and my stomach turns.

Thankfully, the fishmonger walks on, leaving me staring into Derby Street, trying to discern which coach might hold the corpse. I can see the top of the white portico that fronts Pidgeon's home, which seems to sit at the centre of the tumult. The claw of anxiety tightens its grip on my chest.

"Mrs Chancey," a familiar voice hails me from behind. I turn, and look up into Detective Inspector Hatch's pale face. "What are you doing here?" he asks.

"Inspector, who has died?" I hold tightly onto my purse and handkerchief to stop myself from grasping his sleeve. "I have friends — the Pidgeons — who live in that house, there. Please tell me it's not one of them."

Hatch's thin face seems to lengthen as he watches me.

Two gentlemen stroll close by, crane to see into the road. A cab slows down for the driver and passengers to stare out at the commotion.

Hatch steers me by the constables guarding the road, gestures for me to hop up into the police buggy. "Please sit, Mrs Chancey. I'm afraid I have some bad news for you."

I'm glad of the seat because my knees feel weak. I hadn't really noticed how cold the morning was before, but now I feel as if my limbs are made of ice, that my lips are frozen.

Hatch's words are hushed and swift. "I'm afraid your friend, Sir Henry Pidgeon, has been found dead in his carriage."

My mind is awhirl, as though a flurry of snowflakes fills my head. "But how?" I manage to ask. *Please let it be an apoplexy or a lung fever. Not . . .*

The Detective Inspector leans forward and briefly grips three gloved fingers of my left hand. "You must be strong, Mrs Chancey. What I have to tell you is not for the faint-hearted, but I believe I can use your services again. And I know Pidgeon was a good friend of yours."

I'm conscious of how dry my lips are, but can't summon the will to lick them. I just stare at Hatch and nod.

"It appears Pidgeon has been murdered by the fiend who killed both McBride and Lovejoy."

I let out a long breath. I breathe out for so long, my corsets conflate with my stomach. My breath in is too short, and the next, and the next.

"Was he . . . ?"

Hatch nods. "He was murdered in the same manner as the other two men."

Pidgeon. With his mournful, hound-like face. Doting father, loyal friend. The terror he must've felt.

"Mrs Chancey, are you all right?"

I nod. Closing my eyes, I try desperately to think of something pleasant, something reassuring that will help me right my breathing. I try to imagine I'm by a bright fire, that I'm safe, home in Mayfair. I imagine there are strong arms wrapped around my shoulder. I think they might be Hatterleigh's, but no. Cosgrove's? I frown. No. And then I realise they're Amah's.

I open my eyes. "I apologise. This has been quite a shock. For that poor man to die in such a terrible manner." I shake my head. "I can't fathom it." I glance over at the carriage. Three men have unharnessed the horses and lead them away. Two constables guard the carriage doors, and Pidgeon's driver stands close by, staring into the gutter, puffing on his short pipe. "What is it you needed of me?" I dab my lips with my handkerchief and my hands quiver only a little.

"Please come inside and sit with Miss Pidgeon. You will only need to stay with her until her aunt arrives from Croydon. Obviously, she is in quite a bit of shock." He climbs down from the buggy and takes my hand as I take the two steps down onto the road again. "Maybe you can find out if she knows something that can shed light on this affair."

He steers me in a wide semicircle around the carriage so there is no chance I might accidentally see inside, but just as we reach the bottom of the Pidgeons' front steps, his driver greets another man on the pavement, and I hear him say, his voice low yet urgent, "His head had fallen fair in his lap, Roddy. In his lap! I'm not lying to you." The driver lifts his pipe to his lips with shaking fingers.

I almost glance back at the carriage, but Hatch takes my arm, says, "No, Mrs Chancey. You don't want to look."

I look up at him. "Is it true?"

He nods, as he leads the way into the house. "I'm afraid so. One of the more vicious crime scenes I've ever seen."

Isobel appears at the top of the stairs on the first landing. "Heloise. Heloise," she moans. I hurry up the stairs to her.

I wipe Isobel's hair back from her forehead. It's damp with perspiration and tears. She lies along the sofa, and her head rests in my lap. Besides stroking her hair, I don't know what to say to her as her tears seep into my skirts.

Anger builds inside me the longer I sit here. I don't know much about McBride and Lovejoy, but who would want to kill Pidgeon, who was such a harmless, well-loved man? Fury billows up from my stomach through to my chest. Isobel's sobs stoke the rage, until I feel the pressure of it in my head, in my fingertips and my jaw aches. I want to burst out onto the street and scream, "Who did this?" Closing my eyes, I imagine forming a fist and smashing it into the murderer's face. But the picture shifts — the cheekbone, the chin, the eyes — for I don't know yet who is the culprit. Is it really a Chinese person, as Cosgrove and the others suspect, or is it someone else?

I glance back down at Isobel. I won't trouble her with these questions. Her father is dead, and that's all that matters to her, not the how and who.

Picking up her left hand, I gently squeeze her fingers. "Why are your fingertips so orange, Isobel?" She still has an apron over her skirt, and she smells distinctly of something like mutton stew and onion.

She sniffs, wipes under her nose. "I was teaching Cook a recipe for a curry I learnt while we lived in Burma." Rubbing her fingertips together, she says, "It's from the paprika. They don't make curry quite like that at the Oriental Club, and as it was Father's favourite, I . . ." She presses her hands to her face and sobs quietly. I rub her shoulder, helpless.

Isobel's aunt arrives about an hour later, and I leave the two women to weep together on the sofa. The carriage has been cleared away, along with poor Pidgeon's body, and only one policeman remains, stationed on the bottom step leading onto the pavement.

"Where is everyone, Constable?" I ask him.

"The Detective Inspector has returned to the station, madam," he says. He's rugged up in his heavy uniform overcoat, but his cheeks and nose are pink from the cold. "Down on Vine Street."

I thank the man and walk home as swiftly as I can. My eyes tear up against the rising wind, but also from my sorrow for Pidgeon and his daughter. I bow my head as I make my way, wishing my hat had a veil attached that I could pull down over my face.

Flinging open my front door, I call for Bundle. "Can you let Taff know I need the carriage as soon as possible?"

I run up the stairs to my dressing room and sweep through my drawers until I find a short length of Chantilly lace, black with a pattern of roses, that I can swathe over my hat. I then return to the hallway and pace the floors, waiting for Taff.

When I hear my carriage pull up at the door, I hurry out, call up to Taff, who's seated on the driver's box, "Don't bother getting down, Taff. I'll be fine. Take me to the police station in Vine Street, please." A young couple passes by my house at that moment, and the man looks as though he might offer me his hand, but I manage to haul myself and my skirts into the carriage.

I look out the window as we make our way, but I don't really see anything. I'm anxious that Hatch might have left the station before I make it there. I want to know more of what happened and if they've managed to find any clues as to who has done this horrible thing. I feel if I don't keep moving, keep busy, there will be nothing left for me to do except allow the tightness in my chest to dissolve so that I'm capable of nothing but blubbering on my bed.

The police station is hidden behind a forbidding brown façade. The strident windows are covered with black metal bars and a large lantern perches over the entrance. A constable leads me down a dingy corridor and leaves me in a poky room, windowless, and only furnished with a table and four sturdy chairs. I'm reading the names nicked into the table-top when Hatch enters the room.

"Mrs Chancey." His expression is slightly surprised, but without reproof. "How can I be of assistance? I only have a moment, I'm afraid. How is Miss Pidgeon?"

"Not well. But that is to be expected. I left her with her aunt." I watch as he takes a seat opposite me. "Have you any clue yet to who may have done this?"

He takes in a big breath and lets it out noisily. "We are back at the beginning, I'm afraid."

"What do you mean?"

"Well, I first questioned Pidgeon's butler, and it seems Pidgeon received a message earlier in the morning that caused him to finish his breakfast abruptly and call for his coach."

"Did you see this message?"

Hatch nods. "We found it in Pidgeon's pocket."

"And . . . ?"

"What can you tell me of Jedediah Hunt?"

Hunt. I think of the last time I saw the older man — his whiskery face, his loud, querulous voice — in my drawing room the night McBride was murdered on my doorstep. "Not a lot." I tell Hatch that he's just one of the group of explorers who frequent my soirees. "I think there was talk of a time when they were all stationed together in . . . was it Mandalay or Sarawak?" I try to think back to the night at my place, but what with the amount of champagne I'd had and McBride's death, the evening is a bit of a blur. "Why do you ask? Was the note from him?"

Hatch doesn't answer, he just frowns down at the table, traces his finger across the word "hell" that's been etched into the timber.

"And the *kris*," he finally says. "You are sure the *kris* we found is the one from your display cabinet?"

I nod. "Quite sure. But, if you want to confirm that, you are welcome to show it to Bundle, my butler. He will know."

"Yes. I was going to question your servants today, in any case."

"Were you? About the *kris*?" I stiffen a little, wondering how poor Bundle and Agneau will take to being interviewed.

"Yes. See if they saw anyone suspicious around the time of McBride's death." He shifts in his chair. "The thing is, if the *kris* was from your home, then the culprit had access to it. I'm afraid I'll have to question both your servants and your guests."

I swallow. "What of the coachman? Did not he see who murdered Pidgeon?"

Hatch blinks twice as he stares at me. He seems to be weighing up how much to tell me. "He says he was sitting on his box, thought he felt a bit of a commotion below in the coach but put it down to Pidgeon just trying to make himself comfortable. He didn't know anything was amiss until he was pulling out from the kerbside and a man jumped from the carriage and ducked around the corner."

"Could he describe him?"

"Said he looked Asiatic."

I take a sharp breath in. "The Chinaman."

Hatch shakes his head. "I'm not so sure, although I'm no expert on the subject." He's frowning again. "When I asked him to elucidate, he said the fellow was dark and tall, and had a long red cloth of some kind swathed around his head."

I try to picture what he's described.

"Fortunately, at that precise moment, a midwife was leaving a house further down the road and told the constable on duty that she also saw the man lurch from Pidgeon's carriage. Her description was similar. Tall, dark man. Long loose clothing. Foreign. But she called his head covering a turban. Said she'd worked in a household once who employed Indian servants. She was sure the fleeing man was of Indian blood."

I sit back in my chair, flummoxed. "Well, that's a strange twist."

Hatch's frown takes on an irritated cast. "Yes. Just what I was thinking."

CHAPTER
TWENTY-NINE

As Bundle lets me in through the front door, I feel faint, jittery, and I realise it's late afternoon and I've not drunk or eaten since a cup of tea and toast at my dressing table this morning. My face feels flushed, but at the same time as if all my blood is dropping to my feet. As I peel off my gloves, I see that my hands tremble.

"Bundle, Detective Inspector Hatch will be here sometime to talk to you and the staff. Please let Agneau and Taff know. It's about the *kris* that went missing."

"And Abigail, Mrs Chancey?"

I'd forgotten Abigail. "Yes, her too. Although, Bundle, I'm not sure he'll need to talk with Amah."

Bundle just bows and returns to the back of the house. How thankful I am for the man. He always understands me.

Amah appears at the top of the stairs. "What is it, Heloise?"

I beckon for her to follow me into the drawing room, where I sink onto the sofa, and say, "Pidgeon is dead. Murdered."

Amah pauses by the card table.

"Did you hear me?" I say, exasperated. "I said Pidgeon was murdered this morning. Just like McBride and Lovejoy."

She shakes her head slowly. "Terrible. Do they know who did it?"

I shrug. "The coachman and another witness claim it was someone of Asiatic appearance." Asiatic. The general term for a brown foreigner. Lucky the midwife knew a thing or two. Or did she? Really, she might have been as mistaken as anyone.

I stare down at my bag, at the embroidered leaves that match the colour of my skirt. I remember that Amah never liked the Pidgeons. She probably doesn't care. But when I glance back up, her face is as pale as rice pudding, and a small frown flickers between her brows.

I sit forward. "Take a seat, Mama. You don't look well at all. What is the matter?"

"Nothing, it is nothing, Jia Li," she says.

Abigail treads past the open doorway with a heavy pail that swings against her knees. She opens the front door, closes it behind her and we can hear the brush's bristles scrub across the tiles of the front steps. A bit late in the day for that, I would've thought.

"I need to go out, Heloise," says Amah, as she walks from the drawing room. "I might be late home."

"But where . . . ?" She's already trotting up the stairs and out of earshot. I roll my eyes. What bee does she have in her bonnet this time? I pull the box of Turkish delight onto my lap.

Bundle places a cup of tea on the side table, already sugared, and I smile my thanks to him.

"Maybe you would like an early supper, Mrs Chancey?"

My stomach rumbles at the thought, despite my low spirits. "Yes, please, Bundle."

After a few sips of the sweet brew, I can feel my heartbeat settle, my fingers steady. Placing the cup back in the saucer, I pick up a square of Turkish delight and take a bite. Licking the powder from my lips, I am transported back to the night before with Cosgrove.

Cosgrove. I wonder if he's heard from Hatch. If he's heard the terrible news.

I take to my feet, almost upsetting the box of sweets. I quickly sip more of my tea and then pop the rest of the Turkish delight into my mouth as I hurry into the hallway.

"Bundle, Bundle," I call, walking towards the back of the house. "I won't need my supper just yet, thank you. Can you tell Taff I am very sorry, but can he take me out again?"

Bundle appears in the kitchen doorway. "I'm afraid Amah just left with him, Mrs Chancey. I assumed you knew."

I'm nonplussed. Amah must be very flustered indeed to take the coach without letting me know. "Not to worry, Bundle. Can you please fetch me a cab, then?"

The cab passes along a line of identical Georgian terraces in Holborn. Luckily, I know Cosgrove's directions from the frequent times I have needed to address invitations to him, and the driver leaves me outside a house with a door painted the shade of a glossy horseshoe. I rap on the knocker, glancing left and right. The sun has set, and I wonder if Cosgrove would be embarrassed if his neighbours were to see him receiving a solitary, female visitor.

A middle-aged man with short, dark hair oiled flat to his head answers the door, but almost immediately Cosgrove is at his elbow, saying, "Heloise, Mrs Chancey, this is a surprise. Meadowes, there's a good man, fetch us some tea, would you?" He ushers me past his man into a room to the left.

I find myself in a small sitting room that also functions as a study. A desk, piled with books and loose sheets of paper falling to the floor, sits under the front window, next to an overcrowded bookcase, its glass doors ajar. In a semicircle before the fireplace is a setting of two lounge chairs the colour of oxblood, which are divided by a low-set marquetry table. A fine Turkish rug covers the floor. The room smells of smoke, books and leather.

Cosgrove pulls the curtains together across the window to the street. "Take a seat, Heloise." He lowers himself onto the lounge chair opposite to mine. "To what do I owe the pleasure of your company?"

His words are polite, yet the gleam in his eye is cheeky, gives a hint of other pleasures. My chest feels heavy. He mustn't know about Pidgeon.

I reach out, place my hand on his knee. "Maurice, have you not heard from the police?"

A slight frown. "No. Why? What has happened?"

267

At that moment, Meadowes enters the room, bearing a tray of tea things. I draw back into my chair, wait for Cosgrove's man to lay out the cups and teapot, the plate of bread and butter.

When Meadowes finally leaves, closing the door behind him, Cosgrove repeats, "What's happened?"

"Pidgeon is dead." I can't think of any other way to say it. I can't see him appreciating me trying to soften the blow. "He was found this morning."

"But how?"

"The same as McBride." I don't want to describe the ghastly details, give word to how my good friend — our great friend — was murdered. As I watch Cosgrove's head sink, as he covers his face with his hands and groans, "No", I again feel anger rise in me. Who is the bastard who killed poor Pidgeon?

I stare down at the carpet. The white fringe has grubby ends, and in the port-coloured weave there is a patch worn thin from silverfish.

Cosgrove's face is red when he lifts his head again. "What of Isobel?"

"She is fine. She's still at their home but will travel to her aunt's house tomorrow."

Cosgrove's face is haggard as he stares at me. "Where was he when it happened?" he asks, through clenched teeth.

"Outside his home, in his carriage. He seemed to be in a hurry to meet someone."

"Whom?"

"I think it might have been Hunt, but the Detective Inspector wouldn't elaborate."

"Hunt? Do you know where they were to meet?"

"No." I shake my head. "And like I said, I cannot be sure it was him he was called on to meet."

"Surely someone saw the culprit this time? It was morning, you said."

I nod. "They did. Said he looked to be from the East." He opens his mouth to say something, but I cut him off. "No, not the Chinaman, apparently. Someone from India maybe, foreign clothing, a turban on his head."

He stares at me. "What new devilment is this?"

I just shake my head.

"And Isobel? How is she?"

"Not good." I lift the teacup to my lips and am mortified when my fingers tremble so that some tea sloshes into the saucer.

Cosgrove takes the cup from my hand, clasping my fingers. "This must have really distressed you, of course." He draws me to him.

I'm happy to be ensconced in his lap but loath to have him believe I am too weak to cope with this situation. "No," I say, laughing a little. "No, it's just that I haven't eaten today. I'm feeling faint from lack of food." I lean over and take a slice of bread. "I will be right after I eat this, I'm sure. Then we can plan how we are to go about finding Pidgeon's murderer."

I'm torn — I know it's almost indelicate to eat at such a time, but I'm really hungry.

He squeezes me tight, burying his face against my throat. His body is rigid with grief and fury, his eyes are pressed shut. I'm sure he must be thinking of his friend. Like a prickle in my brain, it occurs to me for the first time that he might also be worried for his own safety.

Dropping the bread back onto the plate, I nuzzle into the hollow of his neck, breathe in his scent. His lips find mine and for a few minutes we sink into each other, our unspent rage finding passage in desire. His hands snake up my thighs and I yank his collar apart so his blue lapel pin hangs loose. I kiss his smooth chest, his muscles quivering as I slide my hand across his warm flesh. He lifts me from the chair, lays me down onto the carpet, and we fuck until we're spent and panting amongst the silks of my skirts and petticoats.

He rolls onto the floor beside me and we lie like that, the warm fire crackling next to us. I'm just thinking of retrieving that slice of bread and butter when Cosgrove's head lifts. "Did you hear that? Someone at the door?"

"No, I didn't hear anything," I say, alarmed. I sit up, straightening my stockings and pulling my skirts down. I back up to the armchair and heave myself into it.

"I'm sure I heard something." Cosgrove gets to his feet and walks to the door, buttoning his trousers and readjusting his collar.

I try to neaten my hair, while taking bites of bread. I hope it's not Hatch. Surely, though, Cosgrove wouldn't expose me to another man's censure.

I'm putting an extra teaspoon of sugar into my tea when Cosgrove returns. My hand pauses, the teaspoon mid-stir, when I see his face. "What is it?"

"Meadowes found this slipped through the mail slot. A message from Hunt," he says, showing me the slip of paper. "He wants to meet me."

"When?" I ask, glancing down at the note. *As soon as possible*, is written in neat copperplate. And, sure enough, it's signed, *J. D. Hunt*.

I look up at Cosgrove. "But you mustn't go. It might be another trap."

He frowns down at the note. "By Hunt? I've known him many years now, and I cannot believe he's responsible for these deaths. I cannot. He might be in danger himself."

"But it could be from someone else," I say, following him into the hallway. "It might be the same person who murdered Pidgeon, tricking you into meeting him, by posing as Hunt. At least show it to Hatch first. Let him accompany you."

Cosgrove casts around for his hat, which he finds on a small escritoire. He shrugs into an overcoat. "It says to come now. I must go. You can wait here for me, if you like, or fetch your Hatch and tell him what is going on."

I hurry back into the sitting room and jam my bonnet onto my head. Taking up my coat, which lies on the floor where it was discarded, I pull it on. "I'm coming with you. But first, do you have a firearm we can bring? I've left mine at home, unfortunately."

It takes the cab driver nearly an hour to find the meeting place in the East End. Cosgrove curses, wonders why Hunt or "whoever the damned scoundrel is" who wrote the message chose such an out-of-the-way location to meet.

"It must be a trap," I repeat.

But as we draw nearer to our destination, Cosgrove wrenches the cab window open, peers out at the dreary street. "My God," he says. "I remember this place."

"What is it?" I ask.

"It's where we found a group of those *kungsi* rascals living. Years ago. Tried to bribe Pidgeon, they did. Hunt too."

"The Chinese from Sarawak? Why would they try to bribe Pidgeon and Hunt?"

He's silent for a few moments. We bump against each other as the cab trundles across cobblestones. "I was never quite sure, Heloise. All I know is we rooted them out." By the light of the street lamps outside, I watch his hands clench. "Hunt must've found something."

The cab halts at the corner of a narrow alley. "Far as I can go, sir," calls the driver.

Hopping down into the road after Cosgrove, I repeat my question. "But what on earth did they have on the likes of Pidgeon?"

"I was never quite sure, Heloise," he says again. "Pidgeon, Lovejoy and Hunt — and that fellow McBride — were very quiet about something to do with that riot in Sarawak. I've never been sure of what it was. I was newly arrived in Kuching, and although we have been great friends since . . ." he pauses. He's probably thinking of how those friendships are in the past, now that the others have been murdered, "I was much younger than they, new to their expeditions. I

272

have heard them talk about the wonders of antimony, though, which is mined in Sarawak. They had a good laugh about it, but didn't explain the joke to me. Lately, since these murders, I've begun to wonder if they were hiding something."

"Like what?"

He shakes his head, and lifts his hat to push his hair back from his forehead. "Maybe they knew the Chinese were going to attack. In fact, maybe it was arranged so. With Crookshank and Wilkins out of the way, a negotiator with good business acumen could arrange a tidy deal with the local *kungsi* for the antimony mines. Yes, but maybe the Chinese were double-crossed. Antimony has only increased in value, tenfold probably, in that time. I wouldn't be surprised if that is why the *kungsi* keep sending men in to finish off those that tricked them. Maybe they hope to recover the mines."

"You can't mean Pidgeon was a part of this? He would never!" I say. But then I remember that twice he's tried to tell me of something that was troubling him. If not involved himself, he might have had information against the other men.

We stare down the murky alleyway we must enter. There's a strong whiff of ordure and river rot, and damp stains the walls of the hovels that line the road.

"Damn. I should've brought a lantern," Cosgrove says, glancing up at the sky. The night is cloudy, dimming the moon's glow. "You should have stayed behind, Heloise." His voice is rough and, for the first time, I think that maybe I should have.

"Do we go down here?" I ask, taking the first step into the alley.

"Yes."

I step over a pile of turnip ends and mouldy cabbage and God alone knows what else. I whip the lace from my hat and clamp it lightly against my nose with freezing fingers. Cosgrove grunts and curses as he steps in what I think is human shit and, by the slit of moonlight that finds its way past the ramshackle buildings, I momentarily mistake a decomposing cat for a discarded fur tippet.

The further we walk, the more I can smell something gas-like.

"What a peculiar place to have a pond," I say, walking towards the body of water that marks the end of the alley. By the light of a single lantern hanging from the balcony of a shack on the corner, the water seems to be the shade and consistency of tea. Two rows of houses back onto the pond, while the alleyway snakes off to the right and left, forming the shape of a T. A very low archway leads the way into the lane to the left, its interior swamped in darkness. The lane to the right is a little wider, uncovered, with a long row of terraced shanties on each side of the dirt path.

"He said to wait here."

I wander closer to the pond. It isn't surrounded by any greenery — no grass, no shrubberies — and its banks have been trodden into mud that spreads its sludge onto the path's flagstones. The reek of gas becomes overbearing and I realise what I'm looking at.

274

"It's some sort of cesspool," Cosgrove says behind me.

A faint light glows from one of the houses that backs onto the pool as a woman opens her back door and throws the contents of a bucket into the water. The slopping sound, the fresh, foul stench, leave no doubt as to the contents of the bucket. At the same time, a little girl, maybe seven or eight years old, sidles up to the edge of the pool. Keeping a wary eye on us, she bobs down and dips a tin cup into the water and then quickly turns about, returns to a house several doors down. I gag so strongly that tears form in my eyes.

"Where is Hunt, blast him?" says Cosgrove, taking his pistol from his pocket. "Heloise, it's best if you wait over there." He points to the archway leading to the left. "Hide yourself. If anything is to happen to me, find your way out, alert Hatch."

I know from his voice that there will be no negotiation on this, so I take my place in the dark folds of the tunnel as quickly as I can. As I press myself and my wide skirts against the damp wall, I can just make out two figures walking towards us down the opposite lane. Each of them carries something over his shoulder — shovels, maybe, or rakes? They pause by a doorway, knock, and that's when I see another shadow, taller, solitary, moving up the lane behind them. Cosgrove steps back, by the side of the pool, so that he's out of sight.

The lazy clip-clop of a horse's hoofs draw near. I think the sound is coming from the alleyway we followed from the main thoroughfare. In the distance, a coster, selling some sort of fare, clangs metal together while calling out something indiscernible. The shadowy man in the opposite lane pauses for a moment. A crunching noise behind me. I swing around as a creature scuttles from sight; but not before I see the sheen of its bulbous eye. A rat. Fleeing from a carcase, pink and unrecognisable, that lies not two feet from me, left to desiccate in the open air. Even as I watch, though, two more rats creep close, inspect the mound. A hacking cough echoes down the tunnel, hacking and hacking as the person tries to expel the poison from within, catch their breath. I'm just turning away, pulling my veil across my mouth and nose, when something even darker than the gloom cuts through the air, knocks me into oblivion.

CHAPTER
THIRTY

The first thing I notice when I open my eyes is the smoke billowing around my face. Someone puffing on a cigarette nearby. I turn my head, the uneven cobblestones bumping against my skull. I pull myself up onto my elbows. Not smoking, just my warm breath suffusing the chill air.

The pong of filth and excrement rises around me and I remember where I am. The lane beside the cesspool. Sitting up, my fingers find the ache at the back of my head, carefully prod the swelling that's as big as an egg.

I want to stand, but for almost a minute all I can manage is resting forward on all fours. Trying to ignore the sludge that films my hands and gown, I have to squint against the terrible pain that slices through the right side of my head. I sway like that until I hear a voice cry out. Looking up, I can see that someone is crouched low near the cesspool. I struggle to my feet and lurch towards him, but stop short, my mind whirling, when I see by the feeble light thrown by his lantern that it's not Cosgrove. He's a young man, with beefy shoulders and a flat face and, as I stare at him, a boy steps out from behind him.

The man puts his hands out. "Miss, you shouldn't come any nearer."

"What do you mean?" I manage to croak, stumbling forward until I can see outstretched legs and well-shod feet in the shadows between him and the pond.

"Miss, you really don't want to see this," the man repeats, but as I come closer he steps out of my way rather than touch me.

I look down upon his body. Cosgrove's body. I know it's him, despite the dreadful absence of his head.

"Where's his . . . ?" I whisper.

"It rolled into the pond when we checked on him. Shook him, we did. Thought he was just passed out or something."

The banging in my head becomes unbearable and I fall forward onto my knees again and hack up onto the road, heaving until a line of spittle dangles to the mud. My fingernails scrape the dirt. I wipe my mouth down the side of my sleeve.

The man tries to pull Cosgrove's body away from the edge of the pond. I reach my hand over.

"No, no. Don't touch him," I say. My nose is running and my eyes water from the cold and sorrow. "Fetch the police. Tell them to find Detective Hatch. Vine Street Station."

The man sends the boy, who scampers away down the main alleyway, unperturbed by the dark.

"Did you see who did this?" I ask the man.

He just shakes his head. "By the time me and Jimmy came out, the murdering bastard — excuse my language, Miss — was running down the lane."

278

"You didn't see what he looked like?"

"No ..." The man lifts his cap for a moment, scratches his head. "It was like his head was big, you know? Like too large for his shoulders, if you know what I mean."

As though he had a turban on.

A family of five come out from a nearby house and two men peer from a doorway before approaching. The man holds them all at bay. I hear him murmur the words "murder" and "fell in the pond". A stout woman lets out a short squeal, cups her hands over her mouth, shrinks back into the arms of another woman.

I stay huddled near Cosgrove's body, but I can't look again, not further than the bottom of his right shoe, which I can see out of the corner of my eye. A thin man limps by, lantern swinging, and, by its light, I see a piece of paper screwed up on the ground. I lean forward, pick it up. It's the note from Hunt, but I can barely read it, I'm shivering so hard.

"Here, Miss, take my coat." The young man holds it towards me.

"No, no, I couldn't," I say, my teeth chattering so violently I think I might bite my tongue.

He shoves it towards me again. "Here, take it. Just until the police come."

Relenting, I pull the coat over my shoulders. Drawing it close, I bury my nose into the rough tweed and find comfort in its odour of sweat, ale and tobacco.

By the time the first constable arrives on foot, a small crowd has formed. But by the time Hatch arrives, the lanes are quite clogged with onlookers. Four policemen hold them at bay, push them back from the vicinity of the body.

Hatch draws me to my feet, leads me towards the alley.

"Mrs Chancey, what happened here?"

I open my hand, reveal the crumpled note.

Hatch takes in a sharp breath as he reads. "From Hunt again."

"Yes, but I don't think it could really be from him. I think this whole thing was trickery." I look around for the young man, whose coat I have wrapped around me. "That man over there, the one in the grey shirt, he described the killer to me. Sounds like the man in the turban."

Hatch catches hold of a constable, tells him to escort the witness to the station.

Turning back to me, he asks, "And why are you here, Mrs Chancey?"

I peer hard at him to see if suspicion lights his eyes, but it's too dark, and my eyes are dry and cold, making my vision hazy. I blink, trying to cast my mind back to earlier in the evening. Cosgrove's port-coloured carpet, frayed at the edges. Bread and butter. His heavy body pressed against mine in front of the warm fireplace. "I think . . ." Pidgeon's death. Head toppled off in his carriage. "I visited him to see if he'd heard about Pidgeon. And while I was there, he received that message."

The three detectives who arrived with Hatch gather by the side of the cesspool. They're accompanied by an old man who holds a long rake of some kind.

"Well, you're right about the note not being from Hunt," says Hatch, shoving it into his side pocket. "We've since found out that Hunt is safely away in Bernissart, Belgium. It looks like we are back to an Asiatic culprit. Chinaman or Indian, I still can't place."

A cry of triumph by the side of the pond is accompanied by a hush from the others. The old man lays his pole down, next to a dark, muddy lump. I turn away, gripping my waist, dry retch against the side of a brick dwelling.

Hatch's hand falls onto my shoulder. It's reassuring, but has weight too. "I think you'd better go home, Mrs Chancey. But I will need you to come in for an interview tomorrow. Is that all right?"

I nod. As he escorts me to the main road, we pass Cosgrove's body again. Circles of light from lanterns held high by the police and the many onlookers bob amongst the shadows. As the detectives roll Cosgrove's body onto a stretcher, his gun clatters to the cobblestones from his lifeless hand. By the lanterns' glow, his blue pin glints against the dark, dark stain that has leached into his collar.

CHAPTER
THIRTY-ONE

Taff reins the horses into the kerbside along East India Docks Road. Amah hops down from the carriage, ignoring his loud entreaties to just wait one moment, darn it, and he'll escort her. She turns into the same street she has haunted over the last few days. Despite the late hour, quite a few people stroll up and down the road outside Kung's shop. A group of sailors make their way in the direction of the docks, while a vendor offers sweet buns to others who pass by. A young couple — him Chinese, her white — are seated on the front steps of their home, dandling a thickly swaddled toddler between them.

Amah's heart lifts when she sees the shutters are finally up at Kung's shop. She pushes the door open into a shallow front room. The walls and floors are bare of decoration and the only furnishing is a timber bench that once housed some sort of produce from far away. A bright, lacquered altar sits on the floor to the left. Smoke rises in a wisp from the joss sticks planted in sand next to a sad-looking orange, dimpled and shrunken.

A door opens and a Chinese man steps through. He stares at Amah out of his one good eye; the other is swollen shut, and there's a nasty graze above his brow, which she assumes is a result from his altercation with Sin Hok.

He says something, but she can't understand him. She shakes her head, says, "English?"

"I say Ayah Hostel in Jewry Street. Men only here."

Amah tries to look over his shoulder. "I am looking for Jakub Chee."

He grunts and turns back through the doorway. She peers past him, into the half-darkness beyond. Divans and beds are crammed up against each other, arranged like a maze, with only just enough space to inch around. The man calls out something unintelligible, then, "Chee". Several heads lift, crane around to see Amah, but only one figure, in the furthest corner, rises and makes his way to them. Jakub.

She'd forgotten how tall he is, how fine. His shoulders are slender but strong, his waist trim. She always calls him a boy, thinks of him as a boy, but really he's a man. A young man who doesn't look as pleased to see her as she is to see him.

Taking a seat on the bench, she indicates for him to sit next to her. Jakub hesitates, until he sees her lifted brow. She doesn't like the petulant lift to his mouth, the frown in his eyes, but he must know that she can do testy far better than anyone.

"Why have you been leading me on this merry dance, Jakub?" she says. "We've all been worried about you. Me, your mother, your father."

"Ha," is all he says, staring across at the altar.

"Why do you say this?"

He just shakes his head.

"And what do you have to do with this man, Sin Hok? I was told he's a very bad man. A criminal, in fact. Just look what he did here." With her chin, Amah indicates into the other room to where Kung is playing mah-jong with three other men.

"Who'd you hear that from?"

"A man at the Strangers' Home told me. Cardigan, his name was."

"Cadogan. That weasel." Jakub folds his arms. "He's cross because Sin Hok won't be converted. Sin Hok's just a trader. He's like Kung, in there, or . . ."

"Or who?"

"I was going to say Papa, but I mean Chee. Your uncle."

"But he is your papa. You must call him that. Disrespectful not to."

"Is he? I don't know who anyone is anymore." He clenches his teeth together so she can see the bulge of his jawline.

"Of course he is. Why do you say these things?"

"I know that Miriam is not my mother."

Amah nods slowly. "Uncle Chee said you thought this. Why, Jakub, why do you think this?"

Jakub's dark eyes study the older woman for a moment. He takes a notecase from his coat pocket, flips it open. "Do you remember this?"

He places a photograph onto her lap. The print isn't clear. It's as if the posing couple stands amid a light fog. Amah squints. It takes her a moment to work out who the strangers are in the picture, but then she

284

recognises the tattered pheasant feather poking up from the woman's bonnet, the bonnet that was so cherished because it had once belonged to Mrs Preston. Li Leen. It was a photograph of herself, many years beforehand. Standing next to her, a very young Chee. No gut yet, smooth skin like Jakub's. His hair braided into a long queue, which hangs over his shoulder, snakes down his front, reaching just above his hip.

Amidst the wonder, Amah feels a dip of sadness to see her young face. Oval, like her mother's. "I can't remember ever seeing this." She smiles, thinking of the day Chee corralled her into the stall at the fair, how she'd grumbled that the devil would take their souls. Oh, that day, it was so cold. Much colder than today. Down by the docks in Liverpool it was always icy, even when the sun peeped out and the locals shed their coats and rolled their sleeves up. She can almost feel a shiver tickle up her spine as she thinks of it.

Then her eyes catch what she's holding, bundled in her arms. A baby. Its dark eyes gazing into the camera.

"That's me, isn't it?" he asks, pointing at the child.

There's no use denying it. Even in such an old, faded photo, it's clear that the angles of the skull, the ears as neat as a shell, are Jakub's. "Where did you find this?" she asks.

"In the pocket of an overcoat Papa gave to me to take on my travels. He said the coat served him well when he was on the seas, himself. I suppose he'd forgotten the photograph was in there."

Amah thinks quickly. "Yes, he visited me with you. In Liverpool. To give your poor mother a rest."

Jakub shakes his head slowly. "No, Auntie Leen. Papa didn't even know Mother then."

Amah frowns. "But of course he did."

Again, Jakub shakes his head. He points once more at the photo, this time at Chee. "I've heard Mother say many times that she never knew Papa with his long plait. That he had already chopped it off by the time they met here, in Limehouse."

Amah leans back against the wall. She stares down at the photograph and lets out a long breath. Miriam, and her constant chatter.

Her eyes find Jakub's. "So what do you think this means?"

"I think . . ." His eyes fall from hers. "I think you're my mother."

His mother? Amah? Out of all the scenarios she'd mulled over and over again, she never thought the silly boy would come to that conclusion. "What?" A smile creeps to her face, but she can't help herself, it's so ridiculous.

Uncertainty puckers his brow. "You're my mother."

Taking his hand in hers, she rubs his skin. "No, no, Jakub. I am not your mother." She wants to say she has always loved him as a mother would, that one of the saddest days of her life was when she was parted from him, but the words stick in her throat. Tenderness has never come easily to her; she prefers to use words that bite, that are as sour as a green nectarine. Words that guard her innermost feelings.

The door creaks a little as a gust of wind whistles through, and the men in the next room start up a new game of mahjong, stirring the hard tiles around on the tabletop.

Jakub withdraws his hand from hers and crosses his arms, tucking his fingers into his underarms. "I know the truth, Auntie Leen. Papa told me of the ship you came in. I've been to Liverpool and seen the passenger list."

"But why? What does that prove?"

"I needed to find out who my father was. Even if he is a blackguard."

Amah shakes her head, frowning. She doesn't understand him.

His eyes search hers for a moment, then flick away again. He mumbles something that she doesn't quite catch.

"What?"

"I said, Papa told me of how on that voyage one of the English gentlemen attacked you. Of how you didn't say anything because what notice would they take of two Chinese servants?"

Amah recalls that black night. The sharp stench of smoke-stack fug, the dusty floor, the brandy on his breath as he slobbered against her neck.

"No, no." She goes to grasp Jakub's hand again, but they're still shoved into his underarms, away from contact. "You have it all wrong, Jakub. And in any case, even I am not certain who it was that came to our cabin that night."

"But it must have been one of them," says Jakub. His eyes are red, entreating. "Lovejoy, McBride, Hunt . . ."

Amah covers her mouth with her fingers. Her eyes are wide as she watches him. She thinks again of how he's no longer her boy, her sweet boy, but a man, and what is a man not capable of? "What have you done, Jakub?"

His head hangs low so that his dark hair flops onto his forehead.

The mah-jong players stand from their table, chat to a group of men seated against the wall. They pull coats on and form a straggly procession to the door. Kung is the first through, says something to Chee, mimes the eating of soup. Chee waves his hands, no, and the men go on their way. As they trudge through the front door, cold air blasts through the gap. Amah watches the closed door for half a minute before turning back to Jakub.

"What did you do, Jakub, when you found out about these men?"

"The first one I tracked was McBride. He was still in Liverpool. I hadn't been watching him for half a day before he rushed off and caught the stagecoach to London. I caught it too, and I tried the whole time to build up the courage to speak to him, to ask him of that time, but I couldn't." He stares between his knees at the floor. "He booked into an inn in Soho, but I lost him when he ran for an omnibus. That's when I went in search of Pidgeon. His whereabouts weren't too difficult to discover. I thought I might find something at his house that linked him to that voyage — to you — but just as I was jimmying his window open he arrived home. Scared the life out of me." A ghost of a smile

288

plays at the corner of his mouth. "So I returned to Soho, waited for McBride to come back. The next thing I knew, I was watching him enter Heloise's house." His eyes swivel around to Amah. "And I thought that confirmed it." He holds his hands to his temples. "Why else would he be at Heloise's home, if not to visit you?"

Amah shuts her eyes. "I always knew Heloise befriending those men would lead to trouble." She opens her eyes again, letting out a loud sigh. "She met that Pidgeon first. I don't know where. At one of those ridiculous scientific lectures she sometimes attends. I think she liked that he had visited our part of the world — the East Indies. She's never ventured there, herself, but she's always been fascinated by it. Always pestering me for stories." Amah thinks of the first time she glanced through the peacock's tail into Heloise's drawing room and recognised Pidgeon's long face and Hunt's wiry figure, although his cleft chin was obscured by the grey whiskers he now sported. The shock had shuddered through her body, ringing in her chest, her fingertips, her ears. Later, she'd berated Heloise for inviting them, but that girl always did whatever she wanted. And Amah couldn't bring herself to explain why the men had stirred such terrible memories.

Her mind returns to the evening when McBride visited Heloise's. "I saw you that night, standing on the corner," she says to Jakub. "I thought I was mistaken, and when I saw McBride . . . What did you do then, Jakub?" Her heartbeat quickens. She wills him to get to the point, tell her what he did. But she wants him to not tell her too.

"I waited. When McBride left, he was escorted to the door by another man. I heard him mention the name Lovejoy several times. Another name from that passenger list."

"And then?"

"I followed him back to the main road. He stopped in a coffee house for nearly an hour, writing something, and then returned to South Street — your house — but this time he just stood out the front by a street lamp."

"What was he doing?"

"Waiting for something."

"And you?"

"It was awkward. He was watching the house, I was watching him. And it was bloody freezing. So I loped off home. Spent the night in Limehouse."

She searches his face for signs of a lie. His face is relaxed though.

"And Lovejoy?" That little girl, cut throat. Lovejoy, the blood spilled on the ground. Sliced almost to the bone. The *kris*. Did he steal into Heloise's house and take the *kris*?

He shrugs. "Took me a few days to find out where they lived. I didn't realise that he and his daughter had been murdered." His hands drop to his lap, where they lie open.

"You saw Heloise?"

He looks up at her, surprised. "Yes. I did. That was a shock." His eyes search hers for a moment before dropping to his hands again. "That's when I really thought I was on the right track. That you two were still in touch with these men for some reason." His voice

290

has become tight, his brow creased, he looks sad. "But what I really couldn't understand — can't understand — is why you got rid of me? Why didn't you keep me, like you kept Heloise? Now that I know Papa — Chee — isn't really my father, it makes so much sense. Why he always disapproves of everything I do, that I say, that I think, even. Why didn't you keep me in Liverpool with you? Why did you send me away with him? Is it because you couldn't stand to be reminded . . ."

"No, Jakub, no." This time Amah catches his left hand, presses it in hers. "No. You have it all wrong."

Her eyes follow the fine hair on the back of his hand, the calluses on his fingers. His nails are chewed to the quick, so that the flesh swells bulbous at the tips, and folded into the creases of his skin are fine lines of dirt. At any other time she would flick his ear, ask him if he was a monkey or some other animal and tell him to wash.

She clasps his hand once more, then takes her hand back, and laces her fingers together in her lap. Turning slightly away from him, she stares at the lit joss sticks, at their glowing, red tips.

She'll have to start at the beginning. She'll have to revisit that time on the *Dukano*. She tells him of Chee fetching her from her stepfather's house, of how she became Mrs Preston's maid on the boat. Of the English words Mrs Preston taught her, of the pretty finch she kept in a cage. Her voice falters over the riot in Sarawak, and she doesn't mention the night she was attacked at all. She pauses for a moment as two men return to the hostel, walk through to the back room, closing the door behind them.

"I was a stupid girl, Jakub. Just a stupid, young girl." Amah's voice is hushed. "I didn't recognise what was happening right in front of me. I didn't realise . . ."

"What?"

Amah thinks back to the damp sheets, Mrs Preston writhing in them, tearing the bedding from the mattress. "She was so sickly. So ill, for so long." The stench that came off her skin. Sweet, but not a pleasant sweet. More feral, like the smell of rotting fruit.

"What was she sick with?"

"They were all sick. Dysentery." Shit and vomit everywhere. In the corridors, soaked into the carpets, splattered on the porthole windows from men leaning over the side of the boat.

Everyone's guts bloated with their illness, ready to burst. And Mrs Preston, her small stomach bulging, even though she hadn't eaten or had anything to drink for days. A puzzlement to young Li Leen. "I was so stupid. I knew nothing."

"Nothing of what?"

Of the dark whelp that slipped from Mrs Preston's lower body, wet and shining and mewling.

"She was pregnant. My poor Mrs Preston was with child and I didn't know it."

They're both silent. Someone moves furniture across the wooden floors in the next room, voices are raised on the street.

"You're saying . . . ?"

292

"I'm saying," Amah's voice is heavy, "I'm saying Mrs Preston was your mother."

"But . . ." Jakub lifts his hand, turns it over, gazes at his olive skin that is far darker than Heloise's. Heloise, with her twilight eyes, her golden skin. She'd always taken after her father.

"Chee is your father." She thinks of that morning when her Uncle Chee came into the cabin with a bucket, how he dropped it so water sloshed across the floor, his wide eyes when he spied the wriggling creature in Amah's arms.

Jakub's mouth remains open as he gapes at her. "Papa?" And then, "Mrs Preston?"

Amah nods. "Jane. She was a very special lady. I loved her very much."

"What happened? Where is she now?"

Amah's chest constricts. Mrs Preston's fingers were so cold, so weak, when she took hold of Amah's wrist and whispered in her ear. *Li Leen, my dear friend, you must keep him. Make sure he is safe. My family would never understand our love.* Her hot breath smelt of decay, weeping sores spotted the corners of her mouth. It was the only time Amah had ever seen her Uncle Chee weep, knelt by the bed, his head next to Mrs Preston's on the pillow.

Mrs Preston knew she was dying. Who could survive such a loss of blood, such a high fever?

"She only lived for one more day, Jakub. Luckily we were not far off Liverpool then. I pretended you were mine. Nobody really cared." Except for Luba, the head cook and barber from Africa, who kept them supplied with what little fresh water he had, some flour, a little treacle for the baby. "So, it was not me who deserted you, Jakub, it was your father who wanted you back. As soon as he was married to Miriam, and knew he could look after you, he came and took you from my care." Amah remembers the day, a bright day, the sky almost white it was so blinding. She knows it was just one occasion of many that helped form the fibrous scar tissue over her heart.

She stares down at the photograph again, at the baby's little coffee-bean eyes that are so like his father's. Has he never noticed this?

"Come back to your papa's house, Jakub, and we will tell you all. They have been missing you." She touches his wrist. "We can eat some of your mother's dumplings."

CHAPTER
THIRTY-TWO

The rest of that evening is very bleak indeed. Having returned the kind young man's overcoat with Hatch, I shiver the whole way home in a cab. When I arrive, only one lamp's alight in the front hallway. Before taking himself off to bed, Bundle must have assumed I'd be away all night. It's an occurrence that happens often enough, after all.

I stare up the stairs for a good minute before I can drag myself to my bedroom. Everything feels cold: my feet, the silk of my dress, the banister as my fingers brush its surface. I hold my palm to the tip of my nose. Icy. Pausing halfway up the staircase, my eyes take in the rosy carpet, but really, I see the claret stain again, smeared across the throat I had run my tongue along not five hours ago.

Luckily, when I reach my room, embers still glimmer in the grate, so I throw more wood on top, stoke the fire. Looking down, I can now see clearly the patches of mud — and worse — caked into the skirts of my gown, and a crimson blotch lines the rim of my hem. I tug at the buttons, loosen the stays, until the gown falls to the floor, closely followed by my petticoats and undergarments. Shrugging on my dressing gown, I stare into the flames and think of Cosgrove's hand, drooped over the side of the stretcher, pale, bare . . .

"Heloise, you are home late." Amah stands in the doorway. She has a woollen shawl thrown about her shoulders and her hair is tied in a plait. In one hand she holds an ivory bonnet, and in the other, the silk thread and needle with which she is embroidering it.

I nod, plonking myself down into the armchair. "Why are you still awake?"

Amah walks into my room. "I got home late. I visited Uncle Chee's. Jakub was there."

"He's back? So maybe that was him I saw the other day." My brain is so muddled with weariness, shock, grief, it takes me a moment to realise the meaning of this. "But why would he be in Stoke Newington? Near the Lovejoys'?"

Amah stares down at me for a few moments, then pulls the dressing table chair close by me. She settles into it, her back straight. "It was him. I was very afraid," she says, "very afraid he was involved in your business, but I have found out what was going on. He was only . . ." she thinks for a moment, "sulking. We have talked now."

"Tell me, Mama." My head feels so heavy I rest it against the armchair, the pressure of it reminding me of the bruise at the back of my head. Shifting my head so it's in a more comfortable position, I peer at Amah through half-closed eyes.

She doesn't speak straight away. She rubs her face with the flats of her hands, up and down. "I'm so tired." Picking up the embroidery again from her lap, she pulls the thread taut, ready to sew. "That boy. He's been avoiding me. Us. I thought — I really dreaded — that he was behind the violence against those men."

"Who? You don't mean McBride? Pidgeon?"

Amah nods, then shakes her head. "All that talk of a Chinese man wanting revenge, threatening them all."

"But why would Jakub care about these men?" How silly of her to jump to that conclusion. There are plenty of other Chinese men who could be responsible. "And in any case, if you were with Jakub this evening," I glance at the gilt clock on the mantelpiece. It's almost 1.25 a.m., "it could not have been him."

"Why do you say this?"

"Because Cosgrove was murdered tonight. The same as the others." My hand reaches for my throat and my stomach clenches tight. I will miss him. I will miss the excitement that trembled in my belly whenever I encountered him, thought of him. Such a beautiful man. Wasted. But I can't let my feelings overcome me in front of Amah. She wouldn't understand. Worse, she'll think I'm being ridiculous.

I swallow, glance at Amah. "And we now think that the culprit might be an Indian fellow. Someone who wears a turban. You know these Londoners, they think all us brown foreigners are much the same." My eyes are dry and scratchy, and sadness scorches my chest. I know it's Cosgrove's death that upsets me, but I take my shortened temper out on Amah. "You didn't answer me. What interest does Jakub have in these men anyway?"

Amah adds a few stitches, then rests the bonnet back into her lap. "You know I told you once that I thought I recognised that man Pidgeon?"

"Mmm. From your voyage here? But that was years ago."

"That's correct. Well that Lovejoy, and McBride too, were on the ship."

"No!"

"Yes, they joined us in Sarawak. A whole party of Englishmen set sail with us, fleeing Kuching."

My eyes widen and I sit up again. "I heard them talking of some riot. Was it after that?"

"Yes." Amah's eyes fall to her embroidery.

"What about Cosgrove? Hunt? Were they there too?"

An irritated frown creases her forehead. "I don't know, Heloise. I was very young then. Hadn't seen many white men. They all looked the same to me. Tall, the colour of a knob of garlic, hairy faces." She runs her thumb across the silk thread that forms the petal of a chrysanthemum. "But I know many of them died in Kuching. I saw it with my own eyes. The local overseer, his wife, some miners, the doctor. Mr Preston. Mrs Preston told me it was caused by the local *kungsi* fighting the Englishmen over an antimony mine, but Uncle Chee always said it was over a woman."

"Why is Jakub interested in that time?"

Amah's shoulders lift a little, tense. "You might as well know. You will hear it from your Aunt Miriam soon enough. That woman, she's worse than the local newspaper. Limehouse Bugle I used to call her."

298

"I remember," I say, my voice dry. I've never understood her dislike for Aunt Miriam but, pressed upon it, she always denies it. "What is it she might tell?"

My mother has never spoken much of her journey here, except to say that she was a maid to a British woman, Mrs Preston. She now tells me that Jakub suspected Uncle Chee wasn't his father, that one of these British men were.

"Who did he think was his mother then?" I ask.

Her lip lifts as she meets my eye. "Me."

"But why on earth would he think that?"

A log dislodges in the fireplace, falls to the side with a crack. She hands me her embroidery and then lifts out the poker and prods the log back into place. Settling into her seat again, she says, slowly, "He knew that something terrible happened on that voyage. Uncle Chee had told him — I think to stress to the boy that there might not always be justice at hand for people like us on these long passages."

I can see she's not telling me something. She's choosing her words too carefully. "What happened?"

Her mouth twists to the side as she contemplates me. "A man tried to violate me. One night in our cabin."

I put my hand over my mouth. "Oh no." Oh God, and I remember that night long ago. That carriage. Not my mother too? "But he didn't . . ."

"No." She shakes her head. I think I see a flash of something — fright? apprehension? — in her face. "He attacked me in Mrs Preston's cabin. She was too far gone with fever to hear."

"But you managed to get away?"

And then there's that familiar look in her eye — the unblinking disdain of a black cat, a warning twitch of its tail. She nods.

"Who was he? You must've found out who he was?"

She shakes her head. "No, it was too dark to see beyond a shadow. And we had much more important things on our mind after that. The next morning is when poor Mrs Preston had her baby. When our Jakub first entered this world."

Amah is sure it won't be too difficult to find sleep tonight. She's found Jakub. They have sorted out their misunderstandings. Foolish boy.

Even the reminder of that evening on the *Dukano*, when that scoundrel tried to take what wasn't his to steal, doesn't speed her heart, can't force her heavy eyelids open.

In fact, her lips lift in a smile when she thinks of how that meeting came to an end. Of how her reaching fingers found the handle of her paring knife, how it made a clinking sound against the china plate as she drew it forward. One of his hands held Amah down, pressed against her throat, but his other hand was what . . . ? Untying his cravat? Raised to strike her? All Amah knows is it was at that moment she managed to stab him. She meant to thrust the blade into his chest, but it went straight through the palm of his hand. He reared back, bellowing like a slaughtered ox. Devil. She's never been troubled by the likes of him again.

Amah hears a slight bump below, in Heloise's rooms, and realises that her daughter is still awake, pondering the death of those men. Heloise has never learnt to walk away, to not involve herself. Always has to be part of an adventure. Isn't that how she first came to work in the alley, setting up skittles at only ten years old; how she was tricked away from Amah by that cherry-lipped vixen from the tavern?

When Amah thinks of Heloise, it feels like a snake awakens in her chest, uncoils itself, raises its coffin-shaped head. There are months, years even, of her daughter's life that Amah knows nothing of. Even if Heloise has learnt to protect herself, Amah's afraid that fate's greedy fingers still seek her out, will catch her one day.

CHAPTER
THIRTY-THREE

"Amah," I say, pushing open her bedroom door.

The room is quite dark, apart from a gentle glow from the grate. I pull the curtains apart. It's so overcast, it's almost as if the sun hasn't yet risen, despite it being past the hour Amah usually wakes. It's a very rare occurrence, indeed, that I am up before her.

She lies on her side, nestled into her bedcovers, the blanket pulled up over her ear so that only a narrow strip of her face is apparent. One dark eye blinks at me, and she yanks the covers over her nose. She mumbles something I don't catch, as I light the lamp next to her bed.

"What did you say?"

She flings her arm out and rolls onto her back. "Why are you up so early?" she says. Her eyes scan my gown. "Why are you dressed already?"

"It doesn't matter. I have things to do." I've already had two cups of coffee, but I know it's not just the brew that's left me feeling skittish. In the dead hours before dawn, a jumble of nightmares and tangled images seem to have fermented my blood, so that I can feel it rushing in my fingertips, sparking in my mind. "But first, I can't find my damned atlas. Tell me, do you know where Mandalay is?"

Amah rises onto her elbow, frowns up at me. "Burma. But why . . ."

"Just as I thought. Thank you, Amah," I say, as I leave her room.

At the bottom of the stairs, Bundle helps me into my overcoat.

As I tuck a hat made of sable with silk sashes onto my head, Bundle says, "Taff has the carriage ready outside, Mrs Chancey, waiting your convenience."

I gaze into the mirror of the hallstand. The soft fur tickles the tips of my ears, and although the bonnet frames my face nicely, I can see the bruising under my eyes from lack of sleep. I don't look my best. How could I? Snatching up the matching sable muff, I hurry outside.

First, Taff waits for only a matter of minutes in Holborn as I have a word with Cosgrove's man, Meadowes. Then we make our way to Vine Street. I tell Taff I might be some time, so he jumps down from his box to lead the horses up the road.

A constable leaves me in the same small room from the last time I sought out the Detective Inspector, but it's not long before Hatch joins me.

"Mrs Chancey?"

I stand so fast the chair teeters behind me. "Detective Inspector, do you think I might look at Cosgrove's body?"

Hatch's sandy eyelashes positively flutter with surprise. "You want to see his body?"

I nod. "I think there might be a clue to the killer."

He stares at me. Maybe he's shocked at how unladylike I am, or worried I might faint. He might be offended that I think I can be of assistance. A uniformed policeman passes the open doorway, and one door, then another, slams shut down the corridor. Finally, he blinks, says, "Right you are. Follow me."

I am close on his heels as he makes his way out through the front door and turns to his left. Three doors down, he crosses the road, his arms out to bar oncoming traffic so that I can pass with him, until we reach a low-set building.

"In here, please," he says, bowing me in before him. "You might need your handkerchief to mask the smell."

As soon as the words leave his mouth, a bloody awful odour slams my nostrils. I bury my nose into my muff.

My eyes water, the stench so sharp, so thick, I'm surprised the air before me is clear, not a soupy miasma of filth and poison.

"What is this place?" I ask, wisps of fur catching in my mouth.

"The closest thing we have to a morgue. Be thankful it's winter."

He leads me down a short hallway. We pass three doors, and I can't be sure if I'm just imagining that the closed doors bulge slightly against the weight of gaseous pressure from within. I choke against the fur of my muff.

In the end room, a body is laid out upon a bench, a white shroud across its length. On a table close by, ensconced in liquid like a pickled cucumber, is his head, his longish, dark hair floating like seaweed. I grimace, but I don't back out. Either the sickening smell has faded in this room, or I have become somewhat accustomed, although an underlying scent of raw meat makes my stomach heave. I lower my muff.

Gazing down at the shroud, I ask Hatch to remove it.

Below the jagged flesh at his throat-line, which I take pains to not stare at, the corpse is still attired in shirt and trousers. The lapis lazuli pin is fastened to the filthy collar.

My hand hovers over it as I look up at Hatch. "May I?"

His eyes are bulging, but he nods.

I draw out the pin, slowly, and attach it to my bodice. Then I part the top of his shirt. The flesh of his chest, marble-white, is covered in a robust mat of brown hair. So it's true. I am right.

My eyes find his lifeless fingers. I inspect the neat blue fingertips, stiff now, and note the unblemished skin on the back of his hand. Taking in his other hand, I see that it's much the same, apart from a torn fingernail. I step back from the table. Each time my suspicions are confirmed, it's like a heavy stone is wedged into the pit of my stomach.

I glance up at the head in the jar. Its face is turned away from me, but I've seen enough.

"This isn't Cosgrove."

CHAPTER
THIRTY-FOUR

I expect Hatch to exclaim, to baulk in surprise, but he just nods slowly, frowning. "How do you know?"

I gesture towards the corpse's hands. "Cosgrove has scars on his left wrist, and a knife wound," I point at the unblemished right hand, use my fingernail to indicate where a slice an inch long should be, "on the inside of his palm, and the outside, from the time a pirate drove his knife through." I don't feel the need to mention the smooth, almost hairless skin of Cosgrove's chest. My fingertips find the pin, now attached to my bodice. "This stone, it confused me for a little while. That, and the shock. But eventually last night I remembered his hand," I nodded towards the body, "when it dropped from the side of the stretcher. It was pale and unblemished." Looking up at Hatch, I ask, frowning, "But you are not surprised? You knew it wasn't Cosgrove?"

Hatch ushers me from the room, doesn't speak until we've escaped the stink of the corridor and are standing back out on the side of the road. Taff is still walking the horses, turning them at the next junction.

"I did wonder," he says. "Amongst Pidgeon's papers we found an interesting letter from McBride. Written the night that he died."

"What did it say?"

"That he knew who the rascal was who set up the riot in Sarawak."

"Who? Not Cosgrove?" With each revelation, the heavy sensation of stones in my gut stretches, gathers weight. How had I been so hoodwinked by this man?

Hatch nods. "In his letter to Pidgeon, McBride wrote that he was related to a couple called the Crookshanks, who were stationed out there. They both died in that riot. When McBride returned five years later, he found their diaries, had a word with the servant who was with them at the time. According to the servant, the whole thing was set up to look like a riot over a mine of some sort, but really, a young man — who he said was named Morris," Hatch spells the name for me, "organised it to cover up his affair with Mrs Crookshank, and the murder of Mr Crookshank. McBride wrote that at the time he'd completely forgotten about Cosgrove — his presence in Kuching, and how he joined them at the last moment on the ship to travel home — until he saw him at your soiree. Apparently, Cosgrove, *Maurice* Cosgrove, was very young then, not really a part of their group."

The leaves of a young ash tree rustle above us and two sparrows hop across its branches. I take a deep breath in, wonder at how blank my mind feels.

"Why pretend to be dead? Why murder . . ." I wave my hand in the direction of the makeshift morgue.

"Perhaps he knew it was only a matter of time before we caught up with him. He shut McBride up on impulse with the *kris* from your house and then had to continue with this revengeful Chinese gang subterfuge. And Pidgeon was troubled, obviously, maybe confused as to whether a Chinese man was the culprit or if it could really be his friend Cosgrove. Although he was hesitant to come to us, he did reach out to you and Sir Thomas. Unfortunately, Cosgrove must've clocked his suspicions. And who knows? McBride might have written to Hunt too, but the post missed him before he went to Belgium. In fact, I sent a constable around this morning to check all Hunt's mail."

"This morning I spoke with Cosgrove's servant," I say. "He knew nothing about the note Cosgrove received last night. I think Cosgrove must've written it himself, to lure me to his special denouement. He wanted a witness who would swear the body in the cesspool was his. All Meadowes — Cosgrove's man — knew, was that Cosgrove sent him out with a message for someone else. A man named Thatcher. Cosgrove instructed him to hand it to him personally." I look behind me at the morgue. I think of Thatcher — Cosgrove, Webb and Milly's "friend" — who always leered at me with his wet lips. He was a gross creature, but damn, he didn't deserve to be lying in that pestilent hell. I shudder, clench my fingers together deep in my muff. "The message must have lured Thatcher to the East End."

Hatch turns on his heel and moves back towards the police station. We leap over a pile of horse manure to gain the road, and he says, "Cosgrove must've known it'd only be a matter of time before that man's head would be found and cleaned, identified by someone. So what's he up to?"

That's exactly what Cosgrove needed, I realise. Time. Just enough to make his next move.

"I think I might know."

The police buggy pulls into the kerb of Derby Street before us. As I hop from my carriage, Hatch steps from the buggy. In front of Pidgeon's house is a large travelling coach, and Isobel stands on her front step, directing the driver where to deposit two hatboxes.

"Where are you going, Isobel?" I ask, striding towards her.

Two footmen, wearing bottle-green aprons and long cuff shields over their sleeves, struggle down the steps under the weight of a large trunk.

Fright widens her pretty eyes. "I'm going away. The stress . . ."

Hatch steps close, sends several constables into the house.

"But what are you doing?" Isobel asks, her gaze following the policemen.

"We have reason to believe that a certain Maurice Cosgrove might be upon the premises," says Hatch, his voice heavy. He starts up the front steps to follow his men.

Isobel's eyes fly to her coach. I look too, just in time to see one of the footmen climb into it, leaving his partner to heave the trunk alone. Picking up my skirts, I run to the coach and, just as I reach it, the valet leans out the coach's doorway, shouts up to the driver,

"Leave now, Sharpe! There's an extra twenty guineas in it for you!"

Cosgrove. He's in servant's dress and his hair has been darkened to the colour of boot polish, but I can see it's him. How could I not recognise those blue eyes?

I grab onto the door handle and holler for Hatch, but before I can think, Cosgrove swings out, hauls me into the coach just as it careers out from the side of the road. I push and kick at him, but only manage to get tangled in my damned petticoats as the coach lurches at top speed down the street. Finally, he pushes me into the seat next to him.

"What are you doing here, Heloise?"

"We know everything, Cosgrove."

He rests back in the seat next to me, his body swaying as the coach's wheels grind over uneven ground. "Ah. You think I murdered him? You have it all wrong. I fear for my life. That murdering Chinaman has me in his sights for his next kill. I'm trying to escape, incognito." His handsome face softens. "It was a terrible thing that he mistook that poor man for me. As soon as I knew it was a trap, I fled." He smiles, rueful. "I called for you, but when I received no answer, I figured you'd run off too."

"You're taking Isobel?"

"Well, it's become impossible to retrieve what funds I have, and she has just inherited a tidy sum, after all. She's always had a soft spot for me. Knew her in Mandalay, many years ago, you know. Young thing she was then."

For a moment, I wonder if I should go along with his story, pretend I believe it. Maybe a part of me wants to believe it? But no. I can already feel scorn harden my face. He sees it too, and as he makes a move for me, I hold myself steady against the seat and rake my fingernails down his cheek. He slaps my hand away and lifts a dagger between us.

My eyes are trained on the knife's edge as he pulls me against his chest so that I face away from him. The coach heaves to a stop. I feel the dagger's cold blade against my cheek. By the time the coach pitches forward again, one of Cosgrove's arms holds mine pinned to my sides, the other holding the dagger close to my neck.

"It's a pity you saw through my latest disguise," he says, the tip of his dagger digging into my high collar so that I can feel the prickle of the collar's lace against my skin. "Made a change from being the Indian suspect. Nothing easier than donning a turban, like I did last night. Just wind a scarf around the head and it's done." The coach hurtles left around a corner and the weight of his body slams me against the side of the carriage.

My voice is constricted as I say, "We know about Sarawak, about McBride and the Crookshanks. But why kill Lovejoy? And poor Pidgeon?" I struggle to twist towards him, so he can see the anger in my eyes. I can smell him — his familiar scent, of forest and something musky, and a momentary pinch of regret squeezes my heart.

His grip on my arms tightens. "Had to keep the pattern going, didn't I? The vengeful letters, the *kungsi* murders. I left your *kris* behind when I murdered Lovejoy in the hope the murders would be linked to their ridiculously sinister Chinaman, but I couldn't account for the nightsoil man filching it."

Shouts are heard over the loud rumbling of the coach. Slowly, the coach eases to a stop and, out my window, I can see Hatch's buggy pull in a few metres away.

"Maurice, you have nowhere to go," I say through clenched teeth, straining away from the blade.

"You blasted woman," he breathes, hot against my ear. "Why couldn't you just let things be?"

Hatch runs towards the coach but sees me through the window, sees the blade held to my throat. He halts, flings his arms out, blocking the other policeman from approaching.

"How'd you find out so quickly it wasn't me on the slab?" Cosgrove asks. He taps the glass of the window with the pointed end of the dagger, to ward off Hatch and his men, then returns it quickly to my neck. "I thought the blue pin would trick you. I knew you wouldn't study the severed head. I had the idea that night at the theatre, when you said everyone would recognise you once you donned the red riding cloak. I made sure you knew me from that damned blue pin."

The pin with the lapis lazuli stone. Attached to my bodice. I wriggle against him. His left hand has the dagger firmly pressed to my throat, but his other hand only manages to clasp my right arm tight, leaving my left arm loose. I'm able to bend my left arm at the elbow, slide the pin out from my bodice and hold it firmly between my finger and thumb. I think of jabbing it into his arm but that might not be enough to stop him from sinking the blade into me, so I swing the pin upwards, stab towards his face, feel the sharp end break skin, and then the long, thin shaft slide right through to the hilt.

Cosgrove's scream is high-pitched, sickening, as the dagger clatters to the floor. I wrench open the coach door and, looking over my shoulder, I see Cosgrove clutching his hands over his left eye, as a thin trickle of blood slips down the side of his cheek like a tear.

CHAPTER
THIRTY-FIVE

By the light of an oil lamp, I peer into the mirror, my fingers picking at the lace of my collar where there is a rent in the fabric. Stroking the unscathed skin of my neck beneath it, I think of how much tougher the cotton lace is compared to my smooth flesh; of how lucky I am that the dagger hadn't pressed any closer.

Cosgrove must've become very well-practised at be-heading, after taking so many lives. I imagine his left hand creeping up the back of my neck, his strong fingers running through my hair — for a moment my mind grapples with the pleasures this once evoked — he would've grabbed hold of a large clump of my hair in order to steady my head, as his other hand swept the knife's edge across the front of my throat.

No. No. He would've had to unhand me first to do that. Surely in those precious seconds I would've managed to pull away, defend myself? I close my eyes, concentrate on the blank canvas, blood-red, of my closed eyelids, until the gruesome pictures subside.

"Heloise, what are you doing?"

Amah stands behind me in my drawing room, holding a tray of tea things. As her eyes travel across my face, I feel weary, I feel what she can see.

314

"You need to eat and drink something," she says, placing the tray on the table. She crosses the room to close the curtains against the darkening sky. "And I don't mean whisky."

I glance down at the crystal tumbler in my hand. I'd poured it for myself as soon as I entered the room, but, in truth, I don't have the stomach for it. I place it on the shelf of the china cabinet and pick up the pile of post awaiting me.

"Sit, sit," she urges, taking a seat herself on one of the armchairs. Leaning forward to pour tea, she asks, "You don't have guests tonight?"

Dismay fills my chest. "But what day is it?"

"Wednesday."

I stare down into the teacup she passes me, watching the lazy swirl from where she's stirred honey into the milky tea. "I don't think so. I remember there's a masked ball on Thursday, but . . ."

"What about Hatterleigh?"

I lean back into the sofa, resting the teacup and saucer in my lap. Hatterleigh. I'm not even sure if he's back in town or not. There might be a missive amongst the post before me on the table, but I haven't had the time or desire to check. He'll want to know all the news, about Pidgeon, and Cosgrove. Usually, I take glee in relating my adventures to him, but in this instance, I won't. How do I account for Cosgrove with a straight face? Do I act shocked? Like I'm telling him nothing worse than a ghoulish tale? Or no, maybe better to act like I always knew Cosgrove was up to no good. *Surely you noticed how reserved I was around the man, Hatterleigh?*

"Heloise, what is it? Where were you all day?"

"Hatch and I found out who has been murdering all these men."

"The Indian?"

A scornful "Ha" escapes my lips. "No. And not a Chinaman either. It was none other than Cosgrove, one of the gentlemen of their own set." I tell her of how Hatch had tracked down the incriminating letters from McBride and that latest body wasn't Cosgrove, as we were meant to believe.

She doesn't ask me how I know this, only blinks slowly. "Why was he at Isobel's? I always told you that girl couldn't be trusted."

"Oh, Mama," I say, taking a sip of my tea. "The poor creature had no idea what he'd been up to. That's why I am so late today. I had to accompany her to the police station while she was questioned by Hatch. She thought she was helping Cosgrove escape from the monster. She didn't realise he was the monster; hadn't yet heard he was meant to have been the latest victim. They knew each other in Mandalay when she was young. She had tender feelings for him, I'm afraid." Poor Isobel. Feverish circles on her pale cheeks, nose and eyes almost raw with weeping. She's lost two men she loved in a matter of days.

"Is that why you asked me about Mandalay? And Burma?" Amah asks.

I nod. "I'd heard Cosgrove talk of Burma, and the last time I saw Isobel she mentioned a curry she learnt to make in Mandalay. Cosgrove was great friends with the Pidgeons," my lips compress into a bitter line for a second, "so I thought that maybe they spent time together there. I wondered if he might find shelter with her."

"What did the letter say, that Hatch found?"

"That Cosgrove had arranged the riot to cover up his affair with a married woman, or to finish off her husband."

Amah nods. "So, Uncle Chee was correct. It was all over a woman."

Cosgrove and women. I feel like I should've known. But, of course, I did have an inkling all along; I just chose to ignore it. Didn't I wonder if Milly was his lover? Didn't I fall for him myself? And I consider myself very well-seasoned in such things.

A veritable Casanova, Cosgrove. But ruthless. The dead wife in Sarawak. Prepared to take advantage of sweet Isobel. And that crack he gave me over the head in the alleyway, near the cesspool. Looking back, he must've used his gun to knock me out. My stomach sinks. Fortunate he needed a witness, that he didn't press it to my temple, then and there, finish me off.

Looking up, I find Amah staring at me. "You are troubled?" she says.

I shake my head, more to dispel my horrid thoughts than anything. Amah pours herself some more tea, black, with a squeeze of lemon in it. My tongue puckers at the thought.

"And you, Amah?" I say, reaching for a piece of Madeira cake. "What have you been up to lately, in and out at all hours, I hear." It's only now that I recall her story of Jakub being Mrs Preston's son. Like him, I'd always thought dear Aunt Miriam was his mother. "Chasing after Jakub, I think you said. I cannot believe the cheek of Uncle Chee." I grin, licking powdered sugar from my bottom lip. "Dossing down with the boss's wife."

Amah's lip twists, reprovingly. "He loved her very much, Heloise. We both did."

I pull a face. "Still rather brave, if you ask me." Resting my head back, I close my eyes. "I think we should take some time away, Amah." I open one eye, peep at her. "Maybe Venice? I've noticed the picture book you borrowed from the library." With portraits of canals, grand churches, decaying courtyards. "By the time we are organised, the weather might be more clement there, too, for you. Thaw your bones," I grin. "You can get your sea legs back again on the steamship over."

Her cacao-bean eyes gleam back at me. She doesn't say anything, but I know she's pleased, by her short nod.

I will have a glass of something, after all. Not the whisky; something sweeter. I pour myself a generous portion of sherry, which I sip as I tear open the first letter on the pile.

Hatterleigh.

Dearest Heloise,
I will be back in London by the 3rd. I'm having a devilish time getting away from my estate. Work

work work. Kennard, my foreman you know, will not let me alone. If it's not roofs that need thatching, it's harvests that need collecting. He seems to think he needs my nay or say in everything he does, despite my assurances to him that he is much better suited to making those decisions than I am. I know I must be thankful, though, that he's not a thieving rascal.

It's so horribly cold at the moment, I really think you and I should escape to France for a few weeks when I return. The champagne we can sip! The love we can make! The gougère to grease our lips! I have heard of a wonderful chateau we can stay at in the Loire Valley. And, of course, I know you love the theatre life in Paris. Remember those girls, you minx, in Haymarket, flashing their fannies? Maybe you could learn some of their ways? I am laughing here, my dear. You are far more alluring than they, even covered in yards of silk. What do you say? I say yes! Cherie, mon amour, mon coeur, please say yes too.

Yours
Hatterleigh.

I fold his letter into two, then over again. I glance at Amah, who has thrown my shawl across her knees and calmly embroiders a bird of paradise with yellow silk. Folding the letter once more, my mind races. Paris with Hatterleigh, or Venice with my mother? The tug of loyalty, of obligation, between these two people spirals through my mind. Picture galleries with Amah. Paris

nightlife with Hatterleigh. Love, or riches? Content-
ment, or pleasure?

Or both?

Surely I can manage both. A merry foray into Paris
on our way to restful Venice.

Smiling, I toss the letter into the fire.

Acknowledgements

Thank you, again, to Legend Press and Pantera Press, for your continued faith in my Heloise novels. Special thanks to Lauren Parsons, for her careful, thoughtful editing of my work. Works by Lee Jackson, Liza Picard and numerous others are integral to the research that goes into my Heloise novels, and some might recognise references to George R. Sims' *Living London* (1900).

I would like to thank the Queensland Writers Centre, Sisters in Crime (Aus) and Byron Writers Festival for their ongoing support. Thank you to all those who have helped me shape this book, especially Emma Doolan, Laura Elvery, Kathy George, Vivienne Muller, Fiona Kearney and Andrea Baldwin. Thank you to both Emma and my mum, Margaret Boland, for being the usual suspects (guinea pigs) to read my first drafts. Finally, I am forever grateful for all those who love and encourage me in all my endeavours, especially Jim Riwoe, Mum, Elis, Tina, Liam, Amy, Damien, Dave, Bianca, Jett and Mae.

Finland

a cultural
encyclopedia

Editor-in-chief
OLLI ALHO

Editors
HILDI HAWKINS
PÄIVI VALLISAARI

Helsinki
Finnish Literature Society

Finnish Literature Society Editions 684

Translation: *Hildi Hawkins, David McDuff*
Copy editor: *Miren Lopategui*
Editorial assistant: *Desirée Räsänen*
Picture editor: *Päivi Vallisaari*
Design and layout: *Markus Itkonen*
Maps: *Tuija Jantunen*
Index: *Eeva-Liisa Haanpää*

Photo reproduction: *Euro Pixel Oy*
Printing house: *Vammalan Kirjapaino Oy, Vammala 1999*

2. edition

ISBN 951-717-885-9
ISSN 0355-1768

To the reader

THIS BOOK OUTLINES a culture that is both ancient and in its prime. Its birthplace was charted in Tacitus's *Germania* as early as AD 98. It has been shaped by a history of settlement spanning millennia, Finland's medieval connections with the Catholic culture of Europe and its position between East and West. It came to full consciousness with the national romanticism of the 19th century: a national spirit, national institutions, and a culture recognised as Finnish were born. This development made the declaration of Finnish independence in 1917 both possible and inevitable. *Finland: a cultural encyclopedia* describes the past, but also offers its readers the opportunity to bring their knowledge of Finland up to date as a modern, European country characterised by both a vital and expansive artistic life and dynamic visions of the opportunities afforded by information technology in research and education.

As the book's range of key-word articles shows, the editors have interpreted the concept of culture in its broadest sense. Their country, their *patria*, is, for Finns, an entirety not only in terms of existence of a state, but also of landscape. For this reason, the scope of *Finland: a cultural encyclopedia* includes the forest and snow, the archipelago, the plains of Ostrobothnia and the mountains of Lapland. The Finnish mental landscape is charted in articles on identity, way of life, customs, sex, food, drink and leisure.

The gallery of characters that manifests itself in the book's articles is made up primarily of people whose work is of both national and international importance. Some of the most important figures in Finnish art and scholarship are also among the numerous contributors to the book. Many nationally important names are to be found in the extensive index. We hope that Finnish culture will open up to the readers of this book in its entire polyphonic richness and unpolished diversity. For this, the editors wish to thank the writers.

The editors believe that *Finland: a cultural encyclopedia* will be useful as both a travel guide and a traditional encyclopedia, and that it will find its place both in its readers' luggage and on their bookshelves. The book's reference system has been made as easy as possible. References within the text (▶ sign) have been used to link articles; the index is a comprehensive catalogue of the people, institutions and other matters cited. It has been our aim to present, in *Finland: a cultural encyclopedia*, an information network of Finnish culture.

OLLI ALHO
Helsinki, 1 September 1997

Writers

AA   ANNELI ASPLUND, Research fellow, Finnish Literature Society
MA   MIRJA ALMAY, Textile artist, journalist
MaA   MARIANNE AAV, Curator, Design Museum of Finland
MAo   MATTI ALESTALO, Professor of Sociology, University of Tampere
OA   OLLI ALHO, Programme director, Finnish Broadcasting Company
SA   SUVI AHOLA, Journalist
LAM   LEENA AHTOLA-MOORHOUSE, Senior curator, The Finnish National Gallery
SAo   SAMULI AIKIO, Scholar of Sámi language and culture, Utsjoki
UA   ULLA AARTOMAA, Curator, Lahti Art Museum
HB   HENRY BACON, Music historian
MBy   MARJATTA BARDY, Researcher, National Research and Development Centre for Welfare and Health
NB   NATALIA BASCHMAKOFF, Assistant professor of Russian, University of Joensuu
JE   JARI EHRNROOTH, Sociologist, researcher, University of Helsinki
KE   KAI EKHOLM, Chief librarian, University of Jyväskylä
EF   ERKKI FREDRIKSSON, Cartographic scholar
MF   MARTTI FAVORIN, Archivist, Ministry of Foreign Affairs
AH   AULI HAKULINEN, Professor of Finnish, University of Helsinki
EH   ELIAS HÄRÖ, Buildings historian, scholar
IH   ILPO HAKASALO, Music journalist, Finnish Broadcasting Company
MH   MIKKO HEINIÖ, Professor of musicology, University of Turku
PH   PIM VAN DER HEJDEN, Researcher, Hypermedialaboratory, University of Tampere
SH   SVEN HIRN, Historian
HHlä   HANNU HEIKKILÄ, Historian, director, Federation of Finnish Scientific Societies
MHlä   MARKKU HEIKKILÄ, Professor of theology, historian, University of Helsinki
EHM   ELINA HAAVIO-MANNILA, Professor of sociology, University of Helsinki
HI   HENNI ILOMÄKI, Librarian, Finnish Literature Society
HJ   HEIKKI JOKINEN, Film and comic-strip journalist
TJ   TIMO JÄRVIKOSKI, Professor of sociology, University of Oulu
JK   JUKKA KORTELAINEN, Historian, scholar of games of chance
JKn   JUKKA KUKKONEN, Researcher, Finnish Museum of Photography
JKen   JUKKA KEKKONEN, Professor of jurisprudence, University of Helsinki
MK   MATTI KLINGE, Professor of history, University of Helsinki
OK   OLAVI KOIVUKANGAS, Director, Institute of Migration Studies, Turku
SK   SEPPO KNUUTTILA, Professor of folklore studies, University of Joensuu

TK	TEPPO KORHONEN, Professor of ethnology, University of Turku
ML	MARKKU LÖYTÖNEN, Professor of geography, University of Turku
PL	PERTTI LASSILA, Literary scholar
PLn	PEKKA LAAKSONEN, Director, Folklore Archive, Finnish Literature Society
RL	RIIKKA LAITALA, Information officer, Finnish Radio Symphony Orchestra
SL	SOILA LEHTONEN, Editor, *Books from Finland*
TL	TEUVO LAITILA, Scholar, journalist
PLLH	PIRKKO-LIISA LEHTOSALO-HILANDER, Archaeologist, docent, University of Helsinki
JM	JARI MÄKINEN, Science journalist
IN	ILKKA NUMMELA, Professor of history, University of Jyväskylä
JN	JUSSI NUORTEVA, Scholar of old literature, science journalist
JNn	JAKE NYMAN, Music journalist, Finnish Broadcasting Company
RN	RIITTA NIKULA, Professor of art history, University of Helsinki
EP	EEVA PILKE, Researcher, Hypermedialaboratory, University of Tampere
JP	JUHANI PALLASMAA, Professor of architecture, Helsinki University of Technology
JPn	JUHA PENTIKÄINEN, Professor of comparative religion, University of Helsinki
RLP	RITVA LIISA PITKÄNEN, Onomastics researcher, The Research Institute for the Languages of Finland
AR	AULI RÄSÄNEN, Dance journalist, *Helsingin Sanomat*
KR	KARI RAHIALA, Bank director, collector
KRn	KALEVI RIKKINEN, Professor of geography, University of Helsinki
MLR	MARJA-LIISA RÖNKKÖ, Director-general, The Finnish National Gallery
MR	MATTI RÄSÄNEN, Professor emeritus of ethnology, University of Turku
PLR	PIRKKO-LIISA RAUSMAA, Research fellow, Finnish Literature Society
PR	PERTTU RASTAS, Media curator, Museum of Contemporary Art
ES	ESA SIRONEN, Sports researcher, University of Jyväskylä
HS	HANNES SIHVO, Professor of literature, University of Joensuu
MS	MARTTI SORAMÄKI, Head of media development group, Finnish Broadcasting Company
MSä	MATTI SUURPÄÄ, Publisher, Finnish Literature Society
PS	PIRKKO SIHVO, Folk-dress researcher, National Board of Antiquities
PSn	PEKKA SULKUNEN, Researcher, National Research and Development Centre for Welfare and Health
AMT	ANNA-MAIJA TANTTU, Food editor
ST	SAKARI TOIVIAINEN, Film researcher, Finnish Film Archive
TT	TUUKKA TALVIO, Money and medals expert, researcher, National Board of Antiquities
ESV	EEVA-SISKO VEIKKOLA, Co-ordinator, Statistics Finland
JV	JARMO VITELI, Researcher, Hypermedialaboratory, University of Tampere
MV	MATTI VIRTANEN, Editor-in-chief, alcohol issues researcher, National Research and Development Centre for Welfare and Health
MVn	MARKKU VALKONEN, Director, Retretti art centre
PV	PÄIVI VALLISAARI, Book editor, Finnish Literature Society
HY	HEIKKI YLIKANGAS, Professor of legal history, University of Helsinki
AMÅ	ANNA-MARIA ÅSTRÖM, Folk-tradition researcher

Aalto, (Marsio-Aalto) Aino (1894–1949), architect. From 1924 Aino Aalto worked with her husband, ►Alvar Aalto, in their joint architectural office. Aino Aalto's main contribution appears to have lain in interior decoration. In her design work, Aino Aalto emphasized functionality. In 1935, together with Alvar Aalto, Nils-Gustav Hahl (1904–1941) and Maire Gullichsen (1907–1990), she founded the furniture company ►Artek, of which she was managing director between 1941 and 1949. At Artek, her preferred areas were the interiors of day-care centres and kindergartens. During the 1930s, Aino Aalto also designed utility glass. The most successful of her glassware sets was *Bölgeblick,* a set of pressed glass which won second prize in a glass design competition held in 1934 by the Karhula-Iittala company; in its time, this utility glassware was found in almost every Finnish home. MaA

Chair designed for Paimio Sanatorium, 1935

Aino Aalto

Alvar Aalto

Bölgeblick pressed-glass series by Aino Aalto, 1934

Aalto, Alvar (1898–1976) architect. When Alvar Aalto became a qualified architect in 1921, the First World War was over and Europe open to young people. Aalto discovered Italy, and that country was to influence his entire career: earliest works are elegant variations on the themes of Nordic classicism.

Viipuri Library (1927–1935) developed into a personal masterpiece of functionalism. His first prize in the competition for the design of Paimio tuberculosis sanatorium led to a new kind of hospital architecture in which consideration of the suffering of the patient was as new as the all-embracing nature of the plan and the lightness of the concrete structures. The bentwood chairs used in the sanatorium marked the beginnings of furniture production by Alvar Aalto and his wife, ►Aino (Marsio-)Aalto (1894–1949), and led to the establishment of the ►Artek furniture company.

Friendship with the industrialist Harry Gullichsen (1902–1954) and his wife, Maire (1907–1990), brought Aalto large commissions as a designer of

Auditorium building, Helsinki University of Technology, Otaniemi, 1964–1970

industrial areas. The residential area for the Sunila factory (1936–1939) became Finland's first modern housing estate with which Aalto wanted to promote democracy through architecture. In the Villa Mairea (1938), built for the Ahlström-family at Noormarkku, near Pori in south-western Finland, Aalto presented an experimental laboratory of the new ideals of living.

Säynätsalo town hall (1952) was the first example of Aalto's red-brick architecture, which continued in the main building University of Jyväskylä. The centre of the town of Seinäjoki (1960–1987) is the most monumental of Aalto's urban planning projects: its core is a rhythmic arrangement of church, town hall and library. The House of Culture and the main office of the Social Insurance Institution of Finland in Helsinki, and the small church at Vuoksenniska, are the major works of the 1950s, the Helsinki University of Technology at Otaniemi that of the 1960s. The ►Finlandia Hall remains the handsome conclusion of Aalto's powerful career, even though the urban plan of which the concert hall was to form a part remained unbuilt. RN

Aino Ackté

Ackté, Aino (1876–1944) soprano. Ackté was one of the first Finnish singers to attract international attention. After her debut at the Paris Opera 1897, she performed in many European centres of operatic life and, in 1904–1906, at the Metropolitan Opera in New York. She sang the title role in the first English performance of Richard Strauss's *Salome* in 1910. Ackté was one of the co-founders of what became the Finnish National Opera, and started the first Savonlinna Opera Festival. Her libretto *Juha* was set by two major Finnish composers, Leevi Madetoja (1887–1947) and Aarre Merikanto (1893–1958). HB

adult education As early as the 1970s, the Council of State set as its aim the principle of continuing education, in which all citizens would be offered, at various stages in their lives, the opportunity to self-development through study. Today adult education is divided primarily into all-round education and vocational adult education.

All-round education began in an organised way in 1874, with the founding of the Society for Culture and Education whose task was defined as the provision of popular, inexpensive literature and other activities to awaken a desire for knowledge. In addition to publishing books, the Society became important for its annual calendar, which was published until the end of the 1950s. The Society also supported the founding of libraries and study and hobby circles. This led to the rise of folk college societies in the 1890s, whose aim was the establishment of permanent educational institutions for the regular organisation of cultural work. The first Finnish-language folk high school was founded in 1889 in Kangasala, and its first Swedish-language equivalent in Porvoo the same year. University student societies were of great importance in the founding of many early folk high schools. Models were sought primarily in the Scandinavian countries, particularly in the Grundtvigian folk high schools of Denmark. Many ideological and religious movements have since founded their own folk high schools.

The workers' society and study movement became also active in the late 19th century. In its initial stages, this workers' educational activity was to a large extent directed by intellectuals interested in social questions, but by the early 20th century, as the workers' movement became radicalised, the workers' own interest in developing educational activities increased. The first workers' institute opened its doors in Tampere in 1899, its models taken largely from the workers' institute founded in Stockholm in 1880. As activities spread to the countryside, open colleges were founded which, along with folk high schools, were of great importance in the education and free cultural activities of people who had until then received only a basic education. The Workers' Academy, founded in 1924 in Kauniainen, near Helsinki, is a two-year educational institution whose teaching concentrates on economic and social material.

As education organised by society has increased, different educational institutions have, particularly since the

1960s been forced to seek new modes of operation. The traditional boarding-school type education has gradually begun to decline, and has been replaced by shorter courses on specialities or particular interests. During the 1990s, government cuts have hit funding for workers' institutes and folk high schools particularly hard. Nevertheless, the importance of these educational institutions remains central in adult and continuing education. In 1995 276 open colleges and workers' institutes and 90 folk high schools were active in Finland. 650,000 students took part in the educational programmes of open colleges, and 90,000 in those of folk high schools; 8000 students from the total number participated in long-term education. About one quarter of the education offered by folk high schools was vocational, and 10 per cent was at comprehensive school or senior secondary school.

In recent decades, opportunities for distance learning in general education have also improved. Such tuition is provided by four distance-learning institutions which work in collaboration with educational institutions that approve the examinations taken in them. In language education, the role of radio and television has been significant. General education is also arranged in summer universities and summer senior secondary schools. General language examinations are arranged in Finland; candidates are able to demonstrate their foreign-language skills and to receive a certificate in recognition of them without set studies.

As the demands of working life change, the need for continuing and complementary education has increased. Places for complementary education and re-education for the unemployed were increased significantly in 1996. Most worker education (54 per cent in 1994) now takes place in adult education centres, which are vocational course centres that function on a fee basis. Their services may be bought by both employment officials and individual employers. In recent years, the number of educational institutions offering adult education has increased, and the role played by adult education centres has correspondingly decreased. Adult education offered by vocational educational institutions doubled during the 1990s. JN

Michael Agricola

Agricola, Michael (c. 1510–1557), Bishop of Turku, Finnish reformer, creator of Finnish as a written language. Michael Agricola is one of the most important characters in Finnish history. He first brought the Reformation to Finland, but his influence also extended far beyond the church. The exact year of Agricola's birth is not known, for he was born into an ordinary, if prosperous, farming family. In Finland, where in medieval times there were only five small towns, it was normal for the clergy to recruit from among the ranks of the farmers. For that reason it was not unusual for Agricola to have the opportunity to study first at school in Viipuri, which served eastern Finland, and then in the Turku Cathedral School, which was the only educational institute responsible for the training of priests in Finland.

Agricola was one of the half dozen gifted youths who, with the help of Turku Cathedral Chapter, were sent, in the 1530s, to study in the Reformation centre of Wittenberg. Agricola had already been ordained as a priest, and had acted as assistant to the bishop in the Turku Diocese, to which the whole of Finland belonged at that time. It is known that he was familiar with the basic ideas of the Reformation even before his departure for Germany, for a postilla by Luther that he acquired in 1531 has survived.

Agricola studied in Wittenberg from 1536 to 1539. While there he began to translate the New Testament into Finnish, an unusually demanding task, for Finnish had not previously been used as a literary language. Agricola thus has an important position as creator of the Finnish language. For this reason his use of language remains one of the central subjects of the study of old literary Finnish. His translation of the New Testament was probably completed by the end of the 1530s, but because of the absence of financial support was not printed until 1548, and was preceded by *Abc-kiria* ('The alphabet book', 1543) and *Rucouskiria* ('A prayer-book', 1544), both of which were published by Agricola. *Abc-kiria*, whose first edition probably appeared in 1543, is the first example of Finnish literature. No complete copy has survived; instead, there are incomplete examples of three different editions. The printing of many editions shows that Agricola had absorbed the Reformation idea of improving the reading skills of the people so that every member of the congregation would be able to read the Bible himself or herself.

In addition to the New Testament, Agricola translated more than one fifth of the Old Testament and published, in Finnish, *Se meiden Herran Jesusen Christusen pina* ('The history of Christ's suffering', 1549), based on the gospels, and a *Käsikiria* ('Ritual') and *Messu* ('Missal') for the use of the clergy. Agricola's translation of the Psalms (1551) has been particularly interesting, for in its introduction he presents a list of ancient Finnish gods. It is the oldest surviving source of information about Finnish ▶mythology.

On his return from Wittenberg, Agricola served from 1539 to 1548 as schoolmaster of Turku, with responsibility for training priests in the new Reformation spirit. In 1548 he lived in the official residence of the dean of the cathedral and managed affairs relating to the administration of the diocese. However, he was not appointed to the post, because King Gustavus Vasa was attempting to reduce the number of ecclesiastical offices and to restore church property to the state. For the same reason the office of bishop, which became open in 1550, was not filled until 1554, when Agricola received the appointment. The same year, however, Finland was divided in-

to two episcopies: Viipuri and Turku. The new Viipuri diocese covered the eastern part of the country. In practice, Agricola had been responsible for the diocese since 1550. Even before that, it had been his job to catalogue the property and income of the church and to carry out tasks related to tax reform.

In addition to ecclesiastical and administrative tasks, Gustavus Vasa used Agricola for diplomatic tasks. In January 1557 the king sent Agricola to Moscow to negotiate peace with Russia, with which Sweden-Finland had been at war since 1554. Agricola died on his return journey from Moscow, on the Karelian Isthmus, on 9 April 1557. He was buried in Viipuri Cathedral, which was destroyed during the Second World War. JN

Åland Åland differs from the rest of Finland on account, among other things, of its political autonomy. While there are two official languages elsewhere in Finland, the province of Åland has only one, Swedish. Autonomous rights were granted as a result of a decision by the League of Nations in 1921, and they were confirmed in the autonomy law of 1951, which guarantees language, culture and local customs for the population. The administration of the province is in the hands of an elected provincial government. The Åland flag has, from ancient times, been a symbol of autonomy. At the beginning of 1993 the autonomy law was changed to give Åland citizens better possibilities to determing matters concerning their province. The province governs, among other things, the postal service, radio and television, child benefits, alcohol regulations and agriculture. The Åland passport is like the Finnish passport apart from the cover and personal details page, to which the word 'Åland' is added, in letters of the same size as 'Suomi Finland'.

Åland comprises the main island plus a fragmented archipelago made up of islands, islets, rocks and reefs. To the west, toward Sweden, the border is the Åland sea, and to the east, toward the Turku archipelago, the waters of Kihti. The sea puts its stamp on both the landscape and human activity.

Åland has 6429 islands more than

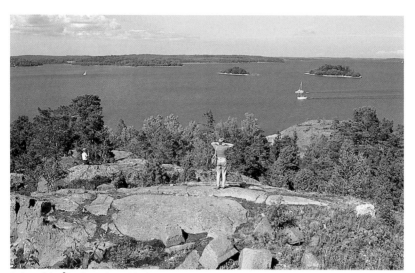

A view of the Åland sea; the archipelago consists of more than 6000 islands

0.3 hectares in area. The proportion of the main island of the total land area is nevertheless two-thirds. The islands are rocky, polished by the continental ice-sheet and washed bare by the sea. The main island is made up of red-brown rough red granite. Traces of rock movement are also visible in the archipelago. The movements follow the numerous cleft lines of the bed-rock, which are generally visible as north-south stripes, but there are also curved formations in the outlines of the islands.

Åland has risen slowly from the sea over thousands of years. Fertile loam has developed in the bays and sounds between the rocky hills. The most extensive loamy plains are on the main island at Jomala and Hammarland. Because the ►climate is milder than elsewhere in Finland, the flora of the area, too, is rich, and includes the northernmost examples of central European mixed deciduous forest. The most remote skerries, however, are very barren.

At the beginning of the 20th century, there were more than 150 inhabited islands, although about 100 of them were inhabited only by one or two families. The number of constantly inhabited islands has continually decreased; in many cases, holiday residence has taken the place of year-round residence. For about a hundred years the population of Åland has remained over 20,000. At the end of 1996 it was 25,257.

Midsummer maypole, Åland. These maypoles, which are rare in mainland Finland, show the clear Swedish influence on the Åland tradition

The town of Mariehamn is the dominant core of Åland, where about half the population of the province lives. People have moved there from the outlying areas. Eighty-five per cent of the population of Mariehamn earn their living from service industries. The backbone of the town's economy is ship-building and navigation.

The countryside of the main island lies close to the core area; it is used for dairy farming and growing wheat, rape and sugar-beet. Fishing and tourism,

13

too, are important sources of livelihood.

The outlying areas of Åland make up the true archipelago, which is suffering a net loss of population. This is to be seen in the narrow age-pyramids of the population, which are evident in its ageing. At the beginning of the 1990s, less than ten per cent of the population lived outside the main island.

Åland plays a transitional role between Sweden and Finland. Traffic between the countries has, since ancient times, passed through the Åland archipelago. There has been much emigration from the archipelago, particularly to Sweden. On the other hand, people have also moved to Åland from elsewhere in Finland. Immigrants receive provincial rights after they have lived in Åland for five years. KRn

alcohol Alcohol is, and has been, an unusually important substance for Finns. This is not because Finns have always drunk, or drink, an unusual amount – rather the opposite. The reason for the special relationship of Finns with alcohol is to be found in their permanent framework of living: Finland is a northern, cold and sparsely populated country.

Nevertheless, the unusual role of alcohol and drunkenness in Finland has, in one sense, a short and well-defined history, arising from the fact that almost total prohibition predominated there for almost exactly a century, from 1866 to 1968.

In 1866 rural farmers were forbidden to distil liquor. Until then, distilling had been both an important source of income for farmers and a tool of social power: excess grain was sold on the markets as distilled liquor, and part of the wages of farm-hands was paid directly in liquor. A great deal of alcohol was also consumed, but regulated by a strict system of normative customs.

In the other Nordic countries, landowners' right to domestic distillation was allowed to disappear through commercial competition with factory production of liquor, but in Finland domestic distillation was actually forbidden by law. The idea was to accelerate the industrialisation of liquor manufacture, so that the government would be able to collect fatter taxes from the liquor factories and merchants than from the farmers. The result was the total opposite. In revenge for the treachery of the government, the rural population refused to buy factory liquor with money, and consumption of alcohol in the countryside began to go into a steep decline. Later, farmers completely prevented the legal sale and dispensation of liquor and beer in the country.

In the late 19th century, because of their position of ownership and the new municipal law, farmers had a great deal of power in local government. Because of this, they were able to instigate a series of municipal alcohol prohibitions. These municipal prohibitions gave rise to a 'dry' countryside in Finland as early as the 1890s – and until the 1950s the countryside was practically the whole of Finland; the towns remained small and of low population.

By the beginning of the 20th century, Finland had, indeed, become Europe's driest country. Consumption was highest in France, with 22.9 litres of 100 per cent alcohol consumed per person. In most of the countries of central Europe this figure was between 5 and 10 litres, in Sweden it was 4.3 litres and Norway 2.4 litres. The Finnish statistic was in a class of its

A national tradition: drunkenness on stage in Simo Hämäläinen's play *Kätkäläinen*

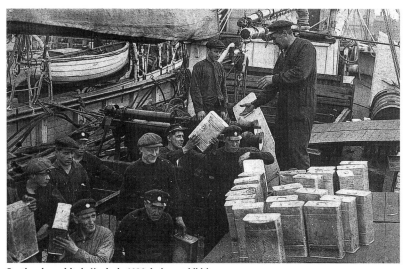

Bootlegging spirits in Hanko in 1928 during prohibition

own: 1.5 litres. From a dry country-side, it was not a big step to demands for total prohibition – which indeed arose in the countryside: if the countryside was alcohol-free, let the towns follow their example.

The workers' movement, which became an organised force at the beginning of the century, threw its weight behind the Prohibition Law – in order to resist 'alcohol capitalism' and the conspicuous consumption of alcohol and the upper classes. Since a large number of the poorest people of the towns could not include alcohol even in their weekly household budgets, banning the joys of liquor from the more prosperous did not cause great difficulties.

The brand-new parliament elected in 1906 decided, as one of its first actions, to pass the Prohibition Law – unanimously and with a standing ovation. However it became law only in 1919, after Finland's independence and the bloody Civil War of 1918.

Once again, the new law brought about a result that was almost the opposite of what was intended. The municipal prohibitions had worked relatively well, but now the total ban on liquors brought about extensive smuggling and trafficking. During prohibition, liquor was cheap and freely available – particularly for common people. Never before, or in fact since, has alcohol had so effective, dense or comprehensive a sales network.

The Prohibition Law was repealed in 1932 – but only in the towns; the countryside remained dry until 1968. A centralised national monopoly was established for the production and retailing of alcohol; with the task (almost explicit) came the restriction and surveillance of the drinking habits of common people, particularly the working populations of the towns.

As a result of the rough treatment of the dry countryside and the monopoly, consumption remained low (around a couple of litres) until 1968, when a new, more liberal alcohol law was passed – which has since been further lifted. By the mid 1970s, consumption had risen to more than 6 litres, at which level it has remained. Since the entry of Finland to the European Union, all that is left of the formerly powerful alcohol monopoly, Alko, is a retail monopoly, operating on a self-service system and stressing service.

To sum up: the chain of prohibition in Finland has proceeded as a kind of revenge process. First the farmers dried the countryside as a reaction to the banning of home distilling, and the workers joined the prohibition front in order to defy the 'bourgeoisie'. When the Prohibition Law came into force, it was characterised in the eyes of common people as oppression by 'white' Finland: the victors of the Civil War were defied by drinking bootleg spirits and by celebrating smugglers as folk heroes. When the monopoly was established, it took common people, intoxicated with freedom from prohibition, as the object of its special surveillance.

The same spirit of defiance, bluster and resistance became, at the same time, a central feature of Finnish drunkenness. First the common folk (the landless farmers and agricultural workers) drank – the little they succeeded in acquiring – as a protest against the driers of the countryside, the powerful dominant farmers and the gentlemen of the state. Then the workers, in their own bars, began to conduct a mental class struggle with the 'bourgeoisie'. During prohibition, liquor became the real power of the oppressed, and remained so – becoming milder with time – for the entire period of the alcohol monopoly.

In drunkenness, the silent resentment and bitterness toward the lords of life and keepers of power became open defiance. Since procuring alcohol was laborious and difficult, it was drunk in great quantities when it could be procured. These features – the depth of drunkenness and the expressions of bitter defiance it produces – form the core of the so-called Finnish drunk.

In the 1950s Finland went through rapid social change. The last structures and modes of thought of the old class society began to crumble; there was large-scale migration from the countryside to the towns; the structure of the labour force became concentrated on the office; the welfare state was under active construction; the standard of living rose; the alcohol monopoly ameliorated its humiliating surveillance. Finland began to become more middle-class, and the chasm between 'gentlefolk' and common people narrowed.

This tendency toward homogenisation was reflected, in the 1970s and 1980s, in the nature of Finnish drunkenness: a number of researchers found that it was becoming tamer. The defiant relationship of the drunken world with order, power and its representatives began to ease.

At the beginning of the 1990s, however, Finland faced serious challenges: changes in the structure of information technology, the deepest recession of the century and immersion in European integration arrived almost simultaneously. The young, fragile Finnish homogeneity has already begun to crack. The worlds of the fortunate and the unfortunate are once more become distanced. As a result of mass unemployment, a class society that is the reverse of that of the turn of the last century is being created: the majority (educated, professional) are in classes, the minority (under-educated, unskilled) are becoming a new kind of urban peasantry. Whether this development is permanent or temporary is difficult to say. If it is permanent, Finnish drunkenness, which has been becoming tamer, will grow wild once more. MV

Allardt, Erik (born 1925) sociologist. Erik Allardt is one of the most widely known Nordic sociologists. Erik Allardt played an important role in reforming the social sciences in the 1950s and 1960s. The subjects of his central studies have been divorce and its causes, the conditions and the consequences of structural changes in society, political radicalism, the dimensions of welfare and ethnic minorities. Allardt has published 20 books and more than 600 articles. His contribution as a scholar, teacher, conveyor of international influences, and contributor to scholarly policy and social debate has been of exceptional importance. He was among the first research professors in the reformed Academy of Finland (1970–1980), and, from 1986 to 1991, was the chairman of the Central Committee of Sciences. He has also acted as visiting professor in many universities of the world (Sweden, Germany, the United States), and his extensive knowledge has been called upon in many international connections. MAo

Anderson, Amos Valentin (1878–1961), artistic patron. Amos Anderson is one of the most important cultural figures in the history of independent Finland. From humble beginnings, he created a financial empire that is still of enormous significance, particularly in Finland-Swedish economic and cultural life. Anderson's fortune – he did not have any direct heirs – is adminis-

Erik Allardt

Amos Anderson

tered by a foundation he established in 1940, the Föreningen Konstsamfundet, the Art Society Association, which assets include the Forum real-estate block, in the centre of ▶Helsinki, the location of Finland's largest Swedish-language daily newspaper, *Hufvud-stadsbladet*, and the Mercator printing press, both of which are also owned by the foundation. A few of the rooms of Anderson's private house have been preserved in the Amos Anderson Art Museum (1965), which is also located in the Forum block. The company also owns a significant part of the Stock-mann department store and, through it, of many other businesses. Söder-långvik manor house on Anderson's home island of Kemiö, which he bought in 1927 and which includes about 6000 hectares of land and more than 100 kilometres of sea shore, is also owned by the foundation. The Söderlångvik manor, where Anderson spent most of the final part of his life, is now a museum.

Anderson's formal education was limited to elementary school and business college. Having completed his business studies in Finland, the easily inspired Anderson continued his education in Göttingen and London, studying economic theory and insurance from 1900 to 1902. On his return to his native land, he soon began to put his new ideas into practice. He edited a magazine on insurance matters and founded the economics newspaper *Mercator* in 1906. Three years later, he set up the Mercator printing press, and soon his influence extended elsewhere in the field of graphics. In 1916 he became the majority shareholder of the Tilgmann printing press and in 1920 the newspaper *Hufvud-stadsbladet* came into his ownership. Anderson edited the paper from 1928 to 1936.

Amos Anderson's activities were wide-ranging. He was member of parliament for the Swedish People's Party from 1922 to 1927, and was a member of the electoral college for three presidential elections, while the same time being a member of the board of many companies.

Anderson is best-known as a patron and amateur of culture. He was an important supporter of Åbo Akademi, the Swedish-speaking university founded in Turku in 1918, and in the construction of the Helsinki Taidehalli Art Gallery in the late 1920s. Anderson financed the renovations to the Swedish Theatre in Helsinki in the 1930s and the restoration of the medieval churches of Parainen, Kemiö and Turku. His legend-drama *Vallis Gratiae* (1923) and his work on Finland's medieval ecclesiastical art, which has been translated into many languages, are witness to his interest in Finland's medieval ecclesiastical culture. Anderson also supported research into classical culture. He was of central importance in the founding of the Finnish Institute in Rome in 1954, and of the purchase of the Villa Lante, on the Gianicolo hill, as its premises. In 1945 Anderson was awarded the title of hononary mining counsellor, and in 1948 Åbo Akademi University awarded him an honorary doctorate. JN

animated films Finnish animation – making movies by filming frame by frame – was extremely scarce until the 1960s, being restricted almost exclusively to advertisements. The first Finnish animated films as such were experimental animations made by the artist Eino Ruutsalo (born 1921) in the 1960s.

Because it is labour-intensive, making animated films is expensive. More cut-out animations have been made in Finland than celluloid animations. Cut-out animation was created as a genre in Finland by Heikki Partanen (1942–1990) with his *Hinku ja Vinku* ('Hinku and Vinku') children's animations from 1964. Camilla Mickwitz (1937–1989) made a number of stylish cut-out animations for children beginning in the late 1960s, among them the *Jason* and *Emilia* films, which also appeared as picture-books.

The only full-length Finnish animated film to date, a version of ▶Aleksis Kivi's classic novel *Seitsemän veljestä (Seven Brothers)*, was made in 1979 by Riitta Nelimarkka (born 1948) and Jaakko Seeck (born 1946). They also made *Sammon tarina* ('The tale of the Sampo'), a series based on the ▶*Kalevala*, between 1971 and 1973. Heikki Prepula (born 1939) has distinguished himself as a maker of chil-

Katariina Lillqvist's Kafkaesque prize-winning animated film *The Country Doctor*, 1996

dren's animations with his versions of folk tales and his *Kössi Kenguru* ('Kössi the kangaroo') character. Children's animations are also made by Antonia Ringbom (born 1946).

The number of animated films made for adults has constantly grown. Marjut Rimminen (born 1944), who lives in England, has made the satirical *I'm Not A Feminist, But...* (1985) and the moving The Stain (1991). Antti Kari (born 1949) is a pioneer of computer animation, and, among other things, won the main prize of the 1982 Zagreb Festival with *Mennyt manner* ('The lost continent') his film about the Finnish poet ▶Eino Leino. Katariina Lillqvist (born 1963) is a member of the new generation of animators. She works in a rare genre, puppet animations for adults; her trilogy based on texts by Franz Kafka, made between 1992 and 1994, is very successful in terms of both technology and narrative. Among the prizes it has won is one awarded by the Tampere Short Film Festival in 1996.

Animation has undergone an explosive growth during the 1990s and is being increasingly used in television, advertisements, multimedia and film.

The reason for this, in addition to the flexibility of animation, is the development of the computer animation technology.

Easier links with a top country for animation, Estonia, have also given rise to new collaborative projects: many Finnish animations are made in Tallinn, the Estonian capital. The Turku School of Art and Communication began teaching the subject in 1995, the first educational institute in Finland to do so. HJ

applied arts ▶design

Arabia ceramics factory, founded 1873. Finland's oldest surviving ceramics factory, Arabia, was founded in 1873 as a daughter company to the Swedish concern Rörstrand to cater for the Russian market. A year later, it became independent, and in 1916 wholly Finnish-owned. In 1948 Arabia was bought by the Wärtsilä conglomerate, and since 1991 it has been part of the Hackman Company.

At first, Arabia used primarily glazed earthenware, but production also included porcelain and stoneware objects. In the 1890s the first designers were employed to raise the standard of the range of products; they were the Swede Thure Öberg, whose task was essentially the design of new decorative designs, and the Finnish architect Jac. Ahrenberg (1847–1914). In 1932 Kurt Ekholm (1907–1975), who had been engaged as Arabia's artistic director, developed a range of household goods to respond to the demands of the time and created the factory's famous art division, whose work soon became an important 'shop window'

Museum of the Arabia ceramics factory

to the world. Development, which had been cut short by the war, was in full swing by 1946, when ▶Kaj Franck was engaged as the factory's new product designer, with the task of modernising its range of household goods. In 1946 he was joined by the designer Kaarina Aho (1925–1990), and in 1948 by Ulla Procopé (1921–1968). Famous designs resulted: Franck's *Kilta* (in production from 1953) and Procopé oven- and flameproof *Liekki* ('Flame') (in production from 1958).

Other designers in the Arabia art department included Friedl Holzer-Kjellberg whose period at Arabia spanned the years (1924–1970), Toini Muona (1931–1970), Aune Siimes (1932–1964), Michael Schilkin (1936–1962), Birger Kaipiainen (1937–1988), ▶Rut Bryk (from 1942), Kyllikki Salmenhaara (1947–1961), Heljä Liukko-Sundström (from 1962) and Kati Tuominen (from 1980). MaA

archipelago It has been calculated that there are 73,001 islands of more than one 1000 square metres in area off the coast of Finland. The Finnish archipelago, which comprises the most south-westerly part of the country, is the most extraordinary and valuable maritime landscape in Finland. It is characterised by complex labyrinths of

The Mikkeli Islands, Vaasa, showing the characteristic labyrinthine arrangement of islands and waterways

Söderskär Lighthouse in the Porvoo Archipelago, 1857–1862

sea and land, composed of skerries, islands, promontories, headlands and stretches of water.

The fragmentary nature of the archipelago landscape derives from the splitting and breaking of the bedrock. The fault lines affect the form and grouping of the bays and headlands. Ever since the Ice Age, the waves have washed the islands that rose from the sea. Thus the glaciated rock polished by the continental ice-sheet has been revealed. On sheltered shores and hollows, plant life has achieved a firm grip. In places such as these, particularly on chalky ground, a luxuriant deciduous flora, rich in species, has established itself.

The habitation of the Finnish archipelago is very old in origin. It is known that many groups of islands were inhabited as early as the medieval period. Important sea-routes brought the Vikings and, later, the Hansa merchants on trading voyages. Numerous ancient relics, foundations and chapel ruins testify to a diverse culture. A typical archipelago village includes, in addition to houses and barns, a harbour and pier and breakwater, and patches of land surrounded by stone walls. Before the advent of the motor-boat, the fishermen's shelters built at the edges of distant fishing grounds were of great importance as temporary dwellings.

Most of the fields, however, have reverted to meadow in recent decades as both individual dwellings and villages have emptied. During the summer months, however, the entire archipelago lives a busy life.

The Finnish Archipelago National Park, comprising some 2000 hectares of land and more than 16,000 hectares of water, was set up in 1983 in the municipalities of Dragsfjärd, Nauvo, Korppoo and Houtskär. KR

architecture Finland's northerly location, severe natural conditions and sparse habitation have regulated the development of its architecture. There has always been plenty of wood or granite; other materials have been taken into use slowly. International building types, technologies, styles and fashions have reached Finland from both West and East and been shaped, here, into highly individual variations. The tension between East and West is, in fact, one of the most interesting strands in the great story of Finnish architecture. The Russo-Byzantine horizontal blockwork technique, or corner-timbering became established in Finland in the 9th century and until the 1930s, it remained almost the only way of building in the Finnish countryside.

Nousiainen Church, near Turku, mid 13th-century

THE MIDDLE AGES – 16TH CENTURY Finland's medieval wooden architecture is lost. The most impressive legacy of building from this period comprises five ►castles and 73 churches. The building of Turku Castle began in the 1280s and ended as late as the 16th century when King John III completed the building to correspond with the requirements of Renaissance court culture and developments in warfare. The ornamental red-brick walls of Häme Castle tell of the arrival of central European technology in Finland. The massive Olavinlinna Fortress was founded in 1475 on a small, rocky island at Savonlinna in eastern Finland. It was the first fortification in Scandinavia to be built, from the beginning, to withstand firearms.

The sturdy stone churches of the medieval period in Finland can be seen as descendants of the European gothic style purely in the height of their roofs and their restrained brick ornamentation. Only the vaults of the Turku Cathedral rise to the heights of their more southerly and easterly neighbours. Hattula church is the only brick church. The age of Finland's medieval churches is currently the subject of debate. Previously, their dates had been set as early as possible. Now it seems that the most important building period took place during the 15th

century, ending when relations between the Swedish church and the Pope were broken off in 1524.

In the 17th century, when the kingdom of Sweden-Finland counted as a great power, the towns founded by the Crown and the first cruciform churches tell of the arrival of renaissance ideals in Finland. The idyllic grid-plan towns disappeared, with the exception of small remnants, consumed at the very latest by the greed of the period of expansion of the 1960s.

THE 17TH AND 18TH CENTURIES The buttressed churches of ►Ostrobothnia are an original example of the skill of Finnish carpenters. Their high gable towers were also an important navigating mark on the shores. The low interior of the sacrificial church of Luoto, Pyhämaa (1647–1652) is unique both as a spatial experience and because of its luxuriant painted decorations. Tornio City church (1686) is the most richly ornamented of the buttressed churches, while the rugged wilderness church of Sodankylä (1689) has been preserved largely untouched.

During the 18th century the Swedish Crown concentrated its forces on the fortification and development of its eastern province. ►Suomenlinna Fortress, built from 1748 on six islands near Helsinki, was the largest building project of the time in Nordic countries. The Great Courtyard on Susisaari Island became the most monumental square in Finland. Contempory architecture was dominated by the baroque style. The town of Hamina, with its circular street-plan, was begun in 1723. The construction of many towns, mansions and ironworks reflect the development of economic life. The professional skills of fortifications officers and stone-masons brought on the art of building in stone.

During the second half of the 18th century, about 120 wooden churches and 130 belfries were built by vernacular masters. Different forms of cruciform church were developed in different parts of the country. The central space was doubled by chamfering in the western part of the country, and by adding corners in the eastern part. At Kuortane, Ylihärmä and Ruovesi, for example, cruciform churches are chamfered at every corner to make 24-sided internal spaces. Lappee Church in Lappeenranta is a fine example of a double cruciform church. A single cruciform church was built by Jaakko Leppänen at ▶Petäjävesi between 1763 and 1765, with a belfry added in 1821.

After Finland had become part of the Russian Empire in 1809, Helsinki became capital of Finland in 1812, and the central Senaatintori Square became, through the architecture of ▶Carl Ludvig Engel, a bold representative model for the early period of autonomy. Engel designed buildings for church, government and the university in a style that made reference to the ancient Graeco-Roman tradition. The ascetic neo-classicism of the Intendant's Office, which Engel directed, became an important factor in Finnish architectural expression as a whole.

THE LATE 19TH CENTURY During the second half of the 19th century, functions, technology and styles diversified, and the number of designers and architects grew. The neo-gothic style gained its greatest popularity in ecclesiastical architecture. According to the plans of C.A. Setterberg, Vaasa became an entirely neo-gothic town. The red-brick architecture of the riverside buildings of Tampere, Finland's only industrial city, reflects the intensity of industrialisation. In the capital, the most visible work in public and private commissions was carried out by the architect Theodor Höijer (1843–1910). The northern facade of the buildings which line the central Esplanade Park show Helsinki being built as a metropolis in the manner of Berlin or Vienna. Höijer's ▶Ateneum (1887) is now the ▶Finnish National Gallery.

In Gustav Nyström's (1856–1917) National Archives of Finland (1890, see p. 24), solemn classicism is combined with modern iron building techniques, while in the House of Estates (1891) the charming spaces are accompanied by plentiful ornamental paintings. In the Helsinki Market Hall (1900), Nyström used rationalism as a solution for the iron structures.

THE TURN OF THE CENTURY At the turn of the century, the young generation of architects, inspired by the Arts and Crafts movement and the Finnish building tradition, rose in revolt against classicism and eclecticism. Lars Sonck (1870–1956), Bertel Jung (1872–1946) and the trio Herman Gesellius (1874–1916), Armas Lindgren (1874–1929) and ▶Eliel Saarinen (1873–1950) created a new, more domestic, freer and more 'authentic' world.

Lars Sonck, Telephone Company Building, Helsinki, 1905

Apartment blocks were built in a romantic style. Stained glass and murals, together with plant and animal motifs in stone, timber and bronze accentuated the atmosphere. The Katajanokka and Eira areas of Helsinki are among the best examples of the new style of living. Villas hidden on lake- or sea-shores or in the forest were the most desirable living places. The most famous example is ▶Hvitträsk, by the Gesellius-Lindgren-Saarinen office (1903). There were attempts to link this ideal with free urban planning in villa towns, for example Kulosaari in Helsinki. This suburb is now divided by a motorway, but here and there remnants of the island community founded in 1907 are still to be found.

St John's Church in Tampere (1907),

Selim A. Lindqvist, Helsinki, 1900

by Lars Sonck, is the most complete Art Nouveau work of art in Finland. The granite of the façades, the spacious vault of the interior, the skilful woodwork, the frescoes and the stained glass are all in mutual harmony.

THE 1920S AND 1930S Asymmetry and wild ornamentation soon ran their course. In the impoverished period that followed Finland's independence (1917), the ideals of architecture turned toward a new classicism, which became the dominant style of the 1920s. The housing shortage was relieved by municipal funding and, gradually, by state support. During the decade, coherent suburbs were built with disciplined harmony, among them the Helsinki areas of Töölö and Vallila. Many churches were built in the same spirit throughout the country. The pan-Nordic elements of the style were most evident in school buildings, which were designed in Helsinki pre-eminently by Gunnar Taucher (1886–1941). The House of Parliament (1931), designed by J.S. Sirén (1889–1961), provided a solemn conclusion to this classicism.

During the 1930s, unornamented functionalism gradually spread. The movement was headed by ▶Alvar Aalto, ▶Erik Bryggman, Hilding Ekelund (1893–1984), Erkki Huttunen (1901–1956) and P.E. Blomstedt (1900–1935). Hospitals and tuberculosis sanatoria

became natural projects for the new design, while the most heated debates took place concerning churches. ▶Olympic Stadium (1938) by Yrjö Lindegren (1900–1952) and Toivo Jäntti (1900–1975) won general approval for functionalism. In city building, open building types and unornamented lamellar blocks became established only towards the end of the decade (e.g. the Olympic Village and Taka-Töölö, both in Helsinki).

POST-WAR RECONSTRUCTION After the Second World War, the project of reconstruction brought international attention to Finnish building. The work of the younger generation of architects raised national morale. Shortages in raw materials and the difficulties of everyday life softened approaches, and colours and free forms came back into favour. Until the late 1950s, many carefully designed houses and suburbs were built. Tapiola became the most famous example of the ideal of a city fused with nature: architects including Aulis Blomstedt (1906–1979), Viljo Revell (1910–1964) and Kaija (born 1920) and Heikki Sirén (born 1918) designed many types of residential building for loose urban plan by Otto-Iivari Meurman (1890–1994); Aarne Ervi (1910–1977) was responsible for the centre.

The 1960s saw large-scale migrations from country to town in search of employment, and the regular grid plan became popular among architects. In houses and element-built

Aarne Ervi, Tapiola garden city centre, Espoo, 1961

Timo and Tuomo Suomalainen, Temppeliaukio Church, Helsinki, 1968–1969, the 'church in the rock'

apartment blocks constructed according to modules, the new aesthetic was linked to the industrialisation of building technique. The results were, at best, light and upright, at worst miserable and massive. Greed spoiled even good ideas, and in the 1980s the concrete suburb became a pejorative term. Unspoiled countryside has tempted people to live at the urban perimeters, and motor transport has choked centres that are becoming dominated by offices.

Fine churches are a strong feature of post-war Finnish architecture: most prominent among them are Kaija and Heikki Sirén's Otaniemi Chapel , near Helsinki; Raili and ►Reima Pietilä's Kaleva Church in Tampere; Simo (born 1944) and Käpy Paavilainen's (born 1947) churches in Olari and Mellunmäki; Kristian Gullichsen's (born 1932) designs in Malmi and Kauniainen; and ►Juha Leiviskä's in Oulu, Vantaa and Kuopio.

In developing new and old residential areas in the 1980s, much attention has been directed toward the quality of the environment. Courtyards, childcare centres, arts centres and care centres for old people have appeared on the pages of architectural magazines. Until the beginning of the economic recession of the 1990s, young architects were still able to gain large commissions through the competition system. Ideals became more colourful, the range of fashions unprecedentedly confused. The recession of the early 1990s, however, put half of Finland's architects out of work. RN

archives The beginning of the documentation activities in Finland was due to the arrival of the Catholic Church, whose administration reached Finland in the latter half of the 12th century. The bishopric, the Cathedral Chapter, the monasteries and the parish churches were the first to draw up and preserve documents. In the 14th century, they were joined by the castle-chiefs representing the Swedish Kingdom. Nevertheless, documents were few, the oldest surviving original document in Finland is a letter of protection given by Earl Birger to the women of Karelia in 1316. Almost all medieval documents concerning Finland have been published in Reinhold Hausen's works *Finlands medeltidsurkunder I–VIII* (1910–1935) and *Registrum Ecclesiae Aboensis*, or the 'black book' of the Turku Cathedral (1890).

During the centuries of Swedish rule, up to 1809, the highest official bodies in Finland were the court of appeal, the provincial administrations and the cathedral chapters. The most important documents, those of the archives of the Turku court of appeal, cathedral chapter and provincial administration, were, however, destroyed in a fire in 1827. The largest and, historically, most important collection of documents are the records of the lower courts of justice, which generally begin in the early 17th century. The tax authorities also kept important registers of population and habitation from the 1550s onwards, and the parishes from the end of the 17th century. Population statistics begin as early as 1749. The National Survey Board began to increase its collection of maps greatly after the introduction of common land enclosure in 1749, followed by land reform. The first estate archives also date from this period, due to the fact that in the previous century estate-owners still lived in Sweden.

During the period of Russian rule (1809–1917), Finland had its own central administration. Its highest body was the Imperial Senate, which was divided into a supreme court and a government, which in turn was divided into committees or ministries. The government was represented to the emperor in St Petersburg through a

Gustav Nyström, The National Archives of Finland, Helsinki, 1890

minister state secretary, and the representative of the emperor in Finland was the Governor-General. The Senate Archives were opened to scholars in 1859. In 1869 it was given the name State Archives of Finland, and from the 1880 it began to accept other official archives, and later also personal archives.

Today the National Archives of Finland form the centre of the public archives network. Their collections comprise 39,000 shelf metres: the archives of the Council of State and the ministries, the central administrative boards, the central organisations of civil societies and of important private individuals. In the peace treaties between Sweden and Russia (1809) and that between Finland and Russia in 1920, agreements were made for material relating to Finland to be transferred to Finland, and these archives are now in the National Archives of Finland. Plenty of material concerning Finland remained in the mother countries, but attempts have been made to obtain copies of them, primarily on microfilm.

There are seven provincial archives serving under the National Archives of Finland. The first was founded in Hämeenlinna in 1927, followed by Turku and Oulu in 1932, Viipuri in 1934 (it was moved after the Second World War to Mikkeli), Vaasa in 1936, Jyväskylä in 1967 and Joensuu in 1974. These archives comprise a total of 43,000 shelf metres material from courts of justice, parishes, district and local administrations and various institutions, most of them from the 19th and 20th centuries.

In addition to the National Land Survey of Finland, already mentioned, Parliament has its own archives, beginning in 1863. The armed forces established the Military Archives of Finland in 1918, which also contains earlier military archives from 1812; and the Foreign Ministry began its activities in 1918. The political parties have their own archives, which are open to scholars. The biggest commercial companies have central archives, and in addition there are, in Mikkeli, the central archives of economic life, which preserve the archives of, in particular, companies that no longer exist, as well as gathering information about economic archives in general.

There are a number of archives connected with culture in Finland. The Literature Archive of the ▶Finnish Literature Society preserves source material for literary scholarship, Helsinki University Library has scholarly archives, and the Sport Archives of Finland has archives concerned with sport. The Finnish Film Archives preserves films and related material.

Official documents are, in Finland, open to the public. Exceptions are documents concerned with national security, which remain secret for 30 to 40 years; those concerned with the economic interests of society, economic life or individuals, which are closed for 25 years, and documents that are kept secret to protect individuals, for which the period is generally 50 years. MF

art THE STONE AGE Early Finnish art is dominated by an aesthetic of austerity. There have been few finds, considering the size of the country, and the objects themselves, although ornamented, are not ostentatious. Functional beauty is best expressed in the design of stone chisels and axes, whether utility or status objects. Simplicity reflects the severe conditions of this northerly culture, and its remoteness from more prosperous centres. This remoteness is an important factor throughout the history of Finnish art: praise for Nordic nature, including winter, formed part of the artistic programme of the patriots of the 19th century, although the European canon demanded exclusive rights for more southerly landscapes.

THE BRONZE AND IRON AGES No art objects as such are known from the Finnish Bronze Age, and other finds, too, are few in number. The Iron Age (500 B.C.–A.D. 1100) is periodised according to imported objects. Animal ornamentation of Germanic origin reached its peak during the period of migration between A.D. 400 and A.D. 600, but the most valuable finds artistically are from the Merovingian period (A.D. 600–800). Ironwork of high quality is represented by swords and the partial decoration in precious metals of their hilts.

Objects from the Viking period (A.D. 800–1100), such as animal brooches, give a picture of a successful peasant culture. Money, crosses and pendants in the shapes of birds were brought from as far away as Byzantium via the Eastern trading routes.

MEDIEVAL AND RENAISSANCE PERIODS Traditionally, the limits of Finland's medieval period are regarded as the 1150s and the 1520s. The first romanesque-style wooden churches were built toward the end of the 12th century. It is believed that they were decorated with paintings.

Mural paintings have survived in around 40 stone churches. The style of the paintings is generally 'primitive', but the early gothic decoration of the ▶Åland churches of the turn of the 14th century represent developed skills.

The 15th-century muralist of Kalanti Church, Petrus Henriksson, is the first whose whole name and influence are known. Bishop Konrad Bitz invited him to Finland from Sweden 1470 to raise the standard of ecclesiastical art.

The decoration of the Church of the Holy Cross in Hattula (1510–1522) is well-preserved and rich in its pictorial programme. Among the achievements of the late gothic are the paintings of St Lauri's Church in Lohja

Virgin Mary, Kalvola Church, 15th-century; the sculpture was imported from Lübeck

(1515–1522) and St Jacob's Church in Rymättylä (1520s).

More than 800 medieval sculptures have survived – mostly figures of saints located in altar cupboards. The most important source of acquisitions and influences was at first Gotland, later northern Germany. The first known Finnish sculptor is the Master of Lieto, who was active around 1320 to 1350.

The flowering of the late medieval period ended with the death of the Catholic Bishop and art patron Arvid Kurki in 1522. The new King of Sweden-Finland, Gustavus I Vasa (reigned 1523–1560), a supporter of the Reformation, appropriated church property to the state. Until the 17th century, the impoverished church allowed many of the old cult images to remain in place, although in 1560 the crucifix and the altarpiece were laid down as the only cult objects.

The paintings of Isokyrö Church, dating to 1560, are among the most important examples of renaissance art in Finland. Renaissance influences are still to be seen in the work of Christian Willebrand (1637–1677), who decorated the churches of Ostrobothnia.

THE BAROQUE AND THE 18TH CENTURY During the 17th century the interior spaces of churches were increasingly filled with memorial plaques, sculptures and coats of arms donated by the aristocracy and the bourgeoisie. The baroque style was best realised in the funeral chapels commissioned by the aristocracy, which manifested the self-assured spirit of the period of Sweden-Finland as a greatpower.

Memorial plaques were often painted in the form of individual portraits, as in the work of Finland's first peripatetic painter, the German-born Jochim Neiman (c. 1600–1673). Among the novelties of the period was landscape as a part of interior decoration. Elias Brenner (1647–1717) developed into the best-known Finnish court miniaturist.

The late baroque continued in, among other things,

the Dutch-influenced work of Finland's first woman painter, Margareta Capsia (1682–1759).

The founding of the Academy of Sweden in Stockholm in 1753 meant great progress, and some of the most gifted Finns, such as the rococo painter Isak Wacklin (1720–1758) settled in the kingdom's capital. The same was true, later, of Gustaf Wilhelm Finnberg (1784–1833) and Alexander Lauréus (1783–1823).

In Finland, artistic capacity was evident in the building and decoration of the churches of Ostrobothnia. The most notable achievements were church paintings by Johan Backman (1706–1768), Mikael Toppelius (1734–1821) and Emanuel Granberg (1754–1787).

The biggest building site of the Sweden-Finland period, the maritime fortifications at ▶Suomenlinna (Sveaborg), radiated Gustavianism, the neoclassicism demanded by King Gustavus III to its surroundings. The best painters of fortification were Elias Martin (1738–1818) and Nils Schillmark (1745–1804).

THE PERIOD OF AUTONOMY 1809–1917 Russia conquered Finland in 1808–1809, and the country became an autonomous Grand Duchy. The change did not at first have any effect on art. Neo-classicism continued, and Finns continued to study primarily in Stockholm.

A favourite project of the new ruler, Alexander I, was, understandably, the monumental centre of the new capital, Helsinki, which created work opportunities for sculptors, but the most important steps forward were taken in Turku. Erik Cainberg (1771–1816) was invited to decorate the auditorium of the new academy building. Between 1813 and 1816 he created six reliefs, which, for the first time, depicted the country's history, and the 'Finnish Orpheus', Väinämöinen.

From the 1830s onwards, nationalists demanded the raising of artistic standards in Finland. The historical and court painter Robert William Ekman (1808–1873) reformed teaching at the drawing school of the Turku Art Society (founded 1846), and, in the 1850s, concentrated on subjects from the ▶Kalevala and on depictions of

Fanny Churberg, *Talvimaisema, iltarusko* ('Winter landscape, sunset'), 1878

folk life. The sculptor Carl Eneas Sjöstrand (1828–1905) also seized on *Kalevala* themes. The painter brothers Magnus (1805–1868), Wilhelm (1810–1887) and Ferdinand (1822–1906) von Wright depicted landscapes and birds in crowd-pleasing, Biedermeier-tinged style, often with elements of German romanticism. Ferdinand was the originator of the idealised image of the Finnish landscape, a lake landscape seen obliquely from above.

The activities of the Artists' Association of Finland bore fruit when Werner Holmberg (1830–1860), sent to Düsseldorf on a scholarship, developed into a competent realist landscape painter. Among other artists to receive the same training was the late-romantic landscape painter Fanny Churberg (1845–1892), the most daring colourist of the day and a pioneer of expressive form.

▶Sculpture was dominated by neoclassicism, under the leadership of Walter Runeberg (1838–1920), until the more realistic approach of Johannes Takanen (1849–1885) broke with the predominant style.

Parisian ideals began to flourish in the work of Albert Edelfelt (1854–1905), who became a pioneer of outdoor painting and an internationally known Finnish artist. Another artist to gain success in Paris was the sculptor Ville Vallgren (1855–1940), who worked in the Art Nouveau style. The growing contribution of women was represented particularly by ▶Helene Schjerfbeck (1862–1945), whose simplified canvases of the 1880s presage modernism.

▶Akseli Gallen-Kallela (1865–1931)

began as a naturalist, but in the 1890s developed a decorative *Kalevala* romanticism from the motifs of folk poetry. Young symbolists such as Magnus Enckell (1870–1925) and Ellen Thesleff (1869–1954) challenged the nationalist style from the mid 1890s. The most individual symbolist painter was ▶Hugo Simberg (1870–1917), who cultivated a naïvist style and themes from folk-tales.

The predominant figure of realist depiction of ordinary people was Juho Rissanen (1873–1950), who combined influences from the early Italian Renaissance and Russia into a rugged style. Pekka Halonen (1865–1933), a more fluid painter, matured, on the other hand, into a master of winter landscapes.

Magnus Enckell, *Lepäävä poika* ('Reclining boy'), 1892

The dynamism of the turn of the century (1896–1906) was a result partly of resistance to Russification, partly of Finland's increased prosperity. A number of landscape painters such as Victor Westerholm (1860–1919) had practised impressionism for a short period in the 1880s, but post-impression was widely influential on the artists of the Septem Group (founded 1910), such as Yrjö Ollila (1887–1932), Magnus Enckell (1870–1925) and Verner Thomé (1878–1953). The Belgian-born Alfred William Finch (1854–1930) had already introduced pointillism to Finland at the turn of the century. The first cubist, Uuno Alanko (1878–1964), made his appearance in 1913.

Early in the 1910s, expressionism began to differentiate itself from 'light-painting' in the work, among others, of Juho Mäkelä (1885–1943), Marcus Collin (1882–1966), ▶Tyko Sallinen (1879–1955) and Jalmari Ruokokoski (1886–1936). Later, the expressionists absorbed the colouristic asceticism of cubism. The November Group, which cultivated this new 'honesty', was established, under the leadership of Sallinen, by, among others, Ilmari Aalto (1891–1934), Wäinö Aaltonen (1894–1966), Alvar Cawén (1886–1935) and Ragnar Ekelund (1892–1960).

AFTER 1917 Alongside the November Group, the avantgarde made its appearance in the work of some artists. As early as 1917, Sulho Sipilä (1895–1949) absorbed influences from, among others, Chagall and cubo-futurism, until he began to paint in a naïvist style. Edwin Lydén (1879–1956) developed his own dynamic, spiritual style from the art of Klee and Schwitters around 1920.

Independent Finland needed elevating monumental works to symbolise the power of the nation. This demand was best responded to by the sculptor Wäinö Aaltonen (1894–1966). At the end of the 1910s Aaltonen created a powerful 'Egyptian' style and later even plumbed the possibilities of art deco and cubism. He, nevertheless, became the most important re-

Väinö Kunnas, *Olavi Paavolainen* (1928)

aliser of the classicising heroic plasticity of the 1920s and 1930s.

A style advocating an international, urban vision became visible in the *Neue Sachlichkeit* painters Väinö Kunnas (1896–1929) and Einari Wehmas (1898–1955), members of the Tulenkantajat ('Torchbearers') group of artists (1924–1930).

The Lhote School influence received support in the 1930s as the number of mural commissions increased. The most daring experiments in painting were represented by the Surrealist Otto Mäkilä (1904–1955) and Birger Carlstedt (1907–1975), who experimented in constructivism and surrealism.

The Second World War was followed by a new, 'angry' wave of expressionism led by Aimo Kanerva (1909–1991), Yrjö Saarinen (1899–1958) and Åke Mattas (1920–1962). The strengthening vanguard of constructivism was made up of Lars-Gunnar Nordström (born 1924), Birger Carlstedt (1907–1975), Unto Pusa (1913–1973), and ▶Sam Vanni (1908–1994). The expressionists' October Group was, indeed, followed by the Prisma Group, which advocated lighter colours and the use of pure geometric form.

Sculptural modernism made its breakthrough at the end of the 1950s in the work of, among others, Kain Tapper (born 1930) and Kauko Räsänen (born 1926). The most violent transition, however, took place with the spread of informalism (beginning in 1960), into a kind of general style. Informalist painters such as Jaakko Sievänen (born 1932) and Esko Tirronen (born 1934) founded the March Group, but soon changed their style in accordance with neo-realism.

The material paintings of Kauko Lehtinen (born 1925) and the object-works of Juhani Harri (born 1939) and Harro Koskinen (born 1945) changed the conceptual horizon of Finnish art. Pop, too, had its supporters, such as Paul Osipow (born 1939), who subsequently became a pioneer of colour-field painting.

Young constructivists sought an ecological and technical ideology, and, in the form of the Dimension Group, fought against the politicised 1970s' demands for realist propaganda art.

Birger Carlstedt, *Mietiskely* ('Meditation'), 1945

Among the most important constructivists were Juhana Blomstedt (born 1937), Matti Kujasalo (born 1945) and the sculptor Raimo Utriainen (1927–1993). The Harvesters Group, for their part, concentrated on conceptualism, performance and the spirituality of the East. The best of the group's painters was Olli Lyytikäinen (1949–1987).

Neo-expressionism became a movement in the early 1980s. The way was shown by Marjatta Tapiola (born 1951), Leena Luostarinen (born 1949) and Marika Mäkelä (born 1947). Intelligent post-modern painting has been represented by Silja Rantanen (born

Henrietta Lehtonen, *Bambino*, 1995

1955), while the sculptor Kari Cavén (born 1954) has examined the verbal meanings of objects.

Among the most important phenomena of the 1990s have been the disappearing projects of Maaria Wirkkala (born 1954), the feminist emphases of the CD-ROMs of Marita Liulia (born 1957) and the video installations of Henrietta Lehtonen (born 1965). The most prominent photographer is Esko Männikkö (born 1959), a Vermeer-like interpreter of the people of the North. MVn

Artek's main showroom in central Helsinki

Artek design and furniture company founded by the art critic Nils-Gustav Hahl (1904–1941), the influential patron of the arts Maire Gullichsen (1907–1990) and the architects ▶Alvar and ▶Aino Aalto in Helsinki in 1935. The fundamental idea behind Artek was to act as a centre for displaying and marketing Alvar and Aino Aalto's furniture and Finnish and foreign objects suitable to their ideas of interior design, and to arrange exhibitions of art and design.

Artek's most important sales items were, from the beginning, Alvar Aalto's laminated-wood furnitures. They were particularly in demand as a result of the Milan Triennale of 1933 and an exhibition held in London the same year, and their triumphal march continued in the Finnish pavilions of the World Exhibition in Paris in 1937 and New York in 1939. As early as the 1930s, Aalto's furniture was much used in the decor of public reception rooms and hotels. Ben af Schultén (born 1939), who was appointed artistic director of Artek in 1976, has added to Aalto's range of furniture with wooden furniture of his own designed in the spirit of Aalto.

In addition to Finnish art, the exhibitions arranged by Artek showed, as early as the 1930s, some of the most famous names of international modernism, including Fernand Léger, Alexander Calder, Henri Matisse and Pablo Picasso. With the diversification of the company, the Artek Art Gallery was founded in 1950, under the directorship of Maire Gullichsen, to organise art exhibitions. MaA

arts and academic administration
Finland's public arts administration is led by the Ministry of Education. The role of the Ministry of Education, and in particular the ministries of Social Affairs and Health, grew significantly with the social reforms of the 1960s. The system of two ministers of education established itself as part of this extension. However, the plan to divide the Ministry and establish a separate Ministry of Culture or Learning, which has been under discussion since the 1970s, has not so far been realised, arts and learning have not proved weighty enough areas in themselves. The most important matters in the Ministry of Education's administrative area have been divided into two spheres: education and learning policies, and, cultural policies. Education, which belongs in the former camp, has long been the biggest area under the ministry's care. Administration of international affairs, which have shown continual strong growth, was centred on its own department as early as 1966.

Higher education developed strongly in the 1960s. A law for the development of ▶higher education passed in 1966 led, in the period from 1967 to 1981, to a more detailed expansion of student numbers, facilities and other resources. The focus was on the development of the natural sciences and technology, but the humanities and the social sciences, too, received their share. The span of the law was subsequently extended to 1986.

At the same time a number of new institutions of higher education were founded. In 1966 a regionally active government established five new units of higher education (Kuopio, Joensuu, Lappeenranta, Tampere and Vaasa). In addition, it upgraded two specialised colleges in Tampere and Jyväskylä to universities. The organisation and funding of the Sibelius Academy in Helsinki were defined in 1965.

At the beginning of the 1970s Finland had 17 academic and art institutions of higher education, which is, by international standards, a large number in proportion to the country's population. Among the reforms of the 1970s were the establishment of a college of applied arts (1972) and the upgrading of the Theatre School to the Theatre Academy (1979). In the 1990s, Finland had a total of 20 academic and art institutions of higher education. In addition, an experiment with vocational colleges was begun in the 1980s; this led to the foundation of the first permanent vocational colleges in the 1990s. The nationalisation of private universities (including the Åbo Akademi University) was also part of the higher education policies of the 1960s and 1970s.

The expansion of higher education, led to the establishment, in 1965, of the Department for Higher Education and Research within the Ministry of Education. The Science Evaluation Group was set up to assist in allocating resources and planning higher education policies; its activities and composition provoked enduring and ideologically coloured criticism in this rapidly developing area. Among the extensive reforms planned by the Department was the democratisation of higher education administration in the late 1960s, an extensive revision of examinations in the 1970s, the allocation of investment to new equipment, extensive educational and social innovations and, in the most recent phase, the implementation of profit-centre accounting in institutions of higher education.

Elsewhere in the academic administration in the 1960s, a mode of thought characteristic of the Organisation for Economic Co-operation and Development (OECD), in which teaching and research were separated, became widespread. In scientific committees it was feared that the development of institutions of higher education would prove detrimental to research. New legisla-

tion was clearly needed. A law passed in 1969 abolished the old Academy of Finland and established a new one, primarily an office of learning with responsibility for administrational matters. Posts as members of the Academy were withdrawn as their holders reached retirement age, and were replaced by research professorships, later academic professorships of limited duration. Research posts and funding increased strongly, at first in the early 1970s, later in accordance with economic trends.

The most recent organisational reform in the field took place from the beginning of 1995, when the Central Board of Research Council was replaced by the board of the Academy of Finland, and the former committees were united into four councils: The Research Council for the Humanities, The Research Council for Social Sciences, The Research Council for Natural Sciences and The Medical Research Council. For the Research Council for the Humanities, this means that projects and posts relating to a total of six faculties (theology, law, the humanities, education, social sciences and economics) are dealt with by one research council. The beginning of 1995 also saw the institution of a graduate school system intended to increase the number and quality of doctorates.

The Academy of Finland, with its research councils, is the most important distributor of public research funding. A significant proportion of public research funding is, however, channelled for the use of research institutions directed by various ministries. The largest of these are the Technical Research Centre of Finland and the Geological Survey of Finland, working with the Ministry of Trade and Industry, the Research Institute of Legal Policy, working with the Ministry of Justice, the Finnish Research Centre for Domestic Languages, working with the Ministry of Education, numerous institutions working with the Ministry for Agriculture and Forestry (including the Agricultural Research Centre of Finland, the Finnish Forest Research Institute and the Finnish Game and Fisheries Research Institute), and the National Research and Development Centre for Welfare and Health, working with the Ministry of Social Affairs and Health.

The information service of the disciplines of technology and the natural sciences and the humanist tradition of the university libraries competed from the 1960s in the development of research libraries. In 1972 the Ministry of Education united the consultative organs of these bodies to form the Finnish Council for Scientific Information and Research Libraries. At the same time the development of a system of central libraries was begun, founded largely on libraries already active in various fields.

The arts received their own office at the Ministry of Education in 1966. This became a department in 1974 and now functions under the name of Department of Culture. Among the innovations of the 1960s was the replacement of the government arts committees, which had functioned rather sluggishly, with arts councils, together with the abolishment of the traditional system of mandates, for greater flexibility. The Arts Council of Finland is responsible for dealing with matters common to nine individual councils: for literature, art, music, drama, architecture, the applied arts, film, photography and dance.

The current system of funding for artists has a long tradition. A regular system of grants to writers was instituted at the beginning of the 20th century. The professional and social position of artists has been much discussed since the 1960s. A committee that sat in that decade drew up a proposal for the development of a support system in this field. In 1969 a law concerning artist professorships and government arts funding was passed, corresponding to the reforms in the area of scholarship and research. At first this reform brought additional funds to the support of the arts, but the national economic recession weakened its subsequent development. The Ministry of Education, indeed, considered full-time artists' posts, in changing conditions dubious in terms of both expense and principle, and instead turned to increasing long-term grants. Artists' retirement pensions were revived in a law passed in 1974.

Attempts were made to renew the main outlines of public arts policy, particularly with the help of a paper drawn up by the Arts Committee that sat from 1971 to 1974 and an administrative body set up by the Ministry of Education. The aim of the political left was the 'democratisation' of the arts, making them available to all levels of society. Because of economic recession and ideological opposition, however, no full-scale programme of cultural policy was ever born, though some progresses had been made. Provincial arts committees had been established in the 1960s and the aims of the reforms of the 1970s were realised: a law concerning municipal arts activities was passed in 1980, which meant an increase in funding and the subordination of municipal cultural administration to the law. The number of lower music colleges grew from the 1950s onward. A law concerning central government aid for them was passed in 1968, and significantly strengthened the teaching of music in the 1970s. The theatre, too, pondered the idea of 'socialisation' in the 1970s. The relevant committee succeeded in supporting the development of regional theatres. On the other hand, attempts to nationalise the main stages and plans to make all theatrical work conform to a comprehensive law were thwarted for ideological reasons. After this, the Ministry of Education favoured supporting more flexible solutions and building projects. The building of a new opera house in Helsinki and the reorganisation of the resources of the Finnish Opera has been the biggest individual project in this area in recent years.

The administration of ►film has constantly been beset by changes of policy. A Government Prize for Film was instituted in 1962 to support Finnish cinema, which fared badly in competition. It proved ineffective, so the Finnish Film Foundation was founded in 1969 on the model of similar institutions in the other Nordic countries. It was funded from cinema taxes. Plans by the Film Board to promote cinema constantly met with difficulties. Public recognition of the field is demonstrated by the fact that the Finnish Film Archive was nationalised in 1979. In addition, the government film inspectors and the film committee function as administrative bodies under the Ministry of Education.

In 1961 Finland received a relatively modern copyright law whose details were subsquently developed in accordance with international changes. The growth of the various forms of electronic media is the great challenge in questions of copyright in the 1990s.

Following international developments has become increasingly important for the arts and education administration. Immediately after the Second World War, the Ministry of Education aimed deliberately, in accordance with new goverment policies, to activate cultural relations with the Soviet Union. Nordic collaboration, too, was gradually activated. On the other hand, in the sphere of education, universities and ►learned societies looked after their own international contacts.

A special department within the Ministry of Education was set up in 1966 to deal with the constantly expanding area of international affairs. In the current organisation of the Ministry, the department comes under the jurisdiction of administrative and headquarters activities. The Ministry itself still deals centrally with organisations, but units of education and arts administration deal with most of their international contacts independently.

In terms of centralised organisations, important matters have included the maintenance of active links with Unesco, collaboration with the OECD, the thoroughgoing revision of Nordic collaboration through a cultural agreement in 1971, and, in the most recent stages, dealing with contacts with the European Union.

Cultural relations between Finland and Soviet Union were defined in the Treaty of Friendship, Co-operation and Mutual Assistance of 1948, in a scientific and technological agreement in 1955 and in an agreement concerning educational collaboration 1960. Finland's growing collaboration with the socialist countries was generally governed by bilateral agreements. Cultural exchange with the Western countries, on the other hand, was realised through multilateral organisations and on a project basis. Bilateral cultural exchange gradually became more commonplace in contacts with western countries during the 1970s. MHlä

Ateneum The Ateneum, named after Pallas Athene, the ancient Greek goddess of culture, is Finland's oldest museum building, and dates from 1887. It was designed, on European models, by the Helsinki architect Theodor Höijer (1843–1910). Originally, this 'house of the arts' housed, in addition to the museum collections, the drawing school of the Finnish Art Society and the school of the Finnish Society for Crafts and Design. Since 1991 it has been the main building of the Finnish National Gallery. On show at the Ateneum are key works of Finnish art from the mid 18th century to the 1950s (including works by ►Akseli Gallen-Kallela, ►Helene Schjerfbeck), and international art (van Gogh, Gauguin, Cezanne). MLR

The Ateneum, which houses the Finnish National Gallery, 1887

B

Paavo Berglund

Berglund, Paavo (born 1929), conductor. Paavo Berglund is the grand old man of Finnish conductors. He began playing the violin at the age of 11 and became a violinist with the Finnish Radio Symphony Orchestra when he was 20. At the age of 33, he was appointed chief conductor of the Radio Symphony Orchestra, following Nils-Erik Fougstedt (1910–1961). In 1972 he became director of the Bournemouth Symphony Orchestra, returning in 1975 to his native country as chief conductor of Helsinki Philharmonic Orchestra.

Among the orchestras Berglund has conducted are the Stockholm Philharmonic and the Danish Royal Philharmonic orchestras; he has also been visiting conductor with, among others, the Dresden Staatskapelle, the New

York Philharmonic Orchestra, the Berlin Philharmonic Orchestra, Leipzig Gewandhaus Orchestra and the European Chamber Orchestra. A central part of Berglund's life's work are his three recordings of all ►Sibelius's symphonies, of which one was made with the Bournemouth Symphony Orchestra in the 1970s and the other with the Helsinki Philharmonic Orchestra a decade later. A third complete recording of Sibelius's symphonies is under way with the European Chamber Orchestra. In recent times Berglund has also worked as director of the Finnish Chamber Orchestra. RL

Bergman, Erik (born 1911), composer, academician. Erik Bergman is one of the central modernists of musical composition of recent decades: in the 1950s he introduced the 12-tone technique to Finland, and in the 1970s he developed his own aleatoric and colouristic style, which is characterised by primitiveness and – partly derived from cultures outside Europe – ritual. Bergman is, in particular, a renovator of choral music, which is apparent in the great synthesis of his work, the opera *Det sjungande trädet* ('The singing tree', 1986–1988). MH

Anna-Lisa Jakobsson, Peter Lindroos and Marianne Harju in Erik Bergman's opera *Det sjungande trädet* ('The singing tree', 1995)

Bible The work of translating the Bible into Finnish originated with the Reformation principle, according to which every individual should be able to read the Bible in his own language. The translation was begun by ►Michael Agricola when he was studying at the University of Wittenberg in the 1530s. The New Testament, in Michael Agricola's translation, was printed in Sweden in 1548. Agricola also translated a

Title-page of the Finnish Bible published in 1685

number of books of the Old Testament, but financial difficulties and other work prevented him from completing the work. Even in its unfinished form, however, Agricola's achievement was considerable, for before him Finnish had not been used as a literary language.

The first complete Finnish Bible appeared only in 1642, or almost 100 years after Agricola's New Testament. This handsome, illustrated, folio-sized Bible was printed in an edition of 1200 copies. Because of the small number of learned Finns and the high price of the work, a number of copies were still unsold at the beginning of the following century.

Erik Bergman

In the early 19th century the Bible was still a rarity in ordinary Finnish homes. Before 1817, only five editions had been printed, and the total number of copies was less than 20,000. A change in the distribution of the Bible came about in 1812 when the Finnish Bible Society was founded on the model of its English counterpart. This, together with the British and Foreign Bible Society, printed hundreds of thousands of Finnish-language Bibles. Thus, the Reformation principle was finally realised in the 19th century, when vernacular Bibles were distributed, practically speaking, into every home.

The Bible's influence on the ►Finnish language has been unusually great, for before the mid 19th century, with the exception of official publications, practically nothing but ecclesiastical and religious books were published, and the language of the Bible strongly marked their linguistic usage. The fourth edition of the Bible, published in 1776, was the official Bible translation of the Finnish ►church up to 1938, and afterwards, until 1992, it remained an alternative version alongside the new translation. The Lestadian ►revivalist movement, however, is still faithful to the 1776 translation.

The current Bible translation was approved for use in 1992. This or earlier approved versions, are used, in addition to the Evangelical Lutheran Church of Finland, by the ►Orthodox Church and the Catholic Church in Finland, and most other Christian denominations. In addition, there is the so-called Bible of the People of God, a linguistically updated edition based on the 1938 translation that is used in small, primarily free-church circles. JN

bibliophilism Until the 17th century, collections of books owned by Finns were still very small. For example, the collection of the rector Henrik Florinus (c. 1633–1705), a known booklover, numbered only 113 volumes at his death in 1705. The Finnish-born Elias Brenner (1647–1717) gathered a collection of 772 books, including skilful bindings and rare illustrated works.

Bibliophilism increased considerably during the 18th century, as did book collections. The most important bibliophile of the century was Carl Fredrik Mennander (1712–1786), Bishop of Turku, subsequently Archbishop of Upsala. His library contained more than 7000 books, among them some real rarities. The increase in bibliophilism is evidenced by a two-part master's thesis written by Pehr Johan Alopaeus in 1791–1792 and entitled *Animadversiones de libris raris* ('Comments on rare books'). It described, among other things, one of the greatest rarities of Finnish literature, the so-called Pälkäne ►Primer, carved on wooden boards in 1719.

During the period of autonomy as a Grand Duchy of Russia (1809–1917), many collections exceeded 5000 volumes. One of the most interesting col-

Book-lovers at the Old Book Days at Vammala, south-west Finland, founded in 1985

lectors was the peddler ►Matti Pohto (1815–1857), whose collection of Finnish books, at more than 3000 volumes, was clearly the largest of his time. The most important collection in international terms was that of ►Adolf Erik Nordenskiöld (1832–1901), the discoverer of the North-East Passage. This collection, which now belongs to Helsinki University Library, contained more than 5000 atlases and books belonging to the history of cartography, among them 14 editions of Ptolemy and 129 incunabula. The collection of Baron Paul von Nicolay (1860–1919) from the manor of Monrepos near Viipuri, containing principally literature of the Enlightenment, is also now part of the collection of Helsinki University Library.

The first organised bibliophilic society was the short-lived Societas Bibliophilorum Fenniae, founded in 1924. The Swedish-language bibliophiles' society was established in 1948, followed in 1951 by the Finnish-language Bibliofiilien Seura. *Bibliophilos*, a periodical for book-lovers, was established in 1942. In addition to these generalist societies, a number of specialist societies are active in Finland, among them societies devoted to crime novels and comics. The most important events for bibliophiles, since 1985, has been the Old Book Days, held annually in Vammala, which attract audiences of around 10,000 people. JN

Björling, Gunnar (1887–1960), writer. The Finland-Swedish Björling was born in Helsinki. His first collection of poetry, *Vilande dag* ('Resting day', 1922) began *an oeuvre* that was eventually to comprise 20 original collections, culminating in *Du går de ord* ('You go the Words', 1955). Björling is the most original, and the most difficult, of the Finland-Swedish modernists. The language of his poems diverges significantly from ordinary language. They are often fragmentary, lacking conjunctions, and they do not follow the rules of grammar.

During the 1920s, Björling was the only notable representative of Dadaism in Finland. For a long time his poetry was read only by a small band of experts; since the 1940s, however, they have achieved lasting recognition in Finland and the Scandinavian countries.

Today Björling is seen as a central modernist in the literature of Finland. A keen explorer of moral and ethical questions in his poems, he was attracted by the ethical relativisim of the pioneering Finnish sociologist ►Edvard Westermarck (1862–1939): moral judgements depend on the judge, not on what is being judged. In the Finland of the 1920s and 1930s, with its tendencies to normativism, Björling's poetry was thus also intellectually alien. With the years, minimalist nature poetry assumed an increasingly important role in his work. PL

book design The most important feature of a book is its content, the message transmitted by the text. Yet a book is also an object, whose external appearance gives rise to images and announces the work's objectives. A book's character is created by its illustration, binding and cover, as well as by its typography and graphic design. The science of book design studies the book as a totality of the above-mentioned elements.

As an object, the book is an item of utility art which narrates the ideals and stylistic orientation of its time. The sole incunabulum of Finnish book history, ►*Missale Aboense* (1488),

is still considered one of its most beautiful printed artefacts. The textural design of its gothic font, which imitates handwriting, is arranged in two columns, and red ink is used in addition to ordinary printer's ink, in order to distinguish large documents, headings and explanations. The woodcut illustrations and initials are inked by hand. The printing is done on sheets of best-quality parchment, and also on ordinary rag paper, which has preserved the book's dignified appearance for more than five centuries.

Before the establishment of Finland's first printing press in 1642, all Finnish-language books and books intended for Finland were printed in Germany and Sweden, and they followed German typographical models. In the Finnish printing presses of the 17th century the choice of typefaces, was by European standards, a limited one. Yet the external appearance of the printed items was not monotonous. By the use of typesetting, red-ink printing, initials, vignettes, ornamental scrolls and picture motifs, the Finnish printing presses of the baroque era sometimes achieved very impressive results. The most impressive printed items are often folio-sized commemorative poems and funeral sermons, in which the decorative elements are hour-glasses, coffins and death's heads.

Gunnar Björling

Animal figures from *De pausepermia rerum* by Petrus Hahn, 1689

In the first half of the 18th century the use of the baroque era's complex ornaments and vignettes diminished, and the appearance of books became more simplified. Illustrations were few until halfway through the century. They became more common, especially in doctoral dissertations after 1750, when the Tallinn goldsmith J.H. Seeliger was employed as the first permanent copper engraver of the Academy of Turku. In the last decades of the century the printing presses acquired new typefaces and a neo-classical style became established in typography. In printed items designed for the ordinary people, Roman type did not replace gothic even in the following century. Literary and scholarly writing were now, however, mostly printed in Roman type.

The typography of Finnish books preserved its neo-classical look until the second half of the 19th century. Illustrations also remained few. A marked change began during the century's last two decades. The neo-renaissance dominated the 1880s, and the 1890s saw the spread to Finland of Jugendstil or *Art Nouveau*, the influence of which continued to be felt during the early decades of the 20th century.

Ateneum, the journal published in 1898–1903, and *Kirjapaino-lehti* ('The typographical journal'), founded in 1907, began a discussion of the aims and expressive methods of book design and typography. Typographical design and the making of book covers and illustrations had interested the leading artists of the age, such as ▶Akseli Gallen-Kallela, Albert Edelfelt (1854–1905), ▶Hugo Simberg, and ▶Helene Schjerfbeck. Because of this, the new European art styles were soon also reflected in book design. Functionalism, which spread during the 1920s, simplifying typefaces and the use of colours, was of special significance for Finnish book designers.

An important step forward in book design was taken in 1946, with the founding in Oslo of the Committee of Nordic Book Design. Its aim was, on the one hand, to improve and develop the technical and artistic standards of book production, and on the other to draw the attention of the public at

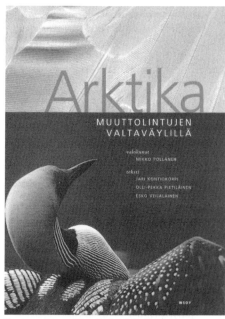

The Committee of Finnish Book Design selected this cover, designed by Martti Ruokonen, as one of the most successful of 1996

large to books also as works of art.

In 1947, with the aim of promoting book aesthetics, the Employers' Federation of the Graphic Arts Industries established the Committee of Finnish Book Design, which included representatives from the University of Art and Design, Helsinki University Library and the largest printing presses, publishing houses and book-shops.

Each year as part of its task the Committee selects what it considers the best and most attractively designed books, which are awarded the Best Book diploma. Since 1988 one of the book choices has been awarded the title of 'Best-Designed Book of the Year'. In 1995, 151 of the books published were sent to the committee for assessment and of these 17 were awarded the title of Best Book. There were 50 entries for the special bookjacket competition, of which five received the diploma. After the Second World War book production was affected by material shortages and the difficult economic situation, which reduced the possibility of economic investment in the artistic appearance of books and the development of printing materials. Since the 1970s a rapid process of innovation in typographical and binding technology has fundamentally altered the basic principles of book printing. In particular, photo-setting and computer-based systems have set new demands in the field. In spite of these factors, Finland has since the end of the 1940s placed much emphasis on the graphical design of books.

The most important book typographers of the post-war era were the printing works directors J.K.V. Paasio and V.A. Vuorio, the latter of whom also wrote a book on the history of style. Later graphic designers who have received numerous awards include Markku Reunanen (born 1933), Reijo Salkola (born 1931) and Urpo Huhtanen (born 1935). Erkki Tanttu (1907–1985), important as a typographer, has become renowned principally for his book illustrations. Other eminent illustrators include Maija Karma (born 1914), Björn Landström (born 1917), Henrik Tikkanen (1924–1984), Ulla Vaajakallio (born 1941) and Seppo Polameri (born 1936). A study of Finnish architecture by Ilpo Okkonen (born 1954) and Asko Salokorpi (born 1935) won the 1986 Leipzig Book Fair's Schönste Bücher aus aller Welt contest, receiving the Golden Letter Award. JN

books Only two books were printed for Finland in the medieval period: the ▶*Missale Aboense* which was the first Finnish book (1488) and the Turku diocesan manual *Manuale Aboense* (1522). The other books in use in Finland at this time had already been published in Germany or France. Book culture was still very limited and was confined almost exclusively to the Church. This situation did not essentially change after the Reformation. The demand for books in Finland was so limited that the Swedish printing presses were well able to meet all the needs of the state. Even rare books in the Finnish language, such as the works of ▶Michael Agricola, were printed in Sweden.

Finland's first printing press was not established until 1642. Its task was to print books mainly for the needs of the Academy of Turku, which was founded in 1640. The Academy owned the printing press and was responsible for supplying its materials and equip-

Title page from the *Piae Cantiones,* a Finnish collection of songs, printed in Greifswald in 1582

ment. The printer was payed a yearly salary that amounted to one quarter of a professor's salary. The academy's printing press was very modest in capacity, and so it was unable to meet demand from outside.

A noticeable improvement in book printing occurred when the Bishop of Turku, Johannes Gezelius the Elder (bishopric 1664–1690) founded his own printing press. Gezelius had the ambitious goal of developing the literacy both of the clergy and of the people as a whole. He even planned the export of books to Sweden, the Baltic countries and Germany, building an entire operational organisation around his press. The clergy and parish clerks had the task of arranging the collection of rags in their parishes for the paper which was made in a paper mill established by the bishop himself. Gezelius produced printed lists of his publications and tried to make the sale of books more effective by marketing them on his ecclesiastical tours of inspection. A peripatetic book agent paid by the bishop also undertook the promotion of the publications of the episcopal press.

The most important productions of Gezelius's book press were textbooks printed for the requirements of the developing school system, catechisms printed for popular education and books and pamphlets intended for the use of the church. Of these, the most remarkable individual work was the second printing in 1685 of the Finnish-language ▶Bible, which was considerably lighter and easier to use than the large edition of 1642. A reflection of the grand scale of Johannes Gezelius the Elder's projects may be seen in the fact that his son, Johannes Gezelius the Younger (1647–1718), complained in an inventory made after his father's death that unsold books were being stored for the needs of several decades to come.

The presses of Gezelius and the Academy of Turku united in 1750, when Jakob Merckell, who had already previously acquired ownership of Gezelius's press, bought the Academy's press. After Merckell's death in 1763 it was transferred to the Frenckell family, which had earlier become a shareholder in the firm, and still owns it today.

Until the 19th century there were only a small number of printing presses in Finland. An important turning-point occurred halfway through the century, when, thanks to the introduction of wood-pulp paper, the development of printing technology and signature binding, the price of books became lower. The improved reading skills of large groups of the population and the increased demand for books brought about by the influence of religious revivalism created the basis for a significant expansion of printing activity. The ▶Finnish Literature Society and its printing press were responsible for the publication of many books of national importance, including the ▶Kalevala (1835), the ▶Kanteletar (1840), the works of ▶Aleksis Kivi, Finnish folk poetry and ▶folklore. Many classics of translated literature have also been published by the society. The most important publisher of Bibles emerged in 1812 with the foundation of the Finnish Bible Society, which received significant support from its mother concern, the British and Foreign Bible Society.

Selling books to the public at large was the task of the bookbinders, who had market stalls where they sold the more common printed items: hymn books, catechisms, almanacs, prayer books, along with unbound broadsheets and pamphlets. The more expensive printed items were sold by the book publishers to advance subscribers, for without enough customers the commercial risk would have been too great.

The first proper bookshop in Finland was founded in Turku by a Swede, Magnus Swederus, at the end of the 1770s. During the first half of the 19th century the number of bookshops grew only slowly, but the end of the century saw a rapid increase. By the turn of the century there were 56 bookshops in Finland. JN

In 1858 the Publishers' Association of Finland was founded, with the aim of making the publication and selling of books more effective. The association's influence on the development of the book publishing trade has been considerable. The most important present-day Finnish publishers, WSOY (Werner Söderström Osakeyhtiö, founded in 1878), Kustannus Oy Otava (1890), K.J. Gummerus Oy (1872) and Weilin + Göös (1872) were founded at the end of the 19th century. WSOY and Otava are also the joint owners of Finland's largest current periodical concern. The firm Kustannus Oy Tammi, founded in 1943 by the Social Democratic Co-operative Movement is the most important book publisher of the labour movement. Its so-called Yellow Library has been one of the most important channels for translated literature in Finland. The most important publisher of Finland-Swedish literature is Söderström & Co. (1891).

The quantity of literature published in Finland has continued to grow throughout the 20th century, both in absolute terms and in relation to the size of the population. Before the Second World War, the annual number of titles steadily rose to approximately 2000, and this threshold was not exceeded until 1945. By 1960 the number of titles was approximately 2500, by 1970 3350 and by 1980 6500. In spite of the weakening of the general economic situation, this increase continued in the 1990s. In 1993 the number of titles was approximately 11,800, of which 9200 were in Finnish, 600 in Swedish and 2000 in other languages. The relative number of titles per million inhabitants has risen since 1960 from 560 to 2300 per year. Although on the basis of Unesco's statistics the numbers of titles are among the highest in the world, because of the smallness of the linguistic area the print runs are low. An important proportion of the books sold each year is represented by non-fiction and textbooks. In 1994 the 65 members of the Publishers' Association of Finland, which includes all of Finland's most important publishers, between them sold just under 20.1 million books. Of these, nearly 60 per cent were non-fiction and textbooks, while fiction and literary works accounted for 19 per cent. JN

bookshops ▶books

Borg, Kim (born 1919), bass singer. Kim Borg is one of the best-known Finnish basses. His active career stretched from the 1950s to the 1970s. An important springboard for Borg's career was his interpretation of the role of Gremin at the Royal Theatre, Copenhagen, in 1952, after which he was engaged by the same house. He made guest appearances at all the important opera houses, among them the Metropolitan Opera House in New York (where he was the first Finnish male singer to perform), the Bolshoy Theatre, Moscow, the state operas of Vienna, Bavaria and Hamburg and almost all the important music festivals.

Borg collaborated with many legendary conductors, including Otto Klemperer, Thomas Beecham, John Barbirolli, Herbert von Karajan and Leonard Bernstein. Thanks to the brilliant quality of his voice, his repertoire of roles was unusually large, including, in addition to the already-mentioned Gremin, the title role in *Boris Godunov*, Basilio in *The Barber of Seville*, Filip in *Don Carlos*, Scarpia in *Tosca*, Sarastro in *Die Zauberflöte*, and Ochs in *Der Rosenkavalier*. His pedagogic importance cannot be considered less than his importance as a performer; he was a professor at the Royal Danish School of Music between 1972 and 1989, and has taught numerous singers in his master-classes. RL

Brummer, Eva (born 1901), textile artist. Eva Brummer is one of the innovators of the ▶*ryijy* tradition in Finland. She designed church textiles and, for decades for the Friends of Finnish Handicrafts, first traditional *ryijy*s, among them floor *ryijy*s and later painterly, primarily dark-toned *ryijy*s whose special effects often include a multicoloured nap. Eva Brummer's *ryijy*s have won numerous prizes in applied arts exhibitions in various parts of the world, and they are on show in museum collections in many countries. MA

Eva Brummer, *Luonnos* ('Sketch'), *ryijy*, 1932–1933

Kim Borg

Bryggman, Erik (1891–1955), architect. Erik Bryggman and ▶Alvar Aalto made Turku into an architectural city in the 1920s. Bryggman designed handsome classical apartment blocks for the town centre and light functionalist villas for the Finnish ▶archipelago. In the book stockroom for the Åbo Akademi University, strict func-

Erik Bryggman

Erik Bryggman, Resurrection chapel, 1941

tionalism made a sensitive neighbour to the medieval cathedral.

The Resurrection Chapel in Turku, completed in 1941, is the mature synthesis of Bryggman's architecture, perhaps one of the most beautiful buildings of its time in Europe. The chapel rests softly in the landscape. Internal and external spaces are interwoven, while a hall spanned by a heavy, free-form barrel vault opens, on one side, on to the light of a spruce heath. RN

Bryk, Rut (born 1916), ceramic artist. Rut Bryk, a graphic artist by training, has worked as a designer at the ▶Arabia ceramics factory since 1942. Bryk's ceramic work divides clearly into two distinct chronological phases.

Rut Bryk

Her work of the 1940s to the 1960s was made up principally of plaques made of chamotte and glazed earthenware, whose figurative subjects ranged from the everyday (oven, fruit-basket) through nature (sunflower, birds, butterflies) to religious themes (madonna and child, holy communion, a Corpus Domini procession). Characteristic of the work of this early period is an intense saturation with colour which is achieved through superimposed layers of glaze. References to Byzantium, the early Renaissance, cubism, folk art and constructivism have been seen in the original visual appearance of Bryk's early work.

In recent decades, Bryk has become well-known for her abstract tile reliefs. In the geometric compositions of the 1970s and 1980s, with their apparently simple modular construction, she plays inventively with variations in scale, detail, surface texture and colour.

The referential starting points of her works are found in both purely abstract ideas and in architectural landscapes or the atmospheres of nature. The rugged countryside of Finnish Lapland has been for Bryk, as for her designer husband ▶Tapio Wirkkala, an important source of inspiration. One high point of Bryk's organic constructivism is the massive work *Kevään tulo pohjoiseen* ('The coming of spring to the North'), commissioned for the Finnish Embassy in New Delhi in 1985. In addition to the applied arts museums of the Nordic countries, Bryk's work features in many European and American collections. MaA

Budde, Jöns Andersson (Johannes) (c.1437–c.1491), Bridgettine monk, translator. The Finnish contribution to the literary culture of medieval Europe was small. Apart from routine documents, it was restricted to a few texts, and they, too, are unexceptional in style and form. Because of the narrowness of this literary culture, a great deal of attention has been devoted to surviving texts. The Bridgettine monk Jöns Budde (or Räk), who translated Latin literature into Swedish, has thus, flatteringly, sometimes been called Finland's first writer.

The exact date of Budde's birth is unknown. According to the estimates of linguistic scholars, he originated in ▶Ostrobothnia. He was ordained as a Bridgettine monk in 1461 or 1462. Working in the monastery of Vadstena in Sweden and Naantali (Vallis Gratiae) in Finland, Budde's greatest achievement was the translation of a few complete books of the ▶Bible into Swedish. His translation work was also of importance in the development of literary Swedish.

Budde's first known work is a translation completed in 1469 of *Liber specialis gratiae*, a work by the German mystic St Mechtilde of Hackeborn. The postscript, in which Jöns Budde describes his own revelation, is the first known personal text by a named Finnish writer.

In addition to the Bible and the text by St Mechtilde, Jöns Budde translated into Swedish an abridged version of St Birgitta *Revelationes* and an anonymous work entitled *Claustrum ani-*

mae, Bernard of Clairvaux's work *Meditationes* and legend literature. Only one volume of texts translated by Budde has survived in his own hand. The famous 'Book of Jöns Budde' created in Naantali between 1487 and 1491 contains a total of ten translated texts. Today it belongs to the collections of the Royal Library in Stockholm. Budde is mentioned alive for the last time in 1491. There is a monument to him in Naantali (1921). JN

building preservation The preservation of cultural remains in Finland dates back as far as 1666, when a law concerning their protection (including ruins of buildings rich in history) in the entire Kingdom of Sweden-Finland was instituted. It was not until the end of the 19th century, however, that the preservation of the built environment in general became a matter of concern.

The extensive reconstruction and redevelopment that followed the Second World War posed a particular threat to the historic building stock. Protective legislation for buildings of cultural and historical interest was not achieved in Finland until 1964. The law then enacted was revised in 1985. Under its terms, valuable buildings can be protected through a decision backed by the Ministry of Environment. Their value in cultural and historical terms is assessed by the National Board of Antiquities. By 1996, however, the terms of the law had been used to ensure the protection of only around 170 buildings or groups of buildings.

Urban planning directives based on the building law, although varying in their application, were of considerably greater importance, and were used to protect more than 10,000 separate urban buildings, of which around 2000 are located in ►Helsinki. The voluntary preservation decisions of individual private owners remained of great importance in building preservation as a whole. Advice on repairs and maintenance and the correct use of old materials became more effective, and had a positive effect on the survival of historically valuable environments. The government made grants to private owners for the maintenance of buildings of cultural value. EH

P. Hansson, *Almanach*, 1678. The vignettes show agricultural tasks for the various seasons

calendars The calendar of saints of the diocese of Turku which, in the medieval period, covered the whole of Finland was based on the 14th-century Dominican calendar, which had been supplemented mainly by the calendars of the Swedish dioceses. Among the Nordic saints, the most popular were St Olaf (feast day 29 July) and the Swedish St Erik (19 May). Finland's own saint, ►St Henry, had two yearly feast-days; the day of his death, 20 January (19 January in Swedish calendar), and the day his saintly relics were moved, 18 June. It is indicative of the bishops' powers of decision concerning saints' days that ►Olavus Magni (died 1460), who had had a long career as rector of the University of Paris, raised Ursula, patron saint of the University of Paris (21 October), and the most important scholastic theologian of the medieval period, Thomas Aquinas (7 March), to a higher liturgical status. Toward the end of the Catholic period, almost one day in three was a holy day, when working was either restricted or forbidden. In the Nordic countries rune-calendars were often used, in which the days of the year and the so-called golden numbers marking the new moons were marked with Scandinavian runes or their derivatives. In Finland, rune-calendars were in use as late as the 18th century.

After the Reformation, the general shape of the church year remained much the same. Saints' days were gradually reduced in number, but their celebration among the people continued long after their removal from the church calendar. After the Swedish Kingdom moved from the Julian to the Gregorian calendar in 1753, the most important saints' days continued to be celebrated, among the people, on their old days until the 19th century. In the contemporary calendar, too, church festivals have retained a strong position. The name-day custom, which has an unusually strong position in the Nordic countries, has developed on the basis of the celebration of saints' days. Of the ten or so festivals that are ordained by law as public holidays, only May Day and Independence Day are not church festivals – although St Walpurgis's Day looms large in the background of even May Day.

The ►*Missale Aboense* (1488) included a calendar section, and the *Rucouskiria* ('Prayer-book', 1544) of the reformer ►Michael Agricola contained a table for the calculation of favourable days for different years. It was only in the late 16th century, however, that almanacs began to be printed, in Sweden. In 1608, the Helsinki-born Sigfridus Aronus Forsius (c. 1550 – 1624) first published almanacs based on the Turku calendar of saints, which were intended for the use of the entire kingdom. Separate calendars for Finnish use were published from 1660 onwards. The first Finnish-language almanac was published in 1705. From 1828 to 1994 the printing of almanacs was the privilege of the University of Helsinki, and their sale brought a considerable income. JN

Minna Canth

Bo Carpelan

Canth, Minna (1844–1897), writer. Minna Canth lived in the small town of Kuopio, 500 kilometres from Helsinki. She was an entrepreneur, a journalist, a dramatist, a feminist and liberal proletarian, and the widowed mother of seven children. Despite her radicalism, however, she was deeply Christian.

Canth's play *Kovan onnen lapsia* ('Hard luck's children', 1888) was banned from the Finnish Theatre after its first night: its anti-clericalism, exaggerated realism and pessimism, it was claimed, shocked the audience. Canth

Minna Canth, *Murtovarkaus* ('The Burglary'), Helsinki City Theatre, 1981, directed by Jouko Turkka

brought the oppressed working classes and women to the stage at a time when the young bourgeois intelligentsia would probably have preferred to watch sublime nationalist hero-stories or harmless comedies at the newly founded Finnish-language Theatre.

Canth's *Papin perhe* ('The pastor's family', 1891), with its psychologically skilful depiction of breakdown in a bourgeois family in the 1880s, is considered her best. In *Työmiehen vaimo* ('The worker's wife', 1885), she describes the shamefully bad social and legal security in the Grand Duchy of Finland. Canth's support of the proletariat originated in a sense of social justice; Marx was not necessary. *Anna-Liisa* (1895) charts how circumstances drive a young girl to murder her child. In the repertoire of the young Finnish Theatre for the first 15 years, Minna Canth's plays were played 164 times, while Shakespeare received only 149 performances and the national writer, ►Aleksis Kivi, 109.

Canth also wrote people's comedies whose popularity among both amateur and professional theatre groups has been immense. SL

Carpelan, Bo (born 1926), poet. After publishing his first collection of poetry in 1945 Bo Carpelan soon emerged as the leading Finland-Swedish poet of his generation, and has achieved a position as one of the central Swedish-language poets of the postwar period. His early work combines the Swedish modernism of the 1940s with the Finland-Swedish modernist tradition of the 1910s and 1920s, particularly the poetic innovations of ▶Gunnar Björling. Carpelan's poetry, often attached to details of landscape or nature and permeated by a strong personality, for example, in the collection *Den svala dagen* ('The cool day', 1960), can be lapidary, but it brings with it a sense of original meaning. In addition to his poetry, Carpelan has also published prose works, for example a fantasy about the end of the world exploring the nature of a nuclear weapons disaster, *Rösterna i den sena timmen* ('Voices at the late hour', 1971), and *Axel* (1986), a novel describing the life of a relative of his who was an eccentric friend and admirer of the composer ▶Jean Sibelius. Carpelan has translated the works of some of the most important Finnish modernists into Swedish, among them ▶Paavo Haavikko. PL

castles Finland's political and social history in the medieval period explains why royal or aristocratic castles were not built here as in central Europe. The oldest surviving aristocratic castles, or ▶manor houses, date from the second half of the 16th century. The building of castles in Finland was part of a project of constructing defensive and administrative centres throughout the kingdom of Sweden-Finland. Six castles of national importance were built in the medieval period, from the second half of the 13th century onwards: Turku, Häme and Viipuri, Raasepori, Olavinlinna and, in ▶Åland, Kastelholma. All of these were official provincial residences. At least three other residential castles, now lost, are known: Porvoo, Kokemäki and Korsholma. During the final decades of the 16th century, two castles were built to administrate and defend the northern wildernesses: Oulu and Kajaani. Of these only the latter survives, in ruins. Kuusisto, the residential castle of the bishops of Turku, also survives as a ruin.

The importance of castles as main bastions and administrative centres disappeared gradually during the 18th century, and from the second half of the 19th century onwards they have

Castles in Finland

been historic monuments and sights. Extensive and thoroughgoing renovations have been carried out since the Second World War at Turku, Häme and Olavinlinna castles. As a result, they have been able to be used for various cultural events, the best-known of which is the annual Savonlinna Opera Festival at Olavinlinna. In addition to various ceremonial uses, Turku Castle is also the centre for diverse museum activities. All three castles are owned by the state, and cared for by the National Board of Antiquities.

TURKU CASTLE The founding of Turku Castle on an island at the mouth of the Aurajoki River probably took place around 1280. It was at first a fortified encampment which, in the early 14th century, was rebuilt as a castle enclosed by granite walls. This comprised a courtyard with accommodation wings grouped in two storeys, linked by wooden staircases, on the north and south side. In the winter of 1364–1365 the troops of Albrecht of Mecklenburg besieged the castle and burnt it. The castle was rebuilt in the gothic style, with vaulted rooms and a chapel. At the beginning

Turku Castle, western Finland, founded around 1280 and rebuilt in stone in the early 14th century

of the 15th century, it comprised around 40 rooms and was one of the largest in northern Europe. During the same century, the main bastion was also equipped with an outer ward protected by ring walls, which was altered in the 1580s in accordance with the demands of the advent of cannonfire. An important renaissance-style modernisation was carried out during the reign of Gustavus Vasa (1523–1560) while his son, John, was Duke of Finland; John lived at Turku Castle from 1556 to 1563 with his Polish-born wife Katarina Jagellonica. To meet the needs of the ducal family, an additional, renaissance-style storey was added. This was destroyed in the bombing of the castle in 1941 and has since been reconstructed in renovations carried out between 1946 and 1962.

HÄME CASTLE Häme Castle was, according to oral tradition cited in the 14th-century *Eric's Chronicle*, founded by the Swedish Earl Birger as a result of a 'crusade' to Häme province. The crusade possibly took place in 1239, but the oldest parts of the building originate from the 1260s at the earliest. The earliest construction phase comprised a quadrilateral fortified encampment with three corner towers. It was built of natural stone, but its transformation, in the mid 14th century, into a residential and defensive castle was carried out using brick as the internal and external surface material, an unusual practice in Finland. Completed toward the end of the medieval period, the castle comprised two accommodation storeys around a quadrilateral courtyard; the buildings contained halls and rooms with barrel- and cross-vaulting, and a chapel. The ground-plan of the castle shows links

with the castle architecture of the Germanic orders of knighthood, and the gothic details can be traced to similar forms in the Mecklenburg area. By the 15th century, at the latest, the castle was surrounded by a brick-faced outer ward. After the Great Northern War (1700–1721), in the 1720s, Häme Castle was made a *place des armes* in the Finnish defensive system, and the main bastion was converted into a grain store. A military bakery was also built on the site. During the reign of

Häme Castle, central Finland, founded in the 13th century, possibly as early as 1260

Gustavus III (1772–1792) the castle's defensive system was modernised with ring walls and tenaille ramparts. When the castle passed into Russian hands in 1808, the building of ramparts continued until, in 1836, the building was converted into a prison, to designs by the architect ▶C.L. Engel. It continued to be used as a prison until 1953. The restoration was completed in 1988. In addition to the medieval spaces of the ground floor, the castle now comprises rooms that have either been reconstructed or left in their ruined state. Exhibitions are staged in the ring-wall building by the ▶National Museum of Finland.

RAASEPORI CASTLE The Castle of Raasepori was founded in the 1370s by the Swedish vice regent Bo Jonsson Grip (died 1386). It was a main bastion for the province of Uusimaa, and its location on the Gulf of Finland took into account the important commercial location of Tallinn on the opposite shore. The original stage of development, at the end of the 14th century, comprised a horseshoe-shaped ring wall, with accommodation towers, built on top of a high cliff. Karl Knutsson Bonde (1408–1470), who was ruler of Sweden on three separate occasions, occupied Raasepori from 1465 to 1467. It was probably during this period that the castle was extended with two accommodation wings. The castle reached its final form in the 1470s, during the period of the Danish-born knight Lars Axelsson Tott (died 1483), when the partially surviving great accommodation wing with its knights' hall was completed. In the late 16th century, the castle was abandoned and left empty. It decayed badly until the 1880s, when its conservation began. The National Board of Antiquities made a careful restoration in the 1970s. The castle's location in the landscape is impressive, and its ruins make a fine setting for theatrical performances in the summer.

KASTELHOLMA The Castle of Kastelholma, in Åland, was also founded by Bo Jonsson Grip, in the 1380s. The location was a good one for monitoring the trade routes of the Gulf of Finland. Following the castle-building practices of central Europe, Kastelholma comprises a main bastion on the south side of the site, and an outer ward, dating from the late 15th century. A modest palace wing is attached to the main bastion. The most notable effect of the exterior is made up of the five-storey Kuuretorni Tower. After a fire in 1619, the outer ward was rebuilt. Åland was a favoured area for royal elk-hunts, and Kastelholma became a kind of hunting castle. Its decay began in the 18th century, and a fire destroyed the castle in 1745, after which only the eastern wing was restored, with the other parts remaining in ruins. Today the castle is owned by the provincial government of Åland and, with the completion of conservation work, has been taken into use for provincial receptions and as a tourist destination. The first Finnish opera, Fredrik Pacius's *Kaarle-kuninkaan metsästys* ('King Charles' Hunt', 1852), is connected with the history of Kastelholma.

OLAVINLINNA Perhaps the best-known of Finnish castles is Olavinlinna. This is partly because of its very impressive location on the extended lake system of Saimaa, on a small rocky skerry. This made it, from the 1870s onwards, an internationally known travel destination, along with the nearby Punkaharju Ridge. The

Olavinlinna Castle, eastern Finland, founded in 1475. The castle is the home of the annual Savonlinna Opera Festival

construction history of Olavinlinna is unusually clear. The year of foundation, 1475, is known from documentary sources. The builder was a Danish-born knight, Erik Axelsson Tott (1418–1481), who had gone into the service of the Swedish crown. The location of the castle in Savo was politically significant – its task was to protect the disputed eastern border of the kingdom from Novgorod, which had conquered Moscow.

Olavinlinna's architecture is characterised by the three surviving round towers, which were designed for defence and accommodation. Originally the castle comprised, as a main bastion, the three towers (of which one was destroyed) and a palace wing connecting them. According to Erik Axelsson's own account, the castle was built by '16 good foreign master masons'. On the basis of details, it is possible to determine that at least some of them came from Tallinn. The castle's defensive capabilities were improved as late as the 1560s by building a thick cannon tower, which was later destroyed. The Russian Emperor Peter the Great besieged the castle in 1714, and it was forced to surrender. After the peace treaty of 1721 Olavinlinna was returned to Sweden-Finland, but was ceded in the peace treaty of Turku 1743 to the Russians. In the second half of the 18th century the Russian forces, under the direction of General Alexander Suvorov (1730–1800), added to the castle's defensive equipment with a chain of bastions designed in a classical style. Having lost its military

45

importance, the castle was almost demolished, but was instead restored, for the first time as early as 1875 on the occasion of the castle's 400th anniversary. A thoroughgoing restoration was carried out between 1961 and 1975, when the castle was also adapted for ceremonial and congress use. The performance of ▶operas began in the castle courtyard, at the initiative of the opera singer ▶Aino Ackté, in 1912. This tradition was revived in the 1960s, and the Savonlinna Opera Festival has become one of the most important cultural events of the Finnish summer season.

KUUSISTO The ruins of Kuusisto Episcopal Castle are a remnant of the residential castle of the bishops of Turku, which was located some 20 or 30 kilometres from Turku on an island in a small sea-bay some 20 or 30 kilometres from Turku. The building of the castle, which was begun in 1317, for the use of the episcopal seat reflected the important political role of the bishops of Turku. The building took place in a number of different stages, and in its final form it comprised a masonry main bastion with a palace wing and three associated outer wards, with a total area of some 110m x 90m.

As ecclesiastical property, Kuusisto fell into the hands of the state after the Reformation of 1527, at which point King Gustavus Vasa ordered it to be demolished. A royal manor was founded on the site of the castle which, in 1690, became a colonel's quarters. The main building, built in the baroque style, survives, and is now in use as a museum.

KAJAANI The last phase in the development of Finnish castles is marked by the Castle of Kajaani. The castle was built 1604–1619. It is located on an island in Ämmänkoski River. Associated with the granite ring walls are two round turrets linked by an accommodation wing. The fortification was continued during Count Per Brahe's (1602–1680) period as Governor General of Finland between 1661 and 1666. The Russians seized the castle during the Great Northern War in 1716 and blew it up. Conservation of the ruins has been carried periodically out since the 1880s. The important Swedish historian Johannes Messenius

(1579–1636) was imprisoned in the castle in 1616 and wrote his work on the history of the Nordic countries, *Scandia Illustrata*, here. EH

Castrén, Matthias Alexander (1813–1852), linguistic scholar, professor. Born one of eight children in a clerical family, Matthias Castrén went to school in Oulu in northern Finland, and proceeded to the Imperial Alexander University in Helsinki. Castrén studied ancient Nordic languages, graduating in 1836. He was appointed docent in 1840, and in 1851 became the first incumbent of the chair of Finnish Language and Literature.

Castrén made numerous linguistic expeditions, at first to Finnish ▶Lapland, Finnish and Russian ▶Karelia (1838–1839), and then to northern Russia and Siberia (1841–1849). On his journeys, he studied numerous Finno-Ugrian languages, and all the Samoyed tongues, some Turkic, Tungusic and Mongol languages and some disappearing and previously unknown languages. On his journeys, Castrén thoroughly charted the living conditions of the peoples who spoke these languages, and made observations important for the study of folklore, archaeology and religion. Most of Castrén's observations were edited for publication some of them on the basis of finished manuscripts by Castrén himself only after his death. ML

censorship In around 1583 Jacobus Finno (c. 1540–1588), publisher of the first Finnish hymnal, banned the use of the ▶*Kalevala* metre in Finnish poetry because he considered it pagan. This can be considered the beginning of the history of Finnish censorship.

After 1809, when Finland became an autonomous Grand Duchy of Russia, a censorship board was established on the Russian model, with local censors. Permission was needed for the publication of newspapers and periodicals, and they were examined in advance. In 1850 a decree was passed according to which only religious and economic literature could be published in Finnish. This was observed particularly strictly in its application to newspapers.

Although censorship was lifted for a

Matthias Alexander Castrén

short period during the 1860s, it was subsequently reinstituted, and the years of strong Russification policies around the turn of the 19th century, in particular, were a period of strict censorship. Many active leftists moved to the United States and published writings that would not have been approved at home.

In 1905 it was announced that advance censorhip would be lifted, but freedom of the press was achieved fully only after Finland gained its independence in 1917. Since then matters concerning the freedom of the press have been attended to by the Ministry of Justice. A law guaranteeing the freedom of the press was passed in 1919.

In the early years of independence, up to the 1930s, however, writers had to be careful about what they wrote, particularly in the newspapers. Leftist, atheist and anti-ecclesiastical literary works and articles were considered the most dangerous. The magazine that published extracts from Jaroslav Hašek's novel *The Good Soldier Švejk* was sued for libel because it was considered to have offended religious values. The same magazine was fined for the publication of socially critical articles by the writer Pentti Haanpää (1905–1955). Haanpää later also encountered difficulties in publishing his short stories describing military life and his novel *Noitaympyrä* ('Witch circle', completed 1931, published 1956), with its critical analysis of life in the North.

War censorship prevailed between 1939 and 1947, imposed first by the Military Headquarters, subsequently by the Ministry of the Interior and, during the Continuation War (1941–1944), the Information Centre of the State, which functioned under the direction of the Prime Minister's Office. In addition to printed matter, war censorship extended as far as private letters.

Between 1919 and 1944, almost 4500 people were found guilty of treason or encouraging treason. Political prisoners were forbidden to read numerous named books. At some points, the works of Marx were permissible, because they had been translated in the past with the Russians Emperor's permission. Pages were excised from some books in prisons.

After losing the Second World War to the Soviet Union, the order was given for the removal of so-called politically dubious books from bookshops and libraries between 1944 and 1946. Bookshops were given an exact list of books to be removed, but libraries were allowed relative freedom in the matter, so the range of missing books was wide. In most libraries the lists featured dozens of names; in larger libraries, their numbers might be in the hundreds. Dozens of pro-German films were also banned. Sixteen million map sheets were ceded to the Soviet Union.

The concept of self-censorship arose in the atmosphere of the postwar years, the period of strong Stalinist foreign policies. In 1948, the editors-in-chief of two Finnish newspapers were arraigned because their coverage of the funeral of a Soviet leader had been inappropriate. The death of Stalin in 1953 was followed by a reaction of strict surveillance, which was one of the factors behind strained Finno-Soviet relations in 1958. Soviet diplomats followed developments in Finland closely. In 1958 a Soviet diplomat protested against a caricature of Nikita Khrushchev by Finland's best-known political cartoonist. Even ten years later the Soviet ambassador objected to the label of a brand of beer called Karjala ('Karelia') – the label, taken from a 16th-century crest, did not fit with the semiotics of the politics of the day. In Finland, these Soviet reactions caused increased sensitivity to matters that might be considered anti-Soviet.

In 1974, Alexander Solzenitsyn's Finnish publisher decided not to publish *The Gulag Archipelago*, arguing that to issue the book was not in accordance with the general interests of Finland. The decision was made some weeks after the writer's expulsion from the Soviet Union. At that time works dealing with non-Russian Soviet nationalities, Soviet Jews or Soviet Christians were not published in Finland; neither were New Left books critical of the Soviet Union. Literature that was considered immoral was also left unpublished. Henry Miller's *Tropic of Cancer* was banned in the United States for 30 years, until 1964. The Finnish translation of the book was confiscated in 1962, and the publisher fined. The book was republished in 1970.

The most significant book-war of the 1960s was caused by *Juhannus-tanssit* ('Midsummer dance', 1964), a novel by Hannu Salama (born 1936), who was found guilty of 'deliberate blasphemy' in 1966. Two years later, the Finnish president overturned the judgement. The original version of the work was published only in the 1990s.

In the 1990s, preventive censorship in Finland applies only to films and videos. According to a law of 1965, a film may not be shown if it is in con-travention of the law or of good man-ners, immoral, brutalising or injurious to mental health; or if its performance constitutes a danger to public order, security or the country's relationship with foreign powers.

Over the years, the Finnish Board of Film Censors has banned a large num-ber of films, among them internation-ally known classics such as Ernst Lu-bitsch's *Ninotchka* (1939), Robert Bres-son's *Pickpocket* (1959), Billy Wilder's *One Two Three* (1961), Fritz Lang's *'M'* (1931) and Ingmar Bergman's *Jung-frukällan* (1960). It has been permitted to show these films in Finland for a long time. Since the 1970s, Finland's relationship with the Soviet Union no longer influenced the work of the Board of Film Censors. In the late 1990s, preventive censorship of films is justified primarily by the protection of children, and its right to continued ex-istence is under consideration. KE

ceramics Finland's first ceramics fac-tories were founded in the 18th centu-ry, and in the 19th century the pace in-creased. Most of the factories, howev-er, lasted only a short while. Their main products were tiles and simple earthenware or stoneware household objects. The most important factory of the period was the Suotniemi earthen-ware and porcelain factory in eastern Finland (1841–1894), the majority of whose production was exported to St Petersburg. ▶Arabia has dominated the field ever since it was opened in 1873. Among other factories and workshops producing utility ceramics, the most important have been Gran-kullan Saviteollisuus/Kera (1917–1958),

Birger Kaipiainen, faience wall tablet, made by Arabia 1965

Kupittaan Savi (1918–1969), the ce-ramist Marita Lybeck's (born 1906) Emel workshop (1938–1957), Savi-torppa (established in 1951) and Anu Pentikäinen (born 1942, established in 1971).

The history of studio ceramics in Finland begins at the turn of the 20th century. The Anglo-Belgian artist and ceramist Alfred William Finch (1854–1930) is considered the father of Finnish ceramic art; he began work as an artist in the Iris factory founded by ▶Louis Sparre in 1897. The Iris factory produced utility ceramics made, in the spirit of the Arts and Crafts move-ment, from Finnish red-burning clay. After the factory had gone bankrupt in 1902, Finch became the first teacher of ceramics at the Central School of Ap-plied Arts. Among his most important students were Maija Grotell (1904–1987), who moved to America and taught at the Cranbrook Academy of Arts between 1938 and 1966, Toini Muona (1904–1987), who worked as an artist for Arabia, and Elsa Elenius (1897–1967), who continued as Finch's successor as teacher of ceramics at the Central School of Applied Arts from 1930 to 1963. From 1963 to 1979, Kyl-likki Salmenhaara (1915–1981), a much respected teacher, was in charge of training in ceramics; informalism made its appearance for the first time in Finnish ceramics in her rough stoneware objects of the 1950s.

From the late 1960s onward, the amount of studio ceramics has been increasing, with small workshops producing utility ceramics throughout the country, among them Kerman Savi and Seenat, founded in 1976. The 1970s also saw the establishment of a number of artists' collectives. Pot Viapori was founded on the island of ►Suomenlinna, close to Helsinki, in 1973, by women potters. In addition to serial production, the art department at Arabia has until recent decades also had a dominant position in art ceramics. Ceramic artists who have worked outside Arabia include, in addition to those mentioned above, Birgit Dyhr (born 1908), Anna-Maria Osipow (born 1935), Ritva Tulonen (born 1941), Outi Leinonen (born 1950) and Kristiina Riska (born 1960). MaA

childhood Perhaps the basic and serene nature of childhood is always rather similar although the time and place of childhood vary strongly, depending on societal and historical developments.

Finland's first law on primary education was passed in 1866, when most Finnish children were needed for agricultural labour, a state of affairs that continued for quite a long time afterwards. Following national independence, with the passing of the compulsory education statutes in 1922, school education became universal. After the Second World War the expansion and development of the school system were important socio-political tasks.

School catering and health care, together with a ►library system that contained a children's section covering the whole country helped to create equality of opportunity for children from different groups of the population. In the 1970s a reform was introduced where non fee-paying comprehensive education was extented to a period of nine years and was made compulsory for all children. In the 1990s two thirds of all Finnish children continued their studies in senior high school or vocational school and more than a sixth at a university or other institute of ►higher education. The period of school education has been progressively extended, and gradually became a part of every child's experience, continuing well into adolescence.

In addition to education, the struggle against child mortality was for many decades one of the most important political issues. In the 1940s infant mortality was 56 deaths per thousand in the first year in all live births, whereas in modern Finland it is 4.4 (1993), the world's lowest after Sweden and Japan. Pregnant women and young children are covered by a free system of regular, basic health care; the law on maternity and child welfare clinics that came into force in 1945 brought about a service network covering the whole country, designed to cater for new generations of children.

The provision of family protection has been an important theme in the

Bird's-eye view: seeing society through the eyes of a child

child policies throughout the 20th century. Child benefit has been paid since 1948. Family benefits and income supplements have become more numerous, and their level has varied. Society's participation in the economic support of the child population is seen as an essential factor promoting equality. Family benefit is paid to both parents for a period of 11 months to an average of 66 per cent of lost salary. In Finland women have traditionally contributed to the family income, and so child care has been an important issue. Political discussion on the subject came to a head in 1973 with the introduction of a law providing municipal day care as an adjunct to home care for all families who need it. Since 1996 parents have had the right to choose either financial support for home care or a fee-paying place at a day-care centre. The reconciliation of work and family life is one of the enduring themes of modern social policy.

In the 1990s one quarter of the population was composed of minors aged below 18. The aging of the population structure was slightly slower in Finland than in many other largely industrialised countries. The birthrate showed a slight increase (with a fertility index of 1.8). Nearly nine children out of ten lived in families with two carers, and over 70 per cent of children had one or several siblings. It was a part of the rights and duties of parents to give their children good care and upbringing. The upbringing of children was reorganised on humanistic principles, and this process was also supported by legislation, which among other things banned corporal punishment of children in 1984.

In 1995 Finland took part in the worldwide 'Give a Voice to the Children' campaign, during which children were invited to write to newspapers with their observations and opinions. The essays by Finnish children concerned environmental issues, the conservation of nature and animals, free time, school, war, peace, violence and human relationships. In some of the essays, children and young people reflected on their own situation and criticised the undervaluing of children and the abuse of power by adults. According to some of the writers, more information about children's rights needs to be provided, so that adults are able to pay children more attention and so that children are able to defend their own rights.

The authors of a recent boom of childhood research have criticised the adult-centredness and asexuality of knowledge concerning children. Reality unfolds differently depending, among other things, on whether it is considered from the point of view of children or adults, girls or boys. It is becoming commoner than earlier for children to be included in studies as informants. Now we are learning anew how the human individual 'makes' his or her everyday reality from an early age. The interest in what a child is not yet turns into curiosity about what a child already is. New perspectives open up to society when it is studied from the point of view of its child population.

Childhood has traditionally been the precinct of medicine, education and psychology. During the period 1992–1995, the child study programme of the Academy of Finland also encouraged research into other areas of the study of childhood.

Even before the growth of modern science, art was an important arena for the quest into the voices of childhood. At the end of the 19th century Finnish literature also learned how to depict authentic child characters and to describe the world through the eyes of a child. At the same time Finnish painters created characteristic images of children and childhood. The depiction of childhood is still a vital, living theme in art of various genres. MBy

Christmas ▶festivals

church The earliest clearly Christian influences arrived in Finland during the Viking period, between the 9th and 11th centuries, as is demonstrated by both grave finds and words entering the Finnish language. The Christian terms of the period are often of Eastern origin. This can be explained on the one hand by influences from the Greek Byzantine culture that arrived via the eastern Viking route, and on the other by the trade routes of Novgorod, which stretched as far as west-

Turku Cathedral, 13th century, originally the centre of the Catholic church in Finland

ern Finland. Features from western Christianity became dominant in ►Åland and south-west Finland in the 11th and 12th centuries; in Häme and ►Karelia Catholic Christianity became established only over the following centuries. Pagan culture did not disappear immediately: the change took place slowly as ecclesiastical organisation progressed.

According to the traditional interpretation, Finland came under the influence of the Catholic Church as a re-

sult of a crusade led by St Eric in the mid 12th century. Information about this so-called First Crusade is based on the legends of St Eric and ►St Henry, and for this reason contemporary scholarship views the historical facts they contain with some caution. The English-born Henry, who, according to tradition, was killed by the peasant ►Lalli, is believed to have been the first bishop of Finland. In the medieval period, St Henry was Finland's national saint, and the anniversary of his death, 20 January (19 January in Swedish calendar), was the highest feast-day in the calendar of saints of the diocese of Turku, which then covered the whole of Finland. A lively pilgrim cult grew up around the legend of St Henry.

The period of organisation of the Catholic Church lasted for more than a century. On the basis of the Finnish medieval episcopal chronicle, the founding of the Cathedral Chapter of Turku has been dated to 1276. The training of priests is considered to have begun at around the same time, and marked an important step in the integration of Finland into the western European cultural sphere. Finnish ►students are known to have studied at the University of Paris from the 14th century onwards. After that, the stream of students to Paris and, later, Prague, Leipzig, Rostock, Louvain and other European universities continued fairly evenly to the end of the medieval period.

Ecclesiastical and cultural influences arrived in Finland from Sweden and Germany and elsewhere on the Baltic coast. Relations with the papal curia in Rome and Avignon, too, were regular; in addition, Finnish believers joined international pilgrimages. New parishes were founded in different parts of the diocese, although the inhabited area was considerably smaller than it is now. The earliest churches were probably built of wood, but surviving ecclesiastical buildings are generally built of grey granite. Most of them date from the 15th century.

The City of Viipuri, founded in 1293 on the shores of the eastern Gulf of Finland, was, after Turku, the second most important in ecclesiastical life. It was one of Finland's five medieval cities, and was the location of both a Dominican and a Franciscan monastery. These orders had convents in Turku, too, and the Franciscans also had one on the island of Kökar in ▶Åland. In addition to the Dominicans and Franciscans, the only other religious order active in Finland were the Bridgettines, whose monastery in Naantali, Vallis Gratiae ('The Valley of Grace'), was founded in 1443. The Dominican influence was important in the liturgy and ecclesiastical literature of the Turku diocese, of which the most significant example was the only printed incunabulum printed specifically for Finland, the ▶Missale Aboense (1488).

The end of the medieval period saw a flourishing of ecclesiastical life in Finland. The Church's influence grew and its economic position improved, a fact that is reflected in the richer decoration of church interiors at the end of the 15th century.

The Reformation began in Finland, as elsewhere in the Swedish kingdom, with the decisions made at the Diet of Västerås in 1527. The Reformation was a process directed from above whose realisation served, primarily, the aims of the state, directed by King Gustavus I Vasa (reigned 1523–1560). The glaring injustices that had led to the Reformation elsewhere in Europe did not exist in the same extent in Sweden-Finland. For the Church, the Reformation meant impoverishment and the severing of traditional connections with areas that remained in the Catholic sphere of influence.

A central role in the realisation of the Reformation was taken by Finnish students who had studied at the University of Wittenberg from the 1530s onwards. Most important among them was ▶Michael Agricola, who is considered the true reformer of Finland. The evangelical faith was already established in the country by the mid 16th century, although priests who had been trained in the Catholic faith went on serving their parishes up to the turn of the century. The changes brought by the Reformation gradually established themselves among ordinary people over a long period; at the beginning of the 16th century customs and beliefs from the pagan period still had a foothold in the country. Cus-

toms associated with the ▶calendar of the saints and the church year, in particular, survived for a long time among the people.

The establishment of the Reformation was also hampered by the interest of King John III (reigned 1568–1592) in Catholicism and the unification of the churches. The sovereignty of the Evangelist Lutheran Church was confirmed only after John's brother King Charles IX (1550–1611) had defeated John's son Sigismund (1566–1632), who had been baptised into the Catholic faith, in an armed dynastic struggle at the beginning of the 17th century.

In the 17th century, the Finnish Church was characterised by a Lutheran orthodoxy that emphasised the position won by Sweden as champion of protestantism in central Europe in the Thirty Years War (1618–1648). It was a clear established Church, and membership was compulsory for every citizen. The ruler was head of the Church, and his position was supported by theocratic arguments.

Among the positive results of the period of Lutheran orthodoxy were an improvement in the training of priests, increasing prosperity for the church and, through these, a diversification of church life and a concentration on education for the people. Hymnals and devotional literature were printed for both clergy and lay people. The first Finnish ▶Bible was, however, not printed until 1642; the New Testament had appeared, in a translation by ▶Michael Agricola, almost a century earlier, in 1548.

German Halle pietism reached Finland at the turn of the 18th century. Pietism manifested itself both as moderate pietism, whose aim was the renewal of spiritual life within the church, and as radical pietism, which was separatist by nature. At first, pietism spread primarily among army officers, artisans and the lower clergy; from mid century onward, in southwestern Finland, it also progressed among country people.

Finland's transfer from Swedish rule to the status of autonomous Grand Duchy within the Russian empire in 1809 did not cause large-scale changes in ecclesiastical life. The Lutheran Church supported the new administration to preserve law and order in the country, while the country's new ruler, for his part, guaranteed the unchanged position of church and religion.

Fear of change was the reason behind the negative attitude of Church and authorities to the religious revivalism – particularly that tinged with pietism– whose area of influence extended from Savo in the south-east to ►Ostrobothnia in the north-west. Legal charges were even brought against the leaders of the ►revivalist movements, and they were fined. This, however, did not hinder the activities and spread of the revivalist movements. The Finnish revivalist movements of the 19th century were not separatist in character, but remained movements for renewal within the church; even today, their influence within the Evangelical Lutheran Church is considerable.

The final decades of the 19th century were a time of considerable change within the Church. The change in world-view offered challenges to church dogma, and other developments fragmented the base of the traditional, agricultural class society. The Church Law of 1869 approved the principle of the freedom of worship, but it was not realised in practice. In the last decades of the century, demands for the realisation of full freedom of worship and the separation of church and state increased from both atheists and a minority of Christians.

The Church responded to these new demands by reforming its organisation and developing new modes of activity. The Finnish Bible Society, founded in 1812 by the Scot John Paterson, concentrated on the distribution of Bibles and New Testaments. It was largely due to this that the Finnish-language Bible, of which there had been a total of only five editions before 1817, was issued in as many as 41 editions between 1817 and 1899. By the end of the century, indeed, the Reformation aim of the distribution of a Bible or a New Testament to every home had been achieved.

The new modes of operation developed by the church in the latter half of the 19th century included internal missionary and lay work. Parish activity was complemented by numerous Christian societies, which offered a channel for many of the new modes of operation. Activity directed toward the internal development of the Church was complemented by the foundation of Finnish Missionary Society in 1859, whose first missionaries began their work in south-west Africa in 1870. By the beginning of the following century, missionary activity extended to China.

After Finland's independence in 1917, the Civil War of the following year was a traumatic experience that estranged the church and the workers' movement. The Church sympathised with the political centre and right wing; in leftist circles, it was thought of as a reactionary force that supported the status quo. The Freedom of Worship Act, which came into force in 1923, demonstrated the traditional idea of the people's church and, despite doubts, succeeded in establishing its position among Finns. By the end of the 1920s the numbers of those who had officially left the Church were limited to just over one per cent of the population. The preservation of the Church's strong position lent support to its role as the established church and to its continued responsibility for population records and burials.

The trials of the Second World War increased national feelings of cohesion and brought the Church and working people closer together. After the end of the war, this was seen in Church circles by an increased interest in social questions. A strong adherence to tradition and national values did not, however, satisfy young people, whose protests climaxed in the late 1960s. They demanded the separation of Church and state, the removal of religious education from schools and the ending of the church's taxation rights.

Alongside the four traditional church revivalist movements there arose, after the Second World War, a movement for spiritual renewal influenced by Great Britain and the United States that is known as the fifth revivalist movement. This emphasised personal religion and took a negative stance toward the ecumenical movement and theological liberalism. Despite its critical stance, however, the fifth revivalist movement, like its siblings, has remained within the Church, although it has also had connections with the free church movement. British and American Christianity has also been of great importance in the development of a youth culture for the church, particularly in spiritual music for young people.

One of the most hotly debated questions in the Finnish Church has been that of women priests. As early as 1976, the Church Assembly decided that women priests were not in opposition to church teachings. Women priests were finally approved, however, only in the Church Assembly of 1986. The Church Assembly approved a new hymnal that same year, which was taken into use in 1987. The renewal of ecclesiastical literature was completed with the adoption of a new translation of the Bible in 1992.

In 1995 the Finnish Evangelical Lutheran Church consisted of 8 dioceses, divided into 80 deaneries and 595 parishes. The Turku diocese had the greatest number of parishes (95). Of the population of Finland as a whole, 85.6 per cent were members of the Evangelical Lutheran Church; the number had decreased by 0.1 per cent since the previous year – about 14,000 people had left the church, and about 10,000 had joined. Leaving the church is at its greatest in the capital and among inhabitants of the big cities. Of marriages registered in 1995, 88.5 per cent took place according to the rites of the Evangelical Lutheran Church. Less than 1.5 per cent of the population belong to the Finnish ▶Orthodox Church.

Of the activities of the Church, its members most easily encounter the parish day-care centres, which care for 58.1 per cent of Finnish children aged between four and six. The most comprehensive activity is confirmation school: in the over 15 age-group, the proportion of participants is 90.8 per cent – more than the percentage of church members. An average of 3.5 per cent of parishioners participated in weekly worship.

The Church's highest decision-making body is the annual Church Assembly, whose members are the 8 bishops of the country and a field bishop who is responsible for ecclesiastical work among the armed forces, a representative of supreme justice, 96 lay members chosen by parishes, and 43 members of the clergy. The Church Assembly presents legislation concerning the church to parliament, approves ecclesiastical books, and passes the budget of the Central Fund. The Episcopal Conference, which meets twice-yearly, can make representations to the Church Assembly. The activities of the Church are directed on a general level by the Church Assembly: beneath it are the functional centres that realise and co-ordinate the different areas of Church activity. The Church employs some 15,000 workers, of whom less than 10 per cent are clergy. JN

circus In its current form, the circus developed in England in the 1770s. Performances at first centred on stunt riding. Tightrope-walkers, clowns, acrobats, jugglers and performing animals completed the programme.

The circus came to Sweden in 1787, and to Finland, in the form of Jean Lustre's stunt riders, in 1802. From then on, as a result of the great magnetic power of St Petersburg, circus troupes travelled continually across Finland and back. There were fine performances throughout the 19th century in Turku, Helsinki and Viipuri.

The famous circus run by the brothers Jean Baptiste and Pierre Louis Fouraux visited Finland in 1828, followed in 1831 by Christoph de Bach and in 1840 by Didier Gautier. The real breakthrough came with Karl Magnus Hinné, whose circus visited Helsinki three times between 1858 and 1871. On his last visit, temporary wooden buildings were erected for the performances, and the music was provided by a 26-piece orchestra. There were more than a hundred artists, and about sixty horses. Thoroughbred horses could be admired freely in their stables, and the enthusiasm of Helsinki citizens reached extraordinary proportions. Later, the director of the St Petersburg circus, the Italian Gaetano Ciniselli, became the Helsinki favourite, visiting Helsinki many times in the late 19th century. Ciniselli's circus artists were skilful and well-known. Through them, Finland also participated in technical fashions. Scipione

The Circus Hinné arrives in Helsinki, October 1871

Ciniselli presented a water pantomime in Helsinki on 5 June 1891, the first of its kind in the Nordic countries. The time was favourable to the circus, which was generally successful. Transport could be arranged conveniently either by sea or by rail.

Ciniselli's circus did not have the monopoly of the Russian market. Performances by Maximiliano Truzzi's circus company were also seen in Finland in 1885–1894. This last, longish, visit is preserved in the annals through the merits of Anatoli Durov – he participated in the programme both as a well-groomed clown and as the famous organiser of the rats' train-ride.

There could be unfortunate encounters between different circus troupes. It is extraordinary that Helsinki citizens could, in the autumn of 1887, simultaneously follow performances by the circuses of Paul Busch and Albert Schumann. These were European stars, even if Schumann's career was only beginning. Competition for audiences was, of course, merciless, and in this connection Schumann resorted for the first time to wrestling matches. This appealed to the robust Finns to such an extent that the real circus acts were in danger of being overshadowed by the contestants' trials of strength.

Finnish circus activity was also beginning. In the summer of 1896, the brothers Carl and John Ducander founded their own company, which toured Finland and travelled in the summer of 1897 to Tallinn. It never returned to Finland, but continued to Odessa, Constantinople and, in 1899, to Copenhagen, where bankruptcy was unavoidable. Carl Ducander nevertheless returned to Helsinki to organise regular circus visits.

A number of obstacles to the success of the circus began to accumulate, most importantly the advent of cinema as a popular entertainment. The outbreak of the First World War in 1914, too, set steep limits on the crossing of borders. In Europe, circus activity withered and shrank. Even the end of the war did not bring back the golden age.

In the case of Finland, the situation became more difficult after the country became independent in 1917. The eastern border closed, and Finland lost its favourable position on the itinerary to what was now Petrograd. War tax was made into an entertainments tax, and conditions for the circus became poor. Only after the Second World War did new and comparatively favourable conditions open up. Trolle Rhodin's Swedish circus and the Danish Brothers Schmidt were surprisingly successful in the late 1940s. The Sirkus Sariola, founded with the 1952 Olympic games in mind, suffered a sore disappointment, and went bankrupt.

In recent years conditions for circus performances have been, with the abolishment of the entertainments tax, reasonably good. There have been visits from Russia and the Nordic countries; standards have been variable, but much has been on offer. A positive development is represented by the Sirkus Finlandia, with its director Carl-Gustaf Jernström, which has for a couple of decades toured Finland.

In the 1990s, the state of the circus has remained weak. The great tradition has been conveyed to Finns largely through the television. A change in atmosphere is, however, anticipated through the enthusiasm among children and young people for traditional circus skills. A number of circus schools have been opened in the country, in which young people practise acrobatics, juggling, clowning and magic. The performances of these schools, directed at children, are popular, and thus the circus seems to be preparing a comeback as an interesting part of Finnish children's culture. SH

classical music The first stylistic period in Finnish musical history that can really bear comparison to developments in central Europe was classicism, which took place at the end of the period of Swedish rule (–1809). The first composers stepped into the limelight – best-known among them Bernhard Henrik Crusell (1775–1838), whose clarinet concertos still form part of the instrument's central repertoire. Public concerts began in the then capital, Turku, in the 1770s, but after the Great Fire of 1827 musical life shifted to the new capital, Helsinki. Frederick Pacius (1809–1891), the German-born 'father of Finnish music', emerged as a central figure, and composed the first Finnish opera, *Kaarle kuninkaan metsästys* ('The hunting of King Charles', 1852), and the Finnish national anthem, *Maamme* ('Our land', 1848). It was not until the end of the century, however, that the classical-romantic tradition received peculiarly Finnish overtones. In 1882 the first full-scale symphony orchestra (the present-day Helsinki Philharmonic Orchestra)was founded in Helsinki, and a music school (now the Sibelius Academy) was established. Both were of great importance in the career of ▶Jean Sibelius.

The national awakening, the ▶*Kalevala* and ▶Karelianism influenced Sibelius's early work. This period, characterised as *Kalevala* romanticism, includes the *Kullervo* symphony (1892), with which the 'Finnish tone' is considered to have been found, the *En Saga*, *Karelia* and *Lemminkäinen* suites and the first two symphonies. The works composed between 1903 and 1919 are in the European classical style (the violin concerto, the string quartet *Voces intimae* and the Third, Fourth and Fifth Symphonies). The works of the 1920s, the music for *The Tempest*, *Tapiola* and the Sixth and Seventh Symphonies are marked by the universality of their style. *Finlandia* (1899) has become one of the most important symbols of Finnish identity. With the exception of the Fourth Symphony, Sibelius did not approach the central European modernism of his time; his music remained tonal. His music's tonal façade – together with the nationalist character of his early work – for a long time hindered appreciation of his contribution as a developer of the Beethovenian symphonic tradition. Although Sibelius has long been probably history's best-known Finn, his music has not gained as firm a foothold in central Europe as it has in Britain and the United States.

Sibelius's status in Finland has always been incomparable: his music has been performed more than all other Finnish music put together. Indeed, it has often been remarked that the Finnish concert-giving institutions and the media have, between them, allowed Sibelius's shadow to fall over even the creative Finnish composition that is not stylistically in any way indebted to Sibelius. Only new Finnish ▶opera has from time to time achieved a similar position in the limelight.

Sibelius's stylistic shadow was cast essentially on the subsequent generation, which continued in the spirit of national romanticism. Nevertheless, these composers of whom the most notable are the symphonic and operatic composers Erkki Melartin (1876–1937) and Leevi Madetoja (1887–1947), and the composer of piano and vocal music Selim Palmgren (1878–1948) show both non-Sibelian stylistic influences (including impressionism) and personal tones of voice. The extensive song *oeuvre* of Yrjö Kilpinen (1892–1959), associated with the German Lied tradition, was born at a distance from the mainstreams of the time, but gave its composer an internationally prominent position. At present Kilpinen is neglected, while the works of the national romantics are much recorded.

The active recording of the 1990s (particularly by the Finlandia, Ondine and Bis labels) has drawn attention – in addition to the music of our own time – to the works of the modernists of the 1920s, which had almost been forgotten. The composers of operatic and orchestral music Väinö Raitio (1891–1945) and Aarre Merikanto (1893–1958) wrote in an expressionist-impressionist style which at times approached atonality. Merikanto's opera *Juha* (1922) suffered the fate of the modernist, and was not performed until 40 years after it had been completed, at which point it was raised to the status of a national opera, alongside Madetoja's *Pohjalaisia* ('The Ostrobothnians', 1924).

From the 1930s to the 1950s, Finnish music was dominated by a Stravinsky-influenced neo-classicism to which even the modernists of the 1920s adapted. Most popular was Uuno Klami (1900–1961) with his orchestral fresco, the *Kalevala* suite. The generation that followed the Second World War also made its appearance in the name of neo-classicism. Among the most important works of the period are the first two, Shostakovitch-influenced, symphonies by Einar Englund (born 1914). The early chamber music of ►Joonas Kokkonen (1921–1996) was inspired by Bártok's motif technique, while the inspiration for Merikanto's students ►Einojuhani Rautavaara (born 1928) and Usko Meriläinen (born 1930) came from Stravinsky's rhythm and colourful instrumentation.

With the exception of Englund, the entire new generation went through a 12-tone period, which lasted until the mid 1960s. For many decades the leading figures of modernism were ►Erik Bergman (born 1911), who developed his own primitive aleatoric and colouristic style in the 1970s, and Paavo Heininen (born 1938) who, after a dodecaphonic period, became the main representative of the post-serial style, after Meriläinen.

While Bergman, Meriläinen and Heininen continued the modernist tradition in the 1970s, many other composers, including Kokkonen and Rautavaara, returned to tonality, a kind of neo-romanticism. At the end of the 1960s Finnish music saw on the one hand a restoration of the traditional values of beauty, and on the other the advent of pluralism, which permitted the combination of very different stylistic effects and borrowings within the same piece. In addition to Rautavaara, such a 'post-modern' style has characterised the work of, among others, Kalevi Aho (born 1949) who, with his ten symphonies, has emerged as his generation's most notable representative of this.

The period no longer characterised by a uniformly modernist style has been favourable to ►opera. With Joonas Kokkonen's *Viimeiset kiusaukset* (*The Last Temptations*, 1975) and *Ratsumies* (*The Horseman*, 1974) by ►Aulis Sallinen (born 1935), a veritable opera boom took place in Finnish musical life in 1975. In addition to Sallinen's five freely tonal operas, there have also been modernist (Heininen, Bergman) and pluralist (Rautavaara) operas.

With Merikanto and Kokkonen, Heininen has been one of Finland's best-known teachers of composition. From his class come the most interna-

Live music: the midsummer music festival at Porvoo Summer Sounds, the Avanti! Chamber Orchestra conducted by Esa-Pekka Salonen tionally successful composers of the younger generation, ►Kaija Saariaho (born 1952) and ►Magnus Lindberg (born 1958), for whom computer technology opened the way to, among other things, the organisation of the inner change of large tonal surfaces. They belonged to the radical Korvat auki ('Ears open') performance group of the early 1980s; other members included ►Esa-Pekka Salonen (born 1958) who has subsequently risen to world fame as a conductor, and Jouni Kaipainen (born 1956), whose current symphonic architecture leans heavily on tradition.

Composition in Finland has a very strong social status. Among active composers of serious music, about a third have been favoured with commissions and government bursaries – in other words, they have been able to practise their profession almost full-time. Since the 1960s, musical life has also strengthened significantly in other ways. The network of music schools giving basic instruction has increased explosively (around 150 schools around the country), and the professional training previously available only at the Sibelius Academy in Helsinki can now be enjoyed in 11 conservatories. Dozens of different music festivals have filled the Finnish summer, the number of large symphony orchestras has grown to five, and Finnish singers and conductors, in particular, have risen to world fame. MH

coat of arms ►national symbols

climate With the publication in 1539, in Venice, of his map *Carta Marina* and the written description appended to it, Olaus Magnus (1490–1557), the last Roman Catholic archbishop of Sweden-Finland, announced to the world that the North is the home of extreme cold. Magnus believed in Aristotle's doctrine that the fauna and peoples of the cold regions are more hardy and courageous than others. As an example, he cited the fact that falcons from the North are sought after because they are more pugnacious than the falcons of the South. Magnus depicted all human activities in Finland against a background of a stern and wild nature, frost, snow and ice. By its

The open road: extremes of climate have their effect on Finnish life and character

location, Finland is indeed a northern country which thanks to the Gulf Stream possesses more favourable conditions than its latitudes would otherwise permit. The matter can also be expressed in a more scientific fashion. Finland belongs to a climatic region of snow and forests with damp, cold winters, in which the average temperature of the warmest month of the year is over +10 °C and of the coldest, lower than –3 °C. Another peculiarity of this climate is that rainfall may occur in every month and that the region always has a short 'real' summer and winter. Above the treeline in the fell region of northern Finland there is also the so-called 'tundra' climate.

Finland's climatic characteristics and the climatic differences between its regions are influenced by three principal factors: its situation on intermediate degrees of latitude, the relatively warm North Atlantic with its Gulf Stream to the west, and the great continent of Asia to the east. Finland's location on intermediate degrees of latitude means that the country lies in the path of cyclones moving from west to north-east. Thus it typically has changeable and unstable weather. In addition, Finland is situated on the so-called polar front – the dividing line between a cold-air mass originating in the polar regions and a warmer, subtropical air-mass. The movements of this front are reflected in the weather.

When the front moves over Finland in a southerly direction, cold, clear polar air comes to the country. But when the front moves in a more northerly direction, the air becomes warmer and moister.

The second principal factor influencing Finland's climate – the North Atlantic, warmed by the Gulf Stream – is experienced by the whole of Nordic countries during the winter. Because of this, southern Finland has an average January temperature some ten degrees higher than points at the same northerly latitude in other parts of the globe.

The third important factor is the influence of the great continent to the east. Because of it, Finland may experience long spells of severe frost in winter and correspondingly hot spells in summer. KRn

coffee According to statistics, Finns are, along with Swedes, among the world's highest consumers of coffee.

Coffee became familiar first to the highest class of society at the beginning of the 18th century, then to the landed peasantry in the early 19th century; it finally became a beverage for the entire nation in the second half of the 19th century. This was, at first, a very urban phenomenon. In 1750 only 1 in 7 coffee-drinkers was from the countryside. By means of comparison, only 1 in 20 was a town-dweller.

Like alcohol consumption, or cigarette-smoking, coffee-drinking spread

Coffee oils the political machine: Jacques Delors, the President of the European Commission, and Esko Aho, then Prime Minister, in conversation in 1994 in Kokkola, north-west Finland

from the west and south to the north and east. One can hardly pay a social visit in Finland without the coffee-table being laid. The ladies, in particular, are apt to ask those who have returned from a visit about the buns, cakes and biscuits. As the use of coffee spread, a hundred years ago, the compulsory dry bun became a part of popular custom in rural areas, too. Until then, coffee bread had generally been eaten when brought as a gift from the towns. During the 19th century, the power of coffee even changed traditional eating habits, and the customary morning dram was replaced by morning coffee. Despite the advice of nutrition experts, most Finns still start their day with coffee.

The triumphal march of coffee in Finland proved irresistible. Before 1809, while Finland still formed part of the Swedish kingdom, it was banned

Traditional respite: a break for coffee while transporting tar along Oulujoki River, 1899

four times and taxed as a luxury. In the mid 19th century coffee replaced salt as the country's most important import. In terms of today's consumption, the 1819 annual figure of 25 grams per head seems ridiculous. In those days a labourer could work for three full days for a kilogram of coffee. By 1840 imports had increased sevenfold and the real price of coffee had halved.

The repeal of the British Navigation Act in 1847 freed competition in navigation, which proved to be to the advantage of Finnish coffee consumers. By 1860 a kilogram of coffee per head was being imported per year, and by 1900 the figure was more than 4 kilograms. At the beginning of the century half a day's work was necessary to buy a kilogram of coffee; today, half an hour is enough. IN

comic strip The first modern Finnish comic strip is considered to be *Professori Itikaisen tutkimusretket* ('Professor Itikainen's Study Expeditions', 1911) by Ilmari Vainio (1892–1955), a series which advanced by one picture per page. Another early example of the genre was *Janne Ankkanen,* written by Jalmari Finne (1874–1938) and drawn by Ola Fogelberg (1894–1952). This anarchistic duck commented on world events in the journal *Suomen Kuvalehti* during 1917–1918. Its publication ceased with the outbreak of the Finnish Civil War (1918). The most famous character of comics artist Ola Fogelberg is *Pekka Puupää* ('Pekka Woodenhead'), character born on the eve of 1 May 1935. Simple, hen-pecked Pekka is a central classic of Finnish comic strip. The series' affectionate popular humour is based on misadventures and the consequences of misunderstandings. *Pekka Puupää* appeared in the journal of the Finnish Co-operative Movement, *Kuluttaja* ('The Consumer', 1925–1970), and from 1943 in special annual albums that were sold in runs of up to 60,000–70,000 copies.

After Ola Fogelberg's death, the series was continued by his daughter Ruth 'Toto' Fogelberg-Kaila (born 1924) until 1976. 13 motion pictures were also made from the series, one more attempt in the 1980s. Since 1972 the Finnish Comics Society has awarded the Puupää Hat as its special prize.

The 1920s was the golden age of the Finnish comic strip. The country saw the publication of a large number of humorous magazines in which comic-strip artists emerged unhindered by competition from foreign comic strips, which had not yet come on to the Finnish market. The main 'idea-bank' was Hillari Johannes Viherjuuri (1889–1949) or Veli Giovanni, who wrote the captions for nearly all the artists and also published humorous magazines.

Kieku ja Kaiku ('Screech and Echo', 1927–1975) by Asmo Alho (1903–1975) was one of the longest-running Finnish comic-strip series. This genial animal strip discussed life in an instructive fashion, and at the same time entertained people of all ages. Its rhyming texts were for the most part written by the author ▶Mika Waltari.

With the arrival of the 1930s, American influence began to be visible. Everyday humour gave way to adventure, comic strips became more action-packed and the text moved from below the pictures into speech-bubbles above the characters' heads. The most prolific comic-strip artist of the period was Ami Hauhio (1912–1955). During the Second World War, Hauhio published strips featuring vigilant border guards and heroic airmen in tune with the spirit of the time. In 1947 war moved into space in the beautifully drawn album *Maan mies Marsissa* ('Earth man on Mars'). Kari Suomalainen (born 1920), later known as a political cartoonist, produced in 1942–1944 the Western strip series *Henkensä kaupalla* ('At risk to life').

In 1949 the first comics magazines appeared, mostly containing foreign work. At the same time, the homespun Finnish alternative also began to disappear from the comic-strip pages of the newspapers. The American comic was something new and fascinating in Finland's traditionally German-oriented culture. It was also less expensive than the domestic variety.

Joonas (1950–1972), by Veikko Savolainen (born 1929), combined humour and adventure in an elegantly realistic personal drawing style. The series also appeared in various German newspapers during the 1950s under the title *Jonas – der lustige Maler*.

The most famous Finnish comic

Ilmari Vainio:
Professori Itikainen
('Professor Itikainen')

Ola Fogelberg:
Pekka Puupää
('Pekka Woodenhead')

Veikko Savolainen:
Joonas

Tarmo Koivisto:
Mämmilä

Erkki Tanttu:
Rymy-Eetu

Asmo Alho:
Kieku ja Kaiku
('Screech and Echo')

Riitta Uusitalo:
Hyvissä naimisissa
('In good marriage')

Kati Kovács:
Vihreä rapsodia
('Green rapsody')

Series of stamps issued in celebration of the hundredth anniversary of the Finnish comic strip, 1996

strip is the fairytale-like ▶Moomin series by ▶Tove Jansson (born 1914), based on her own books. During the period 1954–1960, Tove Jansson produced it for the *London Evening News*, which distributed it to over 40 countries and over 100 newspapers. Tove Jansson's brother Lars Jansson (born 1926) continued the series until 1975. In the 1990s the Finnish-born Dennis Livson produced a Moomin animation and feature film which was shown in several countries. At the same time the comic strip was begun anew. The new Moomin series, designed by an international team, was distributed abroad as a comic magazine, album or newspaper strip.

At the beginning of the 1970s, underground art aroused new interest in the comic strip. During Veikko Savolainen's editorship of the all-Finnish magazine *Sarjis* (1972–1974), many subsequently well-known comics-strip artists made their initial debut. The subjects chosen now extended to cover politics and everyday life. In 1971, the Finnish Comics Society was formed.

In 1975 the new flagship of Finnish comic strip was launched – *Mämmilä*, designed by Tarmo Koivisto (born 1948). *Mämmilä* is a depiction of a vil-lage, without the traditional heroes. The leading role in the series is played by the community as a whole, the changes that affect it, the human relationships within it and the reflection on it of the events of the time. *Mämmilä* gives an accurate mirror-image of Finnish society, showing its ups and downs. Koivisto's realistic drawing style also adds a sense of authenticity. The series, which appeared in the monthly supplement of *Helsingin Sanomat* until the end of 1996, had almost a million readers. Kari Leppänen (born 1945) began his career in *Sarjis*, and quickly became a professional comics artist, designing international series. He also produced work for the magazine *Mustanaamio* ('Phantom') and also his own science fiction stories. Mauri Kunnas (born 1950), well-known as an author of children's books, also began as a comics artist. He produced the thriller parody *Kotlant Jaarti* ('Scotland Yard', 1974) and the rock spoof *Nyrok City* (1975–1985). The multi-faceted work of Timo Mäkelä (born 1951) is characterised by unusually skilful drawing and vitality of line-style.

Näkymätön Viänänen ('Viänänen the invisible', from 1973), designed by newspaper strip writer Jorma Pitkänen (born 1947), is an ironic story about a poor man from a development region who is completely invisible to the fine folk of Helsinki. The work of Harri Waalio (born 1956), which has also been published in Germany, extends in range from children's comics to adult humour. Jukka Murtosaari (born 1963) is a professional strip writer who has designed covers for Disney magazines, Moomin comics and many original series of his own.

The rise of the new wave of music in the late 1970s and early 1980s saw the birth of dozens of privately-funded magazines that gave strip writers a new venue for their work, one that was independent of commercial publishers. Little magazines have remained important recruiting channels for new talent.

Comic strips are also used in education and public announcements. Ari Kutila (born 1961) and Keijo Ahlqvist (born 1955), from the northern Finnish City of Kemi, have specialised in utility strips. In 1985 Kemi published its official municipal annual report as a comic-strip album designed by Ahlqvist, while Kutila's work includes a comics cookbook. Kemi also holds the Kemi Arctic Comics Festival every March.

The artist Riitta Uusitalo (born 1960) makes comic strips that break with old traditions, while the idiosyncratic Rome-based Kati Kovács (born 1963) emerged from the pages of the women's comic strip magazine *Naarassarjat* ('Women comic strips', 1992–1993). The magazine was founded by Johanna Rojola (born 1970) who has studied comics-making in France. Her work is often based on women's issues.

Modern Finnish comics are a complex field, in which there is no one single trend or grouping, but rather several. It covers all kinds of genres, from children's stories to adventure comics and comics soap operas. The dominant feature of the 1990s is the interest of the comics makers in pictorial art – many now have a background in art studies, and there is an abundance of foreign influences.

In 1996 a series of eight postage stamps was published, presenting the Finnish comic strip. The series was designed by the versatile comics artist Pentti Otsamo (born 1967). From be-ing a marginal area of Finnish culture, the comic strip has evolved into an established part of it. HJ

constitution Finland has a written constitution. Of the constitutional legislation, the most important items are the Constitutional Act of 17 July 1919 and the Parliament Act of 1928. According to these, Finland is a republic in which a parliament elected in a public, equal and secret ballot (from 1906) deploys supreme, or legislative, power. For Finland's citizens the constitution defines the basic rights that have been developed since the declaration of human rights of the great French revolution. According to the classical tripartite division of power, supreme jurisdiction belongs to an independent court of justice and executive power to the president and the government. The government is accountable to the parliament.

A special feature of Finnish constitutional laws is the extensive powers accorded to the president. According to the Constitutional Act, he alone 'determines' Finland's relations with foreign powers, appoints governments, judges, university professors and higher civil servants, and has the power, on the advice of the Prime Minister, to dissolve governments. He can also grant unlimited pardons to criminals. The president is elected for a term of six years. Re-election for one further term is possible. The last-mentioned limitation was instituted after the long term served by President Urho Kaleva Kekkonen (president 1956–1981).

The dominance of the president in Finland's constitution is a consequence of the Civil War of 1918. The winning side – 'white' Finland – made Finland a monarchy, but after the defeat of Germany in the First World War it was forced to abandon its plans after complaints about both the planned monarchy and the German prince it had chosen as king. The United States of America and Great Britain refused to recognise Finland unless it instituted a democratic system. Thus, in 1917 Finland, newly independent from Russia, became a republic in which, to counteract the power of parliament, the office of president was invested with considerable power.

Walter Runeberg, Lex statue, 1894. The statue, which symbolises patriotism and the Constitution, shows Finland protecting herself with the shield of the Constitution, and is located in the state room of the president's palace in central Helsinki

The president's exercise of power has been more evident since the Second World War than before, and reached its height with the terms of office of Urho Kekkonen. This was because the president, as sovereign director of his country's foreign policy, channelled the strength of the major powers – first Germany, then the Soviet Union – into use in support of his exercise of internal power. The collapse of the Soviet Union in the 1990s instigated a development in a different direction. The president's prerogatives have been decreased, although for the time being only to a very limited extent. The power of parliament has simultaneously been increased by decreasing the regulations for two-thirds majorities and increasing the use of simple majorities in decision-making.

Finland is a democratic system on the west European model supported by a system reliant on a strong head of state on the east European model. HY

crafts ▶fashion, folk art, folk costume, ryijy, textiles

cultural and research institutes
▶Finnish cultural and research institutes

customs Finland is an easy country for visitors. Its customs and etiquette are European, but their observance is not strictly applied. Details of behaviour are seen as a matter of individual choice and, in part, of personality, irrespective of whether they have the blessing of tradition or the arbiters of taste. No Finnish politician or public personality has seen his reputation suffer because of a lack of manners. The differing social customs of foreigners are viewed with understanding and occasional amusement, but the foreigner does not find himself in the position of committing errors of social conduct that could be fatal.

The 1960s student radicals wanted freedom from traditional customs. The German-Scandinavian social culture that dominated student life broke down and changed into 'new informality', which was linked with a conscious opposition to social norms. Many postgraduates quickly adopted the generally accepted student uniform of jeans and sweater. Participation in official academic degree ceremonies was not considedered important, and doctors' caps were not worn. It is obvious that this generation has found it hard in its old age to commit itself to those forms of traditional behaviour that are required, for example, by contacts of an international kind. Among the younger generation, current trends seem to be ousting the kind of conservative stylishness that is represented by traditional social customs. Exeptions are the ▶Finland-Swedish, whose traditions, especially those connected with celebrations, still live on.

The ideology of 'new informality' was also characterised by the replacement of the formal *Te* (You) form of address with the familiar *sinä* form, a feature which – in many respects intenced by the Swedish equivalent – soon spread to the whole population. The reversion to the *Te* form which began in the early 1990s (also in the universities) is slow, and the use of the *sinä* form does not on the whole encounter resistance or protest. A transition to the use of Christian names soon after an acquaintance has been formed is now usual, especially if the parties concerned consider that they are meeting within the context of an ongoing work or special interest situation. In large companies and concerns it is a general rule that employees address each other as *sinä* higher management included. The 'dropping of formalities' is an attractive and now increasingly rarely encountered custom, in which, with a toast of friendship, a closer acquaintance is strengthened.

The minor details of behaviour and the conventions of physical contact are of North European and, less frequently, Eastern origin. When greeting, a Finn shakes hands and considers it important that the handshake be relatively firm. He does not embrace his companions nor – especially if he is a man – kiss them (the hugging and kissing that necessarily became an important part of the meeting of politicians during the Soviet era was viewed by ordinary Finns with negative amusement or slight irritation). In conversation the Finns looks his partner in the eye and likes to keep a distance of at least half a metre between himself and the other person. Finns are not very 'touch-oriented': their handshakes are short and their greetings are not accompanied by other reinforcing contacts. A Finnish man raises his hat when greeting acquaintances in the street, especially women, and he usually removes his hat when in the same lift as women. Some men open the door for women and old people; but in buses or trams women and old people are offered seats increasingly rarely.

At the meal table the Finn uses a knife and fork (the fork in the left hand). In general, he waits for the host to raise his glass before taking a first sip from his own; after this, he drinks whenever he wants to. From time to time he raises his glass to drink a toast with his neighbour: he looks the other in the eye, drinks, looks a second time, nods slightly and then puts down his glass. This Swedish custom is followed especially when drinking schnaps, and when performing the 'dropping of formalities'.

Finnish ▶sauna culture naturally has its own etiquette. In order to understand it, it is best for the visitor to consult a Finnish sauna companion (and prepare himself for a longish lecture). It is as well to remember, however, that since the philosophy of the sauna is internalised, Finns are of the opinion that in the sauna each person follows his own rhythm and listens to the voice within his own body in order to receive the most enjoyment from the sauna experience. Foreigners often remark that the sauna is the one place where the normally taciturn Finns become talkative and, in their praise of the sauna, almost eloquent; at the same time, these normally closed human beings display an unusual, sometimes even startling openness.

The taciturn Finn may now be a somewhat outdated stereotype, but it is true that the Finnish attitude to speech and words is an unusual one. In Finland, words have a greater weight that in many other cultures; Finns take words seriously. To interrupt someone is considered impertinent, while loquacity is viewed with suspicion; many consider this Finnish attitude an advantage: 'a word spoken is a message delivered' – Finns mean what they say and keep their promises. Silence and pauses in conversation are not viewed as awkward, but as part of normal communication.

The equality of the sexes puts its mark on many aspects of Finnish social customs. Male chauvinist or condescending attitudes towards women are viewed as bad manners, although such attitudes are much in evidence. Women like to be treated with the politeness prescribed by traditional etiquette, but in the last analysis judge men's manners according to the extent to which they reflect attitudes of equality. In money matters women are independent and often wish to take part in, say, the payment of restaurant bills. The man does not necessarily have to consent to this. OA

dance The history of stage dancing in Finland begins in the 20th century. Unlike Sweden and Russia, Finland did not have a royal court that might have influenced the birth and development of dance. Although Finnish culture began to grow in the 19th century, during the period of Russian rule, it was not until the 1920s, after Finland had gained its independence, that the development of dance began in earnest. Until then, dance was essentially a matter for visiting Russian and central European performers.

Finnish dance developed under a combination of influences from East and West. The proximity of St Petersburg influenced the birth and development of classical ballet. The important teachers of classical ballet of the turn of the century came from St Petersburg, and the first generation of Finnish professional ballet dancers also studied in the Russian capital. German physical culture and stage expressionism, on the other hand, appealed to those interested in modernist directions. Their popularity led to so-called free dance, which imitated the plastic models of the classical period.

A strong impulse was given to Finnish dance at the beginning of the 20th century by two important visits. In 1905 the American pioneer of free dance, Isadora Duncan, appeared at the Finnish National Theatre, followed, in 1908, by the ballet of the St Petersburg Mariinsky Theatre, with Anna Pavlova as its brightest star. The Finnish organiser of the Russian visit was the concert manager Edvard Fazer (1861–1943), who became the founder and director of the Finnish Opera. In 1921 he gathered a group of professional dancers together with the best students of the Helsinki ballet schools, with the intention of performing the ballet classic *Swan Lake*. The performance, in 1922, was a turning point, and marked the beginning of regular ballet performances.

Inspired by Isadora Duncan, in 1918, the young Finnish art student Maggie Gripenberg (1881–1976) went to Switzerland and Germany to study dance. Gripenberg became a pioneer of modern dance in Finland. She was the first person to choreograph the music of ▶Sibelius and in 1939, won a choreography competition in Brussels in 1939. Influences from German modernism (Mary Wigman) and stage expressionism (Harold Kreutzberg, Kurt Jooss) entered Finnish dance through Gripenberg's students.

The repertoire of the St Petersburg Mariinsky Theatre formed the basis and model for Finnish ballet up to the Second World War. The ballet masters of the early years were the dancers George Gé and Alexander Saxelin, both of whom had studied in St Petersburg. In the 1930s Gé created the first neo-classical and modern ballets on the model of Diaghilev's Ballets Russes. A third important Finnish ballet master was Elsa Sylverstersson (born 1924), who created her extensive and diverse *oeuvre* between the 1950s and the 1970s. The Russian influence on Finnish ballet continued, and it was only in the 1980s that Western influ-

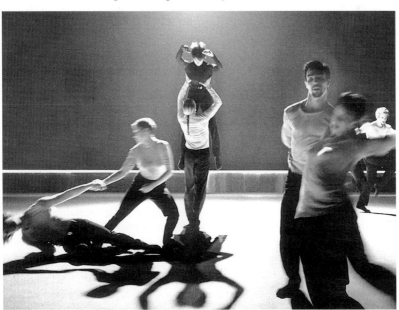

Kenneth Kvarnström, *no-no,* choreography Kenneth Kvarnström, Helsinki City Theatre ences really made their breakthrough, with works by, among others, George Balanchine, Jiri Kylian, Mats Ek and ▶Jorma Uotinen

The slow revival of ballet can be partly explained by the lukewarm attitude of public and critics to the modern dance that first made its appearance in the 1960s. The firebrand of Finnish modernism was Riitta Vainio (born 1936), who had studied in Philadelphia and who began, in the early 1960s, to train the young generation of dancers and to arrange performances. Vainio was ahead of her time as both teacher and choreographer and modernism was generally appreciated only by people from the circles of the visual arts and contemporary music. A kind of dance realism, often dealing with the role of poor people and women from literary base, developed as a counter-reaction to modernism. The most important name in this realistic dance drama of the 1970s was Marjo Kuusela (born 1946), who did important work – her choreography included *Väki ilman valtaa* ('People without power') and *Salka Valka* – as artistic director of the Raatikko Dance Theatre, which she founded, and as a visiting choreographer with the Finnish National Ballet, where her productions included a dance version of ▶Aleksis Kivi's novel *Seitsemän veljestä* (*The Seven Brothers*, 1980).

Influential in the rise of contemporary dance in the 1980s was Jorma Uotinen, a Finn who had danced in the experimental group directed by Carolyn Carlson at the Paris Opera. He began to direct the dance group of Helsinki City Theatre in 1980. An additional influence was the founding of a Department of Dance at the Theatre Academy in 1983. Few choreographers emerged from the Finnish National Ballet, but many came from the very first course held by the Department of Dance.

The 1980s were a decade of breakthrough for the young European-oriented generation of dancers. Many Finnish dancers studied in the Netherlands, absorbing the so-called 'soft techniques' of dance. This young dance characterised by violence, fear and loneliness expressed the feelings of its time. The physical tendency in

dance never became as predominant in Finland as, say, in France, Belgium and Britain. A genuine representative of violent physicality, however, is ▶Kenneth Kvarnström, who studied and began his career in Sweden – his personal language of movement includes influences from Asiatic fighting techniques and rock 'n' roll.

The influence of the Japanese *buto* dance tradition has been strong in the 1990s. Ari Tenhula (born 1964), who has studied in Japan and India, has been influenced by the cultures of Asia, as has Arja Raatikainen (born 1958), who has, in her solo works, also sought the shamanist tradition. Other strong women choreographers include Sanna Kekäläinen (born 1962) and Kirsi Monni (born 1962) both of whom have bravely examined the problems of existence as a human being and a woman in their works. Tero Saarinen (born 1964), an internationally successful dancer and choreographer, has created a distinctive mode of expression, related on the one hand to Samuel Beckett's theatre of the absurd and on the other to silent film comedians and clowns' humour.

In folk dance circles, the 1990s have seen the birth of the so-called new folk dance as a parallel phenomenon to the new folk music. This has focussed attention once more on national characteristics, now interpreted from the often urban perspective of today. Just as urban culture absorbs very diverse international influences, urban folk dance combines often conflicting foreign elements with the Finnish tradition. AR

death In ancient Finnish folk belief, death received, through a sense of transgenerational community, positive overtones. In rituals surrounding death, the departure of an individual took on a cosmic framework which articulated the unique event as part of the cycles of nature. Activities associated with death followed the setting of the sun, the cycle of the moon and the changing of the year. They were timed in such a way that everyone had to be present: the deceased was to be in his or her grave before sunset, or – based on the mythic model of the time between Good Friday and Easter Sunday

Countless candles light the graves at Hietaniemi Cemetery in Helsinki every Christmas Eve

– at least within three days of death. After six weeks, in ►Karelia, came the *kuusnetäliset*, the 'six weeks' provender, recalling the period spent by Christ on Earth before his ascension to heaven. The ►calendar year still has days of remembrance dedicated to the dead in spring and autumn.

For a year after his or her death, the person was a *vainaja* ('deceased'), without individuality or a given name, which the people of old subsequently avoided using. A year was, in Finnish society, the most important milestone; the period of mourning, during which a widow was not allowed to marry or amusements to be enjoyed in the house of mourning. Finnish ►revivalist movements cultivated the habit of meeting for remembrance on the one-year anniversary of death, even when these meetings were forbidden by law, and through them this beautiful tradition has survived to this day.

Encounters with the dead in dreams were expected during the time of mourning, and subsequently feared. The rituals of death aimed at the success of social transference, so that 'the dead would not walk at home'. A flock of waxwings in the rowan tree at home was evidence of a successful crossing of the border. (According to tradition, it was best to return in the form of a bird).

The culture of death was at first different in different parts of Finland, but in the 19th century it became part of the overall Lutheran culture. Differences in the culture of death have survived for ecological and historical reasons. One important ecological factor is connected with the forests and waters of eastern Finland. The eastern distant graveyard is part of the belief-system of the hunting and fishing culture and its mobile way of life, while the western graveyard, close to the village, speaks of the world-view of an agrarian culture that has already settled down.

The old, eastern Finnish tradition was to mark the borderline between village and church, living and dead, by carving a cross and initial on a rowan tree on the path along which the body was carried, in memory of the person whose memorial tree or cross-rowan it was. The memorial tree was a marker which the dead person was not allowed to pass. The eastern Finnish tradition tells of dead people who leave their graves to go home, but return to the graveyard having seen the cross and the mark.

The eastern burial ground gradually became a graveyard, which had in the west been the resting place of the dead since the Middle Ages – first under the church, and then inside it. In the east, graves were long marked with the wooden cross that was the symbol of the Finnish forest culture. This was only gradually displaced by the western gravestone, first for the clergy and persons of rank, then for everyone.

In western graveyards, the more high-ranking the family, the closer the graves are to the church. The wooden cross of the eastern tradition was more egalitarian in terms of both the living and the dead: it disappeared in around the same time as the memory of the person at whose feet it stood. The eastern Finnish tradition reflects a thought that belongs to the Finnish world-view: A person lives as long as he is remembered.

Death had its own grammar in Finland: a vocabulary, the mastery of portents and marks, beliefs, stories and customs. Laments were sacral poetry through which the eastern Finns interpreted death, the journey to the other side and the interaction which the poetry of death is at its profoundest. The lament brought a liberated anarchy to grief as the keener set the pace for each individual's grief. Lullabies of death are known only in Finland and Estonia.

The tradition of death, which also appears in the ►Kalevala, formed a 'book of death' which was passed from one generation to the next. The epic of death tells of the heroes' journeys beyond the Tuonelanjoki River, to cold Pohjola, the underground Manala, the other side or heaven.

The vocabulary of death is the oldest layer in the Finnic languages. The original terminology of the soul of the Finno-Ugrians reflects their conceptions of life and death.

Behind the Finnish tradition of self-destruction or suicide lies, partially, the mythic model of voluntary death that is prevalent in Nordic cultures. This is the right accorded to heroes to determine the way to go, when and where. The Kalevala ends with the judgment of Väinämöinen, in which the hero's death is the exceptional departure of the shaman.

Just as the vocabulary of death is among the oldest layers in the Finnish language, customs associated with death are among the most central elements in the Finnish world-view. Finns' beliefs, attitudes and behaviour in relation to death are still bound by tradition, and they are seldom able to verbalise, still less justify, how and why.

The tradition, in other words, is still primarily part of the mental landscape, but it can also be seen in the cultural landscape, in graveyards, customs and words.

In the family, kinship and village communities of former times, death was a shared experience which had a meaning that supported the community. This culture of death began to change after the industrialisation, urbanisation and emigration that followed the Second World War. Particularly during the accelerating changes of the 1960s and 1970s, links with ecological roots in home parishes were severed, as were the transgenerational links of family and kin in which the Finnish culture of death had its being. The disappearance of many customs, for example viewing the body, expresses the fears of a generation that 'denies death' that it is passing on its own lack of values to its children. The shifting of death from homes to outside life, to the intensive care units of hospitals, is an expression of this. When death visited traditional communities, the entire house and village participated.

Contemporary Finnish culture shows signs of a fumbling towards lost transgenerational roots, for example in the increased habit of family visits to graveyards on Christmas Eve and All Souls' Day to light candles on graves. A peculiarly Finnish cult is attached to the remembrance of military graves on the Day of the Fallen. The military grave at Hietaniemi in Helsinki, centred on the tomb of ►C.G.E. Mannerheim, is a sacred space for a national cult. War veterans play a central part in preserving the cult, through military graves throughout the country and memorials to red and white casualties of the Civil War of 1918. Observing the principle that 'a brother does not abandon his brother', they honour every veteran's funeral with their presence. JPn

design The foundations of Finnish design were laid in the last decades of the 19th century. The liberalisation of economic life and the development of various manufacturing methods demanded by mass production led, in Finland as elsewhere, to rapid industrial growth in the 19th century. The period of Russian rule (1809–1917) was, from Finland's point of view, a time of steady growth. The traditional guild system was no longer suitable to these changed conditions. In Finland, the legislation governing professional activity was repealed in 1864. The reforms, which had the effect of encouraging entrepreneurship, also had their drawbacks. The obligatory master-apprentice relationship was severed, and skills were seen to decline in many areas. Parties concerned about the standard of object-production soon began to organise education and training for both factory workers and designers.

In the field of design, this led to measures that were to have far-reaching consequences. The Sculpture School (now the University of Art and Design) was founded in 1871 to provide education for designers and professionals in the area. A teaching collection was initiated; its first objects were bought directly from the Vienna world exhibition of 1873. Two years later, the Finnish Society of Crafts and Design was founded to support both the school and the museum; its primary task, particularly during the years of reconstruction that followed the Second World War, was the promotion of Finnish design throughout the world. In 1874 what was to become one of the most important factories of Finnish design, ▶Arabia, displayed its first products. Two years later, in 1876, Finland's first exhibition of art and industrial design was held in Kaivopuisto Park, Helsinki, and the Friends of Finnish Handicraft, founded on the initiative of Fanny Churberg (1845–1892), began its activities in 1879: its ideological aim was the revival of the Finnish handicraft tradition and the development of an independent 'Finnish style'.

Raising the standard of industry was linked to the project of raising Finland to the status of a nation among nations, and Finland was represented for the first time by its own pavilion as early as the Paris World Exhibition of 1889. Finding an independent 'Finnish style', however, occurred only in the following decade, in the form of national romanticism, which was based on the international influences of the time, the English Arts and Crafts movement and the continental *Art Nouveau* style, also including a great many designer-specific elements. In the applied arts in Finland, the turn of the century developed into a golden age for which it is difficult to find a subsequent equivalent. In addition to designers with a training in the applied arts, artists and architects became interested, in the spirit of the time, in designing objects in the spirit of the ideology of the *Gesamtkunstwerk*. At the Paris World's Fair of 1900 the Finnish pavilion attracted attention with its interior, which had been realised, according to designs by the artist ▶Akseli Gallen-Kallela, by the Friends of Finnish Handicraft and the Iris Factory. Other large-scale projects of the time which gathered the leading makers together included Tampere Cathedral (1900–1907), designed by Lars Sonck (1870–1956), and three buildings by the Gesellius-Lindgren-▶Saarinen architectural office, the headquarters for the Pohjola Insurance Company (1899–1901), the office and residence ▶Hvitträsk (1901–1903) and Suur-Merijoki mansion (1901–1903), all of which employed the skills of the versatile applied artist Eric O.W. Ehrström (1881–1934), particularly his forging and chasing work.

The early 20th century was a period of active development in Finnish design. The architect Armas Lindgren (1874–1929) became director of the School of Applied Arts in 1902, and diversified the teaching offered by the institution to include metalwork, textiles and ceramics. Industry began to collaborate with designers: in addition to ▶Louis Sparre's Iris Factory, Nikolai Boman (1871–1967) manufactured furniture according to architects' designs, and an up-to-date international contribution was made by the Billnäs Factory, which began in 1909 to manufacture American-style office furniture. The spread of electric lighting created a new need for design, and in 1908 the art forge Koru was founded by the architect Eino Schroderus (1880–1956) to specialise in the artistic design and manufacture of lighting.

Stylistically, the 1910s were, in Finnish design, a decorative post-*Jugend* period, mixed with features from classicism and the revivalist styles. The omniscience of architects that was linked to the *Jugend* idea of the work of art as a whole was called into question. It was believed that the solution to both liberation from imitative styles and the predominance of the architect could be found in specialisation. In 1911 a professional organisation, Ornamo, the Association of Finnish Designers, was founded to protect the interests of those who had received a training in the applied arts.

The period after Finland gained its independence in 1917 saw the creation of symbols for the new nation. The biggest national building project of the period was the House of Parliament (1924–1931), designed by Johan Sigfrid Sirén (1899–1961). Sirén also played a significant part in creating the interior in the spirit of classicism. Also participating in the design of furniture was Arttu Brummer (1891–1951), who was one of the most influential figures in Finnish design from the 1920s to his death. The only exception to the dignified classicism of the House of Parliament was the café, by Werner West (1890–1959), which was furnished with up-to-date tubular metal furniture in the Bauhaus style. In general, the design of the 1920s was coloured by Nordic classicism, and work was on offer to designers essentially on individual projects which were realised as high-quality hand work. Industry in the area still generally satisfied itself with traditional forms. The only exceptions were the ►Arabia Factory, which in the 1920s employed, in addition to Thure Öberg (1872–1935), two young artists, Greta-Lisa Jäderholm-Snellman (1894–1973) and Friedl Holzer-Kjellberg (1905–1993), and the Riihimäki Glass Factory, where Henry Ericsson (1898–1933) devoted himself largely to designing art glass.

The 1930s brought new winds to Finnish design. Sweden's success at the international exhibition of applied arts in Paris in 1925 shocked Finnish manufacturers, too, into understanding the advertising value and importance in competitive terms of new products designed for exhibitions. The glass factories began to hold competitions to create new designs. The Riihimäki Glass Factory organised a design competiton for cocktail glasses, and the Karhula-

Alvar Aalto, *Savoy* Vase, 1936

►Iittala factories renewed their ranges with a glass competition held in 1932, which came to mark the breakthrough of functionalism in the Finnish glass industry. For the 1936 Milan Triennale, the factories held a new competition to generate exhibition objects. The competition was won by the architect ►Alvar Aalto's famous *Savoy* vase. At the suggestion of Kurt Ekholm (1907–1975), the Arabia factory invested in new, contemporary designs and a separate art department. The new strategy began to bite, and Finnish design began to succeed in international arenas.

From the point of view of the breakthrough of functionalism, an exhibition of Finnish design held in the Helsinki Taidehalli Art Gallery in 1930 was important, with a section devoted to the rationalisation of small apartments curated by Alvar Aalto. Furniture in birch and plywood manufactured as a result of experiments in bending and moulding wood by Aalto and the manufacturer Otto Korhonen attracted international attention at the Milan triennales of 1933 and 1936, and the furniture shop ►Artek was set up to market them in 1936, with the additional aim of functioning as a centre for modern art and design. Before the Second World War, the international success of Finnish design continued at the Paris world exhibition of 1937 and the New York World Exhibition of 1939, at both of which the Finnish section was designed by Alvar Aalto.

At the beginning of the 1940s, the war put an end to attempts at innovation. The manufacture of consumer goods was hindered by the lack of raw materials, labour and buying power. Attempts were made to alleviate the material shortages by adapting available materials to the use of design. The wallpaper made of birchbark and greaseproof paper of 1942, designed by Greta Skogster-Lehtinen (1900–1994), has become a symbol of Finnish wartime design.

The promising developments of the 1930s which had been cut short by the war picked up speed in the 1950s. This was a boom period in building, and functionalist ideas were realised in practice. Small apartments set designers entirely new challenges. Standardisation, space-saving and multiplicity of use were keywords in the design of utility objects. The earthenware *Kilta* series by ▶Kaj Franck (designed in 1948; in production from 1953) became a kind of symbol of the period of reconstruction. At the same time, demand for so-called ornamental objects was high. The many new church buildings also offered work to designers. Chasubles, altar-cloths and priests' mantles for numerous churches were made in the workshop of ▶Dora Jung using a skilful damask technique, while altar silverware became an important aspect of the work of the silversmith Bertel Gardberg (born 1916). Active building also brought new commissions to interior architects. The nationalist spirit that had characterised earlier decades now gave way to international cosmopolitanism. An early example of the new thinking was the Palace Hotel building in Helsinki, completed in 1952, whose internationally oriented interior was the work of the interior architects Olli Borg (1921-1979), Olavi Hänninen (1920–1997) and Antti Nurmesniemi (born 1927).

Exhibitions abroad began again in the 1950s. The world success of Finnish design began at the Milan Triennales, of which the 1951 triennale was the first since the war. The ascetic exhibition design of ▶Tapio Wirkkala was rewarded with the highest prize, as were his glass objects and birch-ply sculptures. Other Finns, too, were successful. Their organic, modernist formal language became known worldwide as a Finnish trademark, and the designers themselves became stars. The impressive design, which had at first concentrated largely on art objects, now began to be visible in products intended for everyday use. The design of everyday objects received a theoretical base when Kaj Franck, in the 1960s, began to speak powerfully for the responsibility of the designer and the appropriateness of anonymity in industrial design.

In addition to glass and ceramic design, the textile industry, too, invested strongly in designers. Finlayson manufactured knitted woollen fabrics to the designs of Uhra Simberg-Ehrström (1914–1979), and Dora Jung designed linen and cotton-and-linen damask cloths for Tampella. Together with her husband, Armi Ratia (1912–1979) founded ▶Marimekko/Printex, and began to print cotton fabrics that were colourful and fresh. She employed bold young artists to design them, among them Maija Isola (born 1927)

Birger Kaipiainen, *Paratiisi* ('Paradise') ceramics, 1970

and Vuokko Eskolin-Nurmesniemi (born 1930). The free, painterly style of these hand-printed textiles accorded well with the optimism created by the economic boom of the time, and were highly suitable for the interior decoration of the new architecture, which favoured bare material surfaces.

Teaching of industrial design began in 1961. Two new materials, fibreglass and plastic, had developed into serious alternatives. The influence of pop and op art was visible in bright colours and more daring forms throughout the field, as in the *Pastilli* ('Pastille', see p. 123) chair by Eero Aarnio (born 1932), the experimental acrylic jewellery by Olli Tamminen (born 1944) and in printed fabrics. Marimekko, with its fresh printed fabrics and straightforward clothes, represented a youthful, unconventional life-style. Informalism reached Finland in the late 1960s and early 1970s. In design it was visible in the chamotte goblets decorated with splashes of oxide of Kyllikki Salmenhaara (1915–1981), the *Finlandia* series of glass goblets blown into charred wooden moulds of ▶Timo Sarpaneva and the jewellery designed by Björn Weckström (born 1935) for Lapponia Jewellery.

Nordic democracy, which was emphasised during this period of youth radicalism, could not appreciate the crafts, which were considered elitist, in the 1960s. But the oil crisis of the 1970s and the recession it brought with it raised the value of the crafts once more. Negative values were attached to plastic, and 'authentic' materials were felt to be safe once more. On the other hand industry, struggling in the depths of the recession, could not offer everyone work. Workshops dedicated to individual craftwork and short-run serial production sprang up around the country. One of these was the collective Pot Viapori, founded on ▶Suomenlinna, an island off the Helsinki coast, in 1973, which was the working place of the ceramists Åsa Hellman (born 1947) and Hilkka Jarva (born 1932). The border between the crafts and art began to blur, something that was visible as a new phenomenon as installation textiles in the work of, for example, Kirsti Rantanen (born 1930) and Maija Lavonen (born 1931).

Rauno Sorsa, *Raami* ('Rame') chairs, Pro Finnish Design Competition, 1997

Arni Aromaa, *Discover* computer diskette case, Pro Finnish Design Competition, 1997

The traditional ▶*ryijy*, too, began a process of renewal, liberating itself from its traditional form and becoming more three-dimensional in the work of, among others, Irma Kukkasjärvi (born 1941). Ergonomics and the design of work-spaces became important in furniture and interior design. Blond, natural Finnish wood was popular once more.

Since the 1980s, relationships between industry and design have, in general, strengthened. Design has become a central factor in the success of many companies (for example, the Nokia Telecommunications or the hardware company ▶Fiskars). International postmodernism was visible in Finnish design of the 1980s in isolated experiments, the bolder design of details and ornament. In the early 1980s, everyday objects underwent a rapid re-evalution in design shops and auction rooms as cultural goods. At the same time differences between cheap, mass-produced and high-quality design objects were emphasised. Crafts found their way into the art galleries. The recession of recent years has once more emphasised the value of crafts, and concern for the environment has brought its own ecological slant, for example in the paper jewellery of Janna Syvänoja (born 1960). MaA

documentary films The first Finnish full-length documentary film concerned themes of the ▶*Kalevala* and ▶Karelia. It was a four-part filming of a wedding at Lake Suojärvi, in which, in addition to wedding customs, landscapes, folk types and working habits were presented. Its makers were folklorists. In 1936 Kansatieteellinen Filmi Oy (Folklore Films Ltd) was established; the company produced nearly 50 films before it collapsed in 1941. In addition to experts, Kansatieteellinen Filmi employed high-quality cameramen, such as Eino Mäkinen (1908–1987) who, together with Kustaa Vilkuna (1902–1980) also edited a book of photographs based on the films, entitled *Isien työ* ('Work of our fathers', 1943), on the subject of Finnish peasant culture.

The most important producer of Finnish documentary films was the Aho & Soldan company which, between 1925 and 1950, made more than 400 short documentaries, and a few full-length ones. These ▶short films on ordinary life or newsreels were shown in cinemas before the main feature. Between 1933 and 1964 showing such short films brought cinema-owners a tax reduction. Aho & Soldan's movies were well-filmed and of a high technical quality despite their rapid production schedule.

The new rise of the documentary began in the early 1970s as a result of the strong political commitment of radical film-makers. Many film-makers, it is true, immersed themselves for years in political squabbles and tendencies, but many documentary-makers who were later important emerged during this period. *Ikäluokka* ('Age group'), by Pirjo Honkasalo (born 1947) and Pekka Lehto (born 1948), a film about two Finnish men caught up in the surge of history, received a number of awards at film festivals in 1976. During the 1990s Honkasalo has made fine long documentaries about Estonia and Russia.

The most respected Finnish documentary-maker was Antti Peippo (1934–1989), who made his first film,

Pirjo Honkasalo, *Atman,* 1997. This documentary film follows the course of a Hindu pilgrimage

Viapori, in 1971. Later films have included *Kolme salaisuutta* ('Three Secrets', 1984, 17 minutes), which is based on drawings by schizophrenics; *Graniittipoika* ('Granite Boy', 1979, 10 minutes), which reflects Finnish inter-war history; and his major work, *Sijainen* (*Proxy*, 1989, 23 minutes). *Sijainen* transports the viewer to the first seven years of Peippo's life, his family's conflicts during the war years, and links Finland's history with individual experiences.

Markku Lehmuskallio (born 1938) has, in his long documentaries of the 1980s and 1990s, concentrated on the peoples of the Arctic, their beliefs and life. His quiet style is in balance with his subjects. The Finnish documentary of the 1990s is developing in many directions; it is difficult to find a common factor. The earlier serious social concern and interest in developing countries have been replaced by examination of immediate surroundings and reflection of the experiences of the individual and of the family. The contribution of women directors is still increasing. HJ

dress ▶folk costume, fashion

Easter ▶festivals

E

East–West In Finnish history, *West* means Sweden (Stockholm in particular), Germany and, still more broadly, western Christendom. When what is now Finland was linked to the rest of the world, it was secularly with the nascent Swedish kingdom, which was still a weak system, and spiritually or ideologically with the Roman or *western* main branch of the universal Christian Church. Both the secular and the spiritual power systems extended to both taxation and the judicial system. In a secular sense, Finland (in the present-day terms, or those of the borders of 1809 or 1811) was not a uniform administrative area until the foundation of the Grand Duchy of Finland in 1809; instead, the area's various parts belonged to the Kingdom of Sweden, and were subordinate to its king and central administration without an intermediate administrative level (with the exception of a few short periods under a duke or Governor General, when the administrative area, however, was not equivalent to later conceptions of Finland). In a heraldic and historical sense, 'Finland' was certainly a to some extent indefinite entity made up of different provinces, comparable to the 'Kingdoms' of 'Svea' or 'Göta'. Later 'Finland', 'Svealand' and 'Götaland' were joined as local entities by 'Livonia' (Livonia and Estonia), 'Pomerania' (Swedish properties in Germany in the 17th and 18th centuries) and 'Norrland' – all these were new provinces.

Before the formation of the Swedish state – particularly in the 13th century – the whole of 'Sweden', and Finland too, belonged to both East and West; the Varangians' contacts to the East, as far as the capital of Byzantium, finds of Arabian money in, among other places, Birka and Gotland and other facts demonstrate the importance of the East. The ecclesiastical schism between East and West in the 11th century, the rise of western Europe and the Germanic area in the 12th century and, in particular, the conquering of Russia by the Mongols in the 13th century led to the weakening of Eastern contacts and the strengthening of Western contacts. Some of the Eastern features of the so-called folk culture now extend to Sweden and Norway.

In a spiritual sense, the diocese of Finland (subsequently Turku) was part of the diocese of Upsala, or directly subordinate to the Roman pope and curia. On the one hand in terms of state, and thus legislation, administration and social life, and on the other in terms of church, and thus religion, philosophy and education, as well as morality, Finland thus became a part of the West. The Orthodox believers of Karelia began to call members of the western church *ruotshi* or *ruotsalainen* (Swedish), without regard to dialect or tribe; this appellation was still in use in the 20th century.

The influence of German urban culture began in the 14th century and continued, in effect, up to the First World War. This urban culture was also the birth-place of the Lutheran Reformation, which spread to Finland and bound it to Germany but weakened links with Catholic western Europe. European modes of consumption, for example of alcohol, coffee and fabrics and the way of life of the upper social classes, in particular, spread to Finland at an early stage, and Finnish upper-class life followed the general shifts of orientation of Sweden.

After 1809, Finland absorbed many cultural influences from Russia, but the majority of these were German and west European elements of the culture of St Petersburg, in terms of military culture, technology, architecture, musical culture, as well as furniture and cuisine.

At the same time, Finland's non-Russian tradition was evident as the country's position as a nation and a state began to take a different direction from that of Russia. Russia favoured Finland's Western-style modern development for economic reasons and for its exemplary value, and also favoured its formation as a nation for political reasons, to deepen the divide with Sweden. The entire imperial period, however, was essentially a question of Finland's relationship with the culture of St Petersburg and with the monarch in St Petersburg, not with the broad ranks of the Russian people or the Russian national culture. Differences in language and religion remained acute throughout the period.

Russia's adoption of communism

led to Finland's separation from Russia as a state and the severing of economic and cultural links. The Second World War emphasised the differences between East and West concretely. After the war, links with Russia remained formal and regulated; the language barrier continued to hinder real communication.

A romanticisation of the East has nevertheless appeared from time to time in Finland, an admiration partially for Russian art and partially for the state, too. An important aspect of this romanticism is an emphasis on the eastern nature of the Finnish language, accompanied by a desire to stress difference from the West, particularly Sweden. In this way, the structural and, to some – constantly decreasing – extent, the lexical background of the Finnish language, its 'kinship' with the languages of tribes and peoples who live and have for a long time lived in Russia and Asia, represents the East. This 'kinship' is, however, of an ideological variety, for it does not extend to the semantic layer of language, or to the culture beyond the language. The more firmly Finland was linked with Swedish and German cultural circles, the more firmly its language, in all its aspects, became westernised, particularly in semantic terms. MK

Engel, Carl Ludwig (1778–1840), architect. With its neo-classical buildings, Senaatintori Square in ✐Helsinki forms one the the world's most complete urban works of art. Emperor Alexander I (1777–1825) knew the most impressive way to demonstrate his Europeanness. Carl Ludvig Engel, who had graduated from the Berlin Bauakademie in 1804, found his way to Finland via Tallin and St Petersburg.

Helsinki had been created capital of Finland in 1812. In 1816 Engel was commissioned to design all the buildings required by the city's new status and by the new administration. The formal language of the buildings that line Senaatintori Square – the Senate itself, the University of Helsinki and St Nicholas' (Helsinki) Cathedral – is neo-

Carl Ludwig Engel, Helsinki University Library, 1833–1844, exterior (above) and interior (below)

Carl Ludwig Engel

classicism, which expresses the origin and central importance of the institutions. The city administration, on the south side of the square, is still overshadowed by this trinity. All in all, Engel designed some 30 public buildings for Helsinki; of their interiors, the most impressive are the vestibule of the University of Helsinki and the sequence of rooms in the Helsinki University Library.

As director of the Intendant's Office from 1824 until his early death, Engel designed an enormous number of churches and secular buildings throughout Finland and, through employing them in his office, educated architects in a country that as yet had no other route for entry into the profession. The most original of his churches were built in Ostrobothnia. RN

explorers Although Finland's role in the history of expeditions and voyages of discovery is small compared to that of many other European countries, in terms of organising scientifically oriented expeditions Finnish achievements are considerable. Finnish exploration can be divided into three periods, each of which has its own special nature: the period under Swedish rule (to 1809), the period under Russian rule (1809–1917) and the period of independence (from 1917).

The collapse in the 18th century of a greatpower status based on a belligerent foreign policy and increasing support for Enlightenment ideas in Sweden directed the country gradually towards the quest for material wealth. The businessmen and industrialists belonging to the Royal Academy of Sciences (founded in 1739), realised that science offered the opportunity to conduct this quest more effectively than before. Playing their part in the scientific study demanded by economic activity and growth were scientifically oriented expeditions to all parts of the globe.

Under the direction of Carl von Linné, many Finnish explorers also took part in this work. Among Linné's Finnish pupils, the most well-known were ▶Pehr Kalm, who travelled to North America, and Petter Forsskål (1723–1763), who travelled to Arabia with a Danish expedition. In addition, Herman Spöring the Younger (1733–1771), who was born in Turku and studied medicine and the natural sciences came to London as secretary of Linné's student.

A fourth important 18th-century Finn travelled east. Numerous scientific expeditions of Eric Laxman (1738–1796) took him to Bender and Tsaritsy in southern Russia and as far as Ohotsk on the shores of the Ohota Sea in Siberia. Laxman's travels east were, in a way, a portent of what was to come: Finland's new role under Russian rule opened previously unhoped-for opportunities for Finnish explorers to study Russia from the point of view of folkloristics and linguistics as well as the natural sciences.

The 19th century also marked a diversification in Finnish expeditions in terms of both destination and subject. Instead of wide-ranging natural scientists, specialists now went on expeditions, examining and charting areas from the perspectives of the disciplines they represented. New scientific knowledge was thus acquired about subjects as disparate as the lives, histories and languages of Finnish tribes and the surface formations of the Altai.

The Finnish explorers of the 19th century also set out for other distant destinations: ▶A.E. Nordenskiöld was the first to sail the North-East Passage, ▶G.A. Wallin and his followers created the basis for Arabic scholarship in Finland, and Finnish traders increased their knowledge of the cultures of the Far East in terms of both languages and material culture.

▶Edvard Westermarck's seven years of field work in Morocco and the monographs published as a result provided an example for an entire approach. ▶Gunnar Landtman made studies in Papua-New Guinea between 1910 and 1912, while ▶Rafael Karsten (1879–1956) made three expeditions to South America between 1911 and 1929, and, in 1938, published his major work, *The Head-Hunters of Western Amazonas*. ▶Hilma Granqvist, a rare woman scholar in this company, spent a number of years in a Palestinian village in the 1920s and 1930s, and published five monographs on the material she gathered, among them *Muslim Death and Burials* (1964).

As an officer in the army of imperial Russia, ▶C.G.E. Mannerheim – later Marshal of Finland and President of the Republic – made an expedition from St Petersburg to Beijing between 1906 and 1908. Although this was a military reconnaissance trip, it also became, as a result of Mannerheim's interest, an important expedition. Prophetic in the journey were its military nature and realisation just a few years

Unexpected encounter: three Finnish explorers dressed as Mongols – Sakari Pälsi, G.J. Ramstedt and J.G. Granö – met by chance in central Mongolia in 1909

before the outbreak of the First World War.

The enthusiasm provoked by the ▶Kalevala and ▶Karelia was influential in the late 19th century and early 20th century in creating the movement known as ▶Karelianism. In addition to linguistics, experts and scholars of the folk tradition, and artists of many kinds made expeditions to visit the guardians of the *Kalevala* tradition. The movement was highly influential in, among other things, music, the visual arts and literature.

Finland's independence (1917) was also visible in the new areas to which expeditions directed themselves. The erection of the communist system on the ruins of the Russian empire and the drift of the Soviet Union into political conflict first with Germany and then with western Europe caused many difficulties for Finnish explorers. Although the border was not closed completely, practical difficulties in arranging expeditions eastward increased substantially. The obstacles were felt to be particularly troublesome in the study of the Finnic tribes living in the Soviet Union.

In independent Finland, expeditions were directed partly according to old traditions, for example the expeditions of social anthropologists to various parts of the world. New destina-

tions were sought all over the world, and perhaps the most significant of them was the geographical study of Tierra del Fuego carried out by Väinö Auer (1895–1981). He led a total of 14 expeditions to the area.

The pioneering studies carried out by Finnish geographers, geologists and botanists in the Amazon and in the polar regions, both north and south, are examples of the scientific expeditions of our time. ML

family ▶childhood, man and woman

fashion The distinguishing features of Finnish fashion are top-level design – which largely follows international fashion trends – high-quality manufacture, and the use of natural fibres and colourings. Finnish clothing may be characterised as practical but well-balanced. Fashion trends among the young are also moderate in character. Because of the climate, different clothes are needed for winter and summer, and special intermediate seasonal clothing is also required for autumn and spring. Finnish summer clothing is typified by loose blazers and denim garments, while in winter the streets are dominated by quilted sporting jackets. Other popular winter fashions include modern sheepskin coats and elegant furs. In every season people dress practically and comfortably, and as a result of this colourful sports clothes are coming into everyday use.

The Finnish clothing industry is almost one hundred years old, but original Finnish fashion may be said to date from no earlier than the 1950s, a fact that does much to illustrate the unpretentious ways of thinking, closely attuned to nature, that the northern climate creates.

The first Finnish cloth mills were established in the 16th and 18th centuries. They wove cloth and frieze for the state or the army, which because of the numerous wars had a large need for kit and uniforms. During the 19th century and in the early years of the 20th century, dozens of textile factories were established, along with cotton and flax mills. Their success was based on exports to Russia, as the people of Finland had a natural economy and wore homespun clothes until the end

F

of the 19th century. Many factories became very large: for example, the city of Tampere was built around the Finlayson cotton factory, which for several decades was the largest industrial workplace in Scandinavia. After the 1917 revolution, Finnish exports to Russia ceased for almost 40 years.

The first clothing factories, established at the end of the 19th century, made shirts, aprons, undergarments and working clothes or heavy outdoor garments which were not badly designed. The best clothes were made by tailors and seamstresses, who followed European fashions from the fashion journals. During the Second World War nearly all the clothes factories made kit and uniforms for the army. After the war, a shortage of raw materials, accompanied by rationing, continued until the early 1950s. At that time the only materials available to the factories were army tents, old greatcoats and the like.

Training in clothing design began at the Central School for Applied Arts in 1948 (the Institute was founded in 1871; since 1973 it has been known as the University of Art and Design). Nowadays several art and handicraft institutes also train clothes designers.

►Marimekko, founded in 1951, succeeded because of the originality of its collection: it created a unique image for itself as a manufacturer of designed clothes and was the first Finnish garment house to enter the export market. One of its principal designers of fabrics and garments, Vuokko Eskolin-Nurmesniemi (born 1930), established the firm of Vuokko in 1967. Vuokko garments were skilfully cut, in an architectonic manner. They always quickly acquired great international popularity. In addition to Marimekko and Vuokko, the hand-woven cotton productions of Jyväskylä-based Annikki Karvinen (born 1931) represented original Finnish design and technology, and conferred new status on the traditional rag rugs used in Finnish homes.

Marimekko's success provided a stimulus to Finland's textile and garment factories, which employed trained designers to design their fabrics and clothes, and also in the 1960s to the design collections of some factories,

Unikko-kolmio ('Poppy-triangle'), viscose velvet, design by Vuokko, 1984

which in addition to clothing produced accessories that were much in demand in Europe's centres of fashion. Throughout the whole of the 1970s, the Finnish garment industry experienced a period of intense growth, and many Swedish factories moved their production to Finland, because of its still cheap labour. At the height of this period there were 500 factories, and some 35,000 people worked in the industry.

Some factories specialised. ►Luhta in fashionable sporting and leisure clothes, Torstai, located on the Arctic Circle, in skiing clothes; Terinit in athletic sports outfits, while, in association with textile factories, Reima developed materials suitable for winter conditions. A truly remarkable example of these is enstex, in which the outer surface of the cloth consists of durable polyamid and the inner surface of soft, fluffy cotton. From it are made children's dungarees and special garments such as boiler suits and ice-fishing dungarees. Many factories specialising in men's, women's, tricot and knitted clothing sprang up in the 1960s.

The extensive size of the Finnish clothing industry in the 1970s and 1980s was founded on the export trade. Well over half the production of some factories went to export. The most important countries exported to were the Nordic countries, the countries of the European Free Trade Association, EFTA and the European Economic Community, EEC, and the Soviet Union. Soviet interest in Finnish clothing production manifested itself in the late 1950s. At first the exports were barter transactions – enormous quantities of products were exported, as many as half a million nylon shirts or tens of thousands of overcoats – while the counter-purchases might be wagon-loads of cement or mandarin oranges. Later, this commerce was pursued within the framework of official trade agreements. The Soviet trade was beneficial to the clothing industry, but also had negative consequences. Its long production runs guaranteed full-time working for the factories, but many of them became dependent on this. The trade with the East ended with the collapse of the Soviet Union in 1991, which drove some Finnish factories into bankruptcy.

One of Finland's oldest trades is that of the furriers, who were known as early as the 14th century, when the Nordic lands and Russia were Europe's foremost fur producers. Because of Finland's cold climate, furs have always been necessary items of utility clothing there, and many clothing factories also made cloth coats as well as furs. Finland is still the largest producer of furs in Europe. In the 1970s trained designers began to make furs. They included the mink fur innovator Tarja Niskanen (born 1944), and Tua Rahikainen (born 1944), who made superb post-modern musquash furs. The reversible furs designed by Kirsti Aho (born 1948) represent the most fashionable end of the industry, along with the light sheepskins and ultra-modern leather garments of ▶Friitala.

The footwear industry developed alongside the clothing industry at the end of the 19th century. Original Finnish footwear is represented by the leather-made *lapikkaat* and *huopikkaat*, which are still made in some felt factories. The manufacture of winter footwear has always been a special Finnish skill. In 1930 a Lahti shoemaker developed the 'Mono' ski-boot –

after family name Mononen – which became known abroad. The product was intended as skiing and hiking footwear, but entered into general use for decades. For reasons of climate, rubber boots are also an important item of Finnish work and leisure clothing. In the 1990s the Nokia Footwear Factory, established in 1898, still manufactured a wide range of rubber boots and shoes. Finland's largest shoe factory was Aaltosen Kenkätehdas (Aaltonen's Shoe Factory), founded at the end of the 19th century. The fashionable shoes of Pertti Palmroth (born 1931) have long been famous beyond the borders of Finland.

In the late 1980s and early 1990s the Finnish clothing industry suffered a recession. Production costs rose and many factories went out of business or moved their production to countries with a cheap labour force. Often design and marketing were the only branches of the industry to survive. New trends are represented by the small enterprises established by many designers, an example of which is Kultaturve, making peat textiles. MA

festivals Finnish festivals are both sacred and secular. In an agrarian culture, the annual round of festivals was based on the economic calendar in such a way that the agricultural and religious years merged. As Finnish society has industrialised, the annual festivals have become separated from their origins, and their content has to some extent changed.

As well as their date, much of the content of annual festivals are based on their pre-Christian equivalents. Folk customs associated with festivals independent of season include the interpretation of omens, cleansing, protection against spirits, sacrifice and festival meals, and games of various kinds. Many of these features survive in some form, even if their deeper meaning is no longer believed. The Finnish ▶calendar today includes only four ecclesiastical festivals that do not fall at weekends: New Year's Day, Good Friday, Ascension Day and Christmas Day. In addition, May Day (1st May) and Independence Day (6th December) are legally prescribed holidays.

New Year's Eve: fireworks in Senaatintori Square, Helsinki

NEW YEAR'S EVE AND NEW YEAR'S DAY The beginning of the new year overshadows the old ecclesiastical significance of this holiday: the circumcision and naming of Jesus. It has become a carnival, with fireworks and parties at home or in restaurants. The tradition of making prophecies for the coming year, thousands of years old, lives on in the casting of molten tin into water. Among the contemporary rituals of New Year's Day are watching the Finnish president's address, the Central European ski jumping contest and the Strauss concert from Vienna on television.

RUNEBERG'S DAY (5 February), which commemorates the birthday of the national poet, ▶Johan Ludvig Runeberg is much celebrated as a cultural festival among ▶Finland-Swedes, particularly in the towns where the writer lived: Pietarsaari, Porvoo and Helsinki. At midday, student choirs serenade a statue of the poet sculpted by his son, Walter Runeberg (1838–1920), in 1885 in Helsinki's central Esplanade Park. In honour of Runeberg's memory, Svenska Litteratursällskapet i Finland (The Society of Swedish Literature in Finland) makes annual awards to Finland-Swedish practitioners of the arts and sciences. A Runeberg festival is held in the Assembly Rooms in Porvoo. A Runeberg tart – a small sponge cake decorated with a spoonful of jam – was introduced as early as the 1840s.

Shrove Tuesday: a carneval atmosphere is combined with the traditional custom of sledging

SHROVE TUESDAY The Tuesday before Ash Wednesday is, in Finland, known as *laskiaistiistai*, or 'descent Tuesday' because it marks the 'descent' into the fasting period of Lent. The custom of sledging on Shrove Tuesday originally marked a change in women's work – they stopped spinning, and began weaving, which demanded more light – and its intention was to ensure the growth of linen the following summer. Shrove Tuesday is still celebrated by sledging in Finnish cities on slopes prepared for the purpose by students. The day is also marked by the consumption of sweet buns filled with marzipan or jam and cream, often eaten from bowls filled with hot milk.

FRIENDS' DAY (14 February) The festival of St Valentine – patron saint of lovers and guarantor of happy marriages – became familiar in Finland only in the 1980s through films and cartoon strips and was introduced by young people who had spent time studying in the United States. Despite its commerciality, Friends' Day has grown in popularity every year in the form, for example, of the sending of Friends' Day cards.

THE LAST DAY AT SCHOOL and OLDIES' DAY (mid February). Candidates for the matriculation examination, or abiturients, celebrate their last day at school together before the ex-

Last day at school: matriculation candidates drive round town in lorries decorated with slogans

aminations by disturbing normal teaching at school during the morning and, in the afternoon, driving through the centre of town in lorries whose sides they have decorated with funny slogans and drawings. On the lorry platforms the abiturients, or *abis*, shout and throw sweets to the onlookers who gather on the pavements. In the evening the celebrants go to a restaurant together, or on a boat cruise. When the abiturients have left school, the oldest remaining students are known as 'oldies'. On the day after the abiturients' departure, they can be identified by their 'historic' party dress. Among the customs of Oldies' Day in schools is a formal salon dance.

KALEVALA DAY, or DAY OF FINNISH CULTURE (28 February). ▶Elias Lönnrot dated the introduction to the first version of his ▶*Kalevala,* 28 February 1835. The day has since been celebrated as a festival. The Kalevala Society lays a wreath on the statue of Elias Lönnrot sculpted by Emil Wikström (1864–1942) in 1902, and schools celebrate with activities centred on the theme of the *Kalevala.* The festival was adopted into the calendar in the 1950s, but became an official flag-day only in 1978, when it was also given the additional title of Day of Finnish Culture. The most important national funding body for the arts and sciences, the Finnish Cultural Foundation, announces the recipients of its annual

funding on this day. Since the 1930s, pastries in the shape of the ▶*kantele* have been available in the shops.

EASTER (between 22 March and 25 April) The Easter period starts with Palm Sunday. The name refers to the green leafy branches that were used to decorate churches in commemoration of the palm leaves strewn in Jesus' path on his entry into Jerusalem. In eastern Finland, children used to strike adults lightly with decorated willow-branches, wishing good luck rhymes. Today this tradition has spread, through the influence of schools and kindergartens, throughout the country, and has become mixed with the tradition of the Easter witch. The period between Good Friday and Easter Day, the day of Christ's resurrection, was the

Easter: little girls dress up as witches and strike adults with willow-switches – and receive sweets or money in return

time of evil spirits, when witches or trolls were believed to be abroad, stealing luck from their neighbours. Such witchcraft was practised in Finland as late as the 20th century. The Easter fires burned in Ostrobothnia were a protection against witchcraft, and have recently been revived as a tourist attraction. The dyeing of eggs was a custom in the cities from the early 19th century. Today the skilful painting of Easter eggs is practised in clubs. The characteristically Finnish Easter food, *mämmi,* is sweet rye dough toasted until it is a dark brown-black. It is mentioned in written sources as early as the 18th century.

MAY DAY (1 May) May Day was originally the festival of the Catholic saint Walpurgis, whose celebration was mixed in the north with aspects of the Germanic spring festival. It was designated a workers' festival at the Congress of Paris of 1889. In Finland, May Day has been a workers' festival only

May Day: students in white caps begin the day in Kaivopuisto Park in Helsinki with champagne breakfasts and dancing

since 1902. Since the 1960s, the political parties of the centre and right have also organised their own May Day celebrations, complete with speeches. The May Day march has remained the prerogative of the left.

▶Students in their white caps visit the graves of soldiers killed during the Second World War on the eve of May Day; the dead of both sides of the Civil War of 1918 are also commemorated. Since 1932 students have also set a white cap on the statue of ▶Havis Amanda, which is located at the edge of the main market square in ▶Helsinki. This takes place before a large crowd at 6 pm., and is considered the official beginning of the celebrations. The evening is spent at parties at home or in restaurants, which sometimes last throughout the night. The next day at nine in the morning, the official raising of the flag takes place on Observatory Hill in Helsinki, after which students gather in the nearby Kaivopuisto Park to dance. Since the late 1970s, the street scene has been enlivened by the brightly coloured overalls with which students announce their subject, and others advertising commercial businesses. In addition to making reference to the shared celebrations of students and workers, the overalls are excellent dress for all-night revellers in the cool weather of spring. Traditional May Day comestibles are *sima*, a light mead made with hops, and *tippaleipä*, a pas-

try made of strips of dough rolled into a ball. The drinking of champagne is a more recent innovation. Other ingredients of the Finnish May Day tradition include balloons, May Day sticks and whisks made of brightly coloured tissue paper and, a more recent tradition, masks of various kinds. May Day is spent out on the streets and lunch is generally eaten in a restaurant, with salty Baltic herring playing an essential part in the meal.

WHITSUN (May) The commemorative festival of the coming of the Holy Spirit and the foundation of the congregation of Christ takes place 50 days after Easter. The burning of bonfires, which begins on Ascension Day, is in some places continued at Whitsun. The tradition of game-playing among young people, which was formerly centred on village swings, has been exchanged for the summer's first outdoor dances. Whitsun is – in addition to Midsummer – a popular day for summer weddings.

MOTHERS' DAY (second Sunday in May) This festival, which originated in the United States, was known in Finland as early as the 1910s, but was not accepted into the calendar until 1930; it became a flag-day in 1947. The national Mothers' Day celebrations organised by Väestöliitto, The Finnish Population and Family Welfare Federation awards medals to mothers of particular merit in bringing up their children – and, in some cases, to fathers too. The festival is celebrated within the family, but with a fair dose of commerciality. The most popular Mothers' Day flower is the rose. Children also pick wild flowers for their mothers, and make cards for them at school or in clubs.

SNELLMAN'S DAY (12 May) Snellman's Day is also known as Finnish Day. The memory of the nationalist philosopher and statesman ▶J.V. Snellman is celebrated by flying flags. The Association of Finnish Culture and Identity places a wreath on the statue of the great man located outside the Bank of Finland in Helsinki. Snellman was of central importance in the 19th century in lobbying for a separate currency for Finland, the mark.

FLORA'S DAY (13 May) Flora's Day is a spring festival among students and the final ceremony of the academic year. Around midday, students of the ►University of Helsinki take a tram-ride from the central market to Kumtähti Square in Vallila to dance and raise champagne glasses. This was also the site of the first performance, in 1848, of *Maamme* ('Our land'), which subsequently became the Finnish national anthem.

DAY OF THE FALLEN (third Sunday in May) Unlike many other countries, Finland has no offical tomb of the unknown soldier. Those who fell in the Second World War are buried in the churchyard of their home parishes, so that relationships with heroes' graves are more emotional and individual than elsewhere. On the Day of the Fallen, relatives visit the graves of dead soldiers, and the state authorities also lay a wreath on a hero's grave. Flags are flown at half-mast between 10 am. and 2 pm., and fully raised only subsequently.

SCHOOL-LEAVING (CAPPING) DAY (last Saturday in May) School-Leaving Day is visible in the streets in the form of young people wearing white caps. When the school year ends, some 30,000 young people receive a white cap as a mark that they have passed the matriculation examinations. After a ceremony held at school in the morning, school-leavers have studio photographs of themselves taken with roses they have received from well-wishers and take part in a coffee party with relatives and friends. In the afternoon they visit soldiers' graves, and they end the day by celebrating in a restaurant with their friends.

ARMED FORCES FLAG DAY (4 June) Armed Forces Flag Day was established on this day in 1942, the 75th birthday of the Commander-in-Chief, Marshal ►C.G.E. Mannerheim. The main annual national parade takes place in different garrisons in turn every year. The Finnish president, the defence minister and the Commander-in-Chief of the armed forces award medals and special mentions; promotions among both active and reserve forces are made. These are announced in the newspapers.

MIDSUMMER'S DAY (between 20 June and 26 June) Midsummer's Day, the feast-day of John the Baptist and Finland's Flag Day, has been one of the most important days in the Lutheran calendar. The festival is celebrated on the Saturday that falls between 20th June and 26th June. Many of the customs associated with Midsummer's Day derive from the pre-Christian and pan-European festival of light and fertility that marked the summer solstice. The burning of the Midsummer *kokko* ('bonfire'), originally a tradition linked, in the north and east of the country, with beliefs concerning fertility, cleansing and the banishing of evil spirits, has in the 20th century spread

Midsummer: burning the *kokko* bonfire in the endless white night of the north

throughout Finland. It has become the central element in the programme of commercial Midsummer festivities, along with music and dance. Homes are decorated with flowers and birch-branches. A Midsummer pole reminiscent of an ornamented sailing mast is part of the Finland-Swedish tradition of southern Finland and ▶Åland. Flags are raised at 6 am. on Midsummer's Eve and lowered only at 9 pm. on the night of the following day. Midsummer delicacies include pancakes, new potatoes and salmon.

SLEEP-SPIRIT'S DAY (Unikeonpäivä) (27 July) This festival celebrates the memory of the seven martyrs of Ephesos. In a purely Finnish tradition, the member of the family who sleeps longest on this day is teased and dubbed *unikeko* ('sleep-spirit'). Outside the family circle, Sleep-Spirit's Day is celebrated, in particular, in spa towns (e.g. Hanko, Maarianhamina, Naantali), where noisy processions go through the streets very early in the morning, waking sleepers. Since 1959, there has been a tradition in Naantali of waking up a prominent citizen or spa guest and throwing him into the water in the harbour. The festivities continue with masked balls and other carnival amusements.

ALEKSIS KIVI DAY and FINNISH LITERATURE DAY (10 October) A statue of the writer ▶Aleksis Kivi, sculpted by Wäinö Aaltonen (1894–1966) in 1939, in the Railway Station Square in Helsinki is showered with flowers by students of the Southern Finnish Students' Society of ▶University of Helsinki. A delegation of students also visits the writer's grave in Tuusula. The day was designated Finnish Literature Day in 1978, and it is also the date of the annual festivities of the Finnish Writers' Association. The Aleksis Kivi Society makes an award to a person, named after a character from the writer's most popular play *Nummisuutarit* ('The heath-cobblers'): 'Eskon puumerkki' ('Esko's mark') who has exhibited the Finnish traits of stubbornness and perseverance.

ALL SAINTS' DAY (Saturday between 31 October and 6 November) Behind the celebration of All Saints' Day, in Finland, is the old eastern Finnish festival of the ending of the agricultural

year, *kekri*, many of whose features have subsequently become attached to Christmas. *Kekri* was also the occasion when dead members of the family are remembered. It was easy, from the 1920s onwards, to convert the custom to the taking of candles to family graves. The Centre Party, whose traditional supporters are rural, holds its most important political events on All Saints' Day and encouraged the use of the term Kekri Festival.

(SWEDISH DAY) SVENSKA DAGEN (6 November) Svenska Dagen marks the anniversary of the death of the powerful Swedish King Gustavus II Adolf (6th November 1632). The worldwide interest in minority identities that began in the 1970s has encouraged the celebration of Swedish Day in schools. This generally instigates debate about the position of minorities and minority languages (Swedish and ▶Sámi) in schools. Established flag-day.

FATHERS' DAY (second Sunday in November) Fathers' Day was celebrated in the United States as early as the 1910s, but the festival was adopted by the Finnish calendar only in 1970. There is no officially designated Fathers' Day flower; the chrysanthemum and the cyclamen are the most popular. Fathers' Day has not attained the same popularity as Mothers' Day, and there are no national celebrations. Within the family, the day is marked with small gifts; publicly, it is a flag-day.

INDEPENDENCE DAY (6 December) Independence Day marks the day on which Finland declared itself an independent republic, in 1917. Independence Day was celebrated for the first time in 1919, but it legally become a general festival and holiday only in 1929. Among its customs are official celebrations including visits to graves and monuments, church services, parades, musical matinées and parties. In the early evening, ▶students march through Helsinki in torchlit processions from soldiers' graves to the central Senaatintori Square. Candles are lit in the windows of homes and offices at six in the evening and fireworks light up the dark winter sky. The President of the Republic arranges an evening reception in his residency. High administrative officials, the diplomatic corps, and citizens who have distinguished themselves during the past year are invited. The reception is unique in the world since it is televised direct so that Finnish citizens can all participate in the event.

Lucia's Day (13 December) Lucia's Day is a festival of light commemorating a blinded Sicilian martyr. It has been celebrated in the Nordic countries since the 18th century. In Finland it is a festival among the Swedish-speaking population which has been especially cultivated by schools. Since 1950 Finland's biggest Swedish-language daily newspaper, together with a charity, has organised an annual public vote and collection for a young girl to bear the name Lucia. The winner is borne in a procession at 6 pm. from Helsinki Cathedral to the ▶Finlandia Hall, where she is crowned. In family celebrations, a daughter appears, dressed in white and wearing a crown of candles, as Lucia, and serves coffee and pastries in the morning. The custom is also spreading among Finnish-speakers.

Christmas: the *tiernapojat* ('star boys') enact the Christmas gospel in a tradition that originates, via Sweden, in the Italian *commedia dell'arte*

Christmas Eve (24 December) The celebration of the birth of Christ has, in Finland, replaced the pre-Christian festival of the return of the sun, the dead and the end of the crop year. The Christmas season begins on Christmas Eve and ends with Epiphany on 6 January. Today only two Christmas holidays are kept.

Of all the calendrical feasts, Christmas has most clearly retained its family nature. Among the customs associ-

The Christmas meal – ham, vegetable casseroles, Baltic herring salad – is eaten on Christmas Eve

ated with it are the lighting of candles on family graves, the decoration of the Christmas tree, in which the entire family participates, and, the Christmas meal and the giving of presents. The most important element of the meal is the eating of ham, which originated in pagan times, although turkey has in recent times become more common. Other Christmas dishes include swede and carrot casseroles and a Baltic herring salad garnished with whipped cream. The food is accompanied by beer. Presents are brought by ▶Santa Claus in his sack or placed under the tree, and distributed on Christmas Eve.

Personal celebrations. Name-days Name-days have been celebrated in Finland since the 17th century, but the custom spread widely only at the end of the 19th century. Beautifully scripted and illustrated greetings paintings were given, serenades or comic poems were performed and small presents were given. The person whose name-day it was offered his guests hospitality. The name-day tradition survives both in families and at work-places, where the person concerned offers his closest colleagues coffee and cakes.

Birthdays Since the 18th and 19th centuries, the birthdays of public figures and statesmen (▶J.V. Snellman) and great poets (▶J. L. Runeberg, ▶Z. Topelius) have been celebrated. Children's birthdays are celebrated within the family and, among adults, 'round' birthdays (20th, 30th and so on) are marked. Among the nobility and in cities the habit of solemn celebrations of 50th and 60th birthdays began in the early decades of the 20th century. The custom spread before the

Second World War among rural civil servants and prominent local figures, and thence further afield. Most common is the celebration of 50th birthdays, in which relatives, friends and working colleagues participate. Daily and weekly newspapers include separate columns containing announcements of coming 'round' birthdays and a note of whether there will be a reception or not. The latter option is generally indicated by saying that the celebrant will be 'travelling' whether or not this is a white lie. TK

film As late as the 1980s, around 15 full-length films were made in Finland every year; in the 1990s, production fell to around 10 films a year. Nevertheless, this number is very large for a country with a population of only 5 million and in a market increasingly dominated by imported American films.

Finnish film production has always relied on home markets, and still cannot rely on export. This means that most contemporary films need more than 100,000 viewers to break even. In proportion to the population of the United States, this would mean that films with fewer than 4–5 million viewers would make a loss. In Finland, the profitability threshold is exceeded only by the most popular comedies, or film versions of books that have attained the position of almost national epics, such as ▶Väinö Linna's *Tuntematon sotilas* ('The unknown soldier') or Antti Tuuri's (born 1944) *Talvisota* ('The Winter War'). The Finnish film industry remains alive to a large extent through government subsidy.

The history of film in Finland dates back to the first performance of the Lumière brothers' tour on 28 June 1896. Finnish production began with short documentary films in 1904 and with filmed dramas in 1907. During the silent period Finnish film served to construct a national identity and the drive for independence: national themes were an end in themselves, and the importance, difference and competition provided by Finnish films compared to foreign productions was emphasised. Erkki Karu (1887–1935) can be considered the creator of the industrial and artistic base of Finnish film:

Erik Blomberg, *Valkoinen peura* ('The white reindeer'), 1952. The film won the prize for the best story-based film in Cannes Film Festival in 1953

he was one of the founders and directors of the biggest production company, Suomi-Filmi, and was also one of the most important directors of the entire silent period, consistently following an international line. His adaptation of ▶Aleksis Kivi's play *Nummisuutarit* ('The heath-cobblers') was released in 1923, while his film about the army, *Meidän poikamme* ('Our boys') dates from 1929.

The transition to talking movies in Finland lasted long into the 1930s, but after mid-decade there began a period that could be called the golden age of Finnish film, a boom that even the years of the Second World War could not stop. With the exception of brief interruptions, production remained in full swing during the Second World War, and continued to be even in quantity. Public success was guaranteed, since other amusements were rationed and there were fewer foreign films on offer than usual. Every Finnish film attracted an average total audience of 400,000, or more than 10 per cent of the country's population, and more than ten times today's average.

After the war, when the importation of foreign films and other amusements opened up, Finnish film began to lose its audience base. Production figures, on the other hand, remained as they were or even increased, so that more and more films were competing for a disappearing audience. In the decades that followed this distortion along with the general development of

Edvin Laine, *Tuntematon sotilas* ('The unknown soldier'), 1955

the media and leisure industries – made the Finnish film a constant trouble-spot.

The production system that had developed in the 1930s remained in place until the 1960s. During this period, Suomen Filmiteollisuus (Finnish Film Industry), directed by T. J. Särkkä (1890–1975), and Suomi-Filmi, directed by Risto Orko (1899–1997), were between them essentially responsible for the entire film output of Finland. Särkkä and Orko were both directors, production planners, and owners of their companies. They were strong personalities who were able, even in difficult conditions, to create better conditions for their companies than their rivals. They had at their disposal a consistent troupe of actors, directors, film-writers and technical staff. The 1930s saw the emergence of many of the best-known Finnish film-stars and directors. The directors ▶Nyrki Tapiovaara (1911–1940), Teuvo Tulio (born 1912) and Valentin Vaala (1909–1976), although their subsequent careers took them in very different directions, all received their original artistic inspiration from the Tulenkantajat ('Torchbearers') literary movement in the 1920s. Tulio's genre was melodrama, a stage for grand emotions, contrasts and caricatures in which visual narrative and visual sense replaced the traditional 'literary' values

of nature photography and interaction. Tapiovaara, who was killed in the Finnish ▶Winter War, made five films on the basis of traditional genres, but was able to demonstrate his talent and rebellion in handling them. While Tulio and Tapiovaara worked for small companies, Vaala was, for the whole of the 1960s, the star director at Suomi-Filmi, and worked in, and mastered, genres from comedy to the thriller, film versions of Finnish literature from the epic to the impressionistic. Of the other important directors of the golden age of Finnish film, Edvin Laine (1905–1989) and Matti Kassila (born 1924) made their débuts in the 1940s, but their most mature work was done in the following decade. Laine became the privileged interpreter of the dramas of ▶Hella Wuolijoki and the epic novels of ▶Väinö Linna, and Kassila's best films, too, were of classics of Finnish literature such as the work of ▶F.E. Sillanpää and ▶Mika Waltari.

In accordance with developments elsewhere in the world, a film crisis hit Finland in the 1950s. In the years that followed, audiences shrank, first under the influence of television and then of video, and it was not until the late 1980s that the decrease was halted – temporarily. Government support for film production was understood as a necessity from the late 1950s onwards, and the first grant system was arranged in the early 1960s in the form of government prizes. The Finnish Film Foundation was established at the end of the same decade; its modes of funding have undergone many changes, and are constantly under reappraisal. The Film Foundation does not itself produce films, but it makes funding decisions and regulates loans with finances that come primarily from art allocations but also from taxes on empty cassettes and television rights, as well as from cinema profits.

When the production system dominated by the large companies collapsed at the beginning of the 1960s, the Finnish 'new wave' – once more on the international model – made its appearance: films made by small companies and individual directors. Of this transitional generation, Maunu Kurkvaara (born 1926) and Eino Ruutsalo (born 1921) were former artists whose cinematic work emphasised visual expression at the expense of narrative. In the work of ▶Risto Jarva, the influence of the avant-garde and of the French *nouvelle vague* developed first into social criticism, then in the direction of fantasy and fairy-tale. Jörn Donner (born 1933), too, built his work on the European art film rather than the national tradition, while Mikko Niskanen (1929–1990) developed into an ultra-nationalistic epic film-maker, a chronicler of young people and the countryside. Of the new film-makers of the 1970s, Heikki Partanen (1942–1990) specialised in fairy-tale films, while ▶Rauni Mollberg distinguished himself with his film adaptations of Finnish literature.

A change of generation took place in the early 1980s, and the decade saw first films from about 30 makers, of which many were also their last. ▶Mika Kaurismäki and ▶Aki Kaurismäki emerged as standard-bearers of the new generation and film, but alongside them Veikko Aaltonen (born 1956), Claes Olsson (born 1948) and Markku Pölönen (born 1957) have also made fine personal contributions. In the conditions of the early 1980s, petrified in terms of both production and creativity, the Kaurismäki brothers' first films broke the ice in emulating the liberated and small-scale movie-making of the 'new wave'. Mika Kaurismäki has subsequently grown closer to traditional cinema and its genres in his crime stories, comedies, action and thriller movies, while Aki Kaurismäki has stayed true to his minimalist genre, which is characterised by reduced, disciplined expression and abrupt, often black, humour.

It is to a great extent due to the Kaurismäki brothers and their cult status that the international reputation of Finnish cinema has risen in recent years, and Finnish cinema in general has been recognised as comparable to the production of that of any other country of similar size, in both technical and artistic terms. In the mainstream film market, audiences for the Kaurismäki brothers' films are, of course, very small and specialised, but with reasonable budgets, international recognition and, to some extent, public funding, they have been able to continue their work, which has not always been the case with other Finnish directors. ST

Finland Festivals Finland Festivals is a joint organisation of Finnish art and cultural festivals, most of them taking place in the summer. The organisation, founded in 1968, functions as a lobby group for the festivals with respect to government arts administration, and promotes them at home and abroad.

Finland Festivals

GENERAL MUSIC FESTIVALS
1 Joensuu Festival
2 Sysmä Summer Sound
3 Mikkeli Music Festival
4 Jyväskylä Arts Festival
5 Turku Music Festival
6 Helsinki Festival

OPERA FESTIVALS
7 Ilmajoki Music Festival
8 Savonlinna Opera Festival

Finland on the map Finland is, with Iceland, the world's most northerly country. Although Norway, Russia and Canada have territories farther north, their geographical and demographic focus is farther south. Because of the Gulf Stream, however, the country's geographical location is more advantageous than corresponding latitudes in the northern hemisphere as a whole. For example, ▶Helsinki is located on the same latitude as the southern tip of Greenland. Areas corresponding to northern Finland in Alaska and Siberia are covered in permafrost. Thanks to the warm Gulf Stream, Finland is able to support a population of 5 million people, accounting for approximately 35 per cent of all those living beyond latitude 60° N in the world.

Finland's population is small, but its area is very large, particularly in European terms. Finland's area, and particularly its length from north to

CHAMBER MUSIC FESTIVALS
9 Oulu Music Festival
10 Hetta Music Event
11 Naantali Music Festival
12 Riihimäki Summer Concerts
13 Korsholm Music Festival, Vaasa and Korsholm
14 Avanti! Summer Sounds, Porvoo
15 Kangasniemi Music Festival
16 Time of Music – Viitasaari
17 Kuhmo Chamber Music Festival
18 Crusell Week, Uusikaupunki
19 Oulainen Music Week

JAZZ FESTIVALS
20 April Jazz Espoo
21 Kainuu Jazz Spring, Kajaani
22 Lakeside Blues Festival, Järvenpää
23 Kalott Jazz & Blues Festival, Tornio and Haparanda
24 Imatra Big Band Festival
25 Baltic Jazz, Marine Jazz Festival, Taalintehdas
26 International Pori Jazz Festival
27 Tampere Jazz Happening

ROCK FESTIVALS
28 Provinssirock, Seinäjoki
29 Nummirock, Kauhajoki, Nummijärvi
30 Ruisrock, Turku

OTHER MUSIC FESTIVALS
31 Tampereen Sävel – Tampere International Choir Festival
32 Sata-Häme Accordion Festival, Ikaalinen
33 Tango Festival in Seinäjoki
34 Kihaus Folk Music Festival, Rääkkylä
35 Lieksa Brass Week
36 Kaustinen Folk Music Festival
37 Festival of Workers' Music, Valkeakoski
38 Lahti Organ Festival

FILM FESTIVALS
39 Tampere International Short Film Festival
40 Midnight Sun Film Festival, Sodankylä
41 Oulu International Children's Film Festival

DANCE, THEATRE AND LITERATURE FESTIVALS
42 Mikkeli International Amateur Theatre Festival
43 Arctic Comics Festival, Kemi
44 Kuopio Dance Festival
45 Word and Music in Kajaani
46 Bomba Festival, Nurmes
47 Häme Castle Children's Festival, Hämeenlinna
48 Amateur Dramatics Festival, Seinäjoki
49 Pentinkulma Days, Urjala
50 Tampere International Theatre Festival
51 Pispala Schottiche Dance Mania, Tampere

NATURE AND HERITAGE FESTIVALS
52 Jutajaiset, Rovaniemi
53 Eteläpohjalaiset Spelit, Karijoki and Kristiinankaupunki
54 Joutsa Folk Festival
55 Kymenlaakso Folk Art and Folk Music Festival, Miehikkälä

ART CENTRES
56 ▶Retretti, Punkaharju
57 Salmela, Mäntyharju
58 Pyhäniemi Manor House, Hollola

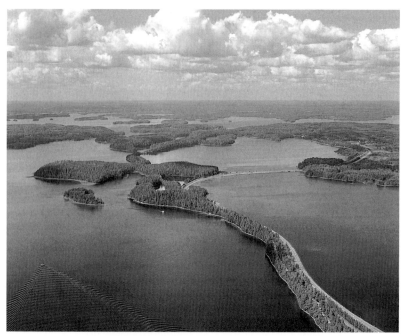

Punkaharju, the most spectacular example of the ridge landscape of eastern Finland

south, make it understandable that there are considerable differences physical and human geography. The long coastline, and particularly the country's southern and south-western parts, have long been the core of habitation. In the interior and to the north, habitation becomes sparser, until, approaching the most northerly regions, it reaches its limits. Thus Finland forms, in terms of regional geography, an interesting strip in the borderland between a cold and temperate climate.

For a long time, Finland was also located in a political and geographical borderland between two societal systems. Of Finland's 2582 kilometres of border, 1269 are with Russia, 727 with Norway and 586 with Sweden. The length of Finland's sea coast is approximately 1100 kilometres, discounting small-scale coastal formations. Finland's waters include the so-called interior and exterior territorial waters along the coast of the Baltic Sea and its bays. The width of the exterior territorial waters is generally set at 4 nautical miles.

It is a result of Finland's geographical position that its borders have varied during the various phases of its history. Changes have been fewest in its sea boundaries. On the other hand, the long eastern border has been subject to many changes. The significance of the borders as a separating or uniting factor has also varied. Borders with Finland's Nordic neighbours, Sweden and Norway, have been so open that it is no wonder that, in the eyes of foreigners, Finland forms a seamless part of Scandinavia.

Finland is a country of varied landscapes, although the general impression is even. Only in ▶Lapland there are hills rising to more than 200 metres. The highest place in Finland is Haltiatunturi Mountain (1328m). The greatest incidence of plains is in the coastal areas of ▶Ostrobothnia. Central Finland has many lakes, and waterways make up more than 25 per cent of the area. The easternmost part is Fjäll-Finland, southern Lapland typically has occasional fells, northern Lapland is characterised by uplands. The Finnish coast has numerous islands (▶archipelago).

Human activity and the increased use of natural resources have, in Finland as elsewhere, led to great changes in nature. Birch and pine forests have spread at the expense of spruce forests. Drainage changes the nature of bogs, and some of the waterways begin to become polluted. The increase of ▶summer cottages brings its own

Counties

Lapland

Oulu

Western
Finland

Eastern
Finland

Southern
Finland

100 km

**Historical
provinces**

Lapland

Ostrobothnia

Karelia

Savo

Satakunta
Häme

Åland   Finland
Proper   Uusimaa

100 km

problems to lakeland Finland. Finns nevertheless have a close and respectful attitude to the nature.

Finland's surface area is 0.25 per cent of that of the globe, and its population less than 0.1 per cent of the total population. In terms of economic and social welfare, Finland belongs among the richest countries in the world.

Forestry is an area in which Finland appears at the head of world statistics. Finland's share in world felled timber is only 1 per cent, but as a wood processor Finland is of greater importance. Finland's share in world production in various sectors was as follows: sawn timber 1.4 per cent, paper and cardboard (excluding newsprint) 3.5 per cent, newsprint 4.0 per cent and pulp paper 5.5 per cent. As an exporter of processed products, Finland's share is even more significant.

In other areas of production, the Finnish share is much smaller. Many other small countries, too, specialise in areas in which its natural conditions and standards of education are advantageous. Environmental determinism also shows its force in the fact that Finland does well in the statistics for skiing medals.

The importance to Finland of the parts of Russia closest to it has grown.

The Kola Peninsula, Russian Karelia and St Petersburg are now accessible in the same way as Sweden and Norway. The St Petersburg area alone has more inhabitants than the whole of Finland.

The independence of Estonia, Latvia and Lithuania brought these countries into closer contact with Finland and the other Nordic countries than before. It is relevant once more to speak of Baltoscandia, a term used as early as the 1920s by geographers to describe the combined area of the Baltic countries, the Scandinavian countries and Finland.

In discussing collaboration between countries, trade and other economic contacts are always mentioned. In recent decades, however, there has been growing appreciation of the extent and international nature of the environmental problem. All the countries of the globe are participants in the great cycle of nature, where changes in one area are also reflected elsewhere. Finns have woken up to environmental destruction both in the Baltic area as a whole and on a more immediately local scale. Finland has until now nevertheless been an ideal place to live. The country is very sparsely populated, so one of Finland's great riches is ▶space. KRn

Finland-Swedes The Finland-Swedes, or the Swedish-speaking minority in Finland, are exceptional in many respects. Consisting of almost 300,000 inhabitants, living mostly in three costal areas and on the ►Åland Isles, these Finns are integrated into Finnish society, but also form a distinct cultural group with some important institutions of their own. The proportion of the Swedish-speaking Finns is now 5.8 per cent of the population as a whole, while at the beginning of the 20th century it was around 10 per cent. Thanks to the constitutional legislation, both Finnish and Swedish are national languages of Finland, and Swedish is an official language on both the national level and at local level in those parts of Finland where the minority is at least 8 per cent of the population.

Svenska teatern ('The Swedish theatre') in Helsinki is the centre of the vigorous Finland-Swedish theatrical tradition

These happy circumstances are due to the fact that the Swedish-speaking Finns formerly constituted the leading layers of the country. In the process of developing language awareness since the 1860s, they constituted themselves as a language group consisting of the old élite and the common folk of the coastal areas. Institutional arrangements in independent Finland gradually secured the interest of Swedish-speakers in Finland with a ►literature of its own, a ►press of its own, schools with Swedish as language of tuition, the minority strove to found new institutions promoting its aims. Society of Swedish Literature in Finland was founded in 1885; the Swedish People's Party 1906.

Since then, two ways of coming to terms with the minority situation have been adopted. One has seen the maintainance of a nationally equal position as important, while the other has favoured one-language solutions, the bilingual ►University of Helsinki and the Swedish Åbo Akademi University being two examples. The non-socialist Swedish People's Party has striven to sit in government, while other political interests have been articulated as distinct parts of the social democrat and left-wing movements.

The culture of the Swedish-speakers in Finland is highly heterogenous and dependent on social class differences. The culture of Swedish-speakers living on the coast, where the earliest towns were founded, or descended from the administrative layers of the country as whole, has long had certain middle-class urban traits. On the other hand, the culture of the farmers and seafolk has resulted in a strong agrarian ►folk culture and a preference for occupations in trade and commerce. Mixing high culture and popular culture is another trait that makes Finland-Swedish culture a microcosm of the national culture. The national loyality of the Swedish-speaking Finns lies with Finland, while a culture of their own, in their own language, also makes them a language group with a strong inner solidarity.

Swedish-speaking areas

100 km

Finland has four permanent Swedish-language theatres. Interest in the theatre is expressed by amateur groups all over the country, and there are numerous summer theatres.

Literary works by Finnish authors in Swedish have spread beyond the country's borders. Through the common language, the spread of literature from Sweden to Finland is also considerable. Finland-Swedish publishing houses also publish translations from Finnish into Swedish. About 200 new titles are published in Swedish every year in Finland.

Finland has always absorbed European influences rapidly through Finland-Swedish literature. Both Finnish-speakers and Swedish-speakers claim Finland-Swedish writers as their own; the Finnish national poet and writer of the national anthem, ▶J.L. Runeberg, wrote in Swedish. In the early years of the 20th century, Finland-Swedish literature was a pioneer of modernism.

Within the Finnish Broadcasting Company, minority programmes for Swedish-speaking people function very well. More than two hours a day a broadcast over TV 1 and TV 2. Children's programmes and the news appear daily at prime time. TV 3 and TV 4, the commercial television companies, do not broadcast in Swedish.

Swedish-speakers have two channels on the ▶radio. The Swedish-language Radio can be heard throughout most of the whole country. This is a full-service channel offering a wide range of programmes, from news to plays. AMÅ

Finlandia Hall The sculptural form of ▶Alvar Aalto's Finlandia Hall glows in solitude among the tattered landscape of Töölönlahti Bay in central ▶Helsinki. The concert hall was completed in 1971, the congress wing in 1975. A new city centre has been planned in the area since shortly after 1910; Finland's grandest urban utopias have disappeared into Töölönlahti Bay as if into a black hole. Between 1961 and 1972 Aalto developed his own model, of which one central feature was a necklace of cultural buildings along the western shore of the bay, while another was a terraced square opening on to the southern end of the bay. Only the

Alvar Aalto, Finlandia Hall, 1967–1971

Finlandia Hall was built. Its interior is made up of the gliding sequence of spaces that is characteristic of Aalto's architecture.

The Finlandia Hall was the venue for the 1975 Conference on Security and Co-operation in Europe. This gave a role to the building in the proud memories of the people; it was also used for the Helsinki Summit of 1997 (see page 151). There has been intense debate over the replacement of the decaying white Carrara marble with which the building is faced. RN

Finnish baseball Finnish baseball is a modernised, faster version of American baseball – at least, according to the developer of the game, Lauri Pihkala (1888–1981). During a visit to the United States before the First World War, Pihkala noted the popularity of baseball and its developed form. In Finland, on the other hand, traditional ball-games were in danger, as athletics was making its appearance and would perhaps do away with memories of the older ball-games. Pihkala began to develop a Finnish equivalent to the American national game.

If Finnish folk-games were confusing and their rules ambiguous, with games often ending in dispute or even violence, Pihkala, with his curious outsider's eyes, also saw shortcomings in American baseball. Its weakness was its moment of triumph, bowling. The game was limited to a duel between pitcher and hitter, with the other play-

Fire and movement: Finnish baseball is enjoying renewed popularity, particularly in Ostrobothnia

Since, in baseball, getting to first base was the most difficult, Pihkala wanted to make the distances between bases gradually more difficult. But that posed a problem, particularly as the broad pitch required by American baseball was not suitable, Pihkala thought, for the more variable Finnish terrain. As a solution, Pihkala had the players criss-crossing the field, rather than touring it base by base in the American style. Thus the relationship of the new game to the American original was like that of a 'war of movement to trench warfare'. Pihkala was delighted.

ers relegated to little more than sentry duty. The pitcher dominated the game, and good bat-strokes seldom occurred. Thus Pihkala replaced the undulating horizontal pitch with a vertical pitch, which was easier for the batsman.

With the help of the army and the civil guard, the fast attack game was made known to Finns and spread throughout the country. In it were crystallised the infantry tactics of a

Finnish cultural and research institutes

New York 1990
Jerusalem 1994
Oslo 1996
St. Petersburg 1996
Stockholm 1970
Tallinn 1994
Copenhagen 1992
London 1991
Berlin 1994
Antwerp 1993
Paris 1990
Madrid 1997
Rome 1954
Athens 1985
1000 km

newly independent small nation, 'fire and movement': accurate grenade-throwing combined with rapid advance on the enemy's dugout. In the Second World War this was, indeed, of significance in the variable forested terrain in which the battles on the eastern front were fought.

Today Finnish baseball is regarded as a fast and tactically demanding game of the intelligence whose audiences compete numerically with football crowds. The best teams have, in recent years, come equally from small towns and the countryside, above all from Ostrobothnia and Savo. In the mid 1990s, the game has been making a comeback in the Helsinki area. Women's baseball is also on the ascendant.

Finnish baseball is played abroad in some parts of Estonia and among Finnish emigrants in Sweden, Germany and even Australia. ES

Finnish Literature Society The Finnish Literature Society (Suomalaisen Kirjallisuuden Seura, SKS), was founded in 1831. Its role in Finland's cultural history is unusually central. Many important collecting, research and publishing projects have originated at the instigation of the Society, as have the basic works of Finland's national literature. Most of the younger organisations and societies active in the area of folklore studies began their lives within the Finnish Literature Society.

A central reason for the foundation of the Finnish Literature Society was the energetic activity of ►Elias Lönnrot. There was a need to fund his research trips and the publication of their results. Ideologically, the project was based on the patriotic national tradition which began to develop in many ways after Finland had ceased to be part of Sweden in 1809. International models were also on offer: numerous literature societies had been founded in the university towns of Europe from the late 18th century onwards.

The most durable projects of the early period proved to be funding of the journeys made by the Society's first secretary, Lönnrot, to gather folk poetry, and the publication of the resulting volumes, the ►*Kalevala* (1835) and the

The Finnish Literature Society in central Helsinki, 1890, exterior (above) and interior (below)

►*Kanteletar* (1840). The Society began to publish, in Finnish, both non-fiction and literature: history, grammars, popular works on the natural sciences, philosophy and law, and translations of the classics of world literature. Writers were sought for stories and plays through competitions. The first novel in the Finnish language, ►Aleksis Kivi's *Seitsemän veljestä* (*Seven Brothers*) was published by the Society in 1870.

The Folklore Archive is the central archive of Finnish ►folk culture and ►folklore research; it administers research programmes, arranges the collection of oral tradition and organises research trips. There are more than 3 million folklore records in the archive's collections; the number of recordings and photographs is also considerable. The Folklore Archive is among the largest of its kind in the world.

The Literary Archive collects and preserves manuscripts by writers and scholars, and photographs and recordings of cultural and historical interest. The Literary Archive contains almost 900 shelf-metres of manuscripts, including 100,000 letters. The manuscripts represent all the decades of the national culture, various literary genres, and hundreds of authors.

The library is the oldest of the Society's institutions, for its founders wanted to build a collection that would contain all material, printed and manuscript, concerning Finnish-language culture. The library contains more than 200,000 volumes. Those acquired earlier are mainly in Finnish. Foreign texts have also been acquired through exchange, particularly ethnological literature. Today the library maintains and adds to collections linked to the Society's activities and at the same time acts as a central library for the field of folkloristics.

The role of the Finnish Literature Information Centre is to increase knowledge of Finnish literature and non-fiction abroad and to promote their translation into other languages. The Information Centre supports performers, translators, literary scholars and critics of Finnish literature living abroad and maintains links with publishers, literary festivals and cultural centres. Together with the ▶Finnish cultural and research institutes in various parts of the world, the Information Centre arranges translators' conferences, literary seminars and events, and exhibitions.

The Finnish Literature Society has some 3000 members in Finland and 200 abroad. They are primarily academics, teachers, writers, translators, artists, editors, civil servants and other professionals in the cultural field, and amateurs of literature and folkloristics. The Finnish Literature Society occupies its own premises, a building completed in 1890, in the centre of Helsinki. PLn

Finnish National Gallery The Finnish National Gallery has functioned under its current name and in its current form since 1990. Its main building is the ▶Ateneum, completed in 1887. The Finnish National Gallery has the main responsibility for the recording, documentation and exhibition of the national art heritage. The collections contain a total of some 20,000 works, most of them paintings, sculptures, drawings, graphics and installations. The organisation is divided into three museums and the Central Art Archives. The oldest is the Museum of Finnish Art, Ateneum, which was opened in 1863 and whose area is Finnish and international art from the period 1750–1960. The ▶Museum of Contemporary Art, founded in 1990, continues from 1960. The third is the Museum of Foreign Art Sinebrychoff, founded in 1921, which specialises in older foreign art (c.1300–1850). MLR

Finns abroad The greatest emigration among Finns has been to America, Australia and Sweden.

AMERICA The documented Finnish presence in America starts with the founding of the 'New Sweden' colony at the mouth of Delaware River, in March 1638. Major contributions made by the early Finnish settlers in America were burn-beat farming, a new way of building log-cabins, and the art of living in peace with Indians. A descendant of these early Finns was John Morton, who signed the Unites States Declaration of Independence in 1776.

In 1855, during the Crimean War (1854–1856), a number of Finnish ships sought refuge in American ports. A few hundred Finns joined the gold rush, starting the Finnish settlements on the Pacific coast. Since 1790, some Finns had settled in Alaska, working for the Russian government. On two occasions a man of Finnish origin was appointed governor of Alaska.

The Finnish settlers of the Arctic Norwegian province of Finnmark were the first to respond to the temptation of the Michigan copper mines and to the promise of free land profferedby the Homestead Act signed by President Abraham Lincoln in 1862. From Norway the tide of emigration spread down south. In the 1870s 'America Fever' took hold in southern ▶Ostrobothia, becoming a mass movement in the following decade. The crest of the wave was reached in 1902, when more than 23,000 Finns applied for passports to emigrate. Emigration continued in a large scale until the outbreak of the First World War. When the US government began to restrict the admission of immigrants in the 1920s, Finnish emigration shifted to Canada and Australia. Between 1864 and 1914, well over 300,000 Finns made their

Postage stamp commemorating 350 years of Finnish emigration to America, 1988

homes in the United States, and another 20,000 across the border in Canada.

The Finnish emigrants to America originated mainly from western parts of Finland. Their reasons for leaving Ostrobothnia were mainly economic and social. Distilling tar had, along with agriculture, been the mainstay of the economy of the Bothnian regions; when the era of sailing ships began to decline after the mid 19th century, the demand for tar declined. Another reason was the rapid increase of population: farms were small, and nearly every household was bursting at the seams with children. The majority of Finns who went to America were young, around 20 years of age. Over 60 per cent were men, most of them unmarried. A main reason for emigration was the desire to earn money enough to redeem the family farm or to buy a house and a piece of land; another was to avoid the draft into the Russian army.

The main attraction, however, was the high wage levels in the United States in certain occupations, this was five times higher than in Finland. Work was available for men in mines, lumber camps, factories and railroads. Employers regarded Finns as good and reliable workers. The homes of wealthy Americans offered employment to women, and Finnish servant girls were in considerable demand.

The Finnish settlements were concentrated in Massachusetts, Michigan and Minnesota. The wish of many Finns to own a farm resulted in Finnish farming communities, especially in the Mid West. In Canada, about 60 per cent of the Finnish population lived in Ontario, especially in Toronto, Sudbury and present-day Thunder Bay.

The Finns in North America conducted an active religious, social and cultural life. At the turn of the century there were some 100 Finnish congregations in the United States, and a few in Canada. Temperance societies were started from the 1880s. The labour movement began to spread in the 1890s, and by 1913 the Finnish Socialist Party could boast 260 local branches. Finns have been a major element in the United States Communist Party, and were trail-blazers in the co-operative movement throughout North America.

The many activities of the Finnish communities included sport, drama, and music, in the form of, among other things, band-playing. The first Finnish newspaper was published in Hancock, Michigan in 1876, and at the turn of the century there were more Finnish language newspapers in America than in Finland. Many were short-lived, but they played an important part as sources of information about the old and new homelands.

Although the Finns formed less than 1 per cent of European immigration to North America, their concentration in, for example, Michigan and Thunder Bay in Canada had a considerable impact on the local population, particularly prominent in the mining communities of Upper Michigan, especially in the industrial strikes. A study made at Northern Michigan University drew the conclusion that American Finns had influenced the English spoken in northern Michigan.

Since the Second World War, Finnish emigration to North America has been quite insignificant: by the 1990s, 15,000 had gone to the United States and 27,000 to Canada. In North America there were about 45,000 first-generation and 180,000 second-generation Finns. Including later generations, there were more than 1 million people of Finnish extraction, a substantial contribution to the ethnic and cultural mosaic of the United States and Canada.

The first Finnish colony in Latin America, Colonia Finlandesa in Argentina, was founded in 1906. Today, descendants of these early settlers, mainly Swedish-speaking Finns, still live there.

AUSTRALIA During the Australian gold rush of the 1850s and 1860s a few hundred Finns, mostly seamen, settled permanently on the continent. The first Finnish group migration to Australia took place in 1899–1900, when the Queensland government offered free passages from London to the colony. Altogether there were some 5000 Finns in Australia before the Second World War, between 1957 and 1973 about 20,000. Finns emigrated to Australia due to high unemployment in Finland and Australian government-assisted passages. The Finns who emigrated to Australia after the Second World War were generally skilled craftsmen, and many were employed in the construction industry. They settled mainly in Sydney, Melbourne and other capital cities. In the 1990s there were about 9000 persons born in Finland and 17,000 second-generation Finns in Australia. Altogether some 30,000 Australians were of Finnish descent.

NEW ZEALAND Since the mid 19th century a couple of thousand Finns have emigrated to New Zealand. A number of Finnish paper mill workers in the 1950s and 1960s were among the pioneers of the New Zealand pulp and paper industry. In the 1970s and 1980s Finns emigrating to New Zealand were generally well-educated, and often married New Zealanders. The major settlement of Finns is in Auckland.

AFRICA The first Finns found their way to European colonies in Africa as early as the 18th century. In the 1860s and 1870s the mining industry caused an economic upheaval in South Africa, in the 1890s emigration to South Africa reached epidemic proportions in Swedish-speaking Ostrobothnia. At the turn of century many Finns participated in the Boer War (1899–1902) on both sides. A total of some 1500 Finns emigrated to South Africa before the First World War. Finnish missionary work began in Ovamboland, present-day Namibia, in 1870. Many of the missionaries settled permanently in Africa. Since the last century a few hundred Finnish adventurers and seamen have served in the French and Spanish Foreign Legions in North Africa. In the 1990s about 2000 Finns were living in Africa. Many of them were in missionary work or employed by Finnish and international companies.

SWEDEN As far back as the 14th century some people from present-day Finland went to Sweden in search of a better livelihood. In the 16th century King Charles IX (1550–1611) invited Finns to Sweden. But the main reasons for the emigration were wars with Russia and crop failures and famines in Finland. Some of these 'forest Finns' of Sweden continued their journey to the colony of 'New Sweden' in Delaware, which was founded in 1638. During Sweden's period as a major European power in the 17th century, Finns belonging to all classes and estates moved to the 'mother country'. Most of them were labourers, sailors, fisherfolk and, last but not least, cannon fodders, but the occasional Finn made it into high office, and many are recorded in the history books as distinguished military men, artists, explorers, scientists and men of letters.

When, in 1809, Finland was wrested from Sweden to become a Grand Duchy within the Russian empire, the flow of emigrants to Sweden was not staunched. Particularly in the latter half of the 19th century, the timber industry and saw-mills along the Swedish coast of the Gulf of Bothnia strongly attracted Finnish labour.

The creation of a free Nordic labour market in 1954 and powerful economic growth in Sweden opened the door for a massive westward exodus of Finnish workers. The flow reached its peak in 1970, when more than 41,000 Finns went to Sweden to work. However, the main reasons for mass emigration are to be found in Finland. A rapid transformation from agriculture to manufacturing made a large number of rural workers redundant. At the same time, the children born in the post-war 'baby-boom' years of 1945–1949 began entering the labour market. Finally, a hefty devaluation of the Finnish mark in 1967 boosted Swedish nominal wages. Many Finns went west in the hope of fatter wage packets.

Since 1533, when the Finnish congregation was founded in Stockholm, Finnish settlers have led active religious, social and cultural lives. The first Finnish society in Sweden was founded in 1830 and after the post-war mass migration the Federation of Finnish Associations in Sweden was established in 1957. In 1987 the Federation had 168 local societies with 46,000 members. Swedish-speaking Finns have similar organisations in Sweden.

Altogether 550,000 Finns emigrated to Sweden after the Second World War. Half of them have since returned to Finland, especially in the 1980s, or moved to a third country. In the 1990s there were more than 200,000 first-generation Finns living in Sweden and nearly 100,000 of the second generation. Nearly half of the Finns abroad were living in Sweden. The Finns in Sweden have been able to find an identity of their own, especially since the Swedish government has acknowledged that the Finns in Sweden are a permanent minority which had lived in Sweden for a very long time.

NORWAY Between the Second World War and the mid 1990s, some 15,000 Finns had emigrated to Norway. Permanent Finnish settlement began to develop in Finnmark, Norway's northernmost province, in the 18th century, mainly due to the famines in Finland. Many of the Finns continued their journey to America. Since the Second World War thousands of Finns have found work in the fish industry of northern Norway and later in the rapidly developing Norwegian oil industry. In the 1990s 5000 Finns were

living in Norway, the majority of them male industrial workers.

DENMARK some 13,000 Finns emigrated to Denmark after the Second World War, and a couple of hundred to Iceland. Most of these, however, have subsequently returned to Finland. In the 1990s there were only about 2000 Finns living permanently in Denmark.

RUSSIA After the Treaty of Stolbova in 1617 Finns began migrating to former Russia. They settled especially around the mouth of the Neva River in the area known as Ingria, where St Petersburg was founded nearly a century later. The number of these Ingrians was highest in 1917, totalling some 120,000 persons.

After Finland was annexed by Russia in 1809, Finns began to emigrate to Russia, and especially to St Petersburg. Finnish settlements were also found in many parts of Russia, including the far East. In the 19th century 3300 Finnish criminals were transported to Siberia, but there was also voluntary emigration across the Ural Mountains.

Because of the lack of statistics it is difficult to estimate the numbers of Finns who have emigrated to Russia. In the 1990s a cautious estimation was 50,000 persons since 1809.

After the dissolution of the Soviet Union in 1991, about 13,000 persons of Finnish origin from Russia and Estonia arrived in Finland. In the 1990s, an estimated 60,000 to 70,000 Finns were still living in Russia.

CENTRAL EUROPE Since the 1960s, Finns have started to settle in central and western Europe. In the 1990s there were more than 12,000 Finns living in Germany, 80 per cent of them women, often married to Germans. As a result of the high rate of unemployment in Finland, the number of Finns in Germany was growing by 1000 a year. About 5000 Finns were living permanently in Great Britain and 4000 in Switzerland. More than 10,000 Finns were estimated to be living in Spain, many of them retired people who come to Finland during the summer. But generally the 'new emigrants' to Europe from Finland were young, well-educated people. This can be regarded as short-term migration, as many of them were employees in projects of Finnish or international enterprises. After Finland joined the European Union in 1995, emigration did not increase, with the exeption of construction workers and nurses emigrating to Germany.

Increased student exchanges have also meant that young Finns find it easy to settle in other European countries. OK

Fiskars, metalwork company, founded 1649.

Finland's first ironworks, Fiskars, was founded in the southern Finnish parish of Pohja in 1649. In the 18th century, copper became the factory's most important product. A purposeful development project began in the factory when it came into the ownership of Johan Julin (1787–1853). First products were, from the beginning, objects that still belong to Fiskars' output: scissors, ▶*puukko* knives, table knives and forks. Fiskars became the founder of Finland's first machine shop in 1836–1837. Among the shop's early products were the country's first steam engine, steam kettles, machines for paper mills and cloth factories and a printing machine. Between 1918 and 1920 Fiskars gained a majority shareholding in the Billnäs Factory, which made various tools.

Since the 1950s, Fiskars has made a particular investment in the design of objects. The silversmith Bertel Gardberg (born 1916) designed an axe for Fiskars and a stainless steel cutlery range, *Triennale*, in the 1950s. In the 1960s the factory's range of products increased with a number of small domestic tools designed by the factory's own group of designers or by the designer Olof Bäckström (born 1922).

Olavi Lindén, Fiskars Clippers, 1996, received the European Design Prize in 1997

The shock-resistant scissors designed by Bäckström in orange plastic and steel, which have, since their arrival on the market, been among the best-known Finnish products, date from 1967. In addition to scissors, tools and gardening equipment have traditionally formed an important part of Fiskars's production.

Since it has ceased to be used for production, the original ironworks area at Fiskars has developed, in the 1990s, into a lively crafts village with exhibition spaces. MaA

flag ▶national symbols

folk art Characteristic of Finnish folk art are functional form and imaginative decoration, combined with strong stylisation and a tendency toward geometrical presentation and symmetry, rhythmic repetition, strong colours and simple colour contrasts, and the depiction of human figures, either head on or from the side.

St George and the dragon, Finström Church, Åland, 16th century

Folk art is defined essentially as art made by peasants and artisans, but it also includes art made for domestic needs and the products of home industries, which are also found in urban culture. Folk art is, to a great extent, applied art. It includes painting and sculpture, ▶furniture and other utility objects, as well as ▶textiles and ▶architecture. It has been influenced by the dominant artistic styles (renaissance, baroque, rococo). The coming of industrialisation greatly atrophied the practice of folk art.

The formal language of folk art varies greatly depending on its location, and its makers' livelihoods, geographical location, influences, raw materials and transport connections. The shaping of the folk art tradition is complex: conceptions of form of widely varying ages and provenance are entwined. Conservatism is, nevertheless, characteristic. Local art traditions often arise during economic boom periods: even after the ending of a period of material flourishing, stylistic and formal features of it are often preserved (for example, in the furniture of ▶Ostrobothnia). Folk art cannot be divided neatly into stylistic periods following one after the other; neither can individual products be dated according to their stylistic features. The same object may exhibit stylistic features of both the 17th and the 20th centuries.

Poor-box, Perho Church, western Finland, 18th century

The most direct outside influences are often derived from churches and their decorations (for example, sun and angel motifs) or from aristocratic houses (for example, the lion) in which members of the lower social classes were in service. Visits to the towns, too, gave country people new ideas.

Sculpture is, in Finland, a rare form of folk art. Rare from a European

Communal beer tankard used at catechistical meetings, 1542

point of view are the poor-boxes that used to stand close to the wooden churches. In smaller wooden objects, too, high artistic standards were often reached. Wooden objects made by a bridegroom for his bride, for example, carved distaffs, spools and rolling boards – demonstrate the skills of their maker. Here and there is some evidence of artistic applied arts. Skilfully made wooden eating and drinking vessels from south-western Finland were sold across the sea as far as the Baltic countries, Stockholm and Copenhagen. The handsomest examples are the wooden feast-vessels, particularly the communal beer tankards, or *kousas*.

Wood-carving generally consists of surfaces faceted with a knife or chisel, which, with the help of light and shade, form strong contrasts. The technique originates in the prehistoric period, but the stylistic origins most often lie in gothic, renaissance or later styles. In addition to carving, perforation is encountered, as well as, to a lesser extent, relief work. Folk forging of

Fish-god, Eno, Marjovaara, north Karelia

metal is represented primarily in the iron locks of doors, chests and cupboards, but village smiths also made candlesticks and grave-crosses.

A liking for ornament is also evident in paintings made on the surfaces of objects. In Finland, folk painting is centred on the decoration of furniture and utility objects. This dates back to the 18th century, but was particularly powerful from the 1860s onwards. In the coastal regions, in particular, greetings paintings carried the names of the people involved in each celebration or festivity with explanatory texts, surrounded with ornamental illustration.

Among the Orthodox sector of the population, the painting of Easter eggs has become a folk art form of its own.

►Ceramics have been of the greatest importance in the east and south-east, where ►food has, historically, generally been cooked in ovens. The manufacturing centre of clay vessels was the Karelian Isthmus, where Russian-influenced crockery was made, decorated with elegant painted and fluted decorations. Through the emigration forced by the Second World War, these skills have been transferred elsewhere in Finland and remained alive.

►Textiles are among the most important and commonest forms of folk art. Trousseau items – involving weaving, embroidery and lace-making – are generally more impressive than everyday items. Among them, in western parts of Finland, are woven ►ryijy rugs, whose motifs – lions, birds, tree-of-life themes – derive, in the last analysis, from the Oriental and Byzantine woven silks of the early medieval period. A tradition of quality lace-making still exists on the west coast, around ►Rauma; through seafaring, it was influenced, among other things, by the Tönder area of Denmark. TK

folk costume Ancient features, some of them dating back as far as in the prehistoric period, have survived in Finnish folk dress, but influences from European fashionable dress have also been absorbed. In the 19th century, with industrialisation and the advent of mass production, folk costumes gradually fell out of use. They survived at their most conservative in southern ►Karelia and the Swedish-speaking areas of ►Ostrobothnia, where they were still in use at the end of the 19th century.

It is customary to make a distinction between western Finnish and Karelian folk costumes. Only parts of liturgical garments from the medieval period have survived. Features traceable back to Renaissance dress fashions include, in western Finnish costumes, a bodice, white smock, pleated skirt and a loose pocket for toiletries.

In the 17th and 18th centuries, dress developed in different parts of Finland into a diverse and varied way of dressing which, freed of regulation in the early 19th century, quickly absorbed fashionable features. Until the 18th century, fabrics were plain and adhered to the dark colour scale favoured by the baroque. Well into the 19th century, red was the predominant colour in the home-woven fabrics from which women's costumes were made. At the end of the 18th century, the freeing of maritime trade increased the availability of foreign fabrics. The red-green colour range of the baroque persisted well into the 19th century.

According to the sumptuary legislation in the Nordic countries in the 18th century, the common people were forbidden to use expensive imported fabrics for their dress. In home-woven fabrics, attempts were made to imitate the stripes of woollen fabrics from abroad. Wide-striped fabrics were popular primarily in the 18th century, after which the stripes narrowed. In southern Ostrobothnia, skirts made from colourful, wide-striped *ikat* fabrics were particularly popular in the 19th century. In Swedish-speaking Ostrobothnia, the *ikat* patterns of skirt fabrics were small and the stripes narrow. In the 19th century, the weaving of cotton and linen fabrics developed in the eastern parts of central Finland and Savo, where the colour blue was adopted for women's dress. Narrow-striped cotton fabrics followed the English fashions in cotton of the early 19th century.

Women's headdresses have played an essential part in dress, and were considered to indicate of social status. From the 17th century onwards in the Nordic countries, the wife's headdress was a white linen headdress edged with lace or a pleated strip of fabric. Fashionable dress, however, demanded a stiffened cap covered with silk, which was sometimes worn over the linen cap. In the 18th and 19th centuries the stiffened cap became the most common folk headdress for women.

Fashionability and expensive imported fabrics characterised the dress of the gentry, while the common people were restricted to clothes made from traditional Finnish and homespun fabrics. Fashionability was also visible in cut. Women's bodices and jackets grew shorter at the beginning of the 19th century as a result of the influence of the empire style. Dresses came into use in the mid 19th century, at first as festive attire, worn with an apron and stiffened cap. At the beginning of the 19th century women's dress in Savo and northern Karelia consisted of a dark blue jacket and skirt made of home-spun fabric, without a bodice. The religious ▶revivalist movement that started in northern Savo adopted the local folk dress as its characteristic costume; the name of the movement, (körttiläisyys) took its name from the körtti, or pleats, at the back of the jacket.

According to European models, Spanish fashionable dress, consisting of knee-breeches, a waistcoat and jacket, was adopted as men's costume. The western Finnish man's breeches were of chamois leather, and knitted socks reached to the knees. The cut of the festive shirt of the 18th and 19th centuries, in particular, has its origins in Spanish fashionable dress.

At the end of the 18th century, to oppose luxuriousness in dress and to balance the national economy, King Gustavus III (1746–1792) introduced in a spirit of national romanticism, the national Swedish costume, which also influenced the appearance of male folk dress. Jacket and waistcoat were made of a narrow-striped fabric, and were worn with a self-coloured coat with a plain long coat with a high stand-up collar, straight back and pleats. Male dress became simpler in the 18th century after the French Revolution, when long, straight-legged sailor's trousers and a short jacket were adopted. Home-spun coarse wool was replaced, under the influence of Swedish uniforms, by broadcloth. Coarse wool,

Magnus von Wright, Karelian folk costume, 1878

however, remained in use as a material for long overcoats and cloaks.

Features of late prehistoric and Renaissance dress survived long into the 19th century in southern Karelia. These included the wife's veil and metal-ferruled girdle. Because of the wars and border changes of the 17th and 18th centuries, European fashion did not affect Karelian dress; the fitted bodice, for example, did not form part of it. It was only in the early 19th century, that innovations in traditional costume were absorbed, and parishes developed their own characteristic costumes. Differences were noticeable – in particular, in girls' and wives' head coverings and headdresses. The headdress of a Lutheran wife was a white veil tied at the neck, whose shape and size varied from parish to parish. The headdress of an Orthodox wife was a sorokka headdress, embroidered in red.

H.J. Strömmer, Orthodox Karelian, 1832

Agathon Reinholm, Girl from Satakunta, 1879

103

Girls' hair was tied with ribbons or twined round supports into buns. In the western parishes of southern Karelia women's costume in the 19th century comprised a straight bodice and skirt made from a unicoloured brown or blue woollen fabric and a linen apron decorated with *nyytinki* lace. The neck opening of the white linen smock, which was fastened with a large silver brooch, was at the centre. In coastal parishes on the Gulf of Finland, the dress was made from brown checked woollen material and originated from the old-fashioned kirtle. The neck opening of the smock was to the left and fastened with a brooch. There was a square embroidered piece at the front, known as the *rekko*. A short linen or woollen cloak was used in summer, replaced in winter by a white coarse woollen cloak with an embroidered collar. The summer apron was of linen decorated with *nyytinki* lace, while the red broadcloth winter apron was decorated with embroidery, fringes and braid ribbons. By Lake Ladoga and in border parishes of Ingria, women wore a woollen skirt of sarafan kirtle type, with long apron tied in the north Russian style high up to the armpits. Male Karelian dress was of grey or white coarse wool, linen in summer. Gradually during the 19th century the colour of men's costume became dark blue. On their heads they wore a felt hat with a high crown and a wide brim.

NATIONAL COSTUMES are a revival of the traditional festive dress used by the peasant population in the 18th and 19th centuries. They were assembled from traditional folk costumes that disappeared from use in the 19th century.

The national costume is a designed and reconstructed costume whose intention is to revive festive folk dress fashions, and which circles representing certain trends of ideas use as festive dress in order to emphasise their links with the past, a particular locality or group of people.

The national costumes of western Finnish parishes are, in a way, examples of types and average versions of the traditional festive dress of their area at a particular period. The costumes used in the conservative areas of Finnish southern Karelia, which were peculiar to particular parishes, can also be called parish costumes.

As their name suggests, the first national costumes were linked with the national spirit in the late 19th century. They were considered to express the national spirit and respect for traditional peasant values. Particular attention was attracted by a group wearing the national costumes of the Finnish provinces during the imperial visit of Emperor Alexander II and Maria Feodorovna in 1885. The wearing of national costumes was promoted and spread by patriotic organisations, societies and choirs. National costumes were made in domestic industry schools and folk high schools in different areas. Most of the designed national costumes are based in the collections of the ▶National Museum of Finland. In 1979 organisations favouring the wearing of national costume founded the Finnish Council for National Costume, which functions as a source of expert advice in its field. PS

ANCIENT FINNISH COSTUMES are not national costumes or folk costumes, although they are often confused with them and are used on similar occasions. While national costumes are revivals of the folk dress of the 18th and 19th centuries, ancient Finnish costumes reflect dress of around a 1000 years ago. They are based on late Iron Age grave-finds in Finland. This reconstruction of funeral dress as festive dress, on the scale on which it has occurred in Finland, is probably unique in the world. These costumes do not exist merely in museum cases, on stage or at meetings of antiquarians, but are used by prominent Finnish women on important festive occasions, including presidential banquets.

Interest in ancient costumes began at around the same time as the use of national costumes. The first booklets of designs also containing patterns, were published at the turn of the 20th century. Although a man's costume based on grave finds was also present, it was the woman's costume, which was called the Aino costume after the ▶*Kalevala* heroine, that became popular. It has remained in production, in various forms, up to the present day.

All the other ancient Finnish costumes in use today are also women's costumes. The Perniö ancient costume was made for an exhibition in the National Museum of Finland in 1925, the Kaukola costume for an exhibition in 1956. The Tuukkala costume was introduced in the late 1930s as festive attire for the mature woman, as was the Ancient Karelian costume, in 1952. A number of different grave-finds were used for the reconstruction of each of these costumes.

The first ancient costume to be based on the finds of a single grave was the Eura costume, which appeared in 1982. This costume was a result of careful scholarship. The grave on whose finds it is based dates from the early 11th century, while the other above-mentioned grave-finds date from between 100 and 200 years later. In the National Museum of Finland, the Eura costume represents the Viking period, while the Perniö costume represents the period of the Crusades.

The 1980s and 1990s have seen the reconstruction of ancient costumes based on grave-finds in the the Masku and Mikkeli areas. PLLH

folk culture Folk culture in Finland is clearly divided between the east and west of the country. At the core of each is prehistoric habitation: in the former, south-western Finnish (Roman Catholic in the medieval period) and in the latter, Karelian (Orthodox in the medieval period). As habitation spread during the medieval period (A.D. 1100–1500) and the early centuries of the modern period, a geographical duality arose in many cultural regions that is still discernible today.

WESTERN SOUTH FINLAND is now known as industrial Finland, but it has always been the functional centre of the country. Half of the entire population of the country lives in this region, and the standard of living here is higher than elsewhere. The region was prosperous from an early period, so that social layering developed strongly, with burghers, aristocratic ▶manor houses and official residences for officers and the clergy. This environment favoured innovation and provided a base for the valuing of achievements and status symbols.

Close contacts with the outside world were cultivated. The influence of central Sweden was felt via the ▶Åland archipelago, which was natural, among other reasons, because the inhabitants of the Finnish coastal strip and ▶archipelago were Swedish-speaking. At first innovations were related essentially to the region's ecology (for example farming methods and types of plough), but later they were associated with features through which it was possible to imitate the example of higher social classes. Innovations were absorbed in building (for example, stone foundations and painting), living (parlours and guest-rooms), ▶furniture (bunk beds, benches with rotating backs), dress (skirts, waistcoats and shoes), folk customs (village weddings) and music and dance. Old traditions are to be found particularly in the area of ▶food management: rye bread, fermented milk, mould cheeses and *mämmi*, a pudding eaten at Easter, and the stockfish eaten at Christmas.

In the ▶Åland archipelago, the enormous importance of fishing, seal hunting and sea faring for livelihoods has emphasised the peculiar nature of the peasant culture. Today it is most clearly to be seen in the building stock, in the boat- and net-houses of small harbours and the Swedish-influenced decoration of houses with wooden cut-out patterns and handsome glass verandahs.

The plain of southern ▶Ostrobothnia is the other main region of western Finnish folk culture. Here, too, the population of the interior is Finnish-speaking, having arrived from the east after the year A.D. 1000, while the inhabitants of the coastal area came from Sweden in the 13th and 14th centuries. The centre of the province is the city of Vaasa, which was founded in 1606.

The population of southern Ostrobothnia was made up largely of peasants. Manor houses were not built here; ▶vicarages were, because of the large size of parishes, few; and ironworks, or industrial enterprises in general, extremely rare. Social differences began to appear only during the 18th century as estates were split up and tenant farms established.

Ostrobothnia has long had close links with the west, with the coastal towns of northern Sweden and directly with Stockholm and, in the past, through trade (including the export of tar) and ship-building, also farther afield, with Denmark, Germany and England. Carving skills learned in ship-building were adapted to joinery for the construction of log cabins and furniture (cupboards, long-case clocks and chairs). The influence of the renaissance and neo-classical styles is obvious here. Among the characteristics of the region are handsome, two-storey houses built in the 18th and 19th centuries with curved fireplaces, and windmills. Two-storeyed store-houses with a loft are also typical. Innovations communicated from the west in boom periods are also evident in dress and textiles (*ikat* skirt-fabrics). A western custom that has been adopted only here is the burning of paschal fires. An Ostrobothnian speciality is *leipäjuusto*, a chewy form of baked milk, which is now available throughout the country. The crown wedding tradition, which used to be a tradition of the entire west of Finland, has, on the other hand, now become an Ostrobothnian peculiarity.

The flourishing peasant culture of Ostrobothnia continued until the end of the 19th century, as bog and burn-beat farming extended cultivated land and brought prosperity. At the turn of the 19th century, the growing population was decanted in the form of emigration to America, for the modernisation of farming here began later than in the south-western part of the country.

The folk culture of central Ostrobothnia is marked by immigration in the 17th century from eastern Finland, and by the activities of the Kokkola-Pietarsaari area as a cultural gateway to the west. Evidence for the latter is present in the form of, for example, the lengthwise-pedestal cradle and the wide-frame housing type, or side-chamber house, which can be seen at the Kaustinen Folk Heritage Centre. Because of the presence of extensive natural meadows, the basis of livelihood lies in cattle-farming particularly in the south. Connected with this is the building of special summer byres and the preference for sweet cheeses which demand a great deal of milk.

THE EASTERN FINNISH region is more homogeneous than the west in

Traditional western Finnish interior, Virrat heritage village, Häme

terms of folk culture, as some of the areas originated very late. At their core are the cultural characteristics of the ancient Karelian population who lived on the shores of Lake Ladoga in the late prehistoric and early historical period, which spread through settlement first to the Mikkeli area and then, in the medieval and modern period, throughout the whole of eastern and northern Finland. A fragment of population also emigrated from the northern shore of Lake Ladoga to northern Karelia. Their descendants form the oldest core of the current Orthodox population of Finland.

The region has been socially homogeneous. In addition to the burghers of the small towns, only the sparse clergy and a few noble manor-house owners in northern and southern Savo could be classed as gentry. Peasant farmholdings were small, but the towns of the south quite large. Social contacts have always been characterised by liveliness and directness.

The main source of livelihood until the second half of the 19th century was burn-beat farming, except in the Kuopio–Iisalmi and Liperi–Joensuu areas, where field-farming gained a foothold early as a result of the fertile clay soil. Old burn-beat land can now be identified by its fine birch copses. After the famine years of the 1860s, cattle-farming was of increasing importance, partly because of the trade in exporting butter to St Petersburg. Excess populations emigrated to the centres of the south and to the industrial centres of south-eastern Finland.

The eastern chimney-less cabin with its high stove, now visible only in museum buildings, traces its origin to the old Karelian tradition. This living tradition includes the raised barn, a type of sickle adopted from the Slavs and soft, loaf-like rye bread, an unsoured, thin barley bread (*rieska*) and many kinds of pie, primitive shoes woven from birch-bark (*virsut*), gloves knitted with one needle, and cloths decorated with geometrical human and animal figures embroidered in red.

Innovations – for example ribbon-braiding from Estonia – were absorbed primarily through the City of Viipuri, at the head of the Gulf of Finland. After the foundation of St Petersburg in 1703, eastern influences increased. Among them were the everyday drinking of tea, the use of mushrooms and sauerkraut in the food economy, the baking of bagels and, in the sphere of leisure-time activities, the popularity of particular dances and the use of the accordion for accompaniment.

Innovations were absorbed on commercial travels, the carrying trade and sailing. The opening of the Saimaa Canal after the Crimean War of 1856 marked a boom in agriculture and the birth of industry: saw-mills and factories were founded on the southern shores of the Lake Saimaa system and in Kymenlaakso in southern Finland.

Northern Finland belongs – with the exception of the ►Sámi culture of ►Lapland – to the eastern Finnish cultural region. Peasant culture here is young: at the beginning of the 18th century, almost all of Kainuu was still inhabited by Lapps. The Savo expansion reached as far as the mountains of Kuusamo. The Finnish habitation of western, central and northern Lapland, on the other hand, originates in the coastal areas of the west, and spread along the great rivers to Muonio, Rovaniemi, Kemijärvi and Sodankylä.

NORTHERN FINLAND is a socially homogeneous region. More prosperous than the peasants are the farmers of the river-banks. Before the building of the hydro-electric dams, they held large-scale fishing rights. Cultural influences were absorbed via the coastal towns, Oulu (founded in 1606) and Tornio (founded in 1621). The basis of the economy was salmon-fishing, cattle-raising and trade, and, in addition in the south, tar-burning. Smoking tar-burning pits can still be seen in Kainuu, north-eastern Finland.

Striking features of the folk culture include the very high ovens of old cabins, the location of a fireplace in winter byres and the use of small, pyramid-roofed summer byres. Often there is still a reindeer meat-drying rack on the roof of one building, proof of the continuing efficacy of this old method of preservation.

The 1860s saw the arrival, in the western part of the region, first of the saw-mill industry, then of the paper and other mass industries. These offered tree-felling and log-driving work to thousands, until the rationalisations of the 1960s. In the landscape, changes have meant the harnessing of the rivers and the building of artificial lakes to meet the needs of hydro-electric power-stations. The economic base of the region has been diversified by building tourist attractions.

The folk culture of the southern part of Tornionjokilaakso Valley shows western features such as the pedestal barn, hard bread, cheeses and fermented milk. Striking in the area's furniture are the lengthwise-pedestal cradle, high-backed sofas with painted decorations, handsome chests and tables. A building-type peculiar to the region is the three-storey barn, the roots of which lie in the warehouse buildings of the traders of the coastal towns.

In the second half of the 19th century, Finland's folk culture entered a period of transition. New influences increased and were rapidly introduced and their absorption no longer took place on a communal, but on an individual, basis. This was because the structure of agriculture itself was changing at the same time as it was beginning to lose importance compared to other sectors, above all industry. The excess population of the countryside moved to factory locations and towns. Working-class culture and even urban culture, however, are still to a large extent based on the old culture, for the roots of their bearers are in the countryside.

The Second World War was followed by a second phase of industrialisation. Its starting points are different, because the countryside, too, has changed. Nevertheless, allegiance to social groups is still almost as strong as before. In recent years, age groups have become stronger than social groups in terms of defining of cultural behaviour and decisions. TK

folk dance Among the oldest items of the Finnish folk dance tradition are the song-dances and song-games, which belong to the medieval European song-dance tradition. Song-dances were performed under the direction of a principal singer and dancer to the accompaniment of the Kalevala metre; later, ballad and other new song-metres were also used. The dancing was generally done in a circle or chain, accompanied by various interweavings and archings, and also in facing rows. The circle games, performed in the metre of four-line rhymed stanzas, which became popular at the end of the 19th century, are the last reflection of this old tradition. The instruments used to accompany folk dancing have been the violin, clarinet and later the accordion, while in ▶Karelia the ▶*kantele* was to some extent used.

The first instrumentally accompanied Finnish dance was the *polska*. This dance of Polish origin had been adopted in Sweden as early as the late 16th century, becoming quickly established and acquiring the character of national dance. It also became naturalised in Finland in the 17th century, and was the most popular dance there until the early 19th century. The *polska* was originally performed as a couple dance, the steps and handholds of which varied greatly. Later, the circular *polska* became common, particularly in ▶Ostrobothnia, where it was danced ceremonially at weddings, and survived until the middle of the 20th century. The minuet, originally a French court dance, was also adopted in Finland as a folk dance. It enjoyed a long and special popularity among Fin-

land's Swedish-speaking population, from the 18th century almost until modern times. The minuet has preserved its place as a ceremonial dance at weddings. The *polska* was always danced after the minuet.

In the 19th century Finland also saw the rise of a new dance-fashion, the *kontratanssi* or contredanse, which was based on the English traditional country dance. This spread from England by way of France to all of Europe. The contredanse is a pattern dance performed in rows, squares or triads, and sometimes also in circles. In the Finnish tradition it is possible to distinguish local and historical versions. The oldest version is the row-dance, in which each couple dance with one another in turn and with all the other couples. This dance is found mainly in Savo and eastern Finland, and this type of dance is also performed in Karelia, to the accompaniment of Kalevala metre songs. In western Finland they apparently gave way to the newer square dance, which quickly spread under the name of the quadrille. In western and southern Finland long, many-rounded quadrilles were danced, while in central Finland a large number of short foursomes with alternating partners was more common. The quadrille was adopted especially by the upper-class social milieu. The short triple dance, on the other hand, spread among the common folk as, for example, sailors brought it with them from abroad. It is most common among Finland's coastal communities. Most of Finland's recorded folk dance tradition belongs to the contredanse category.

The *purpuri*, or potpourri, was a dance-chain in which various different dances were performed in sequence, at first mainly contredanses, but later also couple dances. The common folk learned the *purpuri* dances from the upper classes, but when danced by them these acquired quite a different character. The *purpuri* was danced extensively in western Finland, and existed in more or less differing versions according to region. It had a maximum of 12 rounds. In some localities the *purpuri* was a ceremonial wedding dance in which the entire wedding group took part, and often lasted for several hours. Finland is the only

Folk-dance performances are held at Seurasaari Open-Air Museum in Helsinki

country in which the potpourri was danced by the ordinary people.

In the 19th century a new dance-fashion, the couple dance, gradually began to replace the contredanse. The waltz arrived in Finland at the beginning of the century, but was only gradually adopted by the ordinary people. The polka, on the other hand, became unexpectedly popular in the 1840s and also had a strong influence on the Finnish dance tradition. Many previously well-known dances were also danced to the steps of the polka, for example, the *polska* was sometimes turned into a polka, as were many quadrilles. Many modifications of the polka and miniature polka-dances came into being. The *jenkka* (German *polka*, or *schottische*) arrived in Finland from Germany in the second half of the19th century, and is still danced today. The mazurka was not as widely-accepted as the other dances mentioned, but it too was subjected to various popular modifications.

All the recorded folk dances in Finland are social dances which involve an equal number of men and women; special men's or women's dances and solo dances are, with a few rare exceptions, not found. Characteristic features of Finnish folk dance are variety and variability of patterns and steps on the one hand, and considerable rhythmic monotony on the other. Some 90 per cent of dances have a 2/4 rhythm, while 5 per cent are in 3/4 time and 5 per cent in both.

From the point of view of folk dance, Finland may be divided into three quite clearly distinguishable areas of tradition: western Finland, where new dances always arrived first, eastern Finland, where more of the older dances were preserved and where there was also the influence of the lively Slavic dance tradition, and the Finland-Swedish regions in which there were more contacts with the Scandinavian tradition than in other parts of the country. Folk dancing, approached as an object of study, began to be presented at upper-class social occasions in the 1860s, and in 1901 Finland's first folk dance society, the Finnish Folkdance Association (Suomalaisen Kansantanssin Ystävät) was founded, and still functions. There are estimated to be 25,000–30,000 devotees of Finnish folk dance in Finland today. PLR

folk medicine In Finnish research into folk medicine, attention has been focussed on folk beliefs regarding sickness and health, methods and tools of healing, and the cultural and historical background of these phenomena. The conception of folk medicine thus includes both folk pathology with its numerous names and explanations for sicknesses and its many healing methods.

Finnish folk pathology has, above all, been etiology: in other words, the clarification of the origin of the disease. On the other hand, the definition

Alive and well: the ancient remedy of cupping is still practised in Finland today

of the disease's quality and nature, or diagnosis, was not, in the minds of the folk healers, so important. Diseases were not believed to develop in people, but were thought to come from outside. Most often, the reason was the supernatural world: the dead, the spirits of land, forest or water. But malicious people were also capable of sending diseases. In this case, diseases could originate from the four basic elements of the universe: earth, water, fire or air – or, in the eastern Finnish tradition, also the forest. This demonstrates the central role of the forest in the folk world-view.

Diseases were considered to be living creatures who had brothers and sisters and who, in healing spells, were addressed accordingly. Spells described the movement, running or eating of diseases.

It has been customary to divide folk healing methods into beliefs and methods based on either practical experience (massage, cupping, herbal remedies), or supernatural thought (spells, charms, certain medicines). It should nevertheless be remembered that where our rationalist period sees supernatural activity, people of former times believed they were acting rationally and logically.

The founder of the study of Finnish folk medicine, ▶Elias Lönnrot, in his doctoral thesis, *Om finnarnes magiska medicin* ('Concerning the Finns' magical medicine', 1832), stressed that all healing activity should take into account both *psyche* and *soma*, soul and body. He understood that many illnesses are psychosomatic by nature.

The origins of modern medicine, too, lie in folk medicine and were based on supernatural ideas. For example, the first pharmacopoeia of Sweden-Fin-

land, published in 1686, mentions numerous medicines that are prepared from human or animal body parts, snakes, frogs or swallows' nests.

Modern medicine owes a great debt of gratitude to folk medicine. It has been estimated that one quarter of the medicinal materials known in folk medicine circles were objectively effective. Among them are salicylic acid, cocaine, quinine and ephedrine. In Finland, certain folk remedies still offer alternatives to which people can have recourse if they wish. PLn

folk music Two strands dating from different periods are clearly visible in Finnish folk music. The earlier strand, comprising vocal music, includes rune-melodies and laments, cattle-calling songs and other signalling melodies. The most important instruments are the ▶*kantele* and the *jouhikko* (cf. English *crwth* or bowed harp). In addition, there is a large group of various types of wind instrument that were used by shepherds. Finns regard the *kantele* as their national instrument, but instruments of a similar kind have also been in use among Baltic Finns, Balts, and other Finno-Ugrian peoples.

The most distinguishing feature of the music of this older strand is its restricted melodic character; the scales were often merely composed of a pentachord. The oldest *kanteles* were correspondingly five-stringed, the *jouhikkos* two- or three-stringed. The melodic movement was even, and large intervals were rare. The unceasing variation of the melody did, however, create a diverse musical expression. Clearly defined major and minor keys were unknown, but in the absence of key the third degree of the scale sometimes alternated between a major and minor third.

The most important form of vocal music was rune-singing (or *Kalevala* singing), which could be divided according to content into epic, lyric, wedding and other ritual songs. In former times, rune-singing was a common skill, but in many communities there were also distinguished experts in the tradition, master singers whose skill was superior to that of others.

Rune-melodies were one- or two-line in structure, with a four or five ac-

Kaustinen Folk Music Festival 1996; held in July, the Festival is the focus for the Finnish folk-music revival

cented rhythm. More complex rhythms were in use during the last phase of rune-singing culture at the end of the 19th century. The most common type of rune-melody was the five-accented pentachordal melodic line, the last two notes of which are of longer duration than the two preceeding ones. Melodies of this kind were well-suited to performance as a solo, while the four-accented melodies could be sung as a duet or choral song, creating a kind of antiphon between the soloist and the other singers.

It was typical for one singer not to master very many different types of melody. There was a type of melody for every situation, so that in weddings, for example, only a few different melodies were used, but different villages had their own types of melody, which were varied. This meant that when singing words and tunes there was not the same kind of fixed unity as in classical music. Rune-singing was usually done in unison, although heterophony was sometimes heard in community performances.

Laments were ritual songs performed by women, usually at funerals and weddings. They were characterised by improvisation, both verbal and musical. The lines of verse were – unlike those of the rune-songs – in free metre and rhythm. Their melodies, like those of the rune-songs, employed close intervals moving around the pentachord, but their rhythms followed that of the words of the song.

The curves of the verse-lines were falling ones, and in the last part of the lament the lines often ended with a sob.

After the Reformation, Finnish folk music culture began to acquire new forms. The changes began on the coasts, where new cultural influences arrived more quickly, mostly from Sweden, than they did inland. The old folk music culture survived better in eastern Finland and in the Russian border regions until the 19th century. However, the period of transition was a long one, and produced many new musical manifestations. Ballads and dance songs were borrowed from Scandinavia, at first being blended with the old rune-singing tradition, but in a later phase also preserving the Scandinavian melodies. The new currents in instrumental music spread mostly from Sweden, and in the period of Russian rule (1809–1917) also from St Petersburg.

After the mid-18th century, the rhyming stanza model became established as the most important Finnish song-form. This was the so-called *reki-laulu* (English approx. 'roundelay'), built on a stanza form that combines two couplets which often end with two notes that are twice as long as the others. In musical terms this corresponds to the so-called *kolomeika* rhythm. The *rekilaulus* were mostly sung by young people, and their lyrics were mostly concerned with amorous themes. They also reflected the emotions and attitudes of the 19th century Finnish agrarian community. *Rekilaulus* were most usually sung in association with circle games.

An essential feature of the new song culture, both in the sphere of vocal and instrumental music, was a considerable expansion of the melodic range. The scales changed from pentatonic to septatonic ones, and the melodic range sometimes even exceeded an octave. While the old rune-singing culture had been characterised by an even flow of melodic movement, in the new folk songs the progression of the melody was variable, and there were many large intervals.

There were also many changes in the field of instrumental music. The old instruments began to fall out of use. The ▶*kantele* and *jouhikko* were largely replaced in the 17th century by the violin, which, because of its more audible sound as a dance instrument supplanted the old, softer-sounding instruments. Even where the *kantele* survived as a domestic instrument, it began to be developed and constructed on the model of larger instruments. By the end of the 19th century the *kantele* had over 20 strings, and by the 1920s large chromatic *kanteles* with 36 strings had begun to be built.

The instrumental music of the new strand was mainly dance music, and it was mostly used at weddings and village dances. At large weddings there were usually two or three violin players, while for village dances one player was usually enough. The oldest stratum of fiddle music is represented by the polska, a type of dance music in three-four time (polonaise), which was also known elsewhere in Scandinavia. In addition to the polska, the minuet, a quieter though more nimble dance, was also played.

At the beginning of 19th century the waltz became the new dance of fashion, and the polska and minuet began to be considered old-fashioned. Around mid-century the polka also arrived in Finland, followed slightly later by the schottische and the mazurka. At about this time a new instrument, the accordion, came into use, and it began to replace the violin.

The clarinet, introduced under the influence of military music, became popular, but only in the south and west of the country. Towards the end of the century the mandolin and the harmonica were also played. The harmonium and the double bass did not become widely used in Finland until the 1970s, with the reawakened interest in folk and fiddle music. The most usual combination of instruments was two violins, accordion and double bass.

At present, Finnish folk music is dominated by a blend of various styles. The oldest generation of folk musicians follow the old traditions, while the younger players freely absorb the influence of Irish and East European folk music, rock or pop music. At the same time, however, the old heritage of original Finnish folk music has been revived. Folk music is at its most lively at the Finnish folk music festivals, a rich and multi-faceted group of events, the most important of which is the International Kaustinen Folk Music Festival, held in July. AA

folklore The use and scholarship of folklore, have played a central role in Finland's cultural history. Eyes turn first, of course, to the ▶*Kalevala* and the ancient poems from which it was composed, whose importance in the rise of Finnish national culture has been stressed since the beginning.

Documented Finnish history is relatively sparse, while the unwritten history, folk poetry, has been unusually well-recorded. The reason is known: the young nation needed to seek its past in human memory, in the oral tradition. The Folklore Archive of the ▶Finnish Literature Society is probably the largest of its kind in the world. The collections of ▶*Kalevala* poetry, for example, contain more than 130,000 texts.

The *Kalevala* metre, which forms the basis of the folk poetry tradition, is believed to have originated at the end of the pre-Finnic period (2000–500 B.C.), when the linguistic communities of the eastern Baltic were just beginning to diverge. *Kalevala* metre poetry is encountered, in addition to among the Finns, among the Estonians, Votics and Karelians.

Finnish epic poetry contains a number of ancient mythical subjects, which tell of how the world and the

Finnish Literature Society's Folklore Archive is one of the world's largest of its kind

human environment began. It is now believed that the most ancient elements in the Finnish cultural heritage originate from two sources. One is the common palaeo-Arctic culture of Siberia and North America, which may be the source of the shamanistic features of Finnish folk poetry, its bear-killing rituals, the primitive beliefs and customs concerning the relationship between people and animals, the cult of the dead and ideas relating to the *aurora borealis* and other natural phenomena of the Arctic. The poems may even contain messages from the people known as the proto-Lapps, who are believed to have lived in the area that is now Finland even before the Finno-Ugrians.

The other source of pre-Finnic culture wells up from the high cultures of the east. This is the origin of the earth-egg myth about the birth of the world, but also of the subjects of some Estonian, Finnish and Karelian myth-poems: the great oak, the great bull, the great pike, how fish bring the first spark of fire, how the sea receives its nature and its fish-hollows, how the first human couple is born. They are the strongest Finno-Ugrian legacy of the most ancient layer of Finnish culture; many of them have been preserved only in poem-fragments or the introductions to incantations.

A group of Baltic and Baltic Finnish culture hero poems originated from the period after the birth of *Kalevala* metre. Here, the central subject is the birth or origin of some cultural theme or object: boat-carving, the birth of the ►*kantele*, barley, beer or iron. They show that an agrarian society was already in existence and, at the same time, tell of incipient village life.

The next period is regarded as having begun with arrival in Finland. Here, recent scholarship has suggested a considerably earlier date. Formerly, it was imagined that emigration to Finland took place around the beginning of the Christian period, and that it was only after this that Germanic influences began. Now it seems that the Finns had already been in present-day Finland for some centuries, and subjected to Germanic influences. The many hero-poems about Väinämöinen, including the fine *sampo* poems, which are encountered only in Finland and Karelia, probably originated during this comparatively long culmination period of ancient poetry.

The heroes of Viking epic, on the other hand, were no longer seers and skilled men, but soldiers and adventurers. The mythic plots of the poems became more prosaic: songs began to be sung about journeys, courtships and relationships between men and women. The archipelago epic about the adventures of Ahti and Kaukomieli dates from this period. Characteristic of the poetry of the Viking period are the repetition of lines and the pattern of three questions and answers.

Among the characteristics of the *Kalevala* poetry of the medieval period is an increase in Christian and western influences. Many Christian legends and ballads, but also some of the Väinämöinen and Lemminkäinen poems, date from this period. The most extended of the legend poems is the *Tale of the Creator*, a Finnish messiad, which offers a popular version of the events of Christmas and Easter. The poems *The Great Pig* and *The Great Bull*, which have been interpreted as satirical, are probably from the same period: it has been suggested that at least in *The Great Pig* a representative of the Christian faith is poking fun at pagan myths. Wandering mendicant monks, for their part, influenced the spirit of legend poetry, giving it a strong proletarian and Christian message.

The Reformation and the advent of written Finnish brought the last transition in ancient poetry. Subsequent poems tell of warlike events in Sweden-Finland or of cheerless life in the serf villages of Ingria. Rhymed folk songs, vulgar poetry and broadsheet ballads began gradually to replace the ancient poems.

The *Kalevala* song tradition was longest-lived in the relatively narrow strip of land that began with Russian Karelia and stretched via Olonets, Ladoga Karelia, the Karelian Isthmus and Ingria to Estonia. In the northern poem-area, both men and women sang: men sang epic hero-poems about Väinämöinen, Joukahainen, Lemminkäinen and the *sampo*, while women sang lyrical and epic poems about their own lives, family relations and, at a later stage, about love, too. The songs were monophonous, and could be performed by one or more singers.

In the southern poem-area, on the Karelian Isthmus, in Ingria and Estonia, songs were mainly lyric or lyric-epic, and were performed by women. The singing style, too, was different, based on alternation between chanter and choir. The chanter began with a line or two, which would be repeated by the choir. On Sundays, Ingrian girls would wander the lanes of their home villages in brightly coloured groups, loudly singing their songs, which young men and others were welcome to listen to.

It has been suggested that the lyrical *Kalevala* poem was, at its birth, an entirety of between 4 and 15 lines. Many of these poems were recorded in the northern poem-area; in the south, the songs have generally been concatinated or otherwise extended. The reason for this must surely be the difference in singing styles between the areas.

The *Kalevala* singing style began to disappear from the heartlands in the 17th century with the advent of social changes. The ►church played a central role in this transition. The ancient poems were not, however, replaced just with hymns, but with rhymed or new, or newer, folk songs. But the transition was not easily accomplished. During the course of its long history, *Kalevala* song had grown and developed in its own natural context. Melodies and words had adapted to each other. The new metre and songs were based on a totally different kind of linguistic and musical culture.

Interest in the other segment of folklore, the prose tradition, was at first the province of history, not literary studies. It was believed that folk stories would help cast light on ancient pagan beliefs, the achievements of rulers, habitation history and the development of occupations and trade. Fairy tales could not, therefore, be a very important source. On the other hand, the appreciation of the various genres of folk tale was still very incomplete even when collection of the folk-tale heritage had been begun. Historical memory, stories, legends, myths and creation myths interested collectors and scholars much more, as did *Kalevala* metre folk poetry.

Animal tales have been particularly popular in Finland. More than 130 types of animal tale are known, while Sweden and Denmark have only half this number. Most animal tales derive from the eastern European tradition of the classical period. But it has also been demonstrated that some stories about the adventures of foxes and bears may belong to a 1000 year-old Nordic tradition. The story of how the fox tempted the bear to fish through a hole in the ice with its tail may belong to this tradition. Animal tales often include elements that explain the origin of phenomena: why the bear has no tail, why the tip of the fox's tail is white or why the hare has crossed lips. Later, animal tales became a tradition for children, foregoing their sharpest satire, and often their profoundest symbolism.

In addition to animal tales, there are wonder tales, novella tales, religious tales and humorous tales. Common to all is that they are tales based on the imagination and intended as entertainment. They are not told with the intention of being believed, but may nevertheless reflect conflicts in society.

In Finland, a total of 7000 wonder tales have been recorded, representing 140 different types. Often they are very long: the telling of a wonder tale may last several hours. Repetition, formalism and the repetition of phrases made it easier to remember and tell the story.

Novella tales are often short, and do not feature speaking animals, magic objects or supernatural helpers. They transport their listeners to royal and luxurious surroundings. The king's daughter, however, is not won through supernatural gifts, but through cleverness and cunning. Among these stories are a number of romantic love-stories in which faithfulness and innocence are put to the test, but there are also thrilling stories about thieves and murderers.

The most outspoken and daring stories in the tradition are humorous tales. Ridiculous courtship or marriage situations offer suitable material for the main themes of these stories, the demonstration of stupidity, wisdom or sexuality. In humorous tales, the climax is a series of actions, each more impossible than the last, and the clever hero makes his listeners laugh. Among the best-known humorous tales are those that tell of an exceptionally peculiar village or tribe.

The study of fairy tales brought Finnish folklore studies to world fame as early as the turn of the 20th century. The tales were, in general, loan material, and steady and diverse international collaboration was needed for their study. The situation is made interesting by the fact that this happened at the time when Finnish scholarship in the humanities in general concentrated on research emphasising the national characteristics of the Finns. Folklore scholars throughout the world still recognise the name of the first compiler of a typology of folk tale types, the Finn Antti Aarne (1867–1925). PLn

food TRADITIONAL FOOD As late as the Second World War, it was still possible to distinguish areas of Finland where distinctive cultures of food and drink had developed over the ages. Today these regional foods are encountered in broader areas, for the resettlement of the population of ▶Karelia after the Second World War and the changes in economic structure that followed have brought many regional foods to the consciousness of the nation as a whole.

Historically, Finland was situated between two powerful cultures. To

Karjalanpiirakat – Karelian pasties

Kalakukko, or baked fish loaf

generalise, it may be said that in terms of cultural history the western part of Finland belonged to the Roman-Catholic and Lutheran sphere of influence, and via them to that of Germanic culture. The fasting foods of Easter, for example, derive from the medieval Catholic tradition, although fasting itself was no longer practised in Lutheran countries. The eastern part has been influenced by the Slavic culture of the north-west and the ▶Orthodox tradition.

Another difference reflecting the bilateral nature of Finland's gastronomy is based on technological differences. A closed oven type in which bread and other foods could be prepared by internal simmering, and which simultaneously provided heating for accommodation, reached eastern Finland in the late medieval period. In the west, on the other hand, food was prepared on an open fire, and even bread was still made in external ovens in some places as late as the 20th century.

The most typical example of these differences between East and West is bread, which in the West has been thin, hard and long-lasting, baked only a couple of times a year in large quantities. In the east, however, where the oven was heated almost every day, bread was baked daily and was soft and fresh.

As elsewhere in Europe, innovations in gastronomy began early in the modern period, when trade increased and new influences spread more easily and rapidly. New foodstuffs such as the potato, spices, vegetables, sugar, liquor and coffee diversified food habits in both towns and the countryside from the early 18th century. As a result of the industrialisation, modernisation and demographic mobility that began at the end of the 19th century, the old provincial and regional differences began to even out. Nevertheless, despite this mixing and the new international influences, the basic differences in Finnish gastronomy are still visible.

Traditional food economy was based on the products of arable farming and animal husbandry. These were available, to a greater or lesser extent, throughout the year, although seasonal differences and calendrical and other festivals brought variations. Even now, both in the food industry and in individual families, annual festivals such as Christmas (ham, stockfish), the day of the national poet, ▶J. L. Runeberg (Runeberg tart, ▶festivals), Shrove Tuesday (Shrove Tuesday bun), Easter (*mämmi*) and many other special days with their particular foods.

Even today, it is possible to find traditional folk foods and drinks, either made at home or prepared industrially. South-western Finland once belonged to the sphere of influence of the Roman Catholic Church, and fasting was of some importance. It is not many decades since the traditional food of *mämmi*, a dark-brown malty pudding baked in the oven, was eaten only in this region. *Mämmi* is a black-brown Easter food baked of malt in the oven, which is believed to have originated as a fasting food in the medieval period. It is served with sugar and cream. As a factory product, it is nowadays available during the Easter period throughout Finland, while making it at home has almost completely ceased. The speciality of ▶Åland and the western Finnish coast is black bread, a bread made of rye flour, malt and spices whose preparation takes almost 24 hours.

In the East, in the sphere of influence of Slavic culture, the tradition includes many oven-baked foods and

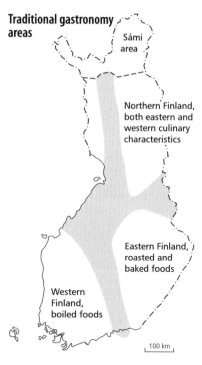

Traditional gastronomy areas

Sámi area

Northern Finland, both eastern and western culinary characteristics

Eastern Finland, roasted and baked foods

Western Finland, boiled foods

100 km

pastries, many of them linked with the eastern traditions of hospitality. The Karelian pasty has become a kind of symbol of Karelia. It has become commercialised in a long, ovoid form, although among Karelians it is still baked at home. Originally a speciality for Karelian holy- and feast-day celebrations, it has now spread throughout the country, but – unfortunately – become commercialised and, as an industrialised product, has almost completely lost its original formal beauty and taste, and in addition the variation of types.

The *kalakukko*, or baked fish loaf, also forms part of the eastern tradition. The fish – most often vendace or perch, which is sometimes replaced by turnip or potato – is enclosed with fatty pork in a rye-dough crust. The tradition reaches beyond the border with Russia, and parallels have even been drawn with the pizza – the difference being simply that one is closed, the other open, and each is filled with materials suitable to the relevant natural conditions and climate. The making of the *kalakukko*, once the province of every housewife, has now been taken over by small, specialised bakeries. And finally, even large food manufacturing companies have begun to make *kala-*

kukkos, which are rarely the original versions. Later foods of the Slavic tradition originating in south-east Finland which have subsequently spread throughout the country include Russian sauerkraut and the use of mushrooms in cooking.

The food of northern Finland is largely based on reindeer. The Sàmi region has a highly individual gastronomy, which has subsequently spread to the south and has to some extent also gained a foothold as exotic on the menus of luxury restaurants. Reindeer has traditionally been used for both clothing and other implements and for food of the greatest diversity. In *poronkäristys,* thin strips of frozen reindeer meat are simmered in a pot, seasoned and eaten with natural products such as lingonberry or cranberry jelly.

Reindeer meat is also dried during early spring on the roofs of buildings and on sunny walls. It is excellent and long-lasting provender. Preserving meat through drying is an old custom in eastern Finland.

From the north to the southern areas of Ostrobothnia, delicious *leipäjuusto,* or cheese-bread, was formerly prepared. Farm cheeses are made in the same way throughout western Finland, but in *leipäjuusto* the whey-mass is pressed into a round, flat cake on a special bread-board, and set to cook before a fire until the surface is flecked with brown. Particularly in its northern areas, it used to be a delicacy for feasts. According to the old custom, the cheese is cut up into the bottom of a coffee cup and coffee is poured on top. The ►coffee is drunk, and finally the pieces of cheese are eaten. This delicacy, too, is now produced commercially and has spread from its original regions throughout the entire country. So-called *kehäjuusto,* or ring-cheese, is made only in south-western Finland; it is an unripened cheese that is made in a mould.

Fish cannot be forgotten in Finland. The most exotic, flavoursome and traditional ways of preparing the salmon and whitefish of rivers include *loistelohi,* or flamed salmon, skewered

whitefish or the Satakunta speciality known as crucified whitefish. Smoked fish is on offer in town markets. Crucified whitefish, on the other hand, can only be obtained by ordering it specially. The whitefish is split in two, cleaned, salted for some time and then spread on a wooden board with the skin underneath, fixed with wooden nails and set in the blaze of a fire until it is golden-brown, a process which takes, depending on size, two to four hours.

Fresh milk was, during the period of traditional agriculture, the drink only of children and the sick. *Piimä,* or soured milk, was made for drinking in the winter when the cows were not milking. Spirits have been part of the Finnish diet ever since it began to be imported in the 17th century, at first as medicine, then as a festival drink and also as an intoxicating liquor. Finns can nevertheless be considered a beer-drinking nation. A unique speciality is the folk malt drink, *sahti.* Its preparation is entirely based on a medieval tradition, and is linked to the medieval German tradition of beer-making. In Finland, however – unlike Germany – it survived as a folk drink in many places in central and western Finland. *Sahti* is strong or weaker according to whether it is offered to men or women. Its preparation and use for domestic purposes were permitted in the countryside despite official attempts to abolish it. When more liberal winds began to blow in alcohol policies in the 1980s, preparation for commercial uses was also allowed.

During the course of the 19th century, the food of common people diversified, and many customs and new foods that had previously been reserved for the gentry and townsfolk were adopted. Coffee began to replace liquor, and the use of wheat increased in, for example, coffee-breads and pastries, the use of vegetables became widespread, and the centralisation of

The sausage is called 'the Finnish national vegetable'.

education of young country girls increased knowledge of foods outside the home village. The foods described above are examples of the most strongly surviving folk foods and drinks. MR

MODERN FOOD Today's Finns no longer themselves know what Finnish food is. During the past 30 years, pizza has become so familiar that it is almost thought of as traditional. Country people know pizzas, pasta and burgers as well as townsfolk. The pleasant cafeterias of petrol filling stations have played their part in spreading familiarity with international pastries. Traditional provincial foods, however, remain important to Finns. In addition, there are a few food combinations that few Finns would willingly give up. They have lasted for decades, throughout the history of Finnish cuisine. Such combinations include ►coffee with buns, pea soup with oven-baked pancakes, pancakes with jam, sausage with mustard, new potatoes with pickled Baltic herring, Karelian pasties with egg-and-butter mix, blinis with turbot roe, crayfish with dill, strawberries with ice-cream, cloudberries with baked milk, and, in autumn, stewed mushrooms, preferably picked oneself, with meat and fish dishes.

By Finnish roadsides private entrepreneurs advertise sausage, hot smoked fish, pizza, pea soup, fresh bread and freshly fried doughnuts, jam and pancakes. The range of products varies from one province to another, with local delicacies such as the pies of eastern Finland or the black sausage of the Tampere area or the reindeer meat of ►Lapland. Roadside sales are generally concentrated in the summer months, from the end of May to the beginning of September. A black-and-white sign reminiscent of a traffic signal indicates a reputable seller.

Finnish berry farms have, in recent years, begun to produce wines and liqueurs on the model of central and eastern Europe, mainly from blackcurrants. Illicit spirits and home-brewed beer are also produced.

Almost every region still has its outdoor or indoor market, a tourist destination in itself. But ordinary food shops give a real picture of everyday Finnish eating habits. Small village shops are already a rarity. Modern

Fashionable summer delicacy: flamed salmon

Finns prefer hypermarkets where there are cheap goods for sale, as well as space and good air-conditioning.

The hurried, working consumer buys convenience products. Prepared foods, salads shredded in the factory, casseroles and meat-balls sell well. It is convenient to buy bread ready-sliced. Finns like dark bread, particularly the long-baked, sour-dough *jälkiuunileipä*. Crispbread, whose newest shape is small and round, and sourdough crispbread are regular items in the Finnish diet. Increasingly, bread is baked on the premises. These in-store bakeries have increased sales of fresh bread, and also its popularity. Salty margarine or butter is spread on bread in greater or lesser quantities.

Low-fat versions of all dairy products are available. Milk comes in full-fat, light, premium and non-fat grades, and as *piimä*, or thick, soured milk. *Viili* – another form of soured, or clabbered, milk – was formerly made at home, but is now generally bought from the shop. New dairy products, which equalise lactic acid levels, and yoghurts flavoured with berries are increasing in popularity. Milk is drunk from the early morning onwards, with porridge or cereals.

Finland produces fine Emmental, cream and blue cheeses, as well as specialist cheeses, but according to statistics Edam is the most popular of all. The originally Ostrobothnian baked milk has become a product that is sold throughout the country, and new, skilful cheese-makers appear every year. Examples have been taken from Switzerland and France, whence cheese-makers originally came to Finland.

In most shops the meat counter has been replaced by cold-cupboards containing ready packed, cut and marinated meats. The few culinarists and traditionalist cooks who wish to choose and flavour their meat themselves must seek out specialist butchers' shops. Pork in its various forms is cheap, as is intensively farmed chicken, which first became popular in the 1960s, at outdoor summer events. Chicken, often ready-grilled, is now part of Finnish everyday life. Competing with it is ring sausage, the number one Finnish food. Sausage is good, and cheap. It is increasingly eaten with vegetables, except at ▶sauna evenings, when sausages are grilled over an open fire and munched with mustard or potato salad.

Because fish consumption is rising, outlets for fresh fish are increasing. Buying fish caught the same day, however, remains a problem. The ice-packed fish counters are dominated by farmed salmon, every Finn's everyday fish. Wild salmon, Baltic herring, vendace, pike, pike perch, whitefish and perch are also increasingly valued, in both shops and restaurants. In many places, fish is available ready filleted. If only they could be marked with the day of catching!

Smoked products such as fish, pork, lamb and sausages are among Finnish basic foodstuffs. If a Finnish restaurant were to be founded, it could feature, in addition to the cheese and dessert trolleys, a trolley for smoked meats, which would tell of the ancient customs of the smoke sauna, where hams and sausages 'bathed' like human beings!

The quality of coffee is of great importance to Finns, although tastes have a Finnish slant. Specialist cafés and restaurants offer espressos and cappuccinos, and an order for coffee will meet with the response, Finnish or specialist?

Family festivities are generally celebrated at home, around the coffee table. Where, in earlier times, coffee and the proverbial seven sorts of pastries were on offer, these have now been replaced by savouries, pies and salads. They are enjoyed first, with non-alcoholic home-brewed beer, shop-bought beer or wine and are followed by coffee and sweet items. Sweet coffee-bread is part of the tradition, as are biscuits and sandwich cakes. A sandwich cake should be juicy and sweet. Layered sandwich cakes are now often replaced with cheesecakes, which are reminiscent of the curd cheese tarts of eastern Finland. Coffee parties are like miniature dinner parties. At large parties, where wedding guests or other important visitors are to be entertained, the tables groan with local delicacies and traditional foods. There are dozens of dishes, and the festivities may last for a couple of days.

Finnishness is least evident today in restaurants, of which most have chosen to offer an international menu. There are few restaurants offering purely Finnish food, although most have a Finnish menu and, naturally, local and seasonal delicacies.

Finnish cuisine has strong traditions. Its raw materials are pure, flavoursome and generally of a high quality. An interest in Finnish food has arisen through different food projects. Finland's special position between the culinary cultures of Sweden and Russia has been exploited. Finland's exoticism as a gastronomic country has been noted, and great things are promised for it in the future. AMT

foreigners in Finland Having lost more than a million people as emigrants during the past hundred years, in the 1990s Finland became a country of net immigration. In the years 1990–1995, the net immigration to Finland was around 46,000 persons by the mid 1990s. Finland had 110,000 foreign-born residents: of these, 75,000 were citizens of foreign countries. Approximately a third of Finland's foreign community is from the former Soviet Union. Of this group, about 15,000 are Ingrian Finns. The next largest group is composed of Swedish citizens, of whom there are around 7000.

Finland's foreign community, only 1.5 per cent of the population, is very small by comparison with other European countries. A considerable proportion of the foreign community are Finnish re-migrants or their children, who have citizenship of another country.

Foreigners have migrated to Finland throughout the whole of its history. They included German merchants and craftsmen. During the period of Russian rule (1809–1917) ▶Russians and citizens of other European national groups, such as ▶Tatars, settled permanently in Finland. There have been refugees in Finland since the 17th century, when the first ▶Romanies were deported from Sweden to the hinterland, Finland. As a result of the Russian Revolution (1917), 41,000 refugees arrived in Finland in the period 1917–1922; of these, 33,500 remained in the country permanently.

Arrangements for refugees in present-day Finland are based on the Geneva Convention of 1951, which defines refugee status and the right to asylum. Finland took its first refugees from Chile in 1973–1977, and from 1979 onwards from Vietnam. In 1996 Finland's refugee quota was 500, but there was pressure to raise it permanently to 1000 persons a year. Most of the country's 13,000 refugees went there as asylum-seekers, particularly from the former Soviet Union after 1992.

For a long time the largest group of refugees was formed by Vietnamese. According to statistics, by the mid 1990s, there were 2000 of them, though the group itself put the figure at 2500. The group was very dispersed and contained ethnic Chinese, among others. Nearly all the Vietnamese arrived as quota refugees or members of disunited families.

The largest group of refugees was formed by Somalis who unexpectedly arrived through the area of the former Soviet Union at the beginning of the 1990s: there were approximately 4000 of them. About 2500 refugees came to Finland from the territory of the former Yugoslavia. From Turkey, Iran and Iraq there were around 1000 immigrants and refugees from each country. There was also an influx of about 700 Thais and 500 Filipinos, most of whom were women married to Finnish men.

Finland's foreigners speak more than 60 languages as mother-tongues and some 45 per cent of them live in the area of the capital. In 1997 the foreign community had trebled in the course of five years and comprised 20,000 people. There was a particularly high density of foreigners in the rented accommodation areas of the eastern part of the city.

Finland also has its share of racism and hostility to foreigners. The most important reason for this has been a period of recession, accompanied by high unemployment. Work is being done on developing tolerance towards immigrants and refugees by integrating them into Finnish society. Instruction in the Finnish ▶language and ▶vocational training are the most essential elements in the integration. OK

forest The forest has been the mainstay of the life of all the Finnic peoples. The forest was governed by a life-sustaining mother who in Finnish folk incantations ultimately inherited the role of the Virgin Mary. The forest is approached with respect, but timidly: man is a guest, who does not have any self-evident rights over the forest.

Sacred is a keyword in the hunter's faith. His faith consists of what he considers to be sacred. It includes the myths about how life began, how the people got its living space and how man learned the limits that can be crossed by means of ritual. The key question of man's relation to nature is harmony, a state of equilibrium between the microcosm of man and the macrocosm of nature. Life patterns conserve, do not dominate. The marked area is made sacred.

The god of the Finnish forest was Tapio. In the context of the time, the hunter's luck was characterised by safety and success in one's livelihood. Luck did not depend solely on the hunter's skills, but also on there being sufficient game for him. Thus, behind the hunter's luck in the forest lay the mythical relationship between Tapio and the woman Tapiotar, who was considered to be the ancestress of game birds. In prayer incantations, Finns had many forms of address for the being who granted happiness in finding game, the most important of which was Tapio: each human being was allotted a 'fate', a word that initially signified the forester's share of the common stock of game.

According to Finnish folk wisdom, 'the forest replies in the way one shouts into it.' At the end of his life,

Birch-forest: where burn-beat agriculture has been practised, in eastern Finland, extensive birch forests are found. They are rich in undergrowth, including wild strawberries and mushrooms

Pine-forest: traditional pine-forests are sparse in undergrowth, typical plants include heathers, mosses, bilberries and lingonberries

man returns to the soil; this takes place at a symbolic level additional to actual burial. The forest is a semantic equivalent of ►death: the forest's peace, quiet, solitude, wildness are part of the theme of death found in the cradle songs and laments that are unique in Finnish folklore. The forest soldier of the later martial poems hopes for nothing better for himself than 'the honour of hearing the whispering of your spruce trees from his grave'.

The eastern Finnish culture of death is still forest-centred: natural cemeteries with Orthodox characteristics in forests or groves, on islands or the opposite banks of rivers, with wooden crosses, shrines and sepulchres above the graves. Until the 1900s it was an eastern Finnish custom to make a memorial tree (*karsikko*) in memory of the deceased. The *karsikko* was a living tree, the lower branches of which were pruned away from below, while the crown and uppermost

branches were left untouched. In the middle part of the tree, two branches were often left as 'hands' in order to show the points of the compass, the way home or the dead person's social status. Trees were also often pruned in order to show the points of the compass to hunters and fishermen, and it is supposed that it was in this connection that such trees came to serve as ritual symbols of the forest and death.

Although a spontaneous consciousness of the forest has faded among modern Finns, and their conscious attitude to it now reflects western ideas of utility, on an unconscious level their relation to the forest is as it was before: the Finn hunts, exercises, skis, rambles and orientates in the forest. Even the mental landscape of city-dwelling Finns is still moulded by Finnish forest archetypes. The Finn likes to spend his summers far away from his neighbour, in a summer cottage by the shore of an untouched woodland lake.

Individualism and the quest for independence are still the basis of the Finnish lifestyle and ►mentality. The settler-archetype lives on strongly in literature and the cinema. In addition to the settler, the free hunter of the wilderness – 'the hero of the wild spruce copse' – and the lumberjack are central images in the Finnish mental landscape.

Forest archetypes are an essential part of the Finnish migrant identity. When migration from Finland to central Scandinavia was encouraged from the 1580s onwards, the aim was to benefit the country by using special Finnish skills to cultivate the uninhabited wilderness. Thus an over 40,000-strong Finnish community was formed in central Scandinavia, and did not die out until the 1970s. Sweden's Finnish forests are still known as 'Finnskogen', and the Finns who live there are called 'Skogsfinne'.

Forestry, lumberjacking, burnbeating, the log cabin and the sauna are features peculiar to the Finnish mentality and repertoire of skills, from which the forest Finns of the New Sweden colony founded in 1638 created the models of the north American pioneer settler culture. The role of the settler, 'Lumberjack Finns', in the forests of the USA and Canada during the 19th century was similar to the lasting and characteristic contribution of the 'Finnish carpenters' who built Australia's Canberra in the 1960s. JPn

Franck, Kaj (1911–1989), designer. Kaj Franck has become famous as an innovator of household ware and of the design educational system. He graduated in 1932 from the furniture-design department of the Central School of Applied Arts and began his career designing furniture and printed fabrics. As designer and subsequently director of the design department of the ►Arabia Factory, and as designer and artistic director of the ►Nuutajärvi Glass Factory from 1951 to 1976, his task was the renovation of utility-ware design to correspond to the changing needs of urbanising people. His design combined the ideals of ascetic functionalism in the Bauhaus spirit with the softness of the material-based Nordic tra-

Kaj Franck with the coffee pot and cup from his famous *Teema* range of utility ware

dition. In seeking new forms, he did not reject tradition, but respected as starting points the forms of Nordic material culture, which were shaped by use. In the 1960s Franck polemically challenged the prevalent cult of the designer, emphasising the integrated nature of industry, in which the designer is only one factor.

Franck's best-known industrial product is the *Kilta* series, which came into production at Arabia in 1953. *Kilta*'s simplified formal language, multiuse and space-saving economy combine the fundamental ideas of Franck's design ideology. In addition to numerous series of blown and pressed glass that continue the *Kilta* mode of thought, Franck designed a large number of unique pieces, among other things reviving for the ►Nuutajärvi Glass Factory its 19th-century tradition of production of Venetian filigree glass.

Franck conveyed his design philosophy to a younger generation as a teacher and subsequently artistic director of the University of Art and Design from 1960 to 1968, and achieved a legendary reputation as innovator of

Kaj Franck, colourful serial-production glassware for the Nuutajärvi Glass Factory

the foundation course and teaching in general composition. MaA

Friitala Friitala Fashion, Finland's best-known manufacturer of leather products, was founded in 1892 near Ulvila in south-west Finland, and began to tan hides for local farmers. The factory, which by the 1920s employed around 150 people, began to make leather clothing whose wearers included engine-drivers, motorists and aviators. From the 1960s, particular attention has been paid to product development and design. Export of leather clothing began in 1964. By the 1970s, there were almost 1500 employees. Friitala has developed the internationally known water-repellent water free leather type, which offers new opportunities for the use of delicate aniline and suede leathers for outdoor wear. Since the end of the 1970s, Jukka Rintala (born 1952) has been chief designer at Friitala. Friitala's clothing consists of practical leatherwear and furs and high-fashion leatherwear. In the 1990s, almost 70 per cent of the company's leatherwear and suede-fur production has been for export. MA

furniture The freeing of the Finnish furniture industry from official regulation in the 1860s sparked a vigorous period of founding of factories. At the end of the century pro-

The peasant tradition: late 19th century chair (above), chest-chair, Yli-Tornio, northern Finland, 1830 (right)

Jukka Rintala, double-faced lambskin with lizard-print finish for Friitala, 1997

fessional architects, among them Sigurd Frosterus (1876–1956) and ▶Eliel Saarinen and artists ▶Akseli Gallen-Kallela and ▶Louis Sparre, began to develop an interest in the development of Finnish furniture. Aesthetic influences from the English Arts and Crafts movement, in particular, strengthened the sensitive relationship with natural materials, above all wood, that had always predominated in Finland. Among

Eero Aarnio, *Pastilli* ('Pastille') Chair, 1968

Antti Nurmesniemi, *Triennale 001* chair, designed for the Milan Triennale in 1960 and in production from 1995

the furniture manufacturers active at this period were Billnäs (1641–1974), Helylä, Iris (1897–1902), ▶Muurame (1903–1991) and Nikolai Boman (1871–1967).

The furniture of the 1920s was influenced by the Nordic inflection of classicism. Tubular metal furniture in the functionalist spirit developed at the Bauhaus school in Germany arrived in Finland in the late 1920s and early 1930s. In contrast to the hardness and coldness of 'metal functionalism' Finland's internationally most important architect, ▶Alvar Aalto, developed wooden furniture, replacing the metal framework with laminated and moulded birchwood structures with curved plywood seats. These were made by the Huonekalu- ja Rakennustyötehdas ('Furniture and construction-work factory'), later Korhonen Ltd., founded in 1910. The early work of Finland's most significant furniture designer of the 1940s and 1950s, ▶Ilmari Tapiovaara, exploits new moulding techniques for plywood.

The 1960s were a period of change in furniture. Traditional forms and materials were rejected, and plastic and fibreglass became widespread. Among the early users of fibreglass was the interior architect Olavi Hänninen (born 1920). With his highly contemporary chairs, the interior designer Eero Aarnio (born 1932) achieved international recognition for both himself and the chairs' producer, the Asko Furniture Factory (founded in 1918). His radical chair designs *Pallo* ('Ball') was exhibited at the Cologne Fair in 1966, and *Pastilli* ('Pastille') was shown in 1968.

The interior designer Yrjö Kukkapuro (born 1933) has been the leading Finnish furniture designer of recent decades. The starting point of his design work has always been comfort. His chair *Karuselli* ('Carousel', 1965) was one of a number of designs that emerged from extensive experimentation. Kukkapuro's chair designs of the 1960s include a number of plastic models, but as a result of the oil crisis of the early 1970s the use of plastic was largely abandoned, and for Kukkapuro, as for many others, the decade marked a shift to engagement with ergonomic questions and the design of office furniture. Brisk trade with the Soviet Union was important for the economic success of the Finnish furniture industry in the 1960s and 1970s.

The ascetic and serious furniture style of the 1970s was replaced, during the economic boom of the 1980s, by a more lively and life-affirming phase whose international trigger was postmodernism. In Finnish furniture design, this meant a new kind of experimentation and colour. A way of designing furniture that is regarded as Finnish persisted, however, as a counterweight to postmodernism. This mode drew on the one hand from craft and folk skills which are still to be found in parts of Finland and on the other, on the industrial production process developed by Alvar Aalto. Since the early 1990s, there have been attempts to increase diverse use of wood in furniture through various design projects. Worldwide concern for the state of the environment has lent additional urgency to an aesthetics of materials and forms that are felt to be close to nature. MaA

Gadolin, Johan (1760–1852), Professor of Chemistry, Academy of Turku. Johan Gadolin's interest in the natural sciences originated at home. His father, Jakob (1719–1802), was Professor of Astronomy and Physics and his maternal grandfather, Bishop Johan Browallius (1707–1755), had, as pro-

G

fessor of physics at the Academy of Turku, instituted the teaching of chemistry there in the 1730s.

Gadolin studied chemistry in Turku under Professor Pehr Adrian Gadd (1727–1797) and, between 1779 and 1783, in Upsala under one of the most famous chemists of his time, the Swede Torbern Bergman. Between 1786 and 1788 Gadolin made an expedition to Germany, the Netherlands, England and Ireland.

Gadolin took an active part in the international debate on chemical terminology and the grouping of indivisible substances. He was invited to be a member of many foreign scientific societies and academies of science, and received a number of international distinctions. Gadolin was Professor of Chemistry at the Academy of Turku from 1785 to 1822. In 1798 he published the first chemistry text-book to be printed in Finland. When the university moved to Helsinki in 1828 he retired to his manor house, where he died at the age of 92.

In a study carried out in Ytterby, Gävle, Sweden in 1794, Gadolin discovered a heavy stone in which he detected the oxide of a hitherto unknown element. The element was later named yttrium for its place of discovery, and the mineral that contained it was called gadolinite or ytterbite. Gadolinium was discovered in 1880 by Jean-Charles de Marignac, who named it after Johan Gadolin in 1886. The yttrium discovered by Gadolin, which penetrates neutrons, has been of importance in contemporary nuclear technology.

In 1936 the Finnish Chemists' Society established a Johan Gadolin medal, which can be awarded to Finnish and foreign chemists. JN

Gallen-Kallela, Akseli (Axel Gallén, 1865–1931), painter and graphic artist. Axel Gallen-Kallela rose to the forefront of Finland's *plein air* artists in a short time in the mid 1880s. He polished his technical capabilities during periods spent studying in Paris between 1884 and 1889.

In his early masterpieces, Gallen-Kallela used a glaring, modern brush technique and consciously sought out corrupt subjects which suited the pro-

Akseli Gallen-Kallela

Johan Gadolin

gramme of naturalism. Before him, naturalism had been experimented with, although in milder form, by Albert Edelfelt (1854–1905), Helena Westermarck (1857–1938) and ▶Helene Schjerfbeck.

Poika ja varis ('Boy and crow', 1884) and *Akka ja kissa* ('Old woman and cat', 1885) established Gallen-Kallela's position. His desire to depict real people un-embellished in real surroundings took him repeatedly to distant country parishes in ▶Karelia, the mythic birthplace of the ▶*Kalevala*. A constant tension between urban culture and the countryside, seen as authentic, is indeed visible in his work.

Finnish arts policy promoted the use of motifs from the *Kalevala*, but satisfactory results were achieved only in the 1890s. Central works among these are Gallen-Kallela's triptych illustrating the Aino story (two versions, 1889–1891), and four works that still dominate Finns' mental images of the world of the *Kalevala*: *Sammon ryöstö* ('The stealing of the Sampo', 1896), *Lemminkäisen äiti* ('Lemminkäinen's mother', 1897), *Velisurmaaja* ('Fratricide', 1897) and *Kullervon sotaanlähtö* ('Kullervo's departure for war', 1901).

The climax of the artist's symbolist phase took place in 1894. Among the

Sammon puolustus ('The defence of the Sampo'), 1896

Joukahaisen kosto ('Joukahainen's revenge'), 1896

Liekki ('Flame'), *ryijy*, 1899

Akseli Gallen-Kallela's studio-home at Tarvaspää, Espoo

works of the period are the two versions of *Symposion*, *Conceptio artis* and *Ad astra*.

In 1895 Gallen-Kallela studied in Berlin, and learned etching and Japanese woodcutting techniques. He held a joint exhibition with Edvard Munch in 1895 and made illustrations for *Pan* magazine. His etchings and woodcuts raised the status of the techniques in Finland and strengthened decorative simplification in, among other areas, book illustration. Gallen-Kallela's dream, the illustration of a *Great Kalevala*, remained unfinished, but the vignettes for the so-called *Koru-Kalevala* ('Ornament *Kalevala*') were completed in 1922.

Gallen-Kallela's vision of a Nordic renaissance of the arts concerned, in addition to painting and graphics, monumental painting and even architecture. Gallen-Kallela designed two national romantic *Gesamtkunstwerken*, the wilderness studio Kalela at Ruovesi in 1895 and the *Art Nouveau* style Tarvaspää studio home near Helsinki in 1913; the latter is now a museum dedicated to the artist. Of his monumental paintings, the most important were the murals for the Finnish pavilion at Paris world exhibition of 1900, the frescos for the Juselius mausoleum in Pori, 1903, and the frescos of the entrance lobby of the ▶National Museum of Finland, 1928.

The Paris pavilion brought Gallen-Kallela fame as a painter of simplicity and soulfulness living in the midst of the forests. In 1905 he was invited to exhibit with the Die Brücke Group in 1906–1907. He also became a member of the group. Gallen responded to the challenges of post-impressionism and expressionism by painting a group of works in glowing colours on his journey to East Africa in 1909–1910. His work continued later in 1923–1925 in the United States where, despite external success, innovation ceased. MVn

games of chance One of the most widespread Saturday-evening rituals of Finnish families is watching the week's lottery draw on television. Finns are a nation of confirmed lottery-devotees:

The Finnish gambling machine, *pajatso*, is to be found in every bar and garage forecourt

around 40 per cent of them take part in the lottery every week, and almost 60 per cent take part at least once a month. Only 17 per cent never take part at all in this gambling game that was established in 1971.

Because of the lottery's popularity, the Finns' propensity for games of chance is said to be founded on the 'pursuit of paradise': people put FIM 5 into the game and hope to win the jackpot of FIM 5,000,000 even though they know that the probability of this is extremely small. It is true that the pursuit of great fortune is part and parcel of Finnish gaming habits, but betting that involves skill and knowledge has also begun to have a greater appeal to this betting nation than before. In particular, in 1996 a draw based on more varied types of sport emerged to join football pools and horse-race betting.

A popular place in the Finnish gambling culture is also enjoyed by slot machines, the oldest and most famous of which came to Finland from Germany in the 1920s, and were followed during the next decade and from then on by the development of the *pajatso* (literally: 'clown'). The secret of its popularity is largely explained by the fact that until the early 1970s the mechanical *pajatso* was the only kind of slot machine permitted in Finland. Later American-style electronic slot machines replaced it alto-

gether in the gaming halls, but the powerful nostalgia associated with the *pajatso* is demonstrated by the fact that a few years ago a electronic version was made for fairgrounds.

In 1996 Finns spent an average per head of FIM 1550 (US$ 310) on games of chance. This figure is relatively high in international terms, and shows that Finns have quite a broad-minded attitude to gambling nowadays.

This has not always been the case, however, something illustrated above all by the fact that the Finnish gambling industry is comparatively young when viewed against that of southern and central Europe. An organised industry based on financial profit has only existed in Finland for less than 100 years, while in many other countries such an industry has been established for centuries.

The youth of the industry is linked to the fact that gambling has been very strictly controlled by legislative means. Legislative control has its roots at the end of the 19th century, when the playing of games for money was so clearly seen to be against the interests of morality that it was criminalised. Only draws with prizes in the form of material goods were permitted.

Not until after Finland had gained its independence, was state legislation affecting gambling altered with an act legalising raffles in 1926. The following year saw the passing of a law permitting sweepstakes at horse races. This was extended to slot machines for the first time in 1933, and again four years later. A law permitting football pools was passed in 1940. Later these laws were supplemented and revised several times. Legal regulations concerning the gambling industry were not drafted until 1965, with the lottery law, which at the time of writing is in the process of revision. Finland's accession to the European Union in 1995 has to some extent made necessary a revision of the tight social controls with regard to the system.

The liberalisation of the gaming laws has been to some extent analogous to the relaxation of legislative controls on alcohol consumption. The prevailing moral view as to whether gambling for money may make a person dependent in the same way as alcohol has proved to be a guiding principle in legislation on the matter. Gambling for money was disapproved of in newspaper editorials as early as the 1930s.

The first legislative measures affecting gambling coincided with the repeal of the prohibition laws at the beginning of the 1930s. The laws that permitted slot machines were of a similar nature to those permitting the serving of alcohol in restaurants, and involved the same factors of age-limits, premises and supervision.

The later extensions of the gaming laws also coincided with further liberalisation of the alcohol laws. At the same time as medium-strength beer was freed from restrictions at the end of the 1960s and early 1970s, Finns were also permitted to play the lottery and roulette, and a whole range of American-style slot machines. In the early 1990s international casino and new forms of betting completed the spectrum of games of chance at the same time as ▶alcohol legislation and alcohol culture were beginning to acquire a more European flavour.

Although the Finnish gambling industry has, with the course of the years, expanded and been freed from many restrictions, it is still subject to the regulation and supervision of the law. A characteristic trend is for various games to be brought under special legislation to promote the possibilities

for fair play, and for strict supervision to be imposed on the game providers and the use to which the profits from the games are put. This has meant that certain games have become the monopoly of the organisations that were founded to promote them, while as a counterbalance to this the net profits from the games have been utilised for purposes of public charity.

The gambling industry in Finland is represented by three organizations, Raha-automaattiyhdistys RAY (The Slot Machine Association), Suomen Hippos and Veikkaus, all of whose operations are based on the above-mentioned special legislation. The functioning of all of them is supervised directly by the Ministry of Interior or by officials belonging to its jurisdiction.

The oldest of the present-day organisations, RAY is a public law institution with approximately 100 member organizations devoted to various charities. As its name (The Slot Machine Association) suggests, it covers the slot machine industry as well as the functioning of casinos and entertainment automats, and also runs Helsinki's international casino. In 1996, RAY's games produced a profit of around FIM 2500 million, of which FIM 1450 million went to a public charity. The government approves the annual distribution of services proposed by the Ministry of Social and Health Affairs.

Veikkaus, which began its operations in 1940, is a company wholly owned by the Finnish state. Among its products, Veikkaus includes lottery, betting and sweepstake activity as well as various games of chance and television games, and the trotting pools. In 1996 the total turnover of Veikkaus's games was FIM 4930 million, of which the net profit ceded to the Ministry of Education was FIM 1680 million. The profits are distributed for the support of science, the arts and sport.

Suomen Hippos runs a monopoly of horse-race track games, of which the oldest and most popular is the totalisator, or 'toto'. Founded in 1973, Suomen Hippos has as its members the horse breeding associations, the race-tracks and other associations connected with horse breeding. In 1996 the turnover of Hippos's games was approximately FIM 860 million, of which the Ministry of Agriculture and Forestry distributed approximately FIM 140 million for the promotion of horse breeding and the support of racing sport.

The very liberal attitude adopted by Finland towards gaming and the wide selection of different games available has provided an adequate outlet for the national gaming instinct. Illegal organised games of chance are almost non-existent, as the legal system offers the opportunity both for large stakes and large winnings. Poker, which Finns prefer to play in its five-card stud version, has preserved its position outside the public games. The game dates from the early years of the Second World War, when *sökö* (cf. English 'check') enjoyed great popularity among soldiers at the front. JK

glass The glass industry is one of the oldest branches of industry in Finland, although its history in comparison to the history of glass in Europe is short. The contry's first glassworks was the Uusikaupunki Glass Factory, which existed in western Finland for four years between 1681 and 1685. Because of restless times and rationing, it was more than 60 years before the next glass factories were founded in Finland. Of the glass factories founded in the 18th century, the first was Åvik (1748-1833). This was followed rapidly by 11 others. Of these, the only one still active today was ▶Nuutajärvi Glass Factory (founded 1793). The manufacture of glass was the only branch of industry that could, during the period of Swedish rule, compete with the industry of the rest of the kingdom. When, in 1809, Finland became Grand Duchy of Russia, a strong period of industrial development began in the country. Twenty-eight glass factories, of which most were small, were founded. In terms of their activities during the 20th century, the most important were ▶Iittala (founded 1881) and Karhula (founded 1888). Up to the beginning of the 20th century, the main products of Finnish glass factories were domestic glass and window glass. Models were copied directly from European designs, or adapted from them, in the 19th century particularly from Belgium, Bohemia and France.

At the turn of the 20th century, the first attempts were made in the Iittala and Nuutajärvi glass factories to introduce original designs. The real change in production came in the 1920s and 1930s. Inspired by the international success of Sweden's Art Deco glass, the Finnish glass industry also began to understand the importance of original designs in promoting sales. In the late 1920s, Riihimäki Glass (founded 1910) held a design competition for cocktail glasses and began using professional designers including, in the 1920s, Henry Ericsson (1898–1933), Arttu Brummer (1891–1951) and Gunnel Nyman (1909–1948). Göran Hongell (1902–1973) designed for the Karhula glassworks. In 1932 the Karhula-Iittala glassworks held a competition whose pressed glass category was won by ▶Aino Aalto. The competition marked the breakthrough of functionalism in the Finnish glass industry. The most famous individual creation of the history of Finnish glass, ▶Alvar Aalto's *Savoy* vase (see p. 70), was the result of a glass competition held by Karhula-Iittala for the Milan Triennale of 1936 .

The late 1940s was the most prolific period of the designer Gunnel Nyman's work. In a spirit of organic modernism, she designed collections of glass for Iittala, *Riihimäki Glass* and Nuutajärvi, creating the base for the

Kaj Franck, two birds, 1971

Oiva Toikka, goblets from the *Pro Arte Vitrea* series, c. 1980

success story of Finnish glass, which ▶Timo Sarpaneva, ▶Tapio Wirkkala, ▶Kaj Franck, ▶Nanny Still, ▶Oiva Toikka and others were to continue in subsequent decades. After the Second World War, glass production centred on the big factories, and between the 1970s and the 1990s a reorganisation has taken place in the field. Since 1976, Riihimäki Glass has concentrated entirely on mechanised container-glass production. Iittala and Nuutajärvi have, as a result of buyouts, formed part of Hackman Designor since 1991.

The first independent studio glass workshops appeared in Finland in the early 1970s. In 1971 Heikki Kallio (1948–1993) and Mikko Merikallio (born 1942) set up their own studio. The designers of the younger generation in the 1990s include the independents Markus Eerola (born 1962), Päivi Kekäläinen (born 1961) and Vesa Varrela (born 1957); Brita Flander (born 1957) and Anna-Lena Hakatie (born 1965) collaborate with factories on a freelance basis. MaA

J.S. Sirén, House of Parliament, Helsinki, 1931

Brita Flander/Marimekko, *Seitsemän veljestä,* ('Seven brothers'), 1984

government In Sweden and Finland which formed part of Sweden until 1809 effective state administration began as early as the 16th century. This was because of the absence of a strong, hereditary landed aristocracy in Sweden; the state was able to build a countrywide organisation early on. The foundation of the pre-modern state was created in Sweden during the reign of Gustavus I Vasa (1523–1560), and the reforms were completed in the reign of Gustavus II Adolphus (1611–1632) at the beginning of the 17th century.

Finland developed a three-tier central state administration. Beneath the Council of State of Finland and the ministers were the central administrative boards, a phenomenon which is really known only in the Nordic countries. The central administrative boards include the National Board of Education, the National Board of Health, the National Board of Patents and Registers etc. The division of labour between the ministers and the central administrative boards has traditionally been arranged in such a way that preparing material for questions to be decided is the responsibility of the central administrative boards, while the ministers present them in their judicial form. The provincial administrations function under the aegis of the central administrative boards.

Constructed in this way, the Finnish administrative system is slow and unwieldy. The same matter is dealt with on many different levels, and often on a fraternal basis. In this system, there is not a great deal of room for local autonomy. Finnish municipalities do, it is true, have publicly elected councils, but their authority is limited, because the municipalities are controlled by the provincial administrations. It has indeed been said that Finnish municipal autonomy is merely a continuation of the state administration through elected officials. There is no intermediate autonomy between the municipality and the state administration. Weak local autonomy is entirely incapable of putting pressure on the state administration in any way, or of influencing it in general.

Recently, Finnish administration has been developed along the lines of continental Europe. The importance of the central administrative boards has lessened, and ministers' say increased. Local autonomy has not, however, essentially broadened, although, in the case of education, powers that formerly belonged to provincial departments of education, the National Board of Education and the Ministry of Education have been delegated to it. Political reform in Finland continues to take place primarily within the framework of the official government administration. HY

Granqvist, Hilma (1890–1972), anthropologist, teacher. A student of ▶Edvard Westermarck, Hilma Granqvist was an important scholar who, as a woman, was not able to influence the cultural debate of her time equally with male scholars. She spent years, during the 1920s and 1930s, in Palestine and used the material she gathered in her books *Marriage Conditions in a Palestinian Village I–II* (1932, 1935), *Child Problems Among the Arabs* (1947) and *Muslim Death and Burial* (1965). She also examined the influence of research into the history of religion on the teaching and meaning of religion. PV

graves, graveyards ▶death

Groop, Monica (born 1958), mezzo soprano. Monica Groop is in the 1990s one of the most sought-after Finnish opera singers in the world.

She studied at the Sibelius Academy in Helsinki and graduated in 1985. Since then she has performed a large number of Mozart roles (Dorabella, Cherubino, Sextus, Zerlina) and has also appeared as Wellgunde in *Das Rheingold* and *Götterdämmerung* and as Waltraute in *Die Walküre*. Groop has also performed a number of Mahler's orchestral songs, as well as a great deal of baroque music.

Groop's international career began with her debut in Wagner's *Ring* at Covent Garden in 1991. She also achieved success in 1993, singing the role of the Composer in Richard Strauss's opera *Ariadne auf Naxos* at the Opéra Comique, Paris. In recent years Groop has also given many concerts abroad, in London, San Francisco, New York, Frankfurt, Cologne, Amsterdam and Munich.

Groop's recordings include solo songs by ▶Sibelius and Grieg, Mahler's

Das Lied von der Erde, and performances in Mozart's *Cosí fan tutte* under Sigiswald Kuijken, Mozart's *Don Giovanni* under Georg Solti, ▶Joonas Kokkonen's song sequence *Lintujen tuonela* ('Birds' Hades') and Sibelius's *The Tempest* and *Kullervo* under ▶Jukka-Pekka Saraste with the Finnish Radio Symphony Orchestra. RL

gypsies ▶Romanies

Haavikko, Paavo (born 1931), writer, member of the Academy of Finland. Paavo Haavikko comes from a family of Helsinki businessmen. His first collection of poetry, *Tiet etäisyyksiin* ('Roads to distances', 1951), was hailed as a modernist breakthrough. Haavikko's poetry is based on a form of expression that uses relationships between things and analogies in complex ways. Through his original imagery and metre, his expression is suggestive. History, property, money, power and love in many mutual relationships are among his themes. Haavikko challenges the study of history and politics, alongside which poetry is an autonomous and equal mode of knowing. In the decades following his first collection, the diversity, quality and quantity of Haavikko's work has given it a unique position in Finnish writing. In addition to poetry, he has written narrative poetry, short stories, novels, stage and radio plays and pamphlets. He has also written libretti for the operas of ▶Aulis Sallinen and the memoirs of the long-serving Finnish president, Urho Kekkonen (1900–1986). In 1990s Haavikko is internationally the most respected Finnish writer. In 1984 he was awarded the Neustadt Prize. PL

habitation and buildings The oldest evidence of habitation in Finland dates back 9,000 years. For a long time habitation was based on hunting as a livelihood and, because of this, changing places of domicile during the year. The advent of agriculture tied people to one place. At the beginning of the 17th century permanent habitation reached as far as the rivers of ▶Ostrobothnia and the lake district of central Finland, spreading into the northernmost parts of the country only at the end of the

Hilma Granqvist

Monica Groop

H

Paavo Haavikko

19th century. Settlement received a new impetus after the Second World War. Through settlements and the division of farms, population densities in the countryside increased and spread, but at the same time began to consist predominantly of small farmers.

The rural population declined rapidly in the 1960s when agriculture began to be rationalised and urbanisation accelerated. Until recent times, towns and their surroundings have still been taking in new inhabitants. Habitation is densest in the southern and south-western parts of the country, which also contain the biggest built-up areas and the country's largest cities, ▶Helsinki, Espoo and Vantaa, which comprise the capital city area, as well as Turku and Tampere. Habitation becomes sparser to the north and east, and the number and size of built-up areas decreases.

Towns Towns were founded on market sites and around fortifications, where traders and artisans settled and began to live permanently. Contemporary towns are characterised by central apartment blocks and, on the outskirts, detached houses. In recent times, urban structures have begun to fragment, with some quite large residential areas, containing urban-style groups of buildings, being built far from town centres.

It is unusual for habitation to be class-based, and in Finland the large working-class districts familiar from central and western Europe hardly exist. There are, however, charming areas of wooden workers' housing in Helsinki, Tampere and Turku. The prosperous urban bourgeoisie attempted to imitate the lifestyles of the aristocracy by choosing to live in park-like suburbs. Examples of this tradition are to be seen in, for example, Kaivopuisto Park and Kulosaari Island in Helsinki.

Village types Finnish villages have generally been shaped by geography, livelihood and history of habitation, but they have also been influenced by the family as an institution. Villages can be divided into agricultural, fishing, industrial and suburban (dormitory) villages. Village centres are generally densely built areas whose inhabitants have come from the surrounding

An Ostrobothnian house from Alahärmä (above) and a house from Ilomantsi, north Karelia (below)

countryside, particularly the more remote villages, since the Second World War. Village populations range from a couple of thousand down to a couple of dozen.

In areas of plentiful common field-land, such as the shores of the Baltic Sea and the rural areas of Finland Proper, rural habitation has taken the form of centralised groups. Clusters of houses built on hillocky ground badly suited to agriculture are still to be seen here and there, although centralised divisions of land have fragmented them, partly to avoid fire risks. More fragmented villages are built in ribbons along roads, canals and, particularly in Ostrobothnia, along rivers, while in northern Karelia they appear on hills. Such elongated villages are more recent in origin than the cluster form. In eastern Finland, more individual, segmented field ownership has separated agricultural land from houses. The dominant form is small villages of one or two dwellings, and individual dwellings.

The farmyard The dwelling-house, cattle byres and storage buildings are situated close together around a courtyard that often contains a small kitchen garden with apple trees and berry bushes. Formerly, the main building dominated the courtyard, but in recent times cow-sheds, pigsties and hen-houses designed for efficient production have begun to play a more visible role. The demands of the ►climate, together with the plentiful supply of ►wood, have shaped the common basic features of traditional building. They include saddle-roofed, planked and painted log cabins. The traditional outer wall colour is dark red, but it has come under competition from paler colours. Red has kept its predominance, particularly in Ostrobothnia, but in other parts of the country it is now used primarily for outhouses. Particularly in the eastern and northern parts of the country, unpainted timber buildings worn silvery grey from exposure to the weather are still to be seen.

FROM CABIN TO APARTMENT The traditional order of rooms is simple and favours large common areas. Since the 17th century, the basic form of Finnish rural building has had a centrally situated vestibule behind which is a chamber flanked by a larger room on either side. The smallish room behind the vestibule served either as a bedroom or a kitchen. One of the larger rooms was an everyday room that functioned as a kitchen, dining room, living room and bedroom. ►Food was prepared in its large fireplace; in one corner was a long dining-table with benches, and in another a bed. The other larger room was a parlour that was used only on festive occasions.

After the Second World War, refugees and the families of war veterans founded a total of 143,000 farms. According to the building plans, their plank-boarded houses generally comprised, on the ground floor, a kitchen and three rooms, and two rooms on the attic floor. This building type, with its central oven, was practical, and was very popular throughout the country.

In the 1960s and 1970s the old building tradition was stopped. Houses were built in the southern European tradition, with flat roofs, and brick began to supplant wood as a building material. The most recent development is represented by bungalow-type buildings.

In the 1990s, the focus of living has gradually shifted from the countryside toward apartment blocks located in cities or built-up areas; at the same time, living space has increased. Statistically, the commonest type of apartment, until the beginning of the 1920s, had one room and 2.6 inhabitants; since the 1960s, the average has been two rooms and a kitchen. In the 1970s, the average floor area was 70 square metres and the number of rooms three, so that, statistically, each inhabitant had his own room. 40 per cent of dwellings are still located in the countryside.

In small towns, in particular, the characteristic rural patterns of habitation are giving way to a more urban style and becoming standardised. In recent times, this development has been consciously resisted, and attention has been drawn to the individual and environmental values of traditional rural building. TK

Havis Amanda The statue called Havis Amanda was created by the sculptor Ville Vallgren (1855–1940). In 1901 people in Finland believed that Vallgren, in Paris, was working on a figure of Aino, a character from the ►*Kalevala*, for a fountain. The result was sur-

The coquettish Havis Amanda, symbol of Helsinki, affectionately dressed by students

prising, not Aino, but a 'French nude coquette', a corrupter of morals. In fact, Vallgren had sculpted, as a personification of the city of Helsinki, a mermaid rising from the Baltic Sea, and surrounded her with 'un-national' sea-lions. Today Havis Amanda ('Beloved by the sea') is a cult destination for the May Day student festivals. The maiden is washed and decorated as in the Venus festivals of antiquity.

The supple, lightly moving elegance of Vallgren's sculpture is pure *art nouveau*, and it found an appreciative audience elsewhere in Europe before it became popular in Finland. Vallgren was rewarded with the rank of officer of the French Légion d'Honneur in 1913. Five years later he was made a professor in Finland. MVn

Hietalahti flea-market has become one of Helsinki's most popular outdoor markets

The Baltic herring market, held every October, dates back 250 years

Helsinki Helsinki has an excellent location at a junction between both east and west and north and south. The predominant element of the 'daughter of the Baltic', as Helsinki is known, is the sea, which surrounds it on three sides and opens up as a shoreless expanse of water from the Market Square and the City Hall, which is situated at the edge of the Market. Of the city's area, two-thirds is water; Helsinki has 96 km of shoreline and 315 islands, of which the most important is northern Europe's most handsome historical island fortress, ▶Suomenlinna (1748–1788).

Helsinki is Finland's door to Europe. The Swedish King Gustavus I Vasa (reigned 1523–1560) founded the town in 1550 on the shores of the Gulf of Finland on the site of a trading port located on the old Viking route to the east, as a competitive partner to Tallin in the south. Thus, Helsinki is the last member in the family of Hansa cities. For the first couple of centuries, however, life was marked by warfare instead of trade. By the early 19th century, Helsinki's merchant navy had grown to be the largest in the Baltic. Today Helsinki harbour is used by the world's biggest car ferries, and more than 6 million passengers pass through it each year, primarily to Stockholm and Tallinn, but also to St Petersburg, Gdansk and Travemünde.

In 1812 Helsinki was named capital city of the country after Finland had, three years previously, become part of Russia as an autonomous Grand Duchy. There were then fewer than 10,000 inhabitants; today there are more than half a million. The city is bilingual: 89.2 per cent of Helsinki people speak Finnish, 7.1 per cent Swedish. 4.3 million travellers visit the city every year, although only 1.2 per cent of inhabitants come from outside Finland.

The symbol of Helsinki as a capital city is its oldest square, Senaatintori Square, which is lined with the neoclassical palatial buildings of the state, university and city administrations and the most important buildings of both the Lutheran and Orthodox denominations. The architecturally minded Emperor Alexander I (reigned 1801–1825) wanted Helsinki to share some part of the brilliance of the imperial classicism of St Petersburg, and commissioned a favourite architect, the Berlin-born ▶Carl Ludvig Engel, to

Helsinki, seen from the South Harbour, with the neo-classical Helsinki Cathedral and Senaatintori Square complex, designed by the German-born architect C.L. Engel, in the centre

direct the planning and construction work (1816–1840). Engel settled in Finland because he was able to design an entire city almost unaided: the 17th- and 18th-century buildings were demolished and Engel designed some 30 public buildings and a large number of private houses. The 'white city of the North' thus received a uniformly cool and pale tone.

The second half of the 19th century was a period of strong economic, technological and cultural development. Low wooden houses gave way to high stone buildings, entire areas of the city received a neo-renaissance, *art nouveau*, national romantic or functionalist appearance. Helsinki became Finland's only metropolis. Its identity, and at the same time that of the whole nation, was reflected in important buildings that were also strong creators of the *genius loci*: the Old Students' House (1870), the Finnish National Gallery ▶Ateneum (1887), the National Theatre (1902), the House of Parliament (1931), the ▶Olympic Stadium (1934–1938), the ▶Finlandia Hall (1971), the National Opera (1993) and the ▶Museum of Contemporary Art (1998).

In 1880 75 per cent of all buildings in Helsinki were still one- or two-storey wooden houses. Today these have almost entirely disappeared. In general, Helsinki has always abandoned the old and adopted the new, which can be considered either a negative mark of the youth of the culture or a positive aspect of progress. Since Helsinki has always striven to be in the vanguard of progress, it is surprising that it is the only city in Finland to have preserved its gas power (1860) and tram-cars (1891). The green tram is, indeed, today one of the best-loved symbols of Helsinki.

The university has been essential to Helsinki's rich cultural life. Founded in Turku in 1640, this was moved to the capital in 1828. Today it is the country's leading university; in addition, Helsinki has seven other colleges of ▶higher education. An orchestral society was founded in university circles in 1845, and Finland's first art exhibition was held the same year. The first real theatre building, to house visiting companies, was opened in 1827; the Finnish-language National Theatre was founded in 1872. Traditionally Helsinki is, indeed, a city of theatre and the visual arts. Close to half the country's artists live near Helsinki. There are 8 permanent theatres, and 1 million people go to the theatre and opera each year. In terms of numbers of museums (64) and libraries (56), Helsinki scores high in world statistics; 7 million loans are made each year.

After Finland gained its independence in 1917, Helsinki's role as a European city and as a meeting-point of

The Academic Quarter – a student sporting event held annually in May in Senaatintori Square

cultures became more accentuated than before. Among the most important star moments were the Olympic Games of 1952 and the first Conference on Security and Co-Operation in Europe (CSCE), which took place in 1975 in the ▶Finlandia Hall. Helsinki, which has been through three wars this century, has wished to work for world peace, and the Helsinki CSCE conference did, indeed, provide a firm basis for collaboration, known as the 'Helsinki spirit'. Today Helsinki is a notable congress city: around 70 international congresses are held here each year.

Closeness to nature is still essential to Helsinki. In addition to the sea, the landscape is characterised by greenness: urbanised areas are split by extensive forests and field areas; there are 1725 ha of tended parkland. The importance of nature is underlined by the changing seasons. Average temperatures vary between –12°C (February) and +20°C (August). The arrival of summer, May Day, has always been celebrated in Helsinki, and in its current form, a 24-hour student celebration, since 1831. Banner parades by working people were added at the end of the 19th century. The celebration of midsummer is concentrated on the Open-Air Museum of ▶Seurasaari Island (founded in 1909). One of the climaxes of the autumn is the Helsinki Baltic Herring Market, a 250-year-old festival to which fishermen from as far

away as the ▶Åland Islands and Estonia now come to sell their wares. The darkest time of the year is brightened by Christmas, which is in Helsinki a real festival of light: the first decorated street was opened in 1930, and the custom has spread everywhere, down to the windows of private houses.

The most important annual cultural event has been, since the 1960s, the Helsinki Festival which, in late August and early September, for a few weeks offers Helsinki people the opportunity to enjoy star moments of art from both Finland and abroad, from opera and art exhibitions to rock concerts and culinary experiences. The climax is the 'Night of the Arts', when the whole city is on the move and cultural institutions keep their doors open until the small hours of the morning. MLR

Hemming (c.1290–1366), Bishop of Turku. The Swedish-born Hemming was one of the most important medieval Finnish bishops. He acted as canon of the Cathedral Chapter of Turku from 1329. He was appointed bishop in 1338 and acted in this capacity until his death.

During Hemming's bishopry, attempts were made to set the Finnish Catholic Church on a European level. In 1352 the first synodal statutes were given, with which canonical law was introduced into the diocese. The statutes governed the life and work of

Bishop Hemming, painting from Urjala church, 16th century

the clergy. The fact that the priests were forbidden, on pain of excommunication, from keeping children with them demonstrates that the law of celibacy had not yet been implemented in Finland; priests often had families. New churches were built, Turku Cathedral extended, and tithing established during Hemming's time.

His personal faith, his friendship with the Swedish St Bridget (1303–1373) and his great importance as a developer of the church in Finland formed the basis for Hemming's fame, which led to the setting in motion of the process of his canonisation toward the end of the 15th century. Its first phase, in which Hemming was proclaimed blessed, was ceremonially concluded in 1514. Hemming's remains were then placed in a reliquary that survives in Turku Cathedral, and in which other relics were later stored. His proclamation as a saint, however, was prevented by the realisation of the Reformation in the Swedish Church in the 1520s. JN

higher education Finland's first university, the Academy of Turku, was founded in 1640. Having suffered severe damage in the fire of Turku in 1827, it was moved to the new capital, ▶Helsinki, in 1828. Until 1918 the University, which was called the Imperial Alexander University in Finland, was the only university in the country. In

1919 its name was changed to the ▶University of Helsinki (*Universitas Helsingiensis*).

The founding of the Academy of Turku was the result of a need on the part of Sweden, which had attained great-power status, for educated civil servants. During the first decade of its existence, about half the professors were Swedes; subsequently the number of Finns grew to such an extent that in 1808 all 15 professors were Finns. During the period of Swedish rule, the Academy of Turku was a regional university whose international importance was slight. In Finland, however, it was the central educational and cultural institution, through which new ideas and international scholarly movements reached Finland.

After the move to Helsinki, the University was expanded rapidly, and new buildings were constructed for its use. The main building of the University of Helsinki (1832), the Observatory (1833), the University Library (1845) and many faculty buildings form an essential part of the harmonious empire-style city centre designed by ▶C.L. Engel.

Despite the existence of new universities established during the 20th century, the University of Helsinki has retained its position as overwhelmingly the largest university in the country. Today, the University of Helsinki has 9 faculties: theology, law, medicine, humanities, mathematics and natural sciences, pedagogics, political science, agriculture and forestry, and veterinary science.

In 1996, the student body of University of Helsinki numbered 32,700, of whom 62 per cent were women. The University is bilingual. There are 27 Swedish-language professorships, and the proportion of Swedish-speaking students is about 7 per cent. There is a total of 2000 teaching and research staff, and 4400 other staff. There are more than 1800 docents, of whom some belong to the permanent teaching and research staff, while others work outside the university and are responsible only for lectures. There are 1250 foreign students, 100 foreign teachers and 620 foreign research staff.

Each year around 3000 final qualifications are gained at University of

Helsinki, and almost 300 doctoral theses are examined. In 1995 the University received its funding primarily from central government (64 per cent), but partly from its own funds (10 per cent), outside funding (23 per cent) and value-added tax (3 per cent). The majority of the outside funding is made up of paid service activities and research funding granted by the Academy of Finland.

Within the Student Union of the University of Helsinki, founded in 1868, which acts as an umbrella organisation, some 200 societies are active, from subject and special interest societies to political student societies. The Students' Union maintains student accommodation, organises canteens on University premises, and publishes text-books. It is also one of the most important property-owners in central Helsinki. The students' health is cared for by a clinic supported by a separate foundation.

The establishment of a second university was already under consideration before Finland gained its independence in 1917. The language conflict between Finnish-speakers and Swedish-speakers, however, led to the foundation, soon after independence, of two new universities in Turku. The Swedish-language Åbo Akademi University (Åbo is the Swedish name of Turku) in 1917, and the Finnish-language University of Turku, in 1920. Both universities were founded using private funding.

From its first decades, Åbo Akademi University developed in a clear-cut manner into a university with many faculties corresponding to teaching in areas from theology to technology. As well as from Finland's own Swedish-speaking population, Åbo Akademi University received both financial and teaching support from Sweden.

Åbo Akademi University was nationalised in 1980, but it was left with extensive autonomy concerning both teaching and economics. Today, the University has 7 faculties, those of the humanities, mathematics and the natural sciences, economics and political science, chemistry and technology, theology, pedagogics, and social work.

Behind the founding of the University of Turku, was the aim, which

Universities

had been current since the mid 1800s, of developing higher education in the Finnish language by establishing a second university in the country. The idea received new impetus during heated debates in the early 20th century at the University of Helsinki concerning increasing teaching in the Finnish language, which did not, in the opinions of Fennomanes, lead to a satisfactory outcome. For this reason the foundation of a private Finnish-language university began to be planned among the Finnish-language intelligentsia. After consideration of a number of alternatives, Turku was fixed upon, and it became possible to found the university in the winter of 1920. The University of Turku opened its doors to students in 1922. With the help of increased government funding, a medical faculty was established in 1943 and it became possible to develop the University in other ways, too. Dentistry training was begun in the medical faculty in 1958, and a faculty of law was founded in 1960. The University of Turku was nationalised in 1974, at which point a pedagogical faculty was established. The University's other faculties are those of the humanities, mathematics and the natural sciencies, and law.

The predecessor of the University

The University of Tampere in Finland's second city acquired university status in 1966

of Tampere, was founded in 1925 in Helsinki. Its aim was to raise the standard of education of those who had completed only their secondary education, or less, and offered training programmes in various professions.

It moved to Tampere in 1960, and became a university in 1966. The University has 5 faculties: social science, humanities, pedagogics, economics and administration, and medicine. The University plays an important role in adult and continuing education, particularly in the areas of youth work, tax adminstration, insurance, municipal administration and journalism.

The University of Jyväskylä, has traditionally specialised in teacher training. The precursor of the University was a training college for primary-school teachers, the first in Finland, founded in 1863. It became a college in 1934, and a university in 1966. Another speciality of the University of Jyväskylä is physical education. The University of Jyväskylä now has 5 faculties: pedagogics, humanities, social sciences, mathematics and natural sciences, and physical education. A language centre and environmental research centre are also active within the university.

The University of Oulu was founded in Oulu on the north-west coast, a town well-known for its schools, in 1958. The University, which is located on its own campus a little way from the town centre, is the country's fourth largest. Particular attention is directed to research into Arctic areas and the biological sciences. The University of Oulu has 5 faculties: humanities, pedagogics, the natural sciences, medicine

and – in contrast to other universities – technology. Unlike the other faculties, the technological faculty offers engineering and architectural diplomas as its basic degrees.

The University of Vaasa originated in the Vaasa School of Economics and Business Administration, founded in 1966. The School was nationalised in 1968, and became a university in 1980. The University of Vaasa has 5 faculties: humanities, commerce and administration, commerce and technology, and social sciences. On the basis of an exchange agreement between the University of Vaasa and the Helsinki University of Technology, a small number of students in the faculty of commerce and technology can gain a diploma in engineering at the Helsinki University of Technology. The University of Vaasa also collaborates a great deal with the Swedish University of Umeå, on the other side of the Gulf of Bothnia.

The University of Joensuu originated on the basis of a teacher-training college that had served the needs of eastern Finland. Its founding in 1969 formed part of the higher education policies of the 1960s, which emphasised the regional development of higher education. The University has 5 faculties: pedagogics, humanities, social sciences, mathematics and natural sciences, and forestry. The theological department, which forms part of the faculty of the humanities, specialises in Orthodox theological education. One of the central focusis of the University is economic and cultural regional studies directed at the environment. The Karelian Research Institute was founded in 1971 to serve this end.

The founding of the University of Kuopio in 1970, was also connected with the development of education in eastern Finland in the late 1960s. The University has 4 faculties: pharmacy, medicine, natural and environmental sciences, and social sciences.

The University of Lapland, based in Rovaniemi, is Finland's northernmost university. It is divided into four faculties: education, law, social sciences and art and design. The Arctic Centre, an institute within the University, interprets the effects of changes in the interaction between humankind and the northern environments. Being the host for the secretariat of the Circumpolar Universities' Association makes the University of Lapland a key actor in international co-operation among the northern universities.

Helsinki University of Technology became a university in 1908. The main building in Helsinki was badly damaged during the bombing of the Second World War. In the late 1950s, as demand for technological education grew, Helsinki University of Technology began gradually to move to Otaniemi, Espoo, to a campus designed by ►Alvar Aalto some 10 kilometres north of central Helsinki. The buildings of the Technical Research Centre of Finland are also located at Otaniemi. Helsinki University of Technology offers education programmes for engineers, architects and landscape architects. The architecture department and cryophysics laboratory enjoy great respect internationally; the latter has achieved records in the attempt to reach absolute zero.

Tampere University of Technology opened its doors in 1965 as an affiliated university of Helsinki University of Technology. It became independent in 1972. In 1985, with the support of the City of Tampere, the University founded a research centre for information technology whose aim is to increase the effectiveness of commercial applications of work done in the University.

Lappeenranta University of Technology began its work in 1969, at first in temporary accommodation. Like the University of Joensuu, Lappeenranta University of Technology has developed from a regional college toward a nation-wide university.

The pioneer of higher education in the commercial field was predecessor of the Helsinki School of Economics and Business Administration founded in 1911. From 1920 onwards it was also possible to gain qualifications equivalent to university degrees, and from 1931 doctorates. The first doctoral dissertation, in 1937, was the first doctoral dissertation to be examined in a Nordic business college. The School moved to its current main building in the Töölö district of Helsinki in 1950. It was nationalised in 1974. Since 1977, the basic qualification on offer has been the four-year

The University of Lapland is Finland's northernmost university

master's degree. It is also possible to study for the international Bachelor of Business Administration and Master of Business Administration degrees.

The Swedish School of Economics and Business Administration offers commercial training in Swedish at the highest level. It was founded in 1909. Since 1980 commercial training under the aegis of the School has also been offered in Vaasa.

The Finnish-language Turku School of Economics and Business Administration was founded in 1950 when the need for people with a commercial training grew after the Second World War. Plans to establish a college had been made as early as the 1920s and 1930s. At this point the aim had been to create a faculty of commerce within the University of Turku. At first private, Turku School of Economics and Business Administration was nationalised in 1977.

In the field of the arts, it is possible to gain a degree in music, the visual arts, various genres of the applied arts, and theatre. The oldest arts college is the Sibelius Academy, founded in 1939, which is responsible for musical education at the highest level. Its predecessor was founded in 1882. There are 8 teaching programmes at the Sibelius Academy: performance, jazz, folk music, church music, musical pedagogics, opera-singing, orchestral and choral conducting, and composition and music theory. Training in church music is also available at the University of Joensuu, where the church music option is part of the training of Orthodox theologians.

Like many other areas, special training in the applied arts began in

Finland in the 1880s. The University of Art and Design was founded in 1973. There are 9 teaching programmes on offer for the honours degrees, 16 for the master's degree. They range from audiovisual media culture to more traditional subjects such as textile design, graphic design and the crafts and applied arts.

Separate training in the visual arts in Finland began in 1848. Today instruction at the highest level in the field is given by the government-supported Academy of Fine Arts, which was founded in 1985. The diploma of arts corresponds to an ordinary university degree, while the final examination corresponds to an honours degree. Teaching is given in sculpture, painting, art graphics and the installation arts, including those using audiovisual methods.

Training in drama was begun by a school set up within the Finnish National Theatre in 1906. In 1979 the School became the university-level Theatre Academy. It offers training in both theatre and dance, in such a way that it is possible to complete an honours and master's degree in both. There are teaching programmes in acting, theatre, directing, dramaturgy, lighting and sound design, music theatre and dance. A qualification in theatre is also on offer at the University of Tampere, which has a Finnish-language teaching programme in theatrical work.

Collegiate officer training began in 1779 in Kuopio and was moved to Hamina, on the south coast, in 1819. The Military College, which functioned there, was closed because of the abolition of the Finnish Army in 1903. After Finland gained its independence in 1917, military training begun again in 1919. Today, military training at the highest level is provided by the Military Academy in Helsinki.

In the 1990s, Finnish higher education has begun to be developed into two sectors, the university sector and the non-university sector. The latter category includes vocational colleges, which have been developed from the highest vocationally oriented educational institutions. The development was begun in a law passed in 1991, after which 20 experimental vocational colleges were set up. The aim is to complete the reform by the year 2000 in such a way that most educational institutions offering post-secondary and higher levels of vocational education will become vocational colleges.

The aim of the reform is to raise the general standard of education and make the vocational colleges more tempting alternatives to the universities and technical universities. It is hoped that the two-sector model will also improve possibilities for reforming and diversifying higher vocational education.

The central aim of development in the technical universities is the internationalisation of research and teaching. Participation is to be increased both in scientific projects within the European Union and in other multi- and bilateral collaborations. Exchange of researchers and teaching staff has been hindered by the central position of Finnish as the teaching language in universities and the rigidity of the hierarchical system, which has hindered the recruitment of top researchers and teachers from abroad. Student participation in international student exchanges has been very active. Around 6500 students study abroad with government support each year. Just as in exchange of academic staff, the number of students wishing to go abroad has been larger than the number of exchange students wishing to come to Finland to study. JN

history The history of Finland as a state begins in 1809, when Finland, as a Grand Duchy of Russia, was given its own state system and central administration, while local administration remained as before. An impressive capital, ▶Helsinki, was built for the new state unit, and its most important institutions, the senate and the university (▶University of Helsinki), formed the administrative and cultural core of a nation which extended to a civil society and economic whole covering the entire country. As a result of the Russian Revolution of 1917, links with communist Russia were severed and Finland became a sovereign state, at first with German support. Having succeeded, in two wars fought against the Soviet Union between 1939 and

1944, in preventing the occupation of the country and in preserving its sovereignty, Finland soon achieved a high economic and social standard in European and Nordic terms. Through skilful politics, it succeeded in creating for itself a politically neutral and economically advantageous relationship with its large and, during the Cold War, dangerous neighbour, the Soviet Union. In 1995 Finland became a full member of the European Union, together with Sweden and Austria.

Until 1809, Finland was, for the entire historical period for which written sources are available, part of the Kingdom of Sweden, in whose framework it was one of three (or, at some stages, six or seven) provinces. The name *Suomi, Finland* originally meant the south-western part of contemporary Finland but, particularly as habitation spread, the concept came to denote all of geographical Finland, the area between the sea and Russia. Neither ▶Ostrobothnia nor ▶Karelia was often, even as late as the 18th century, included in the concept of Finland, and the Viipuri area of Karelia, ceded to Russia in the peace treaties of 1721 and 1743, formed 'Old Finland', which remained distinct long into the 19th century.

The provinces of the period of Swedish rule were merely historical and heraldic, not administrative or economic. Thus the towns, trade and administration of the Gulf of Bothnia and the Gulf of Finland were each in direct contact with Stockholm and, from time to time, with foreign countries through Stockholm, without any intermediate layer in terms of local administration. Passenger and freight transport from Finnish towns generally passed through Stockholm (or sometimes Tallinn). In terms of ecclesiastical administration, on the other hand, the diocese of Turku (after its official inception in the 1220s) included almost the whole of present-day Finland and the area of Karelia lost in 1944. This diocese was, however, divided in the mid 16th century into two independent dioceses, the western diocese of Turku (and Ostrobothnia) and the eastern diocese of Viipuri.

Before the consolidation of the Kingdom of Sweden in the 12th and 13th centuries, the western areas of the country had strong connections with Birka and Svealand, while the medieval 'South Finland' had links with Estonia and Kurland, and, farther south, with Vistula and Pomerania. The simultaneous aim for eastward expansion by Sweden, Denmark and the Teutonic Knights in the early 13th century led to the severing of the southern connections of southern and eastern Finland and the extension of Swedish predominance to Häme and the Gulf of Finland. This was particularly so after the so-called Second and Third crusades (1238 and 1293). The expansion led, in the Treaty of Pähkinäsaari in 1323, to an agreement between Sweden and Novgorod for a border dividing the Karelian Isthmus from the remote areas farther north. The eastward expansion of Sweden consolidated the kingdom and Stockholm's role as its centre; settlers were moved from Sweden to Uusimaa and even to the Karelian coast to support the expansion.

During the Middle Ages, the development of Finland was characterised by the deepening impact of Roman Catholic and European culture, which left as its legacy almost 100 surviving stone churches with their works of art, societal thought according to Roman law, absorbed and adapted in the Kingdom of Sweden, and German urban culture with its technical and consumer novelties (despite the fact that the towns of Sweden did not belong to the Hansa League, and that Sweden and Denmark in general opposed it). In the 14th and early 15th centuries, Sweden was united with Denmark and Norway, but the dominance of Denmark also caused opposition, which led to war within the union and, among other things, the Danish destruction of Finnish towns and coasts. The union collapsed in a civil war as a result of which Gustavus I Vasa (c. 1496–1560), elected King of Sweden in 1523, energetically set about creating a centrally administered monarchical state. An important basis in the formation of the state was the considerable appropriation of church property allowed by the Protestant Reformation. Planned settlement was considered important, particularly in Savo and subsequently, as its offshoot, in Värmland and Dalecarlia in Sweden.

At the Porvoo Diet, 1809, during which Finland ceremonially became an autonomous Grand Duchy of the Russian Empire, Emperor Alexander I promised to uphold the Lutheran faith and constitutional laws and rights of Finland. Painting by Emanuel Thelning, 1812

In the late 16th century the kingdom found itself in civil war once more as a result of a dynastic alliance with Poland formed for reasons of Russian policy. Sigismund (1566–1632), joint King of Sweden and Poland, lost the war against his uncle King Charles IX (1550–1611), the Lutheran clergy and a peasant rebellion in Ostrobothnia and Savo; the result was a significant weakening of the power of the aristocracy in Finland as well as Sweden. In the 1610s to 1630s, during the reign of Sigismund's cousin, Gustavus II Adolphus (1594–1632), the kingdom spread to Karelia, Estonia and Livonia as well as Germany; at the same time central and provincial administration, the judicial system, education and culture were cultivated in the European sense, and the position of Stockholm as capital grew stronger. In the Treaty of Westphalia in 1648, Sweden became a European greatpower, but in the decades that followed it found itself at war against Poland and Denmark, and then, in a long war in the early 18th century, suffered defeat at the hands of Russia. However, Sweden retained its position in relation to Denmark-Norway, and a large part of its German lands. The loss of Estonia, Livonia and Viipuri Karelia in 1721 was connected with Russia's new westward expansion, which was to affect the future of Finland in a significant way.

The question of the security of St Petersburg, which had been founded in 1703 and had rapidly grown into a large city, increased the significance of the Gulf of Finland – always of military importance, in Russian eyes – and both Sweden and Russia concentrated resources on the fortification of its coasts and islands (Kronstadt near St Petersburg, Viapori, ▶Suomenlinna in Helsinki harbour, the fortification of Tallinn). After an alliance between Russia and France in 1807 concerning control of Europe, Russia conquered mainland Finland and Åland in 1808–1809, essentially because of the military importance of the Gulf of Finland. Although the Russian army advanced west of the Gulf of Bothnia, Russia satisfied itself, in the Treaty of Hamina of 1809, with a militarily justified border, and made Finland into a military security zone for St Petersburg.

The Ostrobothnian border was not economically or culturally 'natural', and western Finland was for a long time to come to orient itself toward Stockholm, while eastern Finland was drawn, in terms of economics and demographics, towards St Petersburg. Gradually at first, the Grand Duchy of

Finland, now a single administrative unit, developed into a nation through the centralisation of administration, transport and, in particular, culture. An essential factor was the emphasis on differences both from Russia, with its separate language, religion and history, and from Sweden, whose national development was proceeding in an entirely different direction, but with which the survival of Swedish as Finland's administrative and cultural language continued to form an important communicative link. After the university, established in 1640 in Turku, was moved to Helsinki in 1828, the construction of the national identity began in the circles of the university and the ►learned societies that grew up within it – the ►Finnish Literature Society and the Finnish Society of Sciences and Letters (1838), for example. This identity was built on an idealisation of the people and landscape of the Finnish interior as well as of the ancient past, in material edited from folklore gathered on the periphery. At the same time the architect ►C.L. Engel and the composer Frederick Pacius (1809–1891) created, respectively, the bases for an architectural tradition based on an ancient Greek inflection of the empire style and a musical tradition in accordance with German romanticism.

This fundamental shaping of the national identity took place essentially in a mood of political conservatism, in that it was based on acceptance of the Russian victory of 1808–1809 and its absorption as a national conception. This conception was consolidated through popular education and other dissemination of ideas, and survived into the 20th century and up to the cultural transition of the 1960s. From the Russian point of view, the development was positive because it separated Finland from Sweden and from possible hopes for reunification in states of war; at the same time, Finland could be economically useful, and a model in terms of administration and education. The price for Finland, however, was loyalty in matters of foreign policy and rejection of European revolutionary ideas.

The development of the Finnish ►language was well in accordance with this national project. Like many other European languages (including Swedish), Finnish had become a literary language through the printing press, ►Bible translations and Renaissance culture in the 16th and 17th centuries (and decisively in the 1640s). The development of Finnish language, however, came to a halt in the mid 17th century as a result of progress towards integration, and the Swedish language gained ground, both geographically (western Finland) and socially (the upper, literate classes), until the early 20th century. This development was accompanied, from 1809, by the development of the Finnish language, which, in the new administrative system, had become the majority language of the people. It was, however, necessary first to form and standardise the language; it began to become a cultural language as such only in the 1860s, thanks to the ►press and ►literature, and the fact that intelligentsia began to think and write in Finnish. The Finnish-language literary tradition begins in the 1880s with Juhani Aho (1861–1921), Arvid Järnefelt (1861–1932) and ►Minna Canth. ►Aleksis Kivi, who had been influential 20 years beforehand, was a solitary and isolated phenomenon.

In an administrative and economic sense, Finland became a modern nation-state during the reign of Alexander II (1855–1881), when the introduction of regular meetings of parliament, a separate monetary unit for Finland (the silver mark in 1865, followed in 1877 by the gold mark), railways (1862; the St Petersburg-Helsinki track was opened in 1870), large-scale changes in agriculture after the years of famine, beginning in the 1870s, reform of the education system (1869), a new municipal administration and freedom of trade, among other things, rapidly changed economic and social structures. The condition was still loyalty in matters of foreign policy, which Finland demonstrated during the Polish rebellion of 1863, and again during the Turkish War of 1877–1878, during which the Finnish Guard and many Finns serving in Russian regiments gained military distinctions. The loyalty of the former phase had been 'rewarded' by the introduction of parlia-

The unveiling of the statue to Emperor Alexander II, 1894, in Senaatintori Square, Helsinki: loyalty to the Emperor was a precondition of Finland's autonomy within the Russian Empire

mentary life to Finland (in a revived version of the old Swedish four-estate parliament) and an agreement in principle to raise Finnish to the status of an administrative language alongside Swedish; the loyalty of the latter phase resulted in a separate conscripted army for Finland. During the reign of Alexander III (1881–1894), the special position of Finland as a state continued to develop; at the same time, the demand for loyalty began increasingly to shift to internal policy, in the form of a demand for the rejection of the Russian revolutionary movement. This did not cause difficulties in Finland in general, for both the Finnish elites and the ordinary people were monarchists, and expressed their attachment to the ruling dynasty. No closeness or attachment to the Russian people, on the other hand – or any antipathy, either – developed during the period. Finland's in many senses privileged position was entirely bound up with the monarch, and not with the Russian people, and attempts to change the system of administration in Russia were not in Finland's interests.

In the 1860s, during the early years of the reign of Alexander II, a liberal climate of opinion developed in Finland, supported in the Diet by the majority, made up of the nobility and the burghers; among the clergy and the peasantry, the agrarian and loyalist 'Fennomania' was predominant. The latter stressed the development of the role of the Finnish language, while the former placed their trust in normal, self-directing development – which gradually, as the countryside became more prosperous, did indeed make Finnish-language newspapers, literature and schools economically viable. In addition, there was a small Swecomane group, which was anti-Russian and pro-Swedish, and stressed the importance of the Swedish-speaking coastal population. The liberal European orientation was of considerable importance from the point of view of both Finland's economic development and the orientation of scholarship and the arts. The French orientation of art – Albert Edelfelt (1854–1905), Ville Vallgren (1855–1940), ▶Akseli Gallen-Kallela and others – and the German orientation of scholarship and music thus joined the other external stimuli which the successful careers of numerous sons of the Finnish nobility and civil servant class in the Russian Imperial Army in different parts of the empire had already brought to Finland.

The military alliance concluded be-

Eetu Isto, *Hyökkäys* ('The attack', 1899). This painting, which shows the Finnish Constitution, under attack by the double-headed Russian imperial eagle, protected by the Maid of Finland, became a symbol of resistance to Russification policies and was disseminated, in tens of thousands of prints, to most Finnish homes

previous situation also bound it to conservative political circles, above all the representatives of the parliamentary estates, which the liberal and Swedish-speaking front had refused to reform. The land-ownership question, in particular, demanded reforms. Political opposition at first received support in boycotts of conscription calls, which was regarded as illegal, but the boycott weakened rapidly, and this radicalised part of the opposition into attempting, together with the state enemy, Japan, to foment rebellion, which failed. The Fennomane Party remained in favour of conciliation.

Building a nation: at the Paris World's Fair of 1900, the Finnish pavilion drew attention, at a time of the continuing implementation of Russification policies, to Finland's existence as separate from Russia

tween Russia and France in the early 1890s made Germany a potential enemy in the Baltic Sea area, and when, at the turn of the century, Germany began to equip itself as a great naval power, the Russian navy followed suit with large construction projects. The situation highlighted the question of Russian defence on the Finnish coastline and Finland's part in the Russian defence burden. The protracted obstructions of the Finnish authorities gradually became, for Russia, both a practical and a prestige problem, and the young Emperor Nicholas II (reigned 1895–1917) was forced, in 1899, to attempt to solve it unilaterally with the 'February manifesto'. Although the new principle for a legislative system did not constitute any great change from the existing arrangements, the decision caused a great deal of anxiety which, in a couple of years, grew into real opposition. This was partly a question of promoting Finland's rise as a state by internationalising the position of the Grand Duchy and appealing to the sympathy gained in international forums such as world fairs. At the same time, the fact that the opposition restrained itself to defending the

The Japanese War led, in late 1905, to unemployment and demonstrations in Russia, with a large wave of strikes and political crisis, the result of which was the founding of a lower chamber, or *duma*. The wave of strikes spread to Finland, led to the appointment of a liberal senate, and then to parliamentary reform approved by the emperor in the summer of 1906. The four-estate representation was replaced by a unicameral parliament that was elected through universal suffrage, which also extended to women. Thus the Finnish state was strengthened in an attempt to prevent the Finns joining the *duma*, in which all other peoples of the Russian Empire were to be represented. This succeeded, but the new

СОВѢТЪ НАРОДНЫХЪ
Комиссаровъ.

Петроградъ.
.18.- декабря. 1917 г.

№ 101

Въ отвѣтъ на обращеніе финляндскаго Правительства
о признаніи независимости финляндской республики, Совѣтъ
Народныхъ Комиссаровъ, въ полномъ согласіи съ принципами
права націй на самоопредѣленіе, ПОСТАНОВЛЯЕТЪ:
Войти въ Центральный Исполнительный Комитетъ съ предложе-
ніемъ:

а/ признать государственную независимость финляндской
Республики

и б/ организовать , по соглашенію съ финляндскимъ Пра-
вительствомъ, особую Комиссію изъ представителей обѣихъ
сторонъ для разработки тѣхъ практическихъ мѣропіятій,
которыя вытекаютъ изъ отдѣленія финляндіи отъ Россіи.

Предсѣдатель Совѣта Народныхъ
Комиссаровъ

Народные Комиссары:

Управляющій Дѣлами Совѣта Народныхъ
Комиссаровъ

Секретарь Совѣта

The nascent
Soviet Union
recognises Finnish
independence, 1917.
Among the signatories
are Lenin, Stalin and
Trotsky

parliament did not, in accordance with the emperor, receive any more power than its predecessor, the accountability of government to parliament was not prescribed, and the extensive prerogatives of the monarch remained as before. The parliamentary reform satisfied a large number of political needs and, with its frequently recurring elections, opened the way to the development of modern civil activity. But the Socialist Workers' Party, which, surprisingly, emerged as the largest party (80 mandates out of a total of 200 in the first elections in 1907) was dissatisfied, because social reforms were, through the opposition of the small bourgeois parties or through the emperor's veto, not passed as laws. The socialist vote grew steadily, and in 1916 the party achieved a parliamentary majority.

From 1905 until the Russian Revolution, the chasm between socialism and the right wing grew threateningly in Finland , but favourable conditions and a rising standard of living compensated for dissatisfaction and allowed significant investments in eco-

nomics and culture. The First World War attracted growing numbers to the German side. Finnish scholarship, technology and trade were increasingly aligned toward Germany, which had long been important, and it was believed that Germany would be able to guarantee a non-socialist social system better than that of Russia. This model received increasing support in the summer of 1917 as disorder spread in Russia, and particularly after the October Bolshevik Revolution, when relations between Finland and Russia were severed and the Finnish authorities no longer recognised Lenin's government as successor to the emperor. Urged by Germany, Finland declared itself a sovereign state on 6 December 1917, but only after Lenin's government had recognised its sovereignty did Sweden, France, Germany, Austria-Hungary and some other countries (but not Great Britain or the United States) recognise its sovereignty, from 4 January 1918.

There were still many Russian troops in Finland when, at the end of January, a socialist revolution began,

The Civil War of 1918 left a legacy of bitterness that has been slow to heal. C.G.E. Mannerheim, leader of the White troops, heads a victory parade in central Helsinki in May 1918 (above); the 'Red' general Heikki Kaljunen leads a funeral procession in late winter of the same year

which was followed throughout southern Finland by a Civil War between the Red forces and the White forces of the government. The revolution was quelled, and the Russian troops expelled from the country in three months on the one hand by the senate, which had removed itself to northern and central Finland, and its civil guard army under the leadership of a former lieutenant-general of the Russian army, ▶Gustaf Mannerheim, with the help of volunteers from Germany and Finnish volunteer soldiers who had returned from Germany. On the other hand, the red revolution was put down, particularly in Helsinki and the south, by a German division that landed on the south coast. As a result, Finland became strongly linked to imperial Germany, and the new country chose the brother-in-law of the German Kaiser as its king. The king, however, never arrived in Finland, as Germany lost the war, and Finland now oriented itself with the victorious western powers

under the leadership of General Mannerheim, who became a ruler interested with the powers formerly held by the emperor. He was not, however, able to persuade the rest of the Finnish political leadership to agree to aid the white Russians and besiege St Petersburg, and in the summer of 1919 signed the constitution that is still in force in Finland, which is a compromise between monarchical and republican principles. K.J. Ståhlberg (1865–1952), a social liberal, was elected as the country's first president.

The solution of the problems caused by the Civil War and the settlement of the land-ownership question were the central problems of the postwar period. At the same time the turbulent situation in Russia caused anxiety. The 1920s were, nevertheless, a period of positive development in all respects, until the world economic situation and the leftist – and, in particular, rightist – political radicalism associated with it reached Finland. The Finnish

Finnish children awaiting evacuation to neutral Sweden during the Second World War. A total of 70,000 Finnish children spent the war years in Sweden

social order, however, did not alter, but communist activities were banned. In the 1920s Finland was at first oriented towards the Baltic and Poland, but then put its faith in the security system of the League of Nations, which had guaranteed Åland for it, against Swedish aspirations. The growing strength of Germany and Russia from the early 1930s led to attempts to create a Nordic security alliance; these attempts failed, and when, in 1939, Germany and Russia agreed the Ribbentrop Pact, Finland was left alone as it denied the Soviet Union its territorial demands and, in 30 November 1939, found itself the object of an attack by the Soviet Union.

In the inhuman conditions of the ▶Winter War in 1939, the Finnish defence held its against an aggressor many times its size until the Soviet Union abandoned the puppet government it had instituted and agreed to a heavy but honourable peace with Finland in March 1940. The 'miracle of the Winter War' was based on traditional Finnish loyalty and opposition to the Soviet Union, and on a reconciliation between the Red and White sides of the Finnish Civil War that had been achieved during the 1920s, as well as on the government coalition of 1937. It led to an enormous wave of goodwill throughout the world. When, 1940, Germany expanded eastwards, the Soviet Union occupied the Baltic

Karelian evacuees arrive by train from Parikkala, June 1941. Many of them moved back to Karelia after the Winter War, only to be forced to leave their homes again during the Continuation War

A member of the women's auxiliary volunteer services, or Lotta, tends a wounded soldier at Kiestinki during the Finnish advance through Karelia, 1941

countries and began once more to put pressure on Finland and to amass troops on the Finnish border. Finland now received political support from Germany, and when war broke out between Germany and Russia in June 1941, Finland and Russia found themselves automatically also at war. This war finally ended in September 1944, in the same conclusion as the Winter War; Finland now turned against Germany and expelled its troops from northern Finland to Norway.

After the war, Finland avoided becoming part of the expanding Soviet sphere of influence, essentially because it had avoided occupation, because it fulfilled the terms of the interim peace and the final Paris Peace Treaty of 1947, because it avoided provocative behaviour and because it recieved political and economic support from Sweden and the United States. The question of the security of Leningrad was solved in 1948 by the Treaty of Friendship, Co-operation and Mutual Assistance in which Finland bound itself to prevent the use of its territory as a base for attack against the Soviet Union. The Soviet Union, in the atmosphere of détente of the mid 1950s, agreed to give up the military base it had rented on the Gulf of Finland, the Porkkala Peninsula. At the same time Finland joined the United Nations and the Nordic Council, and then obtained from all the great Western powers assurance that it was regarded as a neutral state, perhaps on the model of Austria (although Austria had been occupied).

It was significant for Finland that Sweden did not join a defence alliance proposed by Denmark and Norway, or NATO, but remained neutral, and that Norway and Denmark, too, declined to house NATO strategic points in time

Pioneering work: as part of the post-war reconstruction, the Finnish government offered grants for the creation of new farms. Finland was the only European country in which the number of smallholdings increased after the war

of peace. This reduced the danger of local conflicts in northern Europe, but the situation was naturally dependent on world politics, and particularly on changes in the position of Germany. Finland's relationship with the Soviet Union became mundane in a significant way once extensive bilateral trade was established soon after the war, and particularly after Finland had, in 1952, paid the war reparations demanded in the Paris Peace Treaty – the only losing power in the war to do so. Finland's exports to the Soviet Union were between 15 per cent and 20 per cent of its total exports, and this did a great deal to stabilise Finland's sensitive economy. Imports from the Soviet Union consisted primarily of crude oil, which was refined in Finland.

In terms of foreign policy, in its constrained but skilfully managed situation, Finland succeeded in securing its position also by increasing prosperity and modernisation: the transition of industrialisation and urbanisation occurred during the 1960s. The multi-party system and coalition governments succeeded in attaining a fairly good consensus; the long term of office of President Urho Kekkonen (1900–1986), from 1956 to 1981, brought important stability. Kekkonen succeeded in persuading the Soviet Union that there was no danger to be feared from the Finnish side of the border. Through the position of trust he had achieved, Finland was able, without endangering its Soviet relations or trade, to join the European Free Trade Association (EFTA) and then gain associate status with the European Community in 1973. When the

The Russian sign is replaced with a Finnish one at the railway station as the Porkkala Peninsula is returned to Finland by the Soviet Union in 1956

Finland has drawn attention to its independence by hosting a number of important international political congresses. Above: (right to left) Bill Clinton, President of the United States, Martti Ahtisaari, President of Finland, and Boris Yeltsin, President of Russia, at the United States–Russia Summit Conference, Helsinki, March 1997; President Urho Kekkonen (left) and Olof Palme, Prime Minister of Sweden, at the Conference on Security and Cooperation in Europe, Helsinki, 1975

situations in the Soviet Union and Germany radically changed between 1989 and 1991, and the European Community became the European Union, Finland, with EFTA, became part of the European Economic Area, another free-trade area, and, after a referendum, became, at the beginning of 1995, a full member of the European Union, together with two other former neutral countries, Austria and Sweden.

Finland's internal development in the post-war period is in many ways reminiscent of that of Sweden and Norway, but from the point of view of identity its successful defensive war and the tradition treated by the dangerous superpower next door were very different. With the exception of a short interim period, Finland has not, unlike in its neighbouring countries, had a leftist parliamentary majority and, compared to Sweden, Norway

and Denmark, had a long-lived Communist Party like that of France. Joining the European Union was also more widely supported in Finland than in its neighbouring countries. The renewed independence of Estonia, from 1991, also influenced changes in Finland's position, both in reality and in terms of identity. The eastward shift in the focus of Europe has had a positive effect on Finland's position. MK

Presidents of Finland	
1919–1925	K. J. Ståhlberg
1925–1931	Lauri Kr. Relander
1931–1937	P. E. Svinhufvud
1937–1940	Kyösti Kallio
1940–1944	Risto Ryti
1944–1946	C. G. E. Mannerheim
1946–1956	J. K. Paasikivi
1956–1981	Urho Kekkonen
1982–1994	Mauno Koivisto
1994–	Martti Ahtisaari

home ►childhood, man and woman

humour Today's Finns laugh at Finnish humorists' stories and songs, farcical films and sometimes really funny, but quite often indifferent, television sketches. National comedy is bound to language and the lived past. Finns, like others, spontaneously tell one another jokes, anecdotes and funny stories that they have heard from one another and on the radio, seen on television or video, read in books or magazines. The great themes of laughter are taboos in general, as well as sex, liquor and religion in particular. As extensive ingredients of life, they appear in all sorts of social relations and well up in the rich landscape of the collective unconscious. The people's laughter is also transfixed by cross-textures of pleasure and death, the holy and the grotesque, the obligatory and the possible.

But with a change of perspective, the Finns can be described as masters of interior speech and soundless laughter. They have long been trained to this self-control, and have learned their lesson well. The rule, in short, has been that in places where speech is forbidden, so is laughter. Finns therefore practised the noble art of silence in all places where they gathered together (church, school, the army, the dinnertable, the sauna, the bus, fishing trips, the forest, artistic occasions). Outside laughter, both sounded-out and soundless, are left those Finns who do not watch the most popular Finnish films, who do not, for one reason or another, have a television, who do not read literature based on folk humour and do not spend time sitting in bars and restaurants. The national writer, ►Aleksis Kivi, would not have meant them when he wanted to claim that the Finnish people were 'the world's most humorous people'.

In any case, the entertaining and comic element of the media is so much in demand that the cultivation of humour in Finland is more extensive than ever. Talk of the thinning or even decrease of humour in the country and the world is nonsense. It is true that, in comparing past and present, it is easy to think that the comedy of the old folk culture was somehow more 'Finnish', or more natural to Finns

The world's most humorous people?: the comedian Uuno Turhapuro (Vesa-Matti Loiri) and his screen wife (Marjatta Raita) in a parody of relationships between the sexes, 1983

than the forms of comedy that are so popular today. But in nostalgia for past Finnishness, it is worth remembering that the grotesque laughter of ancient folk was in many respects of a quality that would today stick in civilised people's throats.

According to the ancient but still influential puritanically Christian peasant ethic, the Finnish man may live an excellent life without ever laughing, a man prone to laughter, moreover, is dishonest or an imbecile. Although laughter itself cannot be counted a sin, laughing for no good reason is a different matter. And since the matter is interpreted in such a way that there is generally no good reason for laughter, the message is clear. The belittling of laughter and the exaggeration of laughter that ends in tears are much in evidence in old proverbs, but on the other hand joy, too, is often praised. Laughter points to a sinful but enjoyable life, joy to a good, ascetic one. Ordinary Finns have a tendency towards the former.

In studies of humour and comedy, it has been popular to operate with so-called 'two-worlds theories', according to which people build 'alternative realities' alongside their everyday worlds; the most often repeated of the theses is that humour contrasts the world as it is with the world as it should be. The master-servant anecdotes of the ancient world, express subordinates' aspirations to seek experiences of freedom, strength and community. From the social perspective, it is significant that the relations of authority described in anecdotes are temporarily broken: narrators and listeners can make contact with real utopias.

In anecdotes, stories and tales, the

co-existence of master and servant (mistress and maid, mother-in-law and daughter-in-law) has been the subject of most extensive consideration. It belongs directly to the basic themes of the folk world-view. In addition to mixed emotions, the stories of this subject-area emphasise the importance of intelligence and the comic aspects of understanding, in which disorder forbids order. Generally speaking, anecdotes about social order are stories about possible events built on a comic foundation: they point towards the common sources of humour, the comic, understanding and pleasure.

In anecdotes expressing a folk world-view, subjecting authority to ridicule does not, for either teller or listeners, signify the illusion that the subordinates could, with their little pranks, crack the social and economic order. For it is common even in the world of anecdote for fantasies to crumble and relations of authority to return to the status quo. According to the extensive evidence of the oral tradition, however, the people's experiences of drunkenness, falling in love and religious ecstasy are nevertheless, experientially, of a similar kind to the short duration of laughter. What is essential is that the realism of concreteness does not destroy the realism of the emotions. SK

Hvitträsk In 1902–1903 the young architects ▶Eliel Saarinen, Herman Gesellius (1874–1916) and Armas Lindgren (1874–1929) built a shared living and studio space for themselves at Kirkkonummi, close to Helsinki. In dark coniferous forest, on a steep slope leading down to the clear waters of Lake Hvitträsk, a lively group of buildings was constructed – of natural stone, brick, logs and shingles – in which private and shared spaces of varying heights encircled a central courtyard. Such wilderness studios represented the flight of architects and artists of the time from the cosmopolitan atmosphere of the city to a solitary life that was understood to be more authentic. Hvitträsk is a perfect *Gesamtkunstwerk*: everything, from landscape to the details of the furnishing, is designed and realised in an integrated style.

Eliel Saarinen, Herman Gesellius, Armas Lindgren, Hvitträsk, Kirkkonummi, 1902–1903

The Gesellius-Lindgren-Saarinen partnership had already attained international fame with its pavilion for the 1900 world exhibition in Paris. The office had been set up in Helsinki in 1896.

The early stages of the group of buildings at Hvitträsk are to be found in Lindgren's sketch-book. Most of the building design work was carried out by Saarinen, who continued to live at Hvitträsk until his move to the United States in 1923. In the summer of 1922 a fire destroyed the north wing of the main building, and the gloomy log tower that had dominated the courtyard was lost. Since 1971, Hvitträsk has been a museum. The best-preserved rooms are essentially a museum to Saarinen. The graves of both Saarinen, who died in 1950, and Gesellius, who died in 1916, lie in the forest at Hvitträsk, amid tall spruces and great, mossy boulders. RN

Hynninen, Jorma (born 1941), baritone, opera director. Jorma Hynninen made his debut at the Finnish National Opera in 1969. Since then, he has made an impressive international career, with a repertoire ranging from various Mozart roles through Verdi and Wagner to contemporary works. He has created many of the leading roles of Finnish operas by ▶Aulis Sallinen and ▶Einojuhani Rautavaara. Hynninen has also contributed to the development of Finnish opera life as the artistic director of the Finnish Na-

Jorma Hynninen in the title role in Aulis Sallinen's opera *Kullervo*, 1992

tional Opera and, subsequently, as the general director of the Savonlinna Opera Festival. HB

hypermedia is the combination of hypertext and media, and is the term used for communication by computers of hypertext via various mediatexts, graphics, sound, animations and video. Hypertext has been defined as an approach to information management in which data is stored in a network of nodes connected by links.

Applications of hypermedia in Finland have been made actively since the end of the 1980s. Among the first hypermedia products was the *Hyper-aapinen* ('Hyper primer', 1994), which originated in the hypermedia laboratory at the University of Tampere and was finished by the Sansibar Company. During the 1990s, information technology has been an important area of development in Finnish society. As the leading information technology business, Nokia Telecommunications has also given Finnish digital contents production a flying start. In the 1990s, Finnish universities and institutions of higher education are pursuing this activity strongly, and businesses of new forms are still expanding. PH, EP, JV

Iittala Glass Factory. The Iittala Glass Factory is the largest glass factory currently active in Finland. Since 1991 Iittala has been part of Hackman Designor Ltd. The factory was founded in 1881 at Kalvola in southern Finland. Its first glass-blowers came from Sweden. From the beginning, the range of goods was large and work-methods modern. Production comprised pressed glass, blown bottle and pharmaceutical glass, simple utility glass and finer glass. A grinding mill worked in conjunction with the mill, and a few years after its foundation products were being decorated with painting, etching and engraving. Iittala's early products, which were largely copies of European designs that reached Finland via Sweden, followed the same lines as Finland's other glass factories. An exception was Alfred Gustafsson's (in Iittala 1894–1923) range of pressed glass, *Suurmies* ('Great man'), which was decorated with Finnish national romantic motifs and was taken into production at the turn of the 20th century.

Iittala Glass Factory museum

Timo Sarpaneva, *I* glass range 1954–1964

In 1917 Iittala became part of A. Ahlström Ltd, which already owned the Karhula Glass Factory. With innovative design centred primarily at Karhula, Iittala's designs remained conservative for a long time, and in the 1920s and 1930s Iittala achieved international recognition for its high-quality crystal objects. Iittala's rise to become one of Finland's leading glass factories received its prime impulse in a glass design competition held in 1946. As a result, the designer ▶Tapio Wirkkala was employed by the factory. In 1950 the designer ▶Timo Sarpaneva also joined Iittala's designers. Iittala's new designs, based on sculptural art-glass objects, made its first international appearance at the Milan Triennale of 1951, where they were much praised, and their success continued in subsequent triennales. The innovation that at first characterised art-glass production soon began to be seen in utility glass too. New thinking concerning diversity of use in drinking glasses was evident as early as 1948 in a range called *Aarne* designed by Göran Hongell (1902–1973), and the borderline between art glass and utility glass was blurred by the arrival on the market in 1956 of Timo Sarpaneva's coloured *I*-range of glass.

Other Iittala designers include Heikki Orvola (born 1943), who brought a fresh look to the factory's products with glass that combined a number of different materials, Mikko Karppanen (born 1955) and Tiina Nordström (born 1957). MaA

image of Finland Since the first descriptions of Finland, Tacitus' *Germania*, A.D. 98 and Procopius' *De Bello Gothico*, the Finns, or fenni, were confused with the Lapps, or 'Skrithfenni', a diminutive, primitive tribe living at the edge of the world and moving on skis. This Lapp mythology was disseminated particularly from the 17th century onwards by Johannes Schefferus' work *Lapponia* (1673).

In addition to *Lapponia*, a fantasy of Bjarmia as a fabulous world on the shores of the White Sea is also attached to the image of Finland. The ancient Scandinavian sagas and chronicles told of Bjarmia, among them Saxo Grammaticus' *Gesta Danorum*.

In world literature, the idea of the Finns' magic powers, which has connections with Lapp ►shamanism, was evident from an early date. Finnish seamen, in particular, were thought to be able to conjure winds and storms. The Finnish seamen in many seafaring novels testify to this. The translations of the ►*Kalevala* that appeared in the 19th century strengthened the image of Finnish shamanism. Rune-singing and magic combined in *Kalevala* fantasies which have reappeared even in the virtual world described by science fiction.

Foreign travellers who arrived in Finland from the late 18th century onwards went at first to northern Finland and Lapland in order to chart the Arctic Circle and to continue still farther north to Nord Kapp. The Aavasaksa Mountain at Ylitornio became a famous travel destination. It has been described by numerous explorers, among them the Italian Giuseppe Acerbi in 1802 and the Frenchman Pierre-Louis de Maupertuis in 1736. The descriptions of Aavasaksa brought

Giuseppe Acerbi's
Travels through Sweden,
Finland and Lapland to the
North Cape, 1802,
made Finland known
for exotic phenomena
such as the sauna

the light summer nights of the far north to European consciousness.

The discovery of the rest of Finland was often connected with the route that led from Stockholm to Turku and thence via Viipuri to St Peterburg; this was followed, among others, by the Scot Andrew Swinton in 1792 and the Englishman E.D. Clarke around 1800.

From Acerbi on, descriptions of the ►sauna as an exotic phenomenon has fascinated travellers. The thousands of lakes, the "green gold" of the forests and the granite cliffs of the sea shore became established as the basic images of books about Finland. Finns, by this time writers were generally able to distinguish between Finns and the Swedes of the coastal areas, were classed according to racial theories as an eastern, Mongol race, although the blonde beauty of Finnish women was praised. The exotic harmony of the Finnish language was also extolled.

Books about Finland were published, in particular, by Britons, among them Mrs Alec Tweedie (1896), Paul Waineman (1903, 1908), Rosalind Travers (1911), A. MacCallum Scott (1906), Mrs A.M.C. Clive-Bayley (1895) and Ernest Young (1912). For Russians, Finland opened up via the Karelian Isthmus. Russian literature offered the same stereotypes as other writing sabout Finland: forests, lakes, granite cliffs. The Imatra area and the ►Imatrankoski Rapids were a favourite destination for Russian travel and travel descriptions.

Finland came to the attention of the world from the turn of the 20th century onward first for its fight for autonomy against the Russian 'bear', then for its independence and finally for its self-defence against the Soviet Union in the ►Winter War (1939). It was at this point that the concept of 'brave little Finland' became established.

Between the world wars, the image of Finland was already coloured by the conception of a northern democracy where the traveller could also encounter the nature of the north.

During the Cold War, conceptions of a magical land between East and West made their reappearance in the image of Finland. In thrillers and spy novels by John Gardner, Len Deighton, Robert Ludlum, Martin Cruz Smith and Desmond Bagley, Finland was like an anteroom to the Soviet Union where international espionage flourished. HS

Imatrankoski Rapids Some 4000 years ago the First Salpausselkä Ridge formed an efficient barrier to the Lake Saimaa system in its descent along many channels to the Päijänne water system. When it reached the land further west, the water level of Lake Saimaa rose at its southern end, until the waters at last broke through the Salpaus Ridge at Vuoksenniska, producing the Vuoksi River, descending to Lake Ladoga. In the upper reaches of the river numerous waterfalls formed, the most handsome of which is Imatra. As a natural sight and an item on the tourist map it is perhaps Finland's most famous waterfall.

In its natural state, the Vuoksi was a fast-flowing river, to which the ►*Kalevala's* Joukahainen's words are well-suited: 'There is no one who has conquered Vuoksi, crossed Imatra.' In summer and winter alike, the Imatrankoski Rapids thundered swiftly. In places the water flowed through a channel only 20 metres wide at a speed of nearly 600m^3 per second.

Imatra attracted admirers early on. It acquired international fame when, among others, Empress Catherine the Great (1729–1796) visited the site with her retinue. In the 19th century tourism developed, and Imatra also became the object of wider attention.

The artists Akseli Gallen-Kallela (left) and Albert Edelfelt at Imatrankoski Rapids, winter 1893

Imatrankoski Rapids. The river is now dammed to provide power for the nearby hydro-electric station at Vuoksi, but remains an impressive sight when the water is allowed to run freely

Pekka Kärkkäinen and Petri Suutari with a team, *Hybrid-Ibana*, a city car manufactured in the Laboratory of Automotive Engineering of Helsinki Institute of Technology

Handrails were built along the edge of the falls, together with an alcove, a shelter hut, and finally also a hotel. The completion of the Saimaa Canal (1856) and the Viipuri-St Petersburg railway line (1870) increased the number of tourists.

Imatrankoski Rapids' popularity as an object of tourism reached its culmination in the period preceding the First World War. When Finland gained its independence in 1917, its eastern border was closed, and the flow of tourists from St Petersburg ceased. An even more significant change was the building of the Imatrankoski Rapids power station, a large project that was brought to fruition in 1922–1928. The waters of the Vuoksi were led to the machine house along a wide upper channel that bypasses the old rapids bed. None the less, the old, derelict channel is still an attractive sight. The fettered Imatrankoski Rapids still foams within its banks during the demonstrations that are arranged on summer Sundays and during the drainage that is carried out in periods of flooding. KRn

Valmet Automotive's product development team designed and manufactured the concept car *Boréal*, 1997.

industrial design The fabulous success of Finnish design in the 1950s and the star cult that followed led to a period of self-reflection in the 1950s. ▶Kaj Franck presented a manifesto in which he demanded the recognition of the anonymous group work involved in serial production and the abandoning of the centrality of the artist. On the other hand, the social activation of the young generation of designers and the attention given to the satisfaction of the needs of different social groups increased interest in the design of serially produced objects. The development of technology and the beginning of teaching in the area in 1963 in the Central School of Applied Arts created the external framework for progress. In 1911 industrial designers founded their own professional organisation, Ornamo, which in the late 1990s has more than 200 members.

In the 1960s, the use of designers was still largely restricted to companies representing traditional areas of applied arts, such as the glass and ceramics industries. In the recent decades, the industrial designer has increasingly been accepted as a member of the design team, and the design of a product is seen as an essential part of both its functionality and its marketing. Among the most significant fields of Finnish

Juha Vainio, series of handles for ABB, 1996.

industrial design in recent decades are telephones, where among others designer Jorma Pitkonen (born 1945) has worked with the Nokia Telecommunications, and sports equipment design, where specialist designers include Pasi Järvinen (born 1951). Various gadgets and machines have been designed for example by Hannu Kähönen (born 1948), Eero Rislakki (born 1924) and Antti Siltavuori (born 1943) and safety equipment by Börje Rajalin (born 1933). MaA

information technology In 1636 a general post office was established in Sweden-Finland, whose scope was extended two years later to include Finland. Various land-owners were appointed whose responsibility it was to forward post at least a league (some 11 kilometres) in two hours 'whether it be night or day or whatever the weather'. A regular postal service began, however, only in 1643, when a postal route was opened from Stockholm via Åland, Turku, Helsinki, Porvoo, Viipuri, Käkisalmi to St Petersburg and on to Narva. Special postal coaches were not used until 1877, the year before Finland adopted the telephone. Telephone exchanges were installed in the largest towns in 1882, and the first automatic exchange opened in 1921.

Perhaps because of its long internal distances, Finland has always been in the forefront of communications technology, so it is no wonder that today's Finns are, along with their Nordic colleagues, among the world's most enthusiastic users of mobile telephones,

and that the use of the modern information technology is surely among the greatest in the world. The new technology arrived in Finland suddenly in the early 1990s, and it would not be an exaggeration to say that Finland is already an information society.

The mobile telephone is perhaps the most visible part of Finnish communications culture. In 1996, one in four Finns, on average, had a mobile telephone in his or her pocket, and not only busy businessmen in the towns, but everyone, regardless of age, dwelling-place or gender. One person may use a mobile telephone to order pizzas for the family, another to book a hairdresser's appointment, a third to say she will be late, and even a child in the playground may telephone his mother to ask to be taken home.

The same is, indeed, true of all of the Nordic countries, for in 1979 the telephone companies of Finland, Sweden, Norway and Denmark agreed a common mobile telephone standard, the Nordic Mobile Telephone (NMT) system. NMT is an analogical mobile telephone system which made the rather traditional radio telephone system rather like an ordinary telephone. In addition, the technology was sufficiently advanced that the telephone could be made portable by 1984, and three years later the first pocket telephone emerged – although at that stage it still had to be a rather large pocket.

NMT spread rapidly because the Nordic countries are sufficiently large a marketing area for it to be worthwhile for telephone manufacturers to invest in product development, and in addition the telephone companies made their network comprehensive and invested in marketing it. Since it was possible to make a call from a reasonably priced telephone in a car, or even one that would fit into one's pocket, from almost anywhere, the popularity of the system was guaranteed, and it was easy to begin developing a new, digital mobile telephone network.

The Finnish company Nokia, which had played a large role in the development of NMT, was the first to succeed in making a GSM-compatible telephone call in 1991. The Global System for Mobile telephones has subsequently made its breakthrough both within Europe and outside the continent, and naturally the digital network in Finland is very comprehensive. Because of its high sound quality and numerous additional features, GSM is very popular, particularly because since 1992 the telephone has been easily transportable – the best models will fit into a shirt pocket and are just a little larger than a pager.

The manufacture of digital telephones is typically appropriate to Finland, as programming is the most important aspect of design. The mobile telephone is, in fact, an effective computer: who ever succeeds in programming it for the greatest diversity and/or simplicity will succeed. The same is true of telephone networks, in which field both Nokia and the Swedish company Ericsson are well-known names.

Mobile telephones are, however, only the visible tip of the iceberg of Finnish communications. Perhaps more important is what lies below ground: information networks. Finland is a pioneer in the information society, for its basic networks were founded on the old ATM technology – in other words, very rapid information networks were taken into use in Finland among the first in the world. In addition, Finns are greatly over-represented on the ►Internet in comparison to the country's size. According to estimates, around 500,000 Finns use the Internet to obtain information, for communication, for leisure and even for shopping. Commerce and marketing on the Internet are a precondition for its expansion to an information channel available to everyone, like television and radio, and in this sense Finland offers a good laboratory: it is important in the expansion of all new technologies to achieve a so-called critical mass, or a sufficient number of users so that revenue is sufficient to fund expansion. Finland is a highly developed country with a highly educated population with an interest in technology, so it is no wonder that in the mid 1996 about one third of all businesses participated in the Internet in some way. They use the net for everything from information and image-building to direct trade and selling of products in Internet department stores.

Electronic mail is, in addition to the fax, the other great blessing of modern technology for often shy Finns living in the far North. The fax may have been developed by the Japanese to transmit their complex written characters, but for Finns the fax offers a good way of dealing with their foreign contacts, in particular, as it is easier to write foreign languages than to speak and listen to them. The above is a generalisation, of course, but nevertheless many people have a fax machine even at home. Electronic mail is still more convenient, because with its help all communication can take place via the computer.

The new technology has already changed Finnish life in essential ways since, for example, the 1970s. And when Finland in the 1990s is compared to the beginning of the century, there can hardly be many countries in the world in which development has been so great: from an agrarian society to a modern information society, where people carry their telephones with them and where mail travels along electric wires at the speed of light. For children, this is all obvious, and even pensioners enthusiastically learn to use computers; in schools, computers are part of everyday life, and in adult education and open colleges large investments are being made in the new technology.

If the changes have already been great, this is just the beginning. The mobile telephone and the computer will combine – and, most important of all, the information networks will soon penetrate every home, either via cable television or through the telephone network, and it seems likely that Finland will be among the first to adopt systems in which television images, telephone conversations, mail and all other information, from general announcements to the news, will reach the user via a single line. All the same: Finland has, in relation to its size, a record number of newspapers and magazines, and nothing seems to threaten them. Even if the Finn reads the Internet and sends electronic mail during the day, breakfast without the printed word is nothing. JM

J

Tove Jansson

Internet

Virtual Finland
http://virtual.finland.fi
Parliament of Finland
http://www.eduskunta.fi
Universities
http://www.edu.fi/koulut/
yliopistot.html
Education
http://www.minedu.fi/
Museums
http://www.museoliitto.fi
Finnish National Gallery
http://www.fng.fi/
Finnish Design
http://www.designfinland.com
Books from Finland
http://linnea.helsinki.fi/bff
Kalevala and Kanteletar
http://www.sci.fi/kalevala
Finland for Visitors/
Finnish Tourist Board
http://www.mek.fi
Finnish Broadcasting Company
http://www.yle.fi
City of Helsinki
http://www.hel.fi
City of Tampere
http://www.tampere.fi
City of Turku
http://www.turku.fi
The Åland Islands
http://www.aland.fi
Finnair
http://www.finnair.fi
Nokia
http://www.nokia.com.

Internet Finns are enthusiastic users of the Internet. According to some accounts, Finland has the world's greatest number of Internet-users in proportion to its population. The use of information networks has been promoted in Finland by both government and business in various areas of society. In the mid-1990s the Ministry of Education declared its aim to install an Internet connection in every Finnish school by the year 2000. Universities and other institutions of higher education offer their students free use of the Internet in furthering their studies. Research and development activity concerning the Internet is the object of particular interest and funding. According to one study (1997, Rissa & Järvinen Oy, http://www.pjoy.fi/tutkimus/kt97/.), active Internet-users in Finland are predominantly young and male. The average age of respondents was 30.5 years and 85 per cent were men. Because of this low average age, many of the respondents were childless (62.7 per cent) and unmarried (46 per cent). Internet-users have higher than average incomes; most earned FIM 150,000–200,000 per year (US$ 30,000–40,000; 23.2 per cent of respondent s), but the influence of students was seen in a large proportion of users earning less than FIM 25,000 (US$ 5000; 20.3 per cent of respondents). A belief in teledemocracy survives: 64.4 per cent of respondents believed that it was possible, with the help of the information networks to improve opportunities for citizens to take part in social decision-making. In addition. 72.9 per cent of respondents felt that Finland should be a pioneer and experiment with teledemocracy in practice. PH, EP, JV

Jansson, Tove (born 1914), writer, artist. Tove Jansson was born in Helsinki, the daughter of a Finland-Swedish artist family. She studied to be an artist herself, and has worked as an artist and illustrator of her children's books. In the 1940s she peopled the fairy-tale world of Moomin Valley with ►Moomins and other imaginary beings. The success of the Moomin books began with her breakthrough work, *Kometjakten* (*Comet in Moominland*, 1946). In both that book and, for example, *Trollkarlens hatt* (*Finn Family Moomintroll*, 1948), the existence of the valley and its family idyll are threatened by a great disaster. Resourcefulness and the strength of the bonds between members of the valley community save them from cosmic or mysterious dangers. Later, the emotional relationships between the characters become more important as sources of tension than external threats. Jansson's Moomins have become part of the collective inheritance that Finns absorb as children. They link children, their parents and even their grandparents in a way that no other Finnish children's writer has achieved since the Second World War. In translation and as television animation series, the

Moomins have become part of international children's popular culture. In her novels and short stories for adults, Jansson has explored people's emotional interdependence. PL

Jarva, Risto (1934–1977), film director. Born in Helsinki, Risto Jarva qualified as an engineer, but worked purposefully to achieve his early ambition to be a film-maker. He absorbed the aesthetic radicalism of the 1950s, which provided fertile ground for his own social radicalism of the 1960s. Jarva's career developed from the avant-garde experimentation of his early short films to the liberated expression of the new wave in his films *Yö vai päivä* ('Night or day', 1962) and *Onnenpeli* ('Game of fortune', 1965); then to the everyday realism of *Työmiehen päiväkirja* ('A worker's diary', 1967) and *Yhden miehen sota* ('One man's war', 1975); the science fiction of *Ruusujen aika* ('The time of the roses', 1969); the modern melodrama of *Kun taivas putoaa* ('When the sky falls in', 1972); and, finally, comedy in *Mies joka ei osannut sanoa ei* ('The man who couldn't say no', 1975) and *Loma* ('The holiday', 1976). Jarva's last film before his accidental death, *Jäniksen vuosi* ('The year of the hare', 1977), strove for a kind of synthesis of its maker's many stylistic genres and themes, as well as a balance between comic and tragic elements. ST

Risto Jarva, *Jäniksen vuosi* ('The year of the hare', 1977)

jazz The history of Finnish jazz begins in the late 1920s. Anglo-American music reached Finland slowly, because dance-music influences arrived from Germany. British jazz was heard in live performance at most once or twice a year, American jazz not even that often.

Nevertheless, a few important Finnish dance orchestras devoted themselves ambitiously also to the jazz of their time. Among the best achievements were those of the Rytmi-Pojat ('Rhythm-Boys'), conducted by Eugen Malmstén (1907–1993), and the Ramblers under Klaus Salmi (1906–1987). After this first boom period, the war years of 1940 to 1944 marked a regression for jazz, although light music was otherwise valued for its capacity to lighten the spirits.

Risto Jarva

When Finland began to recover from the war, jazz had a clear significance in 'opening windows to the world', although it was still far from being music for the general public. The various international movements in jazz were followed enthusiastically among professional musicians. A small but skilful Finnish band of musicians played it to audiences which were themselves not large.

Ossi Aalto's (born 1910) orchestra promoted high-quality swing, Olli Häme's (1924–1984) ensemble more modern music such as be-bop. Foreign contacts remained slight even in the 1950s, and even the best Finnish jazz hardly had an opportunity to perform abroad. Although jazz was in that decade – while the majority of people still lived in the countryside – the music of urban, educated people, the best dance orchestras, such as Erik Lindström's (born 1922) also offered it to some extent outside their 'home territory', performing in dance halls around the country.

It was not until the 1960s that jazz began to be played by musicians who concentrated exclusively on this kind of music. That period saw the beginning of the careers of such influential figures as the drummers Christian Schwindt (1940–1992) and Reino Laine (born 1946), the wind-players Juhani Aaltonen (born 1935), Eero Koivistoinen (born 1946) and Pekka Pöyry (1939–1980) and the pianist Heikki Sarmanto (born 1939). All are also significant composers. The spiritual fathers of the leading Finnish jazz musicians were, as elsewhere in Europe, the modern international artists

Trio Töykeät – Rami Eskelinen (percussion), Eerik Siikasaari (bass), Iiro Rantala (piano) – represent the sound of young Finnish jazz

of the time, but each one created his music from his own, freshly personal material. The originality of Finnish jazz was widely recognised.

By the 1970s, at the latest, Finnish jazz musicians were interesting performers elsewhere in Europe and outside the continent. The percussionist Edward Vesala (born 1945), the multi-instrumentalist Sakari Kukko (born 1953) and the guitarist Jukka Tolonen (born 1952) in particular, have gained fame on international stages. The saxophonist Eero Koivistoinen's Quartet and Vesala's Tuohi Quartet have won the Grand Prix at the Montreux Jazz Festival.

Among the musicians of the younger generation, many have often given concerts abroad: the pianist Iiro Rantala (born 1970), whose Trio Töykeät is one of the most original discoveries of the 1990s, the guitarist Raoul Björkenheim (born 1956) with his Krakatau ensemble, and the wind-player Antti Sarpila (born 1964).

Finland holds around a dozen annual jazz festivals. The largest is the Pori Jazz Festival, held since 1966, which is one of the most important European jazz events. The active organisation for the genre is the Finnish Jazz Federation. IH

Jews Jews in Finland have, since the 19th century, been quite a small minority. In the 1850s they numbered approximately 300; by 1870, 700; by the First World War, 1100; and by the 1990s, 1500.

Although most Finnish Jews originate from eastern Europe, the backgroud of the Jewish population in Finland is diverse in character. The majority of them are still descended from Jewish soldiers in the Russian army and their families. Also great numbers of Jews emigrated as refugees from Russia, Poland and Lithuania during the persecution periods of the 1880s. Another great move took place after the Second World War, when the Jews in Viipuri, along with other members of the Finnish population, were evacuated to Finland, mainly to Helsinki.

The Jews in Finland are a typically urban religio-cultural minority centered in the largest cities of the country: in the mid 1990s there were 1200 in Helsinki, 300 in Turku and 30 in Tampere.

Because of their east European background and the particular nature of Finnish history, Jews in Finland have been multilingual, speaking Russian and Swedish along with Yiddish. This has been quite a natural development, since most Jews emigrated from Russia in the 19th century, and were settled in what were at that time Swedish-speaking territories of the country. As the language conflict between Finnish and Swedish reached its peak in the 1930s, the teaching lan-

Jac. Ahrenberg, Jewish synagogue, Helsinki, 1906

guage of the Jewish School (founded in 1918) gradually started to favour Finnish. After the Second World War the integration of the Jewish population of Finland into Finnish society was eventually complete, and in 1979 the first Jew was elected into the Finnish parliament.

As far as culture is concerned, the Jews in Finland are a minority which has lived in a double, or even triple, identity situation. The double identity is an identification with both the Finnish majority and the religio-cultural minority, with education and other infrastructures shared by the group they belong to. The triple identity concerns those Jews who, have preserved Swedish as their mother tongue and Yiddish as the language of their Jewish culture and religion.

The problem of assimilation into the majority culture still concerns all the 30,000 Jews living in Nordic countries. Apart from mixed marriages, the

vitality of these ethnic groups is diminished by emigration, particularly to the West or Israel. Since marriage between two Finnish Jews is a rare exception, mixed marriages have 'finnicised' the Jewish home, the heart of Jewish culture. In this process most children with Jewish ancestors lose their linguistic, ethnic and religious identity. JPn

Jotuni, Maria (1880–1943), writer. Maria Jotuni began as a short storywriter in 1905 before switching to drama. Her sharply ironic and satirical comedies are aphoristic portraits of her contemporaries; her subjects are often women, marriage, money and various individual attempts to improve social standing, particularly through marriage. Jotuni's apt dialogue seems perennially modern, whatever social class or period her speakers represent, as does the leisurely progress of her dramatic tempo. Although she generally depicts strong women, she does not portray them tendentiously, as heroines on the contrary, they are often unpleasant, corrupt, powerseeking and greedy. It is no wonder that, in an age of conventional manners, Jotuni's portraits of women were considered shocking.

When it was performed at the Finnish National Theatre, *Miehen kylkiluu* ('The rib of man', 1914) provoked doubts among the theatre's

Maria Jotuni

Television version of Maria Jotuni's account of an unhappy marriage, *Huojuva talo* ('The crumbling house'), 1995

board of directors in advance on account of its morality; for it described open man-hunting. *Kultainen vasikka*('The golden calf', 1918) is a satire on wartime speculation, the blinding power of money. *Tohvelisankarin rouva* ('The armchair hero's wife', 1924) provoked parliamentary debate about funding for the National Theatre.

Jotuni's important and extensive novel about wedded hell, *Huojuva talo* ('The swaying house') was published posthumously only in 1963. In 1995 it was made into an acclaimed five-part television adaptation directed by Eija-Elina Bergholm (born 1943).

Jotuni's dialogue has a sharp core. The base of her comedy is cold analysis, of her farce discord which the theatre-goer of the late 20th century, accustomed to cynicism, recognises as close to the truth. And Jotuni's dialogue is not bound to realism; it has been found to allow diverse stylistic experiments in performance. SL

Jung, Dora (1906–1980), textile artist. Dora Jung was among the innovators of Finnish textile art. She designed many church textiles and monumental works, including an illustrative textile for Turku Castle in 1961, *Katarina Jagellonica*, and the stage curtain for the ►Finlandia Hall designed by ►Alvar Aalto. She used the demanding damask technique, rare in Finland. The elegant linen damask cloths and table-cloths designed by Dora Jung are fine examples of the modern utility textiles of her time. MA

Dora Jung, *Katarina Jagellonica*, textile, Turku Castle, 1961, detail

Juslenius, Daniel (1676–1752), Professor at the Academy of Turku, later Bishop of Skara. The fame of Daniel Juslenius is based on his academic works, *Aboa vetus et nova* ('Turku old and new', 1700) and *Vindiciae Fenno-*

Daniel Juslenius

rum ('In defence of the Finns', 1703), and his Finnish dictionary, *Suomalaisen Sana-lugun coetus* ('An attempt at a Finnish lexicon', 1745).

In the manner of the historians of his time, Juslenius painted for Finland a mighty past stretching back into ancient times. According to him, Hebrew and Finnish were related languages, and with the help of etymology he demonstrated how Andalucia in Spain and Vienna in Austria derived their names from the Vandals, whom he interpreted as a Finnic people. Of particular significance was Juslenius's emphasis on Finns and Finnishness in relation to Swedishness at a time characterised by an attempt to homogenise the Kingdom of Sweden-Finland, which was realised to some extent at the expense of Finland's particular position. It was precisely because of his defence of Finnishness that the historiography of the latter part of the 19th century, with its nationalist emphasis, attached attention to Juslenius and made him part of the national consciousness once more.

Daniel Juslenius was born the son of a clergyman near Turku in 1676. He enrolled at the Academy of Turku in 1691, gained his master's degree in 1703, was appointed assistant in philosophy in 1705, Professor of Greek and Hebrew (*linguarum*) in 1712 and Professor of Theology in 1727. Juslenius was appointed Bishop of Porvoo in 1734 and, having fled war to Sweden, Bishop of Skara in 1744. Juslenius died in Skara in 1752. JN

Juusten, Paulus (Paavali) (c.1516–1575), Bishop of Viipuri, subsequently Bishop of Turku. Paulus Juusten, who belonged to a burgher's family in Viipuri, was among the small band of Finnish students who, during Luther's time, studied in the Protestant University of Wittenberg and, on his return, progressed to leading posts in the Finnish Church. Juusten had been ordained three years before beginning his studies in Wittenberg, and had acted as *lector mensae* to Bishop Martin Skytte (died 1550) and as rector of Viipuri's school. When he enrolled in the University of Wittenberg he was already about 27 years old. Juusten studied primarily under Philipp Melanchthon (1497–1560), and received from him, on completion of his studies, a letter of recommendation to the Swedish king, Gustavus Vasa, and to the Cathedral Chapter of Turku.

On his return to Finland, Juusten worked initially as rector of the Turku Cathedral School, which was responsible for the training of priests in Finland. In 1554 he became Bishop of the new diocese of Viipuri, and in 1563 he proceeded to the bishop's seat of Turku, which post he continued to occupy until his death in 1575.

Along with ▶Michael Agricola, Paulus Juusten was the most important church leader of the Reformation period in Finland. In 1574 he published a Finnish-language catechism, and in

Missal published by Paulus Juusten, 1575, title page

the following year a Finnish-language missal. Juusten's most important work, however, was the collection and completion of the Finnish medieval episcopal chronicle, *Catalogus et ordinario successio episcoporum Finlandensium*. Although the book was not printed in Juusten's lifetime, this work has earned him the title of father of Finnish historiography. JN

Kalevala The *Kalevala* is an epic composed by ▶Elias Lönnrot in the 1830s and 1840s from ancient Finnish poems, the most central source of symbols for Finnish culture and Finland's most important contribution to world literature. The roots of the *Kalevala* lie in the collecting activities of Henrik Gabriel Porthan (1739–1804) and his circle. As early as 1817, Carl Axel Gottlund (1796–1875) had cause to forecast: 'If it were desired to collect old folk songs and arrange them into a whole, whether it resulted in an epic, a drama or whatever else, then a new Homer, Ossian or Nibelungenlied could be born.'

Elias Lönnrot realised the romantics' dream. On his ten long collecting trips, he met prominent seers and runesingers, among them Juhana Kainulainen of Kesälahti in 1828, Ontrei Malinen of Vuonninen in 1833 and Arhippa Perttunen of Latvajärvi in 1834.

The *Kalevala* was the result of a complex process. Between 1829 and 1831 Lönnrot published 90 old and 20 contemporary poems in four booklets entitled *Kantele taikka Suomen kansan sekä vanhoja että nykysempiä runoja ja lauluja* ('*Kantele,* or old and newer poems and songs of the Finnish people'). In 1832 he began to arrange separate miniature epics about the hero figures of the old poems, Väinämöinen, Ilmarinen and Lemminkäinen. But having met, in Russian Karelia, singers who performed the deeds of different heroes as consistent narratives, he concentrated the miniature epics in 1833 into a coherent 5000-line *Runokokous Väinämöisestä* ('Poetry gathering about Väinämöinen'), or *Alku-Kalevala* ('Early *Kalevala*'). Into its framework he fitted his poem-harvest of the spring of 1834, so that the result was *Kalevala taikka vanhoja Karjalan runoja Suomen kansan muinosista ajoista* ('Kale-

K

Akseli Gallen-Kallela, *Aino-taru* ('Aino's story', 1891). The triptych depicts Väinämöinen's courtship of Aino, and her suicide by drowning rather than becoming his wife

vala, or old Karelian poems about the ancient times of the Finnish people', 1835).

1849 saw the publication of the *Uusi Kalevala* ('The new *Kalevala*'), a collection of 50 poems to which Lönnrot had added, in particular, the narrative poems gathered by Daniel Europaeus (1820–1884) in Ingria and Ladoga Karelia, including the *Kullervo* poems. *Vanha Kalevala* ('The old *Kalevala*') contains 12,078 lines, *Uusi Kalevala* ('The new *Kalevala*') contains 22,795 lines.

The composition of extended epic from dozens of myth, adventure, ▶shaman, legend and wedding poems, charms and lyric poems of very different ages would not have been possible if a unique special code, the *Kalevala* metre, had not dominated the production of memorable texts for more than 2000 years. It is unlikely that there are any other known cultures in which the use of a particular poetic metre has been so widespread. This facilitated Lönnrot's work: the great majority of his poetic material, so diverse in intended use and age, were in the same poetic metre, and as such could be used in the *Kalevala*.

At the beginning, Lönnrot believed that the events of the old poems described riel events. He sited them on the southern shores of the White Sea and believed that the poems had originated from poems composed by early witnesses of events or people who had heard of them. In passing from one generation to the next, the poems had changed in form to some degree, but had preserved their original content.

Pekka Autiovuori as Väinämöinen and Tiina Rinne as the Mistress of the North in Antti Einari Halonen's adaptation of *Kalevala*, Finnish National Theatre, 1996

In eliminating, in his creative work, the Christian and other late elements, Lönnrot believes he was returning the poems to a likeness of their original content.

In 1835 when it appeared, the *Kalevala* caused enormous enthusiasm among those interested in Finnishness. It was felt that a jewel of ancient song, which was believed to be of European importance, had unexpectedly been added to the sparse genre of Finnish-language literature. Like Homer's epic, the *Iliad*, in Greece, the *Kalevala* in Finland was believed to demonstrate that the Finnish people, too, had their own history and ancient culture. From this perspective, the *Kalevala* became a central source of identity for a nation

The most significant *Kalevala* translations	
1841 Swedish (The old *Kalevala*)	1957 Icelandic
1845 French (The old *Kalevala*, prose translation)	1959 Romanian
	1959 Estonian
1852 German	1962 Chinese
1864 Swedish	1963 English (prose translation)
1867 French (The new *Kalevala*, prose translation)	1964 Esperanto
	1965 Turkish
1871 Hungarian	1967 Norwegian (abridged version)
1885 German	1967 German
1888 English	1968 German (abridged version)
1888 Russian	1969 English (The old *Kalevala*, prose translation)
1891 Estonian	
1894 Czech	1969 Georgian
1901 Ukrainian	1972 Armenian (prose translation)
1907 English	1972 Lithuanian
1907 Danish (abridged version)	1972 Hungarian
1909 Italian	1974 Polish
1909 Hungarian	1976 Japanese
1910 Italian	1976 Hungarian
1914 German	1983 Fulani (abridged version)
1921 German	1984 Spanish
1922 Lithuanian	1985 Dutch
1924 Latvian	1986 Latin
1930 Hebrew (abridged version)	1986 Vietnamese (abridged version)
1930 French	1988 American English
1935 Serbo-Croat	1989 English
1937 Japanese	1990 Hindi
1939 Estonian	1991 French
1940 Dutch (abridged version)	1991 Arabic
1944 Swedish (abridged version)	1992 Swahili (abridged version)
1948 Swedish (abridged version)	1992 Bulgarian
1948 German	1992 Greek (abridged version)
1953 Spanish	1993 Faroese
1954 Yiddish (abridged version)	1994 Vietnamese
	1994 Danish
	1994 Tamil
	1994 Catalan

that was awaking to a consciousness of itself.

The *Kalevala* had inspired great enthusiasm for the collection of folk poetry. Many young men, most important among them D.E.D. Europaeus (1820–1884), set out to continue Lönnrot's work. Europaeus and his travelling companion, H.A. Reinholm (1819–1883), discovered a rich new source of poetry, Ingria. The express purpose of the journeys was the gathering of new poetic material for Lönnrot for the second edition of the *Kalevala*. By the end of the 1840s, ten times the number that had been included in the first edition had been collected. In a letter, Lönnrot did indeed remark that, from the material he now had, he would have been able to put together seven *Kalevala*s, all different.

Lönnrot's idea of the ancient poems changed during his work in creating the new *Kalevala*, and became essentially different from that of a decade earlier. He no longer believed that the folk poems could, even in terms of content, be returned to their originals. Particularly in dealing with lyric poems, he had noticed that the singers combined poems and poem-fragments in many different ways. Since he now knew more poems than even the best rune-singers, he also felt able to proceed as they did, combining poems and their subjects according to his own views. This meant that an aesthetic principle came to the fore, in place of the earlier genetic one. The aim was now the creation of an extended poem comparable to the great epics of world literature.

Lönnrot preserved his records of folk poems – both his own and those he had received from other people – carefully in order that no dispute over the genuine folk poem origins of the finished epic could arise, as they had in the case of J. Macpherson's *Song of Ossian*. As a result of this care, the process of creating both editions of the *Kalevala* and the folk origins of the lines are known very accurately.

The second edition of the *Kalevala*, described as 'new' and complete, soon overshadowed its predecessor, which was forgotten. Today, in speaking of the *Kalevala*, it is the second edition that is referred to. It is recognised as one of the great epics of world literature and, translated, in its entirety, into 45 languages, it has aroused interest all over the world. Although it is Lönnrot's creation, it is considered a poem about distant times that bears comparison to Homer's. The *Kalevala* is, indeed, a Homeric poem, for the *Iliad* was an important model for Lönnrot, and the *Kalevala*, for its part, has been a direct source of inpiration for later poems, including the Estonian *Kalevipoeg* and Henry Wadsworth Longfellow's *Song of Hiawatha*. No other Finnish work of literature has become so well-known outside the country as the *Kalevala*, and no other Finnish work has had so diverse and profound an influence on national and international culture.

The *Kalevala* continues to inspire the best representatives of Finnish literature, the visual arts and music. Kalevala Day, 28th February, is celebrated as the day of Finnish culture. PLn

Kalevala Koru Kalevala Koru jewellery is made by the firm Kalevala Koru Limited owned by a women's association. It is most often designed according to prehistoric ornaments found in excavations in Finland.

There are three different types of Kalevala Koru. The jewellery of the first group closely follows its early models. They are copies of museum pieces, particularly from the period A.D. 600–1200, to which missing parts have merely been added, or technical

Karelian plaited ribbon motif brooch, Kalevala Koru. This design is a copy of a Karelian grave-find from the period of the northern crusades, AD1100–1300

solutions that facilitate their use. The jewellery of the second group has not been copied slavishly: motifs have been varied, combined, adapted for sequences of jewellery or for new connections. For example, all the earrings using motifs from the Iron Age belong to this group, as Finns did not use ear-decorations. A third group is formed by new models created by designers, which nevertheless can have an ancient flavour. Characteristic of these is the combination of Finnish gemstones with bronze and silver, and sometimes gold.

Many of the best-known Finnish designers have, at some time in their careers, worked for Kalevala Koru. For many Finns, Kalevala Koru is synonymous with the ancient jewellery of Finland, and in particular of one's own area. PLLH

Kalm, Pehr (1716–1779), botanist, Professor of Economics, doctor of theology. Pehr Kalm was born into a modest clerical family. He studied at the Academy of Turku and at the University of Upsala. At Upsala Kalm was one of the most talented students of Carl von Linné. When Sweden sought to increase its prosperity by, among other things, importing foreign cultivated plants, the Swedish Academy of Sciences sent experts in botany and the natural sciences out into the world. Kalm made an expedition to the interior of Russia in 1744, to England and North America from 1747 to 1751, and Canada in 1749. In 1750 he was one of the first Europeans to visit the Niagara Falls.

Kalm published the results of his American journey in his extensive travel book *En Resa til Norra America*

Pehr Kalm, *En resa til Norra America,* Dutch edition, title page, 1772

('A journey to North America', 1753–1761). The work was translated into English, German, Dutch, and, partially, French. In his travel accounts, Kalm gives detailed descriptions of social phenomena as well as nature. Kalm also wrote a large number of travel articles and shorter travel accounts and was a supervisor of doctoral theses as a Professor of Economics and Natural Sciences at the Academy of Turku. The practical results of his journeys were the seeds of hitherto unknown plants that were able to flourish in the far north. PV

Kamu, Okko (born 1946), conductor. Okko Kamu's international career began brilliantly when he won the first Herbert von Karajan conducting competition in West Berlin in 1969. Before that he had studied the violin and worked with various orchestras in Helsinki. Since winning the competition he has worked as conductor of a number of orchestras, including the Finnish Radio Symphony Orchestra (as chief conductor), Helsinki Philharmonic Orchestra, the Netherlands Radio Symphony Orchestra, the Oslo Philharmonic Orchestra and, since 1991, the Helsingborg Symphony Orchestra. He has also had long-term appointments with the Stockholm Royal Opera, and the symphony orchestras of Birmingham, Sjelland and Singapore.

In Kamu's recordings, the work of ▶Aulis Sallinen is particularly important, including the operas *Punainen viiva* (*The Red Line*) and *Palatsi* (*The Palace*), Benjamin Britten's piano concerto with Ralf Gothóni (born 1946) and the Helsingborg Symphony Orchestra, symphonies by Schubert and Berwald with the same orchestra, and music by ▶Jean Sibelius, Leevi Madetoja (1887–1947) ▶Joonas Kokkonen and Väinö Raitio (1891–1945) with the Finnish Radio Symphony Orchestra. The conductor, who enjoys sailing and golf, began work as chief conductor of the Finnish National Opera in August 1996. RL

kantele (or **kannel**) The *kantele* and rune-singing both symbolise ancient Finnish culture. In the ▶*Kalevala,* ▶Elias Lönnrot had constructed an image of a mythic *kantele,* made of the jawbone of a pike, as the typically Finnish musical instrument of the epic hero Väinämöinen. In the final stages of the work, the *kantele* is an essential part of the power of Väinämöinen's song. It was thus, through the *Kalevala,* that the *kantele* became, in the 19th century, the Finns' national instrument.

The *kantele* is the oldest Finnish folk instrument, and is classed as a cordophone, that is, an instrument whose sound arises from a string stretched between two fixed points. The other Finnic tribes of the Baltic used similar instruments, as did a few Finno-Ugrian peoples, in addition to the Balts and the Russians.

The history of the *kantele* stretches back a couple of thousand years. There

Okko Kamu

Iivana Bogdanoff-Vihantola and Iivana Shemeikka play the *kantele* at the Helsinki Song Festival of 1900

is no accurate information as to its age. The older type of instrument was made by hollowing out the trunk of a pine, spruce or alder. The strings, of which there were usually five, were attached at one end to tuning pegs and at the other to a metal shank. The instrument was tuned to a diatonic scale between its bass and top notes which could, depending on the tuning of the central string, be either major or minor.

The *kantele* player held the instrument in his lap or on a table, with the shorter side toward him. There were various methods of fingering. Common to them all was that the shortest string was played with the thumb of the right hand, and that the forefinger of the left hand was used for the next shortest string. The fingers were interspersed, so that each string was played with a particular finger. Thus the melody and accompanying chords were constantly interleaved, and the sounds of the accompaniment could appear above the melody. The player created a tonal world, moving within a narrow range but constantly varying. Playing did not result in pieces as such; instead, it produced freely flowing music that progressed through small variations and was based largely on improvisation.

In the eastern parts of the country, particularly in ►Karelia, five-stringed *kantele*s were still in use in the early 19th century, but at the same time changes took place in construction techniques. Larger instruments were made from thin planks of wood, and it became possible to increase the number of strings. In the mid 19th century, *kantele*s of 10 to 14 strings were being played. More strings were later added, and in the end of 19th century big *kantele*s had 20–30 strings. At this point, changes in playing style also took place. The instrument was turned so that the longest strings were closest to the player; the melody was always played by the right hand, and the accompanying chords by the left.

Some areas developed damping technique in which the left hand was used to damp strings while the right hand played the undamped strings. In this case, the instrument was held with the sounding board vertical, not hori-

A living tradition: the Sikiät group of *kantele* players at Kaustinen Music Festival, 1988

zontal as traditionally. With the new instruments and instrumental styles, the music, too, changed, and in the second half of the 19th century contemporary dance music was generally played in those few places where the *kantele* had survived as a folk instrument.

In the 1920s a 36-string chromatic *kantele* was developed, furnished with a mechanism that made it possible to change key easily. Amateurs of folk music today, however, use instruments of all kinds, for since the 1960s, with the new wave of folk music, the *kantele* has undergone a real renaissance. AA

Kanteletar The *Kanteletar*, is ►Elias Lönnrot's collection of lyrical and lyrical-epic Finnish folk poems, published in 1840. It marked the realisation of the second stage of Lönnrot's great folk poetry project, the first being the ►*Kalevala*. The project's third part was Lönnrot's edition of the Finnish magic poems, which appeared in 1880.

After the publication of *Kalevala*, Lönnrot devoted himself to writing down and recording the lyrical folk poetry he heard on his research travels, especially in ►Karelia. In 1838 he completed the first draft of the *Kanteletar*, which he augmented in the same year with new material from his collection. Most of the material for the *Kanteletar* was gathered by Lönnrot himself, but he also took account of earlier published folk poetry. The full title of the work is *Kanteletar taikka Suomen kansan vanhoja lauluja ja virsiä* ('The Kanteletar, or old songs and ballads of the Finnish people').

There are 652 poems in the *Kanteletar* and it contains over 22,000 lines, if the specimens quoted in the preface are included, almost twice the number contained in the first edition of the *Kalevala*. The first part of the *Kanteletar* consists of lyrical songs, which Lönnrot grouped into songs for general occasions, wedding songs, herding songs and children's songs. The songs of the second part are divided by the supposed presenter into songs of girls, women, boys and men. The third part is a collection of historical poems, romances, legends, ballads and other lyrical-epic poems.

The *Kanteletar* is principally composed of Finnish Karelian poetry; the Russian Karelian material is very limited. Information about the songs is scanty. Lönnrot himself mentions the real singer as being Mateli Kuivalatar of Ilomantsi, in addition to whom Juhana Kainulainen of Kesälahti is also to be remembered.

Lönnrot's treatment of the folk poetry material he collected was a relatively free one. In the preface he comments that the *Kanteletar* contains more than just the songs he heard from the mouths of the people. Editing of poems was difficult because different singers sang the same poems in different ways and the poems of some of the singers were confused. The *Kanteletar* contains only a few poems which are based on one or two notations.

Just as in the first edition of the *Kalevala*, Lönnrot standardised the style and language of the poems, but preserved their Karelian flavour. His aim was to create a form of poetry that would also be understood outside the Karelian region, and he hoped that Finland's new poetry would be founded on the cornerstone of the old songs.

In the history of the inception of the *Kalevala*, the *Kanteletar* represents an important intermediate stage from two points of view. Lönnrot freed himself from an excessive dependence on his source material and learned to treat them as a realisation of the aesthetic goals he had adopted earlier more independently. In addition, the *Kanteletar* became an important source of material for the complete edition of the *Kalevala* (1849). At least some 2000 lines were moved from the *Kanteletar* into the epic, the most important influence being felt in the Kullervo episodes and the lyrical interludes.

The *Kanteletar* has been an unfailing source of inspiration for Finnish literary art. It influenced the prose of ►Aleksis Kivi and Juhani Aho (1861–1921), but above all it influenced the lyrical poetry of the neo-romantic era. Many of its poems have been set to music. They have also been translated into English, Swedish, German, Hungarian, Estonian and Russian. PLn

Karelia and the Karelians Karelia is the general name for the area whose westernmost part is still in Finland, the greatest part of which was ceded to the Soviet Union as a result of the Peace Treaty of Paris in 1947. What is known as eastern Karelia, or Russian Karelia, had already, after the Peace Treaty of Tartu in 1920, become one of the republics of Soviet Union. In 1991 the area, now known as the Republic of Karelia, became part of the Russian Federation. The area contains around 10 per cent of Karelians and Finns in a total, multi-national population of some 800,000.

Karelia

Confusion in contemporary Finnish has often been caused by the fact that the Karelians evacuated from their homes during the Second World War use the term Karelia to refer to the ceded areas in which their homes were lo-

The Bomba House, Suojärvi, 1917, an example of a Karelian house for an extended family. A copy of the Bomba House has been built in Nurmes, northern Karelia

Viipuri, once Finland's second, and most cosmopolitan, city. Viipuri was ceded to the Soviet Union, along with most of Karelia, after the Second World War

cated, while the media now use the same term to refer to the Republic of Karelia or the historical Russian Karelia, which has never belonged to Finland.

The national debate about Karelia that arouse during the 1990s concerned the former province of Viipuri, which was ceded to the Soviet Union, and whose return to Finland could be justified in historical and moral terms. Officially, Finland has not adopted the return of Karelia as a subject for intergovernmental discussion.

The concept 'Karelians' is a matter of both ethnicity and identity. Ethnically and linguistically, the Karelians were a tribe that lived in Lake Ladoga area and the Karelian Isthmus as early as the 11th century and which, having become allied with Novgorod and the eastern church, fought against the Finns from Häme province, who belonged to the Swedish circle of power. In 1323 the Treaty of Pähkinäsaari between Sweden and Novgorod divided the Finnish Peninsula from the Karelian Isthmus in the south-east to ►Ostrobothnia in the north-west. Border disputes concerning the wildernesses continued as tribal warfare and divided Karelia between Sweden and Russia.

In subsequent peace treaties, the border moved progressively eastward, and Karelia increasingly became a battlefield for great-power politics between Russia and Sweden. The greatest part of the area inhabited by the Kare-

lians belonged to the West during the period of Sweden as a great power. On the other hand, it was the Peace of Stolbova, signed in 1617, that divided western Karelians from the 'Karelians proper' of the provinces of Archangel and Olonets, with their ►Orthodox faith, Karelian language and epic folk poetry (►folklore), the surviving element of a tradition that had evidently once been common to the whole of Finland.

The centre of western Karelia, or Swedish Karelia, around the City and Castle of Viipuri, lived its great days as the medieval period gave way to the early modern period, and – particularly through its Hanseatic traditions – Viipuri developed into an important maritime trading city. The Peace Treaty of Uusikaupunki, signed in 1721, separated the province of Viipuri from Finland. Attached to Russia, this so-called Old Finland fell in many respects behind the development of the rest of Finland, and a large proportion of the peasants lost their freedom – although they did not sink entirely to the status of serfs. Many of the peasant lands of Lake Ladoga area and the Karelian Isthmus were given as gifts to the emperor's favourites. The building of the city of St Petersburg meant to the peasants of Karelia, in addition to constant burdens of work and taxation, possibilities for making a livelihood.

In 1809 Finland became part of Russia as a Grand Duchy. At this point the province of Viipuri was joined administratively to the rest of Finland. During the century that followed this Finnish Karelia, and particularly the Viipuri area, gradually closed the economic and educational gap with the rest of Finland.

At the end of the 19th century and beginning of the 20th century, the importance of Finnish Karelia gradually increased, particularly in the sphere of influence of St Petersburg. The inhabitants of Karelia, in particular, made their way to St Petersburg as both traders and workers. On the other hand, too, the villas that had spread from St Petersburg to the Karelian Isthmus offered increasing earning opportunities to Karelians. At the same time they also increased pressures for the defence of Russian interests on the Isthmus, which finally resulted in demands to add a few border parishes to Russia after 1910.

In 1918–1919, after Finland had gained its independence, attempts were made to join eastern Karelia to Finland. In the Peace Treaty of Tartu in 1920, the newly formed Soviet Karelia was promised many rights, but the liquidation of the Finnish and Karelian minority of the Stalinist period and after ended national development in the area. As part of Finland, on the other hand, Viipuri province developed strongly; its economy and cultural life were an essential part of the increasing prosperity of Finland. For this reason it was tragic for the entire country when Karelia became a theatre of war and destruction. The ▶Winter War of 1939 was begun by a Soviet attack, while the Continuation War of 1941 was instigated by Finland in an attempt to recover its lost territories. This war, which ended in 1944, was fought across the entire area of Karelia, from the Isthmus to Olonets and Archangel. The massive defensive victories of the last stage of the war were fought by Finland on the Vuoksi front on the Karelian Isthmus and in Ilomantsi, northern Karelia.

As a result of the wars, 450,000 inhabitants were forced to leave Karelia. Their resettlement in other parts of Finland demanded an enormous effort from the nation, which was also forced to pay war reparations to the Soviet Union. The connections of the Karelian émigrés with their lost homes nevertheless continued in the form of family and clan traditions. The amount of literature, memoirs, folk tradition and other documents concerning Karelia is impressive, compared with that of other 'lost' areas, even in world terms. HS

Karelianism Karelianism is a movement in Finnish cultural history, folklore, ▶art, music and ▶literature that had its origins in the late 19th century and remained influential in the early years of the 20th century.

Karelianism may be compared to other ethnographical, artistic, provincial, historical and national romantic movements such as the Celtic revival, Scandinavian Viking romanticism or Dalecarlian romanticism in Sweden, Brittany romanticism in France or the Heimat movement in Germany. At base, Karelianism is the Finnish national romantic version of the myth of a national golden age, the paradisiacal primal home of the Finnish people.

The basis of Karelianism lies in the scholarly and collecting journeys of ▶Elias Lönnrot in ▶Karelia, on either side of the eastern Finnish border. From the folk poetry he collected in Karelia, Lönnrot composed the epic poem, ▶*Kalevala*, which was published in 1835. After the appearance of the national epic, Karelia began to be regarded as a treasure-chest of poetry and an idyllic museum of the ancient world. ▶Students began to cultivate Karelia as an interest. The collectors of folk poetry, folklorists, linguists, artists and writers who travelled to Karelia after Lönnrot were pilgrims, who, inspired by Finland's 'holy book', the *Kalevala*, believed the Karelians, Karelian ▶folk culture, its decorated architecture and crafts, its exotic sung poetry and archaic ways of life to be the last vestige of an ancient culture that had long since disappeared elsewhere. Travel to Karelia was particularly favoured in the 1890s, when the writers ▶Eino Leino and Juhani Aho (1861–1921), the painters ▶Akseli Gallen-Kallela and Eero Järnefelt (1863–1937), and the composer ▶Jean Sibelius were among those who sought inspiration there.

Field trip: folklore scholars enjoy a pause for tea with local guides at Vuokkiniemi, Karelia, 1894

Karelianist art marked the golden age of Finnish art. Via national romanticism, this can also be called the Finnish renaissance. The earlier Greek classical or Viking romantic styles, in art associated with the *Kalevala*, was now influenced by both symbolism and, specifically, by the rich ornamentation of Karelian ▶folk art.

During the cultural struggle of Russian oppression, the *Kalevala* myths and hero-figures of Karelianist art took on the character of political allegory. Karelianist art includes nationally important architecture – public buildings, artists' villas, such as ▶Hvitträsk – great paintings, frescos and sculptures, music inspired by the *Kalevala* and Karelia, *Kalevala*-romantic prose-writing and poetry. The Karelianist and *Kalevala*-romantic tradition has continued, in various forms, to the present day. HS

Rafael Karsten

Karsten, Rafael (1879–1956), social anthropologist. The son of a clergyman, Rafael Karsten was a student of ▶Edvard Westermarck and wrote his doctoral thesis (1917) on the origin of worship. Having first taught philosophy to law students (1910–1911) and published a work on the pagan origins of Christianity, *Kristendom och hedendom* ('Christianity and paganity', 1910), Karsten set out on the first of his many research expeditions to South America. Between 1910 and 1913 he studied questions relating to magic and religion in Argentina. His most important literary work, however, arose from his second expedition, to Ecuador, between 1916 and 1919, after which he published his work *The Civilization of the South American Indian* (1926). His third expedition (1928–1929) resulted in his major work, *The Head-Hunters of Western Amazonas* (1935). His fourth expedition, to Ecuador and Peru (1947–1948), was his last.

Karsten's scientific expeditions and his literary work are characterised by accurate reporting of details and the capacity to describe his subject broadly and diversely. The subjects of his enquiry included the origin of religion, the Inca State and specialist questions of ethnology, such as the function of self-decoration, about which he was in dispute with Westermarck. ML

Kaurismäki, Aki (born 1957), film director. Aki Kaurismäki began his film career as an actor and script-writer in his brother ▶Mika Kaurismäki's films, and as co-director of the rock documentary *Saimaa-ilmiö* ('The Saimaa phenomenon', 1981).

In his own films, Aki Kaurismäki has proved to be consistent, in terms of both style and theme, the characteris-

Matti Pellonpää in Aki Kaurismäki's *Varjoja paratiisissa* ('Shadows in paradise', 1986)

Kari Väänänen and Martti Syrjä in Mika Kaurismäki's *Rosso* (1985)

Aki Kaurismäki

Mika Kaurismäki

tics of which are expressivity, consciousness of tradition and a warped sense of humour. His way of filming his marginalised, underprivileged main characters combines criticism of the prevailing values with a restrained moral pathos, as, for example, in the 'workers' sequence' *Varjoja paratiisissa* ('Shadows in paradise', 1986), *Ariel* (1988), and *Tulitikkutehtaan tyttö* ('The match-factory girl', 1990). *Hamlet liikemaailmassa* ('Hamlet goes business', 1987) is an original, modern version of Shakespeare, and as a result of his international fame his movies, too, have become internationalised: *Leningrad Cowboys Go America* (1989) is set in the United States, *I Hired a Contract Killer* (1990) in London, and *Boheemielämää* (*La vie de bohème*, 1992) in Paris. Kaurismäki's film *Kauas pilvet karkaavat* ('Drifting clouds', 1996) was a great international critical acclaim. ST

Kaurismäki, Mika (born 1955), film director. Mika Kaurismäki studied at the Munich film school, where his diploma project, *Valehtelija* ('The liar', 1981) brought its young maker an immediate breakthrough and Finnish cinema a breath of fresh air. *Arvottomat* ('Worthless', 1982) continued the same liberated and small-scale line, which included playing with roles, gestures, quotations, and the relationship between film and reality. In his later work, there has been a rapprochement with the values and genres of traditional film-making, with starting-points including the thriller in *Klaani – tarina Sammakoiden suvusta* ('The clan', 1984); the road movie in *Rosso* (1985); comedy in *Cha Cha Cha* (1989); the gangster movie in *Helsinki*

Napoli All Night Long (1987) and the adventure movie in *Amazon* (1990), as well as science fiction in *Viimeisellä rajalla – The Last Border* (1993). ST

Kivi, Aleksis (1834–1872), writer. Aleksis Kivi was born, a tailor's son, at Nurmijärvi in southern Finland. He is the pioneer of the Finnish-language novel and drama, and the first significant writer to have Finnish as his mother tongue. His first work is *Kullervo* (1864), a tragedy based on themes from the ►*Kalevala* and influenced by Shakespeare in its dramatic technique. The best work in his extensive dramatic repertoire is the comedy *Nummisuutarit* ('The heath-cobblers', 1864). The plot is based on the unsuccessful marriage plans of the simpleton son of a cobbler's family in a country village. The main character, Esko, is, with the protagonists of Kivi's major work, the novel *Seitsemän veljestä* (*Seven Brothers*, 1870), among the best-known characters in Finnish literature. *Seitsemän veljestä* is a humorous and realistic epic novel that is closer to the work of the Spanish writer Miguel de Cervantes than to the contemporary European literary tradition. The novel

Aleksis Kivi

Martti Kuningas and Helge Herala in Valentin Vaala's film version of Aleksis Kivi's *Nummisuutarit* ('The heath-cobblers', 1957)

describes the difficulties encountered by the seven brothers of the prosperous peasant family of Jukola in adapting to modern society, their ten years of escape into the wilderness, their adventures, their mellowing, and their return to society. Kivi's masterpiece has played a central role in Finns' understanding of themselves. PL

Joonas Kokkonen

Kokkonen, Joonas (1921–1996), composer. Joonas Kokkonen was one of the most important Finnish symphonists and influential musical figures of his time. He was a member of the Academy of Finland from 1963. After a period of neo-classical chamber music, he shifted to dodecaphony and orchestral works, including four symphonies and a cello concerto. The Third Symphony (1966) was followed by a freely tonal, 'neo-romantic' style which reached its climax in the opera *Viimeiset kiusaukset* (*The Last Temptations*, 1975) and *Requiem* (1981). MH

Esa Ruuttunen as Paavo Ruotsalainen in Joonas Kokkonen's opera *Viimeiset kiusaukset* (*The Last Temptations*, 1975), 1994

L

Krause, Tom (born 1934), baritone. Tom Krause's early career was centred mainly on Germany and Austria, but he has gone on to appear in most of the world's major opera houses. He has performed in a variety of works ranging from those of Mozart through much of the standard romantic repertory to modern operas such as Ernst Krenek's *Der goldener Bock* and Searle's *Hamlet*. Krause has also won acclaim with his sensitive *Lied* interpretations. HB

Tom Krause

Kvarnström, Kenneth (born 1963), dancer and choreographer, artistic director of the Helsinki City Theatre Dance Company since 1996. Kenneth Kvarnström represents the voice of the

Kenneth Kvarnström

young generation: his urban contemporary dance works convey the energy and atmosphere of the street. The works are very physical and stir extreme emotions. Kvarnström trained at the Stockholm Academy of Ballet between 1984 and 1987.

He began to choreograph his own dance routines in 1987. In 1990 he was commissioned by the Helsinki Festival to create the work *Exhibo*, which he later adapted for dance groups in, among other countries, Norway and England. Among his most important works are '*... that was all I wanted so I stuck my finger in his eye...*' (1991), its continuation, '*... and the angels began to scream...*' (1995), and *Digger Dog* (1993), *Neste* ('Liquid', 1994) and *Nono* (1996); the last two were created for the Helsinki City Theatre. In them, Kvarnström deals with themes of loneliness and the outsider, as well as violence as a consumer commodity of human relationships. His works have been performed in a number of European countries, and in Latin America. Kvarnström has also created dance works for television; *Duo* (1992) received an award in an international dance video competition in Paris. AR

Lalli (died c. 1157) According to medieval tradition, Lalli was the name of the Köyliö peasant who murdered Finland's first bishop and patron saint, ►St Henry. According to legend, he put the dead bishop's mitre on his head, but when he later took it off, his hair and scalp came with it. In the medieval

Lalli: painting from the inside of the altar-cupboard door of Urjala church, late 15th century

period and for a long time afterwards, Lalli represented paganism and St Henry the victory of Christianity. The figure of Lalli is often used in medieval art, shown lying submissively at St Henry's feet, scalpless.

Subsequently, Lalli's formerly completely negative image has received new overtones. Lalli has been regarded as symbolising the independence and stubbornness of ordinary Finnish people, and their unwillingness to submit to authority. Anti-clericalism, resistance to church and religion, has also been associated with Lalli. Lalli still appears as a man's name, although it is rare and is not included in the calendar of name-days. JN

Landtman, Gunnar (1878–1940), social anthropologist. The son of a civil servant, Gunnar Landtman became a student of ▶Edvard Westermarck at the turn of the century. Inspired by the example of his teacher, Landtman continued his studies in Great Britain (London, Cambridge and Oxford) at various times between 1903 and 1908. His doctoral thesis, which he completed in 1905, examined the origin of the clergy. Between 1910 and 1912 Landtman made an expedition to Papua-New Guinea, the results of which he published in two extended works, *The Kiwai Papuans of New Guinea* (1927) and *The Origin of the Inequality of Classes* (1938).

Landtman acted for Westermarck in the chair of practical philosophy at the University of Helsinki from 1916 to 1922, but lost the appointment to another of Westermarck's students, ▶Rafael Karsten. After this, Landtman worked outside Finland for many years, in Great Britain and Germany. He was appointed professor in 1927. Although Landtman was a student of Westermarck, he declared himself a Kantian teacher representing humanitarian values. As a member of parliament in 1922–1923, representing the Swedish People's Party, he opposed the death penalty. ML

language Of the approximately 5 million inhabitants of Finland roughly 4.6 million have Finnish as their native language. Outside Finland, Finnish is spoken by 1.3 million speakers, mainly

in the United States (616,000), Sweden (450,000), and Canada (91,000).

Finnish belongs to the Finno-Ugric group of the Uralic language family. Finno-Ugric peoples formed the earliest known population of north and middle Russia. The closest relatives of Finnish are jointly called Finnic languages: among these, Estonian has gained a status as an official language.

The speakers of the proto-Finno-Ugric language inhabited a vast area between the Gulf of Finland in the west and the Ural Mountains in the east. During the early phase, these speakers presumably had contact with Indo-European proto-languages; this is attested by loan words like *nimi* ('name'), or *vesi* ('water'). The earlier view that the predecessors of Finns migrated to the area of present day Finland about 4000 years ago has been disproved by archaeologists: there has been uninterrupted settlement around the Gulf of Finland ever since the end of the Ice Age, about 9000 years ago.

During the last 2000 years before Christ, pre-Finnic was heavily influenced by both pre-Baltic, and especially by various forms of pre-Germanic languages. Loan words such as *tytär* ('daughter'), *kaula* ('neck') from pre-Baltic, or *rengas* ('ring'), *kuningas*

Gunnar
Landtman

Finnish dialects

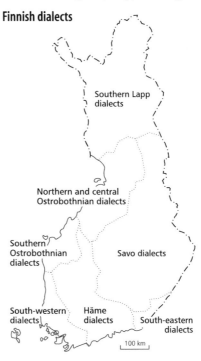

Southern Lapp dialects

Northern and central Ostrobothnian dialects

Southern Ostrobothnian dialects

Savo dialects

South-western dialects

Häme dialects

South-eastern dialects

100 km

('king') and *kana* ('hen'), from pre-Germanic, are evidence of close contact. Towards the end of the first millennium after Christ, a Slavic influence was felt: *akkuna* ('window'), *risti* ('cross'), and *raamattu* ('Bible') attest to the nature of this influence.

No century can be defined as the starting point of something called the Finnish language. As a group of fairly closely related dialects, Finnish began a separate development toward the end of the first millennium after Christ. Until the time of the first written documents, in the middle of the 16th century, early Finnish existed predominantly in an oral form, while Latin and Swedish were used in education and administration. The New Testament was translated in 1548, and the whole ►Bible in 1642. These translations were remarkable achievements considering that the population of the country was only about 300,000 around the middle of the 16th century. In the 17th century, Finnish was quite extensively spoken by learned people as well, but prolonged wars and famines weakened Finnish culture and language in the 18th century.

Being a borderland of the Swedish Empire meant constant involvement in wars, but also an enrichment of the culture and of the vernacular: hundreds of loan words were taken from Swedish and, via Swedish, from other European languages, including Greek and Latin. This meant a Europeanisation of Finnish: *hattu* ('hat'), *lamppu* ('lamp'), *hovi* ('court'), *lasi* ('glass'), *kruunu* ('crown'), *tuoli* ('chair'), etc.

In the 19th century, the national romantic movement took off in academic circles. The historical origins of the nation and the genetic relationships of the language became important. Other texts besides religious ones began to appear; the dialect base of the written language was broadened – of particular importance to the enrichment of the literary language were the findings of the ►folklore collectors in eastern Finland, the basis for the ►*Kalevala* epic.

Finnish gained official status by 1863, Finnish schools were established, and Finnish was accepted as a language of higher education. There is no historical parallel to the 'great language change' in which a considerable proportion of the Swedish speaking intelligentsia opted for the vernacular, adopting it as their domestic language.

The sound system of Finnish consists of 8 vowels: *i, e, ä, y, ö, u, o, a* and, in the indigenous vocabulary, only 13 consonants: *k, t, p, d, m, n, r, l, s, h, j, v*. The system furthermore makes use of quantitative opposition in the majority of sounds: *tuli* ('fire'), *tuuli* ('wind'), vs. *tulli* ('customs'); *tulen* ('I come') vs. *tuuleen* ('into the wind'); *laki* ('law') vs. *lakki* ('cap'). The majority of word stems are bisyllabic; monosyllables include the pronouns (*se* ('it'), *hän* ('(s)he'), or conjunctions *ja* ('and'). Initial consonant clusters are not allowed; consider *koulu* ('school') which derives from the Swedish skola < schola. Words are shaped by what is known as vowel harmony: front vowels *ä, y, ö*, and back vowels *a, u, o*, do not occur in the same words: *saare-ssa* ('in an island') vs. *sääre- ssä* ('in the leg'). The main stress is exclusively placed on the first syllable. Stops undergo a so-called consonant gradation: *katu* 'street', *kadu-lla* ('in the street'); *Pekka* 'Peter', *Peka-lle*' ('to Peter').

Running words in Finnish are on the average polysyllabic, as both derivational and inflectional suffixes are attached to word stems: KIRJA+**sto**-*i*-ssa-**mme**-kin 'in our libraries, too'.

There are between 150 and 180 derivational suffixes in Finnish; less than 10 per cent of them are actively used in coming new phrases. Word formation by the 'domestic' means of deriving and compounding form a counterbalance to the influx of direct loans; the latter, until recently, were at least partly adjusted to the restrictions of Finnish word structure, for example *pankki* ('bank'), *kenraali* ('general').

Finnish has 14 morphological case endings, corresponding to, for example, Swedish or English prepositions. Verbs take suffixes for mood, tense, and person. There are also several means of nominalisation. Neither nouns nor personal pronouns have a category of gender; thus *hän* means both 'he' and 'she'.

As a former subject-verb-object language, Finnish still predominantly uses postpositions and preposed adjectival modifiers: *Suure-n puu-n takana*

('Big-of tree-of behind') for 'Behind a big tree'. Due to the richness of the inflectional morphology, word order is predominantly used for thematic and contrastive purposes: *Poika näki tytö-n* ('Boy saw girl'); *Tytö-n näki poika* ('It was the boy who saw the girl'). Further, sentences may begin with a verb or an adverb, as well: *Sataa* ('rains'), ('It is raining'); *Minu-lla on nälkä* ('Me-at is hunger'), 'I am hungry'. With these features, a third one is related: passive sentences are agentless and subjectless: *Naapuri-ssa nuku-taan* ('Neighbor's-in is being slept'), 'They are asleep next door'. AH

Utsjoki, Tenojoki River

Lapland Lapland was written about as early as Olaus Magnus's *History of the Northern Peoples* (1555) and Johannes Schefferus's *Lapponia* (1673). In the 18th century, it was popularised by many foreign scholars and tourists, whose journeys there usually focussed on the valley of the Tornionjoki River. The best-known of these travel descriptions are the books by the French writer Pierre-Louis Moreau de Maupertuis (1736) and the Italian writer Giuseppe Acerbi (1799) in the 18th century. Although the picture of Lapland gradually expanded, for a long time it remained coloured by prejudices, romantic ideas and clichés.

Lapland is, above all, a land of natural grandeur and mighty landscapes. During the course of the centuries it established itself as a historic province, although its borders were subject to change. Lapland is divided between four states: Finnish, Swedish, Norwegian and Russian Lapland have existed for a long time. In recent times, when speaking of these areas of co-operation, the term *Pohjoiskalotti* ('Northern Calotte') has begun to be used.

The waters of the northernmost parts of Finnish Lapland, also known as Fjäll Lapland (*Tunturi-Lappi*) mostly flow into the Arctic Sea. The only species of tree that grows here is the mountain birch. The peaks of the mountains are, however, treeless and bare. To the south, there are tree and forest lines of birch, pine and spruce. In Forest Lapland (*Metsä-Lappi*) the landscape is dominated by wide string fens. There is also a certain zoning pattern that runs from west to east. The rivers Kemijoki, Ounasjoki and Tornionjoki flow from north to south, and the roads that follow their courses divide Lapland into sectors that also have their own historical background of settlement. The towns of Tornio and Kemi came into being on the estuaries of these rivers, where they flow

Reindeer
round-up, Vuotso
reindeer-owners'
association, 1995

into the Gulf of Bothnia. Rovaniemi, the 'gateway to Lapland', is situated where the rivers cross, not far from the Arctic Circle.

The ▶Sámi, or Lapps, are a people who have their own language and folk culture. In the 1990s the number of Sámi living in Finland was around 7000. The number fluctuates according to how Sámi nationality is defined; defined by language, in 1995 there were 1726. Finland's Sámi-speaking population lives mostly in Enontekiö, Inari, Utsjoki and the northern parts of Sodankylä. Utsjoki is the only province where Sámi-speakers form the majority. In Inari, too, the Sámi were in the majority until 1910. The proportion of Sámi has, however, diminished because Finns have since moved to the centres of Ivalo and Inari. Important Sámi villages in the Inari province are Kuttura, Lisma, Menesjärvi, Angeli, Iijärvi and the Skolt Sámi villages of Sevettijärvi and Sarmijärvi. In Enontekiö notable Sámi villages are Vuotso and Purnumukka. In the Sámi area as a whole, however, Finns are in the majority in the areas of highest population density, with the exception of Utsjoki village. Some small villages are, on the other hand inhabited exclusively by Sámi. In Norway and Sweden the Sámi population is considerably larger than it is in Finland, and even in Russia there are almost 2000 Sámi. Estimates of the total number of Sámi in the four countries vary between 40,000 and 80,000.

Sámi national life is in general associated with reindeer herding. In 1993 there were 215,000 reindeer in Finland. It is, however, notable that Sámi-land is only one part of a reindeer-herding area. In the south it extends into ▶Ostrobothnia as far as Kainuu, north Karelia Reindeer herding is still the occupation of just under half the male heads of Sámi families, although the Sámi have increasingly adopted Finnish occupations. This relinquishing of traditional professions has had the effect of reducing the distinctive character of the Sámi population. There is also an attempt to tend reindeer beyond the borders of the Finnish state.

In spite of the austere soil and climate, agriculture is also of local importance, while in the Inari Basin forestry is practised. Wide tracts of land have, however, been classified as wilderness areas, where wood-felling is mostly impossible. In addition, there are large national and natural parks.

During the last few decades tourism has increased – partly because of ▶Santa Claus. The roads to the Arctic Sea pass through Sámi-land. In spite of national borders, co-operation between all the Sámi peoples of the 'Northern Calotte' has begun to thrive. Sámi identity has grown stronger and demands for the use of the Sámi language and the Sámi region have become more marked. KRn

law and justice Finland is in all essential aspects a western, constitutional ▶welfare state; however, the Finnish legal system has one or two idiosyncratic features that can be understood only through a knowledge of Finnish history. In the context of the European legal tradition, Finland belongs to the Roman-Germanic group. Within this group, it is closer to the Nordic countries, especially Sweden, which is natural considering the long political connection between the two countries, which lasted almost 700 years. From a historical point of view, the special feature of the Nordic legal system is that the influence of Roman law has been noticeably less in the Nordic countries than is generally the case in central, and particularly southern, Europe. This system is characterised by a certain democratic tendency that may be seen, for example, in the traditionally strong position of laymen within the judicature.

The period of autonomy (1809–1917), when Finland was subordinate to the Russian state, did not alter the situation; Russian influences remained minimal in the sphere of justice. The laws which originated in the time of Swedish domination – the most important of them being the codification of 1734 – remained in force in spite of the change in Finland's political status.

During the period of autonomy, the eyes of Finnish jurists turned to Germany, from where positivistic doctrines emphasising the primary importance of written law spread to Finland, as they did to almost all of Europe, in the second half of the 19th century. The German influence on Finnish jurisprudence continued to be strong until the end of the Second World War.

In spite of certain steps towards legalism during the period of Swedish domination, the development in Finland of a constitutional state, 'Rechtstaat', did not begin until the mid 1850s. During the reign of Emperor Alexander II (1855–1881), when the Diet began to sit again after a 50-year interval, a massive program of juridical reforms was implemented in Finland. As a result of these innovations the mercantilistic legal system that typefied an estate society broke down, and a juridical basis for the market economy was introduced. Notable among the innovations were principles concerning freedom of trade and contracts, bank and company legislation and legislation promoting economic activity in general.

In spite of the changes that had occurred in the area of economic activity, the democratic constitutional state was still a long way off. A signpost in that direction was the new Diet Act brought into being on the wings of the tsarist authorities' temporary weakness in 1906. This brought Finland a radical modern unicameral parliament, the members of which were elected on the basis of universal and equal suffrage for both men and women. When the tsarist authorities tightened their grip again, however, the functioning of the parliament was more or less paralysed.

The foundations of the democratic constitutional state were created in Finland during the years following the declaration of Finnish indepedence in 1917. Finland recovered quickly from its bloody Civil War (1918) and the Constitutional Act of 1919 and many other important legislative reforms (including the land reform) paved the way for democracy. The heritage of the Civil WEar was still to be seen, however, in Finland's legislation, including the distribution of the highest political authority in a way that gave the President of the Republic accentuated and wide-ranging powers. In general, control policy was strict in Finland during the inter-war period, although a certain relaxation began to be felt during the second half of the 1930s, when the extreme left had been driven underground by legal means, and when the demands of the extreme right for a replacement of 'rotten democracy' by an authoritarian regime were also rejected.

After the Second World War, and especially in the 1950s and 1960s, Finland developed into a welfare state, with the introduction of social security, free education and health-care. In the 1960s and 1970s the Finnish legal system was also modernised, bringing considerable improvements in legal security in the fields of criminal law and of procedural law and enacting legislation improving the legal status of the ordinary citizen. The laws on free legal aid and consumer protection – just to mention some examples – originated at this time.

The period from the 1980s onward has meant much the same in Finland as elsewhere in Europe: deregulation of legal provisions. Particularly in the sphere of economic activity – largely connected with the process of European integration – obstacles to free competition have been removed. On the other hand, the requirements of international human rights agreements have meant an increasing emphasis on perspectives connected with legal security in criminal, procedural and governmental law.

On the whole, when viewed in the light of the traditional doctrine of the distribution of power, developments may be said to be progressing in the direction of a reinforcement of the role of the courts. This trend is now common throughout Europe.

Lastly, attention should be drawn to one important feature of the Finnish legal tradition: the Finnish tendency towards an allegiance to law, an attitude that may be characterised as legalistic. Although there are obvious breaks in the legalistic tradition (for example, the political trials of the post-Civil War period), law-making and the following of the letter of the law have been firmly rooted in Finland. In Finland the law is taken literally, and the development of justice is viewed as the province of those who make, not of those who interpret, the law. JKen

learned societies During the era of Swedish rule the Finnish scientific community maintained contacts with Sweden's learned societies, the most important of which was the Royal Academy of Sciences, established in Stockholm with the co-operation of Carl von Linné. When Finland became an autonomous part of Russia in 1809, contacts with St Petersburg in the first place became more active.

The oldest of the learned societies founded in 1838 by the Finnish scientific community, is the Finnish Society of Sciences and Letters. It can be compared with international scientific academies in that membership of its departments is limited, and the society appoints its own members. On the other hand, the Society of Sciences and Letters has had only limited means with which to fund scientific research.

In the Society of Sciences and Letters the Swedish language has been dominant, and the main emphasis placed on the natural sciences. When in the early 19th century the Finnish educated classes began to focus their interest on the culture of their own country, the need arose for a society functioning in the Finnish language. The Finnish Academy of Science and Letters (1908) also adopted an active role in wider Finnish society, holding some of its meetings outside Helsinki, for example.

Even before the establishment of the Society of Sciences and Letters, there had been established in Turku the Societas pro Fauna et Flora Fennica (1821), one of the purposes of which was to assemble the most extensive possible museum of Finland's fauna and flora. In 1857 this material was added to the collections of the university, which had moved to Helsinki. Thereafter the society continued its research work with the help of activity involving publishing and presentation. The ►Finnish Literature Society (1831), important in the sphere of national awakening, also works for the advancement of the position of Finnish literature and language in a wider context than that of scholarly research alone. The Finnish Literature Society gave birth to the Finnish Historical Society (1875) and the Finnish Geographical Society (1888).

The Finnish educated classes gradually became predominantly Finnish-speaking, and with them the learned community. This may explain the fact that in several areas of knowledge the founding of a Swedish-language society was followed by the establishment of a corresponding society with a Finnish-speaking membership: e.g. Finnish societies for medical science (1835 and 1881) and for legal science (1862 and 1898). An exception to this rule is the field of economics, where Finnish-speakers founded the Economic Association (1884) before the Swedish-language Economic Society of Finland (1894).

The House of Estates in Helsinki is a meeting place for learned societies

The number of societies has been enlarged not only by the language question, but also by the increasing specialisation of research in new areas. In the late 19th century and early 20th century, societies were founded covering various different areas of science. Frequently, however, alongside these smaller, specialised societies dealing with separate fields of study came into being. Recent years have seen the emergence of new branches of study and the founding of associated societies that gather together members from various primary fields of research. Examples of the latter are the Finnish Society for Women Studies (1988) and the Finnish Society for Environmental Sciences (1987).

For the above-mentioned reasons, rather many learned societies have come into being in Finland – over 200. The majority of them are voluntary, registered associations and operate on a nation-wide basis.

The purpose of the learned societies is to create possibilities for the discussion of scholarship and science.

To this end they publish periodicals, of which there are almost 100. The learned societies are Finland's most important publishers of non-fiction. Each year some 200–250 new titles appear.

Since 1899, the Federation of Finnish Learned Societies has functioned as the co-ordinating body of Finland's learned societies. Through it the member societies are able to obtain premises for their meetings; in addition, the Federation attends to the requirements of their publishing activities. The bookstore *Tiedekirja* sells the societies' publications.

The Federation functions as a publicity organ for research. Every second year a Science Festival is held, at which researchers talk in layman's terms about the results of their work. The journal *Tieteessä tapahtuu* gives information about the meetings of the learned societies and their new publications. The Federation of Finnish Learned Societies was one of the organisations that founded the Heureka Science Centre, whose exhibitions explain by illustration the importance of scientific research in society. HHlä

Leino, Eino (1878–1926), writer, poet. Eino Leino was the most important developer of Finnish-language poetry at the turn of the 20th century, the leading Finnish writer of the early 20th century and now probably Finland's best-loved poet. He published his first collection of poetry in 1896. Leino's *oeuvre* is unusually wide and diverse. He published about 80 original works in addition to translations including Dante's *Divine Comedy*. At its best, Leino's poetry is song-like and sensuous, at its weakest full of pathos and preaching. In his major works, the collections of narrative poetry *Helkavirsiä* ('Whit songs', 1903, 1916), Leino revived expression based on the ▶*Kalevala* and folk poetry, which had been almost exhausted in the 19th century. He combined the archaic and mythic Finnish tradition with a vision of the free, truth-seeking individual based on the work of Friedrich Nietzsche and a conception of art and the artist inspired by symbolism. Leino also attempted to renew Finnish theatre with his symbolically charged 'sacred drama'. In his novels, Leino reacted rapid-

ly to contemporary social, political and ideological questions. PL

leisure In pre-industrial Finland ▶work and leisure were closely interrelated and not always easy to separate. Fishing and hunting for men, knitting and handicraft for women, were leisure activities that also had economic functions. Even the ▶church did not operate purely in the spiritual field; it had important administrative, disciplinary and statistical tasks.

The nation-building era under Russian rule (1809–1917) brought forth a plethora of ▶popular movements and organisations around temperance, womens issues, youth, sports and labour politics that created a large number of clubs with educational and leisure functions. A large network of peoples' educational institutions was founded on them with state support, and many important cultural institutions have their origins in these movements.

Sports, drama and music are part of the curriculum in the Finnish school system but mostly these leisure activi-

Eino Leino

In the wilderness: whether alone, like this ice-fisherman (above), or in company, like these elk-hunters (below), Finns like to spend much of their leisure-time in the peace of the countryside

Work or leisure: one of the pleasures of summertime is washing rugs in natural water, sea or lake. Special jetties are provided in the towns for the purpose such as this one in central Helsinki

ties are organised privately albeit with public financial support. Finland has a nation-wide network of free public ►libraries, and with their help reading has become the most popular cultural leisure activity. About 80 per cent of adult women and 70 percent of men have read books during the past 6 months, which is a very high percentage in international comparisons. An increasingly popular cultural activity is going to art exhibitions (50 per cent of women and 40 percent of men have visited one or more during the last 12 months). In this Finland follows the same trend as other western countries.

The most popular leisure activity is watching television (75 per cent daily).

Today, leisure activities are gender specific, women participating more in culturally oriented and educational hobbies, men more in sports.

In terms of time budgets, domestic work including child-rearing remains the most important leisure activity even in urban settings. The division of labour in the home between the sexes is slowly levelling out, women spending on the average 3.3 hours and men two hours in these activities. PS

Juha Leiviskä

Leiviskä, Juha (born 1936), architect, member of the Academy of Finland. The church architecture of Juha Leiviskä is distinguished from the visual noise of contemporary architecture by its pure development of a clear theme. His churches are rhythmic series of spaces of differing heights. Puolivälinkangas Church in Oulu was completed in 1975, Myyrmäki Church and Parish Centre in Vantaa in 1984, and St John's Church in Männistö, Kuopio, in 1993.

Juha Leiviskä, Myyrmäki Church and Parish Centre, 1984

Myyrmäki Church turns its back on the railway and opens instead on to a slender birch coppice. The rhythm of rising spatial sequences is finished off by spilling-over daylight, groups of small lamps and spatial textiles. In Männistö Church, colour surfaces are reflected in narrow verticals as immaterial colour in the space. Art and architecture are one. Leiviskä himself emphasises the influence of baroque architecture and the environment.

In more everyday comissions, too – for example, the small group made up of a day-care centre and library for the old working-class residential district of Vallila in Helsinki (1985) – Leiviskä has brought joy and value into workaday life.

In 1995 Juha Leiviskä was awarded the prestigious Carlsberg Prize, by the Queen of Denmark. RN

Leningrad Cowboys, rock band. The Leningrad Cowboys, who call themselves the world's worst rock band, hugely enjoy sending up the clichés associated with rock stardom. The trademarks of this band, which cultivates a peculiar brand of humour, include enormous quiffs and half-metre winkle-pickers. The Cowboys' world success has been aided by ►Aki Kaurismäki's cult film *Leningrad Cowboys Go America* (1989), which describes a Siberian rock band's adventures, for

The Leningrad Cowboys (with quiffs) with members of the Red Army Choir

better and worse, on their journey to the New World (where, in fact, they wound up in the Top Ten in Mexico).

In 1993 the Leningrad Cowboys, together with the Red Army Choir, held a massive outdoor concert called the Total Balalaika Show, and this event, in the historic surroundings of Senaatintori Square, Helsinki, was followed by an audience of 70,000. The same elements were present in 1994 in Unter den Linden, Berlin, at the Nokia Balalaika Show, which was at the same time a farewell to Allied troops. In the same year, MTV invited the band to perform at the annual music-video prize-giving ceremony at New York's Radio City. The Leningrad Cowboys have released six discs, of which the most recent is *Mongolian Barbeque* (1997). RL

libraries The Finnish library system is based on co-operation and the division of labour, and the networking ethos that derives from these. Finnish libraries fall into three main categories: public libraries supported by the municipal authorities, universities, research institutes and research libraries work in conjunction with civil service departments. In addition, the private sector and general government operate over 300 information service units providing data that is an important factor in economic competition. The collections of Finnish libraries contain over 54 million bound volumes and periodicals, audio-visual and microfilm material, and material stored on computer.

In the 15th century Finland's churches and monasteries are estimated to have contained collections of thousands of manuscripts. However, religious purges deprived these institutions of their powers, and the books were destroyed or ended up in Sweden, from where some were subsequently returned to Finland. The nucleus of the library of Academy of Turku, founded in 1640, was 21 books belonging to Turku Gymnasium. The earliest catalogue was published in Sweden, in the form of Johannes Schefferus's *Svecia literata* (1680) with its supplement *Appendix, in quo exhibentur Finnicae gentis Scriptores nonnuli*. Anders Anton Stiernman (1695–1765) compiled the catalogue *Aboa literata* in 1719, when the library was evacuated to Sweden on account of the Great Northern War. The collection was also augmented by a gift of books from the royal chancellery. In 1764 Henrik Gabriel Porthan (1739–1804) became the librarian, his aim being to 'gradually collect for the Library of our Academy everything that pertains to the written history of our nation'. This part of Porthan's life work was, however, destroyed by the fire of Turku in 1827; only some 800 books that were on loan elsewhere survived. They were moved to the library of the Alexander University of Helsinki, from which the

Finnish national library, the Helsinki University Library later developed.

The history of the Finnish public library dates from 1794, when the Vaasa Reading Library was founded. The first school library was established at Anjala in 1802, while the oldest completely preserved Finnish library belonged to Porvoo Gymnasium. Parish libraries came into being during the 1830s and 1840s. The most famous private library is the collection of Viipuri's Monrepos Manor, which is now in Helsinki University Library.

In 1856–1857, Fredrik Wilhelm Pipping (1783–1868), chief librarian of the Helsinki University Library, prepared the *Luettelo Suomeksi präntätyistä kirjoista* ('The catalogue of Finnish printed books'), which formed the beginning of Finnish national bibliography; the subsequent parts were made available initially in printed form, and later as microfilm and machine-readable copies. The database contains some 250,000 titles (1995), there is also a CD-ROM version. Helsinki University Library, which is the Finnish national library, maintains the catalogue. The preservation and registration of the national heritage is covered by the law on free copies (1919, revised 1981). In the period when Finland belonged to the Russian state (1809–1917), the Helsinki University Library received free copies of works printed in Russia. This collection formed the basis of the internationally important Slavic Library. The Library of Valamo Monastery (►monasteries) is a valuable collection of Orthodox religious works.

Finland has around 20 university libraries and nearly 800 specialised research libraries, the oldest of which are the library of the ►Finnish Literature Society (1831), the Meteorological Library (1841), the Helsinki University of Technology Library, which originated from the Technical College Library (1849), the Helsinki University Undergraduate Library (1858) and the Forestry Library, successor to the Evo Forestry Collection (1862). The Exchange Center for Scientific Literature (1899) makes available international periodicals, while the National Repository Library contains little-used literature. In 1972, an addition to national

Listening to music at Itäkeskus Library, Helsinki. Finnish libraries function also as meeting-places

work-sharing and self-sufficiency, a central library network was created: ten libraries have the task of developing the data collections and services in their respective fields. They prepared special bibliographies, which form the KATI general database (also available on CD-ROM). This was followed up in the 1990s with the maintenance of the decentralised ARTO article database. The areas of medicine, economics and technology each have their own article database files.

Finland's scientific and scholarly libraries are not covered by any standard legislation. The libraries attend, in the first instance, to the fulfilment of the needs of their own researchers and students. Co-operation and development affecting libraries, archives and museums is co-ordinated by the Finnish Council for Information Provision. An important co-operative project begun in the 1980s is the introduction of a standard computer-based integrated library system and the construction of an information network (LINNEA). The catalogues of the libraries belonging to the system form the LINDA database, which may be used nationwide in order to check the availability of books. The information service is operated by the utilisation of both Finnish and international resources. Through the FUNET network shared by universities and the scientific community, access to Internet sources is made possible. The digitalisation of collections is now in its initial phases. Several research libraries are co-operating in virtual library projects. They are partners also when electronical publishing of Finnish scientifical literature is promoted. The Automation Unit of the Finnish Research Libraries working under the aegis of the Helsinki University Library directs the development of the library system and network communications. It functions in association with the co-operation secretariat, which co-ordinates participation in the European Union's library programs.

The tasks of the public libraries were determined in 1986 by the reform of the library laws. The libraries must 'put books and other suitable recorded items into public use'. The development of information technology is watched alertly, and electronic data storage and information networks have already in part been brought within public reach in Finland's libraries. In every municipality a tax-funded library is provided cost-free to users; in all, there are 2150 service units. Two-thirds of all Finns regularly use the library services and 48 per cent have a library card. Library borrowing continues to grow; in 1994, 102,010,064 loans were made (20.2 loans, 12.4 library visits per inhabitant). Of these loans, 82.4 per cent were of printed materials. In addition to books, audio-visual material is loaned, and in some places works of art are also borrowed. Interlibrary lending also takes the use of the material further afield. In some municipalities computer-based library

systems are in use, while in others the emphasis is placed on solutions involving regional co-operation. The development is directed by the central library, while the regional responsibility is carried by the regional central libraries. The catalogue of their collections makes up the MANDA database, which is intended to incorporate all the municipal libraries within the same network service before the turn of the century. HI

light Dramatically variable light conditions, the light of a summer night, the dark of autumn, the snow-reflected light of a winter day, the brightness of a frosty night, the polar night, the twilight of morning and evening – contribute as much to the atmosphere of the north as the forms of terrain and flora. The scarcity of light in winter and its superabundance in summer make light an important factor in mood; light creates the rhythms of the seasons and of life.

The variations of light in the North have been a central theme in Finnish painting from the outdoor painting of the 19th century to the abstract art of today. Realist paintings, such as those of Veikko Vionoja (born 1909), often show rural Finnish surroundings in a summer night or in the blue-grey light of winter. But even Finnish geometrical abstract art, such as the painting

The play of light on snow in this Lappish forest in late winter brings welcome relief from months of darkness

constructions of the well-known representative of concretism, Jorma Hautala (born 1941), often has as its base the experience of the light of the landscape.

Sensitive depictions of the light conditions of the landscape are also familiar from Finnish literature and poetry. Descriptions of light in literature are often accompanied by descriptions of sound and silence.

A sensitive handling of light is one of the characteristics of Finnish ▶architecture. From the 1930s onwards, ▶Alvar Aalto developed inventive modes of roof-lighting, which became the trademark of his architecture. The contemporary church buildings of ▶Juha Leiviskä are like instruments of light, in which reflected light and colour take on quite ecstatic characteristics. The interest that has been shown in both Aalto's and Leiviskä's lighting has also resulted in interesting designs for artificial lighting. Finnish architects and designers in general have, indeed, liked to design lighting. JP

Magnus Lindberg

Lindberg, Magnus (born 1958), composer. In international contemporary music circles, Magnus Lindberg is perhaps, at the time of writing, the best-known Finnish composer. He began in a post-serial style (the piano quintet ... *de Tartuffe, je crois*, 1981), but his music has since become characterised by the great tonal masses of his orchestral works, first as aggressive blocks (*Kraft*, 1983–1985), then as more harmonic, rapidly moving tonal surfaces (for example *Marea*, 1989–1990, Arena, 1995). MH

Stefan Lindfors

Lindfors, Stefan (born 1962), interior designer, industrial designer. Stefan Lindfors is internationally the best-known of the younger generation of Finnish designers. He graduated as an interior and furniture designer from the University of Art and Design Helsinki in 1988. As early as 1985, he attracted attention with his light, metal-frame chairs, but his true breakthrough came in 1987 with the *Metaxis* exhibition held at the Design Museum of Finland in Helsinki in 1987, at which Lindfors showed thrones dedicated to three leaders of great powers (Gorbachev, Reagan and Ziyang).

Väinö Linna

Stefan Lindfors, 'Hippolyte' table, 1988

Lindfors is a designer of the rock generation: permissive, constantly self-renewing, with a firm belief in himself. His bubbling energy can express itself equally in fine art and in the design of objects and spaces. One important starting-point in his object design is forms originating in the animal world, particularly the structures of insects and other invertebrates. They have given rise, among other things, too the *Scaragoo* lamp (1988), in production with the German company Ingo Maurer, and sculptures made from iron constructions and acrylic, which Lindfors showed at his *Reges Insectorum* exhibition at the Amos Anderson Art Museum in Helsinki in 1991 and at the *Freedom of Speech* exhibition in Kansas City, Los Angeles and Washington in the United States in 1995–1996. Among Lindfors's furniture and interior design projects are furniture for the Finnish Broadcasting Company's television news (1990), interior design for the cafeteria of the Design Museum of Finland (1989) and a shop for the clothing company ▶Marimekko in Helsinki (1993). In 1992 Lindfors received the most prestigious Nordic design award, the Georg Jensen Prize. Between 1993 and 1996 Lindfors was rector of the Kansas City Art Institute in the United States. MaA

Linna, Väinö (1920–1992), writer. Linna was born into a working-class family in Urjala in central Finland. His third novel, *Tuntematon sotilas* (*The Unknown Soldier*, 1954) was a unique success in Finnish literary history:

Aarno Sulkanen as Akseli Koskela in Edvin Laine's film adaptation of Linna's *Täällä Pohjantähden alla* ('Here beneath the North Star', 1968)

more than half a million copies had been sold up to 1990 which, in Finnish terms, the total population exceeding only 5 million in the 1990s, is a large number. This exciting, realistic and humorous novel tells of the fate of a rifle brigade during the war fought by Finland against the Soviet Union between 1941 and 1944. The novel satisifed the need to describe and understand the personal and collective problems caused by defeat in war. The nation recognised itself, both its strengths and its weaknesses, and was thus able to leave behind the traumas of war and refine its experiences into a positive attitude. In his next and last work, the novel trilogy *Täällä Pohjantähden alla* (*Here beneath the North Star*, 1959–1962), Linna presented the members of an ordinary country family as central characters in the historical panorama of the development of Finnish society from the end of the 19th century to the period after the Second World War. The description of the Civil War of 1918, in particular, which is seen from the point of view of the revolutionaries, healed a society that had been divided for decades. Linna's view of history, which is influenced by Leo Tolstoy's *War and Peace* (1869), has had a lasting influence on Finns' conception of the past and of themselves. PL

literacy The development of literacy was one of the aims of the Reformation in Finland, as in Germany. The fact that fragments of ►Michael Agricola's first Finnish ►primer have survived from three different editions testifies to the practical furthering of this aim. In practice, however, the goal remained distant in the 16th century.

Only in the 17th century did regular work toward spreading literacy among ordinary people begin to bear fruit. The ability to read was demanded of the adult population at parish catechistical meetings, and knowledge of the main points of Martin Luther's Catechism. It has been estimated that literacy to this standard had been generally achieved in central areas around the 1640s. In more distant parts, however, complete illiteracy was still widespread. The parish schools that developed as part of the general education system toward the end of the 17th century, in the time of Bishop Johannes Gezelius the Elder (1615–1690), were a central part of education for the people. Increased literacy facilitated the growth of literature directed at ordinary people, primarily hymnals and catechisms, at the end of the 17th century.

Between 1701 and 1721, the Great Northern War weakened popular education, but after the war this was intensified once more. Particularly important was a recommendation given in 1740 concerning the holding of confirmation classes for young people, which was instituted as a clerical duty in 1763. The results of this more effective tuition rapidly became apparent. It has been estimated that the ability to read aloud was attained fairly comprehensively by the younger age groups in the last decades of the 18th century. In many cases the standard of literacy is difficult to estimate, as information is based on parish confirmation records, and criteria for acceptance for confirmation varied a great deal from place to place. The habit of reading increased significantly in the late 18th and early 19th centuries by the ▶revivalist movements, whose influence on independent reading was significant.

The establishment of the primary school system in 1866 continued the development in such a way that by 1900 only 1.5 per cent of 15-year-old children were illiterate. The compulsory education legislation of 1921 decreed that all children between the ages of 7 and 15 should complete studies equivalent to a primary school education. Through the influence of effective and long-term primary education, Finns are among the most active readers of books and periodicals, and library-users, in the world. JN

literature Linguistic conditions, romanticism and Hegelian philosophy have had a definitive effect on the development of Finnish writing.

From the First Crusade (c. 1155) till 1809, when Finland became subordinate to the Russian Crown, the gradually developing Finnish literature, discounting the Finnish-language folk poetry which was preserved in the oral tradition, was part of Swedish literature. Swedish and Latin were the languages of literary culture, education and government, and continued to be so until the end of the 19th century.

The oldest known texts written in Finland are Latin legends from the end of the 13th century. The oldest surviving manuscripts date from the mid 14th century. The first book printed for use in Finland is a missal, the ▶*Missale Aboense* (1488). The Bridgettine monk ▶Jöns Budde or Räk is the first Finnish writer whose name is known. Budde published Swedish translations of Latin legends about the saints and of some books of the Old Testament.

The Lutheran Reformation, which arrived in Sweden with the ascension of Gustavus Vasa (1523–1560) to the throne in 1523, marked the beginning of Finnish-language literature. ▶Mich-ael Agricola published, among other things, the first Finnish-language book and ▶primer (1543), and a Finnish translation of the New Testament (1548). These began the development of Finnish as a literary language.

The foundation of the Academy of Turku (1640) and the country's first printing press (1642), which was established to serve the university's needs, gave new impetus to literary culture. Nevertheless, literary activity in the 17th century, and even the beginning of the 18th, was makeshift in Finland. The most important Finnish-born writers – Jacob Frese (c. 1691–1729), who wrote spiritual poetry in the baroque style, and Gustav Filip Creutz (1731–1785), one of the leading writers of the Swedish rococo – moved to Stockholm early in their lives.

The small amount of Finnish literature from the period before romanticism, in both Finnish and Swedish, is, with few exceptions, of modest quality. Literature as such was born during the romantic period and under the influence of national romanticism in the 19th century. The institutions of literature (publishing houses, bookshops, literary criticism, literary publicity, readership) developed only towards the end of the 19th century.

Romanticism reached Finnish literature in the Swedish-language poetry of Frans Michael Franzén (1772–1847). In the poetry of ▶Johan Ludvig Runeberg, also written in Swedish, it achieved a culturally and nationally pioneering form. ▶J. V. Snellman, a Finnish disciple of the German philosopher G.W.F. Hegel, argued for the organic unity of the Finnish language, the national literature, the national spirit and the development of the state; his thoughts provided a cultural and historic role for the Finnish language, and improved its status at the expense of Swedish.

The ▶*Kalevala* (1835, 1849) and the ▶*Kanteletar* (1840), works by ▶Elias Lönnrot based on epic and lyric folk poems, demonstrated that Finnish was, contrary to what had been thought, an expressive literary language comparable to others.

The Finnish-language novel, drama and art poetry were born and achieved artistically durable results in the hands

'Windows open to Europe': the Tulenkantajat ('Torchbearers') group of young writers in 1927

of ▶Aleksis Kivi. His novel *Seitsemän veljestä* (*Seven Brothers*, 1870) and his comedy *Nummisuutarit* ('The heathcobblers', 1864) are the foundation of Finnish-language literature.

Finnish literature joined the European mainstream when, in the 1880s, realism and naturalism from Scandinavia, France and Russia arrived in Finland in, for example, the socially critical dramas of ▶Minna Canth and the novels and stories of Juhani Aho (1861–1921) and Teuvo Pakkala (1862–1925).

At the turn of the century, neo-romanticism and symbolism displaced naturalism. In the poetry of ▶Eino Leino, international symbolism is combined with the archaic language of Finnish folk poetry in, for example, the collection of ballads and legend-poems *Helkavirsiä* ('Whit songs', 1903, 1916).

The political and social unrest of the early 20th century, the First World War, Finland's independence (1917) and the crisis of the Civil War (1918) gave birth to satirical realism. The short stories and plays of ▶Maria Jotuni examine social and attitudinal changes in ordinary people and the bourgeoisie from the point of view of women's roles. *Putkinotko* (1919–1920), a novel by Joel Lehtonen (1881–1934), reveals, through humour and satire, the conflict between the idealism of the bourgeoisie and the backwardness of ordinary people.

In the inter-war period, with its stresses in both domestic and foreign politics, the novels of ▶F.E. Sillanpää placed a therapeutic emphasis on the durability and beauty of nature in contrast to the rapidity of historical change. Other writers who sought a counterweight to the conflicts of times past, stylisation and beauty were Volter Kilpi (1874–1939) in his novel *Alastalon salissa* ('In Alastalo's parlour', 1933) and Aino Kallas (1878–1956), whose novels were set in the romantic past. The bourgeois cultural hegemony could not tolerate the criticism of contemporary society levelled by Pentti Haanpää (1905–1955) in his humorous and ironic short prose pieces.

Modernism entered Finnish literature, through continental stimuli, in Finland-Swedish poetry. ▶Edith Södergran, Elmer Diktonius (1896–1961) and ▶Gunnar Björling were, in the early decades of the century, leading Scandinavian avant-garde writers. Finnish poetry continued in a post-romantic style until, in the 1920s, expressionism gave it a contemporary air.

At the turning point after the Second World War, poetry turned toward an entirely new mode of expression, emphasising the permanence of the cultural tradition and the value of times past in the poetry of P. Mustapää (real name Martti Haavio, 1899–1973). Aaro Hellaakoski (1893–1952) sought a basis for a world view in Finnish people's relationship with nature, Helvi Juvonen (1919–1959) in the archaic and magical world of religion and folk poetry.

Late by international standards, modernism, mediated by the influence of Ezra Pound, T.S. Eliot and Ernest Hemingway, among others, transformed Finnish poetry and prose in the 1950s. ▶Paavo Haavikko, ▶Eeva-Liisa Manner and Mirkka Rekola (born

191

East meets West: a panel discussion at the biennial Lahti Writers' Reunion. Left to right: Jörn Donner, Mongo Beti, Olli Alho, Antonio Lopo Antunes, Yevgeny Sidorov

1931) reformed Finnish-language poetry; in Swedish-language poetry, the modernist tradition was continued by ▶Bo Carpelan. Prose broke away from realism in *Manillaköysi* ('The manila rope', 1957), a novel by ▶Veijo Meri. Other pioneers of modernist prose included Antti Hyry (born 1931), ▶Paavo Haavikko and Marja-Liisa Vartio (1924–1966).

Traditional narrative retained its influence and its readers for a long time. The historical novels of ▶Mika Waltari, for example *Sinuhe, egyptiläinen* (*The Egyptian*, 1945), interpreted his own time by holding it up against the distant past. In her ▶Moomin books, written for children, the Finland-Swedish writer ▶Tove Jansson dealt with fears of catastrophe. The books have achieved international fame. In his novel *Tuntematon sotilas* (The unknown soldier, 1954), ▶Väinö Linna painted a critical but humorous portrait of the nation and, in his trilogy *Täällä Pohjantähden alla* (*Here beneath the North Star*, 1959–1962), interpreted the country's history in a healing way.

Development after modernism was led, in poetry, at first by ▶Pentti Saarikoski toward speech-like, open, at first political expression. Later, concretist and surrealist features appeared in the work of, for example, Väinö Kirstinä (born 1936), while Kari Aronpuro (born 1940) took his stimuli from semiotics and Arto Melleri (born 1956) from pop music. The minimalism of modernist prose was replaced by a nat-

uralism influenced by Henry Miller, for example in the work of Hannu Salama (born 1936). Various different forms of post-modernism have been visible in the 1970s and 1980s, from the social analysis of Olli Jalonen (born 1954) and the exploration of the possibilities of fiction of Matti Pulkkinen (born 1944) to the philosophical and social interpretations of computers, artificial intelligence and virtual reality of Leena Krohn (born 1947). PL

literature in translation The Number One of best- and steady-sellers among Finnish literature in translation is, unquestionably, the Finnish national epic, the ▶*Kalevala*, of which there are more than 45 translations into different languages.

Next on the list have been ▶Mika Waltari's historical novels, which have, since the 1930s and 1940s, appeared in almost 30 languages, and the work of ▶Tove Jansson, whose ▶Moomin books are available in 33 languages. In recent years the humorous novelist Arto Paasilinna (born 1942) has enjoyed considerable success in France, in particular, where Waltari's books have also been issued in new editions. Finland's only winner of the Nobel Prize for literature, ▶F.E. Sillanpää, who received the prize in 1939, was translated primarily in the 1930s.

A curiosity that reflects Finland's geopolitical position during the 1950s and 1960s is the case of Martti Larni (1909–1993) – whose success in Finland has otherwise been rather modest

– with his novel *Neljäs nikama eli veijari vastoin tahtoaan* ('The fourth vertebra, or, a rogue against his will', 1957), which has been translated into Albanian, Bulgarian, Georgian, Latvian, Lithuanian, Moldavian, Mongolian, Romanian, German, Czech, Hungarian, Russian (the most recent edition appeared in 1992) and Estonian (in addition to Spanish and Greek). The novel is a satirical story about America in the 1950s, poking fun, among other things, at advertising, beauty contests, liberal education and the power of money – humorous criticism of the freedoms of the West was clearly rare and welcome material to the east of Finland. Larni was so popular that his Moscow publisher put out an English-language booklet entitled *Laugh with Larni* (1973), which was distributed free through Aeroflot at Soviet airports.

In 1996 a total of 202 Finnish works were translated into 27 languages – as far as is known: these statistics are from the Finnish Literature Information Centre (which is part of the ▶Finnish Literature Society), and represent only cases where copyright has been assigned.

The greatest number of translations (38 books), were into English. Next came Swedish and German (24), and Estonian (23), followed by French (20). There were, in total, 77 works of fiction, 53 non-fiction works, 22 anthologies and selections, 14 magazines, 13 plays, 9 children's picture books and 14 radio plays.

The Finnish Literature Information Centre makes annual translation grants to translators and publishers; in 1996 the total sum was FIM 868,000 (US$ 175,000) for 74 projects. Of fiction translations, about 80 per cent received translation grants. The centre also advises the Ministry of Education concerning the annual award of the Government Prize for Translation of Finnish Literature. In 1996 it was worth FIM 50,000 (US$ 10,000).

New translations of Finnish literature are also available in an English-language literary magazine, *Books from Finland*, which appears quarterly. *Books from Finland* carries modern and classic Finnish prose, poetry and non-fiction, with extracts, essays and interviews, and sketches the background cultural debates from which the writing emerges. The magazine was founded by the Finnish Publishers' Association in 1967; it has been published in its present form by Helsinki University Library since 1976. *Books from Finland* is distributed to readers in more than 80 countries, and its circulation is 3500. Its editor-in-chief has, since 1996, been the writer Jyrki Kiiskinen (born 1963). In its present form the magazine has published works by more that 200 writers. SL

Luhta (founded in 1907), leisure-wear company. Luhta has been in the hands of the same Luhtanen family for 4 generations. In the early 20th century its products were work-shirts, trousers and sweaters. The first dress-making workshop was built in 1927, and by the 1930s the business employed more than 200 workers. In the 1950s Luhta became Finland's biggest manufacturer of outdoor clothes. In the 1960s, the fashionability of the company's designs was emphasised, trained designers were employed, and export to the Nordic countries, central Europe and the Soviet Union began. By the 1970s the company was manufacturing at factories in four different locations and employed almost 1500 workers.

Luhta's outdoor and leisure wear, and its workwear and clothing for young people, have achieved their

Leisure-wear from Luhta, winter 1997–1998

worldwide fame through the high standards of their design, and as much as two-thirds of production is exported. Luhta's long-standing designer trio, Seija Haapsaari (born 1940), Riitta Kuparinen (born 1948) and Heljä Tenhiälä (born 1944), have won numerous prizes. In addition to them, the company has employed a large number of other designers.

At the beginning of the 1990s, Luhta bought a number of companies: the leatherwear factory Big L, the leisure-wear company Story, the rainwear manufacturer Rukka, the sportswear company Torstai, and J.A.P., which manufactures clothing for young people. MA

Wivi Lönn

Lönn, Wivi (1872–1966), architect. Wivi Lönn was the fifth woman to qualify as an architect in Finland (1896), and the first to set up her own office. Lönn's first major work was the Finnish Girls' School in Tampere (1902). It was comfortably domestic, according to the new principles which she had learned in England and Scotland. Later, Lönn designed dozens of school buildings around Finland. In 1906 she won the competition for the main fire station in the city of Tampere (1906), which provoked rancour among male colleagues, but the building was, in both practical and artistic terms, a success. Wivi Lönn's particular strength were her skilfully laid-out ground plans. The plan of the Estonia Theatre in Tallinn (1913) was a successful exemple. RN

Wivi Lönn, Tampere Finnish Girls' School, 1899–1902

Lönnrot, Elias (1802–1884) collector of Finnish folk poetry, researcher and writer. Elias Lönnrot was, with ▶J.L. Runeberg and ▶J.V. Snellman, one of the most important figures in the

Elias Lönnrot

Finnish movement of national awakening. He was not only a collector of Finnish folk poetry, the creator of the ▶*Kalevala* and the ▶*Kanteletar*, but also a versatile cultivator of the Finnish language – as researcher, lexicographer, translator and hymn writer.

Lönnrot enrolled at the Academy of Turku in 1822. He took the Väinämöinen poems as the subject of his master's dissertation, thus acquainting himself with all the Finnish folk poetry that had been collected at that time. In the spring of 1827, Lönnrot took his master's degree. The fire of Turku occurred in the autumn of the same year. When the university moved its activity to Helsinki in 1828, Lönnrot began to study medicine. His dissertation *Om Finnarnes magiska medisin* ('On the magical medicine of the Finns') was completed in 1832. Soon after this, he travelled to Oulu, on the coast of Ostrobothnia, to take up the post of assistant district medical officer, from where, in 1833, he moved to Kajaani (1833–1852) as district medical officer.

From 1828 to 1844 Lönnrot made over a dozen research and poem-gathering expeditions that were funded by the ▶Finnish Literature Society.

In 1833 Lönnrot began to edit his collections of folk poetry for publication. This work led to the appearance of *Vanha Kalevala* ('The old Kalevala', 1835), *Kanteletar* (1840), and *Uusi Kalevala* ('The new Kalevala', 1849). Lönnrot also edited works that were based, not only on his own gatherings but also those of others: these included a collection of riddles (1833) and another of proverbs (1842). He produced Finnish translations of two guides to health and hygiene, and edited the remarkable, *Suomalaisen talonpojan Kotilääkäri* ('The Finnish peasant's home doctor', 1839).

Lönnrot was also a journalist. He founded the first Finnish-language periodical, *Mehiläinen* ('The bee'), which appeared from 1836 to 1837, and from 1839 to 1840. In addition to specimens of folk poetry it also contained didactic essays on many subjects, including geography, history, arithmetic and law.

In 1853, Lönnrot was appointed to the post of Professor of Finnish Language and Literature (1853–1862) at the ▶University of Helsinki, and continued his intensive work as a practical cultivator and teacher of the Finnish language. As he translated and edited books he created dozens of new words and terms in various fields, and thereby strove to lead the struggle surrounding Finnish dialects along the path of a more peaceful development.

Lönnrot spent the days of his old age in the province of Sammatti in southern Finland editing a Finnish-Swedish dictionary and completing a new Finnish hymn book. In his latter years he also returned to the field of folk poetry, publishing an extensive collection of Finnish magic poems in 1880.

In his old age Lönnrot was the object of numerous tributes. He was the most approachable of the modern state's great founders. The first statue of Lönnrot, by Emil Wikström (1864–1942), was unveiled in Helsinki in 1902. PLn

man and woman There are just over five million people in Finland, 2.6 million women and nearly 2.6 million men. The number of women exceeds that of men by one hundred thousand, although more boys are born than girls. Because of the higher mortality of men, the male majority becomes a minority after the age of 50. The life expectancy of a woman born in 1995 is 80 years, that of a man 73 years. Finnish women thus live on average seven years longer than Finnish men.

EDUCATION Girls and boys study approximately the same amount, but the pattern of their education is different. After comprehensive school, at the age of 16, more boys apply to vocational schools than girls, who go on to senior secondary schools. After successfully completing the senior secondary school at the age of 18, more boys apply and gain entry to institutions of higher education than girls. Girls apply to vocational and professional education institutions a little more often than to institutions of higher education. In Finland applying simultaneously to a number of different educational institutions, for example a university or a vocational and professional education institution, is commonplace. About half of students matriculating from senior secondary schools, both men and women, apply to institutions of higher education. Of the women senior and secondary school-leavers of 1994 (a total of 17,700), 25 per cent took up studies in vocational and professional education institutions and 25 per cent in institutions of higher education during the same year, while for men (12,500) the corresponding figures were 9 per cent and 23 per cent. In 1994, 55 per cent of new higher education students in Finland were women.

Women form the majority of students in vocational and professional education institutions (or 52 per cent, in 1995) a total of 203,000, and they also number more than half (52 per cent in 1995) of students of higher education (133,000) and (56 per cent in 1995) of graduates (13,500). The spheres of education for men and women are, in general, traditional in both vocational and professional education institutions and institutions of higher education. Women's spheres include the caring professions (health care, social work), pharmacy, teaching, trade and office work and the humanist and aesthetic fields, while men choose primarily technology, communications, economics and forestry.

Men still have more education than women. 54 per cent of them have at least upper secondary-level education, while among women the figure is 52 per cent. Women aged less than 50, however, have more education than men of the same age.

FAMILY Cohabitation as young people's first form of life together increased during the 1980s, and mar-

M

riage age rose: women formed their first marriages, on average, at 27, men at 29. Finnish women gave birth to their first child at 27, on average. The increase in cohabitation has led to the fact that marriage is often entered into only after, or immediately before, the birth of the first child. More than 40 per cent of first-born children and 30 per cent of all children are born to unmarried mothers. Cohabitation is, however, less common in Finland than in the other Nordic countries. Cohabitation is the commonest form of living together among young, childless couples, to the extent that childless couples under the age of 40 are more likely to cohabit than to be married.

A Finnish woman gives birth, on average, to 1.8 children. Among European Union countries, this figure was higher in 1993 only in Ireland and Sweden. Today the average size of a Finnish family is 2.2 children. The mother is the lone parent in 15 per cent of families with children under the age of 18. The father is the lone parent in only 2 per cent of families with children. Finland has the lowest abortion rate in Europe. Teenage pregnancies and births are very rare.

WORKING LIFE Men and women enter working life at approximately the same age, generally between 20 and 24 years. Generally young people between the ages of 15 and 19 are engaged in full-time study. The economic recession of the 1990s has increased unemployment particularly among young people who are seeking to enter working life for the first time. Less than 30 per cent of women in the labour force aged between 20 and 24 are unemployed, while the corresponding figure for men is more than a third. Male unemployment in Finland is greater than female unemployment. At the end of 1996, unemployment among men and women of working age was less than one fifth (16.5 per cent of men, 16.1 per cent of women).

Most women between the ages of 15 and 64 participate in working life (about 70 per cent in 1996). Less than one third (30 per cent) remained outside the labour force in 1996. Among women of working age, 59 per cent were employed, 11 per cent unemployed; 12 per cent were engaged in full-time study, 11 per cent were retired, and only 6 per cent were full-time homemakers. Studying and child-bearing decrease the number of women in the labour force particularly between the ages of 20 and 29. Participation in the labour force is at its highest among women between the ages of 40 and 49 (nine out of ten). Waged work begins to decrease clearly among women between the ages of 55 and 59. Among them, however, six out of ten still participate in working life. Among the over-60s, the proportion declines to 20 per cent.

In addition to their own income, participation in waged work means,

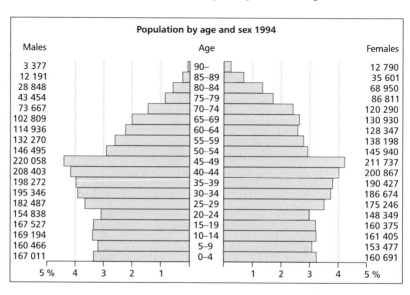

Population by age and sex 1994		
Males	Age	Females
3 377	90–	12 790
12 191	85–89	35 601
28 848	80–84	68 950
43 454	75–79	86 811
73 667	70–74	120 290
102 809	65–69	130 930
114 936	60–64	128 347
132 270	55–59	138 198
146 495	50–54	145 940
220 058	45–49	211 737
208 403	40–44	200 867
198 272	35–39	190 427
195 346	30–34	186 674
182 487	25–29	175 246
154 838	20–24	148 349
167 527	15–19	160 375
169 194	10–14	161 405
160 466	5–9	153 477
167 011	0–4	160 691

5 % 4 3 2 1   1 2 3 4 5 %

Housewarming party, Heinola, 1996: the family remains important in Finland, and family gatherings such as this one are frequent events

for most women, a double working day. Women continue to do most of the household chores. Only about one in ten women (11 per cent in 1996) are engaged in part-time work. The proportion of part-time workers is small compared to, for example, Sweden and Norway, in which between 40 and 50 per cent of women in the labour force are engaged in part-time work. Even mothers of small children are generally in full-time employment. Almost three-quarters of mothers of children under the age of 7 were engaged in wage work in 1993. For mothers, working is made possible by the municipal day-care that is organised for children under school age and by the hot lunches offered by primary schools. In 1996 about 900,000 Finnish women worked as wage and salary earners, in other words in the service of another individual.

The commonest professions for women are in service, educational and care work, such as secretary, office clerk, nurse, laboratory or dental technician, day-care worker, teacher, shop assistant. In other words, at work as at home women are generally engaged in service, educational and care work.

Of Finnish men between the ages of 15 and 64, six out of ten were employed in 1996, 13 per cent were unemployed, 12 per cent in retirement and 11 per cent engaged in study. Men were primarily in full-time employ-

ment. In 1996 only 5 per cent were in part-time employment.

Men's withdrawal from working life also begins after the age of 55. The reason is generally early retirement due to unemployment or disability to work. Three out of four men aged between 60 and 64 no longer belong to the labour force.

In 1996 894,000 Finnish men worked as wage and salary earners, in other words in the service of another individual. Of them, more than half worked in professions such as industry, as chauffeurs or drivers, in construction. Technical professions are highly male-dominated, although the service industries also employ numerically the most men in Finland.

Twice as many men as women work as entrepreneurs. In 1995 there were 304,000 entrepreneurs in Finland, of whom two-thirds were men. The largest group of entrepreneurs is made up of farmers, who form a good third of entrepreneurs (104,000). Two-thirds of them, too, are men, one-third women. In Finland it is the practice in both statistics and taxation that if both husband and wife work primarily on a farm or in farming, they are both considered agricultural entrepreneurs. Of women entrepreneurs in 1995, more than 40 per cent worked in agriculture, one fifth in commerce, and less than one fifth in the service industries. Of male entrepreneurs, 36 per cent worked

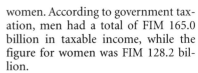

in agriculture, 16 per cent in trade and 12 per cent in the construction industry.

Women's businesses are generally small: shops for everyday needs, hairdressers', laundries, cafés, bars etc. The commonest professions among women entrepreneurs are agricultural entrepreneur, wholesale and retail trader, hairdresser, barber, cosmetologist. The commonest professions among male entrepreneurs are agricultural entrepreneur, company director, driver.

In participating in working life, both men and women also participate in trade union activity: most wage earners belong to the relevant trade union. In 1993–1994 the central wage earners' organisations had almost two million members, of whom more than a million were women. During the economic recession of the 1990s, membership guaranteed an unemployment benefit related to previous income.

WAGES AND INCOMES A divided labour market is a reality in Finland. Differences in wages and salaries reflect it clearly. In 1994 a man in full-time employment received an average wage of FIM 155,000, and a woman FIM 116,000. Men's wages increased nominally by 4 per cent in 1994, women's by almost half that amount, 2.5 per cent. Women's wages levels are thus on average three-quarters those of men. Wages in male-dominated areas such as the metal and paper industries are considerably higher than in female-dominated areas such as the clothing and food sectors. Wages for men and women working in the same area and under the same title are usually clearly differentiated, to the benefit of men.

Looking at taxable income as a whole, the situation is somewhat more balanced. In 1994 the total income of about 1.1 million male wage and salary earners was FIM 116.2 billion. The corresponding figure for women was FIM 86.9 billion. The total income from various types of pensions of women was slightly higher than that of men. This is due to the population distribution. There are about 100,000 women in excess of men aged 65 years or more. The average pension income of men is higher than the average of

women. According to government taxation, men had a total of FIM 165.0 billion in taxable income, while the figure for women was FIM 128.2 billion.

Men had more than twice as much taxable capital income than women. Men's taxable capital income as a whole is more than one third higher, at FIM 283 billion, than women's at FIM 188.1 billion.

POWER AND VOTING In both national and municipal elections, women are more active voters than men: in the 1995 elections, 73 per cent of eligible women voted, as opposed to 71 per cent of men. Women, however, do not stand as candidates in proportion to their ratio of the population. In the last parliamentary election, 39 per cent of candidates were women, and women's share of votes was 37 per cent. Women's share of elected candidates was 33.5 per cent. In municipal elections, women's electoral activity was 72 per cent, and men's 70 per cent; 33.5 per cent of candidates were women, women's share of votes was 36 per cent and of elected candidates 31 per cent.

In the trade unions, power is still concentrated around men. The proportion of women in the leadership of the three largest trade unions in 1993–1996 was between 20 and 33 per cent, although their membership was between 46 and 68 per cent. In working life, men still generally continue to play the leading roles. In 1993 the proportion of women as managers in the private sector was about one fourth, as managers in large firms 11 per cent, and as company and managing directors only 2 per cent. In 1996 the proportion of women among senior management was nearly quarter (24 per cent). ESV

Manner, Eeva-Liisa (1921–1995), writer, poet. Eeva-Liisa Manner is one of the most important modernists of Finnish poetry since the Second World War. Her first collection of poetry appeared in 1944, but it was only with the collection *Tämä matka* ('This journey', 1956) that she broke through to modern, individual expression, and at the same time made a considerable success. In Manner's poetry, a personally

Eeva-Liisa
Manner

felt philosophical and intellectual philosophy, influenced by Martin Heidegger's thought, is combined in a rhythmically and linguistically rich mode of expression. Manner spent long periods in Andalucia, southern Spain, which influenced her work. Her poetry has an important ethical and moral dimension, which is to be seen, for example, in her collection *Fahrenheit 121* (1968). The role and responsibility of the individual in the world are determined both philosophically and politically and lead, in the poems, to both sympathy and anxiety, as in the collection *Kuolleet vedet* ('Dead waters', 1977). Manner also published plays, and a novel, *Varokaa, voittajat* ('Beware, victors', 1972). PL

Mannerheim, C.G.E. (1867–1951), soldier, Marshal of Finland, President of Finland. Carl Gustaf Emil Mannerheim, whose family roots lay in the Netherlands, was born in the ▶manor house of Louhisaari at Askainen southwest Finland, and began his schooling in Helsinki, whence he was expelled on account of his wild behaviour. At his second attempt he gained entry to the Hamina Military College in 1882 but was expelled once more for lack of discipline. Having at last matriculated in 1887, he succeeded in entering the Nikolayev Cavalry School in St Peters-

burg. After graduation, he was appointed to the chevalier guard. He was very much at home in the cosmopolitan atmosphere of St Petersburg.

Mannerheim volunteered for the Russo-Japanese War of 1904–1905, being promoted, for merit on the front, to the rank of colonel. In 1906–1908 the Russian Military Headquarters sent him on a military reconnaissance expedition to Turkestan, China. The strategic and statistical information gathered by Mannerheim remained for the most part unused, but the scientific material he gathered proved very valuable, and is still used in research.

Having worked in Poland on military matters in 1909–1914 and participated in the First World War on the Polish front (1914–1917), Mannerheim left the Russian army after the October Revolution on 1917. On his return to Finland, he led the white army in the Civil War of 1918. During the initial years of Finnish independence (1917–), Mannerheim withdrew from public life, but returned to political activity in 1931, when he was appointed chairman of the Council of Defence. He was Commander-in-Chief during the ▶Winter War and Continuation War (1941–1944), and President of Finland (1944–1946). He was awarded the title of Marshal of Finland in 1942. ML

C.G.E. Mannerheim on a military reconnaissance and research expedition in China, 1906

C.G.E. Mannerheim as Marshal of Finland, 1942

manners ►customs

manor houses The term manor house is used in Finland to denote estates owned by the aristocracy, which enjoyed tax privileges in return for equestrian service. They may be medieval freehold estates, or they may have originated as late as the 17th century as royal gifts. In addition to these ancient estates, there are also manors that originated in a different way, including former *puustelli*s, officers' quarters or the mansions of ironworks-owners. With the passage of time (finally by the 1860s), the difference between aristocratic estates and ordinary estates disappeared, but where manor houses remained in the hands of old families or other members of the aristocracy they preserved features differing from those of peasant village communities and environments. The elegant design characteristic of manor houses also makes them architecturally interesting, and many old manors are classed as historical monuments.

In the medieval period, aristocratic manor houses were built of wood, and none has survived to this day. The Vasa period in the 16th century was a time of expansion for the Finnish aristocracy, and the oldest surviving, stone manor castles date from this period. Among them are Kankainen/Kankas (Masku, near Turku) and Vuorentaka (Halikko, near Turku), both manor houses belonging to the Horn family, which are lived in to this day. The powerful Fleming family built a number of manor castles; Kuitia/Qvidja (Parainen, south-west Finland), Suitia/Svidja (Siuntio, southern Finland) and Sundholma (Uusikaupunki, south-west Finland) survive. In addition it is worth mentioning Karuna (Sauvo, southwest Finland) and Sjundby (Siuntio, southern Finland). The most important parts of all of these date from between 1560 and 1580, although they may also contain older elements. Most of these houses were of two storeys, with the ground floor barrel- or cross-vaulted. In some cases the paired-room system (with rooms on either side of the hallway) was used in the plan. Attempts were made to follow the architectural principles of the Renaissance, although the result is often characterised by an awkwardness attributable to a peripheral view and the difficulty of working granite. The renovations carried out during King Charles's IX (1550–1611) period at Turku Castle, from 1556 to 1563, were highly influential stylistically.

In the latter part of the 17th century, the building of stone fortified buildings as manor houses ceased almost completely. The interest of the great nobles was focussed largely on the defence capabilities of estates in Sweden, and no 17th century Finnish wooden manor buildings survive. The only two significant monuments of this period are Fleming family's Louhisaari/Villnäs (Askainen, south-west Finland), completed in 1655, and Sarvilahti/Sarvlaks (Pernaja, southern Finland), which was taken into use in 1683. Both houses follow the Dutch Palladian style. The buildings' gardens show the regular grouping of the baroque, with their garden paths. Louhisaari is known as the birthplace of Marshal ►C.G.E. Mannerheim; it is owned by the Finnish state and is open to the public as a museum. Sarvilahti is owned by the Society of Swedish Literature in Finland. The main building is still in private use.

After the Great Northern War (1700–1721), from the 1730s onwards, a new flourishing of manor-house architecture begins, during which the baroque Finnish manor house achieves its characteristic form. The first named architect, Chr. Fr. Schröder (1722–1789), also dates from this period; a group of elegant *corps de logis* ensembles were built to his designs, particularly to commissions by rich ironworks owners. Schröder's work includes Fagervik (begun 1762, Inkoo, southern Finland), Lapila (1763, Naantali, southwest Finland), Lempisaari/Lemsjöholm (1763, Askainen, south-west Finland) and Teijo/Tykö (Perniö, near Turku), Viksberg (Paimio, south-west Finland) and Nuhjala (Taivassalo, south-west Finland). All of these are stone buildings, but the large *corps de logis* of Mustio/Svartå (1782–1791, Karjaa, southern Finland) is built of logs. Schröder's design was completed by Erik Palmstedt, city architect of Stockholm, who was the most important designer of the Gustavian neo-

One of Finland's finest renaissance palaces: Louhisaari Manor, Askainen, south-west Finland, 1655

classical style in Sweden. The purest example of the neo-classical style, Jokioinen (1790, Jokioinen, in Häme), is also his design; today it houses an agricultural research centre. Besides these monumental great houses, dozens of modest, single-storey, mansard-roofed, red-painted manor buildings were constructed, their designs often ebased on pattern-books. One example of this type is Pukkila (1760s, Paimio, south-west Finland), which is now a museum.

In the 19th century, manor house architecture received a new appearance with the empire style. Among the most important designers early in the century were Charles Bassi and ▶C.L. Engel. Count G.M. Armfelt's (1757–1814) Joensuu/Åminne (Halikko, near Turku) was renovated to designs by Bassi; the library, in particular, is known as one of the purest examples of its stylistic period in Finland. Engel's architecture is at its most monumental in the main buildings at Vuojoki (1836, Eurajoki, south-west Finland) and Sannäs (1837, Porvoo). The former is now a retirement home, and has thus unfortunately lost its authenticity, and the latter has been unsympathetically restored as a training centre.

The building of manor houses decreased towards the end of the 19th century. Among the few significant examples of this period are Tjusterby (1859, Pernaja, southern Finland), an example of the English gothic style, and Malminkartano/Malmgård (1882–1885, Pernaja, southern Finland), designed by F.A. Sjöström (1840–1885). Saari (in Mäntsälä, southern Finland, now a government agricultural college) was built as late as 1929. Together with Vanajanlinna (1924, in Häme), and the Ruhala manor house (1938, Ruovesi, central Finland), it forms the culmination of the history of Finnish manor house architecture. Changed conditions since the Second World War have led to the disappearance of the surroundings of many manor houses. Nevertheless, in the 1990s around 200 manor houses remained as working estates, and many of their buildings have been designated national monuments. EH

maps The earliest mentions of the existence of Finland in the far north were conveyed to the consciousness of learned men in southern Europe by merchants travelling the northern trade routes. At the end of the medieval period, when the Catholic Church had already extended its influence to Finland, northern areas and their peoples were described in certain maps that were disseminated in manuscript versions.

World-maps preserved as co-ordinate catalogues of Claudios Ptolemy (c. 90–c. 168), a scholar of the Hellenic period, became known to the learned men of southern Europe in the 14th century. The Dane Claudius Clavus published a reconstructed version of Ptolemy's *Geographia* in 1427 with an addition presenting cartographic information about Scandinavia and the north Atlantic. For a century, cartographic information about Finland was to be based on the names *Findlandi* and *Findhlappi*. In Hartmann Schedel's well-known *Liber Chronicarum* of 1493, Finland is cited for the first time in its correct form on a printed European map.

In the Bavarian-born Jakob Ziegler's map of northern Europe, printed in 1532, more than ten names of a recognisable Finland, then part of the Swedish Kingdom, are present. In the map's text appendix, around 100 place-names are cited, with co-ordinates.

The *Carta Marina* published by the last Catholic archbishop of Sweden-Finland, Olaus Magnus (1490–1557), in 1539 presented the geography, habitation, livelihoods, transport connections, fauna and other riches of Finland with exaggerated abundance. The information of Olaus's map continued to influence the cartographic image of Finland, particularly the interior, for centuries. The many variations of this map included in Sebastian Münster's *Cosmographia* conveyed information about Finland to an increasingly large European readership.

A number of Netherlandish cartographers made the far north known in many cartographic publications from the late 16th century. The maps of Gerard de Joden (1570), Abraham Ortelius (1579), Gerard Mercator (1595), Adrian Veen and Jodocus Hondius (1613), and Joannes Janssonius (1645) each marked a gradual improvement in the cartographic image of Finland. The imaging of Finland's coastline became more accurate, but information about the interior continued to be based primarily on Olaus's map.

Andreas Bureus (Anders Bure), who was given the job of directing cartographic work in Sweden-Finland in the early 17th century, was commissioned to draw up a new map of Scandinavia. His map, published in 1626, was based on surveyors' measurements and determinations of position. The many dozens of copies of Bureus's map, among the most advanced of its day, which were published in the next few decades, made Scandinavia and Finland known everywhere where printed maps were published. The *Magnus Ducatus Finlandiae*, or 'Grand Duchy of Finland', published in the Netherlandish cartographer Joan Blaeu's great atlas of 1662, is the first separate map of Finland based on Bureus's map. In this map, Finland, which is de-

Jacob Ziegler, *Qvæ intvs continentvr, Octava tabvla continet Cheronnesum, Schondiam, Regna autem potissima Norvegiam, Sveciam, Gothiam, Finlandiam, Gentem Lapones,* map of the Nordic countries, Strasbourg 1532

Joan Blaeu: Atlas Maior, Magnus Dvcatvs Finlandie ('Grand Duchy of Finland'), Amsterdam, 1662

The first map of
independent Finland.
Finnish Geographical
Society, 1925

picted in some detail, is no longer an eastern province of Sweden among other provinces, but a Grand Duchy comprising seven provinces. Finland was presented in still greater detail in the four regional maps of Finland published by Nicolas Sanson a little later; these, too, were based on Bureus's work.

Throughout the 17th century, the National Land Survey of Sweden drew up increasingly accurate maps, particularly of the southern parts of Finland, but for military reasons these maps were not published. After one of the maps of the Swedish Kingdom had come into the hands of Netherlandish map publishers in the early 18th century, however, information about the Finnish interior became public. In order for navigation to succeed, it had already become necessary to publish sea-charts of all the maritime areas of Sweden-Finland.

S.G. Hermelin, who became director of the National Land Survey of Sweden in the late 18th century, published 30 regional maps of the kingdom, of which five were of Finland. The maps, which were based on geodetic measurements of the terrain, represented the latest developments in the art of surveying.

After the war between Sweden and Russia of 1808–1809, Finland was annexed to the Russian Empire as an autonomous Grand Duchy. Maps of the Grand Duchy, were based geographically – until at least the late 19th century – on Hermelin's maps. After the annexation of Finland by Russia, the area called Old Finland, made up of the government of Viipuri and the province of Käkisalmi, was in turn annexed to the Grand Duchy. This area, entirely inhabited by Finns, had been lost by Sweden to Russia in the early 18th century.

Separation from Sweden also meant, for Finland, disappearance from the map of Scandinavia, on which it had until then appeared. After the annexation by Russia, Scandinavian maps often showed, in place of Finland, some city vignette, other image or map. In the European atlases of the time Finland was from now on to be seen only on a small scale at the north-western extremity of the map of Russia.

In Finland, from the mid 19th century onwards, a number of school atlases with Finnish place-names were published, as well as wall-maps intended as teaching aids. Finnish-language education, which received widespread support, aimed to displace the position of Swedish as the country's official language. The teaching of geography, which developed in many countries as part of popular education, made Finland known in different parts of the world.

At the behest of the Geographical Society of Finland, a collection of maps of Finland and associated statistical information were set out at a geographical congress held in London in 1895. The maps of the exhibition section, which attracted international attention, formed the basis of an extensive atlas of Finland published in 1899. Less than ten years later an extensive social and statistical atlas of the Finnish rural communes, with texts in Finnish, Swedish and French, was published, and in 1910 an entirely new and diversified atlas of Finland, both with extensive explanatory texts. The desire for national independence which strengthened at the turn of the century and the presentation of the Finnish identity in international arenas played their part in the creation of these atlases.

In most atlases published after the First World War, Finland was once more shown alongside Scandinavia. The first atlas published in independent Finland (1925) depicts, in addition to national achievements, a strong western European identity. Finnish cartographic work at that time was based on the latest geodetic surveying techniques of the time.

In the Second World War, Finland was forced to cede, in the peace made with the Soviet Union, the islands of the eastern Gulf of Finland, the Karelian Isthmus and Ladoga Karelia, the Salla area of Lapland and, for a limited period, the Hanko Peninsula.

After the Second World War a great number of new atlases were published throughout the world in which Finland, which had retained its independence, was shown either on a map of its own or with the Scandinavian countries.

In recent decades, many new forms of map and specialist atlases have been published. The rapid development of road travel has led, among other things, to the plentiful publication of road maps showing new roads. Numerous new cartographic methods, with aerial photographs taken from both aeroplanes and satellites, have offered opportunities for many new cartographic applications. The combination of up-to-date satellite information with digital local information systems is opening up new challenges for the cartographic image of Finland in the future. EF

Marimekko In the early 1950s Armi Ratia (1912–1979), who had trained as an applied artist, began to print gaily coloured fabrics on her small printing press in Helsinki. They were enthusiastically received, and the collection of clothes made from them was an immediate success. In 1951 Ratia founded a dressmakers' workshop called Marimekko, for which she employed the young designers Maija Isola (born 1927) to design fabrics and Vuokko Eskolin-Nurmesniemi (born 1930) to design both fabrics and clothes. The clothes were completely different from other clothing of the period. Export

Annika Piha-Rimala, 'Tasaraita' ('Even stripe') T-shirts from the early 1960s, still in production.

Interior, Marimekko-style. Textile *Siren* by Maija Isola, 1967

Vuokko Nurmesniemi, *Piccolo* dress, Marimekko, 1959–1960

markets for Marimekko opened up quite naturally, and the company really took off when the wife of the future President of the United States, Jacqueline Kennedy, bought seven Marimekko dresses from an exhibition held in Boston, making Marimekko an immediate sensation on the new continent. Marimekko flourished, and the dynamic Armi Ratia gathered more talented designers around her. Woollen clothes, knitwear and canvas bags were designed in the natural Marimekko spirit, which for a particular group of people – particularly the academic young and young at heart – became nothing less than a way of life. After an intermediate phase following Armi Ratia's death, Kirsti Paakkanen has continued at the head of the flagship of the Finnish clothing industry. MA

Karita Mattila

Mattila, Karita (born 1960), soprano. Karita Mattila appeared in 1981 at the Savonlinna Opera Festival in W. A. Mozart's *Don Giovanni* as Donna Anna, while still a student. In 1983 she won the First Prize at the Cardiff Singer of the World Competition, and was heard as the Countess in Mozart's *The Marriage of Figaro* at the Finnish National Opera the same year.

Mattila studied at the Sibelius Academy in Helsinki and, from 1984, in London under Vera Rozsa. Since 1986 she has performed regularly with the best conductors in the world. She made her Covent Garden debut as Fiordiligi in Mozart's *Cosí fan tutte*, and has since sung on almost all the world's operatic stages, including the Metropolitan Opera, Hamburg State Opera, Vienna State Opera, Chicago Lyric Opera, the Paris Opéra and the Houston Grand Opera.

Mattila's recordings include Anton Bruckner's *Te Deum* conducted by Bernard Haitink, *The Marriage of Figaro* with Zubin Mehta, Beethoven's Ninth Symphony, *Cosí fan tutte* and *Don Giovanni* with Neville Marriner, Richard Strauss' songs with Michael Tilson Thomas and Jouni Kaipainen's (born 1956) *Stjärnenatten* ('Starry night') with ▶Osmo Vänskä. RL

May Day ▶festivals

medallic art The roots of the Finnish medallic tradition can be found in 18th-century Sweden and 19th-century France. The custom of making medals not only for statesmen and nobles but also for members of the middle classes derives from Sweden, and the first 'Finnish' medals were commissioned from Stockholm by academic circles in Turku around 1800. During the period of Russian rule (1809–1917) they were followed by medals struck in St Petersburg and, from the 1860s onwards, ▶Helsinki. It was, however, the 'renaissance' of this art form in France, with its artistic and technological innovations, that was behind the renewed popularity of the medal in Finland from the late 19th century onward. The issuing of medals to commemorate important persons and events soon found favour among ▶learned societies and other organisations and the Finnish Numismatic Society was founded in 1914, mainly for this purpose. The Finnish Art Medal Society, founded in 1965 has promoted the making of cast medals in particular.

Most Finnish sculptors of note have designed medals. The pioneer was Walter Runeberg (1838–1920), followed by Emil Wikström (1864–1942) and Ville Vallgren (1855–1940). Wäinö Aaltonen (1894–1966), although best-known as a monumental sculptor, made numerous medals between the late 1920s and the early 1960s.

Essi Renvall (1911–1979) established herself in the late 1940s as the most prominent of a new generation of medallists. Her work was innovative but basically traditional. A modern idiom was introduced by Eila Hiltunen (born 1922) and Aimo Tukiainen (1917–1996) in the late 1950s. After a period of non-figurativism there was a return to more conventional forms in the 1970s.

Among the better-known medallists of the recent decades is Kauko

Kari Juva: celebratory medal for the 150th anniversary of the Finnish Literature Society, 1981

Räsänen (born 1926), who has become famous for his 'multi medals', consisting of two or more parts. TT

media art The history of media art in Finland is short – as is that of experimental cinema and art as a whole. From the moment of the birth of video art in the mid 1960s to the beginning of the 1980s there was, with the exception of the activities of the Dimensio Group, which combined scholarship, architecture and art, little interest in the genre. The experimental films (and advertisements) of Eino Ruutsalo (born 1921) and *9 runoa* ('9 poems'), filmed by ▶Risto Jarva in 1957, were a slight base, which was built upon only in the late 1980s and early 1990s in the form of the Helsinki Film Workshop.

Interest in international media art began with the interest of the critic and artist Jan-Olof Mallander (born 1944) in the work of the Korean-born Fluxus artist Nam June Paik. Paik is known as the father of video art. Mallander introduced Paik at the same time as the first media art event was held in Helsinki – Intermedia 1971. At this event, Paik's taped works were shown, as well as a combination of computer and video, DiMI-O built by Erkki Kurenniemi (born 1941).

The DiMI (Digital Musical Instruments) series was made up of sound synthesisers, built by Kurenniemi himself, which could be used to produce audio effects interactively on the basis of video image information. The Di-MI-O version shown at the Elonkor-

jaajat ('The harvesters') event comprised dance filmed by television camera, which produced electronic noises – many of the most important makers of interactive art have used exactly the same idea some two decades later (among them David Rokeby's famous *Very Nervous System*).

In the same year, Kurenniemi pondered the immaterialisation of art in his article, 'Message is Message'. Works 'disappear from the palpable world because they are unnecessary for most of the time', for when 'a work is spoken in programming language, it can be realised whenever and wherever there is an output machine'.

Erkki Kurenniemi's visions of the future did not become concrete only in the interactiveness of DiMI-O. In the mid 1980s he predicted video glasses with which one would be able to watch artificial realities. Soon afterwards the United States VPL company revealed its commercial data helmet and data gloves.

The first images of video art as such were taken in Finland as late as 1982, almost 20 years later than in the international arena. The Turppi Group filmed the performance video *Earth Contacts*, which is now considered the first work of Finnish video art. At the same time, in 1981–1982, in the Old Students' House Gallery in Helsinki began showing of the most important works of European video art. In an exhibition at the Sara Hildén Art Museum in Tampere, in addition to *Earth Contacts*, videos shown included a video of a street performance, *Rahaa*

Marikki Hakola,
Milena-Distanz, 1992

('Money') by the Ö Group. An article included in the catalogue by the German curator Wilf Hergogenrath is the first general account of video art in the Finnish language. Video art came to the notice of a larger public the following year in connection with the ARS '83 exhibition, in which the most important international artists such as Sara Birnbaum and Bill Viola were represented. The same year, Finnish video art was seen for the first time abroad, at the Long Beach Museum of Art in Los Angeles.

In Finnish video culture, the development of video workshops in the mid 1980s – the model was taken from English artists' video workshops – marked an expansion of opportunities for video work and an enormous growth in the number of users. In the 1990s, almost 100 municipal media centres and video workshops were in operation.

Video art played its part in bringing a consciousness of media art as a whole to Finland, at the same time as performance and space-time art were flourishing in the Jack Helen Brut and Homo S groups.

Ambitious works by Marikki Hakola (born 1960) – *PRE* (1984) and *Piipää* (1987) – combined installation and video work (in *Piipää*, also performance and dance) in a way that was already seeking its way out of individual taped works toward a more complete concept of media art. In the mid 1990s Hakola was working with her own production company, Kroma Productions, in collaboration with artists, producing various media works, primarily in conjunction with the Finnish Broadcasting Company.

In 1987 a group of young artists founded MUU, the first artists' association to embrace video art as part of its programme. MUU's name – the word means 'other' – arose logically from the fact that artists working with cross-disciplinary projects and media found themselves having to check the box marked 'other' in applications for government funding and explaining the nature of their work, which is so unlike that of composers, writers or actors. With its active exhibitions programme and debates about inter-disciplinary work and the changed condi-

tions and new opportunities of the changing art field, MUU soon became a very important forum for debate about cultural policies. One of MUU's central projects is the Audio-Visual Ark, which has become the archive and recording centre of Finnish media art.

In the mid 1990s, media art was an essential part of the Finnish art scene and of the art education system. Many museums and galleries consistently showed works and projects by media artists. In addition to MUU and the Audio-Visual Ark, the ▶Finnish Museum of Contemporary Art, focussed on the development of the performance culture of media art. PR

mentality At the core of a historically developing national mentality is an image of humanity, a concept of the Finn. In his book *Maamme kirja* ('The book of our land', 1875), ▶Zacharias Topelius remarked that a stranger arriving to Finland would note that 'the inhabitants of this country are very much like one another'. For Topelius, Finns do not merely present themselves and behave similarly; they are similar. As well as the influence of living conditions, there is also a mark with which 'God has branded the Finnish people'. The Topelian Finnish people have ten characteristics: fear of God; perseverance, toughness and strength; patience, self-denial and vitality; calmness; heroism and fitness for battle; tenacity and stubbornness; obedience to authority; phlegm and hesitation; love of freedom; and thirst for and love of knowledge.

Although, since Topelius, new attributes have been added to Finnishness, there has often been a desire to use them to point to some entirety, either a given national character or a historically developed unified culture, an identity-creating rule of interpretation with whose help a Finn can recognise another Finn. In the most recent cultural research, the assumption of authentic Finnishness has been abandoned, but in popular culture expressions are still used in which a Finnish person's individual self merges with the national self.

Ever since the nation was being formed, in the 19th century, debate about Finnishness has been a structur-

Encounter in the snow: the Finns' egalitarian mentality is in dynamic balance with their love of solitude

al component of the work of creating a national identity and of political rhetoric. In the 1870s, when the Fennomanes – who emphasised Finnish language and culture – created a politically expedient ►image of Finland, they – irrespective of differences in policy – always leaned upon the idea of the existence of an integrated will of the people. A strong link was created between Finnishness and its fundamental homogeneity.

Another component part of Finnishness was created in 1905, after the general strike, when class society gave way before universal and equal suffrage, the new civil societies, the political parties and the unicameral parliament. The modern concept of citizenship was created by those ►popular movements whose ideal was not so much the free individual as the member of a movement, faithfully bound to his own collective. A strong bond of meaning was born between citizenship and collective solidarity. Correspondingly, the link between the individual and citizenship has been weak. In Finland, citizens' rights have, as it were, protected a group of members, not individuals. Even modern equality has been realised within the circle of conformity, demanding groups that cultivate unanimity.

The first phase of the modern civic society ended with Finland's declaration of independence from Russia in 1917 and in the Civil War of 1918, in which the nation was divided into Reds and Whites. The unbroken value of national solidarity was shattered by the bloody conflict. After the Civil War, national conformity was reinstated, but the conflict of 1918 became a national trauma for Finland, which is worked over again and again, and because of which the avoidance of internal social conflict has been one of the cornerstones of the domestic politics of independent Finland.

The cultural articulation of the social order, too, has avoided the expression of over-strong differences. It is not possible to find in Finnish culture a hierarchy that produces recognisable classes of taste. In Finland, very different matters and people can meet on the same level, respecting one another democratically and avoiding open conflict.

In more recent cultural research, Finland is, indeed, considered a homogeneous and 'low-context' culture: the sign-system is small, and the meanings of expressions are unambiguous. People and things are limited as they seem.

A conformist culture has proved no hindrance to modern individuation. Under the moral pressure to conform, however, individuation has been experienced as an exacting struggle for survival to protect one's own separate autonomy. In Finland, there has been a tension between the modern, freely self-fulfilling individual and the nationally binding, conformist cultural ethos; this has even been said to cause depression, anxiety and self-destructive tendencies.

The uniformly constructed Finnish mentality can be described psychoanalytically as a model in which a severe and collectively charged super ego watches over the actions of a weakly independent and fragile ego. This collectivist model has been, in Finland, both a limitation and a great source of strength. It has suffocated individual feeling for life and entrepreneurship. But it has also made possible the unanimous construction of society, the heroic struggle of the ▶Winter War against an overwhelming enemy and a political consensus with whose help one of the world's most highly developed ▶welfare states was created in Finland.

As the 20th century draws to a close, the construction of conformist culture, collective mentality and political consensus has begun to change. The national self and the individual self are distinguishable. Among the generations who grew up in the safe atmosphere of the welfare state, Topelian God-fearingness, self-denial, slowness and self-will are giving way. A new Finnish mentality is developing, believing in individuality, amused, self-assured and sociable. It is a diverse entirety that makes use of its low-context culture as an arena for rapid innovation, primitive creativity and inventiveness.

Although the homogeneous Finnish mentality described by Topelius has indeed crumbled, the stranger arriving in Finland will note that, diverse as the contemporary citizens of this country are, their attitude to one another is driven by one common characteristic: recognition of people's equality. In Finland, the equal value of all citizens is always set above cultural hierarchies. JE

Veijo Meri

Meri, Veijo (born 1928), writer. Veijo Meri was the son of a non-commissioned officer in Viipuri. His novel *Manillaköysi* ('The manila rope', 1957) was a pioneering work of Finnish modernist prose that broke the realist mainstream and questioned with the rational mastery and objectivity of re-

ality. In their place came an unpredictable and sometimes absurdist view of the world. Military life, in both peacetime and wartime, is a theme to which Meri has often returned. *Manillaköysi* is set in wartime, but the war and the stories about it are divested of their nationalist and ideological significance. The same is true of Meri's Civil War novel, *Vuoden 1918 tapahtumat* ('The events of 1918', 1960). The new Finnish prose was influenced both by American literature (including Hemingway) and the new French novel. Meri prefers relatively short narratives, and has written a number of plays that belong among the best of modern Finnish drama. He has also written a large number of personal essays, and published historical books and biographies (▶Aleksis Kivi, ▶C.G.E. Mannerheim). PL

metalwork Before the 17th century, when Finland's first ironworks, ▶Fiskars, was founded, Finnish country smiths obtained the iron they needed largely from pig-iron furnaces using lake ore. The first blast furnaces were taken into use in the 16th century. The manufacture of factory-made tools began in connection with ironworks. Designs were taken directly from traditional, hand-made tools. The first factory to manufacture tools and cutlery was Fiskars. In the 1890s two factories were founded to compete with Fiskars: Kellokoski Factory, which made tools, in 1891, and the Sorsakoski Factory of Hackman Ltd, which specialised in cutlery and other metal domestic goods.

Eric O.W. Ehrström (1881–1934) is considered the pioneer of modern metalwork in Finland. His most important works were carried out in connection with projects by the architects Herman Gesellius (1874–1916), Armas Lindgren (1874–1929) and ▶Eliel Saarinen. Ehrström also designed some jewellery and objects in precious metals. In general, such objects, which were made in small workshops and, from the early 20th century, in factories such as Hopeatehdas, Suomen Kultaseppä and Kultakeskus, followed traditional designs for a long time. A new contribution was brought after 1917 by the goldsmiths who had

Antti Nurmesniemi, coffee pot, enamelled steel, 1958

Bertel Gardberg, cocoa pot, silver, teak, 1958

worked in St Petersburg and moved to Finland after the Russian Revolution.

The first company to produce lamps was the art forge Koru in 1907. Antoher company with design ambitions was Taito Ltd (1918–1953). Taito, whose artistic director was Paavo Tynell (1890–1973), best-known as a lighting designer, manufactured both lighting and silver objects that demanded a high calibre of professional skill. Silver designers before the Second World War include Henry Ericsson (1898–1933), Runar Engbom (1908–1965) and Gunilla Jung (1905–1939).

Since the Second World War, the unquestionable leader in Finnish metalwork has been the silversmith Bertel Gardberg (born 1916). His silver objects and jewellery combine a solid plasticity of design with virtuosic craftmanship. In addition to his unique pieces, Gardberg transformed the design of Finnish cutlery in the 1950s. He worked in collaboration with both Fiskars and Hackman factories. The steel *Carelia* range Gardberg designed for Hackman soon became a classic, and is still in production. Other designers who have worked with metal objects since the 1950s include the silversmith Mauno Honkanen (born 1931), the designers Börje Rajalin (born 1933), Eero Rislakki (born 1924), Antti Nurmesniemi (born 1926), ▶Timo Sarpaneva, ▶Nanny Still and

▶Tapio Wirkkala. Among the designers of the younger generation are Pekka Pietikäinen (born 1945), Olli Tamminen (born 1944) and Karin Bonde Jensen (born 1960). MaA

Midsummer ▶festivals

minorities ▶Finland-Swedes, foreigners in Finland, Jews, Romanies, Russians, Sámi, Tatars,

Missale Aboense The medieval missal of the diocese of Turku, the *Missale Aboense*, is the first example of printed literature in Finland, and the country's only incunabula. It was printed in 1488 by Bartholomaeus Ghotan, who was one of the most important Lübeck printers of the incunabula age and had printed the first missals in Germany in 1479 and 1480. The *Missale Aboense* was commissioned by Konrad Bitz (died 1489) the bishop of the diocese of Turku, and the book contains his foreword. The *Missale Aboense* is a typical Dominican missal; the editorial work was carried out by Daniel de Egher, Prior of the Dominican Convent of Wesel. Finnish features are, in addition to Bitz's foreword, a calendar of the diocese of Turku and an anonymous woodcarving linked with the foreword that shows the patron saint of Finland, ▶Saint Henry, with his murderer, ▶Lalli, at his feet, accompanied by Bishop Konrad Bitz and the

Missale Aboense, illuminated page, 1488

cathedral dean, Magnus Särkilahti (died 1500).

It has been estimated that some 120 copies of the *Missale Aboense* were printed, of which none has survived complete. A facsimile edition was published in 1971 on the basis of the surviving copies, and again in celebration of the 500th anniversary of the *Missale Aboense* in 1988. JN

Rauni Mollberg

Mollberg, Rauni (born 1929), film director, member of the Academy of Finland. Rauni Mollberg went to drama school, worked as an actor and director in provincial theatres and as a director of television drama before his first film, *Maa on syntinen laulu* ('The earth is a sinful song', 1973), which was an adaptation of the forcefully primitive first novel, a ballad of a Lapp girl and her doomed love by Timo K. Mukka (1944–1973). The film became Mollberg's breakthrough, a considerable public success and one of the best-known Finnish films abroad. Mollberg returned to Mukka's world in *Milka* (1980), having made an adaptation of the texts of the brilliant humorist Aapeli (Simo Puupponen, 1915–1967) in *Aika hyvä ihmiseksi* ('Quite good for a human', 1977), and subsequently a new version of *Tuntematon sotilas* ('The unknown soldier', 1985), from the monumental novel by ►Väinö Linna. The individual and nature, the struggle of the individual with forces of nature and with his desires, are among Mollberg's central themes, treated with a realistic and expressive naturalism with which he links people to their northern landscape and strips them of their illusions and of their veneer of culture. ST

Arctic hysteria in Rauni Mollberg's *Maa on syntinen laulu* ('The earth is a sinful song', 1973)

monasteries Both monastic institutions active in Finland at present belong to the ►Orthodox confession: the Monastery of New Valamo and the Convent of Lintula. Both are located in the municipality of Heinävesi in eastern Finland. They were evacuated during the Second World War from ►Karelia, near St Petersburg, the former from an island in Lake Ladoga, the latter from the Karelian Isthmus. At the same time two other Orthodox monasteries that had existed on what was then Finnish soil were evacuated, the Monastery of Konevitsa, on an island of the same name in Lake Ladoga, and the Monastery of Petsamo in the far north, on the shores of the Arctic Sea. Their activities are at present at a halt.

The Orthodox monastic system in Finland is, at its deepest roots, Byzantine. According to ecclesiastical tradition, Byzantine monks were among the founders of the monasteries of both Valamo and Konevitsa. The monasteries' religious tradition and rules nevertheless follow the Slavic pattern.

Scholars are not unanimous as to the foundation date of the oldest monastery, Valamo. Today the most widespread theory is that the monastery was founded in the early 14th century, but a date as early as the 12th century has also been suggested. Konevitsa was founded at the end of the 14th century, the Monastery of Petsamo in the 16th century and the Convent of Lintula in 1895.

The inhabitants of all these monastic institutions were, for a long time, Russian; Karelian or Finnic monks and nuns are hardly known. The Fennicisation of the monasteries began after the Second World War, and only since the 1970s has it been possible to speak of Valamo and Lintula as clearly Finnish monasteries.

This Fennicisation coincided with a strong reconstruction of the monastic institution. After the Second World War Valamo, where the monks of Petsamo had also been evacuated, Konevitsa and Lintula were located on farmsteads that they had bought for their use. Konevitsa ceased to function in the 1950s, but Valamo and Lintula began to be transformed from farmsteads to something more closely resembling monastic institutions. This

The new Orthodox monastery of Valamo (above and below)

construction, in which Byzantine models were used, was completed in the 1990s.

Valamo and Lintula are in many respects very different monastic institutions. Tourism is essential to Valamo, and in addition the monastery offers an open college, a library with research facilities and a conservation institute. Lintula's main source of income is the manufacture of candles for the Orthodox Church. Lintula is not isolationist, but neither does it seek extensive publicity.

The number of inhabitants of each monastic institution has remained constant for the past couple of decades: the number in Valamo is about ten, in Lintula a little more. TL

money The Finnish word for money, *raha*, originally means 'fur', a fact that reflects the importance of fur trade in earlier times. Metallic currency was at first an import commodity, the value of which depended on its intrinsic worth. Swedish rule led to the implantation of the Swedish monetary system, while the Russian period (1809–1917) saw a gradual development toward a national currency based on the silver, and later the gold, standard.

The earliest coins found in Finland are imports from the south: a handful of Roman silver and copper coins, mainly from the second century A.D., and a few late Roman gold *solidi* from the fifth and sixth centuries. During the later Iron Age (800–1150) coinage, still imported, came to play a somewhat more prominent role in Finnish society. Finds from that period consist of some 7000 silver coins, most of them Arabic, Anglo-Saxon and German.

The finds also include a number of primitive imitations of Byzantine and Arabic coins, and some of them are clearly of local origin. Finnish imitations seem to have been made during the first half of the 11th century, perhaps mainly to be used as amulets.

When Finland was incorporated into Sweden during the 12th and 13th centuries, it began to participate in the Swedish monetary system, which was based on the Swedish *mark* and *öre* and, from 1776, the *riksdaler*. In southern Finland, Livonian money was also used in the medieval period. During the 15th and 16th centuries there was a mint in Turku, but minting was not continuous.

From the early 17th century to 1776, Swedish currency was based on both silver and copper. In 1661–1667, 'Stockholms Banco' issued the first banknotes in Europe The bank had a branch in Turku, and so we know for certain that the notes were put into circulation in Finland too. In the 18th century, paper money came to play an increasingly important role, and during the last decades of Swedish rule there were even local notes in circulation in Finland.

After the conquest by Russia in 1808–1809, the rouble was proclaimed the monetary unit of Finland. A bank was founded in 1811, and as there was a shortage of currency, it was given the right to issue notes, at first however only in small denominations. In 1840, following a similar reform in Russia,

One mark 1866, silver. The first Finnish coins were minted in Helsinki in 1864

500-Finnmark note
of 1922, designed by
Eliel Saarinen

Finnish rouble notes became redeemable in silver, and at the same
time the bank assumed the name of
the Bank of Finland. During the Crimean War however, in 1854, the bank
was compelled to cease redeeming its
notes, and in the following years the
value of paper money fluctuated and
metallic currency disappeared from
circulation. The problem was mainly
caused by the Russian rouble notes,
which in Finland had the same status
as Finnish ones. In 1859, the Finnish
Senate appealed to the Emperor and
petitioned that Russian paper money
should no longer be current in Finland according to its nominal but to
its real value. It was also claimed that
even in normal circumstances, the
rouble was too high a monetary unit
for Finland.

The result was that Finland gained a
monetary unit of its own. It was originally conceived merely as a subdivision
of the rouble, but when the notes of the
Bank of Finland in 1865 again became
redeemable for silver and subsequently
for gold, and a corresponding reform
in Russia was postponed to 1897, the
rouble gradually ceased to be legal tender in Finland. During the period of
the gold standard, silver roubles could
circulate in Finland only as change, and
gold roubles and Russian banknotes
were accepted at the current rate. Vari-

ous measures taken by the Russian authorities to re-establish the position of
the rouble in Finland were only partly
effective.

The proposal made in 1859 concerning the value of the Russian notes
was rejected in St Petersburg but,
somewhat surprisingly, the idea of a
new monetary unit met with a positive
response – presumably partly because
the benefits of a smaller unit were at
that time also being discussed in Russia. On 4 April 1860, the mark *(mark-
ka)*, divided into 100 *pennis* and worth
a quarter rouble, was confirmed as the
currency of Finland.

The first mark notes were issued already in 1860, but coins could not be
struck until 1864, when the Mint of
Finland commenced operation. The
coin series consisted of seven denominations in silver and copper, ranging
from one penni to two marks.

A solution to the original problem,
that of the Russian paper money, was
not found until 1865, when Russian
and Finnish silver coins became the
only 'legal' currency of Finland. The
renewed silver standard did not, however, last long: after a decline in the
price of silver, Finland followed the example of several European countries in
adopting, in 1877 the gold standard.
A reform was carried out, giving the
mark the same value as the French
franc – which in practice only meant
the confirming of an earlier *de facto*
parity. Gold coins in denominations of
10 and 20 marks were now put into
circulation, but the redeeming of the
banknotes in gold was suspended after
the outbreak of the First World War.
After 1917 even silver was replaced
with coins struck in cupro-nickel and
later in other base metals.

The present-day 50-Finnmark note bears the
image of the architect Alvar Aalto

Between 1914 and 1920 the mark lost more than nine-tenths of its value, and another period of severe inflation followed during the wars of 1939–1945. The gold standard was restored in 1925, but following the international depression it had to be abandoned again in 1931. The measure was intended to be temporary, but it was extended until the monetary reform of 1963, when the value of the mark was no longer defined in gold. The main purpose of the reform was, however, to introduce a 'new' mark which was equal to one hundred old ones. According to the monetary law of 1993, the external value of the mark is defined on the basis of the currencies of the European Union. TT

Moomin products, Hackman-Arabia

Moomins The Moomins are the imaginary family of trolls created by the writer ▶Tove Jansson. The family's life is followed in eight story books, four picture books and countless comics series (the design of which she later left to her brother, Lars Jansson, born 1926).

The first Moomin was Moomintroll, whose outward form was created in the early 1930s. His initial role was as a *nom de plume* or identification mark in the humorous drawings Jansson made for the political satire magazine *Garm*. During the ▶Winter War Moomintroll acquired his name on becoming the main character in the first Moomin book (*The Moomins and the Great Flood*, 1945). In this story his parents also appeared for the first time.

The Moomins live in a valley, whose landscape is reminiscent of the bushy eastern inner archipelago of the Gulf of Finland. The blue, turreted Moomin house is like a tiled stove. It is a reminder of the Moomins' past, when they lived behind the stoves of people's houses. As confirmation of this, in the book *Moominland Midwinter* (1957) Moomintroll meets one of his forefathers. The latter – clearly more primitive than the pale, velvet fluff-covered Moomins – is a small, black, long-haired creature.

From the 1930s to the 1970s the form of the Moomins changed to some extent on account of differences in drawing technique and thematic development. Their long, sharp noses became rounded, their mouths disappeared beneath them, and their figures grew plump.

Moominpappa is initially an orphan child who is left together with his memoirs (*The Exploits of Moominpappa*, 1950) wrapped in newspaper on the stairs of a children's home. In his youth he roams the oceans of the world. He meets his wife one stormy night when a breaker throws her on to the shore. Soon the couple have a child, Moomintroll, and then the parents are separated by a flood (*The Moomins and the Great Flood*, 1945). Once this has been resolved, they move to Moomin Valley, and soon the family is joined by other members, adopted children, neighbours and friends: Sniff, the wandering Snufkin, Little My, the siblings Snork and Snork Maiden.

The whole Moomin family is largely modelled on examples from Tove

The Moomins at table (clockwise): Moominpappa (in top hat), Moominmamma, Moomintroll, Whomper, Little My, the Snork Maiden, Misabel, *Moominsummer Madness*, 1958

Jansson's own family. The Moomins do not do 'real' work but live on invisible wealth, like the Finland-Swedish patrician and artist families at the beginning of the 20th century. They are tolerant and Bohemian and are not startled by sudden changes in their lives.

Moominpappa is reminiscent of the sculptor Viktor Jansson (1886–1958). Both are melancholic artist types, who are cheered up by emergency situations and take their children to watch fires, thunderstorms and stormy seas. There is a perpetual struggle within Moominpappa between a respectable paterfamilias and a lonely adventurer.

The character of Moominmamma is that of Signe Hammarsten Jansson (1882–1970), who was also an artist (among other things, she designed postage stamps and banknotes for the Finnish state) but who throughout her life took a secondary role for the sake of her husband's work, their home and family. Like her, Moominmamma is both an efficient housewife and loyal mother, and an artist. Usually her creativeness is of an everyday, practical kind, but from time to time (as in the book *Moominpappa At Sea*, 1965) it throws her into a personal crisis, in which she demands her own space as an artist.

Moomintroll may be considered a self-portrait of the writer herself. The character, in the process of growing out of childhood into puberty, is often in its modern, uncertain, illogical intolerance also a prototype of destructive modern man. Moomintroll does not grow any further than adolescence – at that point, Jansson thought it best to end the series and move to adult prose.

Although Moomintroll's parents are clearly sexualised, he himself is a peculiarly androgynous figure, and so are his closest friends. The friendship of Moomintroll and Too-ticky (*Moominland Midwinter*, 1957) is a beautiful portrait of the beginning of the relationship between Tove Jansson and her companion, the artist Tuulikki Pietilä (born 1917), which has lasted for many decades.

In the books the Moomins usually experience adventures or disasters (a flood, a comet that threatens the earth, a hurricane, a sea-monster), which involve a journey and a return home. In the end the lives of the Moomins always settle back into security, and the books invariably end with general celebration. SA

Museum of Contemporary Art The Museum of Contemporary Art was founded in 1990, and is part of the ▶Finnish National Gallery. Its speciality is Finnish and international art, beginning in 1960, which marked the most important turning point in Finnish art after the Second World War. In addition to traditional paintings, sculpture, graphics and installations, the collections contain a large amount of art produced by electronic means (film, video, multimedia) and performances and other events in recordings of various kinds, for example on CD-ROM. The museum's new building Kiasma, which will be completed in 1998, is designed by the New York architect Steven Holl. MLR

Steven Holl, Kiasma, The Museum of Contemporary Art, Helsinki, 1998

museums It is said that Finland has the world's greatest density of museums per capita. In 1990s the number of museums was almost 1000, which means one museum per 5000 inhabitants. Most, however, are small local museums, founded since the Second World War. Four million people visit museums every year; almost half of the population visits a museum at least once a year.

The basis for museum activity began to develop at the end of the 16th century, when the state began to document historical memories. As early as the 17th and 18th centuries it was required that fixed ancient monuments,

Nineteenth-century interior, Kalanti local museum, south-west Finland

ruins, excavation finds and material that had been in the keeping of the church should be declared and preserved, but the first statute for the preservation of ancient memories was passed only in 1883.

In the 1870s and 1880s students at the University of Helsinki participated enthusiastically in the gathering of ethnographical objects, including in the form of an exhibition in 1876. In 1893 it was announced that the collections that had been formed by different bodies would be united to create the Finnish Historical Museum. This received its own building and took the name ►National Museum of Finland in 1916.

Various collections were also begun from the mid 19th century outside the capital. Finland's oldest local museum is believed to be the Raahe Museum, which was founded in 1862 by a local doctor who found his inspiration in Paris and London. It was a couple of decades before Raahe's example was followed by other towns, but by the end of the century 12 towns, or one-third of towns in Finland, had their own museums. Today town and city museums, of which 20 also function as provincial museums, form the backbone of Finland's museological institutions.

The starting point of art galleries was the Finnish Art Society, founded in 1846. It soon began to amass its own collection of art, which was placed on permanent public display in 1863. This also considered the year of foundation of the ►Finnish National Gallery. Finland's first purpose-built museum building is the ►Ateneum, built to house the Finnish National Gallery in 1887.

In 1995 there were 65 public art museums in Finland, providing an even coverage of the entire country. Of these, 16 functioned as regional art museums. After the Finnish National Gallery, the oldest gallery of Finnish art is the Turku Art Museum (1904). Contemporary art, including international works, are the speciality, in addition to the ►Finnish National Gallery, of the Sara Hildén Art Museum (opened in 1978) in Tampere and the Pori Art Museum (opened in 1979).

Fifty per cent of Finnish museums, however, are devoted to cultural history. The commonest museum type is the open-air museum, most often the so-called building museum, which may include, for example, a farmhouse with its farmyard. The core of the museum is generally an 18th- or 19th-century building preserved on its original site, around which buildings from elsewhere have been gathered. There are around 250 museums of this type. The most important is ►Seurasaari Open-Air Museum, founded in 1909 in Helsinki on the Swedish model, which preserves typical buildings from different parts of Finland. Another important group is made up of workers' housing and town areas, which generally represent the beginning of the 20th century. These include the Kuopio Open Air Museum (opened in 1972) and the Worker's Museum of Amuri in Tampere (opened in 1974). An exception is Luostarinmäki Handicraft Museum in

Turku (opened in 1940), a unique 18th-century artisans' city area which survived the fire which destroyed the rest of the city in 1827.

Besides the ▶National Museum of Finland, important museums of cultural history include Turku Provincial Museum (opened in 1881), located in the medieval Turku Castle, and Porvoo Museum (founded in 1896), whose premises are the 18th-century town hall. A curiosity is formed by around 100 small local museums which function in old parish grain stores, generally located close to the church.

In Finland, museum premises are generally old, disused buildings such as castles, barracks, mansions, rectories, schools, banks and hospitals and, particularly from the 1990s onward, industrial buildings. Only about 40 museums are housed in new buildings.

Finnish museums began their strongest development in the 1960s and 1970s, when around 200 new museums were opened and amateurishness was replaced by hard professional skills. Development in the entire area is overseen by the National Board of Antiquities, founded in 1972 and the central museum of cultural history, the National Museum of Finland, which functions under its authority. The museums of natural history of the University of Helsinki were formed into the Finnish Museum of Natural History in 1989. The central national museum for art musems has been, since 1990, the Finnish National Gallery. Matters in common, including information, marketing and training, have since 1923 been the responsibility of the Finnish Museums Association.

Half of the museums are owned and funded by municipalities. Central government contributes around 38 per cent, and provincial museums and regional art museums receive permanent funding. Specialist museums of national importance also receive central government funding. A number of specialist museums are also of international importance, including the Design Museum of Finland (opened in 1874) and the Museum of Finnish Architecture (opened in 1956) in Helsinki, the ▶Sibelius Museum (opened in 1926) in Turku and the ▶Alvar Aalto Museum (opened in 1973), which is located in a building designed by Aalto himself in Jyväskylä, and, the newest arrival, the Finnish Forestry Museum and Information Centre Lusto (opened in 1994) at Punkaharju in eastern Finland. MLR

music ▶classical music, folk music, jazz, opera, popular music, rock'n'roll

Mustonen, Olli (born 1967), pianist, composer. Olli Mustonen is one of the foremost young Finnish musicians. He began studying the piano, harpsichord and composition at the age of five.

Success in the Geneva Competition for young soloists in 1984 was the springboard for an important international career. Among the orchestras with which Mustonen has appeared as soloist are the Chicago Symphony Orchestra, the Cleveland Symphony Orchestra, the Philadelphia Symphony Orchestra, the Los Angeles Philharmonic Orchestra, the London Philharmonic Orchestra and the Tokyo NHK Orchestra. In the spring of 1997 he made his debut with the New York Philharmonic Orchestra.

Composition is, for Mustonen, as important a mode of expression as performance. Among his most important works are the *Fantasia* for piano and strings, the *Toccata* for piano and string quintet, and a work commissioned by the Wigmore Hall, London, the *Nonetto* for strings. A concert of Mustonen's compositions was held at the Helsinki Festival in 1996. RL

Muurame The joinery factory Muuramen Tuolitehdas was founded in central Finland in 1903. The big sellers of the factory's early production were adaptable birch reproductions of Viennese chairs, which were awarded a prize at a national industrial exhibition in St Petersburg in 1908. From time to time most of the factory's products were sold to Russia.

One of the keywords of the design of the period of post-war reconstruction was standardisation. Muurame responded to the challenge in the early 1960s by bringing on to the market the *Moduli* ('Module') range of furniture, which the interior architect Pirkko Stenros (born 1928) had been developing over the previous ten years.

Olli Mustonen

Pirkko Stenros, Muurame, *Moduli* interior of childrens room, 1960s

Marketed as timeless and extremely simplified in form, the *Moduli* range included furniture suitable for spaces of all kinds; the pieces were easily combined or used in different ways as circumstances changed. The range included furniture for children's rooms, living rooms and offices; in the 1960s, with its fresh colours, it symbolised a youthful lifestyle. The *Moduli* range remained Muurame's best-selling line for decades. Muurame, which, in addition to domestic furniture, subcontracted items for public spaces, was felled by the bankrupty of the large Wärtsilä-Meriteollisuus conglomerate in 1991. MaA

mythology In 1551, ▶Michael Agricola published a list of old Finnish gods in the foreword to his Finnish translation of the *Psalter*. In this list are reflected the cultural differences between western and eastern Finland: among the gods from Häme in the west, he listed nature spirits, guardian spirits and human possessions, divinities associated with the sun and lunar phases, as well as a dead child being which haunted the living, Liekkiö. Väinämöinen and Ilmarinen, which also emerge quite visible in the later tradition, appear here respectively as 'the forger of song' and the weather god of travellers.

The Karelian gods, on the other hand, are characterised by a specific link to economic sources of livelihood: rye, oats, barley, various root crops as well as flax and hemp, all had their own patron divinities. The divine pair Ukko and his wife Rauni guaranteed that the grain would grow. Agricola mentions a sowing festival dedicated especially these gods in which a central cult object was 'Ukko's bushel'; the cult itself

was associated with sexual rites and ritual intoxication, the disgracefulness of which was particularly noted by the author. Hunters and cattle farmers also had their own patron divinities. At the end of the list Agricola mentions more generally that the Finns also worshipped, among other things, 'stones, tree stumps, the stars and moon'.

Agricola's fragmentary information has served as the basis for research into Finnish mythology. It was supplemented in the 1700s by Christfrid Ganander's (1741–1790) *Mythologia Fennica* (1789) and Erik Lencqvist's (1719–1808) *De superstitione veterum Fennorum theoretica et practica* (1782). Later researchers were able to use archaeological finds, petroglyphs, and for example the records of witch trial proceedings. An important source is nonetheless the oral tradition which appeared chiefly in poetic metre and which began to be collected for the Folklore Archive of the ▶Finnish Literature Society in the time of A.J. Sjögren (1794–1855) and ▶Elias Lönnrot. The epic which Lönnrot compiled from these poems doubtless reflects the ancient Finnish world view, but as a secondary source it does not qualify as a source for research of a religious studies nature.

In the old Finnish poems, an archaic world view of multiple dimensions can be perceived: conceptualisations of the origin of the world and its structure, the constituitive deeds of cultural heroes as well as those fundamental events to which the current system can return. Incantation poetry and its epic elements in particular appear to have preserved authentic mythic information concerning the origin of things. A central element of the Finnish *tietäjä* (seer's or healer's) expert knowledge was control over and use of precisely this information with regard to both individuals and the community in crisis situations. The Väinämöinen of the ancient poems is, in fact, not only a god and hero, but also a *tietäjä* and shaman (▶shamanism), and as such, moves about in the 'other world' in animal form to search out 'words', i.e. information concerning the origins of objects and animate beings.

The central themes of Finnish mythology are in many ways associated

Fish god, Eno, Marjovaara, northern Karelia, late 19th century

with a universal heritage. The creator god (often Väinämöinen) creates the world from the egg of a water bird, or from the mire brought up from the floor of a primeval ocean by a water bird or devil. At the centre of the world grows an enormous tree, The Great Oak, and the skies are propped up by the world pillar, which is in turn fixed to the North Star. The Tuonelanjoki River separates the world of the living from the realm of the dead. Cultural heroes perform deeds of a creative and fundamental nature: Väinämöinen gives humanity music and lays the foundations for agriculture; Ilmarinen appears as the bringer of fire and as a skilled blacksmith; the story of Lemminkäinen is an Arctic version of the myth of a god who dies and is resurrected. One of the most puzzling mythic subjects is the tale of the Sampo, a magic mill which continuously produces money and wealth. In order to gain posession of this Sampo, the heroes of the ▶Kalevala wage war against the people of Pohjola and their female leader, Louhi.

In scholarly circles there have appeared radically divergent perspectives concerning the issue of whence the elements of the Finnish folk worldview originated. One school of thought emphasises the part played by eastern traditions – the Finno-Ugric tradition and the ▶Orthodox Church, while another points to the Scandinavian tradition and to the old trade links with

central Europe. It is not difficult to perceive that Christianity, in both its eastern and western forms, was adapted easily to a new context and Catholic saints were adopted into the old folk belief tradition in Finland as they were in many other places. With regard to the older elements of the world view in question, questions of dating and influences remain in many cases unanswered – in exploring the historical depths of the Finnish world view, our plumb line does not reach the bottom.

Included in these unanswered questions are those concerning the *tietäjä* institution and the shamanic tradition, the particularly important cult of the dead and the ancient bear rites with their associated concepts of the heavenly origin, death and resurrection, of the bears' female primogenitor. We may assume that these sorts of elements, together with beliefs in the animism of nature, belong to the oldest layers of Finno-Ugric tradition. OA

names PLACE NAMES It is estimated that in the 20th century at least 3 million place names have been in use among Finland's Finnish-speaking population. They have come into being in rural culture, and a considerable proportion of them have been in use among small communities. The number of these traditional place names in different provinces and parts of the country fluctuates. Many names are required where settlement is dense and old. Thus the largest number of names is found in the south-western and southern parts of the country, to an average maximum of around 30 names per square kilometre. In the sparsely populated regions of eastern and northern Finland, the proportion is only a few per square kilometre.

The most common place names are bipartite in structure. The generic at the end of the name is usually a topographical word expressing place-type. It is preceded by a specifier, which expresses the special feature that distinguishes the place from other adjacent places situated nearby. The name's generic may be a suffix, e.g. *Valkea/järvi* (*valkea* ['white'] + *järvi* ['lake'] – *Valkeinen* (*valkea* + *inen*), *Uusi/talo* (*uusi* ['new'] + *talo* ['house']) – *Uutela* (*uusi* + *-la*). Names may also be formed by adding a new qualifier to an existing place name, e.g. *Valkeinen* > *Iso-Valkeinen* (*iso* ['big']) and *Pieni-Valkeinen* (*pieni* ['small']) as the names of lakes situated close together.

The most common basis of Finnish place names is the site of the place, usually expressed by means of another place name. E.g. *Oulujärvi* (*-järvi* ['lake']) > *Oulujoki* (*-joki* ['river']). The next most common basis is the naming of a place after its owner or something in the place (e.g. a building, flora or fauna). A less common basis for names is represented by the properties of the place (for example its size, form or colour, viz. *Valkeajärvi*), its use or the events that have happened at it.

The country's oldest place names are probably those of important natural features, for example large lakes. The oldest strata of settlement names probably date from prehistoric times. On average the youngest and most variable names are those of arable lands.

Finnish place names have two clearly distinct sediments. From northernmost Finland to the country's central regions there are place names with Sámi derivation, for example the parish name *Posio* and the town name *Lieksa*. On the coasts of Uusimaa and Ostrobothnia, and also in the south-western archipelago and Åland the place names are mostly Swedish in origin. Among these medieval Swedish names are the town names *Helsingfors* and the Finnish *Helsinki* that is formed from it, and *Esbo* – *Espoo*.

PERSONAL NAMES The arrival of Christianity in Finland during the Middle Ages completely revolutionised Finnish forenames. Over a few centuries the old, original Finnish names disappeared from use and forenames began to be taken from the saints of the church. In later times, too, foreign forenames were taken, in particular from Scandinavia.

A special feature of Finnish forename usage is the name-day ►calendar, which is based on the saints' day calendars of the Roman Catholic Church. A large proportion of the old calendar names are international names widely used in Europe. The forms of the names are Fennicised, e.g. *Lauri* (< *Laurentius*), *Esko* (< scand.

Eskil), *Liisa*, *Elsa* (< *Elisabet*), *Ni(i)na* (< R. *Nina*). The first Finnish-language names appeared in the almanacs that were published at the end of the 19th century. The name-day calendar is revised from time to time, the most recent being the year 1995. The real-time element is important, as the celebration of name-days is a custom of the entire nation. In the new name-day calendar there are 752 forenames, half women's and half men's; 95 per cent of Finns have names that can be found in the calendar.

The influence of fashion on forenames is significant. In accordance with the fashion elsewhere in Europe, in the early 19th century two or three forenames began to be given, instead of one. In Finland, the use of forenames and surnames was made the subject of legislation, in the form of the name law, which came into force in 1991. According to this law, no child may be given more than three forenames.

While Finnish forenames contain much foreign material, surnames are for the most part linguistically Finnish. The Finnishness of surnames is largely authentic, but is also in part the result of conscious Fennicisation implemented in the 19th century under the influence of the national awekening. The pioneers of this movement were writers who began to use Finnish pseudonyms, such as Alexis Stenvall's ►*Kivi* ('Stone'). Non-Finnish surnames were changed into Finnish ones in two mass alterations effected in consecutive waves: in 1906, on the occasion of the 100th anniversary of the birth of J.V. Snellman, who fought on behalf of Finnish language rights, and in 1935–1937, in connection with the 100th anniversary of the first publication of the *Kalevala*. Fennicised names taken at these times include e.g. *Paasikivi* < Hellsten and *Virkkunen* < Snellman.

Nowadays approximately 85 per cent of Finnish citizens have Finnish surnames. In all, around 79,000 surnames are in use among Finns. A considerable number of the most common surnames are formed with the *-nen* suffix, as for example *Virtanen* (*virta* ['river'] + *-nen*), *Heikkinen* (forename *Heikki* + *-nen*). Names containing the house-name suffix *-la/lä*, such as *Mäkelä* (*mäki* ['hill'] + *-lä*), *Heikkilä* are also common. Other frequently-encountered surname-types are prefixed names containing only the appellative, such as *Laine*,('wave') *Niemi* and surnames resembling place names, such as *Kiviniemi* (*kivi* ['stone'] + *niemi* ['headland']).

Finnish surnames do not necessarily indicate whether the bearer of the name is Finnish or Swedish-speaking. Finnish-speakers may have Swedish surnames, and vice versa. The most common Swedish surnames are *Lindholm*, *Johansson* and *Nyman*.

The name law contains regulations governing the determination and alteration of surnames. For example, people who marry are allowed to keep their own surname (Liisa *Laine* and Lauri *Virtanen*), or adopt the same name as either spouse (Liisa and Lauri *Virtanen*; Liisa and Lauri *Laine*). One spouse may use the shared name in addition to his or her own surname (Liisa *Laine-Virtanen* and Lauri *Virtanen*; Liisa *Laine* and Lauri *Virtanen-Laine*). The official body in charge of surnames is the country's administrative board. The Name Board (*nimilautakunta*), appointed by the Ministry of Justice, functions as an expert body dealing with questions concerning the application of the law. RLP

National Board of Antiquities

The National Board of Antiquities was founded in 1972. Its function is to direct the administration of Finland's ancient monuments and remains, and to oversee the preservation of the cultural environment and heritage. Its task is also to develop museum activity as a whole, to practise associated scholarship and to maintain the National Museum of Finland. MLR

National Museum of Finland

The National Museum of Finland was founded in 1893. It is housed in a granite national romantic castle designed by the Finnish architectural trio Herman Gesellius (1874–1950), Armas Lindgren (1874–1929) and ▶Eliel Saarinen, completed in 1910 and opened in 1916. In addition to Finnish ▶history, the exhibits relate to the history of the ▶Sámi and Finno-Ugrian peoples. Among the most important sights are

Herman Gesellius, Armas Lindgren, Eliel Saarinen, National Museum of Finland, Helsinki, 1916

the presentation of prehistory, which was redesigned in the mid 1990s, the section on medieval ecclesiastical art, the room presenting life in country mansions in the 18th century, the exhibition of costume, armoury and treasury, and a smoke-sauna, which was transferred to the museum as a whole. The collections, which comprise one and a half million objects, include material from outside Europe, including some relating to the Alaskan Indians. A new Museum of Ethnography is being planned for the exhibition of these. In addition, the ▶Seurasaari Open-Air Museum, founded in 1909, is administered by the National Museum, as well as two castles, five country mansions and three museums dedicated to individuals, including the Urho Kekkonen Museum Tamminiemi in Helsinki. MLR

national symbols

The history of Finland's national symbols begins on 13 May 1848 when, as representative of the Finnish people, the Students' Society of the University of Helsinki, at its spring festival, adopted *Maamme* ('Our land'), a song by ▶J.L. Runeberg, as the national anthem; both poem and melody were written expressly for the Students' Union. The students' or Finnish flag – a white ground at the centre of which was the lion of Finland, surrounded by a laurel wreath – was also flown for the first time at the same festival. *Maamme* had a clear contemporary message: directing the political turbulence of the period towards aesthetic and constructive patriotism rather than revolution.

Analogically, in 1831, the time of the previous European revolutionary period, the ▶Finnish Literature Society had been established to develop a politically appropriate patriotic and nationalist ideology; its most important product was the ▶*Kalevala*, compiled by ▶Elias Lönnrot, which, in the spirit of the expectations of the time, was interpreted as the national epic. Runeberg, the national poet, Lönnrot, and the national philosopher ▶J.V. Snellman were 'canonised' in the late 19th century in, among other things, elementary teaching, as national great men to whom streets, monuments and (in the case of Runeberg and Lönnrot) museums were dedicated. Later, the writer ▶Aleksis Kivi was added to the sequence of 19th-century great men, to be honoured with flag-days and school holidays, ▶postage stamps etc. In the 20th century, the composer ▶Jean Sibelius and the politician and Marshal ▶C.G.E. Mannerheim have been recognised as national great men. Such figures were partly the objects of feelings that had previously been directed at members of the Russian imperial family.

The Crimean War (1854–1856), affected Finland directly; during its course, ▶Zacharias Topelius began to champion blue and white as the Finnish national colours. Although there was some historical background for these choices, they were essentially an expression of loyalty towards Russia, whose navy, operating along the

Lasse Viren runs round the track under the Finnish flag at the Montreal Olympics 1976 after winning the 10,000-metre race

Finnish shoreline, had a blue-and-white cross as its flag. The Finnish sailing clubs received the right to use the blue-and-white cross-flag. Against the blue-and-white combination, which soon took on a loyalist and Fennomane meaning, rose a suggestion for red and gold as the national colours, based on the colours of the Finnish coat of arms and supported by the liberals. The Finnish lion coat of arms, which is associated with the title of 'Grand Duke of Finland, Karelia etc.'

The winning Finnish ice-hockey team at the ice-hockey world championship, Stockholm, in 1995, wear the Finnish lion on their chests

adopted by King John III (1537–1592) of Sweden in 1581, is known from the 'prototype' carved by Willem Boy for the funeral monument of King Gustavus I Vasa (1523–1560) for Upsala Cathedral. The lion coat of arms was taken into use in the latter half of the 19th century, and it had appeared in a number of official connections even earlier. The Finnish lion took on the role of a new and central national symbol after Finland became a sovereign state in 1917, particularly in army circles (as an officers' cockade, among other things). In 1942 the Order of the Lion of Finland was founded which, together with the Order of the Cross of Liberty and the Order of the White Rose of Finland (founded in 1918 and 1919 respectively), is a central national symbol and is associated with the Constitution Act of Finland (▶constitution) and, in practical terms, with presidential symbols and power. The crosses and medals of these orders of merit are awarded on national ▶festivals, among which are Indepedence Day, 6 December (the festival of the civilian orders) and Armed Forces Flag Day, 4 June. This last, the birthday of Marshal Mannerheim, replaced an earlier festival held to commemorate the parade for the ending of the Finnish Civil War (1918). In general, these festivals, together with the birthdays of great men, came to replace the earlier imperial festivals. Religious festivals are not associated with an emphasis on national symbols, for example the flying of flags (▶orders and decorations).

The ribbons of the orders of merit are red and yellow (Cross of Liberty) and blue and white (White Rose of Finland), as well as the lion coat of arms (Lion of Finland). The white colour of the government troops in the Civil War of 1918 influenced the decision, made in May 1918, to adopt the blue-and-white cross as the flag of Finland, at which point the red-and-yellow flag, which had been temporarily adopted six months before, was abandoned as too reminiscent of the red colour of the opposing side; only the Swedish People's Party, a continuation of the Liberal Party, supported the red-and-yellow combination (on account of the Fennomane associations of the blue-and-white option). The blue-and-white flag only gradually established itself in general use.

All the central national symbols – flag, coat of arms, national anthem, medals – were taken into active use during the ▶Winter War and the Continuation War (1941–1944), with new methods, using radio and film. It can be said that at this time they became established as national features familiar to everyone and, in Finland, perhaps unusually highly respected. Subsequently, the authority of national symbols has been employed in the 'promulgation' of various national matters through, among other things, competitions for the 'national tree', the 'national bird', and so on. Analogically with national symbols, a series of provincial equivalents has been developed, from songs to proposed symbols consisting of flowers, animals and so on, most of which have appeared on old provincial coats of arms. MK

newspapers The first newspapers in Sweden and the Baltic countries, which then, like Finland, formed part of the Swedish Kingdom, appeared in the mid 17th century, but Finland received its first newspaper only in the late 18th century. Finland's first newspaper was the Swedish-language *Tidningar Utgifne af Et Sällskap i Åbo*, founded in 1771 which, under the title *Åbo Tidningar*, continued to be published until 1860. It was Finland's only newspaper until the end of the 1810s. The first Finnish-language newspaper was *Suomenkieliset Tieto-Sanomat*, which was founded by a vicar, Anders Lizelius (1708–1795), in 1776; because of a lack of subscribers, however, it lasted only a year.

In 1820 the government began publishing an official paper containing news and announcements, *Finlands Allmänna Tidning*, which became a six-day operation in 1831. It was combined in 1917, after Finland gained its independence, with the corresponding Finnish-language publication, founded in 1857, and continues to appear as the government's official organ under the name *Virallinen Lehti – Officiella Tidningen*. The oldest surviving newspaper as such, *Åbo Underrättelser*, was founded in 1824. The quantity of the press increased gradually from the

Åbo Nya Tidningar, 1789

1820s. Its possibilities, however, were restricted by preventive ►censorship, which was particularly severe in the 1840s and 1850s. *Saima*, a newspaper edited between 1844 and 1846 by the nationalist philosopher ►J.V. Snellman, was among the publications forced to close.

The beginning of state activity in the 1860s and the temporary removal of preventive censorship between 1865 and 1867 increased interest in newspapers, particularly in nationalist Fennomane circles. A number of local, Finnish-language newspapers were established in the 1870s, among them *Aamulehti* in Tampere in 1882. The Fennomanes' main newspaper was *Suometar*, founded in 1847, which subsequently became *Uusi Suometar*, and then, from 1919 to 1991, *Uusi Suomi*. The politically liberal Finnish-language party was represented by *Päivälehti*, which began to appear regularly in 1890, from 1904 under the name *Helsingin Sanomat*, which has, since the Second World War, been Finland's unrivalled largest newspaper. *Helsingin Sanomat* still belongs to the Erkko family, which founded it; the family also controls the extensive Helsinki Media Company. The main newspaper of the Swedish-speaking minority is *Huf-*

vudstadsbladet, founded in Helsinki in 1864.

At the turn of the century, the field of political newspapers broadened when the workers' movement's *Työmies* began to appear in 1895, and the rural population received *Ilkka* as its representative in 1906, and *Maakansa* (now *Suomenmaa*) in 1909. Newsgathering was made more effective by the founding of the Finnish Telegram Office in 1887 and the Finnish News Agency in 1915.

The number of newspapers in Finland grew, between 1890 and 1910, from 58 to 116. Party loyalty was strong in the 1920s, but decreased thereafter, although a few strongly right-radical newspapers were established in the 1930s. *Helsingin Sanomat* became politically independent in 1932.

During the Second World War, the number of newspapers had decreased, and during the economically difficult years that followed the war the opportunities for small newspapers, in particular, were weak. Since the war, the political orientation of the press has decreased. Urbanisation and population growth increased the circulations of the dominant newspapers of the large towns, but made the position of the provincial newspapers more difficult in the 1950s and 1960s. Since 1971

Front-page news: *Helsingin Sanomat,* the leading Finnish daily newspaper, runs advertisements on its front page

225

the government has supported the press with funding, but the economic recession of the 1990s, in particular, brought difficulties for the press.

In 1994 235 newspapers were published in Finland, of which 56 appeared between four and seven days a week and 179 appeared on one to three days a week. The total had decreased by 12 since 1980; the most important newspaper to have ceased publication was *Uusi Suomi* (founded 1847), which went bankrupt. Total newspaper circulation in 1994 was a little higher than in 1980, at 3.5 million copies. In the best year before the recession, 1989, total circulation had, however, been 4.08 million copies. Nearly 70 per cent of newspapers sold were daily newspapers appearing between four and seven days a week. The market share of the three largest papers, *Helsingin Sanomat*, the Tampere newspaper *Aamulehti*, and *Turun Sanomat*, published in Turku, was more than 20 per cent, that of the other first papers of the market areas 26 per cent and of evening papers 9 per cent. The largest-circulation newspapers in 1994 were:

Helsingin Sanomat	470,000
Ilta-Sanomat	216,000
Aamulehti	132,000
Turun Sanomat	115,000
Iltalehti	102,000

The biggest-circulation Swedish-language newspaper was *Hufvudstadsbladet*, which reached a daily circulation of 60,000 copies. Among specialist papers, the most important was the financial five-day paper *Kauppalehti*, whose circulation was 76,000. The market share of politically non-aligned newspapers was 88.9 per cent; the figure had been 68.3 per cent in 1986. The share of the two largest newspaper companies, Sanoma and Aamulehti, in the total circulation was more than 30 per cent. Most readers have their newspapers delivered, generally early in the morning. The share of counter sales is about 25 per cent of the total circulation, but for evening newspapers it is 95 per cent. Of Finns of more than 10 years of age, 93 per cent regularly follow a three- to seven-day paper, 33 per cent also read a one- or two-day newspaper, and 51 per cent read free newspapers.

In terms of the content of newspapers, 33 per cent is devoted to home news, 15 per cent to sport, 11 per cent to leisure activities, 9 per cent to radio and television programmes, 8 per cent to economics, 7 per cent to foreign news and 6 per cent to culture. The share of advertisements in the registered columns of newspapers is around 30 per cent. The Finnish Newspaper Publishers' Association is responsible for gathering statistics about newspapers. JN

Nordenskiöld, A.E. (1832–1901), geologist, explorer. Nils Adolf Erik Nordenskiöld, the fourth of seven children of a civil servant, spent his childhood in Mäntsälä, southern Finland. Inspired by his father, who was also a geologist, Nordenskiöld graduated from university with geology as his main subject, gained his doctorate in 1855 and planned an academic career. The project, however, was thwarted, because he had drunk toasts insulting to the Russians and spoken warmly of Finland's previous mother-country, Sweden. Having refused to apologise for what he had said, Nordenskiöld was ordered to leave the country. He moved to Sweden, where he was appointed to a professorship in 1858. Nordenskiöld always considered Finland his homeland, and followed its cultural and political life closely. In his adopted country he took part in political life, participating in two parliaments as a representative of the nobility, and was a member of the second chamber three times.

Nordenskiöld's diverse and notable scientific achievements comprise an extensive literary repertoire, ten expeditions to the Arctic Sea and the development of the mineralogical department of the Swedish Museum of Natural History into the world's best mineralogical collection. Two of his achievements, however, are more important than the rest. In 1878–1879 he sailed the North-East Passage for the first time, thus sailing round the entire Eurasian continent – a feat that raised him to world fame as an explorer. His second achievement was his interest in historical cartography, which led to the compilation of a geographical and cartographic collection containing almost

The Nordenskiöld expedition to Greenland, 1883

A.E. Nordenskiöld

4000 catalogued items, with material dating back as far as the 15th century. The collection was bought by Finland in 1902 and is located in Helsinki University Library, where it is still the library's most valuable special collection. ML

Nurmi, Paavo (1897–1973), runner. For Finns, Paavo Nurmi is a symbol of the country's days of greatness in athletics. As a sportsman, Nurmi was a pioneer of today's science-based training, who was known for the fact that in races he held a pocket-watch in his hand as he ran round the track, glancing at it from time to time.

Paavo Nurmi's career began at the Antwerp Olympic Games in 1920 with

Wäinö Aaltonen, statue of Paavo Nurmi, 1924, Olympic Stadium, Helsinki

2 gold medals. His greatest moments occurred at the Paris Olympics in 1924. Unlike today – for example at Atlanta in the case of Michael Jackson – the essential events for the then superstars, the 1500 metres and the 5000 metres races, took place on the same day, and even within the hour. Nurmi won both, the latter with a new world record. The director of the Finnish team forbade him from participating in the 10,000 metres race in order to give the other Finnish runners a chance.

After the Paris Olympics, Nurmi went on tour in the United States, where he achieved world fame as the 'Flying Finn'. In less than six months, he took part in 55 competitions, losing only 2. President Calvin Coolidge invited him to visit.

Paavo Nurmi appeared for the last time before a sporting audience when he brought the Olympic Torch to the stadium in Helsinki Olympic Games in 1952.

During his career, Nurmi won 9 gold medals. In Atlanta Olympics in 1996 Carl Lewis challenged his position as sportsman of the century by winning his 9th gold medal at his 4th Olympics. Lewis had 1 silver medal, while Nurmi had 3. Nurmi won his medals at 3 Olympics. His career ended at the point where, today, many athletes' begin. In 1932 he was declared a professional on the eve of the Los Angeles Olympics. ES

Nuutajärvi Glass Nuutajärvi Glass Factory, which has belonged to Hackman Designor Ltd since 1991, is Finland's oldest surviving glass factory. It was founded in 1793. Originally, the

O

Kerttu Nurminen, *Mondo,* **1988**

factory produced window-glass, bottles and simple utility glass. In the mid 19th century the factory raised it to one of the most important glass factories in the Nordic countries. Pressed glass began to be made in the factory in 1852, and in 1857 filigree glass. In 1905 the factory made its first attempt to include new Finnish designs in its range by holding a glass-design competition. A few designs in the *Jugend* or *art nouveau*, style resulted, among them a goblet designed by the architect Valter Jung (1879–1946).

In the 1940s, Gunnel Nyman (1909–1948), one of the pioneers of Finnish art glass, designed an important collection of art glass for Nuutajärvi. In 1950 ►Kaj Franck moved from ►Arabia to Nuutajärvi with the task of revising the factory's range of utility glass. In 1952 he was joined by Saara Hopea-Untracht (1925–1984), who, in addition to working on utility glass, also updated the factory's crystal-ware. Franck's and Hopea's simplified formal language was enlivened by a wide range of colours. ►Oiva Toikka and Heikki Orvola (born 1943) began work at Nuutajärvi in the 1960s. Toikka brought with him new, popular, decorative ranges of pressed glass which, from 1968, could be manufactured fully automatically. Kerttu Nurminen (born 1943) has worked as a Nuutajärvi artist since 1972 and Markku Salo (born 1954) since 1982. In addition to serial production, unique objects, marketed since 1981 under the name Pro Arte, have been an important part

of Nuutajärvi's production since the 1960s. In the 1990s, when most production has been moved to ►Iittala, art glass has remained Nuutajärvi's only production sector. MaA

Olavus Magni (died 1460), Rector of the University of Paris, Bishop of Turku. The fame of Olavus Magni rests mostly on his achievements during his period at the University of Paris (1420s–1438). His learning is emphasised as early as the episcopal chronicles of medieval Finland: according to the chronicles, this brought him fame among the French, and particularly among Parisians.

Olavus Magni gained his master's degree in 1428, after which he taught, among other things, Aristotle's ethics at the university. He acted as rector of the university in 1435–1436. The university entrusted him with important positions of trust. During his time in Paris, Olavus Magni was appointed arch-dean and cathedral dean of the diocese of Turku. He succeeded to Finland's only episcopal seat after his kinsman, Magnus Tavast (1357–1452, Bishop of Turku 1412–1449) in 1450 and remained in office until his death in 1460.

Olavus Magni and his work as rector of the University of Paris has been, in academic celebratory speeches, an almost clichéd example of Finnish learning in the medieval period. JN

Olympic Stadium The tower of the Olympic Stadium added a vigorous landmark in 1938 to the low profile of ►Helsinki. The stadium, designed by Yrjö Lindegren (1900–1952) and Toivo Jäntti (1900–1975), made the new functionalist style a symbol of the vitality of the young republic. From the beginning of Finland's independence (1917), sport played an important role in the building of national self-confidence, and the most important sports institutions – the Olympic Stadium, and the Finnish Sports Institute at Vierumäki (►Erik Bryggman, 1936) – became dream commissions for functionalism.

Lindegren and Jäntti received the commission for the Olympic Stadium as a result of architectural competitions held in 1930 and 1933, and the

Yrjö Lindegren, Toivo Jäntti, Olympic Stadium, Helsinki, 1938–1952; photograph taken during the Helsinki Olympics, 1952

first phase was built between 1934 and 1938. The dynamic architecture of the stadium was made possible by new techniques using reinforced concrete. The structures of the high, curving grandstand were light, their forms stable and precise. The Olympics planned for 1940 were thwarted by the Second World War, but in the summer of 1952 the extended Olympic Stadium was the main stage of the Helsinki Olympics.

The artistic effect of the stadium's ascetic architecture rests on refined dimensions and polished details, which extensions and renovations have partially hidden. RN

opera Probably the first operatic performance in Finland was seen when Carl Gottlieb Seuerling's theatre company visited Turku in 1768. During the first half of the 19th century many itinerant opera companies travelled through Finland on their way from Stockholm to St Petersburg or vice versa, performing in the three major coastal cities, Turku, Helsinki and Viipuri.

The first attempts by Finnish composers in the field of opera were performed only in Sweden and in Swedish. Even the first truly Finnish opera, *Kung Karls jakt* ('King Charles' hunt', 1852) was written by Frederick Pacius (1809–1891), a German-born composer who played a major role in creating an institutional basis for Finnish musical life. It took quite some time before new works of any quality emerged, but operatic life received a tremendous boost in 1872 when Kaarlo Bergbom (1843–1906) established the Finnish Theatre. An opera department was set up the next year, with Bergbom himself directing most productions. The reception was generally favourable, even enthusiastic, but because of financial difficulties operatic activities were discontinued in 1879.

In 1896 the ▶Finnish Literature Society held an opera competition which was won by Oskar Merikanto (1868–1924) with his *Pohjan neiti* ('The Maiden of the North'). This was the first opera written to a Finnish-language libretto. Another major work from this period is Selim Palmgren's (1878–1951) *Daniel Hjort* (1910), based on a play by J. J. Wecksell's (1838–1907), and set in Turku Castle in 1599.

During the first decade of the 20th century there were only occasional opera performances. These were so successful, however, that in 1911 Edward Fazer (1861–1943), the composer Oscar Merikanto, the opera singer ▶Aino Ackté, and a number of other singers formed a co-operative to support a new opera company. The pay was nominal, and the founding members often performed free. But already the next year Ackté fell into dispute with Fazer and walked out. The following summer she organised the first opera performances in Savonlinna, the first work to be performed being Erkki Melartin's (1875–1937) *Aino* (1912). This first Savonlinna Opera Festival continued only up to 1916. Meanwhile Fazer and Merikanto's opera company formally became a limited company in 1914, when it changed its name to the Finnish Opera. The company did not receive much state subsidy, but it was given a home in the beautiful but relatively small Alexander's Theatre in Helsinki. Since 1956 the company has been known as the Finnish National Opera.

The most important operas to emerge during the 1920s were *Juha* (1922) by Aarre Merikanto and *Pohjalaisia* ('The Ostrobothnians', 1924) and *Juha* (1935) by Leevi Madetoja (1887–1947).

Leevi Madetoja's *Pohjalaisia* ('The Ostrobothnians'), Finnish National Opera, 1991

The play by Artturi Järviluoma (1879–1942), on which *Pohjalaisia* is based, is an allegory of the struggle for independence during the 19th century, when Finland was a Grand Duchy of imperial Russia. Madetoja employed elements from folk music and, partly thanks to this, the vocal style sounds natural and suits the Finnish language particularly well.

Both *Juha* operas came about because of the untiring activity of Aino Ackté. She wrote a libretto based on Juhani Aho's (1861–1921) novel of the same name and gave it to Aarre Merikanto (1893–1958). But when he submitted his opera to the Finnish Opera, the board asked him to simplify the orchestral texture; Merikanto refused, and the opera remained, unperformed until 1963. When it was recognised as an early masterpiece of musical modernism, Ackté's libretto ended up in the hands of Madetoja, whose *Juha* received its premiere in 1935.

Although modernist influences had began to reach Finland in the 1920s, there was a reaction against them in the late 1930s and early 1940s, which led to a late growth of national romanticism. Even after the Second World War, many composers adhered to a fairly conservative style. The operas of Tauno Pylkkänen (1918–1980) and Ahti Sonninen (1914–1984) exemplify this trend. Tauno Marttinen (born 1912), the most prolific Finnish opera

composer, wrote in a more modern idiom. ▶Joonas Kokkonen, in turn, began in a fairly neoclassical style, but soon adopted a more chromatic idiom. He went through dodecaphonic phase, but eventually returned to a relatively secure tonal base. One of the peaks of this later phase as well as his output in general is his only opera *Viimeiset kiusaukset* (*The Last Temptations*, 1975), a story about the spiritual struggle of a 19th-century religious leader ▶Paavo Ruotsalainen.

▶Aulis Sallinen has used highly intellectual libretti, often written by a leading Finnish poet, ▶Paavo Haavikko. On the other hand, Sallinen's musical idiom is fairly easily approachable and his works have found a public not only in Finland but also abroad. His first opera *Ratsumies* (*The Horseman*, 1975) started a major opera boom in the 1970s. Sallinen's second opera *Punainen viiva* ('The red line', 1978), based on a novel by a major Finnish author, Ilmari Kianto (1874–1970), describes the lives of poor people living in north-eastern Finland, their struggle for political rights and against harsh nature. Sallinen's two subsequent operas, *Kuningas lähtee Ranskaan* (*The King Goes Forth to France*, 1984) and *Kullervo*(1992), were both commissioned partly by foreign opera houses, the Royal Opera House in Covent Garden, London, and the Los Angeles Opera House respectively.

Kullervo, based on the Finnish national epic ▶*Kalevala*, was the first work to be heard at Helsinki's new opera house, inaugurated in November 1993. Sallinen's fifth opera, the satirical *Palace* received its premiere in Savonlinna in 1995.

▶Einojuhani Rautavaara has tried many styles of composition during his career, sometimes even successfully combining them within a single work. His most impressive work in this respect is *Thomas* (1985), based on a story about a medieval bishop of Finland (▶Thomas), who was probably the first to conceive of Finland as a national entity. *Vincent* (1987) is about the agony and ecstasy of the archetypal misunderstood artist, van Gogh.

Many important works have been written in a decidedly modern – even postmodern – idiom. *Silkkirumpu* ('The damask drum', 1984) by Paavo Heininen (born 1938) is defined as a 'concerto for singers, players, movements, images, words…' The composer's own libretto is based on a 14th-century Japanese play about a gardener who is promised the hand of the princess if he can make a damask drum sound. Heininen's second opera, *Veitsi* ('The

Karhunen–Hyvämäki–Parkkinen, Finnish National Opera, 1993

knife', 1988), in turn, is located in modern Helsinki and tells of a poet who suddenly has to carry the crushing weight of success on his shoulders.

Olli Kortekangas (born 1955) often uses very heterogenous material both musically and textually, which allows him to move freely in time and space. His operatic works include *Short Story* (1980) and the television opera *Grand Hotel* (1985). ▶Erik Bergman has been recognised since the 1950 as the leading colorist, both vocal and orchestral, of Finnish music. His first opera is *Det sjungade trädet* (*The Singing Tree*, 1995).

The National Opera moved to a modern, purpose-built opera house in 1993. Savonlinna Opera Festival was started anew in 1967, and quickly became a major international event; it has maintained a policy of performing and commissioning Finnish operas. There are also many active and ambitious provincial opera companies throughout Finland. Singers as well as other musicians are provided with training at the highest level at the Sibelius Academy Opera Studio and other institutions of musical education. Finnish opera life thrives and attracts both popular and critical attention internationally. HB

Esa Ruuttunen in Olli Kortekangas's *Joonan kirja* ('The book of Jonah'), Finnish National Opera, 1995

Pehr Henrik Nordgren's *Korvan tarina* ('The story of the ear'), Finnish National Opera, 1993

Oramo, Sakari (born 1965), conductor, violinist. Sakari Oramo has been conductor of the Finnish Radio Symphony Orchestra since 1994. In the autumn of 1998 Oramo takes up an appointment as conductor-in-chief of the City of Birmingham Symphony Orchestra.

Oramo studied violin and conducting at the Sibelius Academy in Helsinki and gained his diploma in conducting in 1992. Oramo also participated, among other things, in the Ilya Musin

Sakari Oramo

conducting course. He made a number of recordings with the Finnish Radio Symphony Orchestra, and took the orchestra on tour to the Nordic countries, in the autumn of 1996, and to Spain in the 1997–1998 season.

Oramo has often acted as visiting conductor to Finnish symphony orchestras. He has made successful appearances with all the major orchestras in the Nordic countries, as well as the London Sinfonietta, the Scottish Chamber Orchestra and the Deutsches Symphonieorkester in Berlin, and made an extensive tour of Australia with the Sydney Symphony Orchestra and the West Australian Symphony Orchestra. By the end of the century Oramo will have made guest appearances with the BBC Philharmonic Orchestra, the Radio Symphony Orchestras of Frankfurt and North Germany, and the Orchestre de la Suisse Romande. He will also have made his debut in North America with the Avanti! Chamber Orchestra in Toronto. RL

orders and decorations Finland's orders of knighthood are based on the Russian tradition.

Finland has three national orders. There are also numerous other official decorations, such as the Military Medal of Merit, the Life-Saving Medal, the Cross and Medal of Merit of the Finnish Red Cross and the Cross and Medal for Physical Education and Sports, and the commemorative crosses and medals of the Civil War 1918, the ▶Winter War 1939–1940 and the Continuation War 1941–1944, as well as decorations conferred by voluntary national defence organisations and various other institutions.

The Order of the Cross of Liberty was originally instituted for the Civil War of 1918. Revived for the Winter War in 1939, in 1940 it was converted into a permanent order which has a military and a civil division, both with a grand cross and four classes (the first class being further divided into two grades, with and without a star). There are also two medal classes. In addition to these the order has special decorations, the best-known of which is the Mannerheim Cross (two classes) for outstanding bravery and meritorious military operations in time of war.

The decorations of a Finnish civil servant and ex-serviceman: Cross of Liberty, military division, 4th class, dated 1941; Order of the Lion of Finland, knight, 1st class; Order of the White Rose, knight; War Medals of 1939–40 and 1941–45; Commemorative Cross of the Armoured Division; Military Medal of Merit.

Nowadays the Cross of Liberty is awarded, very rarely, for advancing the cause of national defence.

The two other orders, the White Rose (1919) and the Order of the Lion of Finland (1942) are divided into five classes (Commander Grand Cross; Commander and Knight [Member], both in two grades) and conferred for civilian and military services. Both orders also have a Cross of Merit below the grade of Knight.

The Order of the White Rose has a collar which is reserved for the Grand Master (President of the Republic) but can also be given to foreign heads of state. Associated with the order are three medals.

War veterans commemorate the 75th anniversary of the Civil War of 1918 at the Finlandia Hall in Helsinki

The Order of the Lion has no collar, but there is a medal, the Pro Finlandia, which is particularly prestigious and ranks after the Commander. It is a special award for authors and artists. Orders and decorations are worn at national festival, for example the reception of the President of Finland on Independence Day, 6 December.

A fourth order, the Holy Lamb (1935) is semi-official. It is conferred by the Orthodox Church of Finland. TT

Orthodox Christianity There are some 60,000 Orthodox Christians in Finland (less than 1.5 per cent of the population). The great majority (more than 57,000) belong to the Finnish Orthodox Church. In addition, there are small parishes belonging to the Orthodox churches of Russia and Romania.

The Finnish Orthodox Church, or officially the autonomous Orthodox Archbishopric of Finland, is made up of three dioceses (►Karelia, ►Helsinki, Oulu) and 25 parishes. In addition, the church has two ►monasteries. The church's centre is in Kuopio, in northern Savo, where the church administration and the residence of the archbishop, the head of both the church and the diocese of Karelia, are located. Since 1988, the church's priests have been educated at the University of Joensuu. Finland also has the largest Orthodox church building in western Europe, the ►Uspensky Cathedral in Helsinki, as well as an ►Orthodox Church Museum. Differing from general Orthodox practice, Finland's Orthodox Church has, since the 1920s, followed the so-called new, or Gregorian, calendar.

The east of Finland, in particular, has for more than 1000 years been a meeting point for Slavonic and Germanic culture and politics, and eastern and western Christianity. The Karelians, who lived for the most part around Lake Ladoga (to the north-east of present-day St Petersburg), had adopted the Orthodox faith peacefully from the Novgorod Slavs by the 13th century.

For centuries, Orthodox Christianity was primarily the religion of the Karelians, and from the 16th century also of the Skolt Lapps, a small population living to the north of the Karelians. It did not really gain a foothold in what is now Finland, where the predominant religion was first Catholicism, absorbed through Sweden, and then, after the Reformation, Lutheranism.

Orthodox Christianity spread to what is now Finland only after 1809, when Russia annexed Finland. Orthodox Christians were at first primarily Russian soldiers and merchants. The Protestant majority, indeed, considered Orthodox Christianity a Russian religion, equating faith with nationality. For this reason, Finns were often suspicious of Finnic Orthodox Christians living in the Finnish Grand Duchy, such as the Karelians. The situation changed as the 19th century progressed, and scholars of the Finnish tradition and builders of the Finnish identity discovered in Karelia the materials from which the ►*Kalevala*, was born (►Karelianism). As language and the oral tradition became the defining factors of national identity, religious differences began to lose their importance. Nevertheless, in times of crises Orthodox Karelians were long considered Russians.

Russia was made anxious by the Finns' nationalist ambitions, and began to strengthen the role of Orthodox Christianity along its borders, including Finland. In 1892 Finland was made into its own Orthodox diocese, with its own bishop; earlier, the Orthodox Christians of Finland and Karelia had been subordinate to the metropolitan of St Petersburg. Within this new diocese, the Karelians and other Finns, who formed a majority, and the minority Russian-speakers, disputed above all about the language in which worship was to be conducted: Finnish or Slavic. There was also some argument as to whether the Finnish diocese was to have some degree of autonomy within the Russian Orthodox Church, as did the Finnish Grand Duchy within the Russian state. These arguments continued after Finnish independence (1917), and were settled in the latter half of the 1920s, when some of the Russians organised themselves as a registered society into two parishes. Both parishes continue to operate in Helsinki, and are subordinate to the

Procession of the cross, Tuupovaara, northern Karelia, 1989

Russian Orthodox Church. In the mid 1990s they had around 1000 members, among them Russians who had moved to Finland in recent years.

The majority of the Finnish Orthodox diocese transferred to the patriarchate of Constantinople in 1923, and the diocese was made into an autonomous Orthodox Archbishopric of Finland. The autonomy of the Orthodox Church had been recognised by the Finnish government in a statute of 1918. In 1935 the government granted the Orthodox Church the right to impose taxes, like the Lutheran Church. The focus of the church's activities was on the Finnish part of Karelia, where the majority of the church's members lived. Orthodox Christians were, however, a minority even in most of Karelia. The sense of insecurity this caused was visible in, for example, the strength of the bonds between members of the Orthodox Church: in the Orthodox community, everyone knew one another and protected one another from the outside.

After the Second World War, Finland lost a large part of Karelia, and Petsamo in the far north to the Soviet Union. The Karelian population – around 400,000 people, including Finnish-, Russian- and Swedish-speaking members of the Orthodox Church – were evacuated to Finland, as were the Skolt Lapps, who numbered about 450. Only at this point did Orthodox

Christianity spread to the entire country. At the same time, Orthodox Christians became more clearly a minority, for they no longer formed a majority in any area. This factor, in addition to the hostility sometimes shown to Orthodox Christians, language problems and cultural differences, increased the sense of insecurity among Orthodox Christians and led to a desire to merge with the majority. Many Orthodox Christians, indeed, converted to Lutheranism or became secularised. The children of mixed marriages between Orthodox and Lutheran Christians were, almost without exception, baptised as Lutherans.

After the Second World War the Finnish government supported the Orthodox Church, which had been forced into exile. In reparation for the property which had been left behind in Karelia, the church was able in 1950–1960, with government support, to construct 13 new church buildings, 44 smaller chapels and 19 accommodation buildings. Thus the material conditions for the church's activities were created. The position of the church was significantly strengthened by the fact that it was supported by a law, which came into force on 1 January 1970, according to which the Orthodox Church received the same status as an established church as the Lutheran Church.

The attitude of the Lutheran Church

towards the Orthodox Church, like that of the government, has been primarily positive. Ecumenism characterises relations both on official levels and in local parishes. Orthodox art, the painting of icons, has spread among Lutherans. Orthodox Christians, on the other hand, have absorbed from the Lutheran Church elements including confirmation school, which is called the school for Christian doctrine. There appears to be no corresponding education for the young elsewhere in the Orthodox world.

Despite the favourable attitude of the government and the Lutheran Church, Orthodox Christianity in Finland appeared to be, after the Second World War, in danger of dying out. The Orthodox population was growing older, and after the late 1950s the majority of young people seemed uninterested in Orthodox Christianity. The situation changed with Finland's change in social structure and the strong movement from the countryside to the towns in the 1960s and early 1970s, when the traditional Finnish value-system, too, began to change. Initially the urban intelligentsia, who were primarily Lutherans or had no church allegiance, 'found' Orthodox Christianity in rather the same way as writers and artists had 'found' Karelian folk culture 100 years earlier. Orthodox Christianity, particularly the monasteries, mysticism and icon-painting, became a kind of fashion phenomenon and a way of building a new identity for those who had lost their earlier system of values. A number of well-known and highly educated people converted to the Orthodox Church, and were prominently featured in the media. The number of converts has grown significantly in recent years, to a several hundred a year. Consequently, after decades of decline, the membership of the Church began to increase in the 1980s. Membership has also been swollen in the 1990s by immigrants from the former Soviet Union.

Many Karelians who were of Orthodox origin but had been baptised as Lutherans also ventured to acknowledge their roots in the 1980s. They dare once more to be proud of their pasts. The Finnish Orthodox Church's collaboration with the Russian Church, particularly in the Republic of Karelia and the St Petersburg area, has increased.

In becoming part of Finnish society, Orthodox Christianity has simultaneously become internationalised. The Church has good relations with sister churches active in both the former socialist countries and western Europe and America. In addition to Greek, English has been adopted as a church language, and the number of acts of worship conducted in the Slavonic languages, too, has increased. It seems that Orthodox Christianity is becoming a natural part of the Finnish way of life. TL

Orthodox Church Museum The Orthodox Church Museum in Kuopio, northern Savo, founded in 1957, is unique in western Europe. It contains more than 3000 documented objects, of which most are from the Orthodox parishes and ▶monasteries of ▶Karelia and Petsamo, the areas of Finland that were ceded to the Soviet Union after the Second World War. The museum's collections are added to continually through both purchase and donation. Most of the objects date from the 18th and 19th centuries. About 20,000 people visit the museum every year, of whom half are from outside Finland. TL

The Orthodox Church Museum, Kuopio

Ostrobothnia Ostrobothnia is a historic province which in a hereditary sense comprises the present-day counties of western Finland and part of ▶Lapland. As a result of natural conditions and historical development it is, however, divided into several provinces: southern, central and northern Pohjanmaa, together with Swedish 'Österbotten', today bear the collective name 'Ostrobothnia'.

A typical
Ostrobothnian
landscape, with its
'sea of barns',
Kauhava

Ostrobothnia is an area of numerous river valleys, descending in the same direction towards the Gulf of Bothnia. Rivers, meadows and flatland are in fact essential features of the province. They have long attracted settlement, which has spread from the coast to the inland regions. The natural centres of the fertile river valleys were the towns that came into being at the mouths of the rivers, towns through which tar, among other products, was exported to the markets of the world. Later, the extension of rail and road traffic to the inland regions saw the growth of more important centres.

Vaasa, Ostrobothnia's largest town, is the capital of the province and contains a university. It is also a centre for the Swedish-speaking coastal population. Vaasa was founded in 1606 on the site of the old port and trading centre of Mustasaari. From there the town has grown with the geological uplift of the land, and its port has been moved to the west.

Since the land uplift is more preminent on the coast, height differences between the low-lying costal areas and the inland areas are constantly diminishing. This explains the region's annual flooding, which is currently the subject of attempts at checking by means of regulating reservoirs and flood dikes. The spring floods of the Kyröjoki River often cover thousands of hectares of cultivated land, cutting off houses and severing road connections. Then the landscape is literally dominated by a 'sea of barns'.

The nucleus of central Ostrobothnia is the Kokkola region. Other old towns of the Swedish-speaking coastal region are Pietarsaari and Uusikaarlepyy. In this part of the province, as in southern Ostrobothnia, the border between the Swedish-speaking and the Finnish-speaking areas is quite pronounced. On the other hand, the industrialised populations of the coast have been joined by Finnish-speaking people, and have become bilingual.

In many respects, the inland regions of central Ostrobothnia resemble southern Ostrobothnia. The land rises, however, more quickly towards the water divide. This may be seen from the fact that the rivers descend in straighter lines towards the coast. At the same time, the clay plains of the valleys are narrower and there are fewer fields. Kaustinen, on the banks of the Perhonjoki River, is the site of the Finnish Folk Music Institute, with its annual summer music festival.

The landscape of northern Ostrobothnia is largely similar. The nucleus of the region is the region of Oulu. Oulu is the centre for the whole of northern Finland. Oulu's location at the mouth of the Oulujoki River has made it an important trading centre for the large hinterland. In the early 19th century Oulu was Finland's largest exporter of tar. The completion in 1886 of the Ostrobothnia railway, terminating at Oulu, and the manufacture and export of wooden goods created the foundation of the city's later growth. The University of Oulu is the second largest in Finland.

Ever since the Peasant Revolt of 1596–1597, Ostrobothnia has been characterised by various intense popular movements. In the 1850s and 1860s the Knifers (*puukkojunkkarit*) terrorised the life of several Ostrobothnian parishes. The religious ▶revivalist movement also had its origins at this time. In southern Ostrobothnia this acquired the character of an evangelical crusade, while northern Ostrobothnia, on the other hand, was the birthplace of Laestadianism. The Youth Association Movement started in 1881, when the first association was founded at Kauhava. Ostrobothnia also had many enthusiastic members of the jaeger movement and a strong patriotic spirit was also present in the Lapua movement of the 1930s.

Mass movement of quite a different kind influenced the life of Ostrobothnia from the 1860s onwards. At that time the increase in population was more rapid than the growth of economic resources. This led to emigration, mostly to North America. On their return to their home villages, many southern Ostrobothnians built handsome two-storey houses there. Approximately half of the emigrants from Finland between 1860 and 1930 were from Ostrobothnia. In recent decades there has also been a movement out of Swedish-speaking Ostrobothnia, primarily to Sweden. KRn

Pälkäne Primer ▶primers

Pälsi, Sakari (1882–1965), archaeologist, ethnologist, writer. Sakari Pälsi worked in the ▶National Museum of Finland from 1933 to 1946 and collected ethnological material during his several expeditions in Finland. In 1909 Pälsi made an expedition to northern Mongolia and in 1917–1919 to northeast Siberia, collecting ancient and folkloric material. Between the 1920s and the 1940s he also made expeditions to various parts of Europe and North America.

Pälsi is known particularly for his photographic documentation and as one of the first makers of ethnological films. His many travel accounts and essays are complemented by fine photographs. In addition to archaeological and ethnological literature, Pälsi's writing – almost 40 books – includes fiction and humorous books for boys. PV

Petäjävesi Church This church in central Finland, which is included on

Petäjävesi

Jaakko Leppänen, Petäjävesi Church, 1763–1764

Detail of pulpit, Petäjävesi Church

Unesco's World Heritage List, was built under the direction of Jaakko Leppänen the Elder between 1763 and 1765. The cruciform church has a steep shingle roof. At the western end is a belltower, linked to the church by a low corridor. Its master builder was Jaakko Leppänen's grandson, Eerik Leppänen; it was completed in 1821. The unpainted log walls and red-hearted pine plank vaults give the church a unique atmosphere with its unembellished but skilfully carved interior emphasises. The Petäjävesi Church ceased to be used regularly for worship in the late 19th century, when the new parish church was completed. PV

philately ▶postage stamps

photography The first photographs in Finland, as far as is known, were taken in 1842 in Turku by the doctor, Henrik Cajander (1804–1848). Until the 1860s, photographers worked like peripatetic craftsmen. Most of them were foreigners, most often daguerretypists and ambrotypists who worked from the other Nordic countries and St Petersburg. Of the Finnish-born

P

Sakari Pälsi

photographers, only the work of the bookbinder Fredrik Rehnström (1819–1857) is worth mentioning; he, too, worked from St Petersburg.

During the decades that followed, photographers concentrated above all on studio portraits. Distinguished from the mass are Jakob Reinberg (1823–1896), who was born in the Baltic but worked all his life in Turku, and the Kuopio photographer Victor Barsokevitch (1863–1933), who came from a Polish family.

Up to the 1870s the field of photography was dominated by portrait-photographers struggling to break free of their status as craftsmen and photo journalists serving the communication of information. An important influential portrait photographer who worked around the turn of the century was Daniel Nyblin (1856–1923), who preferred to photograph people in everyday surroundings in natural light. His methods were taken further by Alfred Nybom (1879–1963), whose portrait sequences of the early 20th century were of international standard. In the decades that followed, interesting work was done by, among others, Emmi Heldt-Fock (1898–1983) and A.J. Tenhovaara (1890–1945). The former had links with German culture, while the latter had received his training in the United States. Between the wars, most photographers worked extensively in the different fields of photography. Of

Heinrich Iffland, *Ateljeen ikkunasta* ('From the studio window'), Helsinki, 1933

these general photographers, the most important were the German-born Heinrich Iffland (1897–1943), Heikki Aho (1895–1961), also known as a film cameraman, and Björn Soldan (1902–1946). Aarne Pietinen (1884–1946) and Osvald Hedenström (born 1913) are known as pioneers of newspaper photography. Eric Sundström (1866–1933) and Rafael Roos (1895–1972) had long careers as photographers of the developing industry and architecture.

The other focus of photography has been, since the 1890s, the work of amateurs. Its general levels of activity, practical aims and results have varied greatly at different times. In the early stages of photography, in the 1890s, camera clubs functioning along the lines of gentlemen's clubs arranged exhibitions and publications. Later they sometimes became hidebound as a kind of primary school for photographic technique and pictorialism. Of the first generation of amateurs, the shop-keeper Vladimir Schohin (1862–1934) and Colonel Ivan Timirasev (1860–1927), both of whom belonged to Helsinki's Russian minority, are worth mentioning. Schohin's colour still-lifes and landscapes, produced with the Autochrome system, have been preserved from the 1910s with astonishing freshness. Timirasev recorded

Alfred Nybom, Maux Möller, 1898

the small events of everyday life, quick situation pictures and news from the streets.

Among both professionals and amateurs, individual works carrying the hallmarks of art appeared very early, but only a few photographers had the stamina to produce artistic works that were polished enough for exhibitions and publications. I.K. Inha (1865–1939), who worked as a journalist, scientific writer and translator, is considered the first artist in the field. Photography was Inha's most important means of expression; he had learned his trade in Germany in the late 1880s. His spacious landscapes, whose subjects cover almost the whole of the country, and particularly the intimate details of his late period, reflect powerful personal experience of nature. This links him with the national romantic generation of artists and to the exponents of ▶Karelianism. The first extensive book of photographs to be published in Finland, *Suomi kuvissa* ('Finland in pictures'), photographed and edited by Inha, appeared in 1895–1896.

Between the main currents of photographic development, and sometimes within groups, heated debate has often been conducted about the art of photography and the work of the artist. As pictorialism became established, Daniel Nyblin was a highly visible shaper of opinion. From the late 1920s, the photographer Eino Mäkinen (1908–1987) was a champion of the new modernist movement against pictorialism. The influence of the German neue Sachlichkeit, or new matter-of-factness, is visible in an interesting way in Mäkinen's main fields, ethnological fieldwork and architecture. The new aesthetic was linked to the spread of the small camera. It was represented, above all, by the work of Vilho Setälä (1892–1985), who was active in many areas of the arts.

Personal experience and its communication have become central elements of the art of photography since the 1970s. Women photographers have played a significant part in the renewal of the expressive language. More sensitively and bravely than men, women have entered their own inner worlds. Among the large amount by women

Jorma Puranen, from the sequence *Kuviteltu kotiinpaluu* ('Imagined homecoming'), 1992

photographers, the intimate, original images of Ulla Jokisalo (born 1955) and Tuija Lindström (born 1950) are of particular distinction.

The desire to free photography of its links with reality has recurred numerous times from the 19th century onwards. A strong new impulse was given to Finnish photography by Arno Rafael Minkkinen (born 1945) who lives in the United States, and whose forceful self-portraits follow the borderline between illusion and truth in varying forms. Among contemporary Finnish photographers, the best-known are Jorma Puranen (born 1951) and Timo Kelaranta (born 1951), both of whom began as strong documentary photographers. Puranen's work has focussed on the north, on the people and environment of the Arctic. His photographs are part of a process that is under way between the present and history, the periphery and the centre. In his sequence *Kuviteltu kotiinpaluu* ('Imagined homecoming', 1992), he returns the Sámi people of the archives of the south as photographs to the present-day landscape of Lapland. In Kelaranta's abstract photographic expression, the photographic subject is not of great importance. The interest of the image is born purely of the effect of light or surface.

In recent decades, a network of photographic galleries covering almost the entire country has developed in Finland – the Photographic Museum of Finland was founded in Helsinki as early as 1969. The most important achievement in international terms in the 1980s was the extensive publication of picture-books, portfolios and small publications. A key figure in this has been Pentti Sammallahti (born

Pentti Sammallahti,
Solovetsk, Russia,
1992

1950), whose own work represents classic, direct photography. Portfolios made up of tear-sheets of photography by Sammallahti and his many followers link photography with the tradition of graphic art.

During the 1990s, photography has merged with the visual arts. At the same time, the electronic manipulation and recording of images opened up a new phase of development for photography. The link between photographer and camera has loosened, and photographs form only part of the material of new works. These new phenomena have not, however, swallowed up earlier strengths: the hung image and the printed image, installation and new media are juxtaposed and interleaved. JKn

Pietilä, Reima (1923–1993), architect. When the husband-and-wife team of Reima and Raili Pietilä (born 1926) won the competition for the Suvikumpu housing area in the new town of Tapiola outside ▶Helsinki in 1962, a new factor was introduced into the rectilinear mainstream of Finnish modernism. The scheme arose directly from the forms of the landscape. The sculptural group of buildings was completed in 1982. In 1966 Dipoli, the Students' Union's building of the Helsinki University of Technology, and

Kaleva Church in Tampere showed the unbounded freedom that concrete can give to the forms of architecture. The angular concrete castings of Dipoli seem to rise straight from the boulders of the landscape, while the free-form plan of Kaleva Church, with its convex and concave forms, has been interpreted as a fish, the symbol of the early Christian community.

In the mid 1990s Reima Pietilä's last

Raili and Reima Pietilä

Hervanta Leisure and Parish Centre, Tampere, 1979

Presidential
Residence,
Mäntyniemi,
Helsinki, 1993

building remains the official residence for the President of Finland, Mänty-niemi, which was completed in 1993. The massive forms of the granite-clad building continue the soft, angular rise of the boulders of the seashore site. RN

Pohto, Matti (1777–1857), book-collector. The most important 19th-century collector of Finnish-language literature was Matti Pohto, an uneducated wandering ragman of no fixed abode. On his journeys through different parts of Finland, he acquired a collection of Finnish literature of more than 3000 titles. In the mid 1840s Pohto began to assist the chief librarian of Helsinki University Library, Fredrik Wilhelm Pipping (1783–1868), who was attempting to put together a new national collection in place of that destroyed in the Great Fire of Turku in 1827. Pohto donated to the library copies of the publications that it lacked.

Pohto was murdered on a commercial trip near Viipuri in 1857. He left most of his books to the university library, where they still form the backbone of the collection of older Fennica. Pipping recorded Pohto's life-story in a bibliography of Finnish-language literature which he drew up in 1856 and 1857. This was the most comprehensive general bibliography of Fennica literature until 1996. JN

popular movements Finnish popular movements have had a distinctive character: they have borne many characteristics of associations – nonviolent, legal and working in close co-operation with a state power that often strove to influence them. The period of large-scale social activism among Finns began in the second half of the 19th century, with the 'national movement'. Its direction was determined by the educated classes, and was largely concerned with popular enlightenment. It was apolitical in aim, and its function was to unite the nation.

In the 1880s new kinds of associations came into being: temperance and youth societies, in which groups belonging to the lower classes of the population took the initiative into their own hands and tried to influence public opinion. The nucleus of the temperance movement was mostly formed of manual workers and other working people. In fact, until the turn of the century, the organisation and development of social consciousness largely took place through the agency of the temperance movement. Not until the second half of the 1890s did the workers begin to organise on their own. After that, the labour movement quickly increased in strenght, founding the Social Democratic Party in 1899. Four years later, the party approved a social-

Founding meeting of the Finnish Working Women's Association, 1900

ist programme. In 1905, the year of the general strike, the mass unrest swept the whole nation along with it. At the parliamentary elections the following year, the Social Democratic Party became the largest party.

With the birth of an autonomous labour movement and the strengthening of the temperance movement, the significance of the latter for the working population diminished and the movement began to crystallize into a middle-class, feminist-oriented association. After the general strike (1905) it was no longer an important channel for the organisation of the people.

The organisation of women in Finland during the second half of the 19th century was typically done through an alliance of temperance societies, young people's societies and workers' associations. There were no special women's groups as such. Women's participation in the membership of, for example, the temperance movement and the young people's societies had by the end of the 19th century almost attained the status of a political party. After the general strike women's social activism continued to rise and was increasingly channeled into special women's groups, particularly the rural Martha Association. The early 20th century 'women's movement' in the towns and cities and in the contryside was characterised by a common emphasis on the ideology of home and motherhood. The demands of the sufragettes concerning political and educational rights did not attempt to call this ideology into question.

Before the Civil War of 1918, the political movement began to be increasingly marked by organisation: the labour movement had its own sports society and temperance society, a women's and young people's society, and in the cooperative movement there was also a differentiation between peasants and workers. The bourgeois sector was made up of the corresponding organisations, together with the patriotic societies and voluntary fire brigades.

The inter-war years were characterised by rightist movements. These movements, which reached their peak in the years 1929–1932, acted in conjuction with upper-class nationalism and the populist agrarian movement. As a result of advances made by extremist forces, leftist organisations were suppressed. After the Second World War the left once again had freedom of action and the leftist movement experienced a short revival, but was soon restricted within a narrow political framework.

After the 'quiet' 1950s, ▶students and young academics began to engage in socio-political activity again during the 1960s. The peace movement was the first to increase in strength, mainly under the auspices of the Committee of 100, which developed new ideas and organisational practices. The Committee of 100 served as a kind of model when, in the mid-1960s, several movements and organisations emerged, prophesying fresh forms of protest. These movements drew public attention to questions concerning sex roles, business, sexual politics, the Third World, the Vietnam War and social control policy, issues that were new and perplexing in the cultural climate of the time. The universities were the base for the new movements, and there were many social links between them.

International student radicalism did not arrive in Finland until 1968. At the turn of the new decade, the character of the unrest altered from left radicalism towards strict political engagement. The leading role in the student movement was played by the Students' Socialist Federation, which allied itself with the orthodox left-wing communists who fostered close relations with the Soviet Union. Thus the Marxist-Leninist line was stronger in Finland's student movement than in the student movements elsewhere in Europe. In addition to the student movement, the communist educated class and its associations were also influential in cultural life, but had only a small influence on the politics of the state in general.

The student movement laid special emphasis on organisation: at the height of its activity, almost 10 per cent of university students were candidates in university elections. In the second half of the 1970s students' interest in organisation began to fade, and by the 1980s all that was left of the student unrest was its memory.

Demonstration against environmental pollution, Rovaniemi, Lapland, 1990

The women's movement and the environmental movement had been part of the 1960s unrest, but during the period of strict leftist 'class-based' politics they remained secondary. When the student movement showed signs of withering away during the second half of the 1970s, the women's movement, the environmental movement and the peace movement grew and expanded. At the end of the 1960s the central theme of the women's movement had been the right of women to both work and family. People spoke of the equality of the sexes, and one result of this was the establishment of the Council for Equality. Feminism did not start to find a wide response in Finland until the mid 1970s, however. The most important feminist organisation, the League of Finnish Feminists, had already been formed in the 19th century, and was taken over by modern feminists in 1976. Top of the list of the feminist movement's demands were financial equality, day-care places for all children, paternity leave, an end to the reification of women, the right to one's own body, free abortion, etc. The movement quickly spread to all the major towns and cities and received much publicity. During the 1980s the women's movement gradually lost impetus as women's influence on politics and economics increased and progress had been made towards the goals the feminists aspired to.

The environmental movement began to develop when young researchers and students took control of the Finnish Association for Nature Conservation and altered its policy line away from traditional 'nature conservation' towards an emphasis on 'environmental protection'. In the 1970s environmental protection continued to receive considerable support: there was a wide proliferation of local environmental battles both in the towns and cities and in the countryside, and the membership of the Association increased almost fivefold within the space of ten years. The second half of the 1970s saw the creation, mainly within student and academic circles, of small societies and action groups against nuclear power and for alternative technology. At the turn of the decade, the most important of these groups was the Koijärvi movement, which worked to protect a small bird-inhabited lake from a drainage project. The movement received much publicity and skilfully used it to its own advantage. It brought together those who were interested in lifestyle and social questions, young activists who had rejected party politics, and thus contributed to the birth of the Green movement and later the Green Party in Finland.

In the 1980s and 1990s environmental activity has increasingly become the province of official bodies (Ministry of Environment) and independent organisations (The Finnish

Association for Nature Conservation, WWF, Green Party, in the 1990s also Greenpeace), though more spontaneous public action has also manifested itself, particularly, during the last ten years, in matters concerning the conservation of old woodlands and forests. An interest in animal protection and animal rights has arisen especially among the young, a fact that is evidenced by the increase in the membership of associations connected with these issues and the establishment in recent years of new ones, and also, for example, by last year's sabotage incidents directed against the fur-farming industry. These attracted wide attention, as Finnish conservation movements have almost always used legal methods, with the exception of a few cases of 'civil disobedience' (for example, in connection with the Koijärvi movement and the forest protection campaigns.) TJ

popular songs A ten-year gap in issuing Finnish records ended after the mid 1920s; at this point, national radio transmissions also began. These two events formed the basis for the rapid spread of popular songs to a large public.

At the same time traditional, folk-based dance music was finally joined by the new rhythms that had con-

quered the world, such as the foxtrot and the tango. The Finnish word *iskelmä* was invented to express the same thing as hit melody in English and Schlager in German.

Many popular songs, above all German and British songs, were converted into Finnish guises in the 1930s; this was less true, at that stage, of American tunes. The most famous orchestra which played hit melodies and dance music was the 15-piece Dallapé Orchestra. Its conductor was the decade's most popular singer, Georg Malmstén (1902–1981), who was also a prolific composer, and, in the 1990s, is still the most-recorded Finn. Finnish popular music has from its very beginnings been coloured by strong national characteristics. Influences arriving from the West have been combined with Slavonic melancholy.

The most important Finnish popular song writer, Toivo Kärki (1915–1992), won an international composition competition organised by the British magazine *Melody Maker* in 1939 with his song *Things Happen That Way*. He would have gone to work in the United States had the outbreak of the Winter War not forced him to serve at the front. During the two decades that followed, Kärki composed more hit songs for Finns than anyone else.

The Dallapé Orchestra in rehearsal, 1962

The Harmony Sisters, Raija Avellan, Maire Ojanen and Vera Enroth, 1937

Women's contribution as hit singers was almost non-existent until the 1950s. An exception was the singing trio the Harmony Sisters, founded in 1937. The group held concerts in Germany and a number of other European countries.

In the 1950s and 1960s, Finnish recordings were released of every foreign pop song that had gained the least degree of success. Works created in Finland, however, were closer to Finns' hearts. The proportion of home-grown popular music in record sales statistics continues to be higher than is the norm in European countries in general.

Finland's most famous popular singer was Olavi Virta (1915–1972), whose most successful period fell in the 1950s. Like other Finnish favourites, he, too, remained faithful to his own country. Many Finnish singers have performed and recorded abroad, but their visits have remained short.

Ever since Finland's first appearance at the Eurovision Song Contest in 1961, there has been debate about why Finnish success has remained modest. There has been no definitive answer.

Popular and dance music is per-

Tango king Olavi Virta, 1960s

formed and recorded in Finland a great deal. Opportunities for work are increased by the fact that, even though the number of dance halls has decreased, live music is on offer in numerous dance restaurants.

The music of younger song-writers shows influences from many kinds of popular music from other countries, including world music. However, one genre of dance and popular music, which has found its way abroad in its Finnish form, retains its strong position: the tango. It has been exported to festivals abroad by, among others, its most well-known singers, Eino Grön (born 1939) and Reijo Taipale (born 1940). The Tango Market in Seinäjoki, founded in 1985, has become the biggest festival in the country in terms of audience figures. IH

postage stamps Finland published its first postal items in 1845, among the world's first countries to do so. The first postal items were postal stationery. At this point, following the example of Great Britain, Finland introduced a uniform postal rate according to which a postal consignment cost the same regardless of the length of the journey (this had previously formed the basis of the postal charge). Two different kinds of entire were published, a 10-kopeck postal entire for ordinary letters and a 20-kopeck version for heavier letters. Those first postal stationeries are now very rare; only ten surviving examples of the red 20-kopeck postal entire are known.

Although the values of the first postal stationeries were expressed in Russian kopecks, they were published by Finland's independent post office, which was separate from its Russian counterpart, and was founded, covering the entire country, as early as 1638. Finland published its first real stamps, to be glued to the outside of the envelope, in 1856. When Finland introduced its own currency in 1860, postage stamps to the value of 1 *penni* were issued from 1866. In the international fashion, Finnish stamps included, in addition to their value, the Finnish coat of arms and decorative motifs.

During the period of Russification (1899–1905), Finland was forced to accept Russian designs for its postage

The black 20-kopeck entire
of the 1850s is a philatelic rarity

stamps. On 1 October 1917, more than two months before Finland gained its independence, the first postage stamps of independent Finland were published, bearing the Finnish coat of arms.

The stamps of the period of independence provide diverse images of Finnish cultural, economic and social life. An image other than the coat of arms appeared on a Finnish stamp for the first time in honour of the 700th anniversary of the City of Turku in 1929. Since then – in addition to the late Presidents of the Republic – postage stamp images have included influential figures from Finnish music, art, literature and other cultural areas, but only after their death. The representation of living individuals on stamps became possible only in the 1990s. More important than individuals, however, as subjects for stamps are the Finnish folk tradition, history, cultural achievements and landscape. The key works of Finnish art have, naturally, also found their way on to Finnish stamps.

Osmo Omenamäki, triangular postage stamp, 1996

Postage stamps have been designed by some of Finland's best graphic artists. In fact, postage stamp art forms its own field of miniature graphics, demanding special expertise. Many Finnish postage stamp designers have received recognition in the form of international prizes.

Finland's modern and businesslike post office remains, on account of its restrained and well-considered publishing policy, highly respected among philatelists, but for other consumers respect for it is based on the reliability, speed and ease of use of the service. The possibilities offered by the rapid development of technology are fully implemented, but no technology can remove the importance of the ordinary postage stamp in creating an image of Finland and a widely distributed prospectus of the country and its culture. KR

postcards Printed, illustrated greetings, enclosed in envelopes, began to be sent in the second half of the 19th century. In 1871 Finland, as the second country in the world to do so, brought into use postcard stationeries or open letter, as it was later subsequently called in many countries. Such open messages could be sent at a cheaper rate than letters, but only if written on 'correspondence cards' printed for the purpose by the post office. If one wished to send one's own illustrated

UNION POSTALE UNIVERSELLE.
CARTE POSTALE.
FINLANDE.

POSTKORT. | POSTIKORTTI.
FINLAND | SUOMI

ОТКРЫТОЕ ПИСЬМО.
ФИНЛЯНДIЯ.

Sida för adressen. — Osoitteen puoli. — Сторона для адреса. — Côté réservé à l'adresse.

19th-century postcard printed in four languages: French, Swedish, Finnish and Russian

card without an envelope, one had to pay postage at letter-rate. Only in the early 1880s did a separate postcard-rate come into force, after which it was possible to send open messages on cards other than post-office forms or postal stationeries. At the end of the 19th century, however, it was common practice to write only the recipient's name and address on the non-picture side of the card, but no message. For this reason cards of this period often have a greeting scratched on the picture, since the other side could not be used. Only at the beginning of the 20th century was the address side divided with a vertical rule, making it possible to write a longer message on the card.

The explosive growth in the use of postcards in Finland is associated with the nationalist struggles of the period of Russification (1899–1905). When the Russian administration banned the use of the Finnish coat of arms and even the use of the country's name in foreign correspondence and abolished Finnish postage stamps, replacing them with stamps bearing the Russian double-headed eagle, activists produced an extensive and diverse range of postcards. Images of churches, bridges, tunnels, beautiful views, important Finnish buildings and patriotic Finns were now printed on postcards that were sent actively both within Finland and abroad.

Since the postcard struggle, the torrent of postcards in Finland has continued. At that time, postcards were printed abroad, primarily in Germany and Sweden. Despite the rapid and extensive internationalisation and even centralisation of the postcard industry, postcards published in Finland from the end of the 19th century onwards reflect, extensively and diversely, the entire cultural life of Finland, as well as its political and economic development. In recent times, images of the Finnish landscape, its unique flora and fauna and well-preserved national environment have proliferated. KR

In a variation on Eetu Isto's famous painting *Hyökkäys* ('The Attack', p. 146), this postcard shows the Maid of Finland holding the Finnish Constitution safely in her arms as the Russian double-headed eagle flies off into the sunset (left)

Pre-independence patriotism: the text of this postcard, which was sent in 1913, consists of the first words of the future national anthem (right)

posters ▶Akseli Gallen-Kallela was the pioneer of modern Finnish poster art, and his action-packed and myth-inspired *Bil-Bol* car poster of 1907 was a key work in the 100 year history of the poster in Finland. Alexander Federley (1864–1932) and Oscar Furuhjelm (1880–1932) represented the international styles of the turn of the century, particularly the ornamentation of *art nouveau*. The De Tre Group, consisting of Bruno Tuukkanen (1891–1979), Harry Röneholm (1892–1951) and Toivo Vikstedt (1891–1930), was the earliest Finnish graphic design studio. Vikstedt was an incomparable draughtsman, and his exhibition and literary posters in the early years of Finnish independence (1917) are memorable works. The stylised ornamentation of Germund Paaer's (1881–1950) posters for the art metalwork company Koru anticipated art deco, as did the poster designed by the well-known painter Einari Wehmas (1898–1955) for the Tulenkantajat Group ('Torchbearers') of writers and artists.

Jorma Suhonen (1911–1987), with his 1930s posters for air companies, was a pioneer of the futurist period. In 1933 Suhonen began a collaboration with Holger Erkelenz (1912–1983) and Aarno Knuus (1911–1941), and the SEK Group they founded became one of the most important advertising agencies in Finland at the time. Another collaborative partnership, Göran Hongell (1902–1973) and Gunnar Forsström (1894–1958), used the same international modes of expression: their work combines features of futurism, functionalism and art deco.

The Second World War put a stop to the development of advertising graphics and poster design for a decade, but the first important posters were created as early as the end of the 1940s. The decade that followed was a period of strong development for graphics and posters. One of the central innovators was Björn Landström (born 1917). In his works there are present all the features of the new poster: the art of simplification, impact, clever, ambiguous texts, and the combination of image and text. The cheerful drink posters, stylish travel posters and constructivist posters designed for a underwear factory of Erik

Martti Mykkänen, cigarette advertisement, 1956

Bruun (born 1926) created a strong base for Finnish poster design. The carefully considered exhibition posters of Martti Mykkänen (born 1926), influenced by Swiss constructivism, prepared the ground for subsequent work in the field of typography. Mykkänen's posters for the City of Helsinki, his two-part, typographic cigarette poster and exhibition posters for advertising graphic designers are among the basic images of the 1950s poster. Rolf Christianson (1928–1997) also worked in a constructivist mode. P. O. Nyström (1925–1996) designed a few warm-hearted, anecdotal product posters in the 1950s, and his perceptive theatre posters of the 1960s are still remembered. The drawn posters of Raimo Raimela (born 1916), with their supple lines, some of them for the Red Cross, and the posters later designed by Lasse Hietala (born 1921) for the post office and for traffic safety campaigns, are examples of successful public information design.

The 1960s, with their emphasis on participation, took Finnish graphic artists with them: posters were made about hunger, pollution, the peace movement, drugs, tobacco and the misuse of alcohol. Kyösti Varis (born 1933), an inventive visualiser, was one of the leading figures. Varis's posters *Tupakkaristi* ('Cigarette cross') and *Kolariton keskiviikko* ('Crashless Wednesday') are prize-winning classics. Jukka Veistola (born 1946), Pekka Kuronen (1948–1997) and Erkki Ruuhinen (born 1943) also collected awards with their committed posters in Finland and in international competitions. Reima Tahvanainen (born 1946) dealt with similar subjects to Kyösti Varis and Jukka Veistola.

The photographic image and offset printing had displaced the lithographs and serigraphs of the preceding decade. Commercial posters, in particular, were printed using the new technologies. Among them are the masculine cigarette posters of Pekka Martin (born 1925).

Osmo Pasanen (born 1936) is particularly well-known as a designer of exhibition posters, but his bread posters, in which the scent of Finnish bread can almost be sensed, have also been excellent. Theatre posters were the field of the artist Raimo Kanerva (born 1941), who exploited the possibilities of serigraphy, and Kai Kujasalo (born 1950), who played with humour and simplified ideas that hit the nail on the head. One of the most original designers of commercial posters is Herbie Kastemaa (born 1940), who treats products marketed to young people with imagination and humour.

Kari Piippo, poster for Lahti Poster Museum, 1990

Kyllikki Salminen (born 1940) has exploited the power of the advertised product: potatoes, tomatoes, cucumbers and tulips blaze, giant-size, from her work.

Quite the opposite tendency is represented by Viktor Kaltala (born 1943), who is at his most original in his posters for printing companies, with their oriental influences. Among the younger generation of designers are Jouni Luostarinen (born 1957) and Esa Haaparanta (born 1953), whose collaboration has resulted the skilful simplicity of Finnair's posters; Luostarinen has continued the same approach in his beer campaigns.

At the end of the 1980s, Kari Piippo (born 1945), Pekka Loiri (born 1946) and Tapani Aartomaa (born 1934) set up an exhibition group, PILOT, concentrating on the design of theatre, opera and exhibition posters. Common to them all is simplification, the effective use of colour and the use of typography. Through an active exhibitions policy, the group has gained extensive international recognition.

Esa Ojala (born 1948), who specialises in business graphics, has designed posters for cultural festivals whose colours are the blue and white of the Finnish flag and the green of the country's coniferous forests. Aimo Katajamäki (born 1962), Mika Kettunen (born 1962), Antti Rahkiola (born 1956) and Heli Hiltunen (born 1960) have concentrated on fashionable styles of the 1990s. Jonni Kuutsa (born 1966), Vesa Lehtimäki (born 1967) and Vesa Tuukkanen (born 1966) have formed the group Punainen Bodoni, and have exploited the

Lasse Hietala, *Köh!*, 1979

opportunities offered by information technology in posters for cultural institutions. A designer of the same generation is Antti Porkka (born 1965), who specialises in concert posters.

Young competition-winners include Hilppa Hyrkäs (born 1960), Asta Raami (born 1967), Pekka Piippo (born 1973) and Sampsa Voutilainen (born 1973). Their future careers will be worth watching. UA

prehistory Modern research has revealed that the oldest signs of human habitation on Finnish soil are to be found both in the region of the town of Lahti, in southern Finland, and on the present-day eastern border of Paltamo and Suomussalmi, in northern Finland. The remains of these earliest dwelling-sites date from the last post-Ice Age period, possibly more than 9000 years ago. The entire area of Finland was then initially covered by an ice sheet, which gradually melted from the east and south-east, when small groups of people arrived following the receding ice-rim either from the south, or from the east or south-east. These two different directions were the ones from which Finland's inhabitants came, even at this early stage.

People lived by hunting and fishing, and the equipment that has been preserved in the dwelling-sites is made of quartz and quartzite, as the flint that was generally used elsewhere does not occur naturally in Finland. Hunting and fishing tackle was probably also made from bone, wood and other organic materials, but of these only rare examples have survived, such as the world's oldest fishing net.

During the following period (7000–4200 B.C.) groups of hunters learned how to use local stone materials and make them into handy and elegant hunting implements. The dwelling-sites from this time are found all the way from Finland's southern coast to ►Lapland, and are sited on the shores and islands of sheltering bays. The seal appears to have been an important beast of prey during the entire period. Judging from the bones discovered in the hearths of camping places, other objects of hunting were the elk, beaver, bear, hare, wolf, common otter, roe deer and wild boar, in addition to fish-

es and birds. The dog was the only domestic animal.

In the course of the period described above began the most favourable climatic era that northern Europe has known. During the period 5500–2000 B.C. (approx.) the average annual temperature in Finland was the same as in present-day central Europe, and large deciduous trees grew all the way to the northernmost end of the Gulf of Bothnia. During this warm period, around 4200 B.C., the hunting people learned how to make clay vessels, some of which were astonishingly large, containing as much as 70 litres. This is considered to be an indicator that the settlements of these people had become fixed, and that they had changed to a storage economy.

The vessels were decorated with various printed patterns, including comb-markings, and because of this these clay materials are called 'comb ceramics'. Vessels decorated in a similar way are found over a broad area of northern Europe. It is thought that the spread of decorative customs derived from exogamous marriage rules, according to which a woman had to take a husband from outside her own group. Since, during the course of the yearly cycle, the hunting people moved across a wide area, wives and skills moved from one group to another.

About 4500 years ago a new population group arrived in the south-western part of what is now Finland. Clay cups decorated with cord patterns, shiny-sharpened perforated battle-axes, straight-bladed working axes and an absence of hunting weapons from the dwelling-sites distinguish these people from the hunting folk who were their contemporaries. The battle-axe peoples who moved widely around Europe are thought to have been cattle-herders and burn-beaters, and perhaps when they arrived in Finland this group of people practised agriculture. It is possible, however, that they initially had to resort to hunting, for only in the following period, when the comb-ceramic groups and the battle-axe people had intermarried with each other, is there clear evidence of grain cultivation.

The battle-axe people are thought to have come to Finland from the south,

Three Bronze-Age, Scandinavian-style clasps

through the eastern Baltic region, and it its possible that Baltic loans to the Finnish language are a heritage of this group. On the other hand, in the Bronze Age (c. 1500–500 B.C.) a strong Germanic influence arrived in southwestern Finland, which already at the end of the Stone Age had had close relations with the western side of the Gulf of Bothnia. The custom, widespread on the Finnish coasts, of building very large stone tumuli is believed to have come from Sweden with a supplementary population group.

The graves of the Stone Age had been inhumation graves in which the dead person was often covered in red ochre. It is possible that earth burial continued among the hunting people, but during the Bronze Age the practice of cremation spread to the coasts. This continued to hold sway until the end of the pagan era, when the burial of corpses again became widespread.

From the end of the Stone Age onwards, Finland was divided into two divergent cultural areas: west and south-facing western Finland and inner and northern Finland, where the most important influences came from the east. This is reflected, for example, in the diffusion of ▶rock painting, asbestos ceramics and Oriental bronze forms. With the onset of the Iron Age in approximately 500 B.C. a firm border was established between the settled, land-cultivating people and the people of the hunting culture. Evidence of the former is given by cemeteries continuing from one century to the next, while the latter are evidenced by their dwelling-sites.

Material relating to the earliest Iron Age is scanty, but it shows a continuity from the Bronze Age, and thus the idea that the Finns only came to Finland after the birth of Christ is nowadays rejected. The new types of burial ground and the eastern Baltic artefacts dating from the first centuries of the era tell us that people migrated to Finland from the south, but the question is merely one of population increase, not the settlement of whole areas. On the other hand, people may also have come from the direction of Sweden, and with time these western influences became ever stronger. When a specifically Finnish jewellery developed from the 6th century onwards, this took place because of the merging of influences that had come from different directions.

In the period A.D. 600–800 Finnish artefacts were at their most distinctive. Smith-work was of a high quality, and male weaponry reflected influences from the Frankish and Alemanic regions. The swords included products from Scandinavia and even further afield, but the form of other weapons was original and without equivalents in neighbouring areas. The most important material for ornaments was bronze, and they were mostly unpretentious in form. Some items provide evidence, however, that the Finns had their own relations with the East even before the eastern voyages of the ▶Vikings.

By the Viking period (A.D. c. 800–1100) a stable agricultural community had already developed in western Finland against a background of extensive areas of wilderness. By collecting furs from the inhabitants of these, and trading them at the markets of Europe, the coastal population acquired the surplus wealth it needed in order to procure Frankish swords, Mediterranean glass beads and raw materials for bronze and silver ornaments. Finnish smith-work lost its distinctive quality, as Frankish weapons were bought

Halikko cross, Finland Proper, early 12th century

Bronze pendant, Tuukkala, Savo, c. 12th century

with as much care and expense as adults.

ARCHAEOLOGICAL SITES Archaeological monuments in Finland are often in the thick of the forests or covered by earth, but some are maintained for the purpose of sightseeing. The Stone Age past can be seen far inland in embankments that mark the ancient seashore as hut-bases, hunting pits or, on the shores of lakes, as remains of hearths and broken fragments by clay vessels. One Stone Age dwelling-site that is under preservation is at Sarsa, Kangasala, near Tampere. There has also been an attempt to reconstruct a Stone Age village at Saarijärvi, to the north of Jyväskylä. A restored Stone Age area of hunting pits is to be found at Posio in Lapland.

Cairns of the Bronze Age are to be found for the most part on the hilltops of the southern and western coasts. There are preserved areas of cairns particularly near Turku, ▶Rauma and Pori in south-west Finland. Rock-paintings are to be found on the cliff faces near the lakes in central and eastern Finland. The most important of them is in Ristiina, to the south of Mikkeli.

Maintained and marked Iron Age cemeteries exist on the south coast, for example at Karjaa, between Turku, and Rauma at Laitila, and at Hattula and Lempäälä, between Hämeenlinna and Tampere. Of the Iron Age cairn areas, the biggest, Harola, is located in Eura parish, about 30 km to the east of Rauma, and the same parish also contains Finland's biggest burial-ground, Luistari in Eura, where more than 1300 graves have been excavated. This area has now been restored as a park, with a small exhibition.

Ancient hillforts are high cliffs or gravel ridges whose more gently sloping sides were once fortified. Only seldom are the stone foundations of the fortifications so well-preserved that the nature of their construction can be made out. Some ancient hillforts are located close to present-day towns. Near Turku is Vanhalinna in Lieto, which has its own museum, near Helsinki is Puodinkylä hillfort, near Porvoo its own Castle Hill, and around Laitila, Hämeenlinna and Mikkeli several hillforts are found. The most mag-

and imitated throughout the whole of the North. Women's jewellery, on the other hand, grew richer and more independent. Many of the ornaments called ▶Kalevala Koru are designed according to the forms of the Finnish Viking Age.

Scandinavia became Christian during the 11th century, and it was at this time that the first Christian symbols were placed in Finnish graves. In eastern Finland pagan burial rites continued, however, for another 100 or even 200 years. The practice of placing food and weapons in graves was the first to be discontinued, and this was followed by the ending of the custom of dressing corpses in festive clothes. The deceased persons were wrapped in shrouds and the graves lost their archaeological interest.

One of the most interesting questions of the late Iron Age is what kind of society was destroyed when Sweden conquered Finland in the 12th and 13th centuries, and the doctrines of the Roman Catholic Church supplanted the ancient Finnish religion. In the opinion of some researchers, the Finns had not even reached the stage of territorial organisation, with some of them believing in tribal leagues and even in a Finnish monarchy. It is not possible, from the archeological finds that exist, to pick out a royal demesne or royal grave. The finds tell of a rather egalitarian society in which women were also allowed to be honoured by sword offerings and children could be buried nificant, however, are perhaps the exceptional ridge fort at Rapola, Valkeakoski, and the impressive rock castle at Sulkava, between Mikkeli and Savonlinna. PLLH

press ►newspapers

primers The first Finnish-language ABC-book, published by the Bishop of Turku ►Michael Agricola in 1543, was a typical product of the age of the Reformation. It was based on a model shaped by Martin Luther in 1525, in which the alphabet itself played a small role and the main part of the contents was made up by a catechism presenting the main items of faith. Finnish ABC-books remained such a mixture of primer and catechism well into the 19th century.

The primer developed into a true tool for popular education in the 17th century. The transition occurred in the latter half of the century, when Bishop Johannes Gezelius the Elder (1615–1690) developed the education offered by the church and, in 1666, published a primer-catechism suitable for this purpose, entitled *Yxi paras lasten tawara* ('An excellent thing for children'). This became the basic Finnish primer of which, by 1914, more than 100 editions had been printed. The Pälkäne Primer, famous in Finnish bibliophilic history, takes this form. Almost as popular as Gezelius's work was a catechism edited by the Swede Olaus Svebilius, which in 1773 was prescribed as the official catechism for use in teaching.

Through the influence of the Enlightenment, from the early 19th century onwards, ecclesiastical catechisms were joined by educational catechisms, in which the proportion of religious material was decreased and the amount of material concerning education and manners was increased. The publication of illustrated primers began in the 1830s, in which pictures supported the educational texts. In ordinary primers, illustration was represented by a cockerel holding a pointer in its claws, which was generally printed at the end of the primer or on its title page. In addition to printed primers, series of wall-charts were also used which, in addition to educational ma-

Title-page with cockerel, primer, Turku, 1737

terial as such, also included catechismal material.

The traditional primer-catechism began to lose its dominant position after the institution of the primary school statute in 1866. Religious material was now replaced by short stories giving factual information. Black-letter type remained general in primers until the 20th century. From the 1920s to the 1950s a primer drawn up by Aukusti Salo (1887–1951) remained in general use in primary schools; this used large Roman letters and the writing of syllables to teach the elements of reading. During the Second World War, a separate edition was published for the use of schools in the areas of eastern ►Karelia occupied by Finland.

In contemporary Finnish primers, the emphasis is on the teaching of reading skills, and the content and vocabulary are chosen primarily with this end in view. The importance of syllabic structure is lessened by typographical means, for the aim is to preserve word-shapes whole in order to facilitate their recognition. Illustrations are clearly linked to the text. The task of the primer is to support the teaching of Finnish extensively in its various forms.

PÄLKÄNE PRIMER The Pälkäne Primer is a great legend of Finnish bibliophilic history. It was an ordinary ABC-book which the former printer of the Viipuri print-works, Daniel Medelplan (died 1737), carved on a wooden block in Pälkäne during the Great Northern War, from which Finland suffred badly, in 1719. Its publication has been considered evidence of the people's insatiable thirst of culture even in difficult times and it has particularly been accorded great importance in nationalist historiography. In fact, there is only one known copy of the Pälkäne Primer. This belonged to the collection of archbishop Carl Fredrik Mennander (1712–1786) from which the University of Upsala bought it after his death. After many appeals, the Pälkäne Primer was handed over to the library of the Academy of Turku, where it was destroyed in the Great Fire of Turku in 1827. The legendary qualities of the primer have been increased by the stories about known copies that have been lost without trace just as they were to be exhibited in public. JN

publishing ▶books

puukko 'knife' The carrying of the *puukko*, the sheath knife, has, in the North, been since ancient times the symbol of a free man. The iron *puukko* has remained in the hand of man and – on a smaller scale – woman for 2000 years. The *puukko* with its sheath is the last relic of the ▶folk costume of Finnish man. It can still be seen by the side of builders, fishermen, huntsmen and ordinary holidaymakers.

The blade and handle of the traditional *puukko* are both, in length, equal to the width of the user's palm. Since the blade is straight on the back and curved on the cutting edge, the point is asymmetrical (unlike the dagger, whose blade is always symmetrical). The blade of the crafts *puukko* is considerably shorter than the handle. The handle is of ordinary or coloured burr birch; another traditional handle is made of layers birch-bark piled on top of one another, resulting in horizontal stripes. Bone-handled knives have also been made in ▶Lapland. The sheath is traditionally made of birch-bark or

Component parts of the modern *puukko*, Marttiini Ltd, Rovaniemi, Lapland

leather. The Ostrobothnian sheat may have two sections: one for a large *puukko*, and one for a small one. *Puukkos* are still made, as craftwork, in Satakunta, southern ▶Ostrobothnia, Savo, Kainuu and Lapland. Well-known industrial marks of *puukko* based on traditional designs are Iisakki Järvenpää and Marttiini. Industrially produced *puukkos* have been designed by well-known Finnish designers, including ▶Tapio Wirkkala.

The Finnish man practised his skills with the *puukko* from the time he was a little boy, first in play, whittling small objects, but the *puukko* is still the measure of a man. Parents consider carefully when a boy can be given his own *puukko*, and graduates from the Military Academy are given a *puukko* as a memento.

The uses of the *puukko* are wide. It is used for carving and whittling, flaying and skinning, chopping and scraping. In using a *puukko*, serious work becomes fun. In the hands of en expert, a *puukko* becomes a decorative tool that produces beautiful utility objects, earlier even presents for one's bride, whose purpose was to assure her that the maker was not all thumbs. On journeys in the wilderness, the *puukko* is often first aid and only tool. In moments of danger, a *puukko* can act as an ice-pick, it can quickly cut through a rope or strap, it can cut wood for a fire, and sometimes it is needed for primitive medicine.

The Finnish man felt himself to be incomplete without his *puukko*. It was taken off his belt only when he went to a funeral, a wedding or a law-court, in order to prevent the possibility of taking up arms in anger, or to defend one's honour when drunk. In the 1920s and 1930s various rules forbidding the carrying of the *puukko* were issued, concerning cinemas, dancehalls and other public places.

During the Second World War, the *puukko* became common once more. Making *puukko*s with their various metal and wooden sheaths was a popular pastime at the front. The *puukko* industry, too, developed. *Puukko*s and sheaths received more varied forms than before, even exotic ones adapted from far-off countries. Nowadays both decorative *puukko*s and traditional forms are on offer in supermarkets and souvenir shops. Gilded by war romanticism and ideas about life in the wilderness, the *puukko* is an apt present for a man's man, for it is a utility object that represents the best of Finnish arts and crafts. TK

radio Radio broadcasting in Finland is provided by the Finnish Broadcasting Company, which operates on a national and regional basis, and since 1985 by privately owned commercial stations, mostly on a local basis. The commercial sector has two regional chain networks with extensive foreign ownership. In 1997 the first national commercial radio channel started.

Broadcasting in Finland began in 1921 with trials by radio amateurs. In 1923 the first radio concert was broadcast to the public. Regular broadcasting began in Tampere in 1923, and the service went national with the establishment of the privately owned Yleisradio/Finlands Rundradio (since 1994 Yleisradio) which began its service on 9 September 1926. In 1928 the company obtained a high power medium wave transmitter, one of the most powerful in Europe at the time. In the 1930s, as other radio broadcasting ceased, the Finnish Broadcasting Company became the sole broadcaster in Finland.

In 1934, the shares of the Finnish Broadcasting Company were acquired by the state. Since then the Finnish Broadcasting Company has owned the transmitters and the technology required for programme distribution in Finland.

Since 1948 the Administrative Coun-

cil of the Finnish Broadcasting Company has been elected by Parliament. The Finnish government determines the television licence fee used for financing the company's operations.

From the very beginning the Finnish Broadcasting Company's radio and ▶television broadcasting has been founded on the principle of public service. These principles imply a broad and comprehensive service and the performance of special duties. At first the principles were determined by the Finnish government when issuing the operating licence to the company, and later, since 1994, by the Act on Yleisradio Oy.

A strong feature of Finnish radio programming has been its national character. This has also applied to music output, which has nevertheless also been marked by radio's emphasis on classical music. The Finnish Broadcasting Company still maintains its own high-quality symphony orchestra (est. 1927, chief conductor ▶Jukka-Pekka Saraste since 1987). From the early 1980s more attention has been paid to young people's music.

News has always been an important element in Finnish radio broadcasting. News gathered by the Finnish News Agency STT has been broadcast by the Finnish Broadcasting Company since its inception. The Finnish Broadcasting Company founded its own Radio News in 1964.

There has been a steady growth of programme time and a high level of technical quality has been maintained throughout. The Finnish Broadcasting Company was one of the pioneers of FM broadcasting in Europe. The next step is digital audio broadcasting (DAB). Finland is one of the top radio listening countries in Europe with an average of 3 and a half hours daily in 1996.

The Act on Yleisradio Oy requires that the Finnish Broadcasting Company ensure equal treatment in programme policy for both Finnish-speaking and Swedish-speaking citizens, and provide services in the Sámi language. Finland's Swedish-speaking population has a comprehensive radio channel covering the whole country, except for northern Finland, and a regional radio channel in southern and

R

Ilmo Valjakka, Finnish Broadcasting Company headquarters, Helsinki, 1993

Rauma

western Finland. ▶Åland (the autonomous Åland Islands) determines its own broadcasting legislation via its provincial government on the basis of the Autonomy Act for Åland. The Sámi-speaking population of northern Finland has its own Sámi-language radio channel which operates in co-operation with the corresponding radio services in Sweden and Norway.

The present structure of radio broadcasting in Finland emerged in the late 1980s and early 1990s. Since 1985, operating licences have been granted to private commercial local radio stations. In 1996 there were about 60 valid operating licences. The Finnish Broadcasting Company carried out a restructuring of its Finnish-language radio operations in 1990.

The Finnish Broadcasting Company has three national Finnish-language channels. 'Radio Ylen Ykkönen' is devoted to classical music, radio drama and cultural talk programmes. 'Radiomafia' is a popular culture station, which aims to target adolescents and young adults in its choice of music and treatment of subject matter. 'Radio Suomi' carries regional and national news, current affairs programmes, sport and popular music.

An important part of the Finnish Broadcasting Company's service is formed by the external service Radio Finland. In addition to programmes in Finnish and Swedish, there are programmes in English, German, Russian, French and Latin. There is also a news and current affairs service for foreigners living in or visiting Finland, which combines these programmes with services by several foreign broadcasters.

Besides direct terrestrial broadcasts from Finland to the target areas, YLE Radio Finland uses satellites for both direct-to-home reception and for placement programming. Satellite services for Europe, Africa, Asia and Australia are carried out in cooperation with Deutsche Welle. For North America YLE uses the services of the World Radio Network. The most notable placement services are currently a daily half hour in English on the national network of CBC (Canada) and on CSpan Cable in the United States. Russian language broadcasts are relayed on a number of stations in Russia and Estonia and Finnish language broadcasts by FM stations in Estonia and in tourist areas in southern Europe. Since 1996 YLE Radio Finland has also been available as Internet Real Audio Live. In 1989 the Finnish Broadcasting Company launched the only Latin-language news review in the world, 'Nuntii Latini', as a part of its domestic and foreign-language broadcasting.MS

Rauma Rauma is Finland's third oldest town, founded in 1442. Like Old Porvoo and the old town of Naantali, Old Rauma is a representative example of medieval Finnish wood town construction. The street system and layout plan of Old Rauma implemented after the Great Fire of 1682 have not greatly changed.

Old Rauma is Finland's largest area of wooden town construction. Some of the buildings date from the 18th century, but most of the wooden buildings were erected during the 19th century. The ruins and cemetery of the Church of the Holy Trinity, built in the 14th century, are situated in the eastern part of Old Rauma. The 15th-century Church of the Holy Cross once belonged to a Franciscan monastery that was built on the site. It has been Rauma's parish church since 1640. The Town Hall, built in 1776, contains ob-

A street of wooden houses in old Rauma

jects related to marine navigation and bobbin lace-making.

Old Rauma was made the subject of a conservation order in 1981, and in December 1991 was added to Unesco's World Heritage List. KRn

Rautanen, Martti (1845–1926), missionary, Bible translator. The basis for the still close relations between Finland and Namibia were created in the late 1860s when the Finnish Evangelican Lutheran Mission opened its first missionary field station there. Martti Rautanen was one of the first missionaries sent to south-west Africa.

Born near St Petersburg, in Finnish-speaking Ingria, Martti Rautanen came from a very poor family who lived as serfs. He studied at Helsinki Missionary College and settled permanently in 1868 in south-west Africa. He was in charge of the missionary station from 1885 to 1920 – a period during which, after a weak start, its activities became established. Rautanen's greatest importance, however, lay in his work in creating a written Ondongan language and in translating the Bible into it. Rautanen also recorded Ondongan speech and parish activities on wax cylinder as early as the 1910s. For these achievements the University of Helsinki awarded him an honorary doctorate in 1925. There is a reconstruction of Martti Rautanen's office at the Missionary Museum in Helsinki, where his Ondongan recordings are also held. JN

Rautavaara, Einojuhani (born 1928), composer. Einojuhani Rautavaara's extensive work is characterised by a diversity of style, including influences from neoclassicism, dodecaphony, serialism and neoromanticism and a religious and mystical world. Rautavaara studied at the Sibelius Academy in Helsinki, and in the United States and in central Europe. Already in his early work he was using symmetrical structures, and he has returned repeatedly to both these elements in his later work.

In the 1950s and 1960s Rautavaara had a period of intellectual constructivism and 12-tone music. From the late 1960s a diversity of styles and an attempt at synthesis began to take shape in his work. From the mid 1980s,

Rautavaara has concentrated on opera, with works including *Thomas* (1985), *Vincent* (1987) and *Auringon talo* ('The house of the sun', 1990), to which he also wrote the libretti. The composer's linguistic gifts are also to the fore in his autobiography, *Omakuva* ('A self-portrait', 1989), in which he has sketched his work as a composer.

Rautavaara was Professor of Composition at the Sibelius Academy from 1976 to 1990 and artistic professor from 1971 to 1976. His extensive repertoire includes instrumental concertos (including two piano concertos, a violin concerto, a bassoon concerto, choral works, seven operas, among them ▶*Aleksis Kivi* (1997), seven symphonies, orchestral works, chamber music and instrumental works. RL

Rautawaara, Aulikki (1906–1990), soprano. Rautawaara started her operatic career at the Finnish National Opera in the early 1930s. Later in the 1930s and 1940s she won international acclaim, particularly with her vivid interpretations of major Mozart roles. She was the Countess in *The Marriage of Figaro* at the inaugural season at Glyndebourne in 1934, and appeared at the Salzburg Festival in 1938. She also performed and recorded *Lieder*, but unfortunately many of the recordings she made, for Telefunken, were destroyed during the Second World War before they could be released. HB

Retretti Art Centre The name of Retretti derives from 'retreat', withdrawing to rest. This art exhibition and concert centre is open in the summer and it is built in the midst of the most beautiful, protected landscape of lakes and ridges in eastern Finland, near Savonlinna at Punkaharju in 1983. In addition to exhibition, shop and restaurant facilities, the centre includes a concert hall which can accommodate an audience of 1000. In addition to exhibitions of Finnish work, artists including Rubens, Chagall, Repin and Picasso have been on show at Retretti. MLR

revivalist movements In Finland, the term 'revivalist movements' is used to refer to the reform movements within the established Lutheran Church that have connections with pietism or evan-

Martti Rautanen

Einojuhani Rautavaara

Aulikki Rautawaara

Retretti (Punkaharju)

Venny Soldan-Brofeldt, *Heränneitä* ('Revivalist Christians'), 1898

gelist revivalist Christianity. Pietist influences reached Finland by the late 17th century, partly as moderate stimuli to the religious life of the church, partly in radical form. The latter included mystical spiritualism and a strong criticism of the church. The church took a negative attitude to pietism, and in 1726 forbade the meeting of illicit societies or conventicles. The impact of the collision was lessened by the fact that the pietist revival was often headed by clergymen, and for this reason separatist tendencies were few in the 18th century.

Revivalist movements, as such, which continue to be active within the church, originated in the 19th century. The earliest was prayerism, whose area of influence can be seen today in southwest Finland, to the north of Turku. Laestadianism, based on the teachings of the clergyman Lars Levi Laestadius (1800–1861), who was active in Sweden, spread to ▶Lapland, northern Finland and ▶Ostrobothnia. At the end of the 19th century it divided into two separate tendencies, of which the so-called old Lestadianism is the more important. With urbanisation, Laestadianism has, particularly since the Second World War, received support in towns and, through emigration, also abroad. Old Laestadianism is the most severe of present-day revivalist movements. It is strongly inward-looking and opposes, among other things, the ordination of women, birth control and television.

The movement known as revival-ism was at first made up of local variants in Ostrobothnia and Savo. They combined in the 1820s after the lay preacher ▶Paavo Ruotsalainen had risen to become the movement's uniting figure. At first the church's attitude to revivalism was negative, but the movement rapidly gained support, particularly among the younger clergy. Subsequently, the movement has had a great deal of influence within the church, and has not had important dogmatic differences with it.

The fourth of the old revivalist movements, the evangelist movement, is more conservative in nature, and, like Laestadianism, opposes the ordination of women.

The British and American charismatic Christianity that spread strongly in Finland after the Second World War is often called the fifth revivalist movement. It is made up of a number of organisations whose common feature is that, like the older revivalist movements, they function within the existing church.

The most widely noticed activity of the revivalist movements is their summer festivals, which attract tens of thousands of visitors every year. The conservative features of the revivalist movement, such as their opposition to the ordination of women and their criticism to historical and critical exegesis, have provoked public debate. Pietism, which has been the most open in outlook, has had a particularly strong influence on the arts. In addition to literature, it has provided subjects for an ►opera about ►Paavo Ruot-salainen by ►Joonas Kokkonen, *Vii-meiset kiusaukset* (*The Last Tempta-tions*, 1975) and Heikki Ylikangas's (born 1937) play *Kolmekymmentä ho-pearahaa* ('Thirty pieces of silver'), whose first performance took place at the Finnish National Theatre in 1982. JN

rock music Rock music can be said to have arrived in Finland in 1955 with the release of *Mambo Rock* by Bill Haley & His Comets. It did not inspire many young people, but Haley's *Rock Around the Clock*, released soon afterwards, was accorded a considerably better reception. By early 1956, this 'herald of rock 'n' roll' was second on the Finnish chart lists.

In the 1950s, however, rock 'n' roll reached only the young people of the larger towns and cities. In the country-side and in small towns, Finnish and continental popular songs, particular-ly Italian songs, remained popular. Al-though a few 'King of Rock' and 'Elvis Presley of Finland' competitions were held in Finland, the young people who were successful in them did not gain access to the recording studio. The music industry did not believe in the durability of rock 'n' roll. The few rock 'n' roll discs cut in Finland were con-signed to routine session musicians, so that they sounded more like dance and pop music than real youth music.

It was the jazz and dance-music veteran Onni Gideon (1921–1994) who was responsible for the first Finn-ish rock record. His instrumental *Ha-waiian Rock* (1957), recorded using trick techniques, was his own composi-tion. It was a clever and successful per-formance, but it did not achieve signif-icant commercial success.

In 1959 the 16-year-old Kaj Järn-ström (born 1943) was voted the Finnish King of Rock. Järnström used the artistic name Rock-Jerry and, un-like earlier winners, he was able to record; as a result, in the early 1960s, a number of fairly good cover versions appeared of rock standards such as *Long Tall Sally* and *Party*. They also sold reasonably well, and this opened the doors of the recording studios to many other young rockers.

At this time, however, the populari-ty of rock 'n' roll began to diminish. The reason for this was the instrumen-tal music played on electric guitars. The style was launched by the English group The Shadows and the American The Ventures. They quickly acquired many imitators in Finland, although the best results were achieved with original ideas. Among these was an electric arrangement of a Finnish folk song, *Emma*, recorded by The Sounds, a group formed by a Helsinki school-boy. In 1963 it became Finland's top-selling single. This was the first time that music by young people under 20 had been seen at the top of the list. When *Emma* was released in Japan slightly later, it sold more than 200,000 copies.

The flowering of music style re-mained short, because in 1963 Fin-land, like other countries, was capti-vated by pop music of an entirely dif-ferent kind. The Beatles, The Rolling Stones and many other English groups rapidly became popular, and some of the bands gave up completely, while others shifted with varying degrees of success to sung beat music. Among them were the brothers Eero (born 1944) and Jussi Raittinen (born 1943). In 1964 they founded their own group, which they called Eero & Jussi & The Boys. It had the honour of being the first group to record a Beatles song in Finnish – *All My Loving*, which was re-leased in 1964. Later, The Boys had many other hits, and both Eero and Jussi were also successful as solo artists. The Boys, who still exist today, have received the sobriquet 'the uni-versity of Finnish rock', for dozens of famous musicians began their careers there.

In the 1960s, Finnish pop music was still fairly derivative. Most of the popular singers and bands released translations of foreign hits. Some, however, recorded their own songs. Cay and The Scaffolds' *Girls* and Jim & The Beatmakers' *My Only One* (both 1964) were among the first successful attempts. Two years later, the Helsinki band Ernos got into the charts with their own compositions *Harha* ('Delu-sion') and *Yksin* ('Alone'), but the two most popular Finnish bands of the 1960s, Topmost and Jormas – both of which were also successful in Sweden –

primarily recorded translations. Topmost's best-known recordings were Los Bravos' *Black is Black* (1966) and Procol Harum's *A Whiter Shade of Pale* (1967), while among the songs Jormas took into the charts were The Beach Boys' hit *God Only Knows* and The Beatles' *Penny Lane* (both 1967).

The first Finnish group of international dimensions was the Cream-influenced Blues Section, who did not attain significant commercial success, but sowed a new enthusiasm and experimental spirit among young musicians. Results soon began to be visible. The Swedish Theatre's production of the most successful musical of the time, *Hair*, gave birth to Wigwam, who, by the end of the 1970s, became the best-known Finnish group abroad. A similar brand of progressive rock was represented by Tasavallan Presidentti, who also attracted attention abroad, particularly in Sweden and England.

Hector, Heikki Harma

Juice Leskinen

Heikki Harma (born 1947), or Hector, began his career in the mid 1960s with translated versions of foreign folk hits. In the decade that followed, he began to make more independent and personal music, which was also commercially successful. His second album, the sombre-toned and mystical, in places even occult, *Herra Mirandos* ('Sir Mirandos', 1973) was both a commercial and a critical success. Many of its pieces, including *Lumi teki enkelin eteiseen* ('The snow made an angel in the hall'), remain classics of Finnish rock, and from that record on, Hector has been among the foremost Finnish songwriters. Although his music has, over the years, gone through many changes, his popularity remains undiminished. Albums containing social comment, such as *Kadonneet lapset* ('The lost children', 1978), have deservedly attracted attention, and this skilful songwriter has also written large numbers of texts for other Finnish singers.

Juice Leskinen (born 1950), too, has written more than 1000 song-texts. Stylistically, however, he is far removed from Hector, for while Juice, too, often makes social comments, he often uses humour as his weapon. Trusting in its power, this virtuoso rhymer ridicules everything possible from stupid po-

licemen (*Pilvee, Pilvee* – 'Hashish, hashish', 1978) to power-hungry politicians (*Midas*, 1980). But although Juice is indeed often a sharp-tongued blasphemer and a ready taunter, he can also write touchingly beautiful songs such as *Syksyn sävel* ('Autumn note', 1975).

One of the most popular Finnish groups of all time came about through the rock 'n' roll revival of the early 1970s. The Hurriganes (yes, the name is spelt with a g) was a trio that performed straightforward and uncomplicated basic rock. Its first hits were old classics such as *Do You Want to Dance* and *Blue Suede Shoes* (both 1974). The album *Roadrunner*, recorded the same year, is considered the band's best; its hit number is the furious *Get On*. But the old rock 'n' roll tradition was also revived in the Finnish language. Rauli Badding Somerjoki (1947–1987) took, among other things, Chuck Berry's *Reelin' and Rockin'* to Number One in 1973.

In 1977, Finnish rock came once more under the influence of England when punk began to provoke interest in Finland. The new wave inspired large numbers of young musicians, and it demonstrated that Finns, too, had a need for self-expression. While there had been about 200 active and gigging bands in Finland in the late 1960s, with punk that number grew tenfold. The first big name of the Finnish new wave was Pelle Miljoona (Petri Tiili, born 1955), whose songs, such as *Olen työtön* ('I am unemployed', 1978) and *Moottoritie on kuuma* ('The motorway is hot', 1980), accurately reflected the thoughts and feelings of Finnish youth. Pelle Miljoona sang directly and pointed the

Eppu Normaali

finger, dealing with subjects as wide-ranging and serious as the welfare state and the threat of nuclear war in his songs.

Eppu Normaali, a group founded near Tampere, approached similar subjects from a completely different angle. If Pelle Miljoona was sometimes over-serious and pessimistic, Eppu Normaali presented similar themes with humour. An excellent example of the group's style appeared on its first record, *Poliisi pamputtaa taas* ('The policeman bludgeons again', 1978). These songs, however, still often have a serious starting-point, and although *Puhtoinen lähiöni* ('My very clean suburb', 1979), about living on a housing estate, or *Murheellisten laulujen maa* ('Land of sorrowful songs', 1982) may sound light, they are in the end not amusing at all. The group later moved closer to mainstream rock, but this did not diminish their popularity; on the contrary, a total of around a million Eppu Normaali records have been sold to date.

The newcomers of the 1980s included Hassisen Kone ('Hassinen's machine') from Joensuu, and Tuomari Nurmio (Hannu Nurmio, born 1950), with his cultivation of black humour. Both reached the charts and the radio's black-list with their first records. Hassisen Kone's racy *Rappiolla* ('Ruined', 1980) and Nurmio's *Kurja matkamies maan* ('Wreched traveller of the earth', 1979), based on an old hymn, provoked severe anger in conservative circles, but among the rock public such condemnation naturally only increased the popularity of the records. Nurmio has continued his original, stylistically very varied line to the present day, and the leader of Hassisen Kone, Ismo Alanko (born 1960) also remains active. Alanko's most important work is probably *Kun Suomi putos puusta* ('When Finland fell out of the tree', 1990), written to a commission from the Helsinki Festival, in which he uses irony and satire to cut through the history, culture and national characteristics of Finland.

Other groups that made their appearance in the 1980s are Leevi and The Leavings, with their catchy pop tunes, J. Karjalainen & Mustat Lasit

J. Karjalainen

('J. Karjalainen & The Black Glasses'), whose style derives from the blues and country music, and Hanoi Rocks, who have achieved international success. Among the most popular names of the early 1990s were Neljä Ruusua ('Four roses'), now 4R, led by Ismo Alanko's younger brother, Ilkka Alanko (born 1969), the stylist Aki Sirkesalo (born 1962), who derives his influence from old Motown-soul, and Mikko Kuustonen (born 1962), a singer and songwriter a little reminiscent of Hector.

The techno music of the 1990s was greeted in Finland in the same way as all earlier world influences, by first copying the big foreign names. Very soon, however, a local techno, sung in Finnish and to a large extent based on the romanticism, longing and minor key of traditional Finnish popular music, established itself as a separate genre. Its biggest names are Movetron and Aikakone ('Time machine'), both of which, in 1995, sold about 100,000 copies of their debut discs. JNn

rock-paintings Rock-paintings are pictorial representations painted on the vertical walls of shoreline cliffs and boulders, which have been dated to the period approx. 3500 B.C. to A.D. 500. They have so far been discovered only in central and eastern Finland, as far north as Kuusamo, and to the west of Helsinki, in Espoo and Kirkkonummi. The paintings are executed in red earth mixed with some kind of binding material, and they are best-preserved in places where they have been protected either by projecting rock or by the glass-like silicon dioxide that has formed over the painting. Because the image surfaces are often located on walls that fall straight into the water, it is supposed that they were painted either in the winter from the ice or in the summer from a boat.

More than 60 rock-paintings have been found in Finland to date, and they comprise a total of almost 450 images. Most of them contain only one to three figures, but the most impor-

tant painting, at Astuvansalmi, Ristiina, southern Savo has 65 images. The commonest subject is the elk, but the paintings also depict, in various ways, people and ►shamans, boats, dogs, snakes, swans, fish and net-patterns, as well as images of hands, feet and paws. Rarer are the ringed cross, symbolising the sun, and the woman holding a bow at Astuvansalmi. Most of the figures are somewhat schematic, for example all the human figures are shown as some kind of stick-people, but among the elks there are some very graphic examples. The group of elks at Verla, Jaala, has been drawn with real artistry.

It seems obvious that the Finnish rock-paintings are connected with the world of beliefs associated with a hunting culture. They were used to safeguard continued catches and success in hunting. It is possible that the paintings were executed before hunting in order to gain power over the prey or to ensure the catch through the ritual shooting of the images. The arrowheads found beneath the Astuvansalmi paintings would seem to indicate the latter.

The paintings could also be 'return images' with whose help the animals' souls are returned to the species guardian to persuade him to continue to send the huntsmen fat prey animals in the future. Images of palm-prints are generally known protective marks. Perhaps their protection emboldened approaches to the elk guardian, to whom

Stone-Age engraving from Astuvansalmi, southern Savo.
The presence of a woman with a bow (left) suggests that women in ancient Finland hunted alongside men

the shaman was directed by helpers, snakes and other animals that cannot be interpreted as elks. Images of boats could be the shamans' mode of transport to the other world from which the animals' souls were to be fetched.

Most recently, the idea has been proposed that the locations of the rock-paintings may have been sacred *seita* boulders before which sacrifices may have been made by the hunting folk. The amber pendants found below the Astuvansalmi painting support this theory. PLLH

Romanies The first mention of the arrival of the Romanies in Finland is encountered in an account book in the Kastelholma Castle in the ►Åland archipelago in 1559. By the end of the 17th century, an attempt was being made to settle 150 Romanies as farmers in the empty lands of eastern Finland. The intention was also to gather a Romany division for the army to patrol the then troubled eastern border.

At the time it was believed that the immigration of Romanies to Finland had taken place exclusively through Sweden. But it seems that they also arrived via the Karelian Isthmus. In the 1990s there were around 6000 Romanies in Finland.

Of the main dialects of the Romany language, the Finnish Romanies speak the most widespread, the *kaale* dialect. Romanies have been copper-smiths, horse-traders and musicians.

The basic unit of social organisation in Romany culture is the *cherha*, or team. This is a kinship group to which the individual belongs through either his father or his mother. It is named after some ancestor, sometimes after a living person. Old Romanies remember their own families in extraordinary detail, going back for a very long way. The *cherha* is divided into families which are in fact often so-called extended families, comprising more than one generation. In such families, children are protected not only by their parents but by other close relatives. Learning professional and life skills also takes place within the family circle.

Role-allocation within the family has been important, and has closely regulated the behaviour of family members. In the Romany role-hierarchy, old people are at the top, young women at the bottom. Respect for old people and many ideas connected with hygiene are central to Romany customs. Among some Romany groups, the Romany institution of justice, or *kris romani*, is known. Its task is to decide differences of opinion between different groups or individuals.

Traditional occupations approved by Romany culture and in harmony with the Romany way of life have been the same everywhere. Romanies have fulfilled the needs of the society in which they find themselves by taking up occupations for which the local population is unable or unwilling. They have been craftsmen, silver- or tinsmiths, harnessmakers, musicians, artists or other entertainers, merchants, horse-changers, animal-healers and clairvoyants.

With the advent of industrialisation, Romanies everywhere began to

Romany family, Kauhajoki, Ostrobothnia

lose their status. In Finland the situation became critical at the point when the horse, so central to Romany culture, began to give way to the machine.

The external ethnic marker of the Romanies is the tradition-rich costume, which has, however, continually undergone small changes. The old, dark costume of the Romany man has been replaced in recent years by a more plentiful use of Romany-style colours. The woman's festive dress has already been complemented by the fact that there are more material alternatives on offer. The amount of jewellery has been not only a measure of social status but, at least in former times, a practical way of converting excess property into an easily portable form.

Because Romany culture is to a large extent unwritten, the oral tradition plays a central role. In Finland, the most vivid part of the Romany narrative traditon is made up of recollections of the family and its various members, or the unwritten history of the tribe. These, like Romany culture as a whole, are characterised by the extensive cultivation of humour.

Most characteristic, and at least in part best-known outside the tribe, are the Romany songs, which are a part of the oral tradition that is constantly being regenerated. The singing of the Finnish romanies, with its vocal quality and plentiful use of grace notes, may contain elements from the very distant past. The song tradition has been published on CD under the title *Kaale džambena – Suomen mustalaiset laulavat* ('Singing of the Finnish Romanies'). Many Romanies have also been successful popular singers. Finland's first Romany writer is Veijo Baltzar (born 1942).

The Romano Missio was established in 1904 with the task of raising the spiritual and material conditions of the Romanies on a Christian basis. The Romano Missio has, since 1971, published the magazine *Romano Boodos*. The Finnish Romany Association, founded in 1967, is the Romanies' own organisation, and exists to stimulate debate. PLn

Runeberg, Johan Ludvig (1804–1877), writer. Runeberg was born into a Swedish-speaking family in Pietar-

J.L. Runeberg

saari, on the shores of the Gulf of Bothnia. A product of neo-humanism, romanticism and the Biedermeier period, Runeberg wrote his work in his mother tongue, Swedish. He began as a romantic poet with his collection *Dikter* ('Poems', 1831), but soon became interested in the life of ordinary people. His hexametric poem *Elgskyttarne* ('Elk hunters on skis', 1832) presents, with idealistic realism, the life of the country people of inland Finland. Runeberg wrote the work with which he made his breakthrough, the bourgeois Biedermeier idyll *Hanna* (1836), in the spirit of J.H. Voss. *Kung Fjalar* ('King Fjalar', 1840) is a tragic Viking poem. The heroic romances *Fänrik Ståls sägner I–II* ('Tales of Ensign Stål I–II', 1848, 1860), which describe the war between Sweden and Russia in 1808–1809, are Runeberg's masterpiece. They include the poem that has since become Finland's national anthem, *Vårt land* (*Maamme*, 'Our country'). Patriotism arises from love of Finland's nature. It is a holy gift from God, in defence of which soldiers have the right to die. Runeberg is the first Finnish writer to have achieved a broad national significance. PL

Ruotsalainen, Paavo (1777–1852), revivalist religious leader. Paavo Ruotsalainen is one of Finland's most influential religious figures. Born to a peasant family, he experienced a religious awakening at the age of 22, after which he began to appear in the pietist-inspired meetings of his home area as a speaker. Through Ruotsalainen's influence, the formerly separate ▶revivalist movements of ▶Ostrobothnia and Savo combined. The official church and authorities at first took a negative atti-

Paavo
Ruotsalainen

tude to revivalism, and in 1839 Ruotsalainen was fined for illegal meetings
in a court case that attracted a great
deal of attention. The revivalist movement nevertheless soon gained a great
deal of support, particularly among
the lower clergy. This was partly because Ruotsalainen's attitude to the
church as such was positive, although
he was critical of the lack of religious
revivalism among the clergy.

Paavo Ruotsalainen is a key figure
in the understanding of Finnish national feeling and national identity in
the early years of independence (1917).
He was seen as a representative of the
people, the peasants, and of initiative,
as a character risen from among the
deep ranks of the people, who dared
challenge the authorities on the basis
of his own personal conviction. This
characteristic offered a good example
during the period of Russification
(1899–1905) that preceded independence, when attempts were made to
unite the nation to fight against the
Russification that threatened Finland's
own legislation.

The composer ►Joonas Kokkonen
plumbed Paavo Ruotsalainen in his
opera *Viimeiset kiusaukset* (*The Last
Temptations*, 1975). The bass singer
►Martti Talvela achieved great popularity for his interpretation of the leading role. JN

Russians During Finland's period as
an autonomous Grand Duchy of Russia (1809–1917), the cosmopolitan nature of the Russian Empire, its army
and its capital, St Petersburg, radiated
its administrative, economic and cultural influence in such a way that people living in Finland and speaking
Russian among themselves were also

cosmopolitan, multilingual and multicultural. In these people's ethnic de-
marcation of boundaries, however, the
most important aspect was the sense
of their own identity.

There had been a permanent Russian population in the south-east part
of Finland conquered by Peter the
Great, which was known as Old Finland, since the beginning of the 18th
century; extremely few Russians, however, lived in Helsinki at that time – in
1724 they numbered only 13. The
number of Russians living permanently in Finland remained low during the
country's period as a Grand Duchy: in
1910 their number was about 4800,
complemented by some 7000 temporary residents.

The permanent residents were generally tradesmen and artisans. In the
mid 19th century, 40 per cent of
Helsinki's tradesmen were Russian,
while in Viipuri Russians made up as
much as half of the entire mercantile
community. Russians kept ice-cream
and confectionery kiosks, small bread,
grocer's and greengrocer's shops, and
stalls in covered markets. Pickled cucumbers, sauerkraut, ice-cream and
baked goods were among their specialities. But they also owned larger businesses, such as beer, confectionery and
cigarette factories, construction companies, nurseries and market gardens,
and so on. Wealthy merchant families
began, as early as the 1870s, to assimi-
late with the Finland-Swedes. Some
clerical families, too, established themselves in Finland. The potter peasants
of Kyyrölä (Krasnoye Selo) and the
workers of the ironworks at Raivola,
both on the Karelian Isthmus, were also prominent groups of Russians.

A colourful and highly independent
life was lived in the fortress of Viapori,
or ►Suomenlinna, in Helsinki Harbour, which reported directly to the
Russian administration. It remained
very Russian, and was like a city within
a city with its soldiers and servants,
priests and doctors, pedlers and teachers.

The temporary residents included
the army, civil servants, seasonal workers and servants. The number of Russians was at its height on the eve of the
First World War. When, in 1910, the
Russian *duma* approved a proposal to

extend the imperial legislature to Finland, a strong Russification of the Finnish administrative apparatus began. In 1912 Russians received the same rights in Finland as Finns, and the ban on foreign ownership of property in Finland was lifted.

In 1913, less than 800 of the villas of the province of Viipuri were in foreign hands, generally owned by St Petersburg families, and in the best summer seasons more than 100,000 Russians spent their holidays on the Karelian Isthmus. The approaching world war also caused a growth in military fortifications, and their building brought additional military personnel into the country. In 1917 the number of permanent residents was estimated at about 6000 and troops at 125,000.

The government of independent Finland wished to rid itself of the Russian troops as quickly as possible: some of the soldiers had fought on the red side in the Civil War of 1918, and the army was disintegrating. An understanding attitude was nevertheless taken towards the predicament of army officers; they were permitted to return to civilian life and leave Finland as emigrants. In 1918 only 40,000 military personnel remained, and at the end of the Civil War (1918) the remaining Russian soldiers were expelled from the country. By 1920 almost 5000 Russian citizens remained. On the other hand, the number of refugees from St Petersburg and temporary residents in the country grew. In 1921, when the flood of refugees was at its greatest, their number was estimated at about 19,000. Bearing in mind Finland's shared border with Russia, there were, in fact, very few Russian refugees compared, for example, with Syria, where, in 1932, they numbered 131,000, or France, where their number was 400,000.

Most of the Russians who crossed the border to Finland between 1917 and 1921 continued their journeys to the other centres of Europe. Only those with some kind of connection with Finland – property, relatives or job – remained. Over half the Russian population of Finland remained in Viipuri province when the borders were closed. Only with the depression years of the 1930s did people begin to seek work further afield, and the move westward began. The proximity of the border proved fateful for the Russian population in 1939, when many of them became refugees for a second time.

There are a considerable number of bearers of the Russian tradition and their descendants, either those who originally fled Russia as a result of the October Revolution or those who had already lived in Finland for a number of generations – a couple of thousand in all. Their exact number is difficult to estimate, for as bi- or trilingual Finnish citizens they seldom feel that they belong to any ethnic minority, and statistical nets have not been able to entrap them. Thus it is more accurate to speak of Russianness in Finland than of Russians.

During the inter-war period these people, of very diverse roots, felt a need to unite culturally behind the same public organisations, such as the many political and social societies, newspapers, amateur theatres, dance, music, art exhibitions, literary clubs or church activities. Between the wars there were Russian schools on the Karelian Isthmus, in Viipuri and in Helsinki. The balalaika orchestra founded in the 1910s still functions, and a Russian amateur theatre continued until the 1950s.

The Russians in Finland were united by three factors: the loss of their cultural motherland, a common system of values and a common language for public discourse. Later, a fourth feature entered the picture: the feeling that an age had irrevocably ended.

From the 1960s onwards, people speaking Russian as their mother-tongue or home language have moved to Finland from the former Soviet Union. These immigrants, commonly known as 'new Russians', are also by nature heterogeneous and multicultural. The number of immigrants from the Soviet Union – or, after 1991, Russia – is, according to official statistics in the mid 1990s, between 14,000 and 15,000, depending on whether they are identified according to language or nationality. A total of around 23,000 people have moved to Finland from the former Soviet Union or present-day Russia according to 1995 statistics;

Orthodox Ascension Day procession of the cross and blessing of water, Helsinki harbour-front

some of these are Ingrian remigrants and Estonians and other nationalities. Russian-speaking people today live evenly distributed around Helsinki, although the majority of them have settled in southern and southwest Finland. They are at their sparsest in Lapland and the Åland islands.

The society of the Russian-speaking population in Finland publishes a Russian-language magazine, *Vestnik*, whose pilot issue appeared as early as 1993, and an information sheet with news of events of interest to Russian-speakers throughout the country. The society also supports various cultural projects, such as concerts, art exhibitions, seminars, minority meetings and so on. It encourages hobby circles and acts as a consultant in legal matters for foreigners, and helps immigrants to find their way through the officialdom of Finnish social services and business life. The society has set as one of its central objectives the cultivation of the Russian language and its transmission to the next generation.

As the Russian-speaking population of Finland has grown, so have the challenges to the Finnish ▶Orthodox Church and the Finnish educational system. Not all Russian-speakers, however, are Orthodox, and not all Orthodox Christians belong to the Orthodox Church. Helsinki has two private Orthodox parishes that are subordinate to the Moscow patriarchate. The

Finnish-Russian School in Helsinki, founded in the 1950s, and the attached kindergarten, form one channel for cultural connections. In addition, the National Board of Education organises teaching of Russian as mother tongue in schools throughout the country. NB

ryijy Finland's best-known art textile is the *ryijy*, or rug. For the Vikings, the *ryijy* was a coverlet and mantle. In Finland, too, it was originally a utilitarian textile which replaced animal hides. In the coastal regions and the archipelago, the *ryijy* was used as a covering for boats at least until the 19th century. Boat *ryijy*s were woven on narrow looms into long strips, which were then cut and sewn together, two or three side by side. They were often decorated with stripes or cheeks, but decoration was hardly an object of interest. In cold stone castles, *ryijy*s and other textiles such as wall-hangings and double-weave textiles were woven in castle weaving rooms and royal demesnes. Castle *ryijy*s were colourful and decorated with, for example, coats of arms or geometrical patterns.

*Ryijy*s became more widespread among ordinary people in the interior of the country only as they became decorative textiles. From the mid 18th century to the early decades of the 19th century the Finnish folk *ryijy* experienced its golden age – it became an art textile whose harmonious plant-

Traditional *ryijy* rug, southern Finland, c.1790

Uhra (Beata) Simberg-Ehrström, *Yksin* ('Alone') *ryijy* rug, 1966

dyed colourings and original patterns were born at the hand of ordinary women. Among the products of that period were wedding and church *ryijy*s and sleigh coverlets.

The making of *ryijy*s declined as, for reasons of hygiene, they were abandoned as bed-coverlets from the 1820s onwards. At the end of the 19th century the Friends of Finnish Handicraft began to revive almost-forgotten craft skills and collected, among other things, *ryijy*s, whose estimation rose. The *Liekki* ('Flame') and *Miekka* ('Sword') *ryijy*s designed by the well-known artist ►Akseli Gallen-Kallela for the *art nouveau* style room of the Finnish pavilion at the Paris World Exhibition of 1900, and woven by the Friends of Finnish Handicraft, were Finland's first modern art ►textiles. From the early 1920s onwards, the Friends of Finnish Handicraft organised regular design competitions; participation was enthusiastic, and the result was a new *ryijy*, a decorative tex-

tile, freed from tradition and designed, according to the influences of the day in functionalist or lyrically painterly style. During the 1930s and 1940s there was much debate over whether the *ryijy* belonged on the wall or the floor. Among the designers of the time were Impi Sotavalta (1885–1943), ►Eva Brummer and Uhra Simberg-Ehrström (1914–1979), who was the first to knot the pile of *ryijy*s from threads of different colours and lengths. She also wove the nine-metre-long *Metsä* ('Forest') *ryijy* for the Montreal World Exhibition 1967.

The *ryijy* flourished for a third time after the Second World War once the supply of raw materials had returned to normal. *Ryijy*s, now transformed into abstract colouristic works, became world-famous: they won prizes at applied arts exhibitions and were acquired by museum collections abroad. In addition to those already mentioned, Kirsti Ilvessalo (born 1920) was an important innovator of the *ryijy*; her *Palokärki* ('Black woodpecker') was the first *ryijy* acquired by the Victoria & Albert Museum in London.

The design of *ryijy*s also led towards sculptural textile art. In addition to textiles, wood, metal, paper and plastic, as well as natural materials, were taken into use. The length of the pile was varied, and *ryijy*s developed into part of modern interior design. Space-works by Kirsti Rantanen (born 1930) decorate the house of the Finnish National Opera in Helsinki, while Maija Lavonen (born 1931) is known both for her textiles and her sculptural *ryijy*s, which are to be found in many public places. The design of *ryijy*s continues to inspire new textile artists. MA

Saariaho, Kaija (born 1952), composer. Kaija Saariaho is one of the internationally best-known contemporary Finnish composers, who has effectively exploited computer technology and live electronics. Her often dreamlike, static music is made up of extended, shimmering tonal surfaces, like light phenomena (*Verblendungen*, 1982–1984; *Lichtbogen*, 1986), but in her more recent works the dramatic quality is more dynamic (... *à la Fumée*, 1990). MH

S

Kaija Saariaho

Saarikoski, Pentti (1937–1983), writer. For Pentti Saarikoski, classical literature was a tradition of essential importance, which is rare for a Finnish writer. His first two collections of poetry appeared in 1958, and *Runot ja Hipponaksen runot* ('Poems and poems of Hipponax'), which appeared the following year, reveals Saarikoski's early source of inspiration. Hipponax's speaking, daring fragments were new in Finnish poetry. In the speech-like language of the collection *Mitä tapahtuu todella?* ('What is happening really?', 1962), which used quotations and fragments, Saarikoski challenged the preceding modernism with its ideal of perfectly honed expression. He became one of the central artistic figures of the New Left movement of the 1960s, and adopted a new kind of public role as a writer. Saarikoski's works are uneven, but their lasting qualities are intelligence, openness and conversation. His late achievement was the *Tiarnia* trilogy (1977–1983). Among his translations are James Joyce's *Ulysses* and Homer's *Odyssey*, St Matthew's Gospel, and works by Henry Miller and J.D. Salinger. PL

Saarinen, Eliel (1873–1950), architect. As a student, Eliel Saarinen won, together with Herman Gesellius (1874–1916) and Armas Lindgren (1874–1929), two architectural competitions. The sculptural apartment blocks designed by these architects renewed ideas about living and the urban landscape in the spirit of the international *art nouveau* style. Private houses were built as works of art in themselves, bound to the landscape. The trio's own house, ▶Hvitträsk (1903), in Kirkkonummi, close to Helsinki, is a full-blooded example of the ideal.

The Finnish pavilion for the 1900 Paris World Exhibition was the project which secured the Gesellius-Lindgren-Saarinen partnership international fame. The richly decorated soapstone façade of the Pohjola Insurance Company (1901) displays the same joy in story-telling. In the ▶Finnish National Museum, also in Helsinki (1901–1910), Gesellius-Lindgren-Saarinen developed a free-form outline of Finnish history.

With his design for Helsinki Railway Station, Saarinen became a rationalist. His romantic competition entry of 1904 became a vigorous urban transport centre (1914). This project also directed Saarinen towards urban planning – designed extensions for Budapest and Tallinn. In 1912 he received Second Prize for the planning competition for Canberra, which secured him a place in the international elite. His Munkkiniemi-Haaga plan of 1915 implied the radical growth of the City of Helsinki. Working with Bertel Jung (1872–1946), in a general plan attached to the Munkkiniemi-Haaga plan in 1918, Saarinen developed a city design that is known by the name 'Pro Helsingfors'.

Saarinen won Second Prize in the competition for a skyscraper building for the 'Chicago Tribune' in 1922, and in 1923 he moved to the United States. Finland had become too small for the scope of his vision. Work in the Art Academy of Cranbrook promised more. Eliel Saarinen's son, Eero (1910–1961), also attained international fame but as an American architect. RN

Pentti Saarikoski

Helsinki Railway Station, 1914–1919

Eliel Saarinen

Saint Henry (died c.1156), Missionary Bishop, martyr, patron saint of Finland. The English-born bishop Henry is the patron saint of the Catholic Church of Finland and the *primus* of the Finnish episcopal succession. The earliest written sources about Henry are based on the Legend of Saint Henry, which dates from the 1270s. It is the earliest example of written literature in Finland.

The sources reveal that Henry was the Bishop of Upsala and that he came to Finland with the saintly King Eric's crusading army around 1155. Scholars nevertheless approach both St Eric's so-called First Crusade and Henry's activity as Bishop of Upsala with caution. It is believed possible that he was a Missionary Bishop without a definite diocese.

Aulis Sallinen

wards the end of the 13th century. Great masses were said on Saint Henry's memorial day, and Henry's cult and legend have been highly influential on both ecclesiastical art and literature in Finland. One of the most important art treasures of the medieval period in Finland is a cenotaph in Nousiainen Church made of a brass alloy in Flanders in the 1420s. The cenotaph illustrates Henry's life and events connected with his martyr's death. JN

Sallinen, Aulis (born 1935), composer. Sallinen is among the best-known abroad of Finland's composers. His traditional compositional style, which appeals to a wide public, national themes and effective dramaturgy in *Ratsumies* (*The Horseman*, 1973–1974, libretto ▶Paavo Haavikko) and *Punainen viiva* (*The Red Line*, 1976–1978, libretto according to Ilmari Kianto's (1874–1970) novel Sallinen), made him the leading name of the Finnish opera boom of the 1970s. Despite its *Kalevala* theme, *Kullervo* (1986–1988, libretto Sallinen) is a timeless drama of destiny. *Kuningas lähtee Ranskaan* (*The King Goes Forth to France*, 1980–1983, libretto Paavo Haavikko) and *Palatsi* (*The Palace*, 1991–1993, libretto Irene Dische and Hans Magnus Enzensberger), on the other hand, represent lighter, comic expression. MH

Saint Henry is killed by Lalli, who steals his mitre, 17th-century altar-cupboard painting

Information concerning Henry's missionary work in western Finland and his martyr's death on the ice of Köyliönjärvi Lake is considered reliable. The peasant ▶Lalli is named as Henry's killer. The day of the murder is, traditionally, 20 January, which was celebrated in memory of Saint Henry in the medieval calendar of saints of Turku Cathedral (according to the Swedish calendar 19 January). Two different stories have survived as to the motives for the murder, both of which describe Lalli's unwillingness to submit to the actions of the church and its representatives as the reason.

Saint Henry was first buried at Nousiainen. In the 1290s, his remains were removed to Turku, where the bishop's seat had been moved (from Nousiainen) in 1229. Henry's position as patron saint of the country was established at around the same time, to-

Veijo Varpio as the King in *The Palace,* Savonlinna Opera Festival, 1995

Tyko Sallinen

Sallinen, Tyko (1879–1955), painter. Tyko Sallinen was born into a Laestadian (▶revivalist movements) family which would not tolerate any kind of earthly joy, least of all in art. At the age of 14, he ran away from home, earning his living as a journeyman tailor until, in 1902, he enrolled as an art student. Sallinen was interested in the conception of colour in and, having won a scholarship to Paris in 1909, Sallinen discovered fauvism and, in particular, the work of Kees van Dongen.

The first of Sallinen's masterpieces, *Pyykkärit* ('The washerwomen', 1911) caused a stir, and subsequently the 'battle' over Sallinen in Finland was constant. He had become the disputed symbol of modernism and bohemianism, and from time to time had to spend time in America when the situation in Finland became too difficult. In practice this meant that he had become the leading figure of the new art, who finally displaced the masters of the 'golden age', such as ▶Akseli Gallen-Kallela and Eero Järnefelt (1863–1937).

Sallinen's *Hihhulit* ('The fanatics', 1918), which is among his masterpieces, is an act of reconciliation with the artist's Laestadian background. The work is also an attempt to find solace for the terrors of the Civil War of the same year. Sallinen's pungent colourism with its fresh blue gave way, in that work, to Finnish earth-colours. MVn

Salminen, Matti (born 1945), bass singer. Matti Salminen made his debut as Philip II in Giuseppe Verdi's opera *Don Carlos* at the Finnish National Opera. Since then, he has appeared on most major operatic stages. His repertoire includes Wagner's great bass roles all of which he has also performed in Bayreuth. Among his other highly successful interpretations, his Boris in Modest Mussorgsky's opera *Boris Godunov* has received particular praise. HB

Matti Salminen

Salonen, Esa-Pekka (born 1958), conductor, composer. One of the best-known Finnish conductors, Esa-Pekka Salonen became artistic director of the Los Angeles Philharmonic Orchestra in 1992. Between 1985 and 1995 he was chief conductor of the Swedish Radio Symphony Orchestra, and 1985–1994 he was chief visiting conductor of the London Philharmonia Orchestra.

Salonen made a meteoric entry into international consciousness after his successful performance, at very short notice, of Mahler's Third

Pekan Hilma ('Pekka's Hilma'), 1914

Esa-Pekka Salonen

Symphony with the London Philharmonic Orchestra in 1983. Before that, he had worked as a conductor in the Nordic countries and studied composition at the Sibelius Academy in Helsinki and in Italy.

In 1983, with his colleague ►Jukka-Pekka Saraste, Salonen founded the Avanti! Chamber Orchestra, which has given numerous Finnish and foreign first performances and sought alternatives to traditional concert norms. In addition to his work as a conductor, Salonen has continued to write music.

Salonen has become particularly well-known as a skilful conductor of modern music and has won numerous prizes for his recordings. Salonen has recorded, with the Los Angeles Symphony Orchestra, music by composers including Bartók, Debussy, Lutoslawski and Messiaen, as well as, with the Swedish Radio Symphony Orchestra and the London Philharmonic Orchestra, Stravinsky (including *Oedipus Rex*, *Petrushka* and *Le Sacré du printemps*). RL

Sámi The Sámi (their own term is *sápmi*, Sámi person, Sámi language, ►Lapland, *sápmelas*, noun and adjective, Sámi person, relating to *Sapmi*) are a small Finno-Ugrian group in the north-

ern part of Fennoscandia. In their current area of habitation, from Hedemark in Norway and the northern parts of Dalecarlia in Sweden (about 62°N) to the eastern point of the Kola Peninsula (41°E), they are an indigenous people, or the longest-known population with no direct political power.

The total number of Sámi is estimated at between 70,000 and 80,000, but no accurate demographic analysis or population count has been made, except in Finland from 1962. More than half of all Sámi (40,000–50,000) live in Norway, about 20,000 in Sweden, 7000 in Finland and about 2000 in the Kola area of Russia.

People are counted as Sámi by their own confession, usually on the basis of language or birth. These criteria are also important in the official definitions adopted by Finland, Sweden and Norway, which have become necessary with the institution of new, representative organs and institutions of government. Among them are the Finnish Sámi Assembly (*Sámediggi*, from the beginning of 1996) and its predecessor, the Sámi Parliament (*Sámi Parlamenta*, 1973–1996), the Norwegian Sametinget (*Sámediggi*, from 1989), and the Swedish Sametinget (*Sámediggi*, from 1993), all of whose members are chosen in elections held among the Sámi people of each country. In Finland, the Sámi Assembly is of particular importance in the Sámi homelands, among which are the country's three northernmost municipalities, Enontekiö, Inari and Utsjoki, and the Lapp reindeer-grazing association in the municipality of Sodankylä.

Skolt Sámi women, Tenojoki River

The Nordic Sámi Institute (*Sámi Instituhtta*), a cultural and research institute, has existed since 1974, with funding from the Nordic Council of Ministers. Previously, political activity among the Sámi people was possible only through private organisations which sprang up since the beginning of the 20th century, but particularly after the Second World War. Among them, the most important is the Nordic Sámi Council, which, now that the Russian Sámi are present, is called the Sámi Council (*Sámiráđđi*, founded in 1956).

The Sámi have lived in their current location for at least 2000 years, since the beginning of what is known as the Sámi Iron Age, probably longer. In addition, their area of habitation appears to have comprised, in the medieval period, the entire eastern part of Fennoscandia, including areas to the east of the Gulf of Finland, Lake Ladoga, Lake Onega and the White Sea. The more southerly groups were superseded in the medieval period by Finnish-Karelian habitation, and generally merged with the new arrivals. In the current area of habitation, there is no evidence of significant population movement in the older Metal or Stone Ages, so that the Sámi are, by blood legacy, at least partially the descendants of the area's oldest culture, Komsa (c. 10,000–4000 B.C.). The linguistic forms, however, nevertheless originate from the same stock as the eastern Baltic languages, the Finnish-Sámi parent language or early proto Finnish. This is believed to have divided into late proto Finnish and proto Sámi at the time of the coming of the battle-axe culture and early Metal Age (c. 2500–1500 B.C.), when the population of southern and southwestern Finland was subjected to strong Baltic and Germanic influence and became Finns practising cattle-rearing and agriculture. Groups living farther north in the interior, which preserved their traditional way of life and culture based on hunting, and also their language with smaller changes, were the beginnings of the Sámi population.

The earliest historical mentions of the Sámi are from the classical period (Tacitus, c. A.D. 98, under the name *Fenni*) and the Hellenistic period (Ptolemy, c. A.D. 150, under the name *phinnoi*). In the Norwegian Ottar's description of northern Fennoscandia of c. A.D. 890 gives for the first time direct information about Sámi (Anglo-Saxon *finnas*) living in the interior of Haalogaland and Finnmark as well as Kola. Ottar also mentions the decoy reindeer used in reindeer-herding and deer-hunting and describes taxation of the Sámi from which, according to him, the powerful men of northern Norway gained their best income. According to Ottar, the Sámi tended his reindeer herds in the interior, but otherwise they were hunting people, particularly in the coastal areas of northern and eastern Lapland, where he had been on an expedition.

The Sámi still are active in primary economy to a fairly large extent, par-

Sámi family, Enontekiö

ticularly in reindeer-herding, which apparently developed into an extended, nomadic form in the medieval period. It is only in the second half of the 20th century that livelihoods have begun to be obtined more extensively from the secondary and tertiary sectors, particularly the service industries. Today at most 10 per cent of Sámi are engaged in reindeer-herding, but in the cultural tradition this dominant way of life of the historical period remains strong.

The linguistic and cultural division of the Sámi into different groups does not follow state boundaries; the largest linguistic group, the northern Sámi, for example, is the dominant group in all the Nordic countries, but there are none in Russia; around 80 per cent of Sámi-speakers speak northern Sámi. The strongest linguistic boundaries are between the eastern (Inari and Skolt Sámi in Finland) and western languages, and on the other hand the southern (the forms of southern Sámi, including Umeå Sámi) and central dialects. In practice, there are six Sámi languages, each with its own written language; only some of the very smallest groups (Umeå, Turja/Ter and Akkala/Babinsk Sámi) lack a functioning written language of their own.

Different orthographic traditions have been used in the different written languages, for example the Russian Kildin Sámi is, with a few exceptions, written in the Cyrillic alphabet. Earlier, the same linguistic forms were written differently in different countries,

but the Sámis' own linguistic bodies, the Sámi Language Board and the Sámi Council, succeeded in uniting the different forms of northern, Luleå and southern Sámi, each separately, by the early 1980s. The homogeneity of the largest group's language, northern Sámi, is sustained by the joint Sámi Language Board (*Sámi Gielialávdegoddi*, established in 1971). The Inari Sámi area (about 300 speakers) is entirely within Finland, while Skolt Sámi is spoken in both Finland and Russia (a total of about 800 speakers).

The Sámi language, which is similar to Finnish in structure, shows a strong adaptation both to the surrounding Arctic and semi-Arctic nature and to the adjoining peoples. The developed terminology for landscape forms, natural and weather conditions, and the reindeer vocabulary, are formed from systematic constructions from basic terms.

The material and spiritual phenomena of folk culture vary considerably from southern to northern Lapland, and moving east. The borderline between eastern and western cultural traditions continues from the south (Finland), through Lapland, and is visible, among other things, in building technology. Beneath it, however, the forms of the older, unbroken Sámi culture are discernible (buildings – for example the *goahti* hut and the *lávvu* shelter – and various store-sheds). The relatively late state boundaries have also caused differences: for example the memory of the *siita*, or Lapp village, is best-preserved in the areas of the former Sweden-Finland and Russia, where for a long time (c. 1500–1900) state administration was forced to rely on the structures they formed. There is also an important boundary between the Orthodox and Lutheran churches on either side of the Finnish-Russian border. In addition, some vestiges of the Catholic period have survived in northernmost Lapland.

Schefferus's work *Lapponia* (1673) conveyed the first examples of Sámi folk poetry to the rest of the world. Many Nordic scholars of the 19th and 20th centuries explored the subject in more detail. These folklore collectors were often also linguists and ethnologists. In the 20th century, a greater quantity of material has appeared. The *juoiggus* tradition of singing has appeared in sheet music and texts, but since the development of recording technology it has also become possible to preserve and publish audio material.

Analytical scholarship of the oral tradition was earlier directed toward religious subjects; this tradition is at its strongest in Sweden. More recent folkloristic and ethnological research has been carried out in Turku, Finland.

Some of the memoirs and reports written by Sámi authors contains a great deal of traditional knowledge. The work of J. Turi, *Muittalus samid birra* (1920; English translation *Turi's Book of Lapland*, 1931), is particularly well-known, but many other pioneers of Sámi literature have also chosen traditional subjects, or conveyed Sámi tradition in their own original ways. Today the greatest amount of Sámi literature is published by small presses in Norway, although many writers are born in Finland, for example Pedar Jalvi (1888–1916), H.A. Guttorm (1907–1992), P. Lukkari (born 1918), Nils Aslak Valkeapää (born 1943) and Kirsti Paltto (born 1947).

Tradition has also had a strong influence on Sámi art, theatre, music and cinema. Nils-Aslak Valkeapää, who has worked in all these areas, has also used thematic images from other Arctic indigenous peoples. The modernisation and strong expression of traditional themes, in both graphics and painting, are natural to many contemporary artists: Iver Jåks (born 1932), Aage Gaup (born 1943), Hans Ragnar Mathisen (born 1945), Rose Marie Huuva, Synnöve Persen (born 1950) and Merja Aletta Ranttila (born 1950), and the same colourfulness and adaptation of new techniques is visible in the well-known songs of Mari Boine Persen (born 1956), and even more in the techno-influenced adaptations of Wimme Saari (born 1960). Cinema has been more traditional in its narrative, but Paul Anders Simma (born 1959) has addressed contemporary problems boldly using diverse means in *Let's Dance* (1992) and *Duoddara árbi* ('The Legacy of the Tundra', 1994), *Beatnat eallin* ('Dog's life', 1995) and *Sagojoga ministtar* ('The Minister of Sagojohka', 1996). SAo

Santa Claus Nowadays Santa Claus, or Father Christmas, is famous all over the world, though he is exclusively indigenous to Europe. The prototype of the continental European Father Christmas is thought to be the 4th century Bishop Nicholas of Myra in Asia Minor, who, with his red cape and bishop's hood, was also the model for the American Santa Claus.

The roots of the Finnish Father Christmas lie in rural tradition. In the days after Christmas young men dressed in furs and wearing horned masks, moved from house to house, amusing and frightening the inhabitants and collecting food and beer. When this goat-like creature (hence the name *joulupukki*, or 'Christmas goat') was crossed with the distributors of mysterious gifts – they were central European in origin, and the most important of them was the above-mentioned St Nicholas – the Finnish *joulupukki* was born.

Father Christmas's most important task in children's eyes, at least – is to bring presents. In addition to the legend of St Nicholas, in the background there is also the present-giving ceremony of the Roman New Year and the Biblical story of the Three Wise Men who brought gifts to the infant Jesus. A Finnish upper-class custom dating from the 16th century involved giving presents to those in the higher ranks of the hierarchy in order to strength social relations, although various kinds of poor aid were also given to menials and tenants. By the early 19th century,

No goatee: Santa Claus, Finnish-style

presents were distributed by a Father Christmas in urban and upper-class families. The Finnish Father Christmas brings the presents on Christmas Eve and hands them out in person.

The belief, originating in America, that Santa Claus lives at the North Pole is supported by the international idea that he lives in a winter environment. Since, as is well-known, he drives in a sleigh drawn by reindeer, it is natural that his home should be thought to be ►Lapland. Even before the First World War, Finnish teachers told their schoolchildren that Father Christmas lived in Lapland's Korvatunturi ('Ear Mountain'). From there he was able to find out if children were good and deserved their presents. In the 1960s, commercial enterprises built Father Christmas's 'gift forge' on the outskirts of Rovaniemi, a place easier of access than Korvatunturi. Rovaniemi is also the location of Father Christmas's post office, where with the aid of his gnomes he answers the letters that arrive for him from all over the world.

Only in the last few decades has the grey-haired Finnish Father Christmas turned into the internationally famous Santa Claus, with red costume and white beard. At the same time, the 'goat' has become domesticated and has left the jokes that referred to the punishment of naughty children out of his sack. The bag, (or woodchip basket), he used for carrying the presents is now changing into a sack on international lines, and even Christmas stockings have made their arrival in the Finnish Christmas tradition. TK

Jukka-Pekka Saraste

Timo Sarpaneva

Saraste, Jukka-Pekka (born 1956), conductor. One of the most talented conductors of his generation, Jukka-Pekka Saraste, received notable international recognition in the 1990s. He was appointed chief conductor of the Finnish Radio Symphony Orchestra in the autumn of 1987. During his period as chief conductor, he has developed the Finnish Radio Symphony Orchestra into a strong international orchestra. In the autumn of 1994 Saraste was appointed musical director of the Toronto Symphony Orchestra.

With the Finnish Radio Symphony Orchestra, Saraste toured successfully in Japan, Hong Kong and Taiwan as well as Europe. In a tour to England in 1991 the orchestra also appeared at the London Proms, and was much praised for its intepretation of ►Jean Sibelius's Fourth Symphony. Saraste has also conducted the orchestras of Detroit, Cleveland and Minnesota, the Boston Symphony Orchestra, the Deutsche Kammerphilharmonie, the Vienna Symphony Orchestra, the Radio Orchestra of North Germany, the Finnish Chamber Orchestra and the Rotterdam Philharmonic Orchestra. From 1987 to 1991 Saraste was artistic director of the Scottish Chamber Orchestra. In 1983, together with ►Esa-Pekka Salonen, Saraste founded the Avanti! Chamber Orchestra. Saraste is also artistic adviser to the Finnish Chamber Orchestra.

With the Finnish Radio Symphony Orchestra, Saraste has recorded all Sibelius's symphonies and his other important orchestral works. He has recorded, with the same orchestra, Mahler's Fifth Symphony and a Stravinsky album and, with the Scottish Chamber Orchestra, Mozart's symphonies. Aarre Merikanto's (1893–1958) opera *Juha* and Sibelius's *Kullervo*, both released in 1996, have been favourably reviewed internationally. RL

Sarpaneva, Timo (born 1926), designer. Timo Sarpaneva's work includes glass sculptures, paintings, graphics, art and utility glass, porcelain, cast iron, stainless steel, silver, textiles, ►ryijys, lighting, theatre sets and exhibitions. He is best-known for his ►glass sculptures. Sarpaneva graduated from the Central School for Applied Arts as a graphic artist in 1948. Since 1950 he has worked as a designer for the ►Iittala Glass Factory.

Sarpaneva often takes an innovation in production techniques as the starting-point for his design. The first of these in the field of glass was the so-called steam-blowing method, which resulted in the glass sculptures *Kayak* (1953), the *Orchid* vase (1954) and the so-called 'glass watercolours' or plates with coloured borders. In the mid 1950s Sarpaneva designed the so-called *I*-range for Iittala (see p. 154). The objects of the *I*-range, whose simplified, homogeneous formal language was supported by a range of four re-

Timo Sarpaneva, *Marcel* vases, 1993

strained, compatible colours, represented new thinking in terms of price range, and were placed between art glass and traditional cheap utility glass. Other products Sarpaneva designed on the basis of new production techniques include the *Finlandia* range of bases, blown into a charred wooden mould from the mid 1960s, cotton fabrics dyed using the ambiente technique (1964), the *Archipelago* range of glass (1978) and the *Claritas* art-glass objects (1984).

Sarpaneva played an important role, as both designer and exhibition architect, in presenting an image of Finland based on design to the world in the 1950s and 1960s. Among the numerous exhibitions he designed were the Finnish section of the H55 exhibition held in Helsingborg, Sweden, in 1955, which, together with the surrounding countryside, formed a dazzlingly beautiful installation and the Finnish section of the 1967 Montreal World Exhibition, in which the exhibition tradition of joint installations culminated in a monumental work representing five different materials. MaA

satellite and cable television Satellite television began in Europe in 1982, when Satellite Television plc (which subsequently passed into the ownership of Rupert Murdoch, as 'Sky Channel'), began transmissions, via the European Space Agency's OTS satellite. Finland's HTV network transmitted these programmes right from the start together with just a few other countries (Norway, Malta).

Finland was a pioneer of cable and satellite television in western Europe, but this sector of the television industry did not develop commercially in the 1980s and 1990s.

Cable television operation refers to the broadcasting of programmes on cable networks built for this purpose. Satellite television operation refers to the broadcasting of programmes for relay via cable television networks or for direct reception in households (Direct-to-Home, DTH).

The Helsinki-based cable television company HTV, nowadays part of the Helsinki Media Company (one of the Erkko family companies), was founded in 1973. The company opened its subscription-based entertainment channel in 1978, one of the first such companies in Europe to do so. The entertainment channel closed in 1994 because of poor viability.

The Nordic public broadcasting companies (in Finland, Yleisradio) have had plans for pan-Nordic satellite projects under various names (Nordsat, Tele-X, Nordstjärnan) ever since the 1970s. These projects have not been realized.

Yleisradio is a partner in the Eurosport (opened 1989) and Euronews (opened 1993) satellite channels, which were founded by members of the European Broadcasting Union. Finland's only domestic satellite channel is Totoline (opened 1995), run by the racecourse betting company Suomen Hippos. In 1997 YLE launched a digital satellite channel to Europe, TV Finland.

The cable TV penetration in Finland, as in the other Nordic countries, is among the highest in Europe. Cable TV households amount to 38 per cent of TV households (1996). The smaller networks for satellite reception (Satellite Master Antenna Television, SMATV) account for 8 per cent of TV households (1996). The number of Direct-To Home satellite households is small (3 per cent in 1996).

The cable networks transmit mainly the cable-only basic channel PTV (a subsidiary of the Helsinki Media Company) and foreign satellite channels, the most important of which are Eurosport, NBC SuperChannel, TV5, MTV Europe and Filmnet Pay-TV. Domestic programming accounts for only a fraction of what is transmitted. Pay-TV has some 50,000 subscribers (2 per cent of TV households, 1996). MS

Finnish idyll: relaxing by a lake after the sauna

sauna There are more than one-and-a half million saunas in Finland. Here the sauna is a central and characteristic part of the culture of everyday life. For Finns, the sauna is more than a washing-place. It is a complex of many traditional customs and beliefs.

The sauna is not, however, only a Finnish invention, it is known among many Finnic peoples. On the other hand, Finns can, with good reason, be considered a special sauna nation. In Finland, the sauna has preserved its role and at the same time continually adapted to cultural change. The traditional smoke sauna has been joined by the electric sauna and apartment sauna. The Finnish sauna is seen to combine the best traditions of two bathing traditions, hot-air baths and steam baths.

As a symbol of identity, the sauna is like the ▸*Kalevala*. It, too, has been institutionalised, it has its own society, postage stamps and band of devotees. On the other hand, the sauna is alive and well irrespective of its offical cultivators – like the *Kalevala*.

The special Finnish nature of the sauna was understood at an early date. At the opening ceremony of the Academy of Turku in 1640, Mikael Wexionius (c. 1608–1670), Professor of History and Politics, stressed that all Finns used the sauna assiduously: 'Even in severe frost they dash out to the sauna and draw water, enthusiastically and with laughter, from well, river or lake, and pour it on their bare skins. But this hardens their bodies and makes them able to withstand effort.'

The *Kalevala* established depictions of the sauna and bathing as part of Finnish literature. In the national epic, the men bathe and converse; the women ensure that the sauna is warm and that clean shirts are waiting. The same *Kalevala*-like arrangement is conveyed by contemporary sauna postcards. Thanks to the writer ▸Aleksis Kivi, the Finnish sauna culture can also be approached humorously, and the Christmas sauna has become the object of both numerous descriptions and of lasting worship.

From early on, doctors began wisely to stress the importance of the sauna in terms of both hygiene and general health, and were concerned at the decrease in sauna-bathing. Beginning with ▸Elias Lönnrot in the mid 19th century, there have been great sauna-champions in medical circles. In addition to writers and doctors, the development of the Finnish idea of the sauna has also been influenced, of course, by folklore scholars.

Sport has made the sauna known throughout the world. At the Paris Olympics of 1924, the Finns already had their own sauna, and it was to this that the brilliant success of Finnish runners was attributed. In the United States it was said that the champion runner ▶Paavo Nurmi trained in the sauna. To try this art, the long-distance runners of Harvard University, together with a reporter from one of Boston's biggest newspapers, experienced an American-Finnish sauna. After this experience they were able to opine that if Nurmi did indeed spend two hours a day in such a bath and then went on to break records on the track, he must be physically the most robust man in the world.

Earlier the sauna was not considered the kind of speciality that could be offered to visitors. It was foreigners who found their way to the sauna. In many travel guides, the sauna, and with it Finnish hygiene, began to be described in glowing terms. In a German magazine, the sauna was advertised as follows: 'If you want to experience heaven and hell simultaneously, go to a Finnish sauna.' Thus the word *sauna* entered the German language. In travel literature published by the Finns themselves, the sauna features only from the late 1930s, in connection with swimsuited sun-worshippers. This was the origin of the three 's's' of Finnish tourism: ▶*sisu*, sauna and ▶Sibelius.

Sauna is the best-known Finnish word internationally. According to the predominant etymological theory, the word *sauna* is linked with a word in the Lapp language meaning a sleeping hollow made in the snow by a willow grouse or wood grouse. The earliest sauna was a hollow made in the ground in the centre of which was a pile of hot stones; the hollow was covered with animal hides.

The Finnish Sauna Society was set up to foster sauna culture in 1937, and in 1986 the sauna was allotted its own celebratory day, the second Saturday in June. PLn

Schjerfbeck, Helene (1862–1946), painter. Helene Schjerfbeck was admitted to the classical class of the Finnish Art Society's drawing school in 1873, at the age of 11. The young talent astonished her public for the first time in 1880 by making a successful entrance into the very masculine genre of historical painting. She caused an even greater sensation by showing her work *Pikkusiskoaan ruokkiva poika* ('Boy

Self-portraits: Helene Schjerfbeck in 1895 (above), 1915 (below) and 1946

feeding his little sister', 1881), painted in Brittany. The new 'realism' of the painting, naturalism experienced as ugliness, offended viewers.

During her period in Paris, Schjerfbeck developed farther than any of her 'sister painters', Maria Wiik (1853–

1928), Elin Danielsson (1861–1919) or Helena Westermarck (1857–1938). Schjerfbeck's geometrically but sensitively reductive style soon approached modernism, for example in *Ovi* ('The door', 1884). The artist's mature style has points of contact with sythetism and the art of Whistler and Manet, the latter of whom was much admired by the artist. The first example of Schjerfbeck's mature style is *Ompelijatar* ('The seamstress', 1903), where the subject is seen from the side.

Schjerfbeck concentrated on portraits and, in the absence of models, on self-portraits. The self-portraits form an unbroken series in the artist's stylistic and psychological development. Schjerfbeck became an observer who, even on her death-bed, was able to depict the closeness of the end with a few simple and convincing brushstrokes. These works are among the most important art-historical documents of death. MVn

schools Finland's first school, Turku Cathedral School, was founded at the end of the 13th century to train priests. Education was also provided by the Dominican and Franciscan schools of Turku and Viipuri, which were also open to students from outside those orders. At the end of the medieval period, small town schools were founded to meet the needs of the burghers in Viipuri, Rauma and Porvoo.

It was not possible to realise the Reformation aim of improving the ▶literacy of common folk, in order that everyone should be able to read the ▶Bible, in the 16th century or the early 17th century. Popular education was hampered by the impoverishment of the church as its property was returned to the crown, and the absence of printing works in the country. For this reason, the three Finnish-language ▶primers published by Bishop ▶Michael Agricola were printed in Stockholm.

The rapid development of the education system began in the 1620s. The development led to a new, multi-level education system which was made public in 1649. Its foundation was laid in grammar schools, which were founded in every town. The grammar school was followed by the four-class *trivium* and the *gymnasium*, also of four classes. Turku Cathedral School became a new-style gymnasium in 1630, in addition to which a new gymnasium was established in Finland's second largest town, Viipuri. With the foundation of the Academy of Turku in 1640, the Turku Gymnasium was closed down and youths went straight to university from the trivium.

In the countryside, where 95 per cent of the country's population lived, educational provision was weaker. Responsibility for education lay with the church, and its minimum requirement was the ability to recite Martin Luther's Lesser Catechism. Learning was controlled through regular tests. Confirmation classes were held in parishes from the 18th century onwards in order to teach young people; attendance at confirmation classes was a prerequisite for confirmation and marriage. In addition to priests, teaching was given by parish clerks, whose level of learning varied greatly. Although development was slow, it can be estimated that widespread literacy was achieved at the end of the 18th century, although local differences were large.

The number of schools increased evenly in the early 19th century, but teaching was still governed by the old educational system of 1724. After 1809 when Finland became a Grand Duchy, development slowed in comparison with central Europe and the other Nordic countries. A new law regulating primary schooling, which aimed at universal education, was passed only in 1866. After this, primary schools rapidly became the norm in towns, but in the countryside forms of education were homogenised only at the end of the 19th century and at the beginning of the 20th. Primary schools were at first divided into separate girls' and boys' schools, but comprehensive education became established from the 1890s onwards. The first private comprehensive secondary schools were founded in the 1880s, and this became the commonest form in the early 20th century. In state schools separate teaching survived for a long time, until the early 1960s.

After the Second World War there was an increased need to both widen and deepen basic education given in schools. Above all, opportunities to continue education after the 6 year primary school were required. This need was met by, on the one hand, extending primary school education by a year and, on the other, increasing opportunities to continue education in municipal secondary schools and vocational schools.

Under a new school law passed in 1958, primary school was extended to 8 years, of which the last or last two years took place in a civic school. From the 4th class of primary school it was possible to move to the more theoretical secondary school, which was divided into the intermediate secondary school and the gymnasium, or 6th form, that followed. In the 1950s and 1960s, increasing numbers of school-age young people chose secondary school. In 1945, 8 per cent of school children continued their studies to gymnasium, in 1970 35 per cent.

A thoroughgoing revision was made in the Finnish schooling system between 1972 and 1977, provoking widespread debate. There was a gradual transition to an integrated, 9 year comprehensive school system based primarily on models from Sweden and German Democratic Republic.

Finnish children start school at seven. The comprehensive school consists of 6 years at the lower level and 4 years at the higher level. After comprehensive school, pupils have the opportunity to go out to work (►vocational training) or to continue their studies in the 6th form or other educational institutions of the middle level. The popularity of the senior secondary school or sixth form has grown continually. In 1990, 55 per cent continued to the sixth form after comprehensive school. From 1982, the 6th form education gradually became course-based, which means that work is concentrated in periods of 5 or 6 weeks. In 1990 the classless sixth form model was adopted, which makes it possible to take courses individually according to varying study plans. At the end of the sixth form, pupils take the student examination (►higher education).

Responsibility for teaching in comprehensive schools has been shifted from the government to the municipalities. The highest administrative organ is the Ministry of Education and the National Board of Education, whose more important role is the development of teaching aims, content and methods. The Board of Education is responsible for both comprehensive schools and sixth forms. JN

sculpture Modern Finnish sculpture can be said to have come into existence in the early 19th century, when Erik Cainberg (1771–1816) created six neoclassical reliefs on the subject of Finnish history for the assembly hall of the

Academy of Turku. The reliefs were executed in plaster. Cainberg had been a pupil of the Swedish sculptor Johan Tobias Sergel, and Sweden was also the origin of the sculptor Carl Eneas Sjöstrand (1828–1906), who is known as the father of Finnish sculpture. He taught the first generation of Finnish sculptors, and was the maker of, for example, the earliest outdoor public statue, of the historian Henrik Gabriel Porthan (1739–1804), completed in 1864 in Turku. Sjöstrand also created sculptures in neo-classical spirit of characters from the ▶*Kalevala*.

Walter Runeberg, the statue of Johan Ludvig Runeberg, 1878–1885

Walter Runeberg (1838–1920), son of the national poet ▶J. L. Runeberg, became the first successful Finnish sculptor. His fame, like that of this predecessors, was restricted largely to Finland and Scandinavian countries, but he was able to support his family in comfort through his work as a sculptor. His colleague Johannes Takanen (1849–1885) had a more difficult time of it: he rose directly from the ranks of the people and had the enthusiasm of the Finnish Art Society and certain private patrons to thank for the discovery of his talent and the opportunity for training. This period also marked the appearance of the first Finnish women sculptors, Aline Forsman (1845–1899) and Eveliina Särkelä (1847–1939). After completing their education in Finland, they all studied in Copenhagen and, with the exception of Särkelä, they were all able to study and practise their profession in Rome too. Marble was at that period the most highly valued material, but because of Finland's harsh climate outdoor sculptures were cast in bronze. All these sculptures began in the spirit of neo-classicism and its idealism; realism began to make its appearance in their work from the 1870s onward. Different subjects received different stylistic treatments. Neo-classicism was considered suitable for mythological subjects, salon realism for genre-painting like sculptures for the homes of the bourgeoisie and realism for portraits. Takanen and Forsman lived abroad for most of their lives, Takanen in Rome and Forsman in Germany. The statue Walter Runeberg sculpted of his father for the Esplanade Park in Helsinki (1878–1885) and Runeberg's collaboration with Takanen on the statue of Emperor Alexander II (1818–1881) in Senaatintori Square, ▶Helsinki (1884–1894) are representative sculptures of this period and at the same time examples of the growing need of the nation to honour people who had influenced its history.

The sculptors of the next generation completed their studies in Paris. Ville Vallgren (1855–1940) became the first internationally recognised Finnish sculptor; he received a gold medal in the Paris World Exhibition of 1889, and a Grand Prix in the corresponding exhibition of 1900. His most characteristic area was miniature sculptures and the emotionalism of *art nouveau* and symbolism. The fountain sculpture ▶Havis Amanda (completed in 1908), which has become an emblem of Helsinki, is his creation. Sigrid af Forselles (1860–1935) also represents symbolist sculpture, and her large religious reliefs can be seen in the interior of Kallio Church in Helsinki.

The more realist approach of Robert Stigell (1852–1907) and Emil Wikström (1864–1942) contrasted with the Parisian work of Ville Vallgren. Stigell is well-known as the creator for the *Haaksirikkoiset* ('The shipwrecked') sculpture on Observatory Hill in Helsinki (1891–1898). Wikström became the most popular sculptor of national monuments of his period. He sculpted the tympanum for the House of Estates (1893–1902) and the memorial to ▶Elias Lönnrot (1899–1902) in Helsinki. The public accepted his realism because his models were recognisably Finnish and his approach unsentimentally direct. The unaffected nature of Finnishness was also underlined by the young Eemil

Halonen (1875–1950) in his wood reliefs for the Finnish pavilion at the Paris World Exhibition of 1900.

Felix Nylund (1878–1940) brought a simplified, vigorous classicism into Finnish sculpture. The *Kolme seppää* ('Three smiths') statue (completed in 1932) in central Helsinki expresses this sculptural purification. Gunnar Finne (1886–1952) and Viktor Jansson (1886–1958) also represent stylised classicism, and Finne in particular, with his monument to ▶Zacharias Topelius, *Taru ja totuus* ('Fiction and Truth', 1929–1932) in the Esplanade Park in Helsinki, also shows elements of the formal ideals of international modernism.

Wäinö Aaltonen, *The Maid of Finland*, 1925

Gunnar Finne, *Fiction and Truth*, 1929–1932

The most important sculptor of the period immediately after Finland gained its independence in 1917, however, was Wäinö Aaltonen (1894–1966). With his reductionist monumental style, he succeeded in creating monuments that are still considered icons of Finnishness. The statue to the runner ▶Paavo Nurmi (1924–1925), *Suomen neito* ('The maid of Finland', 1928–1929) and the statue to ▶Aleksis Kivi (1930–1939) are impressive monuments. He was also able to work Finnish granite so that it became a truly sculptural material. Aaltonen was the only Finnish sculptor who was able to take up the challenge of mod-

ernism, for example futurism and cubism, although he interpreted them in an idelistic way. Aaltonen was made the first member of the Academy of Finland for sculpture in 1948. He also raised the standard of sculptural portraiture in Finland to the highest level.

Monumentality and solemnity are characteristic of Aaltonen's work, but so also are drama and expressivity. Aaltonen's monument to the crew of an S2 torpedo boat who drowned accidentally, *Myrsky* ('The storm', 1929–1930), in Reposaari, near Pori in south-west Finland, gave the starting shot for Sakari Tohka (1911–1958), who developed expressionist sculpture with symbolist overtones. Characteristic of Finnish sculpture between the First and the Second World War, was, indeed, the presence of great emotions and grave questions. The only exceptions were sculptors in wood such as Hannes Autere (1888–1967), who in his popular subjects, cultivated burlesque themes.

The period of the Second World War gave rise to a serious ethos developed by Oskari Jauhiainen (1913–1990) and Aimo Tukiainen (1917–1996). The end of the 1940s, however, saw a certain loosening up, and joyful subjects made their appearance, particularly in miniature sculptures. Mikko Hovi (1879–1962) created primitive figures in a humorous vein which also contained surrealist features. Carl Wilhelms (1889–1953) developed female figures of an oriental balance, and Ben Renvall (1903–1979) sculpted sensual female figures emphasising the flowing nature of bronze. Michael Schilkin (1900–1962) created colourful and warm ceramic art.

Memorials to the war dead dominated the 1950s numerically, but sculptural innovation took place mainly in miniature sculpture. A new generation of sculptors made its appearance. Pekka Aarnio (1930–1960), Kain Tapper (born 1930), Laila Pullinen (born 1933), Harry Kivijärvi (born 1931), Heikki Häiväoja (born 1929) and Kauko Räsänen (born 1926) were inspired by the humorous and informal nature of Italian figurative design and casting. The greatest subject of debate was the competition for the equestrian statue of Marshal ►C.G.E. Mannerheim in 1954, in which the first prize was awarded jointly to Wäinö Aaltonen and Heikki Konttinen (1910–1988), but the statue was finally executed only after a revised competition was held, and was finally made by Aimo Tukiainen (erected in Helsinki in 1960).

A crisis in public sculpture was evident in the early 1960s, and the abstract monument to ►Jean Sibelius (1962–1967) by Eila Hiltunen (born 1922) in Helsinki became its trigger. The monument is also modern in the sense that viewers can walk inside the sculpture and participate in its musical atmosphere. A strict geometricality, on the other hand, characterised the kinetically impressive aluminium lattice works of Raimo Utriainen (1927–1994). Irma Laukkanen (born 1958) has developed her airy, almost immaterially oscillating sculptures into a new kind of music of space which represents contemporary lyrical sculpture.

Wood sculpture has developed, in particular, into a Finnish mode of sculpture – one can even speak of a Finnish school. Kain Tapper is the best-known of these sculptors internationally. He trusts to the innate aesthetics of wood, and, apparently at least, merely helps to accentuate its natural characteristics with his sensitive treatment of the surface of trunkline forms. Mauno Hartman (born 1930) bases his work on structures, joints and human treatment or consumption of wood. A third approach to wood sculpture since the 1960s is the decoratively painted work of Heik-

Martti Aiha, *Rumba*, 1992

ki Virolainen (born 1936). His interpretations of the figures of the *Kalevala*, in particular, are fresh, and combine modernism and Indian totems in a new way. Of the younger generation, Radoslaw Gryta (born 1955), Martti Aiha (born 1952), Kari Cavén (born 1954) and Anders Tomren (born 1965) are interested in wood in a more conceptual way.

The animal sculptors Helena Pylkkänen (born 1945), Pirkko Nukari (born 1943) and Nina Terno (born 1935) celebrate the importance of nature in their work. Modern surrealism is represented by Tapio Junno (born 1940) with his pinstripe statues, and humour characterises the bronze and steel sculptures of Kari Huhtamo (born 1943) and the assemblages of Reijo Hukkanen (born 1946). The work of Martti Aiha is very diverse; he is one of Finland's post-modern sculptors. His work *Rumba* (1992), built of aluminium, is one of the sculptures best-suited to the urban landscape of Helsinki. Another is the four-pillared *Stoa* by Hannu Sirén (born 1953) in eastern Helsinki.

Since Wäinö Aaltonen's pioneering work, stone has continued to mean a great deal to Finnish sculptors. Harry Kivijärvi, in particular, has concentrated on diorite, and his best-known work is the abstract stone monument to President J.K. Paasikivi (1870–1956) in Helsinki (completed 1980). Ukri Merikanto (born 1950) also uses stone and steel with solemn elegance. Matti Peltokangas (born 1952) has made a monument to President Lauri Kr. Relander (1883–1942) in grooved granite cubes, while the kinetic plotters of

Osmo Valtonen (born 1929) combine technology and a natural material, sand, into a hypnotic whole.

Younger sculptors such as Lauri Astala (born 1958), Jan Erik Andersson (born 1954), Kimmo Ojaniemi (born 1957), Markku Kivinen (born 1961), Jari Juvonen (born 1963), Pasi Karjula (born 1964), Marko Vuokola (born 1967) and Jyrki Siukonen (born 1959) begin with a thought, feeling, situation, and give it material expression. Astala is often like science fiction traveller, Andersson playful and participatory, Siukonen solves philosophical problems, Helena Hietanen (born 1963) knits structures out of plastic thread.

In the 1990s, Finnish sculpture has become diverse and unpredictable, as elsewhere in the western world. The intelligent humour of the youngest generation is something new in the serious tradition of Finnish sculpture. Often it is also based on Finnishness and its special characteristics, although in the background are international trends. LAM

Segerstam, Leif (born 1944), conductor, composer. Leif Segerstam is chief conductor of Helsinki Philharmonic Orchestra and the Stockholm Royal Opera. He was chief conductor of the Finnish Radio Symphony Orchestra from 1977 to 1987 and the Danish Radio Symphony Orchestra from 1987 to 1995.

In 1962, Leif Segerstam won the Maj Lind piano competition and gained his diplomas in violin and conducting from the Sibelius Academy in Helsinki. He continued his studies in violin and conducting at the Juillard School of Music in New York.

Segerstam's career as a conductor began with an appointment to the Finnish National Opera, which was followed by the Stockholm Royal Opera and the Deutsche Oper in Berlin. As an operatic conductor he has visited, among others, La Scala in Milan, the Metropolitan in New York, Covent Garden in London and the State Opera in Vienna. Segerstam has worked as chief conductor or artistic director in Finland, Sweden and Denmark, as well as with the Austrian Radio Symphony Orchestra and the Rheinland-Pfaltz Philharmonic Orchestra.

Segerstam's extensive compositional *oeuvre* comprises 19 symphonies, numerous concertos, orchestral poems and songs and chamber music. RL

Seurasaari Open-Air Museum In the 19th century the study of Finnish ▶architecture progressed from castles and churches to vernacular architecture, which was rapidly disappearing. Typical examples from different areas were preserved in open-air museums, which formed the basis of the idea for the huge open-air museum at Seurasaari Island, near Helsinki.

In the beginning of the 20th century, the young architects who were designing the ▶Finnish National Museum, Hermann Gesellius (1874–1916), Armas Lindgren (1874–1929) and ▶Eliel Saarinen, dreamed of creating an open-air museum on the shores of Töölönlahti Bay in central ▶Helsinki. It was, however, founded according to the plans of the museum curator, Axel O. Heikel (1851–1924), a little further from the centre of Helsinki on Seurasaari Island in 1909.

Over the decades, almost 100 buildings from different parts of Finland have been transferred to Seurasaari Open-Air Museum. The wooden church of Karuna is the sole example from the 17th century; the other buildings are more recent. Standing in the small courtyard surrounded by the grey log buildings of the Niemelä crofter's cottage, one realises how frugal the everyday life of poor people was even at the beginning of the 20th century. The most handsome log buildings – the im-

Leif Segerstam

The atrium mansion of Antintalo, 18th and 19th century, was brought to Seurasaari from Säkylä, Satakunta.

pressive atrium mansion of Antintalo, the Karelian house of Pertinotsa and the Kahiluoto mansion – tell of variations in the Finnish building tradition and of the ways of life of the different social classes. A particular attraction of Seurasaari is its abundant flora and fauna. RN

sexuality The sociologist ▶Edvard Westermarck, whose thesis on the origins of marriage, and his subsequent *The History of Marriage* (1891), which proposes monogamy as the original form of marriage, is the pioneer of Finnish sex research. His empirical studies focused on cross-cultural comparisons; he did not conduct research on sexuality in Finland.

Sexuality in Finland has been studied mainly by ethnographers, sociologists, and physicians. K. Rob. Wikman's (1886–1975) work *Die Einleitung der Ehe* ('Introduction to Marriage', 1937) attracted international interest. It described the courtship of youths prior to marriage in Nordic agrarian societies. Wikman discussed groups of youth by age group organisation and described nocturnal visits by boys to girls' living quarters, 'night courting', as a pre-marital institution.

Young people were allowed considerable sexual freedom, indirectly and effectively overseen by adults and peers. Various rituals were associated with night courting. Undressing and lying positions were regulated by norms. Boys went from barn to barn in groups, but gradually a boy might visit a favoured girl alone. The choice of sexual partner and future spouse was from a limited group of the farming population. When a girl became pregnant, her sexual partner was generally known, and a wedding could take place with the parents' approval.

A lively public debate about sexual questions developed in Finland in the late 1960s, including sex teaching in schools, abortion and women's sexual rights. As a result of the debate, the law was reformed and research work into sexual matters began. At first research was carried out principally among young people. In the early 1970s adults became for the first time the subjects of research. In the early 1990s information was gathered about the sexual

Destroy Aids! campaign poster, 1987

lives of 2250 Finns between the ages of 18 and 74. With the help of an autobiography competition, qualitative information was gathered about an additional 161 individuals.

CHANGES IN SEXUAL LIFE The reformist and liberal spirit in the 1960s and 1970s led to legislative reforms and to livelier public debate on sexual behaviour. The contraceptive bill was approved in 1961, cohabitation without marriage started to increase in 1968, women were entitled to decide on abortion in 1970 (a physician's certificate is necessary, but in practice it is a mere formality), and the criminalisation of homosexuality ended in 1971. The Evangelical Lutheran Church accepted family planning in the early 1970s.

Comparisons with Europe in the early 1990s demonstrated that the age of first sexual experience in men and women between 18 and 54 is the same (around 18 years), while in southern Europe men begin sexual intercourse several years younger than women. In Finland, girls still refrained from sexual intercourse for longer than boys until 1971: at that time girls became sexually active at 20, boys at 18.

As early as 1971 Finland could, on the basis of opinions representative of the population, be considered an egalitarian society relatively tolerant in sexual matters. By 1992 opinions had become more freer and egalitarian. Premarital relationships, sex without love and homosexuality were more easily tolerated than before, and similar behaviour was expected of men and women. On the other hand, extramarital relationships were regarded more negatively than 20 years ago.

The greatest societal changes influencing sexual behaviour are the development of contraception and sex education. These have almost eliminated unwanted and teenage pregnancies. The fear of Aids now causes demands for responsible, safe sex.

According to Finnish sex surveys in the 1990s, the number of sexual partners, women's initiative, varying positions and the use of alcohol in intercourse, as well as masturbation, have increased during the past 20 years. Sexual satisfaction has greatly increased, particularly among women, as sexual life has become more diverse. Young age, a sexually unrepressed and non-religious childhood home, the early start of sexual activity, high education, high sexual self-esteem, appreciation of sexual life, reciprocal feeling of love, use of sex materials (erotic literature, videos and films), frequent intercourse, versatile sexual techniques (oral, anal and manual sex, different positions in intercourse) and frequent orgasms correlate with finding sexual intercourse pleasant. The high value given to sexuality, love, and the use of sexual materials are directly connected to physical sexual satisfaction among men, but only indirectly among women. For women but not for men, young age and an early start of sexual life directly counted for pleasurability of intercourse.

HOMOSEXUALITY AND BISEXUALITY
Homosexuals were the subject of a study in 1982 in Finland. More than 1000 homosexuals responded to an extensive questionnaire. Two thirds of the respondents were men, and one third women. About 60 per cent of the respondents reported that they were exclusively homosexual in their feelings, and about 70 per cent in their behaviour. Finnish homosexuals were quite similarly distributed into Alfred Kinsey's categories. Feelings and behaviour were in most cases consistent.

In the Finnish sex survey of 1992, homosexual identity was measured by a five-point scale ranging from exclusive homosexuality to exclusive heterosexuality. According to representative sample surveys of the population aged 18 to 54 years, the proportion of persons interested only or mainly in people of the same sex was 0.8 per cent in 1971, and 0.6 per cent in 1992. When one takes into consideration all people who have at least some interest in people of the same sex, the proportions were 7.6 and 6.5 per cent respectively. Men identified themselves as homosexual more easily than women, whereas there was no gender gap in the proportion of bisexually oriented people. Homosexual experiences are more common than homosexual identity. According to the 1992 survey, 4.0 per cent of Finnish men and 3.8 per cent of women had had homosexual partners during their life.

The lower sexual satisfaction of homosexuals shown by the survey results may be related to the prevailing conceptions about the superiority of heterosexual love and sex. It may be more difficult to enjoy homosexual experiences as freely as heterosexual experiences because of their ambivalent status in sexual culture. This can be concluded on the basis of the fact that 28 per cent of men and 38 per cent of women interested in their own sex have sometimes been bothered personally or feared or worried about their own sexual deviation. This is three times as common as in the population as a whole. This fear still prevails, even though attitudes towards homosexuality have considerably liberalised during the last 20 years. EHM

shamanism Early sources do not include a great deal of data about the uses and meanings of shamanic materials in comparative societies. As far as ►Sámi shamanism is concerned, the earliest account of a shamanic session was recorded before A.D. 1200 and was followed by accounts of trials arranged by the spiritual and secular authorities against shamans. Many *noaiddis* (Lapp shamans) were sentenced to death in the courts, following the wave of witch trials entering the Nordic countries from Continental Europe in the 17th and 18th centuries.

Ostyak shaman; photograph taken by the Finnish explorer Uno Harva on an expedition to the Yenisei River, Siberia, in 1917

Shaman's drum, Kemi, Lapland, 19th century

The trials, led by the Swedish and Danish-Norwegian crowns and churches, however, led to the criminalisation of only the visible elements of shamanism. The most important manifestation of Sámi shamanism was the 'troll-drum', with hammer, rings and other attachments. Its significance is complex, representing the seasonal variation of the universe. Packed with mythical references, the drum is a kind of cognitive map for the trip of the shaman's ego-soul between the three levels of the universe. It might also be interpreted as a star chart including such astral phenomena as the 12-star constellation of the Zodiac.

In the course of the missionary period from medieval time to the 18th century, shamanic knowlegde became a private property of the Sámi mind, or an esoteric ritual practised secretly for good luck in fishing, hunting, reindeer economy, health, happiness in marital life, etc. In delicate matters concerning the fortune of the clan, in the painful comparison of its limited resources against other clans, shamanic skills became a means of attacking members of the other clans and of disturbing their economic and other efforts.

Typically enough, the shaman in Finnish is both the *noita* (witch) or *tietäjä* – literally, 'the one who knows'. ▶Mythology is the key word of Finnish shamanism. Its core is expressed in the most ancient layer of epical and ritual poetry centered around such figures as Lemminkäinen, Ilmarinen and Väinämöinen. Many runes are shamanic in their contents for example, 'Antero Vipunen's Rune', 'The singing competition', 'Väinämöinen's journey to the Abode' etc. Some other songs emphasise Väinämöinen's role as an Orphic singer with his ▶*kantele* rather than as a shaman.

The ancient Finnish epics are a clear testimony of the existence of shamanism in spite of the fact that no drum has been found in Finland outside Sámi territories. Finnish ▶folklore also coincides with Siberian traditions in that shamanic competence is said to be inherited, both physically and mentally. Part of it lies in the genes of the shaman-to-be, who seems to be psychologically more apt than others to communicate with the 'other', the extraordinary, the supernatural, the exceptional. Dreams and supernatural experiences are the most important criteria of the choice of the shaman. According to Finnish and Siberian shamanism, he has been chosen by the spirits, not his fellowships. JPn

short films The golden age of the Finnish short film was from 1933 to 1964. During this time cinema-owners received tax deductions if they showed a Finnish short film before the main feature; and so almost 7000 short films

Jon Andreas Utsi in the Sámi-Finnish director Paul-Anders Simma's short film *Tunturin testamentti* ('Legacy of the Tundra', 1995)

were made in this 30-year period. These were generally either current affairs films or parish portraits. The arrival of television had an adverse effect in short film making, but in the 1970s the short film was re-invented; the form began to be used, among others, by politically active circles for political ends.

From the point of view of cinema as a whole, short films are very important. Undemanding in production machinery and finance, and independent of commercial films, they create possibilities for experimentation, the search for the new and the entry of new talents into the field.

►Documentary films have always made up a significant proportion of short films in Finland; fiction has risen strongly only in recent decades. Finland is the biggest producer of short films in the Nordic countries. In 1996, 232 films were entered for the short film competition held annually in Tampere. Not all of them were of a professional standard, but many competent film-makers have found their mode of expression in short films.

The Finnish short film that is best-known and most recognised abroad is probably the satirical *Elsa* (1981), by Marja Pensala (born 1944), who specialises in very short documentaries. The irony of its romantic admiration of the countryside and the division of labour between men and women is so biting that *Elsa*, which runs to all of five minutes, retains its freshness.

Non stop (1987), by Kari Paljakka (born 1958), which follows the scheme of a circular chain story, is another Finnish short film that is well-known abroad. *Plain Truth* (1993) by Ilppo Pohjola (born 1957) is a more recent success, a strong visual account, making use of new technology, of what it is like to live in a body of the wrong sex.

Of the Finnish Film Foundation's grants, 20 per cent, or about FIM 7 million annually, goes to short films. The Promotion Centre for Audiovisual Culture in Finland, receives its funding from a levy on blank videocassettes, and contributes some FIM 10 million annually to support for short films. In addition, the television companies support films through advance purchase. The most important distributor of short films is the Finnish Film Contact, a non-commercial distributor established by film makers in 1970s, whose films have about 200,000 viewers a year.

In practice, the fate of most short films is a single showing on television. The increased importance of television as a channel for showing short films also influences their approach and visual expression, and squeezes durations into lengths suitable for television schedule slots.

The central forum for independent short films is the Tampere International Short Film Festival arranged annually in March. The festival's domestic and international series of events present new films and in special screenings and retrospectives one can see films on various subjects made by renowned film-makers. The Finnish Film Contact arranges annually in November the Fox Days in Helsinki, where new Finnish short films and documentaries are presented. HJ

Sibelius, Jean (1865–1957), composer. Jean Sibelius is the best-known Finnish composer both nationally and internationally. Sibelius was born to a ►Finland-Swedish family but graduated from a Finnish-language lyceum in Hämeenlinna. He studied violin and composing in Helsinki and then, 1889–1891 in Berlin and Vienna. Sibelius wrote his most important works for orchestra – seven symphonies in 1899, 1902, 1907, 1911, 1919, 1923 and in 1924, a violin concerto in 1905, orchestral suites, symphonic poems – in addition to which his vocal music, par-

Jean and Aino Sibelius and their daughter, Ruth, at home at Ainola, Järvenpää, near Helsinki, in 1915. Ainola is now a museum

Jean Sibelius

F.E. Sillanpää

ticularly the solo songs, have become a standard part of the repertoire.

Sibelius's starting point lay in romanticism (Bruckner, Tschaikovsky, Grieg) and symbolism, but also partly in Finnish ▶folk music. He created a national musical tradition almost from nothing, inspired by the national awakening and ▶Karelianism of his time – and in a way that has made a lasting mark on Finnish musical culture. In that spirit Sibelius composed scenic music of which the most noteworthy work is the symphonic poem *Finlandia* (1899). This work became a symbol of protest against oppression and censorship during the period of Russification 1899–1905.

In his middle period, however, Sibelius distanced himself from national romanticism in inward works (the string quartet *Voces intimae*, 1909)

which at times come close to European expressionism (the Fourth Symphony). His late works, whose masterpieces include, in addition to the last three symphonies, his music for Shakespeare's *The Tempest* (1926) and his last great work, *Tapiola* (1926), are classicist and universal in their nature, and their innovation lies in their formal structure rather than in the surface of the tonal language.

The home of Jean Sibelius from 1904, Ainola (after his wife, Aino) in Järvenpää near Helsinki is the composer's home museum. MH

Sillanpää, F. E. (1888–1964), writer. Born in Hämeenkyrö, Satakunta, western Finland, into a modest farming family, Sillanpää achieved success with his first novel, *Elämä ja aurinko* ('Life and sun', 1916), a romantic story of summer, nature and young love.

He became a writer of national importance with his novel *Hurskas kurjuus* (*Meek Heritage*, 1919), the workaday life-story of the phlegmatic and modest farm-hand and tenant farmer Juha Toivola. In the Civil War of 1918, Toivola joins the ranks of the revolutionaries, and his life ends in execution after the red defeat. The novel emphasises the human value of even a primitive individual and his share in the eternal cycle of life, a conciliatory message in a country inflamed by internal strife.

Love and nature: Matti Oravisto and Eila Pehkonen in Valentin Vaala's adaptation of Sillanpää's novel *Ihmiset suviyössä* ('People in a summer's night', 1948)

Sillanpää achieved success in the Scandinavian countries and in Germany with his novel *Nuorena nukkunut* (*Fallen Asleep While Young*, / *The Maid Silja*, 1931), the emotional story of the life, first love and death from tuberculosis of a young serving girl.

Sillanpää's strength is in his exact but lyrical descriptions, in which nature and the individual are closely linked. Short stories form a significant part of Sillanpää's work. In 1939 he became the only Finnish writer, to date, to be awarded the Nobel Prize for Literature. PL

Simberg, Hugo (1873–1917), painter and graphic artist. ▶Akseli Gallen-Kallela wrote of his student Hugo Simberg that he worked 'quite in the style of the old masters of the 14th and 15th centuries. And it is real (and not acquired) naivety. His work looks like prophecies that everyone should listen to and bear in mind.'

Gallen-Kallela was perfectly right. Hugo Simberg became a highly distinctive artist who visualised folk stories and tales. He did not, however, illus-

Halla ('Frost'), 1895

Elämänköynnös ('The garland of life'), fresco, interior of Tampere Cathedral, 1906

Hugo Simberg, self-portrait, 1914

trate stories, but created apt images of the movements of the unconscious. Simberg's works made good and evil relative and brought some real humour to Finland's very serious symbolism. Simberg admired Arnold Böcklin, the Swiss artist (1827–1901), but did not adopt his robust *Götterkomik*, instead developing the world of his gouaches and water colours from, among other things, the frescos of the early Renaissance and the art of Albrecht Dürer and Hans Holbein. MVn sisu In 1995 Finland played Sweden in the ice hockey world championship. Before the match, a Swedish newspaper wrote that *sisu* was not enough: skill was also needed in the game. The next day's paper carried a smaller headline in which it was remarked that *sisu* had indeed decided the outcome. *Sisu* is Finland's national trademark in sport, but in practice all Finns know the meaning of *sisu* (inner strength) as a psychophysical characteristic.

Sisu large and small: the famous icebreaker (above), and traditional tar-pastilles (left)

Many other words, too, have suffered the same fate as *sisu*, which has, from its literal meaning *inner*, begun to signify a certain natural characteristic, a mental dimension. In terms of the word and the development of its sphere of meaning, it is interesting to note that it is only in the 20th century that *sisu* has begun to be defined as peculiarly Finnish. In ►sport and warfare, it was subsequently considered a special characteristic of the Finnish ►mentality, which is not encountered among other peoples. The belief in *sisu* as a peculiarly Finnish phenomenon is not only a common-sense interpretation: it has been wholeheartedly also supported by certain scholars of Finnishness, according to whom, for example: 'other peoples can appear in some circumstances to have *sisu*, but Finnish *sisu* has a particular characteristic: Finnish *sisu* is inflexible and stiff'.

As *sisu* became conceptualised, its meanings also became complicated, to the extent that many who have written about it have complained about how difficult it is to explain this indigenous trait to foreigners, especially since the word has no equivalents in other languages. Perhaps it is worth commenting in this connection that concepts al-

ways demand interpretation and explanation when translated from one culture to another. Many people in Finland especially today, are also of the opinion that Finnish *sisu* is a myth, or merely a myth, or an intentional product of the imagination. Presumably few of them, however, know how ancient and complex in meaning *sisu* is.

At the first time in a Finnish dictionary, published in 1826 *sisu* was presented as a derivative of *sisä*, or 'inner'. *Sisu* was considered to be the same kind of word as *sisus* ('interior'), it was also mentioned to have a special meaning of 'a mood, particularly bad, evil, hatred'. According to the dictionary *sisu* must originate in the common period of Estonia, Livonia and Finnish, the so-called proto-Finnic. Thus we come to a very interesting, and even surprising, conclusion, according to which *sisu* has, since ancient times, betokened a state of mind.

This history of meaning can be traced back to the writings of ►Michael Agricola in the 16th century, according to which *sisu*, in the sense of the innermost character of the individual, means his physical and spiritual nature. In ancient religious writing, the commonest meaning of *sisu* was evil.

Strange *sisu*: 'The Finnish dragoon has strong teeth. Dragoon Janne Salo can walk 200 metres holding 16 rifles in his teeth', 1930s

Bad *sisu*, which tempts a person to sin, was stubbornness, lewdness, pride and hardness of heart. As early as the 1580, Jaakko Finno (c. 1540–1588), the first Finnish psalm writer, prayed in a psalm: 'All that is bad *sisu* in us, may the dear Lord take away from us'. In the early 18th century, ▶Daniel Juslenius surmised that *sisu* meant the inner organs in which different movements of the mind were born; this interpretation itself refers to the ancient pathology of the humours and the doctrine of the temperaments.

In the mirror of ordinary language, the word *sisu* has had the following meanings: (a) raw, ruthless; *sisu* is, it is true, expressed in an individual's (b) courage and daring, but on the other hand also in his (c) indifference, craftiness and bad temper; *sisu* can also mean (d) perseverance, capacity to survive or endure trials, patience. It is in this last meaning that *sisu* is so often encountered in the names of ice breakers, trailer lorries, sweets and sporting societies.

Although it is true that *sisu* is today generally interpreted as positive perseverance, its negative connotations continue to live a life of their own. *Sisu* appears in children as disobedience, stubbornness, waywardness, which is not good for them and which does not bode well. It is also worth noting that extreme *sisu* easily conceals a subsidiary hint of stupidity or simplicity. For example, in Pentti Haanpää's (1905–1955) novel *Sisu* (1947), a wife's nagging aggravates Ville Vehviläinen's *sisu* so badly that he goes outside in his bare feet and unclothed to get a moment's peace. But Vehviläinen decides to tease his wife by staying outside in the frost, even if it means he freezes to death. 'But the wife is merciless, she has no human feelings. She does not seem to care what happens to Ville.' Vehviläinen creeps inside only to hear his wife's declaration that it's only an idiot who will let himself freeze. When Vehviläinen gradually warms up enough to speak, he says: 'It wouldn't have done you any harm to say, Ville, come inside!' Thus does the wife's *sisu* subdue her husband's. As well as in unyieldingness, *sisu* also manifests itself as extra strength, the kind of secret reserve that can drive a person to incredible achievements even when he believes that he has used up all his strength. Perhaps the most important interpreter of the old bad *sisu* and the new, active version is ▶Aleksis Kivi who, in his novel *Seitsemän veljestä* (*Seven Brothers*, 1870) describes the transformation of his characters' individual *sisu* into collaborative strength. SK

Sjögren, Anders Johan (1794–1855), member of the St Petersburg Academy of Sciences and director of the Academy's ethnographical museum. Born the son of a village cobbler, Sjögren studied at the Academy of Turku and received his magisterial and doctoral papers in 1819, having carried out the

Anders
Johan
Sjögren

Johan
Vilhelm
Snellman

tasks of an assistant in the University Library. Sjögren's career took an impressive upward turn with his arrival the following year in St Petersburg.

Sjögren's first work, *Über die finnische Sprache und ihre Litteratur* (1821), dealt with the Finnish language and literature. During the 1820s and 1830s, Sjögren published a number of monographs on Finnic peoples and some historical studies. Between 1835 and 1838, funded by the Academy of Sciences, he made an expedition to the Caucasus, where he studied the Iranian Ossetian language and its main dialects. The studies he published in 1844, attracted international attention among linguists. It brought Sjögren, who had been appointed a member of the St Petersburg Academy of Sciences in 1844, the Volney Prize of the Institute de France in 1846. In 1845 Sjögren was appointed director of the Museum of Ethnology of St Petersburg, and was granted the title of Councillor of State. After publishing, in 1848, a work on the relationship of Ossetian to the Indo-European languages, Sjögren concentrated on studying the languages and peoples of the Baltic. The ▶University of Helsinki has a foundation named after Sjögren, which distributes funding for the study of the Altaic languages. JN

Snellman, Johan Vilhelm (1806–1881), philosopher, statesman. Born the son of a sea-captain in Turku, J.V. Snellman was the leading philosopher in the national awakening that took place in Finland in the 19th century. He was, nevertheless, no mere theorist, but an active statesman who was of central importance in the devel-

opment of economic conditions in Finland in the 1860s to 1880s.

During his student days in the 1820s, Snellman had come under the strong influence of the Hegelian philosophy that was then spreading to Finland. He acquainted himself also with the work of French, English and Italian philosophers, and gained his master's degree in philosophy in 1831.

Snellman belonged to a debating society founded in 1830, the Lauantaiseura, or Saturday Society, which was of central importance in developing the national culture of Finland and the status of Finnish language in the 1830s and 1840s. The Saturday Society also gave rise to the ▶Finnish Literature Society, which was one of the strongest institutional champions of Finnish culture.

In order to secure his appointment as a university lecturer, Snellman published, in 1835, his doctoral thesis on Hegelian philosophy and, in 1836, a study of the philosophy of Leibniz. Soon after this, however, he found himself embroiled in an argument concerning the right of the authorities to intervene in internal decision-making within the university. Having been fined by a court of law for professional misconduct as a result, Snellman went abroad in 1839.

During his travels, Snellman published his central philosophical works. His work on academic freedom (1840) was published in Stockholm, on the ideas of personality written in Tübingen in 1841, and *Läran om staten* ('The origin of the state', 1842), published in Stockholm.

On his return to his native land, Snellman gained a position as rector of a school in the town of Kuopio in 1843. He influenced opinions through the ►newspapers he published, which were often censored because of their opinions.

The general mistrust of philosophy is indicated by the fact that in 1852 the chairs of philosophy were abolished in all Russian universities, including those of autonomous Grand Duchy of Finland. During the reign of Alexander II (1855–1881) official attitudes to philosophy changed, an in 1856 Snellman was appointed Professor of Philosophy. In 1863 he was appointed a senator and director of the Ministry of Finance. In this role, he achieved, in 1863, an ordinance concerning the development of the Finnish language and, in 1865, the introduction of the mark as Finland's own monetary unit. Snellman made an important contribution, too to the development of the railway system in Finland.

He was active in politics, and was influential, among other things, in founding the national army in Finland in 1878. In honour of his economic activity, Snellman's memorial statue from 1923 by Emil Wikström (1864–1942), is located in front of the Bank of Finland, in the centre of ►Helsinki. JN

snow The importance of snow in the Finnish ►way of life is demonstrated by the existence of dozens of words in the Finnish language to describe the various characteristics and states of being of snow.

Winter and snow conditions have developed specialised ways of life, means of livelihood and tools. The skier in the snow-covered forest, the ice-angler on the frozen lake, the winter seine-netter by his hole in the ice and the snow-suited soldiers of the ►Winter War are the mythic images of Finnish reality. Every Finn remembers the snow-castles and lanterns of his childhood, the sledges and skates, and the creak of snow under the soles of his feet on a frosty day.

The snowy landscape, and the formations of snow and ice, have inspired Finnish artists from national romantic, snow-covered forest landscapes of Pekka Halonen (1865–1933) and spruce copses of Aimo Kanerva (1909–1991)

Snow church, Senaatintori Square, Helsinki, February 1997. The church, which was a model of the Ulrika Eleonora Church, predecessor of the Helsinki Cathedral (visible in the background), lasted for about a month before melting

to ►Tapio Wirkkala's glass objects, born of the forms of ice. Images of winter and snow are equally common in Finnish literature and poetry, from ►Aleksis Kivi to present-day writers. The atmosphere of the arctic landscape also appears in music, as in ►Einojuhani Rautavaara's orchestral works.

Winter and snow have naturally influenced building forms, although the stylistic ideals of Finnish architecture have always originated in the cultures of warmer climates. A covering of snow results in lighting that is reflected from below or seems directionless, and this has been used in the treatment of light in Finnish architecture. A white covering of snow also influences choices of colour in buildings; buildings either aim to distinguish themselves against the snowy landscape – as in the red ochre colour of farmhouses, or the rich coloration of wooden towns – or they merge with the winter landscape in the whiteness of Finnish modernism, which brings the cool gleam of snow into the summer landscape, too.

In the winter of 1996 the world's biggest snow building was at the first time erected in the northern City of Kemi. The snow city became a popular travel destination, but it also provided an opportunity for carrying out serious technical tests concerning the feasibility of building with snow. JP

Södergran, Edith (1892–1923), poet. Edith Södergran was born in St Petersburg into a Swedish-speaking bourgeois family. She attended the German Petri-Schule in St Petersburg and be-

Edith Södergran

gan to write in German. Although she later switched to Swedish, 'Germanisms' remained a permanent feature of her language. Södergran contracted tuberculosis early and, before the First World War, spent long periods in sanatoria, including that at Davos. There, she became acquainted with continental European, and particularly German, literature. Her family lost its property in the Russian Revolution of 1917 and since lived in Finland.

Södergran's first collection of poetry, *Dikter* ('Poems', 1916), was the most avant-garde of the Nordic countries. Her poems are original in their imagery and free in their metre. The most important influence in her early period was the philosophy of Nietzsche. Her Dionysian euphoria climaxes in her collection *Septemberlyran* ('The September lyre', 1918). In her best collections, *Rosenaltaret* ('The rose altar', 1919) and *Framtidens skugga* ('Shadow of the future', 1920), declarative pathos gives way to a more complex expression. Södergran is, in the literary history of Finland, the decisive pioneer of Finland-Swedish modernism. PL

space Anthropological studies show that the dominant features of landscape and environment have their influence in the use of space, in both everyday life and in art. The Finnish conception of space originates in the multiform and multirhythmic topological spatial formations of the forest landscape, to which the clearly delineated geometry of the urbanised European cultures is in sharp contrast. The use of space natural to the Finnish forest culture is also evident in certain characteristics of the Finnish language.

In a forest culture, built space is not the opposite of nature; instead, the architect reflects the spatial structures of the landscape. In Finnish ►architecture, space does indeed often have a nature-romantic or pantheistic nature, and spatial constructions are in a sense diffuse compared with clearly defined and geometric urban space. The Finnish-language word *tila* means both 'space' and 'a state of mind'; this double meaning undoubtedly also plays its part in the ambiguous nature of the Finnish conception of space.

Louis Sparre

Alvar Aalto, interior of Finnish Pavilion, New York World's Fair, 1939

'Forest space' is characteristic of the architecture of ►Alvar Aalto. His Finnish section for the New York World's Fair (1939) and Villa Mairea (1938–1939) are masterpieces of freeform and ungeometrical space. Metaphors of forest, natural forms and natural rhythms appear often in Aalto's work.

The starting-point of the architecture of ►Reima Pietilä lies in studies of the morphology of the Finnish landscape. Pietilä's spatial forms and constructions reflect the geological constructions of the landscape, the formations of water and ice and the forms of plants.

The spatial character of the work of many contemporary Finnish architects, too, originates in the spatial forms of nature. In the work of ►Juha Leiviskä, the rhythms, textures and light of the forest combine with the dynamic spatial ideals of the baroque and de Stijl.

The spatial forms and ►light conditions of the forest often appear in abstracted form in Finnish painting and ►sculpture. The paintings of Tor Arne (born 1934) and the sculptures of Kain Tapper (born 1930), for example, convey images of landscape spaces. JP

Sparre, Louis Louis Pehr Sparre of Söfdeborg (1863–1964), count, artist, graphic artist. The Swedish artist count Louis Sparre studied painting in Paris at the Académie Julien. Having become acquainted with Finland through the painter ►Akseli Gallen-Kallela, he took up permanent residence in the

Table, chairs and ceramics manufactured by the Iris factory, 1898

country in 1891. In Finland, Sparre worked first as an artist, illustrating books. In accordance with the spirit of the time, he also made a number of journeys to Russian ▶Karelia, where it was believed that authentic and 'unspoiled' life in the manner of the ▶*Kalevala* was to be found.

In 1897, at Sparre's instigation, the Iris Factory, an applied arts company was set up in the small town of Porvoo in southern Finland. Inspired by the English designer William Morris, the factory aimed to produce contemporary utility objects of high artistic quality. Louis Sparre worked as the firm's managing director, artistic director and furniture designer. The Anglo-Belgian painter and ceramist Alfred William Finch (1854–1930) was appointed artistic director of the ceramics section. Sparre designed furniture both in the international *art nouveau* style of the time and in the so-called Finnish nationalist style, which was expressed in the abundant use of ethnographical ornaments and woodcut decorations. The greatest international success of Iris Factory was its collaboration with the Friends of Finnish Handicraft at the Paris World Exhibition of 1900. After Iris Factory had gone bankrupt in 1902, Sparre continued designing furniture and interiors in his own drawing office with his wife, Eva Mannerheim-Sparre (1870–1958). In 1908 Sparre returned permanently to Sweden, where he continued his artistic activities. MaA

sport The idea of 'the Finns as a nation of athletes' is almost a cliché, yet Finland's gradual emergence as a nation at the end of the 19th century, the popular movement associated with it and the country's ultimate independence from Russia in the aftermath of the First World War advanced in pace with the spread of European 'sport'. The Finns' concept of themselves as a nation was early on reflected in a collective self-image of an international sporting movement in white shoes.

The earliest Finnish coup in competitive sport took place in the winter of 1892, when Finnish skiers won a triple victory in the Nordic 30 kilometres' ski-race held near Stockholm. The winning time was 2 hours 23 minutes 13 and two-fifths seconds, as the precise time-keeping of even those early days reported. In a newspaper, the event was described under the headline 'Finland's ski-ing heroes'. The idea that people of this kind could also be heroes was new at the time, and opened the eyes of many small boys. When at the end of the 19th century the foreign-derived word sport was Fennicised, after several experiments it became established in the form *urheilu*, which for a long time was felt to have a certain tinge of primitive defiance of danger.

In the newspaper reports of the heroic feats of skiers that stigma of foolhardiness and superfluity associated with the word *urheilu* shone like a positive ideal to be aspired to, the

Start of the Finnish skiing championships, 1962. Skiing competitions, followed by large audiences, are held all over the country

sporting philosopher and developer of ▶Finnish baseball, Lauri Pihkala (1888–1981) recalled. The basic experience was national and individual at the same time. Boys began to ski competitively, both outdoors and in their imaginations.

Finns had to wait some time before their next skiing success. The domination of the slopes of Oslo's Holmenkollen was not achieved until 1922. In their footsteps followed Veikko Hakulinen (born 1925), Siiri Rantanen (born 1924), Eero Mäntyranta (born 1937), Veikko Kankkonen (born 1940) and the other stylish heroes and heroines of Falun, Zakopane and Innsbruck. Their exploits were followed with suspense on radio and later television, and were remembered many times. Such is the function of sport on Finnish society: to create an image of 'us' for others and above all also for themselves. The answer to the question raised in many books on sport as to what attracts Finns to ski-ing and ski-jumping (Matti Nykänen, born 1963), long-distance running (▶Paavo Nurmi, Lasse Virén, born 1949), javelin-throwing (Seppo Räty, born 1962 and Heli Rantanen, (born 1970) and rally driving (Juha Kankkunen, born 1959 and Tommi Mäkinen, (born 1964), and makes them successful in these types of sport, is paradoxically, the existence of those same books and the stories they are telling.

The model is to be found in 1912, when the Finns for the first time took part in the Stockholm Summer Olympics, seriously and in a large team. Suspense was in the air right from the start, for Finland strove by every means to stand out from Russia, to which it officially belonged. At the opening ceremony the Finns marched behind the Russian team, but at a very telling distance. In the wrestling, a dominant branch of sport at that time, the Finns had 37 entrants. Great was the wonder back home in Finland when people read in the newspapers how a certain Asikainen wrestled with one tenacious opponent for 11 hours 40 minutes and even then the match was not decided.

The Finnish hero of the games was, however, the long-distance runner Hannes Kolehmainen (1889–1966), whose three gold medals and a silver were infinitely important to the identity of the nation that was dreaming of its independence. 'Finland runs on to the map of the world' was the story Finns told themselves there.

Thanks to wrestling, general athletics and, above all, regular, modern training, Finland was for a long time one of the Olympic great powers. At Paris in 1924 the Finns came third in the total number of medals won, in Amsterdam in 1928 fourth, and in Berlin in 1936 fifth, with the United States generally winning the country-by-country comparison hands down.

After the Second World War, Finland's success became confined to long-distance running, and by the mid 1990s it was almost solely associated with javelin-throwing. At the Summer Olympics at Atlanta in 1996 Finland occupied 23rd place on a country-by-country comparison. At winter competitions Finns have to this day regularly won gold medals in ski-ing, and especially ski-jumping.

The Stockholm success story was repeated again when in the spring of 1995 the Finnish team won a gold medal in the world championships of the popular modern winter sport, ice-hockey. For a moment this threw the whole of Finland into confusion and produced a national carnival spirit rather untypical of the Finnish ▶mentality, a feeling one quite lacking in the dark side of sport, the hostile fervour against 'the other side'. This in spite of the fact that the Finns took over almost as their second national anthem the victory song that had been composed for the Swedish games – *Den glider in* ('It goes gliding in'). ES

stag-nights and hen-parties (Wedding Eve) On summer weekend evenings in the centre of Finland's larger towns one may encounter cheerful groups of girls or young men who are getting ready to see their friends get married. In recent years the celebration of *Polterabend*, or Wedding Eve, has become more widespread and has turned into an important mini-carnival.

In Finland the tradition dates from the 19th century. The close friends of the same sex as the bride or bridegroom say goodbye to them before the

Stag-party: the bridegroom is dressed as a corpse, and the end of his bachelor days mourned by the 'cortège'

wedding by amusing themselves together. The occasion may also be attended by the brothers and sisters of the central figure, irrespective of sex divisions. There are usually about 30 participants. The organisers of the party plan the event well in advance and agree among themselves who will supply or arrange this or that.

Part of the *Polterabend* tradition consists of a 'kidnapping' of the celebrant. He/she is carried off into the midst of the party while on the way to work, or is persuaded to visit a plausible-sounding place, where the party guests are waiting. The 'kidnapping' tradition enjoys great popularity in the Finland-Swedish (►Finland-Swedes) social milieu, as does the so-called 'bluff': the celebrant is transported during the course of the evening from place to place with a blindfold over his/her eyes, ending up, according to custom, in unexpected surroundings and company.

Ever since the end of the Second World War a central feature of the *Polterabend* has been its public character, and its drawing as much attention as possible to the celebrant's external appearance. The idea is that he/she or the entire company must be distinguished from the ordinary man in the street by arousing attention, by demonstrating the nature of the event and also by permitting a small amount of foolery.

The celebrant is usually made to take a sauna, after which dressing begins. Use is often made of props and make-up. The design of the celebrant's 'profile' follows one of three models. In the first, the celebrant is moved out of the group of unmarried people into the group of those who are married. This change may be expressed by the celebrant dressing as a child: he/she may wear nappies and have a dummy or lollipop, with a sign hung round the neck, reading 'Give me the breast, change my napples'. Conversely, the whole group of party guests may dress according to themes, with the celebrant dressed as Tellus from the *Peanuts* cartoon strip, and the rest of the group as the other kids from the comics. The character of transitional rite may also be observed in cases where the celebrant's loss of freedom entailed by his/her marriage is emphasised. The bride or bridegroom may be given a sign reading 'While I'm still free', encouraging people to kiss them either for a fee or gratis. Dressing up as an angel is a part of the same category. Another tradition quite often encountered is for the celebrant to be made up as a corpse, with the rest of the group forming a solemnly dressed funeral cortège. The reason for their grief is that they are losing one of their members.

The second commonly encountered carnival profile for celebrants is based on changing sex. With the help of make-up, costume, padding and wig, the bride is dressed as a young man and the bridegroom as a girl.

The third group of dress-models is formed by profiles that are well-known and amusing. The celebrant is presented as a clown, a Finnish maiden in national costume or, in mid summer, a skier with skis, etc. The fitness culture of recent years has also led to celebrants being made to perform real physical feats in the form of running, rowing or cycling.

The Wedding Eve celebrations involve trips around town. First the celebrant is driven to places where there are as many people as possible, such as the railway station, markets, shopping centre and so on. For the celebrant, the public attention and ridiculousness of the situation make the event unforgettable.

From outside, the party moves to a restaurant, where the male guests do their best to get drunk. Some restaurants keep a special glass shoe for champagne to be drunk out of, or serve special dishes whose external appearance hints at aspects of sex. Items on the menu at the restaurant may also be associated with the theme of the celebrant's disguise in, for example, food usually given to children. Although special events are arranged for both bride and bridegroom, in the evening the guests of the couple may meet by chance or prior agreement at the same popular restaurant. TK

Still, Nanny (born 1926), designer. One of Finland's leading post-war glass designers Nanny Still began working as a designer for Riihimäki Glass (founded 1910) in 1949. The collaboration continued until 1976. The items Still designed for Riihimäki consisted of both mass produced and art glass. Her designs of the 1950s can be said to have shared the reduced formal language typical of Scandinavian modernism. Still took an early interest in the use of coloured glass, and in the 1960s the formal world of her work, as well as its colour, became more abundant and decorative. Still's best-known glass range internationally is *Flinderi* (1963).

In addition to working with glass, Still has continually been active in other areas of design. In 1954 she won a medallion of honour at the Milan Triennale for her wooden salad-servers.

Nanny Still and her jewellery range *'Lumihopea'* ('Snowsilver')

In the 1970s she designed crockery for the Finnish Hackman company, including the *Mango* range in 1973, and in the 1990s a range of cast-iron pots.

Still has lived in Belgium since 1959, and her collaboration with manufacturers has extended to include central European factories, including Rosenthal in Germany, for which she has designed both studio-line glass and ceramics, Heinrich Porzellan in Germany, and the Cérabel porcelain factory in Belgium. The starting-point of all Still's design work is a feeling for materials and their adaptation serve its purpose as well as possible. Her work combines a personality brimming over with ideas and a liking for richness of colour and form with solid professional skill, and her designs are often planned for adaptation to industrial mass production. MaA

students Students took on a very important role in Finnish society at the beginning of the 19th century, initially following the German example. In other parts of continental Europe, too, students played an important role as instruments of the free formation and expression of opinion. In most European countries, students adopted and expressed, at least periodically, anti-government liberal and leftist political opinions, as a result of which student organisations and activities came under close monitoring and surveillance.

'Revolution in the University has begun': the occupation of the Old Student House Building, 1968

Because of their widespread influence, students have been the object of extensive historical research. At the same time, the ideological, everyday, ceremonial, festive and traditional elements of student life are the objects of continual study: students manifest social mobility, formation of an elite, the social problems of the 'educated poor' or the 'white-collar poor', bohemianism regulated by background or future expectations, or, correspondingly, conformism. After the acceptance of women in the universities at the beginning of the 20th century, student life took on new dimensions as a field of social life between the sexes.

In Finland in the early 1820s, student life was taking on the Germanic form of political opposition, but, as a result of government interest, the year 1822 saw a turning towards, on the one hand, the use of alcohol and rowdiness and, on the other, the loyal patriotic forms that became dominant in the 1830s when the university had moved from Turku to Helsinki and the so-called Lauantaiseura (Saturday Society), led student life. The increasing pan-European politicisation was also evident in the 1840s, and led, after a revolutionary phase, to the temporary banning of traditional student societies in 1852; the government wanted to replace them with faculty societies

Independence Day parade: students visit military graves by torchlight

in order to prevent the pursuance of political interests. Nevertheless, student life flowered again at the end of the 1850s, beginning with the project for a student building led by Fredrik Cygnaeus (1807–1881) and ▶J.V. Snellman; in 1868 the societies (subsequently the Student Union of the University of Helsinki) were constituted as public corporations, and the Old Students' House was completed in 1870. It was followed by the Student Union Building and many large society buildings (particularly between 1904 and 1910), which have played a significant part as stages for Finland's intellectual, political and social life.

In the second half of the 19th century the Student Union was divided into opposing ideological groups. Student societies were equivalent of political parties, but were at the same time constantly active lobby groups and cadre schools for the parties of the parliament; in fact, they constituted Finland's first party organisations. The inspectors of the societies were generally important government figures. Thus, the close connection of students and student organisations with the creation of a national ideology and its expression remained important, particularly during the period of intense political activity that began again in 1899.

The importance of students in Finland was greater than that in many other countries because in Finland there was only one university in the country. At the beginning of the 20th century other institutes of ►higher education and universities were founded, but it was only in the 1960s the traditional role and importance of Students' Union as the leading representative of academic youth weakened. At other times, student activity was very political, particularly in the late 1920s and 1930s, during the period of the dominance of and resistance to the fascist-type Academic Karelia Society. During the 1940s and 1950s, however, social activity to improve student conditions by, among other things, building residences, was to the fore.

During the 1960s, under demographic pressure from the generation of 'baby-boomers', the political influence of students – perhaps above all their desire to question and shake cultural structures – was felt all over the world, and very clearly in Finland. At the end of the 1960s, this generation became dominant and changed many traditional forms of student life, generally from a bourgeois to a more proletarian direction. In the decade that followed, a kind of Stalinism achieved a conspicuous but not major role, as the 'silent' majority concentrated on their studies and small-scale cultural activities. In 1976–1977 the trend turned back towards more traditional forms of student life, ceremonial festivals and dress and so on. Choir singing, which had been central to student history, was revived as an artistic activity, and in international connections the links with Upsala and the rest of Sweden, built particularly during and after the Second World War, received a new emphasis. MK

summer cottages In the 1960s sociologists began to speak of the escape from the countryside. In Finland in the 1990s, foreigners may be surprised by the escape to the countryside, as the towns and cities empty at weekends in summer.

With the Romantic movement in the 19th century, the countryside began to be considered as offering a true experience of beauty. In the countryside, even nature was more authentic. In Finland it was necessary to experience it in summertime. In the late 19th century the upper classes began to build themselves villas in the countryside, but nevertheless close to towns in which life was conducted in a way, which corresponded to their social status.

Between the First and the Second World War, the number of villas quadrupled, as the upper classes of the towns acquired them. In civil servant families this meant that the family moved to the country in summer holidays at the beginning of June and returned at the end of August.

Summer cottages became available to all after the Second World War along with the simultaneous strong urbanisation. As car-ownership increased, cottages could be built on distant sites.

Finns like to own their summer cottages. Part-ownership and renting are rare. The rental market is directed to foreigners, primarily Germans.

One in four Finnish households has a second home. Considerably more, however, have experience of summer cottage life through visiting family and friends. Owning or building a summer cottage has long been a dream second only to owning a home of one's own for Finnish families. Cottage fever is shared by all social groups, even farmers.

For a long time, summer cottages were sparsely equipped. Water came and went by carrying, electricity was a dream and the lavatory was at the end of the garden. A certain traditionality was an essential part of summer cottage life, with the women busying themselves with household chores and the men building something. It was even better when one ate potatoes from one's own garden and fish one had caught oneself.

It is possible to live in summer cottages all year round, and at the same time, the opportunity to return to one's roots is now possible all year round. Thus an increasing number of people who earn their livings in the towns and cities spend an increasing part of the year in their own cottages. This is also evident in the celebration of festivals, when a real, authentic Christmas is spent at the cottage, in a modest way in accordance with the agrarian Finnish tradition. IN

Suomenlinna, (Sveaborg, Viapori)

The building of this sea-fortress, which is located off the shore of ▶Helsinki, began in 1747. Around 60 hectares in area, the fortress comprises six islands equipped with a system of five separate bastions. It was part of a chain of fortifications that was originally intended to be larger, but apart from Suomenlinna itself, only a small part on the mainland, in what is now the Helsinki area, was completed. Operatively, the fortress was also connected to the fortified island of Svartholma, off the shore of Loviisa. In addition to the bastions and troop shelters, there was also a dock. In its time, the building of

C. Hårleman, King's Gate, Suomenlinna, 1754

the fortress was the biggest construction project in Sweden-Finland. The work was financed through a loan granted by the French state. The new fortress was called Sveaborg ('fortress of Sweden'), in Finnish Suomenlinna ('fortress of Finland').

The intention behind the building of Suomenlinna was to provide a stronghold for both offensive and defensive warfare close to the Russian border. In this sense, however, the importance of the fortifications remained modest, and the surrender of Suomenlinna in the war against Russia in 1808 has remained its best-known military event. In 1855, during the Crimean War (1854–1856), the fortress suffered severe damage from shelling by the British navy.

As a monument of fortress architecture, Suomenlinna is one of the most important of its kind in Europe. Its builder, Augustin Ehrensvärd (1710–1772), followed the principles of fortress-building of French Sébastien le Prêtre Vauban, but adapted them in an original way. The stylistic ideals of baroque classicism are visible in the articulation of squares, the façades of the barracks and the architecture of

The image of the King´s Gate, Suomenlinna appears on the current 1000-Finnmark note

the fortress gates. The main gate of the fortress, the King's Gate, was completed in 1754. After Ehrensvärd's death, the direction of the project was continued by Nils Mannerskantz (1738–1809), during whose time a group of monumental barracks, workshops and defence installations were constructed in the Gustavian neo-classical style that was then in favour at the Swedish court. The English garden of Susisaari Island also dates from this period. The fortification was continued while Suomenlinna was under Russian command (1809–1917), and an Orthodox church was built.

In addition to its importance in terms of architectural history, Suomenlinna is also significant for its cultural history. Art and music were particularly active there. Ehrensvärd himself was an accomplished landscape painter, and the well-known Swedish painter Elias Martin (1739–1818) worked here between 1763 and 1765, painting views of the fortifications under construction.

Suomenlinna has also been a centre for the dissemination. Among these are the stone-built cow-sheds – these spread throughout Finland as the soldiers who had participated in the construction work returned home – and lilac trees, whose presence in officers' manor-house gardens can be traced back to the gardens of the fortress.

Since the 1960s, Suomenlinna has been a cultural site in the hands of a civilian administration which is at the same time part of Helsinki: the islands have a population of around 1000. To satisfy the need for housing, the old building stock on Suomenlinna has been added to as late as the 1980s.

Suomenlinna was declared a World Heritage Site by Unesco in 1991. The Nordic Art Center has been active in premises on Suomenlinna since 1978. EH

Ilmari Tapiovaara

Talvela, Martti (1935–1989), bass. Martti Talvela started his career as Sparafucile in Verdi's *Rigoletto* at the Finnish National Opera in 1960. The next year he took the role of the Commendatore in Mozart's *Don Giovanni* at Covent Garden and soon afterwards in Bayreuth. Thanks to his sonorous, immense yet flexible voice, he was

Martti Talvela

soon recognised as one of the great basses of the century. In addition to major Wagner and Verdi roles, he was acclaimed particularly for his both vocally and dramatically imposing performances as Boris Godunov in Mussorgsky's opera of the same name, Sarastro in Mozart's *The Magic Flute* and ►Paavo Ruotsalainen in ►Joonas Kokkonen's *Viimeiset kiusaukset* (*The Last Temptations*). He was also highly successful as the director of the Savonlinna Opera Festival. HB

Tapiovaara, Ilmari (1914–1999), interior designer. Ilmari Tapiovaara is one of the central names of the post-war reconstruction period in terms of the design of furniture and interiors for homes and public spaces. One of the first proponents of the 'Design for Need' ideology in Finland, Tapiovaara has always stressed the designer's social and ethical responsibilities, and his design starts from needs dictated by use. In 1948 three designs by Tapiovaara received awards in an international competition for low-cost furniture held by the Museum of Modern Art in New York.

After graduating, Tapiovaara worked as an assistant in the Swiss architect Le Corbusier's office. Between 1938 and 1951 he worked as artistic director in Finnish furniture factories. Tapiovaara has also had his own interior design office.

Tapiovaara has always liked to use wood for his furniture, and often in natural colours. Another characteristic, particularly of his early work, is the adaptation of technical innovations concerned with the moulding of plywood to mass production. Tapiovaara's

Ilmari Tapiovaara with a range of his chair designs

best-known design project is Domus Academica, a student residence for the University of Helsinki, carried out in 1946. The aim was to create a pleasant environment for living and working, using cheap furniture that could be mass produced. The central element is the stacking wooden chair *Domus*, which later became a popular item of furniture for schools and public spaces. In 1950s and 1960s, Tapiovaara designed many other popular chairs. In addition to furniture, he has designed lighting, church silver and tableware. MaA

Tapiovaara, Nyrki (1911–1940), film director. Nyrki Tapiovaara was born and brought up in the home of a civil servant in Hämeenlinna, near Tampere. He became a cultural radical and leftist intellectual, who, having worked as a film critic and theatre director, received in 1937 the opportunity to make a film version of Juhani Aho's (1861–1921) classic novel *Juha* in 1937. Before his death in the ►Winter War, Tapiovaara made five films, all of which transcended their conventional starting-points, the thriller *Varastettu kuolema* ('Stolen death', 1938), the farce *Kaksi Vihtoria* ('Two Victors', 1939), the musical comedy *Herra Lahtinen lähtee lipettiin* ('Mr Lahtinen makes himself scarce', 1939), and ►F. E. Sillanpää's *Miehen tie* ('A man's way', 1940).

Tapiovaara's talent and vision are evident in the way in which he made literary classics his own, cultivated experimental features within the framework of traditional genres, turned the thriller into a social statement, and transformed farce into critical satire. ST

Tatars The small Tatar minority in Finland is the oldest Moslem group in the Nordic countries. Its first representatives appeared with the Russian army soon after the war against Russia 1808–1809, as a result of which Finland was annexed to the Russian empire. The majority of the Finnish Tatar community are so-called Mishars, who emigrated in the latter part of the 19th century and up to 1925.

Most of the newcomers came from almost the same village, and were farmers who traded during the winter. Since Finland offered them successful temporary business opportunities, their visits became increasingly frequent, and some of them decided to settle in the country. Now merchants only, they chose to take up residence in larger conurbations such as Helsinki, Turku and Tampere and their neighbourhoods.

Finnish Tatars have been officially defined by their Islamic religion. The first Islamic association was founded as early as 1830 by the few Tatars who then lived in Finland. After the 1922 freedom of religion act came into force in 1924, the Finnish Mohemmadanic (Islamic) Congregation was established. It included all Moslems living in Finland until 1943, when another congregation was formed in Tampere.

Nyrki
Tapiovaara

Tuulikki Paananen, (left), Ahti H. Einola and Ralph Enckell in Nyrki Tapiovaara's *Varastettu kuolema* ('Stolen death', 1938)

The total number of Tatars in Finland never exceeded 1000, and in 1992 was 867. Their social structures are based around the mosques which have been built in Helsinki, Tampere and Järvenpää. Tatar efforts to retain their cultural characteristics have been quite successful. Their language, which belongs to the northern Turkish dialect, has almost exclusively been the first language spoken at home. They have a rich literary tradition, still mostly transmitted in the traditional Arabic script. JPn

television Television in Finland is based on a public service system made up of the public service company Yleisradio Oy (the Finnish Broadcasting Company YLE), and the privately owned MTV Oy (MTV Finland) and, since 1997, Oy Ruutunelonen Ab, both of which are financed by advertising revenue. Like the Scandinavian countries, Finland has a strong tradition of public service broadcasting, but also differs from them in its early development of commercial television.

The term 'public service' is defined in the Act on Yleisradio Oy of 1994, as a comprehensive broadcasting service including special duties and covering the whole country. MTV Oy and Ruutunelonen pay a public service fee to YLE.

Television operation refers in this instance to the terrestrial broadcasting of television programmes. Another way of broadcasting television programmes is via ▶satellite and cable.

Just like ▶radio, television in Finland began as a private project. The first television broadcast in Finland was made by a television club of professionals and amateurs on 24 May 1955. Commercially-funded programme operations were initiated by the Foundation for the Promotion of Technology (Tekniikan edistämis-säätiö) in 1956, under the name of TES-TV. In 1960 this became organized as the commercial company Tesvisio.

The Finnish Broadcasting Company began television test transmissions on 13 March 1957 and a regular service started on 1 January 1958 when television licences also became compulsory in Finland. In 1957 the com-

mercially-funded Oy Mainos-TV-Reklam Ab (which in 1983 changed its name to MTV Oy) was established, initially in order to assist the Finnish Broadcasting Company.

In the mid-1960s the success of MTV Finland in attracting television advertising meant that the Tesvisio group experienced financial difficulties, as a result of which Yleisradio took it over in 1964, and then launched its second channel, TV2, based in Tampere.

The Finnish Broadcasting Company began colour television test transmissions in 1969. In the same year the colour television licence was introduced, in addition to the black-and-white licence. The adoption of colour television in nearly all Finnish households meant that a single television licence system could be adopted in 1996, also providing finance for radio.

Since the beginning, the Finnish Broadcasting Company's television programmes have been broadcast in two languages. The Swedish-language programmes are provided by Finlands Svenska Television (FST), which transmits 880 hours of programmes a year. The programmes are broadcast on TV1 and TV2 (11 per cent of programming). The proportion of FST's own productions is 67 per cent. ▶Åland determines its own broadcasting legislation including television broadcasts on the basis of the Autonomy Act for Åland.

In the mid-1980s, arrangements were made in Finnish television which led to the reorganisation and extension of YLE's and MTV's operations at the beginning of the 1990s, and to the enactment of the Act on YLE. In 1985 the Finnish Broadcasting Company, MTV and Nokia (electronics company) founded the company Oy Kolmostelevisio Ab to provide a third television channel covering the whole of Finland. Kolmostelevisio's operations were made possible by the alterations that were made to the operating licence of the Finnish Broadcasting Company in 1986. Kolmostelevisio began regular broadcasts in 1987. The company was founded with the aim of developing Finnish television so as to compete more effectively with the satellite and cable channels that were gaining an in-

Finnish Broadcasting Company television tower, Helsinki

creasing foothold at that time (▶satellite and cable television.)

A major reorganisation of the television channels was carried out at the beginning of 1993. At that time MTV's programming in its entirety was moved to the third television channel and the Finnish Broadcasting Company began to run the TV channels 1 and 2 completely on its own. Even before this, in 1990, MTV had acquired a majority shareholding in Kolmostelevisio, which thus became a subsidiary of MTV.

MTV was granted its own operating licence in 1993. Since 1994 YLE's operation has been based since 1994 on the Act on Yleisradio Oy (1993). Previously, until the end of 1992, what was known as a single operating licence system was in force in Finland. This meant that MTV (and subsequently Kolmostelevisio) broadcast programmes on YLE's television channels until the end of 1992 on the grounds of the operating licence granted to YLE.

In 1996 programme hours per channel were as follows: TV1: 4598 hours (88 hours per week); TV2 3517 hours (67 hours per week) and MTV3 4487 hours (86 hours per week).

Finland and Sweden have an important co-operative agreement concerning television. An edited channel composed of Swedish programming from Sweden's two public service channels (Sveriges Television) is retransmitted simultaneously in unaltered form via the television broadcasting network that covers the southern part of Finland (construction began in 1988). Correspondingly since 1986, an edited channel of domestic programming from YLE's two channels and MTV3 has been retransmitted over the Stockholm area.

This Finnish programming is also available on some Swedish cable networks (in 24 localities) as part of an extended basic package. Swedish television broadcasts can also be received as 'spill-over' on Finland's west coast. In addition, there is a special organisation, Nordvision, devoted to co-operation and programme exchange between the Nordic countries.

Finnish television broadcasting is national in character, but international influences may be seen, for example, in entertainment and games programmes. News and current affairs coverage occupies an important place in the schedules of both the Finnish Broadcasting Company and MTV. As a commercial station, MTV is, however, more oriented towards entertainment and drama.

Although the television companies produce or commission from domestic independents over 50 per cent of their output, Finland is one of those small countries that import many programmes from abroad. The Finnish Broadcasting Company buys a major share of its programmes from the United Kingdom and the United States, while MTV imports mostly from the latter.

There is not much exporting of Finnish programmes abroad, although some have been distributed to dozens of countries. Special mention may be made here of Kalle Holmberg's (born 1939) mini-series *Rauta-aika* ('The age of iron', 1982) based on Finnish mythology and the ▶*Kalevala*, and the animation series based on the Moomin characters created by Finland's Swedish-speaking author ▶Tove Jansson (1990). The latter was a coproduction with television companies in several other countries.

The high level of Finnish production skills has been internationally recognized and used in the production of television signals for major international sporting events. The staff and skills of the Finnish Broadcasting Company were used during the Albertville Winter Olympic Games of 1992 (cross-country skiing, biathlon), the Lillehammer Winter Olympic Games of 1994 (biathlon) and the World Athletics Championships at Gothenburg in 1995 (marathon, walking). Finnish know-how was also used in the production of the television signal for the Atlanta Summer Olympic Games in 1996. MS

textiles The roots of Finland's vital and internationally recognised textile design lie in the folk tradition of this austere country and in women's handicrafts. The training of textile artists is of a high quality, and is directed towards both industrial design and free work of art.

No finds of prehistoric textiles have been made in Finland. The best-preserved art fabrics are 15th century church textiles from Turku Cathedral, and an altar-cloth, which may have been made by the first known textile artist, a nun from a Bridgettine convent which functioned in Naantali, southwest Finland, in the 15th and 16th centuries. Nuns practised a great deal of textile work and also taught handicrafts, including making socks and gloves, to lay people.

The ►*ryijy* is the best-known Finnish art textile. *Ryijy*s developed from utility textiles to art textiles in the late 18th century. During this period, wedding, bench and church *ryijy*s were made, as well as sleigh-coverlets.

Making bobbin lace and knitting became widespread in Finland at the end of the 16th century and bobbin lace centres developed in various parts of the country. As early as the 17th century, making bobbin lace became a livelihood in ►Rauma; it has been revived in the 20th century, and the Rauma Bobbin Lace Weeks, which take place every summer, are evidence of enthusiastic amateur bobbin lace making.

In many places, socks were knitted as an additional source of income, and original knitted sweater patterns developed in the parishes along the coast of the Gulf of Bothnia. Among these is a rarity, the Korsnäs sweater, which combines crocheting and knitting.

The Friends of Finnish Handicraft, which had a decisive influence on the development of modern Finnish textile design, was founded at the initiative of the artist Fanny Churberg (1845–1892) in 1874. Its intention was to foster a Finnish sense of style and handicrafts. The organisation collected old patterns and, from the early 1920s, arranged regular design competitions which attracted enthusiastic participation, and as a result of which the new *ryijy* was born. Throughout its existence, the Friends of Finnish Handicraft has encouraged and employed designers, and almost all textile designers have, at some point in their careers, worked for the organisation.

Training for textile designers as such did not begin until 1929, and, until the 1960s, was highly based on handicraft. The handicraft school of Wetterhoff has taught textile work since 1885, and has also been a significant trainer of textile designers. There are, in addition, some 50 handicraft schools in Finland.

Numerous cloth factories, and cotton mills that grew large, were established in the 19th and early 20th centuries. At first these factories took the European pattern-centres as their models, but at the beginning of the 20th century they began to work in collaboration with Finnish artists. The first permanently employed designers began work in the textile industry in 1937.

After the Second World War, leading textile designers designed patterns for factories, but the artistic printed patterns designed by Maija Isola (born 1927) for ►Marimekko in the 1950s began a flourishing of printed fabrics. During the 1960s and 1970s printed fabrics by designers including ►Rut Bryk, ►Timo Sarpaneva and Kirsti Ilvessalo (born 1920) shone with brilliant colour. Later designers include Anneli Airikka-Lammi (born 1944) and Markku Piri (born 1955). ►Dora Jung's refined linen damasks were symbols of the modernism of the 1960s and 1970s. At the same time, Marjatta Metsovaara (born 1927) made innovations in woven fabrics for inte-

Eeva Anttila, *Työ ja elämä* ('Work and life'), detail, tapestry, 1949–1951

Maisa Tikkanen, *Mustavalkoinen* ('Black-and-white'), matted wool, 1979

Ritva Puotila, paper-thread textiles for Woodnotes Ltd., 1987

rior design. The Marimekko phenomenon also gave rise to small printing workshops for utility fabrics, such as Pohjanakka and Puolukka.

The shift towards freer, more painterly and sculptural textile design came from the *ryijy*. The materials used by Kirsti Rantanen (born 1930) are often taken straight from nature. The textile sculptures of Irma Kukkasjärvi (born 1941) show daring choices of material; her installations can be seen in, for example, the House of Parliament and the president's residence at Mäntyniemi, in Helsinki. Because of the abundance of materials, techniques and three-dimensional shapes, the line between textiles on the one hand and painting and sculpture on the other is often uncertain. The image language of art textiles is close to nature, clear and reduced. In addition to *ryijy*s, the delicate image-textures of Eeva Anttila (1894–1993) reduced the distance between textile art and painting.

Experimental textile art, whose forms range from mini-textiles and embroidery to large scale installation works, is represented by many contemporary artists' twig-weavings, textile sculptures, installations, quiltworks, paper rugs and artworks, as well as imaginative woollen sweaters and quilts on natural themes. The textiles and knitwear produced by ►Kalevala Koru, founded in 1937, also represent the rich handicraft tradition of Finland. MA

theatre There are 5 million Finns, and 2.7 million theatre tickets were sold in 1996. In the mid 1990s in a country recovering from a severe economic recession and penetrated by television and video culture, theatres are full. Attendance figures are very high in international terms.

During the 1960s and 1970s a significant number of old workers' organisations and civil guard buildings that had been used as theatres were replaced by new ones, funded on average 75 per cent by municipalities and central government. Of the so-called commercial theatres, only a few are acknowledged to have any real standing. The theatre is like the library system: it is a service institution in which ticket prices are so highly subsidised that everyone, in principle, can afford to attend. Finland has around 40 theatres, fairly evenly distributed in towns; the most northerly theatre is in Rovaniemi, to the north of the Arctic Circle.

Finnish theatre has been called a theatre for everyone. The reasons for this are partly historical. Because Finland lacked both a court of its own – either imperial or royal – and aristocracy, the theatre never became an amusement for the upper social classes: instead, it was something to be enjoyed by both factory-owners and workers. Another important reason for this popular appeal is the fact that the birth of the theatre in Finland coincided with the development of Finnish language and culture. The first Finnish-language theatrical performances took place in the 1840s: until then, theatre had been only occasionally seen in sparsely populated agrarian Finland, where it was performed by touring companies in Swedish, German or Latin. ▶Aleksis Kivi wrote his plays in the 1860s, when the Finnish language achieved its capacity for artistic expression. A theatre company led by Kaarlo Bergbom (1843–1906), performed Kivi's *Lea*, based on the Biblical story, in 1869. This event is regarded as the beginning of the history of professional theatre in Finland.

Kivi was followed, among others, by ▶Minna Canth; after having been left a widow, with seven children, this enlightened woman became the central writer of the newly founded Finnish Theatre in the 1880s and 1890s. With their radical view of the wretched position of women and working people

Onni Tarjanne, Finnish National Theatre, Helsinki, 1902

and of the double moral standards of society, Canth's social plays caused a stir.

At the turn of the century, during the period of Russification (1899–1905), national feeling strengthened and Finnish-language culture grew. The working class, too, embraced theatre, particularly in its active form: the importance of amateur theatre in Finland as a form of artistic education is significant, since almost every village had its own amateur theatre group so that Finns, irrespective of social class, learned to regard going to the theatre as a natural form of entertainment.

After Finland gained its independence in 1917, the success of theatre continued; foreign plays and artistic movements began to make themselves evident in Finnish repertoires. Finland also became, officially, bilingual, and there are still five Swedish-language theatres in the country, of which the Swedish Theatre in Helsinki has the role of national theatre.

Three writers are of particular importance in the history of Finnish the-

Sturdy traditionalism: Eino Jurkka's classic production of Aleksis Kivi's *Seitsemän veljestä* (*Seven Brothers*) at the Finnish Folk Theatre in 1934

atre: Minna Canth, ▶Maria Jotuni and ▶Hella Wuolijoki. *Tohvelisankarin rouva* ('The armchair hero's wife'), a satirical folk comedy by the dramatist and prose-writer Jotuni, resulted, in 1924, in a parliamentary debate about the level of the play's sexual morals; further performances were banned. In 1933 the Estonian-born Wuolijoki shocked the authorities with her play *Laki ja järjestys* ('Law and order'), which offered a sympathetic interpretation of the losing red side in the Civil War of 1918. But Wuolijoki's well-constructed, dramatic *Niskavuori* plays, which tell of generations of life in a country mansion, with strong women figures, have been a permanent feature of theatre repertoires since the 1930s.

In 1957 the Finnish National Theatre was the second in the world to present Samuel Beckett's *Endgame.* That avant-garde act provoked widespread astonishment in both audience and critics, some of whom saw in Beckett's threatre the signs of the apocalypse; the journey from safe, naive, rural idyll to a fragmented world-view had lasted a little more than a century.

One historic milestone is *Lapualaisooppera* ('The Lapua opera'), a musical play presented by self-proclaimed young leftist theatre-makers at the Student Theatre in 1966. Written by Arvo Salo (born 1931) and directed by Kalle

New generation: the musical play *Lapualaisooppera* ('The Lapua opera', 1966), crystallised the radical values of the 1960s and marked the beginning of political, socially committed theatre in Finland

Holmberg (born 1939), the play questioned the values of the generation that had fought the Second World War and opened up for the theatre a new possibility of being a social commentator and critic. Participants were, in the main, members of the generation born after 1945, of whom many have later made their mark on both professional theatre and cinema in the late 20th century.

The late 1960s and early 1970s were in Finland, as in many other European countries, a period of, among other things, Brecht, politicisation and radical leftism: a number of theatre groups independent of the 'institutions' were also founded by young people according to whose vision democracy in the theatre meant communal decision-making. Many of these toured extensively also abroad. Of these, the most important is probably the KOM Theatre, which celebrated its 25th birthday in 1996. Among its leading lights are the composer and musician Kaj Chydenius (born 1939) and the director Kaisa Korhonen (born 1941). Ryhmäteatteri ('The group theatre') has also established a firm presence, after undergoing some formal changes; it reached a renaissance in the 1980s through the work of the director duo Arto af Hällström (born 1952) and Raila Leppäkoski (born 1950). The latter later became a dramatist and rector of the Theatre Academy.

In the 1970s Turku City Theatre was, for a few years, at the forefront of Finnish theatre under the leadership of Kalle Holmberg and Ralf Långbacka (born 1932), directing artistic triumphs particularly with classic texts (including Brecht, Büchner, Shakespeare and Aleksis Kivi, whose *Seitsemän veljestä* (*Seven Brothers*) was directed by Holmberg; the production remained in the repertoire for years, and was recorded for television).

In the mid 1970s a new theatrical generation stepped forward, turning against politics and wishing to make theatre according to its own aesthetics. A performance entitled *Pete Q* (*Nuorallatanssijan kuolema eli kuinka Pete Q sai siivet*, 1978) ('Pete Q, or, The death of a tightrope dancer or how Pete Q got his wings') was remarkable for its antirealism at a time when realism was at its peak. Since then, Finnish theatre has bifurcated many times: audiences specialise, seeking what will please them, and many new temporary or more permanent theatre groups have found their supporters. Among them is, for example, the Q-teatteri ('Q theatre'), where Antti Raivio (born 1962) has acted as founder, writer and director.

Since the late 1960s a fairly permanent place as *enfant terrible* has been occupied by the director and writer ►Jouko Turkka: his period at the Helsinki City Theatre in the late 1970s is remembered both for his iconoclastic habit of *épater le bourgeois* and, in particular, for his exciting reinterpretations of Finnish classics. His own plays, which he also directs and designs, are mischievous games of unrestrained imagination.

The Theatre Academy, of which Turkka was rector between 1983 and 1985, gained university status in 1979, and trains actors, directors, dramatists, technical designers and dancers. The National Ballet has its own school. In the Theatre Academy there is also a Swedish-language department, as well as continuing education, which offers a diverse programme. The University of Tampere has a drama department which trains actors. The University of Art and Design trains set and costume designers.

Every generation of this theatre-loving nation has had its own favourite actors. The great diva of the early part of the 20th century was the actress Ida Aalberg (1857–1915), whose effect on audiences of her time was notable. The actors of the Finnish National Theatre became widely known as stars of Finnish films; of them, the most well-known and best-loved is probably Tauno Palo (1908–1982), who succeeded in being brilliant and believable even in the mass-produced melodramas of the film industry. He is commemorated by a monument in a Helsinki park.

Although climatic conditions are doubtless part of the reason why street theatre is hardly seen in Finland, natural conditions do not, nevertheless, prevent the blossoming of summer theatres: from Midsummer to August, people gather in their hundreds by lake sides, rained on and bitten by midges, for both amateur and professional performances. Generally the repertoire consists of light folk comedy, but artistically serious theatre, too, is seen every summer throughout Finland. Tampere has a summer theatre whose speciality is a revolving auditorium: for dozens of summers plays have been performed there, particularly with themes taken from Finnish history and 'national' subjects.

Finland's only international theatre festival takes place in August in Tampere. Its director in the early 1990s was Vivica Bandler (born 1917). In the 1960s she made the Swedish-language Lilla Teatern ('Little theatre') in Helsinki famous, and was later the director of the Stockholm City Theatre for many years. Her international contacts have brought many fine productions to Tampere. She was followed as director of the Lilla Teatern by Lasse Pöysti (born 1927), who was a popular child-star in the 1940s; later he also became director of the Dramatiska teatern in Stockholm and the TTT Theatre in Tampere, and an actor best-known for his interpretations of classic roles.

Because culture, language and the arts are young in Finland, speech is of central importance in the short theatrical tradition. Theatre has been considered to be a form of communication, even information, whose success is ensured by plentiful speech. The short expressionist period of the 1920s and 1930s brought with it a few experiments, but realism is the stylistic base on whose sturdy (and, at worst, dully naturalistic) representation of reality theatre has traditionally rested. Street theatre, spontaneous improvisation, the fascinating adult puppet theatre of eastern Europe and wordless, antirealist theatre have hardly been practised in Finland. The dramatist first polishes his text to the last comma – and the theatre performs it faithful to the score, without seeking space behind and beneath the words. But the tradition is changing; cross-disciplinary artistic experiments are helping theatre to detach itself from the word and use gesture, image, sound, light: the enchantment of the theatre, which originates in the experience of presence. SL

Bishop Thomas at Neva River by Aarno Karimo, 1930

Thomas (Tuomas, died 1248), Bishop of Turku. The English-born Thomas was, according to the Turku Episcopal chronicle, the fourth leader of the diocese. Thomas, who belonged to the Dominican order, had worked in Sweden as canon of the diocese of Upsala before his appointment to the episcopal seat at Turku in the late 1220s.

Thomas's time was marked by the eastward spread of Catholic Christianity. A rebellion in the Häme region, which was still largely pagan, was suppressed by a crusade directed there at the instigation of the pope around 1237. This northern crusading age also includes an attempt by the Earl of Sweden at the head of a crusading army to extend the sphere of influence of the Catholic Church eastwards, into the area of the Orthodox Church. Bishop Thomas is thought to have given his active support to this policy. The crusading army, however, suffered a crushing defeat at the head of the Gulf of Finland, at the mouth of the River Neva, in 1240. The victory achieved by the Grand Duke of Novgorod, Alexander Yaroslavovitch (Nevsky), established the border between the churches in the north and had a decisive influence on the shaping of the eastern border of Finland, even though the first peace treaty was not ratified until almost a century later, in 1323.

Thomas gave up the episcopal seat in 1245 because, according to a letter of resignation accepted by Pope Innocent IV, he was guilty of torturing a man to death and of forging a papal letter. After leaving Turku, he withdrew to a Dominican Convent in Visby,

Gotland, where he spent his last years. Part of his important library, which he donated in atonement for his sins to the Dominican convent of Sigtuna in the year of his death, 1248, is preserved in the library of University of Upsala. JN

Toikka, Oiva (born 1931), designer, glassware artist. After training as a ceramist, Oiva Toikka worked from 1956 to 1959 in the art department of the ▶Arabia Factory, attracting attention with his expressive human and animal figures. Toikka is, however, known above all as a glassware designer. Since 1963 he has been a product designer for ▶Nuutajärvi Glass. His work for the factory includes both mass-produced series of pressed and blown glass and art glass objects and glass sculptures. Toikka's first successful design was the pressed glass series *Kastehelmi* ('Dewdrop', 1964). Other popular designs have included the mould-blown *Flora* (1966) and *Fauna* (1967), and the pressed-glass series *Pioni* ('Peony', 1976), which is one of Nuutajärvi's best-selling products of all time.

Characteristic of his glass design is a bold desire for experimentation, colourfulness, luxuriance and playfulness. As with the studio-glass movement that spread through the United States in the 1960s, he was attempting already at that time to free himself from all the functional aims traditionally demanded of all glass objects, thus approaching the role of the free arts. The so-called lollipop sculptures and vases of the late 1960s are early exam-

Oiva Toikka amid his *Otz* vases

Oiva Toikka,
vase, coloured
glass, 1969

ples of this, and the colourful stars and imaginary castles and columns the most recent. MaA

Topelius, Zacharias (1818–1898), Professor of Finnish history, writer.

Almost no one has had as great an influence on the shaping of the Finns' conception of history and their national self-understanding as Zacharias Topelius. He was professor of Finnish history between 1854 and 1879, and rector of the University of Helsinki from 1875 to 1878. Despite that, he is not considered a historian as such. This is because Topelius did not, in his works, use original sources with the dedication that the positivist philosophy of history of the time demanded. He was, rather, a populariser whose writing-style was dominated by romantic idealism and moralism, strong patriotic fervour and a belief in a fate that directs human activities. As he grew older, Topelius's religious orientation became more obvious. He also became known as a hymn-poet, and some of his hymns remain among the all-time favourites. Among Topelius's achievements, too, together with the theology professor Arthur Hjelt (1868–

Zacharias Topelius

1931), is bringing of Young Men's Christian Association to Finland.

Topelius began his literary activities as a journalist for a Swedish-language Helsinki daily, *Helsingfors Tidningar*, which he edited between 1841 and 1860. In it, between 1851 and 1860, he published, as a serialised story, the account of a family from the 17th to the 18th centuries under the title *Fält-skärens berättelser* ('Tales of a barber-surgeon'). That series, with its depiction of social betterment and class conflict, was later published in a number of editions.

Topelius's works are light, romanticised and idealised as narratives. In addition to his novels, he published a great deal of children's literature, including the eight-part series *Läsning för barn* ('Reading for children', 1865–1896) and a collection of stories entitled *Sagor* ('Stories', 1847–1852). Topelius' novels and his numerous children's stories and children's plays were popular in Sweden as well as Finland. Particularly important was a patriotic book on Finland's history, people, countryside and geography, *Boken om vårt land* ('A book about our country'), which Topelius published in 1875. For many generations it was an essential primary school reader, and it has been through more than 60 editions.

Topelius wrote almost all of his literary work in Swedish. His vision of one nation with two languages led to a prolonged polemic with the Fennomane professor ►Johan Vilhelm Snellman, who represented a Hegelian national philosophy and was also one of the figureheads of the nationalist movement. Topelius's command of the Finnish language and his interest in developing it as a literary medium are demonstrated by the fact that he wrote the libretto to the first Finnish-language opera, *Kaarle kuninkaan metsästys* ('King Charles' hunt'), which was given its first performance in 1852. The music was composed by Fredrik Pacius (1809–1891), who also wrote the Finnish national anthem. JN

Turkka, Jouko (born 1942), theatre director. Jouko Turkka has been influential in Finnish theatre, as a director, dramatist, teacher and television pro-

Jouko Turkka

ducer. He began his career at the end of the 1960s and worked at the Helsinki City Theatre in the 1970s, where among the plays he directed were works by Brecht, Strindberg, in addition to Finnish comedies. In his work, forms break with conventional patterns. It is resolutely theatrical. Turkka always has a tale to tell, with a dramatic structure.

In 1980 Turkka made a delightfully vivid interpretation of ▶Minna Canth's folk comedy *Murtovarkaus* ('The burglary', 1881), dispensing entirely with dialogue; the performance employed gesture, music, objects and wordless ploys to tell the story.

The plays Turkka has written, directed and designed for example *Hypnoosi* ('Hypnosis', 1986), *Presidentin dementia* ('The president's dementia', 1994), *Rakkaita pettymyksiä rakkaudessa* ('Dear deceptions in love', 1996) have been driven by unlimited imagination, ironic theatrical games in which the real and the invented are confused, objects take on significant roles, the illusory mystery of the theatre is revealed and political taboos are broken; Finland has no real tradition of political theatre.

Turkka's important television work

Heikki Kinnunen (right) and Heidi Krohn in Nils Holberg's play *Jeppe Niilonpoika*, Helsinki City Theatre, 1985

was his adaptation and direction of ▶Aleksis Kivi's *Seitsemän veljestä* (*Seven Brothers*) in 1989. This 12-hour production provoked extensive and heated media debate: Turkka's brothers were not the conventionally amusing figures 'familiar to the entire Finnish people', but corrupt (if, also, humorously viewed), weeping and squealing, dripping with spit and snot: men living primitive emotional lives in the primitive, if beautiful, Finnish landscape.

Turkka did important work in the 1980s in the Theatre Academy in educating an entire generation of young actors whose psychological and physical capacities are extraordinarily strong. His theatre was also criticised for its narrow conception of humanity, and his educational and directional methods were considered oppressive: only 'strong' actors survive being directed by Turkka. Turkka's Finn is surprisingly Latin in temperament: the folk-theatre clichés of slow, silent men who become wild only when drunk are cast aside. Turkka's work has been important in creating a new mode of expression in a theatrical tradition which, because of its youth, is conventionally conservative. SL

Unesco's World Heritage List ▶Petäjävesi Church, Rauma, Suomenlinna, Verla Mill Musem

universities ▶higher education

University of Helsinki The first university in Finland, the Academy of Turku, was founded in 1640. After suffering extensive damage in the Great Fire of Turku (1827), it was transferred to the new capital of Finland, ▶Helsinki, in 1828. Until 1918, the university, known as the Imperial Alexander University of Finland, was the only university in Finland. In 1919 its name was changed to the University of Helsinki (*Universitas Helsingiensis*).

The Academy of Turku was founded in response to the increased need for educated administrators by the Kingdom of Sweden, which had grown to superpower status. During its first century, about half the professors were Swedes; subsequently, the number of Finnish staff grew to such an extent

U

The University of Helsinki, Senaatintori Square

that in 1808 all 15 professors were Finnish. During the period of Swedish rule, the Academy of Turku was a local university whose international importance was small. In Finland, however, it was a central educational and cultural institution through which new ideas and international scholarly influences entered the country.

After its move to Helsinki, the university was developed energetically, and new buildings were constructed for its use. The main university building (1832), the University Library (1833), the University Observatory (1845) and its many faculty buildings form an important part of the harmonious empire style centre designed for Helsinki by the German-born architect ►C.L. Engel.

When the university opened its doors in Helsinki, it had a total of 337 students on its books, whose tuition was provided by 21 full professors and a number of other teachers. It was not

until the 1880s that the number of students exceeded 1000. Women were allowed to study at the university by special permission from the early 1870s. The language of tuition in the university throughout Finland's period as an autonomous Grand Duchy of Russia (1809–1917) was, with a few exceptions, Swedish.

The international importance of the university in the 19th century remained small. Among the few exceptions are the Orientalist ►Georg August Wallin, who received a Royal Geographical Society medal, and the state counsellor ►Anders Johan Sjögren, who was first appointed a member of the St Petersburg Academy of Sciences (1844) and later became director of the Academy's ethnological museum.

Despite the founding of new universities that has taken place since Finland gained its independence in 1917, the University of Helsinki has retained its undisputed position as the largest university in the country (►higher education). At the time of writing, the university has nine faculties: theology, law, medicine, humanities, mathematics and natural sciences, education, politics, agriculture and forestry, and veterinary science. The university has continuing education units in seven locations in different parts of Finland. It also has biological stations at Lammi, Tvärminne near Hanko, and Kilpisjärvi in Lapland, for field study and research in the faculty of mathematics and natural sciences.

In 1995, the number of students was 32,000, of whom 61 per cent are women. The University of Helsinki is bilingual. There are 27 Swedish-language professorships, and Swedish-speakers make up about 7 per cent of the student body. There is a total of 2300 teaching and research staff, and 3400 other staff. There are 1851 docents, of whom some belong to the university's permanent staff of lecturers and scholars, while some work outside the university and visit it to give lectures. There are 1250 foreign students, 100 foreign teaching staff and 620 foreign research staff. About 3000 qualifications are given annually in the university, and more than 200 doctoral theses are examined. The university receives its funding (1995) principally

Entrance lobby, University of Helsinki

Graduations
old and new:
doctoral graduation
ceremonies, 1919 (left)
and 1996 (below)

from central government (64 per cent); the remainder is made up of its own funds (10 per cent), outside funding (23 per cent) and value-added tax. Most of the outside funding is made up of fee-basis services and research funding granted by the Academy of Finland.

The work of the University of Helsinki is supervised by the chancellor, who also has the right to participate in meetings of the Council of State where matters concerning the university are to be discussed. The university's administration is headed by the rector, who is appointed for a term of three years, and two deputy rectors, of whom one must be a Swedish-speaker. The university's highest decision-making is the senate, which is made up of the rector and deputy rectors, the faculty deans, three other members of the teaching and research staff, three representatives of the other staff, and seven students.

Some 200 societies operate under the aegis of the Students' Union of the University of Helsinki (founded in 1868), from subject societies to special societies and political student societies. The Students' Union funds student accommodation, runs canteens within the university and publishes textbooks. Student health is cared for by a clinic run by a separate charitable foundation. The Students' Union of the University of Helsinki is one of the most important property-owners in the centre of Helsinki. Its property includes some of the most important commercial buildings in the centre. The Old Students' House (1870), also owned by the Students' Union, is among the best-known buildings in central Helsinki. The text on the wall of the building, *Spei suae Patria dedit* ('Given by the fatherland to its hope'), bears witness to the great importance that ▶students have had in Finnish history as the vanguard of new ideals. JN

Jorma Uotinen

Uotinen, Jorma (born 1950), dancer, choreographer. Jorma Uotinen has been the most influential figure in modern Finnish dance since 1980, when his work *Unohdettu horisontti* ('The forgotten horizon') received its first performance at the Helsinki Festivals.

Uotinen has created a poetic, strongly visual dance theatre in which lights are of essential importance. Uotinen studied at the ballet school of the Finnish National Ballet and under the direction of Serge Golovine in Switzerland. His appointments include: Finnish National Ballet 1970–1976; Groupe des Récherches Theatrales de l'Opéra de Paris (GRTOP) 1970–1976; Teatro La Fenice 1980, 1981; dancer and choreographer, Helsinki City Theatre, 1980–1986; artistic director of the Helsinki City Theatre dance company 1987–1991; director of the Finnish National Ballet from 1992. Uotinen has worked as a teacher on dance courses and as a workshop co-ordinator in many countries. He has created his central work for the dance company of Helsinki City Theatre and for the Finnish National Ballet, where he made his debut at the age of 24 with his choreography *Aspekteja* ('Aspects'), to music by ▶Aulis Sallinen.

Uotinen's works created outside Finland include his solo work *Jojo* (1979) for the Paris Opera, choreographies to Arnold Schönberg's *Pierrot Lunaire* (1983) and Franco Donatoni's opera *Atem* (1985) for La Scala, Milan, *Frozen Dreams* (1987), based on ▶Magnus Lindberg's orchestral work *Kraft*, for the modern company of the Paris Opera, and *La Nuit gelée* (1995) for the Vienna Dance Festival. AR

Uspensky Cathedral The Uspensky Cathedral in Helsinki is the largest ▶Orthodox Church building in western Europe. At the same time it is one of the city's most important sights, and is visited every year by hundreds of thousands of tourists and pilgrims. The church was completed in 1868, partly to meet the needs of the growing, largely Russian, Orthodox population, and partly as a 'shop window' of imperial power for the West. The designers were the architects A. M. Gornostayev and Ivan Varnek.

A. N. Gornotayev and Ivan Varnek, Uspensky Cathedral, Helsinki, 1868

Stylistically, the Uspensky Cathedral is a combination of Russian, Byzantine and romanesque architecture. Its main cupola, which rises to a height of 42 m, and the 12 smaller cupolas symbolise Christ and the apostles, and the onion shape of the cupola itself the Holy Spirit. The church is consecrated to ascension of the Virgin Mary (Russian *Uspenie*).

Inside, the church is, in the Byzantine fashion, cruciform, with all the arms of the cross of equal length. At the centre of the cross are four massive granite columns, which support the cupola. The east wall has a semi-circular apse where the altar is located, with a smaller apse on either side. The front part of the apse is made up of an iconostasis with two rows of icons. The cupola and the vaulted roof of the apse are painted with a blue starred sky-pattern. The part of the altar behind the iconostasis also symbolises the sky, the kingdom of God.

Until 1990, the Uspensky Cathedral was the centre of worship in the Slavonic languages in Helsinki. Since then, services have been held for the most part in Finnish. In recent years, however, the number of Russian-speaking Orthodox Christians in Finland has grown, so that it seems likely that the number of acts of worship in the Slavonic languages will also increase. TL

V

Anita Välkki

Välkki, Anita (born 1926), soprano. Anita Välkki made her debut at the Finnish National Opera as Brünhilde in Wagner's opera in 1955. She also sang this role in her first major international engagement at Covent Garden in 1961, and it was to become her principal role. Välkki received acclaim also in other major Wagnerian operas as well as Strauss and Janáček roles. HB

Contrapunctus, mural, City of Helsinki Adult Education Centre, 1959

Vanni, Sam (1908–1994), painter, member of the Academy of Finland.

Sam Vanni's artistic starting point was the Paris school of the 1930s. This liberated his treatment of colour, but acquaintance with the new artistic movements in Paris after the Second World War made his way of thinking increasingly structural. Vanni finally rejected representative form in 1952. In different phases his models were Edgard Pillet, Richard Mortensen and Victor Vasarely.

Vanni greatly admired Wassily Kandinsky's book *Über das Geistige in der Kunst* ('Concerning the spiritual in art', 1911), although it was far from being a collection of instructions for him. Vanni created his own style, whose mobile elliptical forms exhibited a great deal of freedom within the constraints of architectonic discipline.

Vanni's compositional thought was regulated by collaboration with architecture, and his masterpieces include a mural for the City of Helsinki Adult Education Centre entitled *Contrapunctus* (1959). His work and charismatic teaching style inspired a younger generation of artists. It is, indeed, largely to his credit that constructivism became an unusually strong movement in Finland. MVn

Vänskä, Osmo (born 1953), conductor. Osmo Vänskä's international career began after he won the Besançon international conducting competition in 1982. In the 1990s, he has conducted a number of different orchestras in Europe and Japan. Vänskä has worked as chief conductor of the Lahti Symphony Orchestra since 1988, in which capacity he has recorded ▶Jean Sibelius's complete works. Of these, the recording of both versions of the vio-

lin concerto (with Leonidas Kavakos as soloist) won *Gramophone* magazine's prize for the best concerto recording in 1991, and *The Tempest* the Francophone world's prestigious Charles Cros Academy's Grand Prix du Disque in 1993.

Vänskä made his debut at the London Proms with the BBC Scottish Symphony Orchestra in 1995, and the following year appeared with the Iceland Symphony Orchestra in New York's Carnegie Hall. Vänskä has been chief conductor of the former orchestra since January 1996; he fulfilled the same role with the Tapiola Sinfonietta in 1990–1992 and with the Icelandic Symphony Orchestra in 1993–1996. After graduating from Sibelius Academy in 1979, Vänskä studied privately with Rafael Kubelik and ▶Paavo Berglund. He also fits playing the clarinet, as a soloist and a chamber musician, into his busy schedule. RL

Verla Mill Museum This ironworks village, old cardboard factory and pulpwood factory, recreating a unique factory environment of the late 19th century. It is located in the parish of Jaala in south-east Finland. The area was designed by the architect Eduard Dippell between 1885 and 1895. The red-brick factory buildings and the

Sam Vanni

Osmo Vänskä

Verla
(Jaala)

Eduard Dippell, Verla Mill, 1885–1895

wooden factory manager's house are in the central European style, which was typical of Nordic industrial building of the time. The Verla pulpwood factory began production in 1872, and continued in operation until 1964. Verla was opened to the public as Finland's first mill factory museum in 1972. It is the first location representing wood processing to feature on the Unesco's World Heritage List. PV

vicarages In the medieval period, priests' houses were generally built close to the parish church. In addition to a dwelling-place of a certain size and other necessary rooms, they included, as emoluments, a plot of farming land with the necessary buildings. In large priests' houses, the number of separate buildings sometimes reached many dozens.

The building of vicarages was carefully controlled: the first building regulations date from as early as the second half of the 16th century. The building material was, almost universally, logs: the only exceptions are in the Åland archipelago and Maria Vicarage near Turku, which dates from the 1780s.

The oldest surviving vicarage is Kaarlela Vicarage (1736), in Kokkola, Ostrobothnia. The Swedish court style of Gustavian neo-classicism from the 1780s and the empire style of the early 19th century were reflected in vicarage architecture, and the buildings also received their characteristic garden settings. At this point, trained architects and significant folk builders began to be active in the design of these buildings; earlier buildings generally form part of the local vernacular building tradition. The new building type is well-represented by Iisalmi Vicarage (1790), which is now in the ►Seurasaari Open-Air Museum near Helsinki. Examples of the vicarages of the empire period include those of Ostrobothnian Vöyri and Isokyrö, and Lohja and Porvoo in southern Finland. In the latter part of the 19th century, the architecture of vicarages often followed that of large country villas.

The importance of vicarages in terms of cultural history, however, is not primarily based on their physical characterstics, but on their general cultural influence on their surroundings.

C.L. Engel, vicarage, Utsjoki, 1843. The Utsjoki Vicarage is the northernmost in Finland

For centuries, vicarages were homes where a significant proportion of educated Finns were born and brought up. Reforms of the salary system for clergymen have, since the 1970s, meant that vicarages have lost their historical role, and a large number of those that have not been demolished are now used for other purposes. EH

Vikings The term Vikings originally meant the Nordic sea or coastal priates who sought suitable booty in bays and fjords or attacked trading ships on the open seas. The first 'Viking expeditions' were probably to steal sheep from neighbouring fjords. Vikings entered the consciousness of western Europeans at the end of the eighth century, when they plundered the rich monastery of Lindisfarne on the east coast of England (A.D. 793). After that, for almost 300 years, these Nordic seafarers travelled in their light ships throughout Europe, sometimes plundering and exacting taxation by force, sometimes conquering and settling. This period, from about A.D. 800 to

Swords from the Viking period, with hilts decorated in silver and bronze. Their Scandinavian influences point to the existence of a common Nordic culture

1100, is known, in Finland as in the other Nordic countries, as the Viking age.

In recent decades, and particularly in popular archaeology, the term Viking has been used to mean Nordic in general. Thus the question has arisen as to whether the Finns, as inhabitants of one of the Nordic countries, are included. Since the Finns have, almost without exception, participated in the large-scale Viking exhibitions that are arranged from time to time, the question has been asked aloud.

The answer depends on what source material is used. Documentary mentions of the Fenni are extremely rare, and can be interpreted in many different ways. It has even been claimed that all the mentions of Fenni or Finni in Scandinavian sources mean ▶Sámi. According to this argument, the Scandinavians had very little to do with the Finns.

The evidence given by archeological material is ambiguous. Extremely little material that can be interpreted as plundered booty has been discovered in Finland, and treasures including only Arab money are absent from the Finnish mainland. This has been considered proof that the Finns, with the exception of the inhabitants of ▶Åland, did not participate in Viking expeditions, even eastward, although the Viking route to the east skirted the south coast of Finland.

If, on the other hand, Finnish material from the Viking period is examined as a whole, it is evident that weapons in Finland were exactly the same as in the other Nordic countries; only Norway has a greater incidence of so-called Viking swords. Finnish men also dressed in the same way as Scandinavians. Women's jewellery was original, but the basic structure of their costumes was closer to Scandinavian examples than to that of other neighbouring areas.

The funeral goods of Finland's biggest burial ground, Luistari in Eura, imply that Finnish men had close contacts with, in particular, the men of central Sweden and Gotland. The background to the shared forms of weaponry and dress no doubt lay in joint exploration and trade expeditions, in other words a common Nordic way of life. The Finns had plenty of space in their own country, so they did not have to seek new localities to settle, but the desire for adventure inspired them to expeditions along the Viking route to the east in exactly the same way as other inhabitants of the coastal regions of the Baltic Sea. PLLH

vocational training The traditional trade institution, with its masters, journeymen and apprentices, collapsed as a result of the industrialisation of the late 19th century and the freedom of trade that was instituted in 1879. The organisation of vocational training in its broadest sense did not keep pace with this development, particularly since the rapidly growing industrial institutions did not take responsibility for vocational training in the same way as countries that had industrialised earlier.

In Finland, vocational training began to be given in the late 19th century according to the Sunday school principle of Germany and Britain. The idea was that industry should provide practical training and society theoretical teaching in workers' free time. As the elementary school system became established at the turn of the century, Sunday schools lost their importance.

Vocational training as such was provided by two-year industrial schools, of which the first was founded in 1886 to train technicians in management tasks. Training in handicrafts and home industry was given in various educational institutes, including elementary schools and folk high schools. Because Finland remained a predominantly agrarian country long into the 20th century, agricultural educational institutes played an important role in vocational training. The oldest agricultural school was founded as early as 1840 at Mustiala, Häme. It had a separate section for women, dealing with cattle-rearing and dairy skills. In 1865 a two-year dairy college was founded at Mustiala; students qualified as agronomists. Mustiala was the top agricultural college until 1907, when teaching in agriculture began at the ▶University of Helsinki. From 1862, university-level teaching of forestry was provided by the Evo Institute of Forestry, which was merged with the University of

Helsinki in 1908. Training in agriculture at local level was provided by agricultural schools and colleges.

In the early decades of the 20th century, vocational training in industry was generally provided by private colleges founded by businesses. The first vocational training law, which guaranteed 65 per cent funding for private and municipal institutes of education, was passed only in 1939. After the Second World War, the number of municipal vocational schools increased, particularly after the passing of a law in 1958 which ordained the establishing of vocational schools in all municipalities whose population exceeded 20,000 people. Between 1982 and 1988 vocational training was reorganised, to a large extent on the model of the German Democratic Republic. As a result of the reforms training, which was divided into a basic period and a period of specialisation, led to the so-called training professions which were set as goals.

In 1995 there were 485 vocational educational institutes in Finland, of which 323 were municipal, 52 run by central government and 110 private. Opportunities for further study for people who have graduated from vocational educational institutes have been improved during the 1990s. Technical colleges have been developed as a new form of education. In 1995 there were 22 temporary technical colleges and 83 experimental educational institutions. The image of vocational training as a whole has also been altered by vocational adult education, whose quantity almost doubled between 1990 and 1995. JN

W

Wallin, G.A. (1811–1852), orientalist, explorer, professor of oriental literature. Born in the parish of Sund in Åland, Wallin began to study oriental languages as his main subject at the University of Helsinki in 1829. It is not known, why he made such a choise, which was unusual at the time. He was talented linguist, and among other languages he learned to speak Arabic at least to some extent from a Tatar Mullah in the fortress of ▶Suomenlinna.

After making his dissertation for lectureship about Arabic in 1839,

G.A. Wallin

Wallin spent two years in St Petersburg learning more oriental languages. St Petersburg was the centre of oriental studies of the time. Between 1843 and 1849 Wallin conducted expeditions to Egypt, Arabia, Mesopotamia, Palestine and Persia. He devoted himself entirely to his research; merging with the society and environment under study became an end in itself to him. He returned to Finland via London, where he published some of his studies concerning oriental languages, literature and phonetics. His *Notes Taken During a Journey through Part of Northern Arabia* (1848) was published by the Royal Geographical Society in 1851. In 1850 Wallin was awarded the gold medal of the Royal Geographical Society in London, the most respected scholarly distinction of the time on his field.

In 1851 Wallin presented his doctoral thesis in Helsinki, *Carmen Elegianum Ibnu-L-Faridi cum commentario Abdu-L-Ghanyi*, and soon after this he was appointed as professor of oriental literature. Some of Wallin's diaries and studies have been published in Finland in Swedish, but most, because of Wallin's early death, still exist as manuscripts in archives. PV

Waltari, Mika (1908–1979), writer. The son of a Helsinki civil servant, Mika Waltari, achieved great success with his very first novel, *Suuri illusioni* ('The great illusion', 1928), which interpreted the feelings of the new generation and their enthusiasm for the urban and the cosmopolitan. Waltari's repertoire is extensive and diverse. One of the most popular Finnish novelists and dramatists, he wrote short prose, detective novels, story-books and dozens of film scripts. Already before the Second World War, Waltari had dealt with

Mika Waltari

Finnish history in some of his novels. After the war, he made his international breakthrough with *Sinuhe, egyptiläinen* (*The Egyptian*,1945), a novel set in the time of the pharaohs; the book was made into a Hollywood film in 1954. An interesting plot, vivid historical description and easily intelligible characters were the ingredients of his success. Amid the post-war changes, the novel's conception of culture and of the essential unchangingness of human nature appealed to many people. Later, Waltari published a number of long historical novels, some of them set in Byzantium.

The problem with Waltari's narrative is the superficiality of his language; paradoxically, however, it is turned to advantage when juxtaposed with his interesting plots and well-realised local colour and atmosphere. Waltari's central novels have become evergreen entertainments. PL

way of life The rapid changes in the structure of society that followed the Second World War in Finland, urbanisation, the rapid rise in the standard of living, the growth of the mass media and the explosive increase of international influences, changed the Finnish way of life very quickly. The foods Finns ate, their clothes, the decoration of their homes and their leisure activities began, to a constantly increasing extent, to conform to those of other developed countries. Nevertheless, the Finnish way of life retained some essential characteristic features peculiar only to it.

Some of these basic lifestyle features derive from the rapid structural change in society. Characteristic of the structural change that followed the Second World War was a large and simultaneous growth in the size of the working class and groups of officials. Plentiful opportunities for social betterment were available to those who left the countryside. The change was rapid; it occurred within one generation. Thus a rural, peasant way of life was close by and in the blood. This combined with the strong social changes and the demands brought by the new living environments.

The values of rural society and the new achievement pressures of work and living environments that stood in the background open up an understanding of the core of the Finnish way of life, which the scholar Matti Kortteinen (born 1953) has aptly characterised as 'the ethos of survival'. According to Kortteinen, Finns experience the world as a hard place in which it is necessary to survive. And those who survive with credit feel a great deal of pride.

Another of the basic characteristics of the Finnish way of life is connected with the uniqueness of the physical environment. The basic elements of the Finnish landscape, the stark variations of the seasons and the sparse habitation, have exerted their own particular influence. The ▶forest, the abundant islands of the coast (▶archipelago), the tens of thousands of lakes, the variation between summer and winter,

Summer auction: Finns mix their needs for solitude with popular social gatherings such as this one

►light and darkness, and the abundance of space provide a different framework for life from, for example, the urban cultures of central Europe.

The result is a complex and internally contradictory ►mentality in which rusticality, individuality, pride and vigour co-exist with urbanity, the hierarchical nature of working life and the social skills it demands, and the sociability presupposed by leisure activities. The result is independence, defiance and self-sufficiency, but also lack of self-esteem, social insecurity and maladjustment. Finns live in towns or built-up areas, but are perhaps able to relax only in the countryside, beside water or in the ►sauna. Finns are closed and weigh their words carefully, but, when they have indulged themselves with ►alcohol, become noisy revellers and, eventually, fanatics. Although Finns, who are highly mobile in summer, populate summer events, agricultural shows and sporting fixtures, and take part in package tours, they are perhaps almost happier gathering berries in the forest or in the solitude of a lake or island.

Nevertheless, the Finnish way of life is changing. The characteristics described above no doubt best characterised the way of life of Finns born in the first half of the century. If the centrality of the home is added to the equation, this also becomes a description of the way of life of the working class and farmers.

The rapid structural change of the past few decades resulted in an increase of the middle class, in particular, and gave rise to completely new professional groups. On the other hand, as the standard of living rapidly rose, the material and educational starting-point of the new generations was considerably higher than that of their parents. This has given rise to not one but perhaps a number of new life styles.

According to an analysis of Finnish life styles by the sociologist J.P. Roos (born 1945), it is possible to define within the middle class a kind of cultural middle class, whose life style is characterised by a kind of asceticism, concerts, theatre, reading and other cultural activities, and travel and concern for the environment. The life style of the economic and technical middle class, on the other hand, stresses care for material well-being, consumption and fashionability, but also attachment to one's own professional group, exercise and spectator sports.

Common to both middle classes, however, is the fact that their life styles are characterised by the cultural capital created by knowledge and skills acquired through education and training. This offers the facility for decisions concerning new life styles, and also implies openness to new winds and international influences. With these, ways of life and life styles can very rapidly be changed. International fashions and trends are followed more closely than before, and they are quickly seen in the interests of the middle classes and in many everyday activities. MAo

wedding The institution of the wedding has reflected the division of Finnish folk culture into an eastern and a western sphere. In eastern Finland the wedding was a family celebration, while in western Finland it was an occasion when the families of bridegroom and bride were able to show their status to the rest of the village community. This latter tradition survives most strongly in the traditional grand wedding (*kruunuhäät*) found in ►Ostrobothnia.

Many of the old traditions have been preserved, even though, particularly in urban communities, church weddings were not fashionable during the 1960s and 1970s, when civil wedding and marriage were typical among the young. More recently, however, there has been a marked revival of Finnish wedding tradition. Couples who have lived together in civic matrimony for years now consecrate their union in church with the arrival of their first child. Even though marriage has lost its social, judicial and economic significance, church weddings have acquired a new value. They emphasise the importance of a relationship and demonstrate that it has now come into its own right. The increased popularity of marriage may be seen in the advice given on the subject in weekly magazines, and in the growing number of tuxedos and wedding dresses for sale or hire in the shops.

The doorways are decorated with birch boughs in celebration of this early summer wedding

In addition to the bride and bridegroom's kinsfolk, the young couple's friends also take part in the wedding. The wedding guests are invited by sending out printed or handwritten cards. Midsummer is still the most popular time for weddings though long weekends at any time of the year are now also chosen.

As part of her wedding accoutrements, the bride wears a white or pale-coloured wedding dress, while the bridegroom wears either a tuxedo or a dark suit. The bride's female companion, the *kaaso*, helps her. The bride's outfit traditionally contains elements that are supposed to bring good fortune: something old, something borrowed, something new and something blue. The bride's bouquet of flowers is chosen and paid for by the bridegroom. At the marriage ceremony he also puts the wedding ring on the bride's ring finger, next to the engagement ring. The bridegroom's engagement ring usually serves as his wedding ring. The solemn sense of occasion at the marriage ceremony is increased by the bridesmaids and the best man. The latter no longer has the same role as the *puhemies*, or marriage broker of former times, who arranged the marriage with the bride's family.

The bride's kinsfolk and friends sit on the right-hand side of the aisle, viewed from the altar, and the bridegroom's on the left. In recent times foreign influence has played its part, in that women now attend the service in brimmed hats.

After the marriage service the newly wed couple are driven away from the church in the American style, in a lim-ousine or horse-drawn cab festooned with silk ribbons and heart-shaped 'Just Married' signs with tin cans and old shoes tied on at the rear, to the photography session and then to the wedding reception held either at the bride's home or at a rented banqueting hall. The programme consists of coffee or lunch, speeches, performed music and dancing, which the bridal couple begin with the wedding waltz. In former times the wedding reception was arranged by the bride's family, but nowadays the costs are shared between both families. The guests bring wedding presents to the event, and these are placed on a side table. Wedding present customs are in many ways rather down-to-earth: the friends of the bridal pair may give them a gift cheque, or the couple may leave a wish list of presents at a shop which the wedding guests then visit, choosing gifts to suit their pocket. A stubbornly surviving tradition is the bridegroom's morning gift to the bride usually a piece of jewellery. This has a courtly rather than an economic value.

The bourgeois custom of the honeymoon is now so popular that travel agents have begun to advertise services tailored especially for newly married couples. The bridal couple may receive a honeymoon as one of their wedding presents, paid for by several people. TK

welfare state Like Denmark, Norway and Sweden, Finland is a Scandinavian welfare state based on social benefits for all citizens, extensive redistribution of wealth, diverse public-sector services and universal waged work for women. The Scandinavian welfare state differs from the corporatist welfare state of the continent in which social security is based on the breadwinner's position in the labour market, in which the majority of services are private, and which waged work for women is not so widespread. The liberal British and American welfare state, on the other hand, emphasises the individual's position in the labour market, and redistribution of wealth and public services are not as developed. Compared to those of industrialised Europe, Finland's welfare state was a late developer. Its breakthrough occurred in the decades that followed the Sec-

Children's day-care centre: since 1996 parents have had the right to choose either financial support for home care or a free-paying place at a day-care centre

ond World War, at the time of wide-ranging structural change in Finnish society.

Although debate about social politics and the question of the working class began in Finland – following German influence – at approximately the same time as in the rest of Europe, for a long time the focus of social reforms was on alleviating the living conditions of the lower rural social classes and organising land-ownership relations. The slow progress of the welfare state was due to the predominance of agriculture, which was further consolidated by land reforms. Before the Second World War, the focus of social politics had been on municipal relief for the poor, although there were attempts to protect industrial workers, too, by legislation of a general nature.

The Pensions Law that came into force in 1937 was the first reform in social politics to affect the entire nation. Old age and disability pensions, however, came into force only gradually. On the eve of the Second World War, welfare state in Finland was, by European standards, undeveloped, and only a small proportion of the population was protected from social risks such as illness, disability and so on.

The extension of the welfare state began at the end of the 1940s and 1950s as changes in the structure of society began to accelerate. The Child Allowance Law, which came into force in 1948, brought all children under the protection of the state. The Pensions Law was revised in 1956 and the private-sector pensions system began in the early 1960s. A universal Sickness Insurance Law extending to all citizens came into force in two stages in the 1960s. In the 1970s the public sector was strongly expanded with national health legislation (i.e. health care centres) and a Child-Care Law. As the result of these and numerous smaller reforms, social security and public services were made available to the entire population. At the same time social security expenditure grew rapidly. Finland became a Scandinavian welfare state.

The development of the welfare state affected society in many ways. International comparisons demonstrate that in the 1970s and 1980s Finland was among the countries where there was little poverty, where income differences between different social groups were small, where women's work outside the home was widespread and where new labour was recruited in large numbers for the public sector and, in particular, its service sectors. Opinion polls showed that the welfare state enjoyed widespread support among citizens. The obverse of this development was the growth of taxation. The system was built on conditions of full employment.

From the end of the 1980s, however, the mainstays of the welfare state began to buckle, and the Finnish economy found itself in what was perhaps the most serious crisis of its history. Trade with the Soviet Union, which had flourished in the preceding decade, shrank rapidly, and the rapid liberalisation of money and credit markets resulted in over-heating of the economy, the years of 'casino economics'. When, in addition, the growth of exports to the West came to a halt, the Finnish economy was driven into the worst spin of its history. Economic growth was negative, foreign debt grew, the balance of payments was badly shaken and the entire banking system entered a deep crisis. Among the results was the growth of unemployment in Finland to record levels – one-fifth of the work-force. Mass employment, in its turn, raised social security expenditure very rapidly.

Economic development and the strengthening of neo-liberal thought broke the earlier consensus. The development of the welfare state, which had since the late 1960s been based on extensive agreements between the state, the political parties, the strong trades union movement and the employers, ran into difficulties as that unanimity disappeared. Public-sector activities were pruned and various income transfers cut. Although there was an upturn in economic development in the middle of the decade, extensive unemployment and the growth of public debt enforced additional cuts in social security. At the same time social problems, poverty and social differences increased rapidly. Nevertheless, the welfare state has fulfilled its basic functions, and public support for it has not disappeared. MAo

Westermarck, Edward (1862–1939), sociologist, philosopher. After gaining his master's degree at the University of Helsinki, Edward Westermarck made his way, with the help of a bursary, to London to continue his studies. The work of Darwin prompted him to consider the question of the origins of marriage. His doctoral thesis, *The History of Human Marriage*, published in 1891, made him internationally famous.

The Origin and Development of the Moral Ideas appeared in 1906. After the publication of this work, Wester-

marck was appointed professor of practical philosophy at the University of Helsinki (1906–1918), and simultaneously at the University of London (1907–1930). From Helsinki he moved to Åbo Akademi University, where he was rector from 1918 to 1921.

Edward Westermarck

In addition to his work on marriage and moral concepts, Westermarck is known for his numerous field trips. Between 1889 and 1925 he spent a total of seven years in Morocco developing field study methods in social anthropology and adapting them to his own thoroughgoing studies. The resulting works *Ritual and Belief in Morocco I–II* (1926) and *Wit and Wisdom in Morocco* (1930) are still known as classics in their field. Many of Westermarck's students followed their teacher's example, carrying out exhaustive field studies of many research problems in different parts of the world.

As a result of Westermarck, sociological research became rooted in Finland comparatively early. In 1940 the Westermarck Society was founded, which is still active in publishing a journal entitled *Sosiologia* ('Sociology') and organising research seminars. ML

Winter War The Winter War is the name given to the short but bitter conflict that took place between Finland and the Soviet Union between 30 November 1939 and 13 March 1940. The war lasted, in other words, only 105 days. Nevertheless, the losses it caused were enormous. There were almost 25,000 Finnish dead – killed either in battle or in air raids – 43,000 wounded, and more than 400,000 inhabitants of ▶Karelia were moved from their homes to other parts of the country. Finland lost about 10 per cent of its territory to the Soviet Union. Most important was the loss of Karelia, including Viipuri, Finland's second-largest city.

The fundamental reason for the conflict was the so-called Molotov-Ribbentrop Pact, signed by the Soviet Union and Germany on 23 August 1939. In a secret codicil, Germany agreed that the Baltic countries and Finland belonged to the Soviet sphere of influence. As a result of the agreement, the Soviet Union procured mili-

A Finnish ski patrol on duty at Märkäjärvi, Lapland, 1940

tary bases in the Baltic area. Finland received an invitation to negotiations in Moscow on 5 October. In order to protect Leningrad, the Soviet Union demanded from Finland a base at Hanko, part of the Karelian Isthmus and a few of the islands of the Gulf of Finland. In return, it promised to cede areas of a bigger total area in eastern Karelia.

Finland did not agree with the conditions, and broke off negotiations on 13 November. Why did it behave in this way? Did it hope it could win a war? No, because it was estimated that defence would last only a couple of weeks. Did it believe that it would acquire allies? No, because Sweden refused to give military aid and Germany advised Finland to agree to the conditions. The Allies were too far away. Why, then? Because the strong man of the Finnish government – the foreign minister, Eljas Erkko (1895–1965) – believed that the Russians were only bluffing. A country that had for 20 years been saying 'peace, peace', simply could not attack its small neighbour. If this should nevertheless happen – this is clearly how the argument went – Moscow would have to give an ultimatum. Then Finland, saving its face, would agree to the proposed demands for exchange of territories.

These calculations were not entirely based on wrong premises. The Soviet Union really did not wish to appear to

the world as an aggressor. For this reason it never gave an ultimatum, but tried by other means to make clear to Helsinki that it intended to get what it wanted. The Soviet press used threatening language: on 26 November it accused Finland of artillery fire across the border, and two days later it cancelled the non-aggression pact between the two countries.

When no assent was forthcoming from Helsinki, Moscow severed diplomatic relations with Finland on 29 November, and the next morning gave permission to its armed services to begin military operations against Finland. The declaration of war was delayed in the hope that Finland would agree to the Soviet demands.

Foreign Minister Erkko nevertheless considered even the military operations to be mere diplomatic pressure. The rest of the government was of a different opinion: the Prime Minister and Foreign Minister were replaced on the night of 1 December, and in the morning it was announced on the radio that a new government led by Risto Ryti (1889–1956) was willing to continue the negotiations for territorial exchange on the basis of positive proposals. It was, however, too late. Moscow had already informed the world that it no longer recognised the Helsinki government. It recognised only the government in exile the Russians had established in Terijoki, close to the eastern border of Finland, the so-called Terijoki government, in response to whose plea for help it wished to conquer Finland.

Thus the war began. Against all expectations, the Finnish defence lasted until the beginning of March. The Red Army suffered enormous losses. Finally the Russians succeeded in forcing their way across the frozen Viipurinlahti Bay and thus threatening both the Finnish army on the Karelian Isthmus and Helsinki. Although France and Great Britain offered Finland military aid, Finland was forced to sue for peace under heavy conditions. (It was not certain whether the auxiliary forces would come from further away than the Gulf of Bothnia.) Fearful of involvement on the part of the Western powers (this is how the matter was generally interpreted), the Soviet Union abandoned its plans for conquest and the Terijoki government, and made peace with the Finnish government led by Risto Ryti.

The Winter War resulted, for Finland, in the loss of Karelia. The idea of winning it back led Finland to wage war against the Soviet Union at the side of Germany between 1941 and 1944. The Finnish success in the Winter War was partially influential in Hitler's decision to attack eastward, for the Finnish defensive victories were generally explained in terms of the weakness of the Red Army. It can at last be said that the war united the Finns, whom the Civil War of 1918 had badly devided. HY

Wirkkala, Tapio (1915–1985), designer. Tapio Wirkkala is internationally the best-known of Finnish designers. From 1946, after a winning a competition for glass design held by the ▶Iittala Glass Factory, he worked as a designer for Iittala until his death. In addition to this, however, he collaborated with a number of different manufacturers and offices.

The formal starting-points of Wirkkala's sculptural objects are often found in nature. The marks left by the forces of nature are also visible in the surface structures of the objects. Wirkkala was an artist-craftsman for whom continual contact with the material and knowledge of it were the entire ba-

Tapio Wirkkala

Finlandia-vodka-bottles, 1978.

Vase, glass, 1974

sis of creating. His glass objects were born of a close collaboration between glass-blower and artist. Among Wirkkala's best-known crystal objects are the soft-lined, elegant *Kanttarelli* ('Chanterelle', 1946). During the 1950s and 1960s, in addition to serially produced utility items, Wirkkala designed a number of monumental crystal objects, including the *Jäävuori* ('Iceberg') vases (1955) and the *Paadarin jää* ('The ice of Paadar') sculptures (1960), which took their name from a Lappish lake. The expressively rugged surface of the *Paadarin jää* sculptures recur in his popular serially produced glass ranges *Ultima Thule* (1968) and *Luna* (1970), and in the *Finlandia* vodka bottle (in production from 1978).

Wirkkala's sculptural training at its purest is evident in his birch-laminate sculptures. The first laminate sculptures were created in 1951. During the 1950s, Wirkkala also designed plywood-intarsia tables. The climax of his plywood sculpture was the 1967 relief, *Ultima Thule*, for the Montreal World Exhibition, which was intended as a symbol of Finland's wood-processing industry.

Wirkkala's contribution to the Finnish success in the Milan Triennales of the 1950s was decisive. His exhibition designs, which received the Grand Prix in 1951 and 1954, opened the way for the triumphal march of Finnish design in the wider world. MaA

wood In former times, wood was the first important resource in the lives of the Finnish peasant: it took the form of buildings and furniture, transportation and hunting equipment, household implements and working tools, and decorative and art objects. The forest and timber offered the possibility of survival even in hard times: in years of famine, nutrition was derived from wood in the form of bark-bread, and as recently as the last war wood was used as a raw material for, among other things, textiles and the soles of shoes, and as fuel for cars.

The forest is still an important source of prosperity, Finland's green gold, and in today's ways of life and art timber retains a central role. One feature of the development of Finland's formal culture, throughout the ages, has indeed been the adaptation of stylistic themes developed in European urban centres to the forest environment and wood as a material. The courtyard of the peasant house, lined with buildings, and the wooden vaults of the churches of the peasant master-

Wooden scoops in the shape of birds were used traditionally throughout western and northern Finland

builders are distant reflections of the architecture of Renaissance Europe. The classicism of the 1920s and the pure ideals of modernism that followed it were similarly transformed, here, into an aesthetics of wood.

The reconstruction that followed the Second World War was realised in large part in wood, but the international style that emerged in the 1950s was also transformed, in Finland, into a regionalism employing natural materials, rhythms and forms – a regionalism that achieved worldwide admiration for its humanity and its links with tradition.

The original Finnish urban model, too, is the wooden town; the oldest surviving timber urban environments, such as Luostarinmäki in Turku and the cathedral area in Porvoo, date from the medieval period, but most were built according to the neo-classical pattern books of the 18th century. A peculiarly Finnish urban model is the post-war 'forest town', an attempt to combine the forest and the town.

Among the best-known masters of the use of wood in Finland are ▶Alvar Aalto in architecture and furniture design, ▶Tapio Wirkkala in design and Kain Tapper (born 1930) in ▶sculpture. Forest themes are also characteristic of the visual arts, literature and music; one could speak of a 'Finnish forest art'.

With the ecological way of life and building, new uses for wood are being explored systematically at present. In the fields of design, crafts and sculpture, too, interest in the use of wood is growing once more. JP

Traditional timber constructions are still extensively used in summer houses

Re-roofing: joint projects, in which neighbours receive their 'wages' in the form of a good meal, are still common in Finland

work Work in Finland has been largely rooted in the economic structure of the country, dominated until very recently by agriculture, forestry and the wood-processing industries. In 1959 almost half the labour force was employed in agriculture and forestry. The retarded modernisation of employment structures was related to land reform, which continued to create small and technologically primitive farms until the 1960s. State subsidies to smallholders were important partly to secure provision of agricultural products, and partly to secure labour requirements of the forest-related industries. The cultural impact of the smallholding tradition on the Finnish work ethic is still apparent today.

Industrial growth in the 1960s and 1970s was rapid, and coincided with the mechanisation of agriculture and forestry. Industrialisation was concentrated on high-technology, low-employment fields, with a high degree of automation. Consequently industry today employs only about 20 per cent of the labour force, and agriculture (including forestry) about 8 per cent.

Today, most Finnish people work in middle-class occupations, and almost half of the labour force works in the public sector. Female participation in paid labour has always been higher than in other western countries, and continued to increase until the recession of 1990. Women and men participate about equally in paid employment. Women represent slightly more than half of salary- and wage-earners, but men are more frequently entrepreneurs. The Finnish ▸welfare state has both facilitated this expansion and provided employment in female-dominated occupations such as caring work and education. About 60 per cent of employees in the public sector are women. Women represent 90 per cent of all employees in the health-care system and in social work, including child care. The gender segregation of professions has increased. The continuing, even slowly increasing wage differences between men and women are not accounted for by educational level.

The work ethic in Finland still bears traces of the logging-camp and farming life of earlier generations. Extreme tenacity (▸*sisu*) was required to perform strenuous physical work facing all the hardships nature can offer: cold weather, long distances and almost impassable terrain. The classic literary description of this ethos is the novel *Seitsemän veljestä* (*Seven Brothers*) by ▸Aleksis Kivi, but it is also a central theme both in the realist and national romantic tradition of painting. PSn

Georg Henrik von Wright

Wright, Georg Henrik von (born 1916), philosopher.

Georg Henrik von Wright, the most internationally important Finnish philosopher this century, studied philosophy before the Second World War in the universities of Helsinki and Cambridge, where he was influenced by logical positivism and empiricism. He published his doctoral thesis, *The Logical Problem of Induction,* in 1941, and a work on logical empiricism in 1943. Von Wright was appointed docent in philosophy at the University of Helsinki in 1943. Having worked from 1946 as professor in Helsinki and at the Swedish-speaking university in Turku, Åbo Akademi, in 1948 he was invited to succeed Ludwig Wittgenstein as professor of philosophy at the University of Cambridge. Von Wright returned to Finland in 1951, and was professor of philosophy at the University of Helsinki until 1961, and a member of the Academy of Finland from 1961 to 1986. He was visiting professor at Cornell University in 1954 and 1958, Andrew D. White Professor-at-Large from 1965 to 1977, Gifford lecturer at the University of St Andrews in 1959 and 1960, Tarner lecturer at Trinity College, Cambridge in 1969, Woodbridge lecturer at Columbia University in 1972 and Nellie Wallace lecturer at Oxford University in 1978, and visiting professor at the University of California Los Angeles (UCLA) in 1963, at the University of Pittsburgh in 1966, and at the University of Karlsruhe in 1975.

Von Wright is a prominent representative of analytical and applied logic. His studies have included the concept of probability and induction, deontic and normal logic and the logic of action and change. His most important works internationally are *A Treatise on Induction and Probability* (1951), *An Essay in Modal Logic* (1951), *Logical Studies* (1957), *The Varieties of Goodness* (1963), *Norm and Action* (1963), *The Logic of Preference* (1963), *An Essay in Deontic Logic* (1968), *Explanation and Understanding* (1971), *Causality and Determinism* (1974), *Freedom and Determination* (1980), *Philosophical Papers I–III* (1983–84) and *The Tree of Knowledge.* Von Wright has also written about Wittgenstein (1982) and is one of the executors of his literary estate. In books published in Swedish and Finnish, and in his numerous articles, von Wright has approached questions of scientific knowledge and philosophy in a populist way. He has also been one of the most important influences on Finnish scholarly policies since the Second World War. Von Wright was a member of the Finnish Academy from 1968 to 1970 and chancellor of Åbo Akademi from 1968 to 1977.

Von Wright is a member of numerous Finnish and foreign learned academies and societies, including the Institut international de philosophie, Paris (member 1953, chairman 1975–77), Kungliga Svenska Vetenskapsakademie (member 1960), the British Academy (member 1961), Académie Internationale de Philosophie des Sciences, Brussels (member 1962), International Union of History and Philosophy of Science, IUHPS (chairman 1963–65), Trinity College (honorary member 1983), and an honorary doctor of 11 universities. Von Wright received the prize of the Alexander von Humboldt in 1986, the great prize of the Academy of Sweden in 1986 and the Selma Lagerlöf literary prize in 1993. JN

Hella Wuolijoki

Wuolijoki, Hella (1886–1954) The Estonian Ella Murrik married the Finnish member of parliament Sulo Wuolijoki (1881–1957) and took Finnish nationality, worked as a businesswoman and an active member of the Finnish workers' movement, a writer, member of parliament and farmer in the capacity of mistress of the mansion of Marlebäck. She knew both Maxim Gorky and Bertold Brecht (who spent his period of exile in Finland at Marlebäck, and whose *Herr Puntila und sein Knecht Matti* ['Mr Puntila and his servant Matti'] is a version of Wuolijoki's play *Ison-Heikkilän isäntä ja hänen renkinsä Kalle* ['The master of Iso-Heikkilä and his servant Kalle', 1947]). During the Second World War, she was involved in diplomatic negotiations for peace with the Soviet Union, but was sentenced to life imprisonment for treason in 1944. There she wrote her memoirs; she was freed in 1945. Hella Wuolijoki ended her colourful career as director of Finnish Broadcasting Company.

The hundredth performance of Hella Wuolijoki's popular play, *Niskavuoren naiset* ('Women of Niska-vuori'), Helsinki Folk Theatre, 1936. The author is seated, left

Wuolijoki wrote 16 plays. Of these, *Juurakon Hulda* ('Hulda of Juurakko', 1937), a kind of Eliza Doolittle story about a poor girl's path to education, provided the subject for the Oscar-winning film *The Farmer's Daughter* (1947); the writer, however, did not become world-famous. *Laki ja järjestys* ('Law and order', 1933) made reference to the Civil War of 1918 and, because of its leftist sympathies, provoked widespread polemic in the press. As a result of this episode, Wuolijoki began her five-play series about the country house of Niskavuori, and its power-struggles and generations from the 1880s to the 1940s under the *nom-de-plume* Juhani Tervapää.

The *nom-de-plume* was revealed, but the *Niskavuori* plays have been among the most often performed of Finnish theatre. *Niskavuoren naiset* ('Women of Niskavuori') was also seen in London, in 1937, under the title *Women of Property*. Wuolijoki's psychological eye and characterisation are so convincing that even the plays' solidly realist form does not seem burdensome from the perspective of modern theatre. Wuolijoki's old women often have will and power in far greater measure than her young men, whose fate lies in young women. Maids and mistresses, servants and masters live their lives in Finland as it works towards independence and wages war. Wuolijoki's feeling for drama and narrative and the aptness of her dialogue make the plays of this Estonian-born writer classic Finnish plays – so much so that Wuolijoki is, after ▶Aleksis Kivi and William Shakespeare, Finland's most often performed dramatic writer. SL

Index

Photo sources

Amos Anderson Art Museum 28 (top)
Arabia's Museum 18
Artek/Jussi Tiainen 29
Design Museum of Finland 9 (centre left), 39 (centre right), 48; Jean Barbier 122 (bottom), 123 (bottom), 126 (bottom left); 129 (top); Wärtsilä-Foto 129 (bottom); 130 (left), 154 (bottom); Aimo Hyvärinen 164 (left); Kari Holopainen 188 (top); 205 (left, bottom right); Rauno Träskelin 21(bottom left); Lars Rebers 211 (top); Otso Pietinen 219; 268 (centre); Indav 277; Ulla Paakkunainen 297 (left), 309; 314 (top), 329
Finnish Broadcasting Company TV2/Antero Tenhunen 163 (bottom); Kalevi Rytkölä 256 (top), Seppo Sarkkinen 307
Finnish Design Centre 72, 158
Finnish Film Archives 86, 87, 152, 161, 175 (top left), 175 (top right, centre margin, bottom), 189, 212, 291 (top left), 305
Finnish Film Foundation 73
Finnish Literature Society, Folklore Archive 25, 33 (top) 46, 81 (left); Simo Rista 95 (top); Juha Jarva 95 (bottom); 100 (right), 101 (top, right), 110, 111, 113, 123 (top), 169 (bottom), 170, 174 (top), 225 (bottom); Pekka Laaksonen 263; Antti Hämäläinen 273, 268
Finnish Literature Society, Literature Archive 42 (top margin), 160, 175 (bottom margin), 183 (margin), 188 (bottom margin), 191, 194, 225 (top), 264, 265, 269 (top margin), 290 (left margin), 294 (right), 296 (margin), 314, 323 (top)
Finnish Music Information Centre Maarit Kytöharju 33 (margin), 176 (top margin), 188(top margin), 257 (centre), 268 (margin)
Finnish National Gallery, Central Art Archives 26, 27 (left), 166 (top), 207, 216, 258, 279 (centre), 291 (top right)
Finnish National Opera Kari Hakli 33, 39 (top margin), 176 (left, centre margin), 230, 231 (left), 271 (margin), 318 (bottom); 154 (top left); Maarit Kytöharju 169 (margin); 206, 304 (bottom margin); Pasi Haaranen 318 (top margin)
Finnish National Theatre Leena Klemelä 166 (bottom), 310 (bottom)
Fiskars 100 (left)
Friitala Fashion 123 (left)
Gorilla Petri Kuokka 14, 131 (bottom), 136, 315 (top), 318 (top); Esko Männikkö 58, 85 (left), 331; Johnny Korkman 62, 182, 187; Tapio Vanhatalo 89 (top); Matti Niemi (bottom), 92; Ari Jaskari 127, 261; Jyrki Luukkonen 133; Sari Poijärvi 210, 260 (bottom); Hanna Hentinen 234; Jaakko Heikkilä 243; Petri Kuokka 332
Gösta Serlachius Museum of Fine Arts 283 (right)
Kari Hakli 20, 51(bottom), 75 (top), 93, 130 (right), 237 (bottom right), 310 (top), 315 (bottom), 316 (bottom)
Helsinki City Art Museum 319 (top)
Helsinki City Museum 290 (top)
Helsinki City Theatre Kari Hakli 42 (top right)
Helsinki Institute of Technology 157 (top)
Helsinki University Library 35 (bottom), 37, 41, 155, 253
Seppo Hilpo 279 (bottom)

Iittala Glass Museum 154 (top right); Gero Mylius 228
Kalevala Koru 168
Kinoproduction 18
Kuvaliiteri 13, 19, Ilkka Toivonen 44 (right), 106; Arto Vuohelainen 45; E.J. Laamanen 82, 134 (bottom); Heikki Ilaskari 83, 115 (bottom); Veijo Vilska 115 (top); Matti Ylätupa 117; Jari Tuiskunen 118, 183 (top); Tero Pajukallio 126 (right bottom), 134 (top); Tapio Heikkilä 150 (right), 157 (left) 179 (top), 236; Sakari Parkkinen (bottom); Tauno Santaoja 213 (top); Matti Koivumäki 278; Martti Lintunen 282; Mattias Tolvanen 295
Lahti Art Museum 248, 249
Lehtikuva 28 (bottom), Sari Gustafsson 57, 186; Heikki Sarviaho 59 (top); Heikki Saukkomaa 67, 70 188 (centre margin), 223 (bottom), 232 (bottom); 94, 97; Vesa Klemetti 122 (top); Martti Kainulainen 71, 215 (top); Markku Ulander 151 (top), 176 (bottom margin); Kimmo Mäntylä 162, 240 (bottom); 163 (top left); Marja Seppänen-Helin 175 (top margin), 240 (centre right), 260 (top); Ilkka Ranta 184 (margin), 313 (right); Peter Jansson 185; Sari Niemi 192, 223 (top); Ensio Ilmonen 231 (top), 283 (left); 244, 245 (top), 267; Soile Kallio 270 (right); Matti Björkman 284; 286, 291 (right bottom), 296 (right), 299, 300; Mikko Oksanen 301 (top); Ari Ojala 301 (right); Matti Kolho 302; 303 (bottom); 304 (right), 311; Sanna Liimatainen 317 (bottom); 329 (margin)
Luhta 193
Marimekko 205 (top)
Petter Martiskainen 213 (bottom left), 235
Museum of Finnish Architecture 9 (top right,bottom right); P. Ingervo 9 (bottom margin), 21; Teuvo Kanerva 22; Ä. Fethulla 23; 24, 39 (bottom), Kari Hakli 75 (bottom), 194 (bottom); H. Havas 153, 229; Simo Rista (right); N.E.Wickberg 201, 303 (top); István Rácz 237 (top); Juhani Riekkola (bottom right); Eric Sundström 269 (right); 285
Museum of Ostrobothnia Erkki Salminen 271 (left bottom)
National Board of Antiquities 35 (margin), 81 (right), 103, 131 (top), 146 (left), 151 (bottom), 156, 174 (margin), 177, 194 (margin), 199, 206, 220, 227 (top, centre), 257 (top), 270 (left), 313 (top)
Nature Photo Agency 90
Old Book Days Markku Mäkinen 34
Otava 10, 11, 15, 16, 39 (bottom margin), 40, 42 (bottom margin), 59 (bottom), 75 (bottom), 101 (bottom); István Rácz 123 (centre), 330; 125, 137, 143, 145, 146 (right), 147, 148, 149 (top), 149 (centre, bottom), 150 (left), 163 (margin), 164 (top), 171, 172, 176 (right),198; Eero Troberg 237 (margin); 241, 245 (bottom), 251, 252, 257 (bottom), 262, 268 (top), 269 (bottom margin), 270 (margin), 271 (top), 279 (top), 291 (bottom left), 292, 293, 294 (left), 297 (right), 304 (top margin), 317 (top), 319 (top margin), 320 (bottom), 322, 327, 328, 332
Photographic Museum of Finland 238, 239, 240 (top)
Postal Museum of Finland 246, 247
Pressfoto Urho Antero Pietilä 32 (right), 44 (left), 51 (top), 85 (right), 121 (bottom), 132, 135, 179 (bottom), 184 (top left), 197, 222, 227 (bottom), 254, 256 (right), 274, 275, 316 (top), 320 (top), 323 (bottom), 326
Raatikko Dance Theatre Kari Hakli 65
Radio Symphony Orchestra 32 (margin), 131 (centre), 218, 231 (margin), 276 (top), 285 (margin)
Eeva Rista 49, 121(top), 209
Seurasaari Urpo Salo 109
Paul-Anders Simma 289
Sinfonia Lahti Eastpress Seppo J.J. Sirkka 319 (bottom)
Studio Nurmesniemi Max Petrelius 78; Teemu Töyrylä 124
Theatre Museum 332
Turku Art Museum Kari Lehtinen 126 (top left). 126 (top right)
Turku Provincial Museum 217
University of Lapland 140
University of Tampere 139
Valmet 157 (bottom)
Verla Mill Museum Kimmo Rekimies 319
WSOY Seppo Hilpo 27 (right)